WORKHORSE

Caroline Palmer

4th ESTATE • *London*

4th Estate
An imprint of HarperCollins*Publishers*
1 London Bridge Street
London SE1 9GF

www.4thestate.co.uk

HarperCollins*Publishers*
Macken House, 39/40 Mayor Street Upper
Dublin 1, D01 C9W8, Ireland

First published in Great Britain in 2025 by 4th Estate
First published in the United States by Flatiron Books in 2025

1

Copyright © Caroline Palmer 2025

Caroline Palmer asserts the moral right to be identified as the author of this work in accordance with the Copyright, Designs and Patents Act 1988

A catalogue record for this book is available from the British Library

ISBN 978-0-00-873220-2 (hardback)
ISBN 978-0-00-873221-9 (trade paperback)

Interior art by Olga Zakharova/Shutterstock

This novel is entirely a work of fiction. The names, characters and incidents portrayed in it are the work of the author's imagination. Any resemblance to actual persons, living or dead, events or localities is entirely coincidental.

All rights reserved. No part of this publication may be reproduced, stored in a retrieval system, or transmitted, in any form or by any means, electronic, mechanical, photocopying, recording or otherwise, without the prior permission of the publishers.

Without limiting the exclusive rights of any author, contributor or the publisher of this publication, any unauthorised use of this publication to train generative artificial intelligence (AI) technologies is expressly prohibited. HarperCollins also exercise their rights under Article 4(3) of the Digital Single Market Directive 2019/790 and expressly reserve this publication from the text and data mining exception.

Printed and bound in the UK using 100% renewable electricity at CPI Group (UK) Ltd

MIX
Paper | Supporting responsible forestry
FSC
www.fsc.org
FSC™ C007454

This book is produced from independently certified FSC™ paper to ensure responsible forest management.

For more information visit: www.harpercollins.co.uk/green

TO ESTEP

Thank you for talking to me at the library.

Do you not know that those who run in a race all run, but only one receives the prize?
Run in such a way that you may win.

I CORINTHIANS 9:24

Part One

NEW YORK CITY
2001 to 2003

1

I do not yet exist.

I am not on the masthead and, as such, I do not exist.

When your name is not on the masthead—which is the list, in order of importance, of who works at a magazine printed on the inside of a magazine—the workday begins earlier than it does for the other girls. There is no one to tell you this, of course, no official orientation, but the right kind of girl can sense it, like you can sense the weight in a yellowing sky.

I am the right kind of girl.

On this particular morning, like every morning, I stop to swap my shoes before I enter the office. I perform this humiliating task in a dank little inset I discovered during my walk from the subway on my second day of work, and today, like every day, I sneak a furtive glance down the street to make sure nobody is watching me. Then, I slink backward into the timid autumn shadows.

Next, I lift a pair of black high heels out of my large leather handbag and place them neatly on the sidewalk. I rest one hand on the cool concrete wall to steady myself before I wriggle a foot out of a black flat before (and with an almost astounding lack of physical elegance) I attempt to insert myself into the resistant leather of one of the high heels. Some days, this operation goes off without a hitch. Other days, the heel tips over and I must use my big toe—cursing, desperate, my armpits warming—to set it right again. This morning: I lose my balance, and my foot hits the ground with a gummy thud. I grimace, yanking it back up in the air.

"Fuck," I whisper.

I steal a quick look over my shoulder, only to confirm nobody has caught me out in this most pathetic act, and I try again. This time, I am successful: My damp flesh squeaks into the body of the shoe. Next, with my balance precarious, I lift my other leg into the air before I slide into the other shoe. I quickly bend over and, with two fingers, I hook the back of the flats lying on the ground and toss them inside my handbag. This, of course, is disgusting, but it wasn't until I arrived in New York over the summer that I discovered the actual "use case" for the soft cloth bags that came with a new pair of fancy shoes, which is, apparently, to keep the revolting things one walks through on the streets of New York from sloughing off onto all the items in your handbag.

The heels on these shoes are too high—I bought them off a friend of a friend who had purchased them at a Manolo Blahnik sample sale, only to decide they were too pointy—but I don't care: They make me feel almost obscenely able. *You look very competent*, the girl sagely said, handing her new shoes over for the bargain price of $100. Truth be told, they are basically impossible to walk in, but when I stand utterly motionless, I am nearly six feet tall and a force to behold. When they came into my possession, my very first pair of designer shoes, I bought one of those sponge kits from Duane Reade, and I buff the leather before bed every night to keep them looking new. Occasionally the heels get nicked on one of those metal grates that pock the neverending flesh of the city, but I am diligent about taking them to the shoe repair storefront in my neighborhood because, in this fresh new world, I am learning it is diligence, not cleanliness, that is next to Godliness. Armed with this new knowledge, I now spend half my days placing girls into categories. On the train to work, I search for any small sign or signal of other people's failings. The girls with nicked heels or chipped manicures are lazy. The girls who cross their legs at the knee on the subway are trashy. The girls with big silver hoop earrings or skirts with handkerchief hemlines are tacky. The girls with Kors by Michael Kors bags are cheap.

Today, when I clip unevenly past a still-shuttered corner restaurant en route to my office, there is a paunchy, unshaven man aggressively washing down the mottled sidewalk, water blasting out of a thick black hose. He releases his grip on the handle at the last possible second to let me pass without getting wet. I don't look at him, and he doesn't look at me, but like dancers, we dance. It's strange: I am always unnerved by the odd, oppressive silence of midtown Manhattan in the early hours. Every footstep sounds like it has been amplified, but the actual people passing by me seem strangely insulated from the world, like they are incubating inside their own bubble, readying to be reborn. I look at them with a suspicion veiled as harried indifference, and they do the same to me.

I push through the revolving doors of my office building.

The lobby feels sacred, somehow, glacial and hushed at this hour, as everyone shakes off the missteps of yesterday, shedding their crumpled old skins at the door. I pull a week-old copy of *The New York Observer* from my bag and hold it performatively to my chest as I stride across the marble floor. I ride the elevator alone. The head receptionist for our magazine has yet to arrive, so I pull out my badge and let myself through the oversized glass doors. *I am arriving to work at a magazine in New York City*, I narrate. I am young enough that I still live in the movie of my mind without knowing that we always live in the movie of our minds. I don't yet know that we will never arrive anywhere. I don't know we will always think someone is watching.

I learn all this much later.

I proceed down a carpeted corridor hung with black-and-white archival photographs and land at my shared cubicle space, which includes two large white desks arranged in front of a spotless floor-to-ceiling window. I left my desk a mess on Friday, as usual, and I instantly hate myself for it, my obvious inelegance. There are haphazard piles of unrelated papers, stacks of magazines, coffee cups with congealed milk, and, to my horror, a few stiff, crumpled tissues, one with a light green stain, resting like popcorn across the computer keyboard. I notice the lower drawer of my filing cabinet hangs half open. The coated metal bars that hold up the filing system have long collapsed, and there are a few topless pink Covergirl lipsticks rolling around the bottom. Their noise is muffled by a wadded-up pair of thong underwear. They are beige cotton, which strikes me as somehow worse than if it had been black lace, which is a funny distinction because it's still dirty underwear balled in my office desk drawer. I slam the drawer shut.

I am disgusting.

On my swivel office chair rests a folder overfilled with crumpled receipts; it reminds me of a rising cake. It is light blue because, at the magazine, we do not traffic in manila folders. We do not traffic in standard yellow sticky notes. We do not traffic in gummy, blue ballpoint pens with eraser caps or yellow legal pads. This is because our individual office supplies, like everything else, must reflect who we are and what we stand for in matters of taste. My boss Marie Clarice likes everything to be light blue, and in this light blue folder are her belated September expenses, which she clearly dropped off after I left on Friday night. Marie Clarice (or MC as everyone calls her) is French from France, which means she is thin, blows her nose loudly into cloth handkerchiefs, and is completely and utterly unreasonable. She has prune-hued bags under her eyes that signal a sophistication I have yet to understand, some sort of social cue we don't seem to have in America. She wears a large signet ring on her pinkie finger and the gold bracelets on both of her wrists clatter as she stalks around the office like a slender, angry human wind chime. A slender, angry human wind chime who, as of Friday, knows I keep dirty underwear in my desk drawer.

I walk across the hall to open MC's office to get her ready for the new day. I snap off the overhead lighting left on by the cleaning service and turn on the modern-looking lantern-style lamp she keeps on her desk. I start up her desktop Mac computer, and I drum my finger pads lightly as I listen to it hum to life with a protracted yawn. Next, I head to a small mail room on the far side of our floor to collect her newspapers, magazines, and mail, which I take back to my desk and slice open with a real silver letter opener, a task that never fails to feel impossibly elegant. I organize the mail into piles (press releases, invitations, pitches), and then I quickly page through the newspapers. With my own sticky notes (which are white because any other color felt dangerous), I flag all the stories relevant to her work as the entertainment and culture editor and then I carry everything to her office and arrange it in a perfect fan across her desk. I stand back and survey my work. While it is too soon to pitch any ideas of my own, I do want MC to know I am on top of the news and could, perhaps, one day, be trusted to write captions or a short piece for the front of the book.

The "book" is what we call the magazine.

Lastly, I refill the features department printer and take a small stack of plain paper back to my own desk, where I sit down and open MC's light blue expenses folder.

I begin to tape receipts down on the paper with Scotch tape, one by one, playing a game in my mind to see how many of these small slices of paper I can fit on a single page. In the almost three months I've been employed at the magazine, I have established an impressive system. The long restaurant receipts take center billing, flanked by taxi receipts along the edges, which I affix like fringe on a homemade pillow. The ones from the office cafeteria are uniform in size so they receive pages of their own; you can fit nine to a page if you snip the bottom off with scissors. Some receipts have identifying details, but for the blank ones, I usually consult the calendar to see what MC did that day. If there is no notation, I ask things like: *Who did you go to Babbo with last Thursday? Was this the cab home from that midday movie screening?* If no one remembers, which is most often the case, I make something up. It's easy enough when nobody checks the veracity of these expense reports. In fact, I feel almost heroic in my thoroughness. After all, I am new and my time on the field, thus far, has been limited, so I must shine where I can. As I sort through the receipts, smoothing them into neat piles, I quickly calculate that MC's taxi receipts have almost tripled since August. I mean, not that I blame her. Personally speaking, the fact that I, myself, have already devised and mentally executed twenty ways to blow up the New York City subway system does not inspire me to have much confidence in any form of public transportation. But the truth is I suspect no one feels safe anywhere. Not yet. That said, we still ride in crowded elevators, and dine in subterranean restaurants. We dance in overflowing nightclubs and walk arm in arm through Grand Central Station at rush hour. As we continue to move through our lives, we never break pace, even as we pass by familiar altars: chain-link fences puckered with rotting paper flyers of the missing, dried carcasses of grocery store flowers, and rows of abandoned votive candles, their waxy insides overrun with old rainwater from another time. To me, the entire city behaves as if someone dropped dead at a dinner party and the hostess has put on a stiff smile that makes it clear we had better play through. For love of country. For solidarity. For something.

You'll want to expense a lot early. This was the first piece of advice from my new cubicle mate, Davis Lawrence. At the time, she was leaning over my shoulder, showing me how to use the entry system for expenses on the computer. She smelled like Ivory soap. Or my memory of Ivory soap.

Establish a high baseline so, after a while, you start to look frugal when you have a slow month. But not too much because they are watching you. Basically, around month two, start tacking on your dry cleaning and shoe repair and blow-outs. Lunch with friends, that kind of thing. If you make it to the masthead, you've made it for at least a year. You're on the team, so to speak.

Davis Lawrence was born on the team. She graduated from Princeton two years ago and, after a brief stint working for a fashion designer, she landed without effort at the magazine, like the final piece in a toddler's puzzle. She didn't send in her résumé; she didn't complete the edit test or endure an interview. Her mother is from an old New York family, a famous socialite turned Broadway actress turned television actress, a series of details that everyone knows, but no one talks about, and Davis is, in the simplest of terms, rich, smart, and beautiful. She dresses like an early '90s J. Crew model, her clean-limbed body accepting an almost impossible amount of clothing without adding a hint of bulk. Her hair—which she wears both pin-straight and gently wavy, depending on the day—is long, thick, and a glinting golden blond. Her nails are short, round, and buffed to a seashell shine. She has wonderful lips. She wears one prominent piece of jewelry that was clearly passed down by some equally prominent ancestor. She takes an excellent photograph. She has dinner with the right people. She knows how to handle a lobster. She was built to be admired; she was bred to be a winner. Sometimes, I will observe her while I am buying my lunch in the crowded office cafeteria. Most days, she sits at a table with a few other girls from the magazine, and I will linger as I get my napkins or lemon wedges. I am too afraid to sit down in the cafeteria, its tables full of well-known editors and other important people I have yet to recognize, but I want to buy myself a few moments to imagine what it must be like to be a part of her circle. Or, frankly, of *any* circle. I am still floating around the edges, both seen and unseen. The magazine, you see, is staffed by two kinds of people, known as Workhorses and Show Horses, and Davis Lawrence is undeniably a Show Horse—the true blue-ribbon kind—while I learned just last week that Bal Harbor and Bar Harbor are, in fact, two different towns.

As the nine o'clock hour rolls past, I listen to the wall clock ticking and the soft hum of the various machines warming up around me. In the distance, a few phones start to ring, and MC's expenses are finished and placed neatly to my right. With nothing else to do until people start to arrive around ten, I spin in my chair to look out the window. The light is bright and unremarkable by this hour and, thanks to a recently demolished building, I can see straight through to the next street, where the bulbed edge of a Broadway marquee blinks back at me. It's a nice enough view, here at the center of the world, but mostly I am just grateful my windows don't face south.

Another hour rolls by, and I remain idle, although anxiously so. This feeling of uneasiness isn't special. It is standard and, quite possibly, by design. You see, at the magazine, there are so many assistants that we are often in search of more to do, some additional way to establish our value. We are always eagerly turning over rocks, dutifullly searching for some unknown treasure.

"Good morning, sunshine."

This is the magical voice of Davis Lawrence. I turn around to see her drop a tiny black satchel bag on her spotless desk. She is wearing a pair of three-inch high heels, and her sumptuous, weighted wool coat is open, creating an impeccable, somewhat triangular volume.

I am completely obsessed with her.

"You're here early," I say.

"Remember, no staples," she says, pointing to my receipts. "We are a paperclip people."

She takes off her coat and hangs it up on a hanger, which I somehow never remember to do, and shakes out her long, obscene hair, which today looks air-dried after an ocean swim. Like most girls at the magazine, the only makeup she wears to the office is a lipstick bold enough to contrast her peachy-pale skin.

"Also, I take offense," Davis continues. "Remember that being too early means you had nothing interesting to do last night."

"Guilty as charged. I went to the gym," I say, getting up casually to hang up my coat, as if I, too, have just walked into the office and am not a slovenly pig with poor breeding. "So, did you have nothing interesting to do last night?"

"Depends on how you define *interesting*," she replies with a wry smirk.

I open my mouth to say more (probably something inappropriately sexual in nature because I've decided my best chance to worm my way into Davis's heart is to make her laugh, and with great regularity) but, thankfully, I catch MC out of the corner of my eye. She approaches our desks looking even more weary than usual.

"Good morning," I say, sitting back down. "I didn't see you come in. I was just working on your expenses."

I tap the light blue folder competently and fold my hands.

"Thanks," she says dully. "I have a few more receipts in my bag. I finally went to Danube on Saturday."

"How was it?"

"Eh." She shrugs. "How was your weekend?"

We both know this is not a question, but we also both know I should endeavor to answer.

"Oh, it was lovely. I decided . . ."

"I need you to FedEx this for me," she interrupts, holding out a medium-sized black velvet jewelry box affixed with a light blue sticky note.

"Not a problem," I say efficiently. I glance at the note. "Is this the address?"

"Yes," she says. "It's my engagement ring."

I don't look up. As the box grows slowly warm in my hand, I understand I have just stumbled into dangerous territory. I have quickly come to understand that the assistant/editor relationship is, on a good day, a peculiar one. You pick up their antidepressants, read all their personal and work emails, and slide their office doors closed with maternal affection when they are sobbing on the phone about their fertility. At the same time, however, you must *also* pretend they are strangers to you. Fascinating strangers. Fascinating strangers you cannot believe walk among mere mortals like yourself. Strangers you aspire to become one day. They need this kind of assurance, and your ability to provide it to them with the right combination of competence and awe is, in and of itself, an entirely marketable skill. As such, I decide to treat this as a totally standard request from my boss.

"Okay," I reply. "Do you want to include a note?"

"Well, I called the wedding off before he flew back to Miami yesterday, so I think he will get it."

"Okay."

She looks at me for a beat. Her narrow face is a disconcerting mix of gratitude for my discretion and petulance that she can't throw something at my head like an angry child. Then, without comment, she turns and walks back to her office.

I sit for a second, stunned.

"Get the insurance," Davis says flatly without turning around, her elegant fingers moving quickly across the keyboard in front of her computer.

2

The company mail room is located in the basement of our building, and it looks like what I imagine to be the hull of a transatlantic steamship. It's gray and cavernous, with pipes snaking across the ceiling like an answerless riddle, and it smells both overwhelming and cheap, like boat gas and floral perfume. However, despite the many unsavory aspects, the mail room also gives off the magical energy of a Broadway musical during the big set change; I watch in fascination as everything—racks of clothes, floral arrangements, cases of wine, oversized black trunks—moves around me in the bewildering, yet wonderfully efficient, choreography of unyielding success. I approach the shipping window and set down the black box. A woman wearing an orange vest over her normal clothes raises her eyes at me wordlessly.

"Good morning," I say very politely, pulling a triplicate form out of the cardboard box sitting in front of her. "I'm going to need to get the insurance."

I fill out the form neatly, making sure my writing impresses all three pages before I slide it over with a bright smile that she does not return.

"What's your name?" she asks annoyed, looking down at my writing. "Claw? Clo . . . Clo Do?"

"Oh, sorry. It's Clodagh. It's pronounced *Clo-dah. Clo-dah* Harmon," I say. "It's Irish. I mean, technically. My mom is Irish."

The woman says nothing, and I feel a queasy imbalance, like I need to fill the air.

"Just my mom. Is Irish, I mean," I continue. "Not my dad. He's

American. From Philadelphia. So not too far. From New York, I mean. Not too far from New York."

She finishes filling out the form, and hands me the yellow receipt. I watch uneasily as she drops the velvet box inside a padded envelope and seals it.

"So, I hate to be a pain, but maybe we should put it in a proper box?" I suggest. "With, like, that Bubble Wrap?" I point to a shelf of packing supplies behind her.

The woman looks like she might kill me.

"Sorry." I lower my voice to a conspiratorial whisper in an attempt to entice her into compliance with a tantalizing secret. "It's just that it's a *gigantic* diamond engagement ring. Like giant. The diamond is legitimately the size of my thumbnail."

I hold up my thumb to provide a visual as if she is not in possession of two perfectly functional thumbs of her own, but she just glares at me. I start to wonder if maybe she doesn't speak English, but I am pretty sure she just hates dealing with people like me all day. I don't like her either because for some reason she is allowed to be bad at her job, and I am supposed to feel guilty for asking her to do the one idiotic thing for which she is paid.

"You know what? You *obviously* know what you're doing," I say finally, and I let my voice lilt with a cheerful menace. "I mean, we would *both* have hell to pay if an engagement ring of this value got lost."

"It has tracking," she answers slowly, looking at my face closely for the first time. She knows what I know, which is that only one of us will have that hell to pay if an engagement ring of this value gets lost, and it won't be me. She takes the ring out of the envelope and places it inside a box. Satisfied, I give her a tight, toothless smile, and turn back to the elevators. As I walk away, I allow myself to luxuriate in the feeling of her fury—a fury fueled by her too familiar lack of recourse—searing a neat hole in my back.

Fuck her.

When I return to the lobby on my floor, I see the graying head of our receptionist, Rita, which barely clears the desk. I am about to dole out a hearty and profoundly inauthentic morning greeting, as one does, when I see Davis waiting by the glass doors. She motions at me frantically, and I walk toward her quickly, ecstatic to be needed by her in some capacity.

"Where have you been?" she hisses.

"The mail room? In the basement? With a, like, fifty-carat diamond ring having a full-blown anxiety attack?" I say. "Davis, you saw me leave five minutes ago?"

"Holy. Fucking. Shit."

"What?" My eyes dart around, and it takes my brain a long second to understand that I am unconsciously searching for the fire exit.

"No. Not that," she says in a dismissive tone. "Come with me."

She grabs my elbow and spins me around with a false smile suddenly stitched across her perfect face. My heart beats wildly as she hustles me down the hallway and pulls me into the ladies' bathroom. She quickly marches the length of the stalls and flips her blond head upside down to confirm they are all empty.

Then, Davis starts to speak to me conspiratorially:

"MC just quit. Or got fired. It's hard to say," she begins. She leans her hip against the vanity. "She went to L.K.'s office, she came out crying, and then she got her bag and left. She didn't even take anything out of her office. I just looked."

It's worse than I thought.

"Oh my god," I exclaim. "Am I going to get fired?"

"No."

"Oh god. I *am* going to get fired," I say, my voice raising. "You told me that new editors always bring in new assistants."

"Watch your volume," she says sternly. "You will be fine."

"How do you know I will be fine?" I whisper, but now through gritted teeth.

"For starters, there is a hiring freeze because, you know, *everything.*" She gestures to the sky with both hands which is now the universal sign language for planes flying into skyscrapers.

"So you are saying I won't be fired *for a few weeks?*" I say sarcastically. "Wonderful."

Here, Davis looks at me incredulously, like I am missing the greater point of her story, and I oblige her by shutting my mouth and looking down at the floor.

"You know she is, like, over forty," she says before adding: "It's like the Ghost of Christmas Future."

"Forty-two," I say. "I saw her passport when I booked that flight to London."

"That's terrifying," Davis continues. "Can you imagine? What is she going to do? It's not like she has a husband or children or anything. Or a book deal."

"So you can just, like, *get fired*?" I ask.

Davis nods, and we stand together in a thoughtful silence.

"I think I am going to take the flowers from her office," Davis says finally with a little clap. "They're from Miho."

I hold up the yellow receipt from the mail room.

"Should I messenger the receipt to her apartment?" I ask before adding: "I got the insurance."

Davis shrugs and takes a quick look at herself in the mirror before she walks out of the bathroom. I follow wordlessly behind, only to feel my heart pitch when she takes the dreaded shortcut through the fashion department. The hallway is banked on both sides with metal racks, which are swollen with clothes. We must turn sideways to fit down the narrow passage as all manner of silks and tulles and taffetas brushes against our bodies. While Davis moves with great confidence, I feel like I'm trespassing and that—at any moment—someone is going to demand to see my badge. This is the quadrant of our floor where the most famous editors work, the kind of people you hear coming long before you see them, thanks to things like velvet capes and layered gold chain-link necklaces. Now, while a good portion of the magazine's editors are elegant and well-mannered, there are others who snort cocaine and throw temper tantrums over things like using the wrong kind of pen in their line of sight. My friends with corporate jobs find this behavior horrifying, but they are wrong. It is exhilarating, albeit often in a patently scary way, to be a bit player in such an unpredictable cast of characters. While some people worship singers or actresses, I have always been far more fascinated by the kind of people who walk these hallways. When we finally make it back alive to the editorial side of the office, Davis strides into MC's office and hoists up the large flower arrangement that sits on her desk.

"What if she comes back for those?" I ask nervously.

Davis checks the card on the flower arrangement and looks up at me: "She won't," she replies.

There is a rap on the door.

We turn around to see Elinor, who is one of our fellow assistants. She leans on the doorjamb but does not look up; her eyes are fixed on the thick manuscript that rests heavily on her upturned palm. In her other hand, she twirls a gold pen. Elinor is the assistant to our executive editor, L.K. Smith, and she is best described as a super bored teenager. Today, she is wearing a miniskirt and motorcycle boots, and her black eye makeup is, as it always is, adroitly smudged. When I see her arrive each morning, I like to imagine she got blazingly drunk at a fabulous party, jumped into the pool, and then passed out, face down, on a pile of silk pillows only to be awoken in the morning by a servant as they placed a clattering coffee service tray on her little lap.

"L.K. wants to see you," she says.

"Me?"

"Yes."

I look to Davis for emotional support.

"Lip gloss," she says.

3

L.K. Smith is the second-in-command at the magazine, a role she has held for twenty-five years, during which time no one has figured out for what the L or the K in her name stand for, or even in what city or town she grew up. The prevailing rumor is, generations ago, the Smith family sailed to America on the *Mayflower* (or some other *Mayflower*-adjacent ship) and they were one of the hearty few who survived that first cold and possibly cannibalistic winter in a strange and unforgiving new world. It adds up: L.K. Smith is one tough broad. She oversees the major staffing, writing, and business decisions on the editorial side of the magazine, and she controls all access to our editor-in-chief. In my mind, she functions as a super classy Miss Hannigan. She has a frighteningly keen eye and exactly zero tolerance for even the lightest suggestion of bullshit. She spends her days walking the halls and appraising us girls in her unending effort to preserve and protect the throne. We fear her because she is quick to prune, selectively removing anything or anyone that might be inhibiting our growth, but we also worship her because one good word from L.K. Smith to the powers that be can make or break any girl in this town.

Trust me. It has happened before.

When I arrive at her office door, L.K. sits at her computer with her back to me. She has blond chin-length hair and she generally wears it blown out in a bob or smoothed back in a large gold clip. She is tall and poised with polished shoes and facial features so utterly perfect they look like they were hand selected out of a bin. Elinor has not returned to her post, and because I am petrified to announce my arrival, L.K. remains entirely unaware of my presence for a good long while. I let my eyes drift around her corner office, which is awash with light, even on the dreariest of days. She has a pristine white couch, and her shelves are lined with books and personal photographs, all of which are framed in tarnished sterling because, as it turns out, if you're really "old money"—as we all assume L.K. Smith to be—you don't bother with polishing the silver.

Finally, I fake a delicate cough.

"Ah, Clo," she says without turning around. "Thank you for coming down."

She has a clipped crispness in her voice that I sometimes mistake for an accent; on my first week I asked Davis if she was South African.

"Of course," I respond as I clasp my hands below my waist in a posture of ready servitude.

She turns to regard me.

"You may not have heard, but Marie Clarice will no longer be with us," she begins.

For background, L.K. likes to state facts as questions because she knows better than anyone how quickly gossip travels her hallways. As such, she wants to ensure she isn't suffering any fools so I nod because I understand that to look *surprised* by this information, information we *both* know I am already in possession of, would be a catastrophic mistake.

"She wasn't a good fit," she continues.

At this truly dire pronouncement ("not a good fit" is the worst of the bunch while "pursue other opportunities" comes in at a close but deeply distant second) she removes her thick-framed black reading glasses and holds them loosely in her hand.

I stand silent and wait for my orders.

"I need you to keep things organized until we can get the new senior editor in place. You know how particular everyone is about the culture pages." Here, she gesticulates gracefully toward the ceiling with her glasses because naturally, our boss, the editor-in-chief, resides on a plane higher than mere mortals.

"Of course, L.K," I respond with competence. "That is absolutely not a problem."

"Thank you," she says. "It shouldn't be very long. We have someone in mind, but sometimes these things can take longer than I would like."

"Of course," I say.

Here, she vaguely looks me up and down, and while I can sense she feels some indistinct disappointment, she makes no further comment; she just circles back to her computer. She starts typing but then stops. She knows I am still lurking in her doorway.

"Is there anything else?" she asks.

"No, nothing," I say, but too quickly, unsure if I am expected to exhibit remorse for the loss of my boss as a show of loyalty to the magazine. "I *do* feel badly about MC, though."

L.K. slaps her hands flat on the desk in a manner that is either exasperated or angry—I can't tell—before she spins herself back around to look directly at me. She is frowning.

"Clodagh, you cannot feel *badly*"—here she downright hollers this at me; there really isn't another word for it—"You can only feel *bad*."

"Right," I say reflexively, but without having any idea why. "Bad. I feel bad."

"Well, my dear," she says. "You should with that horrendous grammar."

As I slink, hot with humiliation, out of L.K.'s office, I see that Elinor has returned to her desk. She pretends to write on a pad of paper, but she has arranged her tiny body in such a manner that I can see her eyebrows are ever so slightly lifted toward the heavens. Maybe it doesn't sound like much, but it's getting the job done: I feel wretched.

This—the occasional yet humiliating social punishment doled out by a slightly more senior peer—is extremely effective training for new assistants. It all but ensures my future cooperative behavior. I will take my lumps, of course, because I am inexperienced, and I know it's only a matter of time (if I play my cards right) until I'm called upon to discipline others in the same wonderfully subversive manner. For now, however, I am only a student, and it's vital to my future success that I make it clear my spirit can be broken. You see, the lessons for a new hire at the assistant level at the magazine are piled on fast and thick, and it is critical one establishes themselves a ready learner.

You do not complain. You do not explain. You don't point out when you are treated unfairly. You do not ask your superior to repeat the garbled name of the person she wants you to telephone. You don't chew gum. You don't eat hot sandwiches. You don't wear flats. You don't slouch. You don't carry around a plastic water bottle. You don't show cleavage. Ideally, you are not in possession of cleavage. You don't wear pantyhose. You don't bring in "leftovers" for lunch. You don't introduce yourself first. You don't interrupt. You don't offer your opinion. If asked, you never took Accutane nor have you resided in a home with aluminum siding. Furthermore, you don't let anyone know you were born with curly hair, an unmarried mother, or a weight problem. You immediately learn to pronounce the following: *trompe l'oeil*, *atelier*, *décolletage*, *La Grenouille*, and *minaudière*. You silently puzzle out what the actual *fuck* makes something a d'Orsay heel and the first (and only) time you refer to a garment as having an empire waist, you will receive a much-deserved public shaming ("it's *ahm-peer*") from which it will take you weeks to sufficiently recover. When introduced socially, you don't say "nice to meet you" but rather you say "nice to *see* you" because it's how you indicate that, among a certain class, *we are all friends here*. You buy monogrammed stationery so thick you could cut cocaine with it. You develop an entirely unreadable signature. You call your underwear "underpinnings," you call your ass your "backside," and you add an additional syllable to the word *jewelry*. You are not political. You don't "take vacations" because that phrase conjures up pedestrian images of cruise ships to Disney World and undulating plastic glasses brimming with piña coladas. No, my dear, you go "on holiday." And if you aren't in Telluride or your family home in Palm Beach, you had better be in Europe, and by Europe we mean France.

You do not ask your boss for career development. You do not ask for a raise. You do not ask for a promotion. In the world of magazines, there are only two grades: A or F, and your annual performance review, such as it is, is simply *not getting fired*. If you fail in one of the dizzying myriad of ways it is possible to fail, there are no warnings. There are no opportunities to redeem yourself, no helpful conversations with your "HR representative" on ways to improve your performance. You are simply shown the door, and the person you sacrificed so much to become will never be heard from again.

If they want you to cut your hair, you cut your hair. If they want you to lose weight, you lose weight. If they want a longer hemline because your legs are the wrong shape, you drop the hemline. Of course, no one gives you these instructions directly because being direct is *vulgar*. We are never vulgar. In most cases, you just absorb information like a sidelined houseplant that, when given even the slightest sip of water, feeds off the available nutrients with the wild-eyed panic of a shipwreck survivor. Or, maybe, someone at your own level is dispatched to say something in a friendly, offhanded manner, but if you are the right kind of girl, the message is clear.

Not everyone is the right kind of girl, of course. The assistants who are floundering or have a do-gooder streak or an outsized notion of their creative talents will talk about taking the LSAT or getting their social work degree, or—god forbid—their MFA in some Western town because, you know, fashion is so just so *banal*, or so *empty*, or so *discriminatory*. In your low moments, you will root for them. You will understand what they are trying to project. They want to believe this magazine, and by extension this lowly job answering phones and talking academically about table settings or the vintage of a particular pair of blue jeans, is just an off-brand pit stop on their way to greater, more meaningful things. At times, you will wonder if there isn't something special about you, too. You'll research the Peace Corps. You'll *almost* book a spot in a surf camp in Costa Rica. You'll buy a breathtakingly expensive hardcover book about constitutional law at the Union Square Barnes & Noble only to use it as a coaster for the rotating cast of Diet Coke cans and seashells full of cigarette butts that litter your studio apartment. You'll briefly rustle up an unsuitable long-distance boyfriend and talk about moving to his newly hip, *totally not New York town* that has good hikes and *great* coffee. You watch some weird art films alone at the Angelica and romanticize the way the subway thunders under your feet. You'll spend hungover Sunday afternoons shooting profoundly moody black-and-white photographs of the West Fourth Street subway station, clutching the manual camera you bought from a silent Hasidic guy at the B&H on Ninth Avenue with a coupon you clipped out of the newspaper. But you always come back to the magazine. For reasons that can be hard to articulate, the magazine is your home. Maybe this is because, deep down, you can't believe a girl like you made it this far in the first place. Or maybe you have accepted a truth that other girls don't want to face: That, at this age and in this industry, all your value is derived solely from your associations. You are smart enough to know you have no merit on your own, you have not had enough time to build up any brand equity on which you could plausibly trade. There is no reward for playing by your own rules because, to win, one must play the game how it was meant to be played.

What it means to win is somewhat unclear.

What is certain? You do not want to lose.

Davis is ravenous for the gossip by the time I return to my cluttered desk. She, quite literally, bounces on her toes like she's waiting to receive an invisible tennis serve, and I find myself delighted, as ever, to have her full attention.

"So? Did she quit? Was she fired?" she whispers, her blue eyes bright.

"Unclear," I respond as I sit down. As I rub my eyes, I realize I am drained by all the drama in my brief morning. "But she is definitely gone."

"Wow."

"I know."

I pick up a pen and twirl it between my fingers.

"She said she would take me to that benefit at the public library in a few weeks, which would have been good," I say finally. "But whatever."

I hope I sound indifferent to this change in plans, but the truth is that I had been riddled with excitement about attending my first black-tie benefit in New York, even if MC made it clear my primary role in the proceedings would be that of her silent, dumpy handmaiden.

"You should just go," Davis says with a shrug.

"Really?" I ask.

"Yes. Use her invitation."

"Really?"

"Really," she says with a tiny shrug. "You work here. You can do anything you want."

I consider this for a moment.

"I don't know if my ego can handle finding a dress," I joke.

"Well, suck it up," Davis says. "There will be good people to meet. You can *network*."

Here, she uses air quotes around the word *network*, but this is mostly because Davis Lawrence has never had to network a day in her life, and she seems to find my plight charming. Since I started at the magazine, she has taken me under her wing on occasion—offering me advice or introducing me to someone in another department—and although I don't understand her motivation, it is also one I have no intention of questioning.

I am desperate for allies.

"Oh, I almost forgot to tell you," I say suddenly, straightening up.

"What?"

"I saw Oliver Barringer on the subway Friday night. I was—wait for it—reading an *Us Weekly*."

"Oh no," she gasps, covering her mouth with both hands. "Noooooo."

Oliver Barringer is a journalist—not just an assistant like us—and he is employed by another more literary magazine at our company. In fairness, he's a decent writer, but he is equally renowned for sleeping with all the new hires in the office. Not that they aren't trying to get his attention, of course, because to be having sex with someone like Oliver Barringer opens far more professional doors than to be someone wholly unknown by a man like Oliver Barringer. In my recently formed opinion, to have the dexterity to straddle an identity somewhere between these two poles is the most powerful position for a woman in our industry. In fairness, it is also the most arduous to attain.

"Oh yes, my friend," I continue as I slip into the familiar role of self-deprecating storyteller in, yet again, another bid to elicit some laughs. "He, of course, was reading a paperback by someone named Edward Said, who I have never heard of."

"*Say-eed*," Davis corrects.

"What?"

"His last name is pronounced *Say-eed*," she explains. "He went to Princeton."

"Right," I reply with a light roll of my eyes since sarcasm is, quite literally, the only way I know how to manage the terrible, near constant reminder that I did not, in any capacity, attend Princeton.

Everyone at my office seems to have gone to Princeton.

Davis waits.

"Anyway, it wasn't even like he was reading it," I continue. "He was like, holding it? There was sort of a theatrical element to it. *Oh, hello. I live in Brooklyn. Oh, hello. I have glasses and am deeply thoughtful. I am a thoughtful, literary journalist. I read William SAY-EED on Friday nights.*"

"Edward," Davis corrects.

Here, I hear L.K. Smith's disappointed voice in my head.

"Edward," I say out loud. "I feel *bad* about *Edward Say-eed*. I feel *bad* about *Edward Say-eed*. I feel bad about *Edward Say-eed*."

Davis looks confused by my recitation but not interested enough to probe.

"So what did you talk about?" she asks. "He is *such* a dick."

"Talk about? He has no clue who I am," I say. This comment makes Davis wrinkle her forehead almost imperceptibly, like she is trying to recall a time where someone didn't know who she was but is coming up short.

"I got off at York Street hoping he hadn't spotted me," I say. "I walked the rest of the way home in a deep, *deep* shame spiral."

Davis looks at me kindly, her beautiful little head lilting lightly to the side.

"Is York Street in Brooklyn?"

4

At the end of the week—after the senior editors and stylists head out to their afternoon appointments—Davis marches me down to the fashion department like a teenager still being taken to the pediatrician by her mother. As I am not a fashion assistant, I feel immediately conspicuous, like I took a wrong turn into the cheerleader's locker room. We pass through more racks of clothes before we stop at the desk of two girls, one blond and one brunette. It is immediately clear to me that the brunette is in charge. I think it's her posture, or maybe it's the magnificent girth of the all-white, "tightly packed" garden rose arrangement (still wrapped up in the delivery cellophane) resting at her elbow.

"Hi, girls," Davis says casually before she starts to parse through a rack of clothes pushed up against the wall. She pulls out a blouse and shows it to them. "This is pretty."

"I know," the brunette sighs. "They make it in a beautiful dark olive, but it's kind of jumpsuit. But without being a 'jumpsuit' jumpsuit."

"That's genius," Davis enthuses. She is fluent in fashion's shared language of superlative nothings, a language I have yet to master. I am still trying to find a way to slide the line "You know I'd die for you, right?" into a serious work conversation. During my first week at the magazine, I heard one girl say this to another girl after she successfully changed the toner on a fax machine.

"Clo needs a dress for the library benefit in November," Davis continues. "Can we call some in?"

The ease in which she makes this request astounds me. It's like people who are unapologetic when dressing down their cleaning ladies for some minor failure. I still clean in advance of my once-a-month cleaning lady's arrival. The reason is twofold: One, I don't want her to think I am a lazy, spoiled brat, which is how I was taught to feel about having a cleaning lady, and two, I have been known to leave things like half-eaten yogurts, period underwear, and saliva-encrusted mouthguards under the sheets on my bed.

"Cocktail or evening?" the blonde asks.

"Evening," Davis says.

Both girls—and they are always called girls here, never women—fix their attention on my body and, although they don't touch me or spin me around, I feel they are providing me with an expert appraisal. They make faces like they *really like* what they see, which makes me feel shyly happy. I feel like I am in good hands, and I start to understand why this—whatever it is they are technically doing—is considered a very real skill.

"I don't think we have anything *here*," the blonde says finally. She turns to the brunette.

"Polly. Honey. I think we will need to call somewhere that does *sizes*," she says delicately. "Maybe Oscar or Carolina. I think they will have something from last year."

At this moment, Polly turns around and picks up her desk phone. She doesn't put it on her to-do list; she doesn't say she will do it later. Within seconds, she is speaking warmly into the receiver, although I cannot hear what, precisely, is being said.

"We will call you when we have things to try on," the blonde says, turning back to me with a genuine smile.

"Thanks, girls," Davis says. "Love you."

I suddenly realize I have not uttered a peep during this entire transaction, and somehow, I cannot remain silent. I feel like I can't walk away without letting them know that I am *in on the joke*, that I know they are doing me an *enormous, possibly impossible favor* because I have a *terrible body*, and I am an *embarrassing person*.

"Good luck! I know it's a challenge," I quip, doing some weird finger salute against my forehead and stomping.

These girls are very well trained, however; they do not break character.

"You'll look *amazing*," the blonde says reassuringly, which is almost—no, definitely—worse. I feel like a fat child.

Here, Davis takes my elbow and leads me away and, although I could be mistaken, I think I catch her toss an apologetic smile into our dim wake.

After Davis leaves the office that night for "a dinner" (as we call them because somehow adding the article elevates the whole event), I stay behind to fake skim a copy of *The Economist* before I force myself to read another page of that grammar book *Strunk and White*, a copy of which was left on my desk by whomever sat here before me. Of course, I can't absorb anything out of context—I just sit wielding a freshly sharpened pencil—but this charade feels like penance for my repeated grammatical missteps. In the unknown distance, I hear the yowl of an ambulance siren, which is one of the new sounds in my life (sirens don't yowl in suburbia) that makes me instantly despair. I look out the office windows into the blackness of the night. This is the most lonesome hour for me, the time of day I am reminded of how small I am against the complexity and enormity of the world outside. This is when I allow a profound homesickness to fill up my body, and when I must question if I made the right decision by moving to New York. It is also when I agonize over the logistical impossibility of a proper city balancing on such a little strip of land: Can it really be safe to drink the tap water? I mean, the 200-year-old pipes must be full of rust and cancer-causing chemicals by now, right? I'm no dummy: I watched *Erin Brockovich*. I also wonder where stuff really goes when I flush the toilet. I think about air quality and earthquakes and tsunamis. I think about subway bombs, low-flying planes, and I even trot out some old tropes to worry about, like dying alone in a studio apartment full of indifferent cats. I decide that if I could just make some real friends or, even better, borrow the glamorous lot amassed by Davis Lawrence, I would cease to feel so unmoored. As it is, New York still feels like an extremely long layover in a nice airport. I am always half listening for someone to announce my departure gate over the loudspeaker.

I pick up the receiver of my desk phone and punch in the number to my parents' house. I want to be soothed by familiar voices, but after ten rings, nobody answers, and I find myself feeling unchaperoned in a most dangerous place. I put down the receiver, and I promise myself that I won't live here too long. I won't allow myself to become vulnerable to Manhattan's ruinous charms. I will find my way home one day, wholly intact.

My desk phone rings, and I startle: It's Polly. She wants me to come to the fashion closet. I look up at the wall: It's almost eight o'clock.

I weave down the darkened halls, which smell distinctly of stale cigarettes even though we are not supposed to smoke in the office anymore, per a light directive from the building manager that dissuaded exactly nobody from smoking in the office. While not everyone smokes, it is not uncommon to see a stylist in the hallway, parsing through a rack of clothes with a Gauloises perched between her lips. Or catch the bookings editor offering up a cigarette to a famous model who has come to the office for a fitting. You see, most of the more senior editors began their careers in magazines in the early 1990s, a time when smoking was still wonderfully cinematic, and did not definitively kill you. I am fascinated by these girls. They are uniformly tall, rangy, and sometimes English, with doe eyes and razor-straight hair. They arrive to the office late every morning wearing nipped, sumptuous clothes that look perfectly starched, and if you can get close enough, you will find they smell incredible, like they are brimming with secrets from the night before. While these girls are less than a decade older than me, I feel like they all hail from some magnificent planet. They are mysterious and everywhere, like a happy pack of barefaced boarding school girls, roaming a world with no limits.

I cannot imagine what it must feel like to be them.

Most of the desks are dark at this hour, but I notice that one of the fashion editors has left her door half open. I peek through the little gap, which feels indecent and thrilling, like rifling through someone's lingerie drawer. There is a wide, white desk on which a vase of wilted fuchsia peonies sits next to an open hardcover planner and an ashtray. The walls are decorated with an artful collage of signed art and framed photographs and there is a large white bulletin board pinned with dozens of handwritten notes from all the celebrities and models with whom this particular editor has worked. Rounding out the space is an assemblage of strange artifacts (a piece of a saxophone, a mannequin in a deconstructed blazer, an enormous metal film canister), and I reckon this display is all part of a vigorous intellectual and social life that I can still only imagine. There is also a pile of high-heeled shoes—at least a dozen pairs—crumbled haphazardly against the wall.

I hear a vacuum in the distance, which is another one of my sad sounds, and I pull my head back to discover that Polly is watching me snoop. She stands by the door next to the fashion closet, and her expression indicates she was dispatched by her brunette boss to take care of this nightmare. She's brought along another blonde—a lanky French girl with blunt bangs named Capucine—for what I imagine is moral support. Capucine is wearing skintight leather pants, unlaced stiletto black boots, and an emerald green sequined blazer. It looks like she hasn't washed her hair in weeks, and her lashes are thick with lazy mascara. Otherwise, her beautiful face is completely without makeup.

"Okay," Polly says, getting right down to business. She leads me into the closet, which is a small, surprisingly inelegant room full of clothes, disorganized wall units of shoes, and handbags piled on tabletops. I see a rolling rack against the gray wall. There is a piece of paper hanging off it with my name written down in capital letters.

"Try this one first," Polly instructs as she unhooks a black dress from a hanger and passes it to me. I stand there looking around for somewhere private to undress, maybe a curtained-off area or a large chair I can crouch behind.

"So . . ." I start.

"Just here is fine," Polly says reassuringly. I am not reassured. I wonder if this is a good time to tell my new friend Polly that I didn't put underwear on under my tights this morning because it feels bulky. I realize I have no idea if people, in general society, wear underwear with tights. I have kind of always assumed that white crotch pad is supposed to take the place of underwear, but I don't really want to find out I am wrong today.

"Just here is fine," she repeats.

I reach behind my back to unzip my plum-colored shift, taking extra care to cover the tag with my hand because it's from the house line at Macy's. I take the black dress from Polly—it weighs at least ten pounds—and pull its leaden form against my chest like a bashful child. I drop the flimsy work number, which puddles around my feet, and step carefully into the dress. It makes it up to my mid-thigh before I hear the zipper start to rip away from the fabric.

"Stop," Polly says. "That's not going to work."

Thanks, Polly.

"It's not you," she says warmly. "Valentino samples are just *really tiny*. Also, take your bra off."

I self-consciously remove my bra and fold my arms across my heavy breasts, ineptly trying to prevent one of my enormous areolas from tumbling into view. I can feel goosebumps sprouting on my legs and arms.

We try a few more dresses and, honestly, the whole process feels like trying to stuff a redwood tree into a toddler's one-piece snowsuit. I have entered a whole new realm of "clothes not fitting" and public nudity and all I can do is profusely apologize for being five feet, ten inches tall and 150 pounds with, as they delicately put it, "a little to deal with on top." Finally, they produce another Oscar de la Renta, this one navy blue, and we get it over my hips and up to my chest.

"This will work," Polly says turning to Capucine, who is slouched fantastically against a table, watching the process with a disinterest that is somehow both bemused and disgusted. "Cap, can you go get Margot from accessories? I think she's still here."

While waiting for "Cap" to produce "Margot from accessories," Polly gently turns me around.

"Put your body up against the wall," she instructs, and I dutifully comply. "Okay. Now, I want you to try *as hard as you can* to touch your elbows together behind your back."

I try as hard as I can to touch my elbows together behind my back.

"Good," Polly cheers. "Now, I want you to *try harder.*"

At this point, Capucine has returned with Margot who, to my surprise, is a Black woman about my age. How have I never seen her before? Is she new? She says hello in a British accent, and I flash her a humiliated smile because, the fact they had to call in reinforcements to zip my party dress is, well, humiliating. I do the thing with my elbows again, only this time I am aided by Polly who cups my arms with formidable force for a girl in her weight class. At this point, Capucine gets involved: She digs the fat out from between my shoulder blades and rearranges the sides of my breasts in a desperate attempt to find the slightest bit of give.

"Now tip your tailbone, honey," Polly commands, pushing me against the wall with her kneecap.

I tip my tailbone, and immediately feel a panicked third set of hands around the base of my rib cage. It's Margot, and her fumbling urgency indicates she has been unfairly tasked with dismantling a bomb and time . . . is . . . running . . . out. I am about to call it, about to say *I'll just go buy a dress and let's all pretend this never happened,* when I feel the zipper start to creep up my back, inch by horrifying inch, and squeeze the life out of me.

"The corset is up," Polly exhales as she pats my shoulder with relieved affection. "That's the hard part."

She pulls up the shell of the dress, yanking it a few times to straighten it out at the chest, and she bends over to fluff the bottom.

"Okay. Let's have a look."

I turn around very gingerly to present myself to them, namely because I already feel a little dizzy from the unanticipated absence of oxygen to my brain. They all lean back and observe me in silence before Polly steps forward to tuck some of my bulging armpit fat back into the dress.

"Now walk," Polly commands, and I shuffle around the room like someone has bound my feet.

This receives no comment.

"That works," Polly says. "You're so tall we won't even have to hem it!"

At these words, I am half expecting confetti to fall from the ceiling.

"Thanks," I mumble.

"Take a look," she suggests, pointing to a wall mirror. I expect a train wreck, of course, but instead I am knocked sideways by my own reflection. My body, which I feel is usually best described as a "soft rectangle" in clothes is suddenly a tantalizing mix of twists and turns, of angles and hard edges. I turn in a full circle, which requires approximately fifteen tiny steps, so I can see myself from behind.

"Wow," I say. I am mortified to be caught in the extremely unfamiliar position of liking what I see regarding my own body. "Thank you. You guys are, like, legit miracle workers."

"Of course," Polly says. "Now, take it off so Cap can steam it."

"Okay," I say uncertainly, because there is no fucking way that I am going to be able to put this dress on again without a pit crew, and I was hoping I could just stay in it until the benefit in two weeks.

"And you'll need a bag and jewelry," Polly advises. Here, she claps her hands together like a gymnast who has picked up too much chalk and the briskness of tone indicates she is ready to move on to her next routine. "Get earrings *or* a necklace, okay?"

"Okay," I say.

"Not both," she says more plainly. "Okay? Just pick one."

I instantly understand that part of Polly's job is to make sure the staff is presenting well to the outside world. She needs even me—the lowliest of assistants with absolutely no business borrowing designer gowns at this early stage in our career—to preserve the fantasy we all work so hard to sell.

"Okay," I say dutifully.

I am the right kind of girl.

5

After the library gala, on a piercing November night, I pull up in front of Milady's, which is a dive bar on the corner of Prince and Thompson Streets in Soho. The entrance is draped in colored Christmas lights, and from the safety of my chauffeured black town car, I scan the loose knots of smokers huddled near the door in search of a friendly face. People trail down the street like human ellipses, talking and laughing, and some of them look up at my car with narrowed, suspicious eyes. A thin haze of cigarette smoke catches in the blue and green lights of the neon beer signs that hum from the windows of the bar and this evening, like so many New York nights, is crackling with suspense. It's one cliché about New York that is entirely true: It always feels like something wonderful is about to happen.

"Here?" the driver asks.

"Yes, but can you just pull up a little bit?" I am suddenly self-conscious that I am wearing a ballgown on a Monday night. I have just left the long-anticipated library benefit, an uptown kingdom in which this costume was required, but now, down here in the land of normal people, I feel absurd and out of touch with my subjects. I also have a scorching Charlie horse in my left calf because I can't fully sit down without ripping the dress in half, so I have been supporting half my body weight for the past twenty minutes on one leg and both arms. The driver eases the car up a few feet, but I still don't move. He eases up a few more feet.

"Thanks," I whisper as I finger the heavy Swarovski drop earrings

I borrowed for the event, confirming with relief they remain attached to my tender lobes. I inform the driver that I don't have a car voucher (I have been told repeatedly to *take a car voucher*, but as far as I can tell no one ever takes a car voucher) so he hands over a clipboard with a blank one for me to fill out. Honestly, I am grateful for the extra time. As I scribble down the vague details of my trip, I have no idea how much riding around in this car costs; I don't even know who signs off on this expense. I was just made to understand in my first week of work, although indirectly, that it was perfectly fine, and even preferable, for me to call a town car ("as directed" I was told to say) should I need to travel anywhere for any reason. I hand the clipboard back to the driver.

"Can you just wait here for me?" I ask.

"Of course," he replies.

I get out of the car carefully, and double-check to make sure I didn't leave anything in the back seat. It's cold, but I am not wearing a coat because I don't have a coat that is nice enough for black-tie events. I don't even have one that is nice enough for work. As I hobble past the smokers, I hold up the edge of my dress, which makes me feel both insanely feminine and positively ridiculous at the same time, like a grown-ass woman who works at Disney World but gets to be the "best" princess. The dress is strapless and constructed from whale bone–like scaffolding over which a layer of navy blue silk mesh organza has been artfully draped. It has a two-foot train, which I know will be trampled and soaked in beer by the end of the night, namely because I have already been dragging it around like an old rope mop for hours, but I don't care. I already feel entitled to ruin it. Entitlement, it turns out, when encouraged comes with an astonishing swiftness. I can feel curious eyes on me as I open the door to the bar. They are wondering: *Is this someone I should know?* I want to be someone they should know.

Despite the thick, jostling crowd inside, I see my friend Allie has a seat at the bar, but I am not surprised. Metaphorically, Allie Blum always finds a seat at the bar. She sits with her back to me in front of the beer taps, which sprout skyward before her like a glittering metallic garden. As I push closer, I see a half-empty martini glass sits in front of her, peppered with condensation. She wears an unfamiliar newsboy-style hat from which her pin-straight black hair trails down her back.

The room smells like days-old beer and freshly lit cigarettes. Connie Francis plays in the background.

This is my heaven.

I make my way through the final patch of warm bodies and lean over to whisper seductively in Allie's ear:

"What the *fuck* is that hat?"

Hearing my voice, Allie exhales a violet plume of cigarette smoke up to the ceiling, and her mouth breaks into an enormous smile. It crinkles her dark brown eyes.

"Goodbye, corporate world!" she explains, tipping the cap in my direction. "Hello, new academic life I am performatively entering!"

After nearly three years working at a bank to pay the proverbial bills while also trying to become a singer (long story) Allie decided last spring to pursue a doctorate in Renaissance literature at Columbia University. I think she sorted this career change out over a long weekend and, by the following week, was in possession of a full scholarship. You see, Allie Blum is blessed with that relaxed, ambidextrous ambition that makes normal strivers like me want to tear their hair out. Everything—and I mean everything—seems to go her way.

Allie has been my best friend since the second grade. We met after my family moved from Northeast Philadelphia to one of the newly built suburban developments that started to ring our hometown metropolis, that City of Brotherly Love. Her family is Jewish, valued education above all else, and her mom walked around the house, chattering away without a nip of self-consciousness wearing a nude-colored bra. My Irish Catholic family valued emotional forbearance, and I have yet to inform my mother that I got my period, which happened in the eighth grade. Allie won "Most Likely to Succeed" in high school. I won—I kid you not—"Class Clown," an honor for which I was required to wear a colored wig and plastic, oversized polka dot bow tie for the yearbook photo. Allie went to the University of Pennsylvania on a full academic scholarship while I did not go to an Ivy League school, nor did I receive a scholarship of any kind. It makes sense: In high school, which I found to be a nearly unsolvable obstacle course, Allie was always bored. She was bored by the lack of academic rigor in our public school system. She was bored by the boys, all of whom she labeled as having "low-earning potential" thanks to their obsession with playing hacky sack and acceptance letters from what she deemed to be subpar colleges like Millersville or Penn State Altoona. That said, she *really* reserved her contempt for the girls in our class (the girls *outside* our immediate circle, that is) who thought these same boys, with their wallet chains and Beastie Boys ringers, were somehow prizes to be won. By the time we were seniors in high school, Allie spent the bulk of her weekends taking the train to New York to attend concerts or watch the independent movies we couldn't get in our town. She bought marijuana in Washington Square Park and knew a place in Chinatown that served free white wine with lunch in little porcelain jugs. When she graduated from Columbia, she got an apartment on Bedford Street in the West Village and insisted I join her, but I reasoned it was far wiser to sit tight in my hometown rather than lend credence to the ridiculous notion that I might have some unique talent on which I had yet to shed the appropriate light. Also, New York was terrifying to me. Frankly, by that point, Allie was terrifying to me. She was working at a bank called Lehman Brothers and making more money in a year than I could imagine making in an entire lifetime. She took morning runs. She got her nails painted in a polish called Mademoiselle every week. She told me she sometimes slept under her office desk while business deals were being finalized. She went on blind dates. She told me drinks in New York cost fourteen dollars and her rent was $1,400 a month. She signed up for salsa dancing lessons, ate sushi, and, most bizarrely, informed me that the girls in New York don't even think about getting married until they are at least thirty.

In Philadelphia, as I crept toward the age of twenty-five, they were already dropping like flies.

It took me two years post college, but I finally came around to her way of thinking after a series of embarassing romantic entanglements. I arrived in the city at the end of June, which was just in time to watch the fireworks show over the East River from a random, patently unsafe rooftop on the Lower East Side. I wore flip-flops, which I quickly came to understand was the wrong choice, and the small gathering was mostly guys from Allie's class at Penn who now worked in finance. They all wore waffle shirts and hair gel and, to my eye, were spectacularly short in stature, and I couldn't help but wonder where the poets and fashion models and wacky piano-playing gay guys I had long been promised were frittering away their own evenings. As I sipped on my bottle of beer that night, I wondered if I hadn't made a terrible mistake but I also knew it was too late. Sure, I could make a change, but I was worried any new choice would yield even more disappointing results, only this time colored by the far more public failure of having the audacity to try something new in the first place.

For my first month, I slept on Allie's plywood futon couch as I networked in vain for both a job and an affordable apartment in Manhattan. While I was happy to be close to Allie, I was deeply disappointed to discover her first blush of city living had long since faded. She was no longer interested in taking the ferry to Ellis Island or waiting in line for cupcakes at Magnolia Bakery on a Sunday morning. In fact, in those very early days, I felt like her loudmouthed country cousin as I homed in on the neat little world she had already established.

Tonight, I give her tweedy cap a closer look.

"It's not bad, actually," I say. "Does Columbia give them to all their PhD candidates?"

"It's how we recognize each other on campus. We also got quill pens."

"Smart."

"So how was your party?"

"Party?" I reply as I throw my shoulders back with indignation. "Why, it was no simple party! It was a library benefit."

"My apologies," Allie replies with a smile.

"Please understand that while I may be fashionable, I am also a patron of fine literature and the institutions that support it. I give of myself, Allie. I am a *giving person.*"

"You are a giving person," she affirms with a nod.

"It was *fine*," I continue, deflating just enough that my dress doesn't split open at the sides. "Awkward. Marginally successful."

Here is another thing: This is a lie.

The truth is the gala I just attended—my first proper black-tie event since Lisa Rubin's bat mitzvah in seventh grade—has left me uncynically awestruck, which is not a register I had been familiar with until I moved to the city. Until tonight, I had never ventured inside the main branch of the New York Public Library on Forty-Second Street; I didn't give it much thought, figuring, like I did with everything else "important" or "cultural" in the city, I would get to it on some future day because, in your twenties, time remains an infinite resource. Tonight, however, as I alighted the wide concrete staircase that led up to the library's front doors, I felt like I was dropped into an Edith Wharton novel or, maybe, one of those PBS miniseries I used to watch with my mom in middle school. When I passed into the main foyer, I staggered under an unexpected sort of vertigo, surely triggered by the sheer magnitude of the space. I guess I had not been expecting the room itself to be so magnificent. Frankly, I am not sure if I had been expecting anything at all. There were soaring stone arches, all etched with unfamiliar, yet surely historically significant names, and the cavernous lobby was banked on each side by marble staircases bookended with golden busts of very distinguished-looking men. There were candles and flowers, and I could hear string music being played from parts unknown, and it was the most grown-up, most elegant thing I had ever seen outside of the movies.

Of course, I was unsure what to do so I trailed behind a few older women, all of whom were clutching tiny, beaded bags and wearing swishing gowns with tidy jackets, as they made their gentle way to the second floor. As I nervously alighted the candlelit stairs behind them, I lifted my chin like I was balancing a book on my head. I hoped this might convey the deportment of someone who had attended finishing school or, at the very least, had been taught how to ascend a staircase in heels without falling down. Once I made it to the second floor, I was greeted by a row of young men in crisp white shirts, all of whom were offering glasses of wine and sparkling water off silver trays. I picked up a glass of white and took a small sip; it tasted thick, like the chardonnay at a wedding. I looked around. All the men wore tuxedos (with the exception of one bearded man in a tartan kilt, which is apparently a "thing" in certain upper class circles) and with the exception of the willowy girls around my age who chair the late-night party, I took note that most of the guests at the benefit were older and more distinguished-looking than the guests at the parties I usually attend. By my second drink, I started to unearth the courage required to make conversation, and I was greatly relieved that talking to older people was a lot easier than making conversation with the girls my own age. I liked the way the women nodded at me with familial approval when I told them I worked at the magazine. I liked the way the men kindly offered to make additional introductions, strolling me across a room to meet this friend or that acquaintance. I liked the velvet chime that signaled it was time for us to move to dinner. I liked eating soup out of a hollowed-out pumpkin. I liked sitting under centerpieces so tall and made of flowers so foreign, they looked like Truffula trees. I liked having my glass refilled by a man wearing white gloves. I liked clapping at the speeches with a warm, regal approval.

I liked being one of them.

Honestly, I had no idea a world at this scale existed, and I wasn't sure how to capture it in words for Allie or, more accurately, how I felt about being seduced by something so utterly obvious.

All I know is that the seduction—in the span of hours—was complete.

"What are you drinking?" I ask her instead, nodding toward her now nearly empty drink.

"A gin martini, which I think is wonderful," she says, running her finger seductively around the wet rim.

"I would be crying hysterically about how you don't love me anymore if I drank gin," I say. I place my elbows gingerly on the viscid bar and smile up at her. "Or in a fist fight about the Eagles with a bunch of investment bankers."

"Ah, the Eagles," Allie responds with solemnity.

"That just made me a little bit sad," I admit, and I turn my head quickly in the direction of the bartender, mostly because I want to hide my face until the brief, unbearable cramp in my throat subsides. I don't know why I bother. By now, Allie is quite familiar with my waves of homesickness, the gnawing sense that I have no idea what I am doing in New York. When the bartender spots me, I order a vodka and club soda, and then I close my eyes and take a long inhalation.

The bar smells wonderful, like winter in the city.

I turn back to Allie.

"So how do we feel about this dress?" I ask to change the subject. I place my hand on my hip.

"I feel this dress is a very positive step in your world domination plan," she responds.

"Why, thank you," I say in a bright, self-deprecating manner. "Sadly, I did not get my picture taken by Patrick McMullan despite some profoundly desperate hanging around the step-and-repeat pretending I was 'looking for someone.' It's on my 'You Have Arrived' bingo card."

"What's a step-and-repeat?" Allie asks.

"It's that wall with all the logos that famous celebrities pose in front of at red carpet things for magazines. Like vodka sponsors or gyms or magazines or whatever."

"I'm surprised they didn't take your picture. You look great in that dress," she says. "Where did you buy it?"

"The dress? Please. It's a borrow."

"A borrow?" Allie asks.

"It's borrowed from a designer for the night."

"I can't believe you can just borrow dresses at your job," she says. "That is so awesome."

"It's actually horrifying," I say. "I'm not a sample size, so nothing fits."

"You are so thin," Allie says, which would be true in every industry *except* fashion where I'm classified as morbidly obese. "How small is a sample?"

I hold up my pinkie. She smiles.

"Your body looks amazing, though," she says.

"I know," I say.

Over by the pool table, we simultaneously catch the telltale rustle of people extinguishing cigarettes and putting on coats.

"Oh, they are leaving," Allie says. "Can we grab that table?

"I can't sit down in this dress," I admit before brightening. "Thus, we must stand and get very drunk."

"I wanted fries," she says, frowning.

"We can't eat in *public*," I reply in mock horror. "We are working on our image."

"So does that mean now is a good time to tell you that you are drinking out of the cocktail stirrer there, Grace Kelly?"

I look down at my glass and frown: I had no idea this was a cocktail stirrer. I thought it was a straw designed to ensure you couldn't drink alcohol too fast. I pluck it out of my drink and lay it with reproach down on the bar.

"Any thoughts on what you want to do for your birthday?" she asks.

"Ignore it?" I reply.

"I wonder what the young kids are doing these days," Allie jokingly ponders.

"I don't know," I reply. "I can ask them at work tomorrow."

"Please do not tell me you are still pretending you are twenty-three?"

I smile and say nothing.

"There is nothing wrong with being twenty-five," Allie says, and she seems genuinely annoyed, like I am violating some second-tier feminist principle.

"I don't have a choice; twenty-five is too old to be a first-year assistant in magazines. I don't do whatever it is you did at your last job."

Allie lays her chin upon her fist with a dreamy smile.

"Get propositioned by a bunch of Duke graduates in Vineyard Vines ties?" she offers with a mock wistfulness.

"Yeah, that."

I laugh, and she laughs, and as I take another sip of my drink, I feel content, like I have been relieved of some heavy sensation I can't quite pinpoint, almost like how it feels to release a balloon and watch it rise to the sky. It is satisfying to let it go, but it's strange not to know where it is going, not to know where it will land. Maybe someone will find its bright corpse—gummy and deflated—and wonder where it all began, and where it hoped to go.

But in this moment: I feel entirely alive.

6

For assistants in the magazine business, there are properly glamorous work events every night of the week. Maybe it's a book reading at an art collector's Soho loft or, perhaps, a smattering of "small plates" to celebrate the opening of a restaurant. It could be a dressy gala to benefit rainforests or New Yorkers for Children (cue the perennial joke about the benefit for "New Yorkers *Against* Children") or, maybe, it's a boy band singing exactly one song at a Midtown club with bottle service and purple uplighting. The main point here is this: There is always something to *do* and *doing* is an essential requirement of the job. You do not want to be caught out *not doing*. Not doing is death.

Tonight's event is a party for a new handbag (because accessories get their own overdone parties in New York, just like children), and I share a car downtown with a few other assistants from the office. The ride is the fun part: We are still feeling each other out, and this ritual includes sharing everything from grievances to gossip to lipstick. We are nervous and, maybe, a little guarded; we are keenly aware that only a few of us will survive the first years on this arduous voyage through magazine publishing for the simple reason that there are, by meticulous design, not enough lifeboats.

While many of the parties we attend are lavishly orchestrated and full of famous people, the retail-focused ones are strangely identical (white rental couches and Lucite tables, "signature cocktails" passed around by professional waiters, and a famous-enough DJ to spin dance music for a bunch of white girls preening around a blazingly overlit clothing shop), but they are also my favorite kind of compulsory event because, if nobody talks to you, which is often the case for me, you can leave after ten minutes. Tonight, however, Davis Lawrence rides with us in the car to the store, which is a rarity. She sits next to me in the back seat, so close I can feel her warmth. Out of the corner of my eye, I watch her run a brush through her hair and put on lipstick. Then, she wiggles her shoulder out of her shirt.

"Clo," she says, and the directness of her address startles me. She looks down at her newly exposed skin. "Is there a pimple on my back?"

I look. Her shoulder is dusty with white, downy hair.

"Uh, I think so?"

"Is it white or just red?" she asks.

"Just red," I say.

She slides the neck of her shirt back up and smiles at me gratefully. Her closeness is paralyzing.

"Thanks, you," she says, and she wrinkles her nose at me.

My insides freeze up like pipes in winter.

Blessedly, tonight's event is located near an F train, so—after awkwardly making the rounds and being ignored by both Davis and the photographer—I start to strategize my exit. I suspect some of the other girls have plans from which I have been excluded, but I don't blame them; I still don't quite fit in. On my way out, however, I run into Davis, who is smoking with a handsome man on the sidewalk.

"You leaving already, Clo?" she asks sweetly, and I feel myself flush at the way her voice sounds when she says my name.

"Oh, yeah," I say, before quickly adding: "I am meeting some friends for a dinner."

"Do you know Harry Wood?" she asks, pointing at her companion with the cigarette that sits between her fingers. I glance at him, and I notice there is a camera slung over the shoulder of his blazer.

"No," I say, and while this is technically true, I *do* know the name. Harry Wood is a society reporter for the big newspaper, and I have regularly seen his byline. He not only writes the articles, but he also shoots the photographs, which sets him apart from the other up-and-coming journalists in our general cohort. I like his pictures; they are a little more candid, and a lot less polished than the standard posed variety that usually get published. He also recently started his own blog, which is darker and funnier, in my opinion, anyway, than what he is permitted to write at his day job. He regards me with a half smile before he leans over and extends his hand.

"Harry," he says, but the cigarette bobbing between his lips muffles his voice.

"I'm Clo," I say softly, but, as I stand there, I can think of nothing else to say. Something about their beautiful glow makes me feel childlike and pathetic. I excuse myself with a little wave, and turn to walk quickly down the street with my hands jammed into my pockets.

A little while later, while humming along on the subway under the influence of the single saccharine glass of prosecco I drank at the party, I reflect on the strange regularity with which I meet (or at least *see*) people with some semblance of a reputation in New York; it lends the luster of possibility to even the smallest of excursions, and I wonder if that magic exists in other places. I pull a paperback novel out of my bag, and take another stab at reading a few pages, but when the train pulls out of the Jay Street station in Brooklyn, I close the book. I decide what I *really* need is another drink.

I get off at the next stop, which is Bergen Street, and I stand on the cold, quiet corner for a minute, wondering what I should do. I decide to cross the street and poke my head into Boat, a dim bar I have been known to frequent in my later, drunker hours, mostly because it has cute boys and the best indie-rock jukebox in my neighborhood. Tonight, however, it is too early: There is only one person at the bar, and a couple plays the sole tabletop video game, their flaccid, pale faces bathed in an eerie blue glow. I back out the door and onto the sidewalk just as it starts to rain. I hold my hand out for a moment to gauge its severity before I lift my book over my head and dash across the street. The drops start to fall harder, and I duck under every available awning until I make it to Dean Street where I slip into a reliable little French place on the corner called Bar Tabac.

The restaurant is busy and there are no seats open at the bar, but a nice waiter lets me sit at one of the small red tops usually reserved for people eating dinner. I order a glass of pinot grigio and place my damp novel strategically on the edge of the table before I light up a cigarette.

I sit there for a good long while. As I listen to the rain and strain to untangle the threads of conversation around me, I decide to fancy myself an observer of the world. I'm like Hemingway or Fitzgerald or whoever that guy was who spent all the time in cafés in Paris. I drink another glass of wine, and make thoughtful expressions as I evaluate the people in the room, trying to make up their life stories. It is all is going quite well until a large form moves into my line of sight. I look up: It is Oliver Barringer.

"Don't I know you?" he asks, leaning over with a smile. He has his thick dirty blond hair pulled back into a surfer's messy bun, and he looks taller than he did on the subway. Up close, I notice he has a space between his two front teeth and one tooth looks slightly beige. He is not wearing his glasses.

"I don't know," I reply with a comic little raise of my eyebrow. His grin expands, which pleases me. He seems to enjoy a little game.

"I'm Oliver Barringer," he says gallantly. "I think we work for the same company?"

"We do?"

"Magazines?"

"Ah, yes."

"Ah, yes, indeed," he says with a laugh. "Aren't you friends with Davis Lawrence?"

I feel myself break into a little smile at the mention of her name.

"Yes," I say, and I tuck my hair behind my ear. "I'm Clo."

I stand up and extend my arm, which I instantly regret. The gesture feels too masculine. He regards me with interest before we limply shake hands.

I extinguish my cigarette to be polite.

"Can I bum one of those, actually?" He points to the pack on the table.

"Sure," I say, grateful for something to do. I sit down and he pulls out a chair to join me, which I find surprising in a good way. I promptly scan the bar to see who else is there, hoping someone sees us, but I don't recognize anyone. He pulls a plastic lighter out of his plaid shirt pocket and gives it a light shake.

"A white lighter," I comment. "Very bold."

"What do you mean?" he asks, still smiling.

"I was told they were bad luck," I say. "White lighters."

"Bad luck?" He tilts his head in confusion.

That's it. *That is it, Clodagh,* I think. I will never be considered a serious person because I will never be a serious person. I'm too stupid. Our city has endured a terrorist attack, people are getting anthrax in the mail, and—here I am—gossiping about a superstition I heard in high school with a guy who just wrote a story on Afghani women fighting for an education. I say nothing in response to his probing; I choose instead to simmer in my own mediocrity. I deserve every terrible thing that ever happens to me.

"Ah," he says finally. He holds out the lighter and observes it in a very studied manner. "First time I heard that one."

He shrugs and lights the cigarette. He takes a deep drag, smiles with his mouth closed, and then—without warning—exhales the smoke through his nose and directly into my face. Reflexively, I shove my chair back, and it slams into the wall behind me. My face contorts as I blink in a frantic attempt to stamp out the searing sensation that has sliced into the damp meat of my eyeballs. Within seconds, a few greasy, protective tears roll down my cheeks.

"Oh my god!" Oliver exclaims.

My eyes are still closed, but I can feel him rest his hand on mine lightly. As my vision returns, I see he is assessing me very intently, almost lovingly. It is here I take note that he has otherworldly brownish yellow eyes.

"I am so sorry," he continues. "That was a *total* accident."

I sense, oddly, that it was not an accident. I get the distinct impression that he wants to find out what kind of girl I am, how much load I can bear.

"No worries," I say. I ruffle the front of my hair coolly with my fingers. I remain desperate for the heat to fully pass, but I am also intent on keeping my eyes wide open to make it seem like I am okay. "It's totally fine."

Without breaking his gaze, he leans back in a smarmy, satisfied manner, but I am not sure if I have passed this test or failed. The bartender comes over to our table, wiping his hands on his jeans. He has a shaved head and the lightest trace of a French accent.

"Hey, Oli," he says. "How's it going?"

"Good, man." Oliver says nodding. "Very good."

"What will it be?"

"I'll just have a Stella."

Oliver glances down at my glass, which is almost empty, but says nothing about a drink for me. The waiter waits an almost imperceptible beat to see what will happen before he walks away.

"So do you come here often?" I ask, quite seriously, until I hear it fall out of my mouth.

"Sort of. I live in Fort Greene. You?"

"I live in Carroll Gardens," I say. "It's down that way about ten blocks?"

"I know where Carroll Gardens is," he says.

"Right. Sorry."

"Not too many of us around here," he observes, taking another deep drag.

I turn my head to the side for self-protection before I respond, but I am both unsure and thrilled by what he might mean by "us."

"No, I guess not," I say. "I definitely work with a more Upper East Side crowd."

"I saw you a while back on the subway," he says.

"You did?" I ask, feigning surprise. "When?"

"I don't know," he says. "A month ago? I was with my girlfriend."

Point of fact: He was *not* with his girlfriend. This statement is what we single girls call a "girlfriend bomb." It is how a guy drops the fact he has a "girlfriend" two minutes into a perfectly innocent conversation, almost like they feel morally compelled to let your desperate ass down easy. Once they deliver this information, however, they swiftly resume flirting with you again, only now more aggressively. If you're a confident woman, you find a quick way to excuse yourself from such a loser. If you are me, this sounds like an invitation to compete for attention, so you drink too much to restore your confidence and then do gymnastics to compel them to take you home with them. With no strings attached, of course, because, you know, they just told you *they have a girlfriend*. Despite winning this game several times, I am still unclear about the prize.

"I'm usually in another world on the subway," I say before I take the remaining half sip of my wine. "Sorry."

"You're pretty new, right?" He takes a sip of his beer.

"Yeah, I started in August," I say.

Here, I turn my body to favor my breasts and nudge my coat open slightly. His eyes fall to my neckline, and then back up to my face.

"Who do you work for?" he asks.

"I used to be Marie Clarice's assistant in entertainment and culture, but she left. So now I am just waiting for them to hire a new editor."

"Oh man, right," he says. "I heard all about *that* one."

"I know," I say conspiratorially, and we both nod as if we are on the inside of something of substance, even though neither of us know anything whatsoever about the departure of Marie Clarice.

"I heard she was kind of a mess," he offers hopefully.

"I guess that depends on how you define *a mess*," I say. "She once asked me if there was a way to secretly record a phone conversation with her fiancé."

"Totally standard journalistic practice," he says, smiling.

"Totally," I rejoin, giddy that he used the word *journalistic*.

"Do you like it?"

"The job? Definitely." Here, I start to fidget as I strategize how I can elegantly get my hands on the alcohol necessary to fuel this conversation. "In fact, before you got here, I was meeting with a writer I'm going to profile."

This easy and entirely unconfirmable lie serves two purposes: One, it makes it clear I am a serious person, not just one of those assistants who only make photocopies or returns shoes, and two, I am not the kind of girl who gets drunk alone in bars. What's funny is that he is not even remotely compelled to explain himself to me.

"Writing profiles already? Well done," he says approvingly. "Who's this writer?"

"Oh, I can't tell you that," I say girlishly as I slide out of my coat for the big reveal. "Who's to say you won't steal it for *your* magazine?"

Oliver steals another glance, which pleases me more than it should, namely because my breasts, which are nothing but a detriment at my chosen place of business, are oftentimes effective bait when trying to catch the attention of men.

"Now I am intrigued," he says, although he doesn't sound especially intrigued. He taps the book sitting between us on the table with his index finger:

"How are you liking this?"

I have read exactly one chapter of this book. A little drunk. On the subway. An hour ago. You were with me.

"I read it in high school," I lie. "But I am doing this thing where I am rereading books, checking in on how they hold up."

"I loved it," he says.

"I remember loving it, too," I say.

He seems to consider this comment kindly as he takes a long last drink of his beer. He sets his empty bottle down on the table. He picks at the loose flap on the label, clearly considering his next move, and I hold my breath.

"Well, I should get going," he says, which reveals my abject failure in keeping his attention, even with my boobs out. "I have a big day tomorrow."

With this, he stands up and, with imitation sheepishness, plucks another cigarette out of my pack. I watch as he sticks it between his lips.

"Next one's on me, kid," he says.

Next one is on me, kid. I almost vomit, but instead I beam up at him. I blink sweetly, like a teenage doe, tiptoeing innocently through a dappled forest. Why? I want Oliver Barringer to like me. Correction: I need Oliver Barringer to like me. It doesn't matter if I like him, which I don't particularly, because we girls don't get to make these distinctions. Our only advantage comes from two things: One, being cheerfully subservient (and, thus, unthreatening) to the women in power, and two, being sexually desired by the men in power. The fact that men behave in this fashion toward us bothers me far less than the women who insist we be judged on our merits or manners or good personalities. First of all, we are not judged on those things and asking to be judged on them won't make a bit of difference. Secondly, I've never understood why so many women don't grasp the potential to be found on both sides of this dynamic. If men like you, they will give you things. You can use those things to get more things. Why play the angry victim and get nothing when you can have fun playing along and get, well, everything?

Within reason, of course: It's a sin to want too much.

"Sounds good, Oliver," I say with a tiny wave. "Have a nice night."

After he leaves, my surroundings sharpen into focus, including a new table of loud, guffawing drunk girls about my age. They all sport the same low-slung boot-cut jeans and have wrapped oversized knit scarves quite cleverly around their necks. I envy their ease. I have yet to find my own group of friends outside of the post-college crowd Allie has assembled, all of whom seem to think the weekend is not complete without everyone chipping in for a $300 bottle of Grey Goose in a club, and I am aching for a moment of real friendship. There is also an older couple, maybe early forties, sharing a bottle of red wine over a silent, seething dinner and—to counteract them—a young, blushing pair sitting head to head in a trance so adoring that it makes me want to stick a gun in my mouth and pull the trigger. I turn my gaze out the foggy windows and watch wonderfully fat drops of rain splatter on the empty sidewalk tables; each one glints like a diamond in the weeping streetlights. It's a nice place, this bar, especially when it's tricked out like it is tonight with lights and people and that feeling of Christmas being right around the corner, and for a moment I am infused with a feeling of warmth and belonging. The bartender ambles over to my table and starts to gather up the empty glasses.

"Another drink?" he asks. His tone—or perhaps it's my own insecurity—informs me I am not the first woman to have unwittingly bought Oliver Barringer a drink in this bar.

"No, I'll just have the check."

I open my handbag and fumble around for cash, but I don't have enough, so I locate my debit card, which rests among bits of trash and cookie crumbles in the bottom of my bag. I hand it over with a smile, but after a few minutes the bartender returns to inform me that my card was declined. I am about to insist he run it again when I remember: It is Thursday. I get paid on Fridays, which means I get paid at midnight. I look at the vintage clock that hangs over the rows of dusty bottles lined up behind the bar. It's 11:40.

"That's weird. It just worked next door," I lie. "Can you give me a second?"

I need to buy myself some time.

"Sure," he says easily, walking back toward the bar.

I sit for a few minutes going through my options (none) before I collect my belongings and walk to the bar, which is now deserted except for a middle-aged couple who is not speaking English or French. I slide into an empty seat and sheepishly signal the bartender.

"Hey," I say to the bartender as he walks over. "Can I have another glass of wine?"

"What was it again?"

"Pinot grigio"

"You good for it?" he jokes, and I think I pick up on a little energy from him.

"I get paid at midnight," I admit, returning his energy with an intentional helplessness. "So this is all a *little* embarrassing."

While I wait for him to laugh, I briefly imagine this is the part of the movie where the handsome bartender is charmed by a hapless girl on a rainy night, and we get to talking and fall madly in love and it turns out he's not only a bartender, but an heir to a grand New York fortune who also happens to be in medical school studying to be a pediatric heart surgeon. Obviously, we get married, and everyone back home learns that uppity Clodagh Harmon, now a famous Pulitzer Prize–winning journalist, is married to a handsome, humble, and totally loaded doctor who saves the lives of children.

It takes me a long moment to notice that he doesn't, in fact, laugh. He doesn't even pour me a drink. Instead, he is already on the other side of the bar talking to one of the waitresses. When he finally remembers me, he pours my wine so quickly that the neck of the bottle nicks my glass and knocks it over; I watch in slow motion as it smacks against the bar top and breaks into pieces. I lunge for a handful of cocktail napkins to stem the spill, which is racing toward my lap, but when I look up for my future husband's assistance, I discover with great irritation that he is back talking to the waitress. He did not even notice my predicament. Annoyed, I grab another handful of napkins, and as I carefully pick up fragments of glass, I can't help but think that these kinds of things never happen to Davis. When Davis Lawrence spills a drink, someone calls the fire department.

When he comes back to check on me, he asks if I would like another glass of wine. I say yes because it's easier than to explain that the first one shattered and, when he wasn't looking, I stuck all of it—the gelatinous wad of napkins, the broken glass, the intact stem—inside my handbag so as to not inconvenience anyone.

I was just going to throw it all out when I got home.

He pours me another glass, correctly this time, and then he runs the debit card at 12:05 and again at 12:45, when it finally goes through. I have been paid.

By now the rain has subsided and I have finished my most recent drink, which was at least one drink too many if the way I stumble toward the door is a good indication. I button up my coat with clumsy fingers, and glance back over my shoulder.

I whisper a quiet goodbye to nobody.

7

I survive Christmas at home. Correction: I survive Christmas at home save a pathetic crying jag at midnight mass that is manifestly ignored by everyone in my family, of which I am the second youngest of four children. There is also a fight with my brother about the whereabouts of the remote control (his fucking problem), a fight with my sister about the truly revolting things I can inflict upon a perfectly innocent tube of toothpaste, and a fight with my mother because she put my only pair of expensive jeans in the dryer.

Despite this, in the weeks leading up to Christmas, the first one since I moved to New York, I had allowed myself to be seduced by a memory that, almost certainly, never existed. In my mind, this holiday break would include clinking cocktail glasses and roaring fires. My family, all aglow, would gather around our tree, which was historically so massive that it left happy scratches in the ceiling paint, and I would finally be permitted to shake the ache of homesickness, if only for a few days.

Instead, my parents—to their great and strange delight—purchased a small, inexpensive tree from the local gas station. Furthermore, there was no singing or roaring fireplaces (they converted our fireplace to gas without informing us), and my youngest brother seemed even more fucked up than usual. For the occasional escape, I take power walks with Allie who, thank god, was also home for the holidays. We borrow our mom's elastic ankle sweatpants and wear the oversized T-shirts we left behind after high school (GO MUSTANGS!) and perform laps around our upper-middle-class development. We pump our arms like old ladies as we make deeply informed and thoughtful commentary on the various styles of Christmas lights, the indignation of the Bush presidency, and the unfortunate life trajectory of several formerly hot classmates, like Trevor Flynn, who *still* works at the local convenience store. We see him when we buy cigarettes and Diet Cokes and take great pains to ask him questions about his life, as if he is a real person. I also talk to Allie about my brother, who I suspect is using cocaine a bit more than recreationally these days, and about Davis, who is spending the holidays with her mother in Aspen.

I always find a way to bring up Davis in conversation.

To me, there is just nobody like her in the entire world.

On Christmas day, I drive alone to a strip mall drugstore to buy my own toothpaste. After browsing the card aisles to kill a little time, I make my way back to my dad's Lexus, toothpaste in hand, where I see a middle-aged homeless-looking woman wandering the parking lot and muttering. She wears a dingy pink sweatshirt that falls off one shoulder and her hair is matted in the back. I watch her walk in circles for a few minutes, gesticulating wildly to nobody, from the flank of my car.

"That's just *so sad*," I overhear someone say, and I turn to see a mother buckling a toddler into the car seat of her black SUV. While she is ostensibly speaking to her three-year-old, I suspect she's actually trying to establish a little "concerned white lady" solidarity with me. I smile at her, but all I can think is: What's so sad about it? I would love to be able to meander through a parking lot and babble about nothing all day.

Instead, I ran my big fat mouth, and now I must go forth and make something of myself.

A couple of days before the New Year, my dad drives me to the train station. I am going back to New York early because a small group of us bought very expensive tickets to an open bar party at an enormous B-list nightclub. We already know it is going to be terrible, but we can't think of anything better to do; clubs are sort of a thing at this moment in time. Our apartments are too small for parties, so it seems that everyone at our low level of society is attending some ticketed affair while everyone above us in the pecking order is, well, still in Aspen or St. Barth's. On our car ride, my dad doesn't talk very much—I suspect my brother's unacknowledged troubles take up most of his available brain space at the moment—but he does slip me some much-needed cash. This is, ostensibly, to cover my train ticket and a cab home to Brooklyn (my parents are collectively terrified for me to take the subway after dusk) and as he doesn't seem to know my mother did the same thing as I was leaving the house, I do nothing to educate him on the topic. I just say goodbye, gather up my bags, and jog down the stairs, two at a time, because I am running dangerously late for the train. I slide through the doors just as they are closing, and I dump my belongings on the first available seat. As I sit down, I realize my heart is beating hard—almost too hard—and I wonder if my "social" smoking (which is up to about ten cigarettes a day) is having an impact on my health.

I decide it is not.

After all, everyone smokes in their twenties. How could we all possibly die?

As the train jerks out of the station, I lean back on the sticky tan seats and try to settle myself down with long inhales and exhales. The Christmas presents from my parents, mostly clothes and a coffee table book, sit in a brown paper bag next to me. For a long moment, I debate putting my suitcase on the overhead rack, but I don't; inertia has overtaken me. I look outside as chain-link fences, small houses, and aboveground pools speed past, and I feel drowsy.

The train ride is only a little over an hour, and the sun sets as the minutes creep by slowly. I was too late to grab a magazine at the newsstand so there is nothing to do but look out the window or watch people get on the train. At each stop, they clamber up the steps, red-cheeked and happy, and they bring with them that fresh, unmistakable woody smoke smell of a suburban Christmas. *They are probably going to the city "for the night,"* I think, and it pangs me to see them: It's like watching a more innocent version of myself.

When the train pulls up to the platform in Secaucus, it hisses to a halt, and I physically feel the carriage settle deeper into the tracks for what feels like an extended stay. *This is not good,* I think. I straighten up and look around so I can casually read the other passengers' faces for any signs of anxiety. After all, this is the last stop before the train enters the tunnel into New York, and who knows what is happening on the other side? I am always scanning crowds for suicide bombers these days. I have learned to search for blank-faced boys wearing backpacks instead of older men in turbans, but honestly none of it feels good. It feels like a shitty thing to do, but it also feels like we have been instructed that this kind of vigilance is our duty as American citizens. So, I look around the car. I don't see any obvious terrorists, and the other passengers seem unperturbed by the possibility that the train is stopped because someone just blew up Penn Station. I turn around and face the seatback in front of me, but my pulse is racing. After a few long minutes, the train starts to move again, indecisively at first, but then it picks up the tempo, faster and faster. We enter the tunnel at what seems to be a great speed. The lights inside the car flicker, and everything goes black; it's like someone has thrown a blanket over the carriage and is trying to smuggle us into the city unseen. I close my eyes and feel warm air blowing through an open window as I pray, over and over, in my head:

Please God, let me make it to the other side.

8

When I return to my office those first days of January, I am greeted by a colossal pile of weeks-old mail on my desk. There are also stacks heaped haphazardly on the floor around my chair. I place my bag down and unwrap my scarf. The mess is both miserable to contemplate and gives me a disconcerting feeling of purpose. *This is a mess I can handle*, I think. I get on my knees and start sorting the piles, which include press releases, letters, outdated newspapers, and a score of polybagged magazines. When I stand up to drop the first armload of trash into the bin, I catch sight of a large brown box sitting squarely on my chair. *How did I miss this?* I walk over and, with both hands, I lift the box to gauge its weight. It is heavy, which confirms my hopeful suspicion that it contains the advance copies of our next issue. Unable to locate my own scissors amid the chaos on my desk, I snatch a pair from Davis's perfect workspace. I slice the packing tape neatly down the middle and then, less elegantly, I force my fingers inside. I pry the box open with such force that I rip the edges of the corrugated cardboard, leaving the flaps so jagged, they look like they are panting. I peer inside.

I was right: It *is* the advance copies of our next issue, which will hit every newsstand, mailbox, and hair salon on the planet in less than two weeks. We get copies early so we can messenger them to our contributing writers and celebrity agents, generally with a handwritten note from each particular editor on magazine stationery. When that is done, the assistants fight over the leftover copies so they can cut out their own little articles and paste them down into very elegant clip books. I don't have any published articles, so I just carefully stack each issue on the shelf above my computer, like a museum exhibition. It is my visual timeline of each month I have spent at the magazine.

It's a small display.

I look into the box again and take a deep breath. Then, I wedge my hands inside to retrieve the top copy and, honest-to-god, you can almost smell the weight. It is nearly two inches thick, and it is sturdy and perfect; there are no scuffs or dog-ears yet, and the high gloss of the cover is wholly undimmed. I run my thumb against the flat white binding on which the magazine's name is printed and then against the crisp edge of the pages. I remember the feeling, as I do every time a new issue comes out, of receiving my own magazine subscriptions as a kid. I would see the mail truck pull away and sprint down the short, sloping yard, praying that the new issue of *YM* or *Seventeen* had come out. Maybe the delivery would also include my mother's *Vanity Fair*, *Vogue*, *Redbook*, or *Ladies' Home Journal*. There could be *Highlights*, *Sports Illustrated*, *Car and Driver*, *Traditional Home*—we Harmons were a magazine family. I would gather all the issues in my arms and squire them upstairs to my pink-wallpapered bedroom. There, I would lie on my bed and go through each issue, page by page, back to front. To this day, I only read magazines from the back to the front, always back to front. I read the celebrity articles, looked at the clothes, and took the quizzes. I did the at-home hair treatments and devoured the advice columns, although the agonizing social scenarios presented always seemed simple to solve, which I took as a clear sign of my emotional sophistication. I would secretly read about sex in *Sassy*, which was an act as implausible to me as stumbling upon a field full of unicorns, and by college I had added *Jane* to my list of subscriptions. I'd lie in the top bunk of my shared, cinderblock dorm room and imagine the articles were written by a group of older girls in a *really cool* apartment who would think—if they ever met me—that I was *really cool*, too.

Now, I never saw myself in the photography or the clothes, of course, but I didn't have that expectation. Instead, magazines permitted me to *finally* envision a better version of myself. Despite the fact I was too tall with bad skin and distressingly large boobs by the eighth grade, magazines *never* made me feel like a loser. Quite the opposite: They made me feel optimistic. Magazines were my window into an exciting future. Each page impressed upon me that, with enough hard work, an acne-busting yogurt mask, and a better nighttime thigh routine, all things were possible, even for a suburban nothing like me. Do you want to know what *did* make me want to slit my wrists? The real world. In the real world, I would travel with uncertainty through the crowded halls of my public school only to be bombarded, at every turn, by girls who were prettier or skinnier or more popular than me. These were the girls who could tease and spray their bangs with artistic proficiency. These were the girls who could stay within the boundaries of very strict diets, counting out how many cheerios they could eat for lunch while I absently inhaled Tastykake two-packs before meekly checking the calories and subsequently berating myself for the next three hours for being "fat" and "disgusting." These were the girls with divorced moms who let them have boys over on the weekend and attend the night ice hockey games, which was the not-so-secret code for a "slut" by my (completely virginal) high school years. In this arena, I could never compete, and I felt that failure keenly, even though Allie's mother routinely assured us that those kinds of girls invariably grew up to be things like "smokers" or "part-time aerobics instructors" in some hard-to-fathom world she *swore* existed after high school. So, in the absence of a more glamorous real world, I savored the promise of my magazines. After I read them, I would sit on my bedroom floor and cut up old issues by the dozens. Then, I would assemble my own magazines using the white cardboard I would routinely fish out of my father's work shirts when they came back from the dry cleaners. As I glued down the images, I would weave incredible tales in my head, which I would write out with my nicest markers. In my bedroom all alone, I could create a girl, and I could create her life: her friends, her house, her dog, her boyfriend, her wardrobe—all of it. When I was finished, I would sew them along the binding and prop the finished products on my desk, occasionally paging through them as I waited for the next round of magazines to appear. The fact that I am now employed at a real magazine (and, honestly, I wish there was a better, more *erudite*, way to phrase it) feels like a dream that has come true.

So, this morning, after I have sufficiently fondled the smooth exterior of the magazine, I open it, and the binding cracks like a dry stick in a deserted forest. I press my nose into the valley of the pages and inhale the smell, which is a tangled bouquet of perfume strips and freshly printed paper. To me, this is a most sacred scent, and one so biologically imprinted upon me that, so long as I live, it will encourage me to recall a deep and happy past. It smells like my mother's bedroom sheets when I am home sick. It smells like the night before the first day of school when I am quite certain my new outfit will translate into a whole new me. It smells like doctor's offices and airplanes and middle school dances in yellow gymnasiums. It reminds me of the spongy purple carpet installed in every young girl's bedroom in the sea of freshly built suburban colonials that I would bounce between during weekend sleepovers with my new elementary school friends.

It smells like starting over.

I lick my finger and turn to the final page of the issue. Then, I begin to backtrack in a nervous search for the masthead, which I locate about two-thirds of the way through the magazine. My eyes cascade down the list of names like a doomed pinball until I see it, right there, in black and white:

Clodagh P. Harmon, Editorial Assistant

I exist.

9

It is a most brutal winter.

In fact, as I get dressed for work one February morning, the television news informs me it is the longest streak of below-freezing temperatures since 1989: twenty-nine days in a row, to be exact. Not that I need to be told; the season has been so primal in its intensity that I'm often convinced my internal organs start to fail during the short walk to the subway. Despite the cold, I still switch my shoes in the same secret spot, only now the task is infinitely more difficult because I wear Uggs, which are enormous, unspeakably hideous shearling-lined boots. While they are wonderfully warm and do not require socks, they are so cumbersome that concealing them in my handbag is no longer a viable option. As such, I pack a large cotton tote (from the Strand, naturally, because I would like people to know I am a lover of literature!) each day in which to hide them. I stash the bag with an apologetic smile behind the receptionist's desk and, when the coast is clear at the end of each day, I collect it with the same overdone gratitude. I understand this risky footwear selection raises the reputational stakes considerably, but it's not like there is another, better boot that everyone wears in my office; there is simply the *absence* of winter boots. New York could get ten feet of snow, and everyone would still arrive in the lobby of our building with their coats unbuttoned and wearing three-inch high heels. Shoes, in our world, are an extremely important indicator of a person's overall well-being, financial and otherwise. They are also a sign of respect. Case in point: Rumor has it a girl arrived for an interview recently wearing flat black boots that were splattered with street salt, and—if the assistant who relayed the tale is to be believed—it wasn't the fact this candidate had "been underground" that was a deal-breaker, although that wasn't ideal. No, she was summarily rejected because you must be a special kind of stupid to interview at the most famous fashion magazine in the world with shit all over your shoes.

And we don't hire a special kind of stupid.

So, I get off the subway, and trudge up the stairs in my Uggs, only to realize I miscalculated my exit; I am on the east side of the street, which places me at the entrance of Bryant Park. On normal days, this is no big deal, but today it borders on disaster because *today* is the first day of New York Fashion Week, and I am standing at its main entrance dressed like an extra from *The Clan of the Cave Bear*. I quickly scan the immediate area. The trees that line the park are bare, and they stretch their brittle, rangy branches into the mackerel sky. Over the past week, a series of sturdy white tents have bloomed open across the winter grass. These tents, which are erected every September and February, are a soothing marker of time, but their inner workings are as mysterious to outsiders as Stonehenge. As I have not been invited to attend a fashion show, I must be content with the secondhand stories I overhear in the office, and courtesy of the lineups that circulate, all brimming with our upcoming stories about runway looks and heretofore unseen accessories. I console myself by rationalizing I am in the culture department (and, thus, not a "fashion person") but so is Davis, and that never stops her from receiving a stack of invitations so thick she must tie them up in bundles with ribbon.

I start toward the office when, to my horror, I see a group of our editors waiting for the light to change on the other side of the street. I scuttle down a few subway steps, like a trapped animal, and hope that I wasn't spotted. I leave just enough headroom, however, to observe them from my little trench. Regular commuters are banging against me as they make their way out of the subway, but I don't concede an inch.

They can walk around me.

The light changes, and I watch the editors cross the street in a set formation (four rows of girls, three across) like a gaggle of beautiful geese flying south for the winter. They have perfectly straight hair, wear magnificently tailored coats, including some furs, and their four-inch heels clip on the sidewalk in a manner that makes my little heart ache with longing. Davis is in the back row. She is wearing a tall brown fur hat (like a Russian) and her arms are folded thoughtfully across the chest of her double-breasted, gold-buttoned peacoat. She converses easily with the girl next to her. Her legs are long and rail thin, but appealingly so, more athletic than sickly, and she is wearing high stiletto brown suede boots. Once the group glides past my hiding spot, I look down and realize my mittened hands grip the railing, like a kid staring into a toy store window at Christmas. I feel the newly scattered salt crunching under my weight as I haul myself up the grimy stairs, and my eyes strain to follow Davis as she makes her way through the clusters that have assembled near the tents. She shakes hands and kisses cheeks before she is stopped by a photographer. She places her hand on her hip and turns slightly to the side, and, from a million miles away, I can almost hear the adoring flutter of camera shutters. Once she disappears from view, I tuck my chin into the collar of my jacket and make my way toward the sorry little cranny where I switch my shoes, each day. As I jam my boots into the canvas tote, I feel left out, which makes me feel mad. Why am I due at my desk while everyone else is going to spend their mornings at fashion shows and an endless stream of champagne lunches? Anger is my preferred default emotion because I find that it is thick enough to spackle over the weaker, more pathetic emotions I cannot admit experiencing, like shame or envy. I want to direct these feelings toward Davis. I want to believe, somehow, that she is the one holding me back, but I know that to be ridiculous. If anything, I owe her a debt of gratitude for being nice to me. I hoist my bag over my shoulder, and I push through the doors into the warm lobby of my building.

Even though it is Fashion Week, we are in the middle of shipping the next issue, which means late nights and some early mornings (for me at least), so, on this particularly bleary day, I pick up a half dozen sausage links in the office cafeteria. I figure why not? I will be one of the few people in the office for the next hour. For starters, features assistants are always late. Secondly, the fashion assistants will be out all day. As far as I can tell, their main job during Fashion Week is to follow their bosses around the city and divvy out show invitations one-by-one, from the overstuffed envelopes they keep protectively pressed to their chests. This system was designed to spare our editors the indignity of appearing sloppy or overburdened. Afterall, who wants to see a fashion editor lugging around a sensible handbag? I decide that, with the office so quiet, I have earned the right to eat whatever disgusting breakfast I want in relative peace. When I step into the elevator, however, I discover that it is occupied by Mark Angelbeck, who remains a man I usually only see from afar, and two other men in suits. One is our company chairman, who is old, famous, and wouldn't know who I was if I held him up at gunpoint in broad daylight wearing a name tag. The other man is much younger, and I have never seen him before. He wears an extremely unflattering pair of eyeglasses that—as best as I can describe it—make him look like a computer programmer from the 1980s who molests little boys in his wood-paneled basement.

He should absolutely, positively get new glasses.

"Sorry," I whisper.

"No problem," Mark Angelbeck responds.

Now, by this juncture in feminist history, it has been well established that women say *sorry* too often, and it's usually when they have nothing to apologize for, like, you know, riding the elevator at their place of business. What I can't decide—despite all the hand-wringing and article writing—is if this is simply a conversational tic that ultimately means nothing or if I should be taking to the streets with a flaming torch to demand an immediate end to the patriarchy. The elevator stops before I can decide, and the company chairman steps off on the executive floor with a gruff goodbye. The doors close softly, and we start to ascend. I am wearing a black wool dress with a belt, and—in the absence of our chairman—I can physically feel two sets of eyes roam over every inch of my back. Like fingerprints. I hold my breath and hope my thong hasn't bunched up on my hip.

"Big fan of sausage?" Mark Angelbeck asks, and the deepness of his voice startles me. I look down at my hands. As luck would have it, the top of my Styrofoam container has popped open and exposed my shameful breakfast secret. I feel my cheeks warm with embarrassment, but it's not from the sexual connotation implied by his comment. I mean, I have obviously heard far worse. No, I'm embarrassed because I can't seem to generate a quick and witty retort; I want to throw something full of sexual innuendo right back at him, like a modern girl Friday. I want him to know I'm not easily offended, that I *like* to play the game because I am *different* from the other girls. However, nothing comes out of my mouth, and I start to panic that this unbelievably long pause will make me seem prudish, which, quite frankly, is exactly how I feel.

"I'm kidding with you, sweetheart," he says finally. "Relax."

He pats me on the back reassuringly, like I am his poor, slow cousin.

"No, of course," I say quickly, even though the way he said the word *relax* just made me feel a little queasy. "I know. I *know* you were kidding."

I laugh, but I can feel the slow singe of tears.

"Good," he says, and although I cannot see his face, I think he sounds quite satisfied. "Because *sausage* is *good* for you."

At this comment, his bespectacled companion lets out a small, uncomfortable bleat of laughter, and I understand that I have failed. Mark Angelbeck has put me to the test, and I have failed. As I feel my body swell with self-loathing and shame, the elevator comes to a stop on our shared floor.

"Have a good day," Mark Angelbeck says, very professionally, once we are in the lobby and within earshot of our receptionist. She beams at him over her desk.

"Thanks," I manage to say, but I can't bring myself to look in his direction. "You too."

"Oh, I will," he drawls out, which causes the other guy to laugh again.

I head to the glass doors, and I clutch my breakfast with both hands. I can feel them watch me as I walk away. I can feel their bemusement. I can feel their control. They know that I will toddle back to my little desk and eat my little breakfast, and I will never utter a single word to anyone about our interaction.

Why? Because I am the right kind of girl.

10

I wake up to the din of a pummeling rain and the familiar sorrow that can accompany, for me anyway, the mere act of regaining consciousness on a Saturday morning. I am always alone in my studio apartment, of course, but on some days, I feel more alone than others. Especially weekends. On weekends, I rarely have anything to do, even at night, and while I debate going to a museum in the city, I usually just end up wandering the bookstore in my neighborhood and feeling sorry for myself for not having more friends or a beach house or a date. I have decided that being alone must be akin to running a marathon. I practice every day. I practice *every day* because I believe that one day, there will be a big race for which I am exceedingly well prepared. I'll cross the finish line, people will cheer, and then—like magic—I won't mind being alone anymore. Or that being alone won't feel so alone. After all, are we not told that striking out and seeing the world is the brave thing, the thing that makes you stronger? But all I want to do with every breath in my body is go home. I want to go home, but I have too much pride or, more accurately, too little self-confidence, to go home. I also have the gnawing self-knowledge that, if I go home, I will never forgive myself for selecting an easier path. I'll have to take another job as a medical textbook editor. I'll drink bottled domestic beer and cheap gin and tonics in plastic cups in the same old bars, laughing at the same old routines, everyone playing their same old roles.

Here is the thing: I know that if I give up, I won't ever travel the world. And even if I don't travel the world, I certainly never would have lived in an apartment all by myself, an oftentimes scary place where I am forced to deal with late electric bills, the possibility of being murdered, broken faucets, and the late-night scattering of mice. I know I won't read difficult books. Or try (and fail) to learn another language. Or make new friends that are nothing like me. I won't endure the confusing aftermath of a one-night stand with a man I'll never see again or get butterflies during a promising blind date. I won't lift a glass of ice-cold champagne off a sterling silver tray and marvel at a world that I, Clodagh Patricia Harmon, had the courage to create instead of settling for a world I could, without any effort, inherit.

Maybe these moments will seem small or meaningless one day, but from my current vantage point, I suspect it is precisely these odds and ends that add up to a life. So, yes, I want to go home, but I will stick this out. I will stay here in New York and wake up every morning with this searing, starving, relentless ball in my chest in the hope that one day it will dissipate, and that, one day, this strange and harsh and lonely land will feel a little bit more like a land that belongs to me.

11

"Are you good?" Davis Lawrence yells over the music.

"I am good," I yell back, and I give her a double thumbs-up that I instantly regret.

The truth is that I am not good. In fact, every second of my night has been mortifying beyond comprehension.

You see, I have spent the last two hours dancing in a bar called APT (a bar in which I don't belong, mind you, because it's a bar that, quite clearly, belongs to cool people) and while I cannot dance, I did it anyway because I could tell Davis wanted me to dance. As it happens, Davis wanted *everyone* to dance and, so, at a certain point in the evening, she rounded up her little gang, her arms wide and smile encouraging, and snow-plowed us onto the floor. We all danced, primarily, I suspect, because it would make Davis happy, but our heads and long legs moved in the strangest of ways. Nobody made eye contact, and with every agonizing minute, I realized that not a single one of us had any business on a dance floor.

We kept dancing anyway.

My presence at APT was accidental at best and charity at worst. Earlier in the evening, Davis saw me standing alone at the elevator on her way out of work. She was with a group of girls, and they were all in clubby conversation, so I arranged my face to look both cheerful and distracted by the zipper on my bag.

"Clo," Davis called in my direction, and I had looked up. "What are you doing tonight?"

I started to speak, but she just interrupted me.

"Cancel it," she said. "Come with us to dinner?"

She glanced over at the other girls for confirmation, and, after a beat, they all nodded vigorously. I smiled back, but all I could think was how much I hated my outfit.

And so, I went with them to a corner bar called the Spotted Pig in the West Village, which was long part of the city's lore, but somewhere I had never been before because I was saving it, I suppose, for a special occasion. When we arrived, we were quickly ushered upstairs by a man who seemed to know all the girls, kissing them on both cheeks and sending over a round of free drinks. I ordered a salad. Everyone else ordered cheeseburgers, which I found encouraging until they barely touched anything (except for the fries) and every time I thought of adding to the conversation, I thought better of it. I figured my time was more advantageously spent quietly studying their language patterns and table manners. I took note that they all held their knives with their right hands (not switching back and forth as I was taught to do) and, even more fascinating, nobody spoke unless their silverware was resting on the plate. When dinner was complete, everyone placed their napkins to the left of their plate and nobody seemed particularly surprised when we were not presented with a bill. There was some rattling on about where to go next—Passerby in Chelsea (which everyone inexplicably was also calling "Gavin's") and some guy's loft on Spring Street were thrown around—before Davis decided we would go to APT. I followed the girls outside onto the street and, when nobody tried to shove me into a cab, I figured I was permitted to tag along.

Once inside the darkened bar, we all got drinks, although I have no idea who paid, and Davis would glance over at me occasionally, almost to confirm I was doing okay. I would nod but quickly look away. I didn't want her to notice I had been staring at her, marveling at the way she moved through people like liquid. Her clothes didn't bunch. She didn't pick at her sweater or play with her hair. She never approached anyone, nor did she look away from the person to whom she was speaking; her rapt attention lent her a near religious aura. People hung in little clusters at her elbow, me included, like planets waiting for their moment to cycle closer to her blazing greatness. As the night wore on, all kinds of people came out of the woodwork, and many of them were the same people one reads about in the papers. There were princesses, socialites, actresses, artists, and douchebag heirs to great financial and political fortunes, most of whom, to my legitimate astonishment, behaved like normal people. They rattled on about mundane things at the office. They complained they couldn't get cell service inside the bar. They questioned their choice of shoes. They spoke unkindly of the innocent. They had to be somewhere early in the morning.

For me, it was like discovering I could speak to the animals.

Of course, I was completely out of place, but because I had arrived with Davis Lawrence, everyone made some general assumptions about me, the clearest of which was that I deserved to be there. I did a lot of nodding and smiling. I did a lot of drinking.

Just when I decide I cannot dance for another minute, I feel Davis suddenly cup her hand around my ear.

"Get your coat!" she yells.

"Okay," I yell back. "Are you tired?"

"No," she replies, grabbing my hand. She leads me toward a pile of coats on a table. "I want to take you to Florent."

"What is Florent?" I ask as I search for my black coat in the jumble. I am so sweaty, the idea of putting on an extra layer feels immediately oppressive. I run my palm along the back of my neck and wince; I can feel damp curls starting to swell.

"Oh, my love," she replies. "It's only the most wonderful diner in the whole world."

"You don't say?"

"I *do* say," she says, her eyes widening. "And I am *starving*."

As we push our way toward the door, everyone begs Davis to stay. They are rightfully concerned that her departure will release all the air from the room, but Davis will not be dissuaded. I watch as she extricates herself from the swarm in an earnest cloud of air-kisses, and then she grabs my hand again and pulls me out to the street.

It's quiet outside except for the searing ringing in my ears, and my dank clothes seize in the bitter air. I notice that Davis's hair has curled up in little ringlets at her temples. Her cheeks are flushed.

"Thisaway," she sings, and I realize, with nervous wonder, that she has not released my hand.

We clack down the cobblestone streets of the Meatpacking District which, as the name may indicate, is a forlorn and foul-smelling corner of the city. I rarely find myself here. After all, it has only a good bar or two to recommend it, one of those being APT, while the others are Pastis, which I can't afford, and Tortilla Flats, a tacky, glittering Mexican restaurant with low, frantically adorned ceilings and really cheap tequila. There is also the Hells Angels' biker bar Hogs and Heifers, which looks intimidating, but generally lets girls like me inside, so long as we agree to shimmy on the bar and throw our bras into the crowd, both of which I am generally more than willing to do.

We turn down Gansevoort Street, and I see the glowing sign for Florent. I wonder how I never noticed it before; it's green and pink and illuminates one side of an otherwise nearly unlit street. We walk under the green awning and when we push through the door, the heat vent blares down on our heads. The diner is packed at this hour, and so we linger for about five minutes before a waitress points out two newly vacated spots at the counter.

"Best seats in the house," Davis says, and we quickly shrug out of our coats and sit down.

The countertop is wet from the gray rag a bus boy just slopped over it, and our plastic menus stick to the surface. While Davis peruses the late-night offerings, I look around. To me, the room feels electric, like I have stumbled into a land that time forgot. Beautiful people laugh over tables or nestle into the red banquettes, and I decide this moment has the weight of the ages. I look at Davis just as she runs her fingers through her tousled hair and smiles up at the man ready to take our order behind the counter. She chooses for both of us, and because it is so loud, we must talk with our faces mere inches apart as we wait for our food to arrive. When the drinks arrive, I marvel at the way Davis sucks down a Diet Coke in one long draw while holding a lit cigarette delicately over her head, her eyes never leaving my face.

After we drunkenly demolish a plate of fries, bacon sandwiches on toast, and a second round of soda, we head back onto the street in search of cabs to take us home. This quickly proves to be an impossible endeavor, but I don't mind because, quite frankly, I would prefer this night—my first real social outing with Davis Lawrence—to never end. We continue our search for a few blocks, but we don't see another human until a few old guys in white coats start to holler at us because we might, at this point in the evening, be singing the first act finale from *Les Misérables* at the top of our lungs. Their voices startle us out of song; they boom from deep inside one of the many cavernous warehouses that line the street, all trimmed with weather-beaten aluminum signs that say things like EAST POINT PROVISION, INC. or DIAMOND MEATS or MAGGIO BEEF. When we stop walking to peer inside, we see a pair of skinned cows hanging from hooks, and Davis squeals and grabs my hand. She pulls me behind a short line of refrigerated trucks that idle against the curb, breathless with laughter.

"I think I just became a vegetarian," she says.

As we continue unevenly along the street, we see a tow truck roll slowly in our direction, and Davis—because she is Davis—flags the driver down by waving her arms in the air and hopping on one stilettoed boot. When he sees her, the driver slows the truck to a stop and unrolls the window with a smile.

"You ladies need a ride?" he says.

"Sure do!" Davis laughs, and we both climb inside the warm cab, which smells like tobacco and aftershave. We keep singing at the top of our lungs, much to the driver's delight, until he kindly deposits us, at our request, at the subway station on Fourteenth Street and Sixth Avenue. Davis raises her hand to flag a passing cab.

"See you tomorrow, roomie," she calls out sweetly before she ducks inside the waiting car.

"See you tomorrow," I reply, my hands balled into exhilarated fists inside my coat pockets. I look up at the sky.

Maybe this doesn't sound like magic.

But it is.

12

The next morning, the subway rattles me awake. When I roll over and slowly open my eyes, I see it is barely dawn; the sky outside my window is as purple as a new bruise. I sit up and reach for the plastic gallon jug of water I keep on the floor next to my bed. I take a few large gulps as I watch a train lumber around the bend from the Smith and Ninth Street station. Its lusterless hull crawls inchmeal past me in the direction of Manhattan, and because the track structure runs so close to my apartment, I can sometimes make out what people are reading on their commute if I sit at the far end of my bed.

The week I moved into my studio, the landlord, who inhabits the apartment below with his wife and grown daughters, informed me that the house sits under one of only two concrete overpasses in the entire city. This, he explained, is why the subway produces a soothing, muted rumble rather than the typical hair-raising screech that emanates from the "standard-issue" metal tracks. I have no way of knowing if this is true, but I repeat this story to people all the time with great confidence.

It's cold in my apartment, and, apparently, I passed out in nothing but a tank top. As I sit cross-legged and work my way through the water, my heavy breasts rest on the wide roll of fat that encircles my rib cage. I know should put on something warm, but I can't seem to move. The pounding in my head has marshaled all my available resources and while I am often hungover, this is one for the record books. I cannot recall how many vodka sodas I drank the night before.

Not that it matters: I would not change a thing.

I lay back down for a few minutes, feeling thick and doughy, and an anxious insecurity wafts around me as I try to recall all the many ways in which I surely embarrassed myself in front of Davis and her friends the night before.

I had planned to take a run before work, but as I drag myself from the covers, this proves to be a challenging endeavor. As I pull on an oversized T-shirt and leggings, my skin is so sensitive that I become convinced I am running a fever, which I immediately diagnose as liver failure or, more likely, leukemia. Furthermore, a cystic pimple broke ground on my cheek while I was sleeping, and it seems to have established its own circulatory system; a regular thumping now radiates up the side of my face. Once dressed, I grab my yellow Discman off the counter and, without checking the CD, head down my crooked stairs and out onto the street. The sun has just risen above the buildings, and the new light is agonizing. By the time I make it to the corner of my street, a wave of nausea overtakes my entire body. I double over before I fall to my knees and crawl toward a sewer grate where I dry heave like a cat failing to bring up a hairball. My body is cold and hot at the same time, and I feel my upper lip mist with perspiration. I never handle sickness well but, as I start to vomit in public, I suddenly feel so spectacularly alone that I think I might cry. And then I see them: a young couple pushing a baby stroller. They are chatting, coffees in hand, with rosy cheeks that burst with health and prudent decisions. When they spot me, the troll person climbing out of the underworld, the wife covers her adorable mouth with an equally adorable mitten in a mix of concern and laughter. I can see that, despite having a good-looking husband, a baby, and the wisdom not to drink herself into an early grave last night, she doesn't look much older than me. As I have no idea how to feel about that piece of information (Am I jealous? Is *she* jealous?), I simply wipe my mouth with the back on my hand, and put my head back down. For a long time, I gaze into the sewer and feel a sad curiosity about the strange castaways (rubber glove, ice-cream sandwich wrapper, tube sock, one-dollar bill, orange pill bottle) that have been marooned on its marshy bottom. After another—seemingly final—round of fruitless gagging, I understand I will not be able to physically rid myself of this despairing feeling with exercise or throwing up, so I will have to do it the only other way I know how: I go to church.

Fortunately, I live in Brooklyn, where there is a Roman Catholic church on every block, including mine, so redemption always feels close at hand. This morning, I plod up the concrete steps and, with two hands, I manage to haul open the massive wooden door. I slip inside, and release the door. It closes protectively behind me, so slow and soft it feels like I am being vacuum sealed in the Lord's understanding embrace. I start to walk down the carpeted aisle. The interior of this church is standard-issue extravagant—carved arches and pillars and soaring panes of stained glass—and it smells like an extinguished candle and the fresh crack of a pepper grinder. I kneel in the penultimate pew, fold my hands, and rest my forehead on my knuckles to pray. I stay very straight because I have been told, since childhood, that resting your backside on the pew is a sin. Growing up, we were never an explicit "church on Sunday" family, but you could reliably locate the Harmon clan at midnight mass, Ash Wednesday, and Easter Sunday. We didn't go to Catholic school, but we did attend CCD every Monday night from kindergarten until sixth grade when we made our confirmation, an event that signified (to whom, I do not know) our faith was forever sealed. So, while I was raised in such a manner that I have a belief system deeply rooted in Catholicism, it is uniquely my own interpretation. My Catholicism is replete with pound cake from the "good" Philly bakery (Stocks), red coolers jammed with cans of Miller Lite, First Communion parties, highly-functional alcoholism, Class E government savings bonds, and the regular appearance of no less than a dozen cousins, all named things like John and Jack and Patrick and Tara. That, to me, is being a good Catholic.

The crazy doctrinal stuff, on the other hand, is a nonstarter for me, and while I have not been wholly faithful to the Ten Commandments, I don't allow this to trouble me. I don't believe that I am going to burn for all eternity for my sins, such as they are, but rather I believe there is a God that created the world, and he loves every single person with his whole heart. While my God hopes we refrain from bad decisions (like murdering people), he also knows we are human and, as such, we are going to fuck things up royally from time to time. The God I pray to designed me for a reason, and he wants to support me on that journey and, on occasion, even go so far as to answer my prayers. As such, I've been in a quiet conversation with God my entire life. Sometimes I will observe another person moving their lips—maybe on the subway or across the aisle at the grocery store—and I will think: *Are you talking to God, too?* Not that I would ask anyone this question, of course, and certainly not here in New York; I'm not a complete idiot. But I suspect, even in this land of facts and reason and cross-dressers, that there are a lot of people who believe, just like me.

By the time I return to my street—my sins forgiven and nausea at bay—I know I'm running late because the Italian ladies are congregated on my corner. Honestly, it's like they were hired from Central Casting for my explicit benefit. They wear faded floral housedresses and their exposed ankles are covered with age spots, large bruises, and bleeding scabs. As I smile at them, I cannot help but think: What on earth happens to their legs? Or, more distressingly, does your body begin the process of disintegration in the years before you die?

Every single day, these women lumber out of their homes in yesterday's hairdo to reveal what type of meat they have chosen to defrost that morning. Will it be the pork? Brisket? What about the veal cutlets Anthony's niece drove over from that butcher in New Jersey? This chosen meat will be braised or marinated, and, in twelve hours, it will serve as the backbone to whatever complicated meal they are cooking for their family. I think it's bizarre they go to the effort because they clearly find no joy in this lavish culinary planning. In fact, they seem miserable about the whole ordeal, and I am often tempted to reveal that a sleeve of saltines is a perfectly acceptable, even pleasurable, option for the occasional dinner.

They tolerate me, an obvious mick with my blue eyes, shapeless legs, and the rosacea that creeps up my cheeks like unrepentant ivy. Some even say hello on occasion as they look me up and down and shake their heads inscrutably. I've been told I rent the "marriage apartment" and that every girl that moves in gets engaged within the year, but much like the elaborate menu planning, they don't deliver this news with any hint of enthusiasm. It's more like they feel obligated to warn me that marriage and making a nightly dinner for my family are just part of the drudgery I must endure as a woman and, the sooner I accept this fate, the better off I will be. I often entertain the idea of announcing that I am *divorced* or a *giant lesbian* or an *ardent vegan*, but I know it would rob them of the tepid dream that allows them to tolerate me, an interloper on their street. I prefer them to think I am a churchgoing, hardworking girl of modest means, and not, say, a borderline drunk who just received an ominously worded letter regarding a recent, somewhat suspicious Pap smear from her gynecologist.

My landlord Saul sits on the stoop. I like Saul. He has kind eyes, and I get the sense that, despite all his gruff behavior to the contrary, he is genuinely looking out for me. This morning, he smokes a cigarette as he observes a pair of portly pigeons prance across the sidewalk. They peck with fantastic enthusiasm at nothing. Saul is quiet, skinny, and Jewish with an affinity for unfiltered Camel Regulars, plaid shirts and baggy faded blue jeans. His wife is loud, round as a buoy, and Italian, with an affinity for screaming at Saul. He looks to be in his mid-fifties, but his face is mottled and creased, like a thirsty cowboy. He gives off the impression that he has been long resigned to never having a new experience for the rest of his life.

The pigeons will have to do.

I slow to a stop and smile, but mostly because he is blocking the door.

"Another coffee from the shop?" he says, looking at the paper cup in my hand.

"Yes, I know. I am the worst," I admit with faux shame before adding: "I picked it up on my way out of church."

"How much do they charge you for that again?"

"A dollar fifty for the large."

He lets out a long whistle.

"I know, but it's my only joy in life," I protest to both keep the mood light and move along the small talk so I can get ready for work. He must sense my impatience because he scoots out of the way, making room on the narrow concrete landing.

"When you're old like me, you'll wish you made your own coffee," he can't help yelling over his shoulder as I move past. "You're throwing away money you'll need later."

I briefly wonder if that is true, but not for long enough to do math in my head.

"I'll work on it, Saul," I call, and then I shut the front door and race up the uneven, carpeted steps to my one-room apartment.

I shower quickly, shaving nothing, and wrap my wet head in a towel turban. Then, I fish around my underwear basket, but I only find a pair of cotton briefs, which are flowered and a size too large. I glance at the digital clock next to my unmade bed. I don't have time to pick up my clean clothes from the laundromat, a joyless place down the street that folds my underwear into appetizer-sized triangles, so I root through my hamper sniffing around for a not-too-dirty pair. Then, I parse through my small closet and kick through the piles of clothes on my floor looking for something to wear, only to remember, as I remember every morning, that I hate everything I own. I try on my new pair of expensive, incredibly low-rise jeans, which slim down and elongate everything, but I cannot wear them: Jeans aren't approved for general audiences at my office yet. They are still in clinical trials with a handful of very serious, very tall fashion girls. It's probably in the public interest because when I sit down in them, you can see my entire thong. I toss the jeans on my bed and put on a standard calf-length black wool skirt and gray turtleneck which, in my opinion, could be mistaken for something Carolyn Bessette might have worn from Calvin Klein. I look in the mirror and notice that the skirt has a chalky spot on the side, which I decide is just a testament to my larger failings. I run a dirty sock under warm water and blot the stain—over and over—until it fades. Next, I go to the bathroom to brush my teeth, drop Visine in my eyes, moisturize, and dab a spongy drugstore concealer wand on my pimples and broken capillaries. These activities, of course, are just warm-up exercises. I am about to undertake the most strenuous event in my daily routine: Blow-drying my hair to some approximation of pin straight. This task requires I remove my turtleneck, primarily so I don't sweat through it during my exertions. As I stand before my bathroom mirror in my skirt and bra, I hold my round brush in one hand and blow-dryer in the other, and I contemplate all the girls with sleek, shiny hair in my office. I wonder how early they must set their alarms to get it to look so perfect. Do they have a different system? Better product? At this stage of my life, it honestly does not occur to me that they pay someone else to do this for them three mornings a week.

When, I am finished, I pull on my coat. I check to make sure I have my keys, wallet, and lipstick. I put my heels inside my bag.

The sky is spiritless as I jog past the abandoned basketball court next to my apartment and continue along the graffitied subway overpass on Smith Street, the crumbling base of which perennially sprouts weeds, dented beer cans, and the occasional used condom. As I get closer to the subway station, the gritty wall morphs into a charmingly faded mural that was painted—clearly long before my time—by a handful of elementary school children; their names and ages written in stilted handwriting. I wonder how old the artists are today, and where they are in the world. What are they doing? If you start your life in New York City, is there anywhere else to go? At the entrance to my subway station, I hand a quarter to the kind-looking man selling papers off a red milk crate in exchange for the *New York Post* before I drop down into the strange subterranean darkness, only to emerge, yet again, into my bright new world.

13

The office is usually quiet when I arrive, but today I can immediately sense the presence of another, almost ghostlike entity. I walk cautiously past the rows of empty white cubicles, all of which are plastered in tasteful collages designed to communicate each girl's intellectual and aesthetic ethos. You can reliably expect things like ripped-out magazine pages of fashion shoots, black-and-white personal photographs with shingled houses and hydrangeas in the background, and—depending on the girl—a picture of Virginia Woolf/Babe Paley/Stella Tennant/Eleanor Roosevelt tacked up with prominence. I round the corner to my desk, and there she is: Lydia Saintclair-Abbott. She is fiddling with the printer. Liddy assists our arts editor, Maya, a brilliant bird of a woman who only employs daughters of the truly elite. Apparently, they are the only ones she trusts to protect her secrets, which are rumored to be wonderfully legion and profoundly scandalous. Now, Lydia Saintclair-Abbott, whom everyone calls Liddy, is a very familiar type around these parts. My understanding is she is the daughter of a Dallas banking heir and his well-appointed philanthropist wife. Apparently, her extended family is rich and connected enough to have done things like endow museums and hospitals in Texas. She graduated from Vanderbilt in May, and, in an unfortunate twist of fate, we started at the magazine on the same day. Here is the thing: Liddy is so pretty and so rich and so thin that, if there was any justice in the world, she would be stupid. In the movie version of life, she wears a crop top and sucks on a bulbous lollipop. In the real version of life, however, Liddy seems to have majored in

Russian history and economics, speaks three languages, and worked one summer with poor kids in Africa. She also randomly knows sign language. She is a living, breathing reminder that whoever tells you that you can accomplish anything in life with enough hard work is lying to you: You are not Lydia Saintclair-Abbott. Today, Liddy wears a fitted blazer, extremely low-cut jeans, and spike-heeled sandals. To look at her makes me feel matronly in a long skirt and turtleneck, like the Polish cleaning lady who empties out our trash cans at night.

"Hi, Liddy," I say with a forced insouciance. "You're here early!"

I want my chirpy enthusiasm to make it clear that, as someone who is always here early, early is my turf.

"Good morning," she responds, but without looking up. "I know. I am trying to finish something I'm writing, and I *cannot* write in my apartment."

"*Totally*," I affirm. "It's impossible."

Now, it is important to note that I have seen *both* the Saintclair-Abbott estate (which is a ranch that rests on thirty acres outside Dallas, Texas) as well as the family's Manhattan town house, and its two dozen meticulously designed rooms complete with a conservatory (whatever the hell that is) because both have been photographed by *Architectural Digest*. As such, I can imagine any apartment in which Liddy has been installed in New York is perfectly fine for writing. I nod sympathetically, however, because I want her to think that she and I are members of the same class and, thus, share similar burdens in this life.

"Of course, the printer *here* isn't working," she says with annoyance as she slams the paper drawer shut on the machine. "I am going to try to print again. Can you let me know if anything comes out?"

"Sure."

As I wait, I pick through the random stack of mail piled up next to the printer. I am looking for a *Star* or an *Us Weekly*, which is about all I can handle at this hour, but I settle on the new issue of *W*. The printer whirs to life and I watch as a two-page document slowly rolls out. I pick it up and throw it into the nearest trash can before returning to my magazine.

"Did anything come out?" Liddy asks. Her hands are tucked into her back pockets, and she saunters toward the printer like she's the star of a Nickelodeon show about high school.

"No," I say. I flip over another wonderfully oversized page without raising my eyes.

"Okay. I'll try again."

"Sounds good."

From the outside, it is comforting to believe the delta between Workhorses and Show Horses is wide and that I, Clodagh Harmon, am just a wide-eyed Nick Carraway, fumbling along unfamiliar terrain guided only by a finely tuned moral compass. The reality, however, is far more nuanced because, once you hit a certain echelon of society, an immense distinction can be created by mere degrees. A few ticks of the dial—just a little to the left or a little to the right—can produce an entirely different set of circumstances, a shifting kaleidoscope of privilege and power. In my short time in New York, I have come to realize the ways in which people self-select are far trickier to tease out than simply the "rich versus the poor" or "good versus evil" or "black versus white." Around these halls, we employ only two types of people: the privileged (Workhorses) and the super-privileged (Show Horses) but we all go through a prescribed set of motions to affirm that HR's approach to hiring is representationally sound by tossing in a Black British person or a fashionable Asian person here and there. And then the games begin.

A Show Horse is an Ivy League–educated (or appropriately Ivy League adjacent, e.g., Kenyon, Colby) white girl who was born into some variation of generational wealth (nannies, trust funds, private schools, an emotional understanding of Maine) whose pedigree and connections burnish the reputation of the magazine and confirm it as a safe space for their fellow elite. Things like salary, insurance, and whether the company will match her 401K contribution are not on the list of things she considers when accepting the job.

Honestly, a Workhorse is not much different. She is also (most often) a white girl who hails from a thriving public school system located in a tidy little corner of suburbia who has been promised that, with enough hard work, she will be eligible for some variation of upward mobility. She is in possession of a college degree and a set of skis, and she has endured the sweltering horror of at least one landlocked tennis camp. Her mother didn't always *have* to work, but often did in professions like real estate, medical administration, or teaching. Historically speaking, a Workhorse's privilege is new; it generally dates back only a generation, and while she has worn it out a few times, she hasn't quite figured out how it fits. When a Workhorse looks for a job, the salary matters because, while she doesn't usually have much (if any) college loan debt, it is her family's expectation that she will support herself after graduation. However, when the offer comes in far below a living wage (which is the "family money" litmus test), she accepts it immediately and without negotiation because if it all goes to hell, she can fall back into her parental safety net by moving home. However, this kind of girl rarely falls into the parental safety net: She is a Workhorse.

What becomes interesting within this setup is that it creates a dynamic in which Workhorses are so desperate about fitting in among the Show Horses that they will do nearly anything to assimilate. They will behave as expected. They will exceed expectations. They will keep their mouths shut. They will put their heads down. They will forget, with astonishing swiftness, that there may be someone who sits below them on the socio-economic ladder; they quickly come to believe—with their whole hearts—that they are the lowest of the low. Workhorses have a secret code, however. We can recognize each other across rooms by the smallest of symbols, like the presence of dust on the ankles of a re-worn pair of black tights or the telltale green of a Clinique pressed powder compact peeking out of a nondescript purse. I am often reminded of that line from the children's book *Madeline*: *They smiled at the good and frowned at the bad and sometimes they were very sad.*

Until I got this job, the apex of designer clothes for me were collared Polo shirts from Ralph Lauren and my annual sweatshirt from Benetton. I had never heard of Bowdoin College. I didn't know the opera had *so many intermissions* or that "sweetbreads" were organ meat and not a fancy New York City word for French toast. Yet, here I was, elbowing for a seat on the bench and bemoaning the fact that while I was good and privileged, I was just not good and privileged *enough*.

Additionally, I feel it is important to note that I have long suspected I possess an astoundingly shitty moral compass. Unlike other people, I'm not powered by a set of values on which I can intuitively fall back on in times of uncertainty. In my short lifetime, I've gotten away with nearly every questionable behavior in which I most willingly participated (shoplifting, cheating, lying about my whereabouts, selling people down the river for my own benefit) and—outside the super obvious ones (hitting a kid, robbing an old lady)—I don't subscribe to the notion that actions are empirically right or wrong. I think it depends on the situation, and in this new world, my situation is constantly shifting. Also, if I am being honest, it's incredibly inconvenient to always do the right thing when you are busy looking out for your own interests.

And I am always looking out for my own interests.

I don't have a choice. I am a Workhorse.

That is my lot in this world.

The editors are all in a long features meeting, so I am at leisure to whittle away my time watching Liddy stalk angrily to and from the "broken" printer as I nurse a purple Vitamin Water, a case of which—as well as a case of San Pellegrino and a case of liter-sized Poland Spring water bottles—are delivered to our desks each week, ostensibly provided to take the edge off our collective, work-related hangovers. I have no idea who places this order, nor who picks up this expense, but I drink them every day nonetheless. When Davis finally arrives around ten o'clock, she smells, improbably, like cinnamon. Her hair is unwashed and pulled back in a tight bun, which—because she is Davis—makes her look even more gorgeous, like a Robert Palmer girl.

When I see her, I feel my body tense up.

"Hey, Davis," I peep in the most nonchalant tone I can muster.

"Hey, roomie," she responds.

Here, she scoops up her phone and dials her voicemail, and I watch her out of the corner of my eye. I think that if I keeled over right now, it would be totally fine. After a minute passes and I don't die, however, she hangs up, and settles down in her seat. She doesn't say anything and, as such, I feel obligated to fill the air between us, and ideally with something funny.

"I don't get that sweater on Liddy," I say finally.

"What sweater?" asks Davis, but she doesn't look up from the piles of paper in front of her. She is rushing to complete long-neglected photo research for the society pages. Her assignment is to select the best-dressed women from the previous few weeks and illuminate their common sartorial threads (ball skirts, statement necklaces, bejeweled flats) with punchy yet authoritative fashion copy. There are neat stacks of printouts from the photo services covering her desk, and I keep hearing her sigh.

"That sweater." I tip my chin toward Liddy who is now conversing with our IT guy. "It's like (A.) You can only wear it once because it's so distinctive, and (B.) Everyone knows how much you paid for it. I know I am not a *fashion person*, but I just don't get it on an intellectual level. It's like buying a Stephen Sprouse bag."

Davis glances up.

"Hmmm. I see I still have much to teach you," she says. "Incidentally, I heard she was trying to pitch Isobel a center-of-book piece."

"Are you fucking kidding me?" I blurt out. I feel the inside of my heart catch on fire. "*Her?* About what?"

A center-of-book piece (also known at lesser publications as a "well feature") is far more prestigious than a front-of-book piece because it's longer and the spreads of copy and imagery are not broken up by advertising.

"I have no idea," she says dryly. "But you sound like my mother."

"Which is why I would like your mother," I say. "Surely, she understands most women are stupid, conniving bitches."

"You should make that into a button."

"I am just saying, your mother must see things clearly. She's been around some blocks."

"My mother would immediately tell you that you're wearing the wrong bra for such large breasts."

A truly gross cackle escapes my lips before I realize she isn't kidding.

"You have a big chest," she continues. "You don't need those Victoria's Secret T-shirt bras with all the padding. You need support on the straps, but not padding. It looks lumpy under your clothes."

I gently cup my left breast with my right hand and give it a little jiggle.

"And where do they sell these magical bras?"

Here, I struggle to pretend I am not completely put to shame by this conversation.

"You need a fitting."

"A what?"

"A fitting."

"For a bra?" I laugh in genuine disbelief. "That's ridiculous."

The only time I have ever been fitted for anything was my Communion dress in the second grade. I stood on a pine box in a tailor shop in South Philadelphia wearing baggy underwear and a white undershirt while an old man repeatedly measured my chest, waist, and hips as he conversed with my mother about things like fabric and trim. He smelled like the plaid couch in my nana's living room, and his hands were craggy and capped with thick, frightening yellow fingernails. Even though this was a completely standard practice in my extended family, I still recall something about the experience feeling indecent, like a violation from which someone should have protected me. Even thinking about it today fills me with a strange unease.

When Davis doesn't respond, I walk over to the printer with my shoulders slightly slouched to hide my, apparently, *lumpy* chest, and I stand next to the IT guy. He looks relieved to have rid himself of Liddy.

"Hi," I chirp.

I say this sort of jokey, but I immediately wince. I don't know why I insist on always making things awkward.

"Hi," he says in a normal tone. Because he is a normal person.

"I am just waiting for something to print," I lie.

"So the printer *is* working okay for you?" he asks, his eyes wide.

"Me? Yep. Perfect."

I flash him a thumbs-up just as the printer hawks out Liddy's pages another time. I pluck them up and stroll back to my desk.

I scan Liddy's document, which seems to be an in-person interview with an Indian American author whose new novel is about immigrants, a blind cat, and a long bus ride in Texas. *Since when does Liddy conduct interviews?* She references Dante in the first paragraph and, because I have never read Dante, I have no way of knowing if this name drop is brilliant or utterly pathetic. I throw "circle of hell" into conversation occasionally, sure, but if pressed I would not be able to articulate its actual provenance within the text or, more critically, its meaning.

I hate Liddy.

"There are better ways of getting ahead, you know," Davis clucks when she catches what I am reading.

"Easy for you to say," I reply with comic bitterness. This is sort of our schtick. We are not yet real friends, but we are also definitely more than merely work acquaintances at this stage.

"You know, our little *My Fair Lady* routine is not going to work if you insist on being so negative," she continues with a small wag of her finger.

"My recollection is Audrey Hepburn turns out okay in the end," I mumble.

At this comment, Davis snaps her fingers.

"On that note, the Louboutin sample sale is this week on Thursday," Davis says. "I'm ordering a car. We need shoes."

"I need shoes," I say. "You have shoes."

"Okay. You need shoes," she responds. "Want to swing by my apartment after for a drink?"

I perk up.

"Will I get another glimpse of the great Barbara Lawrence?"

"One can always have hope," she replies.

"Then count me in," I say.

Barbara Lawrence is Davis's mother, and I have met her exactly one time, briefly, outside our offices one evening where she was waiting in an idling town car for Davis. She peered kindly out the half-open window at me, but said little. She's the kind of actress who was genuinely famous when I was a kid, transitioning from singing and dancing to great acclaim in big Broadway musicals in the 1970s to her hit role as the daffy mother on a comedy my own mother used to watch religiously in the 1980s. Even at her absolute height, Barbara Lawrence was never popular because she was beautiful. Despite her Anglo-Saxon lineage, she had a wide forehead and curly brown hair that lacked the golden luster seemingly required from the leading ladies of that era, like Cybil Shepherd. That said, she stood out. She had these large, expressive eyes that were always lined with dark liner, and her training as a dancer translated into a real talent for physical comedy. She moved easily, and she had ways of gesticulating that would leave my mother doubled over laughing on the couch at night. When the sitcom ended after three record-breaking seasons (including the one in which Barbara won an Emmy for Best Supporting Actress in a Comedy) and a limping fourth season after the main male character departed to do a movie, I don't think she ever had another major role. I guess it was hard to imagine her as anything else and now, over a decade later, she is famous for, well, being famous when I was a kid.

And Davis Lawrence is her only child.

"Excellent," Davis says. "Now, excuse me, but I must move on to my next assignment, which is to find out if there are any lady scientists in the world that are neither old nor ugly."

"Or fat."

"Or fat."

"You can do it, Davis," I say with a smile. "You went to Princeton with William Say-eed."

14

On the afternoon of the Louboutin sale, magnetic clusters of impeccably dressed women draw together on the wide sidewalk in front of our building at exactly three o'clock. These are our editors, and they chat amicably as they stand next to a long line of double-parked black cars, their destinations exciting and unknown. I take note that some late-season fur—collars, jackets, coats, vests—is still being trotted out, and the usual suspects—Balenciaga motorcycle bags, Fendi baguettes, Chanel 2.55s—dangle deliciously from their long arms: I even see one of those tacky Dior pony-hair saddle bags, which strikes me as strangely off-brand until I realize, with a modicum of pride, that the editor in question doesn't work at *our* magazine. As I survey the crowd, I cannot overstate the genius of our company's hiring process: Every employee is a tool in our brand marketing toolbox, but unlike subscription cards or taxi tops, we are all made of flesh and blood. The fact that you can tell which magazine every girl works for when they step into the elevator is completely by design. We are the fantasy. Are you about five foot five, well-dressed, but hopeless at layering? You work at the *other* fashion magazine. Are you heavy on top, wear one-carat diamond stud earrings, and commute to the office in running sneakers? The fitness magazine. Are you holding a mint-condition Ligne Bowler, have sandblasted skin, and are rocking not one but two Cartier Love bracelets? Beauty magazine. Curly hair and glasses? Researcher. Over forty-five and in a sensible wool coat and ballet flats? Copy editor. Wearing a perfectly nice Prada dress like it's a hog-feed sack and carrying both a cloth tote *and* a Chloé Paddington? Literary magazine assistant. Endlessly trying to lose the last ten pounds, expose your toes too early in the spring, and get a kick out of what you call *fun jewelry*? The shopping magazine.

The mind reels.

Davis and I are the only assistants waiting for a car, so we stand a few respectable feet apart from the group. We know not to mingle. It doesn't take long, however, for a senior editor to wave Davis over and offer her—and only her, I assume—a ride. Although I can't hear what is being said, I imagine Davis is explaining that she previously made a promise to accompany me to a sample sale as a gesture of public service. At this news, the editor squints briefly in my direction (she has clearly never laid eyes on me before) then she releases Davis back in my direction. Davis says nothing of the interaction; she simply looks down at a sticky note, which hangs delicately from the edge of her middle finger.

"My car is number four hundred twenty-two," she says, lifting her head up to scan the cars. The full-time dispatcher our company employs to keep everything running smoothly is racing toward the corner with a walkie-talkie in his hand, clearly in search of the car of someone important. He rises on the balls of his feet and barks into the receiver.

"Not seeing it," I say. I am trying to keep it light, but I feel, yet again, terribly out of my depth. I subtly mimic Davis's elegantly bored body language to see if that is an effective antidote to my searing awkwardness, but, alas, it is not; I feel like a hunchback. I straighten up.

"Ugh. Is he circling? Why are they always circling?" Davis whines.

Davis draws out her black flip phone and starts to dial with her thumb. This everyday motion releases a tendril of hair from her bun, and it falls so seductively across her cheek that I feel the need to look away.

For a while, I watch the double-parked town cars jockey in and out of the tight spaces with great precision and efficiency, but I do take note that one car has been idle for a while. An older, gray-haired driver in a black cap and loose suit leans limply on the back door. He is motionless for so long that I start to wonder if he has fallen asleep. At just that moment, two men exit the building and stride toward the car with great jocularity. The driver snaps to attention as if someone has, quite literally, jerked his strings. I immediately recognize one of the men as Mark Angelbeck. He has not troubled himself with an overcoat or briefcase, and his companion is wearing a black suit, white shirt, and no tie.

I watch as Mr. Angelbeck gestures magnanimously to the other man in conversation, and then they both duck into the car. The driver shuts the door with a satisfying thwunk, and I watch as they disappear into the traffic.

"Well, *that* was definitely *not* your car," I inform Davis cheerfully. "But do you think Mark Angelbeck is going to the sample sale? Should we hitch a ride?"

Davis smirks at me, the phone still to her ear, before turning away to pace the sidewalk. I can hear her speaking in a tone both regal and patronizing to the dispatcher, and I wonder if I could ever speak to anyone in a way that was so effectively frightening.

Another minute or two passes before another car pulls up. This one has a large white sign in the window that says 422.

"Our chariot has arrived," I announce, and Davis, greatly relieved, snaps her phone shut mid-sentence.

We settle close together in the back seat. While the interior is overheated, it feels more soothing than oppressive; it's like we have nestled our overtaxed little bodies into a sensory deprivation chamber. I sneak a glance at Davis. She has closed her eyes. To me, she looks both angelic and utterly exhausted, like a benevolent cherub who stayed up all night, shooting sharp arrows at the deeply lonely. On her lap rests a plain manila folder. I look down at my own lap only to be dismayed by the emergence of a tiny, round hole in my tights, right above the knee. Davis's tights are completely unblemished, and it is oddly these moments, of all the ridiculous moments, that make me the most worried that I won't make it. My only reassurance is Davis. Her sporadic attention permits me to believe, if only for a moment, that I am on the cusp of something better.

"What's in the folder?" I ask. Davis flutters open her eyes.

"Sketches," she says as she opens the folder with a sigh. "For my dress. For the gala."

The gala of which she speaks is an event the magazine hosts each

April at the Boathouse in Central Park; it's our big party each year—full of celebrities, politicians, singers, brand-name athletes—but only the thinnest, most attractive girls in our office are invited to work the event. They are dressed by the fashion department and a Polaroid photograph of each girl wearing her dress is sent to our editor-in-chief for approval weeks before the big night. If you are not invited to work (and, to be clear, I have not been invited), you are to understand that you, quite simply, do not look the part or would be, due to some defect in your physical form, too difficult to dress. Now, Davis, because she is Davis Lawrence, is a special case. She attends the event as an actual guest, which is a very rare distinction for someone at our level.

"Oh," I say as I peer over. "Do you like them?"

She shrugs.

"They are fine, I guess," she says, and she runs her finger along the paper. "Nina Ricci."

Frankly, the sketches are a little inscrutable. I don't think I would be able to tell you what, exactly, Davis's dress would look like in person based upon looking at them, but I also have learned these sketches to be an early step in the process. There will be fabric draping and proper fittings and amendments over the next few months, and while Davis may not love the outcome, that really isn't the point. The point is a famous designer made a one-of-a-kind dress for Davis Lawrence to be photographed wearing at the biggest party of the year before she shuffles it into the massive collection of one-of-a-kind dresses that already reside in her closet.

Davis closes the folder. She rests her head back on the seat.

Maybe it's the heat-induced delirium, but I suddenly feel moved to say something meaningful to Davis, although I don't know exactly what, because, while I am desperate to endear myself to her, I also don't want her to think I am trying too hard.

"I really, um, appreciate how nice you have been to me," I venture.

Here, I genuinely try to be earnest in my delivery, which is out of character, and it comes out as sarcastic, which is entirely in character, and I fear my tonal misstep will sully my good intentions. I look over for any kind of reaction, but Davis hasn't moved. I briefly suspect she has fallen asleep.

"No problem," she says finally, but without opening her eyes. "Sorry if it's all a big disappointment."

"Yeah," I say. "Sitting in this chauffeured car on the way to a shoe sale sucks so bad."

A light smile draws up her lips.

"I almost hesitate to tell you this, Clo," she says.

"Tell me what?"

"The shoe sale thing?" Here she takes an exaggerated breath. "It gets old fast."

"Maybe for you," I say.

"Yeah," she says softly, and I think I hear a flicker of sadness in her voice. "Maybe for me."

We don't say anything for a few minutes.

"So if you weren't doing this, what would you do?" I ask. "I mean, for work. You can pick anything you want."

"I know. That kind of makes it worse," she replies, and her eyeballs move behind her rosy, translucent lids. "All these *endless opportunities* . . . and all I want to do is buy my own teakettle one day."

"You really should pick a more reasonable goal," I joke.

She smiles at this comment, but not really.

"And what is keeping you from this teakettle?" I ask.

"Nothing, really," she says quickly, and she shifts in her seat. "My mom just had a rough couple of years, so, when I graduated, I thought it would be better if I lived with her for a while, just to keep an eye on things."

"Does she have a nice teakettle?" I venture, but all I can think is: *What does she mean by a rough couple of years?*

"Top of the line," Davis says. "But I am just trying to figure out the right time to get my own place."

"That's exciting," I say, but I am hoping she says more about her mother.

She doesn't.

"How about you?" she asks instead. "What do you want to do?"

"Me?"

Davis nods, but she is still leaning back with her eyes closed.

"Well, initially I just wanted to survive long enough to get my name on the masthead," I respond.

"You ticked that off the list," she says. "What's next?"

"Okay. I would like to write a real article," I say with a pantomime of wistfulness. "But that doesn't seem to be on the table."

"It's normal," she replies. "The first year they are just watching you. They want to make sure you're a good fit."

"So what happens once they decide you're a good fit?"

"In our department?" she asks, and I see her brow wrinkle slightly. "Well, you've gotten stationery, right?"

I nod. The week after my name appeared on the masthead, Elinor stopped by with proofs of both my business cards, as well as letterhead and notepads, my name in black print across the top. It's so beautiful that I am afraid to use it.

"Well, you'll get to write an article at some point," she says. "And people will start to know your name, which means you'll get invitations to things," she says.

"Then what?"

"Then?" Davis says, and she seems to think about this for a long moment before she responds. "Then, you are the girl who owns the city."

"What does that mean?"

"It means the doors that are closed to everyone else will be thrown wide open for you."

"That's very poetic, Davis."

"Thank you."

"I can't imagine that being my life, however," I add, but mostly for good measure.

"Neither can I," Davis says jokingly. "But I *do* like a project."

"Well, I am happy to be that project," I say.

Over the past few months, Davis had gone from quietly steering me away from landmines at work to behaving as if she is my actual friend. She confides in me at times and occasionally she will invite me to parties with some of the more seasoned girls, but I can't help but feel there is an almost deliberate unpredictability about her behavior. There have been agonizing days she has barely spoken to me.

They hollow me out with paranoia, but I sometimes wonder if that isn't the point.

"My pleasure," Davis says. "I mean, if I can get you to say *water* instead of *wooder*, my work here is done."

"I do not say *wooder!*" I exclaim.

I do not—for the record—say *wooder*.

At this, she finally opens her brilliant blue eyes and laughs at her own joke. This is a joke, mind you, for which I gave her the material as, Lord knows, Davis Lawrence has never set foot in Northeast Philadelphia. But it is this smile, this very smile, that has pulled everything anyone has ever wanted directly into her universe, and her universe alone. She is like a beautiful black hole into which I, too, am only too happy to surrender.

"You give my life meaning, Clo," Davis says wryly.

It sounds funny. We girls are always trying to be funny. Funny is how we beat life to the punch. Funny is how we inform the world we aren't a threat, that we won't try too hard, that we understand our place. I laugh with her, but, deep down, I know what she is saying to be true. That's the thing about Davis: It is her one wobbly wheel, and I have been playing it to my advantage since the moment I met her. You see, Davis Lawrence, as magnificent as she is to behold, seems to be utterly and hopelessly lost.

And, maybe, I am her last chance at a North Star.

Less than forty-five minutes later, Davis and I drift down Madison Avenue on foot. It's dusk, which has started to descend earlier these days, like a disorienting fog. The cars are nearly invisible except for their lights, which jig cautiously along the street as they wait for the sharpness of a darker hour. My arms are folded against my chest to discourage a deepening chill, and I have the handles of a flimsy brown paper shopping bag pinched in the crook of my elbow.

I keep waiting for the bottom to fall out.

"I don't know why I even go to those shoe sales," Davis says as she stops to peer into the window of a clothing store. "Nothing ever fits me."

"This is the benefit of being almost six feet tall and *not* a model," I reply comically. "I have a sample-sized foot. I wear a ten."

"European sizing, please!" she corrects. "That is a forty-one to you now."

"Forty-one," I say obediently, and Davis laughs.

"So why didn't you get those amazing red sandals I picked out?" she inquires.

"I can only get black right now," I reply.

At the sale, I bought a pair of calf-high black boots with a kitten heel and pointy toe. I get paid $24,000 a year, which, after taxes, breaks down to $700 a paycheck. My rent is $850 a month, and these boots cost me $350. As I will need to be buried in them to justify the enormity of this expense, I remind myself to specify to Allie (who is my emergency contact) that I want a fully open casket, not one of those half ones.

"Why? Black is so boring," Davis says.

"I figure it's hard to tell where your clothes are from if they are all black?"

"It's not *that* hard," she replies, rolling her eyes. "Plus, you always look like you're going to Rosh Hashanah services."

"I didn't know you were such an authority on the High Holidays, Miss Lawrence."

Davis snorts softly without looking at me, but then stops suddenly and gasps with great theatricality.

"What?" I yelp.

"That coat," she says, pointing into a store window. I look: There is a headless white mannequin wearing a red, somewhat military-style, below-the-knee winter coat.

"The coat?"

"Clo, this is it," she announces. "This is your coat!"

"In that color? Really? I'm so ruddy."

"Yes, really," she says, pulling open the door. "Let's go try it on."

The store is aggressively bright, to my eye anyway, and it seems to sell very few pieces of actual clothing. This merchandising tactic, however, makes it easy for Davis to locate the red coat that hangs with two of its siblings on an otherwise empty rack. She checks the sizes, pulls one off the bar (*probably the large*, I think), and holds it up for inspection. I can see the salesperson is sizing us up.

"Oh, I love her things," she says, satisfied with the designer. "Put it on."

She pulls out the hanger and watches me as I struggle my arms into the stiff sleeves without any hint of grace or coordination. It's almost like this coat wants nothing to do with me.

"Oh my god," she sighs once I manage to wrest it onto my body. "It's so well done. Look at the shoulders!"

Davis touches and tugs at the coat approvingly. She pulls at the buttons and smooths away imaginary lint. Satisfied, she turns me around to face a full-length mirror, and I look like a perfectly proportioned, extremely expensive, and very intimidating toy soldier.

"Oh, wow. It *is* nice," I whisper.

"Now put on your new shoes," Davis instructs.

She hands over the brown paper bag. I am taken aback by the absurdity of this request, but something tells me that I shouldn't protest because maybe this is how proper shopping is done by people who have the money to enjoy proper shopping in a proper neighborhood. And I'd like to be mistaken for someone who has enough money to properly shop. I sit down on a tufted maroon velvet couch and flip open the long white box. I kick my shoes off and allow myself a few seconds to admire my new boots. They are nestled in tissue paper—all red soles and a healthy shine—and I cannot believe they belong to me. I slide them on, one by one, and pull the zippers up my calves with a luxurious ease previously unknown to me in the footwear category.

"Stand," Davis says. I straighten up and return to my reflection in the mirror. Davis stands behind me with her mouth parted in a near religious fervor: She has found God in a coat.

"Yes," she hisses.

"Yes?"

"Yes," she affirms. "My mother says you should get a good coat and never take it off at parties. It saves you from having to buy too many clothes."

"A big concern for your mom, eh?"

Davis chooses not to hear me, but instead does a very Davis thing: She hops up and down and starts clapping and squealing.

"You're buying it," she exclaims loudly. "You are buying it!"

This is the fun part where I get to check the price tag, which informs me this life-improving garment costs $1,200. I briefly imagine my mother's limp, disapproving body splayed out between two overstuffed winter clearance racks at a Marshalls.

"It's twelve hundred dollars," I reveal with the assumption that truly shocking information ends the conversation.

"Really? That's not bad *at all*," she says, reaching for the price tag in disbelief.

"For a coat?"

"This is New York City, baby," she says, clapping. "Your coat is your car. Especially since you are getting it for half price. I have an editor's discount here."

I'm quickly learning that most magazine editors seem to have an editor's discount everywhere and, with a flick of a business card, someone like Davis Lawrence gets everything at half price, if they make her pay for it at all.

"At the moment, I don't have half of twelve hundred," I say, but I immediately regret this admission. I don't want to come off as completely pathetic and poverty stricken, just disadvantaged enough to gin up a little sympathy and a free dinner now and again.

"Don't you have an emergency credit card?" she asks.

"No."

"Hold on," she says with her hand up. "Your parents let you move to New York and didn't give you a credit card for an emergency?"

In truth, my parents *did* give me an emergency credit card, but they would also murder me with their bare hands if I used to it buy a $1,200 winter coat. I shake my head.

"I have *more* than one," she says with a conspiratorial smile. "I have *all kinds* of emergencies."

"Yeah, I don't think my parents would be terribly pleased to pay for that kind of emergency."

"In fairness, my mom doesn't pay *my* credit card bills," Davis replies dryly. "She pays *her* credit card bills. I just conveniently keep a few of *her* cards in *my* wallet."

"How does that even work?" I ask as I attempt to slide the coat off my shoulders.

"She has a lot of credit cards, and our accountant pays all the bills. You know her, she can't be bothered with details," she explains, waving the notion away with her hands. "He only flags purchases over five digits. If it's under $999.99 he doesn't bring it to her attention."

"You are amazing," I say.

"I know," she says with a shrug and a smile.

She lifts my black handbag up off the couch.

"Think of it as an investment, Clo," she says, and she is about to hand over my bag when her face clouds over. I feel a sharp prick of panic when I realize she is staring at the compass I pinned to the strap on my bag.

"Why do you have this?" she asks, and she points at it with her eyes wide. Frankly, I am surprised this is the first time she noticed it; it's been hanging there for months.

"Oh, that," I say as I search for the least gloomy explanation. "When I come out of the subway, I never know which way is north or south since the, uh, Towers went down. I was always getting lost."

I grimace after the words depart my mouth and I'm just praying the salesperson—especially if she has a bunch of dead friends—didn't hear me.

"Jesus Christ," Davis cries out. "That's morbid."

We face each other wordlessly for a few beats before Davis recovers her cheerful animation.

"However," she says, holding up her finger like she is teaching me yet another very valuable lesson. "Perhaps this compass should *also* remind you to live your life to the fullest."

I am half listening. I am still looking in the mirror. Davis follows my gaze.

"I know. It's impossibly good," Davis says, just as her cell phone starts to ring. She opens her purse and pulls it out. "It's Grant."

Grant is Davis's boyfriend. They met the summer after freshman year in college at a camp they both worked for in Maine. He went to Harvard, of course, and he's rich, tall, and perfect. He is also an investment banker, which means he works all the time, so I never see him. As a single person with a limited number of friends, I rate this as Grant's finest quality.

"Honey, hang on a second," Davis coos into the receiver before turning back to me. "Take my bag. There's a business card in my wallet. It will get you the discount."

"Davis," I start to protest, but she is having none of it.

"You better buy that coat by the time I am off this call," she commands, and she jabs her finger at me before disappearing out the front door.

I stand there. Admittedly, I am resplendent in this red coat and my high-heeled boots. I can sense the saleswoman is trying to figure me out. She wants to know what, if anything, I can afford, and I suddenly feel the need to explain myself. I walk up to the counter, and place both handbags—mine and Davis's—in front of me. I start to shrug out of the coat because I have every intention of explaining that, while I *adore* the coat, I'm going to come back and get it *another time.*

"You don't have to take it off," the saleswoman says.

She holds up a scanner and points at the price tag dangling from the cuff. Instinctively, I raise my arm, and there is a gentle, wonderfully sedating beep. *There, there,* says the little voice in my head. *This will all be over soon.*

"With tax, that will be twelve eighty-eight seventy-five," she informs me.

Tax, I think bitterly before I remember the business card in Davis's wallet.

"Oh, I get a discount here," I say before adding: "I'm a magazine editor."

I stumble over my words as I open the top of Davis's bag and pull out her wallet, which is constructed of soft red leather and has her initials (D.D.L.) monogrammed on the front in gold. I unzip it only to discover it is so organized (the dollars are crisp and grouped by value) that I experience a wave of self-loathing wash over me for my own persistent disorganization. True story: Last week, I found a chewed piece of gum matted in the zipper part of my own wallet and when I couldn't dig it out with my nails, I gnawed it off with my teeth. Then I chewed the cool, pink wad for a minute to see if it had retained any flavor before I spit it into an old receipt.

I pull out one of Davis's thick, white business cards and slide it across the counter for inspection. The saleswoman glances down and then her eyes, once dismissive, meet mine, and she offers me what I can only describe as a nervous smile. You see, by the simple act of handing over a business card that states I work at a fashion magazine (and thus, I am the blazing hot center of the known universe in New York), I have magically transformed this woman into the lesser partner in our interaction. I have put her on the back foot, and I have made her feel gangly and poor and conspicuous. I have made her feel, quite frankly, like me and, instead of feeling empathy or camaraderie, I feel awesome. I feel better than her, and I so rarely feel better than anyone lately.

"So your discount makes it five hundred," she says. "I own the store so we can just, you know, forget the tax."

"You own the store?" I ask.

I am now, for some reason, speaking in a British accent.

She nods.

"Do you have a business card?" I continue, still British. "I am putting together a roundup of the best independent boutiques in the city. I *might* like to feature you."

"Of course," she says as she pulls one out of a holder on the counter. "That would be amazing. I mean, you guys are like . . . everything."

I smile at her in a patronizing fashion as I pull a credit card out of Davis's open wallet. I am about to hand it over to her when I stop short.

"Oh," I say, flustered by the mistake. I jam my other hand into my own bag in search of my wallet.

"Is everything okay?" the saleswoman asks, and I pause.

I look down at the piece of plastic pinched between my fingers. It's gold and rectangular. The name on this card reads: Barbara W. Lawrence. I glance over my shoulder. Davis is still outside talking to Grant on the phone, but she catches my eye and offers me an enthusiastic wave through the front window. I smile and give her a thumbs-up back. I now feel I have been given full permission to do what I already knew, on my deepest level, that I was going to do anyway. I turn back to the woman with a smile:

"I'm sorry, it's just this credit card belongs to my mother," I say finally. "Is that a problem?"

My head feels like it's suddenly packed in a dense, protective cotton. I have shifted into another, yet not wholly unfamiliar gear.

"Not a problem," she replies easily before making a crack: "Everyone's cards belong to someone else around here."

I pull in my breath as she swipes the card. Then I watch her work the little black machine with her fingers, and I am unable to exhale until I hear the receipt start to print out.

"Thank you, Davis," she says as she hands over my receipt, which is tucked neatly into an elegant black envelope. Then she pulls out a pair of scissors and snips off the tag. "It was an honor to meet you, and I hope you come again soon."

Here, she hands me back Barbara Lawrence's credit card and I decide, without really deciding, to slip it into my own wallet.

"No, thank *you*," I say warmly.

15

It is completely dark by the time we arrive at the apartment Davis shares with her mother, which is housed in one of those formidable buildings that line Central Park East. There is a long green awning under which sits a tasteful arrangement of potted evergreen trees. The doorman is smoking a cigarette, but when he sees Davis, he flicks the pink button onto Fifth Avenue. It lands halfway across the street where it is immediately flattened by the tires of a passing taxicab.

"Good evening, Miss Lawrence," he says with a courtly tip of his hat. He looks to be in his fifties and, unlike most doormen in the city, his accent is as American as apple pie. There isn't even a hint of New York in it; he's like a movie doorman.

"Good evening, Hatch," Davis responds placidly.

Hatch walks across the newly vacuumed carpet and, with a white-gloved hand, pulls open the heavy wooden door. Before we can enter the lobby, however, a young man rushes out. He pushes past us roughly, which jostles our bodies, and I see that his fists are pushed down hard in his coat pockets. He has spiked blond hair and light eyes that look rimmed, every so subtly, in black eyeliner.

"Sorry. Excuse me," he murmurs in our direction, both unconvincingly and after the fact, and then he dashes to the curb and raises his arm for a passing cab. To me, he looks a little rattled, like he's trying to get away from something unpleasant. Fortunately, his escape is easily made; a taxi quickly obliges him, and just like that, he vanishes into the night.

I turn back toward the lobby only to notice that Davis's attention is still very much focused on the now-empty street. Her jaw is shunted forward, and her eyes are narrowed in a way that makes it clear to me she has seen this young man before. Finally, she shakes her head and walks into the building.

I follow her, but not without profusely thanking Hatch for his service. I feel both a kinship and pity for him and, as such, I decide it is of vital importance that I nonverbally communicate that I do not have a doorman. I want him to know I am just a simple girl from simple means. Sure, fifteen minutes ago, I was a British heiress with money to burn in an upscale boutique, but this is just how my addled brain works. I am always trying to adapt myself to circumstances; I am always the mutable element. Hatch smiles at me and winks, and I wink back. *He gets it*, I think.

Davis and I trundle into the elevator, which is small, with an antique mirror and upholstered bench, and I quietly steep in Davis's furious silence as we ride up six floors. I stand behind her as she unlocks the door to her apartment, which sways open to reveal a colossal, octagon-shaped foyer with twelve-foot ceilings and parquet wood floors. In the middle of the room, there is a brass sculpture of a curvy woman on a concrete pedestal. It has an engraved plaque on the base, but I figure it's tacky to be caught trying to read it. When Davis starts to close the door, I notice that it is two feet thick.

"Whoa," I say reflexively. "Why is your front door like that?"

Davis looks at the door, almost as if she is seeing it for the first time.

"Oh, my dad bought this apartment in the seventies before my parents got married. He totally did a number on it for security for all of his art," Davis says.

"Ah," I say.

Davis Lawrence's parentage is one of those long-speculated-upon urban mysteries; it pops up in the *New York Post* every now and again, which is the only way I know about it. Well, that and from my mother. The official story is that Davis—tall, blonde, and clear-blue-eyed Davis—is the product of a brief marriage between Barbara and an unnamed Mexican businessman and art collector who died mysteriously when Davis was a newborn and left behind a truly obscene pile of money. The gossip, however, is that this tale was concocted by multiple PR teams to cover the fact that Davis is, in fact, the daughter of an extremely famous, equally blond, and still *very much alive* actor in Los Angeles with whom Barbara had a controversial love affair during the same period.

"There are all kinds of security things," Davis says with a bored shrug. "There was a panic room, but my mom turned it into cold storage for her clothes collection."

"I don't know what that means, but it seems deeply wise," I offer.

"Dresses from her premieres and stuff," she explains with a laugh, taking off her coat. "And one must not keep fur at room temperature, of course. It's not its natural habitat."

I nod slowly and pinch my chin as if I am deep in thought. Davis laughs. Again, our shtick: I am the funny friend.

"Davis? Davis? Is that you?"

This unmistakable baritone belongs to Barbara Lawrence, and I must strain to subdue the nervous excitement that jolts through my body when I hear her call for us. I already cannot wait to get home and call my mother.

"Yes, it's me and Clo," Davis calls out, straight up into the air.

She hands me a thick wooden hanger from the coat closet, but I decline. I am not ready to part with my new red coat just yet, and, frankly, I want Barbara to see me in it and approve. I am also a little curious as to when I'll start to feel guilty about what I have just done, especially because it hasn't kicked in yet. I've had just enough therapy (two sessions) to know what *disassociation* means, and it's like I am conducting my own little experiment in which I am both the subject and the scientist. More broadly, I am finding it's hard to feel that bad about stealing from a very rich person who will, if Davis is to be believed, never even notice.

"Ladies!" Barbara Lawrence sings as she enters the foyer with an excited double clap. At the sight of her, my mind involuntarily conjures up the image of a trained seal, possibly made of velvet, wearing a triple strand of pearls and tooting on a golden trumpet. "Ladies!"

"Did I just see young Nathan in our lobby?" Davis asks with a false innocence.

"Nathan is just a new friend, Davis," Barbara responds with boredom. "He came over for a little drink."

"Let me guess? Is young Nathan still aspiring to be an actor?" Davis presses, her voice raising slightly. "And you haven't tired of him yet?"

She bats her lashes as if she is joking, which she clearly is not, and

Barbara, for her part, simply ignores her with what strikes me as a devastating elegance. She walks over to me with her arms lovingly outstretched in greeting, like she has been waiting for this moment her entire life. She wears black high-waisted trousers, a silk blouse, and leopard-print Belgian loafers that make a slightly sticky sound on the wooden floor. She looks so much smaller than she does in my childhood memory, half watching her on her show, sleepily nestled in the armpit of my mother's maroon velvet bathrobe. On television, the pieces of her body struck me as graceful and quick, but up close she seems compact and clicked together, like a plastic toy. Her dark hair is now generously highlighted with blonde, and blown-dry straight, but her brown eyes look as I remember them. They are lined on the top and bottom with her signature black pencil, but up close, they are wet and curiously wanting, like she lives with the forever fear of being the last kid picked for the team. She kisses me on both cheeks, which is an awkward formality I still fail to anticipate properly, and then she steps back to admire me:

"It is so lovely to see you again, Clo," Barbara says. "And what a wonderful coat. I just love a good red."

"Oh, thank you," I say before adding, "I just bought it."

Apparently, I am a monster.

"You girls have excellent timing!" Barbara continues with another giddy clap. "I just put out a *gorgeous* tray of cheese and crackers. Let's have cheese and crackers for dinner, yes?"

"Oh, you don't have to make us dinner," I insist.

"It's cheese and crackers, Clo," Davis deadpans.

"Cheese and crackers and wine," Barbara corrects. "And grapes. And some fig jam. No, no, it's not jam. It's *must*. Grape must?" Barbara places a manicured finger to her lip and looks at Davis. "Davis, is *must* a *jam*?"

I, of course, don't know the backstory of young Nathan (or how many other "Nathans" parade through the lobby, although my guess is quite a few), but it's clear Davis wants to make her displeasure known without, you know, having to say anything specifically about her displeasure. It's even more clear that Barbara is aware of this tactic and has no intention of validating her daughter's feelings in any capacity.

"I think not technically, but it's the same idea," Davis answers finally. She looks down at her hands, her expression defeated.

I continue to have no idea what is going on, but I understand my role is to be agreeable, so I just smile as Barbara leads us into her vast kitchen. The room is almost entirely white, and it has a bank of floor-to-ceiling windows overlooking Central Park. I look down at the reservoir, which is dotted with lights at this hour, and its undulating shape reminds me of a middle school diagram of a uterus. I think I can just make out little bodies running around it.

"I guess Betsy has the night off?" Davis asks her mother. Betsy, I gather, is the cook. I already know Marta is the primary housekeeper because Davis is constantly calling her from work, asking her to *do something* or *order something* or *call someone* in an impatient tone.

"Yes, I gave Betsy the night off, you brat," Barbara retorts as she signals for me to make myself at home on one of the upholstered stools that line the marble island. "But I think this looks very elegant. I may have a second career in catering."

Barbara waves her hands over a half-eaten cheese board; her stubby fingers are laden with gold rings and her bracelets jangle in that unrelenting way all older women's bracelets jangle.

"Voilà!" she pronounces. "Please help yourself."

Amid a well-assembled sea of melted, blue-flecked, and other completely revolting cheese options, I search for something resembling a cube of cheddar before I settle on a thick brown cracker. I nibble the edges carefully as I watch Davis rattle around the cabinets before she produces a large bottle of Belvedere vodka. When she clanks it on the marble island with a thud, Barbara frowns.

"Clo, what would *you* like to drink?" Barbara asks, turning her attention back to me. "Red? White? I also have some champagne in the fridge."

"Oh, whatever is open," I say.

"To begin with, nothing is open," Barbara says, and her voice peaks with irritation. "Secondly, what the *hell* have I been fighting for all these years?"

I sit, briefly startled.

"Here we go," Davis murmurs as she pours vodka into an empty cut-crystal tumbler.

"Girls, you must have an opinion. I tell this to Davis all the time," she says as she shakes her head at me. "It's a new century! Ask for what you want. You know what a man would say?"

I sit silent. I have no idea what a man would say.

"Do you know what he would say? *Do you?*" she continues, only now she jabs her finger in my direction with anger. "He would say: 'a glass of red.' Or, better yet, he would ask for a whiskey, which I don't even have out, and he would *get a glass of whiskey.*"

I sit there holding my half-eaten cracker, and I can feel Davis smirk out of Barbara's line of sight. It's almost as if she is enjoying watching someone else get dressed down for once. She puts two ice cubes in her glass and takes a sip.

"I swear," Barbara continues, "Davis would shrug her way through life if I let her. So let's try this one again: What do you want?"

"Hot food," Davis quips.

"Champagne," I answer at the same time, but very quietly.

"Hot food? Oh, I am going to smack your pretty little face, Davis," Barbara says, and while she smiles, her eyes smolder with warning.

Oh boy, I think.

"My mom just says she is going to smack my face," I interject, quite loudly, hoping to throw a little cold water on the situation. "She usually leaves the 'pretty' part out."

While my mother, of course, has never said anything like this to me in my life, I hope this limp joke reduces the rising mother/daughter tension, which I suspect is more of the young-Nathan variety than the temperature of our dinner. Otherwise, I am strangely besotted by the two of them. We don't have family conversations like this where I come from and, like almost everything else about New York, I decide to file it away in my mind so I can enjoy it later.

"Oh, I love that you didn't fix your nose," Barbara takes this opportunity to inform me. "No one has distinction anymore. I mean, I had Davis's fixed in, what was it, honey? Ninth grade? But her nose wasn't interesting. It was just bad. Bad, bad, bad."

Here, it is only Barbara who laughs, and, in my general unease, I turn to Davis. She gives me a creepy full-watt grin:

"I never had my nose fixed," she says brightly.

I have to say, despite her nose's remarkable symmetry and general adorableness, I am inclined to believe her; she doesn't have one of those "nose job" noses. What leaves me more unsettled, however, is that her own mother would make this bizarre assertion in the first place, even if it *was* true, but it is clear there is—between them, anyway—a familiar dynamic at play. I debate responding with something clever or "body confident," but my attention diverts to what is wrong with my nose. I mean, I have always thought it was too big, especially at the tip, but no one has ever said it was too big (to my face, anyway) so I hoped I was just being, as usual, too hard on myself. But alas, now I must sit here and think about my nose on top of everything else.

"Is Grant working late tonight, Davis?" Barbara asks sweetly, entirely unaware she may have hurt my feelings.

"Yes. You know Grant," Davis replies.

Barbara rolls her eyes at me in a comic fashion.

"And to what do I owe this pleasure of Clo?" Barbara inquires. She flashes me another enormous smile, and I notice for the first time that her teeth are very white and all the exact same size. Like Chiclets.

"There was a sample sale, and . . ." Davis pauses for effect. "We have something to celebrate!"

I look at Davis curiously and I catch Barbara doing the same thing. Apparently, we are both secretly hoping this announcement, no matter how small or stupid, is about us because we are both, as it happens, appalling narcissists. I wonder if this is the reason—more than her fading celebrity or bizarre enthusiasm for me—that I feel so immediately drawn to Barbara Lawrence.

"Clo has survived over six months at the magazine!" Davis reveals. She starts clapping.

For her part, Barbara is almost impossibly delighted by this bit of information. She screams and covers her eyes, and I start to wonder how drunk she might already be after her little cocktail hour with young Nathan.

"Now you can do anything!" Barbara exclaims before she, too, starts to clap and bob up and down.

These Lawrence women and all their clapping, I think, but the truth is I feel happy; I am so rarely the object of anyone's attention, let alone praise.

"Really, honey," Barbara insists. She does that believe-me-you thing adults do where she points at me with her wineglass, the stem of which is pinched delicately between her thumb and forefinger.

"I guess time will tell," I murmur nonsensically before looking around the room for a new topic. "This is a really incredible kitchen."

As anyone new to New York City will attest, there is something transporting about encountering a big, suburban kitchen. It's like thwacking through dense vines with a machete only to come upon a lost civilization you cannot believe existed all this time without your knowledge.

"Thank you," Barbara responds after a perplexed beat. She looks around the space, taking measure of the high, hammered-tin ceiling. She stares up in silence for so long, in fact, that it seems she is considering her kitchen for the first time.

"I was never sure about that ceiling color," she says finally.

"It's too white," Davis agrees quickly. "It reads violet in the wrong light."

"Ugh," Barbara says. "And you *know* I *hate* violet."

"I think it's sort of nice that you two live together," I interject.

They turn in unison to look at me with surprise. Then, Davis smiles strangely.

"Well, then I'll have you know that we used to sleep in the same bed. Until like eleventh grade," Davis says. She reaches across the island and draws a cigarette out of her mother's chain-mail pouch. I watch as she places it between her long, perfectly shaped fingers. "Sometimes we still do. My therapist says it's all *very* healthy."

"Oh, and how I will miss it," Barbara says with a theatrical sigh as she watches Davis strike a match on the side of a battered yellow box from Sant Ambroeus. "Pretty soon you'll get married, and I will be all alone. Who will come to all my parties with me?"

All I can think about during this brief exchange is how horrified my parents would be if I ever lit up a cigarette in their presence.

"I don't think Clo and I are destined to marry young," Davis protests, waving out the match and exhaling cigarette smoke into the air. "I think we have a few things to do before all *that* nonsense."

"Oh, I'm not talking about Clo," Barbara says plainly as she weaves a square cracker through what resembles a dish of hummus. "But you'll get married young, Davis."

Davis looks very offended by this comment. I feel very offended by this comment, but I don't let my countenance betray me. What's wrong with me? Am I too ugly to get married? Too poor? I take a second sip of my champagne, which goes down easier than the first. I take a greedy third.

"Oh, don't give me that face, Davis," Barbara continues, popping the cracker in her mouth. "There are life stages. You've got a bunch of children ahead of you. And a country house. Tennis club. Wallpaper, fabric, a big dog with a vaguely nautical name. It's a whole thing."

"It's a comedy routine that never ends around here with Mom," Davis says to me, refilling my glass. "She's always working on a new bit."

"Ah," I manage.

"And where are you in these life stages, Mother?" Davis asks.

"I am currently in what we call 'Shirley MacLaine,' which is a lot of chunky jewelry. A lot of Lincoln Center. Gays. Turtlenecks. The Jews call it Mary Tyler Moore, but it's the same thing."

"What's next, pray tell?" Davis asks.

"Turbans, lefty activism, caftans, death."

"Can't wait," Davis says, and she hoists her drink overhead. We all clank our glasses together and laugh, but it feels forced. There is something unsettling in the air that I cannot quite wrestle down.

After a few more drinks, I assure everyone that I am going to take a taxi home, but I ride the subway back to Brooklyn instead, which means I have to switch trains three times. I keep the twenty dollars Barbara gave me for cab fare in my purse. I have another novel in my bag, another one of those classics everyone seems to have read except me, and I like reading on trains; I think it looks very cinematic. However, as I try to metabolize the first few pages, it turns out my vision is blurry, and my mind is porous and loose. I end up reading the same paragraph, over and over, and I can't seem to pull any meaning out of it; it's like working a dry lime. I hold the book open for the rest of the trip, however, just in case anyone is watching me, and I use the time to daydream about Davis. If I turn my nose to the collar of my new coat, I think I can make out the faintest touch of her perfume. I close my eyes and allow myself to wonder what her bedroom looks like, and if she has her own bathroom.

What brand of makeup does she use? Shampoo? Does she eat breakfast in the kitchen each morning with her mother? Do famous people stop by for tea? Do they get ready together for parties, laughing in the same mirror, passing a tube of mascara back and forth? When I get out at my station, I walk the long way home down Court Street. The quicker route down Smith Street is generally considered to be unsafe at this hour; a girl got held up at gunpoint there just last week, and I somehow always hear my mother's voice when I even so much as consider it. When I get to my apartment building, I climb up the short stoop and open my bag to retrieve my house key, and that is when I discover I accidentally still have Davis's red wallet.

The next morning, I must force myself to wait for the perfect moment to return the wallet, which finally comes around 10:30 when I see Davis talking to Margot from accessories in the lobby. I walk past them, ostensibly on my way down to the cafeteria to get a coffee, and I toss off a casual hello before I stop short:

"Oh, Davis, I almost forgot," I say, as I fish around in my bag and produce my accidental piece of contraband. "I somehow ended up with your wallet last night?"

Davis says a quick goodbye to Margot before she turns to me. She extends a soft, upturned palm, and I place the wallet gently in her hand.

"Typical," she murmurs.

"What's typical," I retort with a smile. "That you didn't notice your wallet was missing until right now?"

"Don't be cute," she says, smiling.

"I can't help it," I say with a joking shrug. "I was just born cute. Anyway, I must have kept it after I used your business card for the discount."

"The coat is great," she says. "I'm so glad you bought it."

"You know I cannot bear to disappoint you, Davis," I say with mock solemnity. I depress the circle button for the elevator.

"Let's keep it that way," she responds as the doors part and I step inside the carriage. "Because I really go crazy when people disappoint me."

* * *

When I return ten minutes later—newly purchased hot coffee in hand—I am horrified to discover L.K. Smith lingering next to my desk. She is frowning, with her arms folded across her chest, as she takes a thoughtful yet profoundly dismayed inventory of my cluttered workspace. As usual, she wears an utterly perfect suit: a nipped, gray flannel number that makes her look like a whip-smart lady detective from the 1940s who just got the better of her handsy, good-for-nothing boss.

"There you are," she says, but she does not look up. She is fixated on the hairbrush I left on my desk.

It is matted with hair.

"Good morning," I say, but when I hear my voice tremble, I make a mental note to join Toastmasters and then kill myself directly after work. Then, L.K.'s eyes flutter over my shoulder.

"There you are, Davis," L.K. says, and while she uses the exact same tone of voice for Davis, I decide it sounds less harsh.

I turn my head to see that Davis has, indeed, arrived.

"Good morning, L.K.," Davis says sweetly as she twists her shiny hair into a bun and secures it on top of her head. She, of course, is completely unperturbed by this surprise visit while I have begun to sweat through my shirt.

L.K. gestures toward me with the black reading glasses she holds in her hand.

"That's a very good coat," L.K. says to Davis. "It's a good coat, isn't it?"

"It's a *great* coat, L.K.," Davis rejoins.

"You needed a good coat," L.K. says to me with approval. "Good."

I stand there with a dumb, shy smile before it slowly comes into focus that Davis was instructed by management to take me shopping for shoes and a proper coat.

Like an orphan.

I remember the red sandals that I didn't buy at the sample sale, and I close my eyes in silent reproach and wonder over how many other clear messages I have, somehow, already failed to hear.

16

I decide to wear sunglasses on my commute to work one Monday morning. I bought them for five dollars off a table in Soho over the weekend, and I figure why not? After all, the older girls in my office wear them like a second skin but, like so many things in my life, it feels immediately inauthentic. I wonder, however, if constantly wearing sunglasses is akin to, say, sleeping with a mouthguard, and that, at some juncture, the awkward discomfort I am currently experiencing will become something I simply cannot live without.

I wonder this about a lot of things lately.

The first person I see when I get to the office is Davis, which is strange as she is reliably a late arrival. This morning, she stands absently by the printer, which allows me to take a long look at her unnoticed. She wears a short gray flannel skirt and tight navy sweater with thick cuffs. She balances on one leg, and her opposite foot is tucked against her slim ankle; the point of her leopard print Christian Louboutin heel hovers a few inches above the ground.

"Why are you here so early?" I ask finally.

"I had to get out of my apartment," she says tonelessly, but she doesn't look at me.

After a few beats, I cough and she turns around.

"Oh, good morning, Audrey Hepburn," she says with a little smirk, and her pale skin looks even more luminous than usual, like a kindergarten boy who has just been kissed on the cheek. I find myself wondering how she spent her weekend. I find myself wondering if she regularly wears sunscreen. I find myself wondering if she thinks about me at all.

"The sunglasses look so chic, right?" I joke, but Davis doesn't respond. She just turns away from me and continues to stare in the direction of our glass-walled conference room. I follow her gaze. There is a small pod of bodies clustered around a woman I have never seen before. I take off my glasses to get a cleaner look.

"Who is that?" I ask.

"That, my friend, is your new boss. Isobel Fincher."

My heart sinks.

"Oh god. She's so elegant," I groan.

"Beautiful," agrees Davis. "And, like, famously smart."

"She's wearing a brooch."

"It's pronounced *browch*," Davis says absentmindedly. "It's a long O, like *roach*."

"Browch," I repeat. We stand quietly for a moment. "On that note, why do some people say *boo-fey* instead of *buff-ay*?"

"I feel like that's just Southern people, but I find they have incredibly weird weddings," she says. "If you're very rich, you make sure there aren't enough chairs for everyone at dinner. They just go to the *boo-fey* and wander around with their plate looking for a place to eat."

"Huh," I say. You really do learn something new every day.

"She has a book coming out, you know," Davis continues, her eyes still fixed on Isobel. "A historical novel. I think it's about women during the Revolutionary period in New York."

"Super."

"They are excerpting it somewhere."

"Even better." I slip my sunglasses back on my face. "If you need me, I'll just be at my desk cracking this cyanide tablet with my teeth."

I point to my cheek, and Davis laughs.

Suddenly, L.K. Smith exits the conference room. She walks toward us briskly, but somehow without any hint of urgency, and I scramble with my ridiculous eyewear, which obliges me by landing on the floor with a cheap plastic clatter. I lean over to pick them up, and when I rise, the look on L.K.'s face makes it crystal clear that, short of a total solar eclipse or her confirmed death, I may never wear sunglasses in the office again. I slide them into my coat pocket.

"Good morning, ladies. I want to introduce our new senior editor, Isobel Fincher," L.K. says with a microscopic gesture that indicates we should follow her. "Clo, for now, you will be assisting her."

Davis locks eyes with me and mouths *for now*, as if I could have missed it, and I shrug my shoulders miserably in response. We follow L.K. into the conference room where she presents us, like obedient schoolchildren, to Isobel Fincher.

The first thing I notice about Isobel Fincher is that she is tiny, *maybe* five feet tall, which is extremely uncommon around these parts. She compensates, to some degree, with her intimidatingly erect manner; it's like she forgot to take the hanger out of her shirt when she got dressed this morning. She looks to be in her early thirties. Her face is smooth, and her features are lovely and generous. Her skin is pale and strangely ethereal, like a baby in an Italian painting, and her hair is long and dark red. It is parted severely down the middle and tied back with a black grosgrain ribbon at the nape of her neck. She wears red lipstick, which shouldn't work with her hair color but does to magnificent effect, and she has enormous, oddly shaped eyes. They are caramel-colored and look like they belong on a much larger face. She reminds me of a Modigliani painting, or a very pretty, very tiny, very serious Mr. Potato Head.

"Isobel Fincher, I want to introduce you to Clodagh Harmon," L.K. says. "She will be assisting you."

"Hello, Clodagh," she says, and her voice is infused with a dignified warmth. "It's a pleasure to meet you."

"No, the pleasure is all mine," I respond. "I have heard *so* much about you."

Of course, I have heard exactly nothing about Isobel Fincher from my superiors, least of all that she was hired, but why bother to inform me of anything if I am only here *for now*. I can sense my left armpit has started to work overtime, and I'm relieved I, yet again, have not removed my coat.

Isobel smiles at me serenely, and I smile back, which gives way to a conversational lull that settles on my chest like an X-ray blanket.

As I stand there with a dumb smile on my face, I wonder, as I always wonder, at what age I will cease to be the custodian of all the awkward pauses on earth.

"You should call me Clo," I continue, my voice nervous. "Everyone does."

She nods approvingly, like a priest after he has given you the Communion wafter, and this benediction emboldens me to continue speaking:

"We should get lunch or a coffee or something," I say. "I can, you know, get you up to speed."

I cringe as I hear myself: I can, *you know*, get you up to speed.

"That would be lovely," she says.

"I can make a reservation. Do you have a place you like?"

"Why don't you pick a place *you* like?"

"Of course. Twelve-thirty?"

I understand that my first official assignment—this picking of the lunch spot—is part of the evaluation period. Isobel looks down to check her watch, which is Cartier, the square gold one with the brown snakeskin band, and she wears an antique-looking cluster of sapphires and diamonds on her left ring finger.

"Let's say one?" she suggests. "I am still getting the tour from L.K."

"Absolutely," I say. "Lunch it is."

L.K. smiles at me with tepid approval before she places her hand on Davis's lower back, and gently nudges her forward. I catch Davis's eyes flash at the intimacy of this unexpected gesture.

"And this is Davis Lawrence," L.K. announces. "*Barbara Lawrence's daughter.*"

Isobel's mouth parts just slightly with uncertainty, but then she breaks into a gracious smile.

"Oh, of course!" Isobel says. "It is so lovely to meet you. Your mother is a *wonderful* actress. So funny. A real *comedienne*."

"Thank you. I'll be sure to pass along the compliment," Davis replies, but her voice is so oddly monotonous, it sounds as if someone pulled a string.

"Davis assists Kate Grant on the fashion news pages, but she has also done work for the society pages," L.K. continues, and she keeps her hand fixed on Davis's back as she proudly lists her accomplishments. "She's very talented."

Davis shifts her weight back and forth, which is an uncharacteristic show of discomfort from a girl who I have yet to see ill at ease a second in her life. She seems irritated or uncomfortable with the attention L.K. heaps upon her, and while I want to feel bad for her, I only feel annoyed. For starters, she is not particularly talented. She is constantly leaning over to my desk, asking me how to spell something or help her gin up a little copy for her captions. Secondly, what is wrong with a little attention? All I want in life is to be Davis Lawrence. I want to be beautiful without trying. I want to be rich without effort. I want to be paraded around the ring and applauded for doing absolutely nothing and I don't know what bothers me more: That I am forced to toil for an occasional fistful of crumbs, or that Davis seems so intent on denying her birthright?

Finally, and probably sensing Davis's displeasure, L.K. removes her hand from her back.

"So, let's keep going with the tour," L.K. says. "Ladies, thank you for your time."

"Our pleasure," I gush, and, although I cannot be entirely sure, I believe I curtsy to Isobel Fincher before I leave the room.

Davis and I walk down the hallway with our heads down.

"I have never felt more enormous in my entire life," I mutter.

"Why?" Davis whispers back, and I get the sense she is relieved to shift focus back to someone else's shortcomings. "You don't even look fat today."

17

The worst part about going to lunch with someone you don't know well in New York City is the actual walk to the restaurant. It's like getting through airport security two hours before a flight. By the time you board the plane, you have read all the magazines and eaten all the snacks, and you must now endure the journey with nothing to do but watch the little white plane make progress on the seatback screen in front of you. When Isobel and I alight the short steps of the Royalton Hotel, a mere block east from our office (and highly recommended by Zagat!) she is up-to-date on how I feel about the weather (it's been mild for winter!), if I have been to this restaurant before (no, but I have been meaning to try it!), and why we didn't cover a particular tennis player last month (I tell her it's because we are waiting to see what transpires at the Australian Open, but I overheard it was actually because she has no clear distinction between her chin and neck).

The inside of the restaurant looks like what I imagine a pirate-themed mini-golf course looks like in China. The decor is brown with hanging globe lights and what looks to be fishing nets, and I get the unsettling sense there may be a shark swimming menacingly somewhere above me. The hostess takes an inscrutable flight path through the half-full dining room, but I quickly realize that is by design: Heads lift from their plates to see if we are someone they should know. A table briefly stops Isobel for a quick hello, and I realize how badly I want to be someone they, too, should know.

After we are settled at our table, a waiter appears and hands us menus. I listen to him fill our glasses with ice water as I scan the lunch offerings.

"Everything looks delicious," I say agreeably. "I'm a sucker for a lunch omelet."

"Anything to drink?" the waiter asks. "The wine list is on the back."

"Café au lait, please," Isobel says, handing back the menu without opening it. "We are just going to get some coffee."

I thought we were having lunch. I made a reservation for lunch. This feels like a bad start.

"Uh. I will just have a regular coffee," I say. "Thanks."

"Sorry," Isobel says apologetically as she lays the napkin across her lap. "I was just asked to sit in on a meeting this afternoon, and I have been instructed to *be early*."

"Good tip," I say, and I quickly place my own napkin on my lap.

"I'm so glad you picked a spot that is quiet," Isobel comments as she glances around quickly. "This place used to be such a scene."

"I know," I say, but I feel my neck get hot. I thought I had selected a fashionable restaurant, a place that would belie my understanding and access, but now I must play it off that I selected this location for the agreeable acoustics.

Isobel says nothing in response.

"So where did you grow up?" I ask.

"In Los Angeles," she responds. "But I spent the summers with my grandmother on the Upper East Side, and I went to boarding school at St. Pauls."

"It's so nice there," I say.

"Where?" she asks. "Concord?"

"The Upper East Side," I say quickly. I have no idea what she means by "Concord."

"Yes, but it was different then," she says. "It wasn't, you know, *the Upper East Side*."

I nod, but I know very little about the Upper East Side except that that the *New York Post* recently crowned 10021 as the "hottest zip code" of the year. That, and there are some half-decent Irish bars up there.

"Where do you live now?" I ask.

"Tribeca. My husband and I just bought a place. We moved in last month so it's all still coming together, but I love the neighborhood. I keep feeling like I am discovering things."

"It's great," I say.

I don't disclose that, despite nearly nine months living in New York and spending many an evening in the various bars and restaurants located in Tribeca, I remain unclear where, exactly, it is located (and, no, the "TRIangle BElow CAnal" thing doesn't help because I have no idea where Canal Street falls into anything). I also don't know if there is an official *geographical* difference between "Alphabet City" and the "Lower East Side" or if people just call the same neighborhood by two different names. Lastly, I took the E train not once but *twice* last month and ended up on something called Roosevelt Island. I climbed all the way up the deserted subway steps, and when I got outside, I saw Manhattan shimmering in the gloaming across the river.

"Where do you live?" Isobel asks.

"In Brooklyn," I say.

"Oh," she manages, but I decide to switch topics rather than do the whole Brooklyn thing. After all, there are only so many times a girl can marvel about butcher shops, small-batch coffee, and the Yeah Yeah Yeahs in mixed company.

"So, have you been married a long time?"

I instantly realize this is a bizarre, possibly creepy question.

"I got married two years ago. In April."

"April is so nice. I mean, as a month." I laugh awkwardly as the waiter returns with a crowded tray. He sets an oversized teacup and saucer in front of Isobel before he places what I can only describe as a large, clear 1960s coffeepot with what *looks like* a plunger on top at my elbow. I lean back in my chair, expecting the waiter to pour the coffee, but he refills my water glass instead.

"Anything else, ladies?" he asks.

"No, thank you," Isobel replies as she demurely lifts her spoon. She is so delicate in her motions and so dignified in her bearing that I feel an urge to leap over the table and devour her, like some crazed Cookie Monster of a person. Instead, I adjust my napkin so I can avoid dealing with my alleged coffeepot.

"Where?" I ask.

"Where?" She looks confused.

"Sorry," I clarify nervously. "I mean, *where* did you get married?"

"Oh. In Upstate New York?" she responds evenly, but I sense she's dismayed that *this* is the topic I have chosen to so ardently pursue. Clearly, someone of Isobel's caliber expects to discuss things like architecture and early Balanchine, but now, on top of everything else, I've made her worry that her new assistant is one of those single girls who subscribes to *Brides*, gets everything monogrammed, and totes around a Vera Bradley weekend bag.

"Where?" I ask. I cannot seem to help myself.

"In Rhinebeck. Do you know it? We rented a big barn. It was raw, but it had beautiful light. You rent everything when you do it that way, though, which makes it a bit of a hassle."

"Wow, that's a lot," I say. *Wow, that's a lot.* Because, in addition to all the other attributes that make me especially well-suited to this role, I would also like Isobel Fincher to know that I am, as evidenced here, a thrilling conversationalist.

We fall silent.

"So how about you? Where are you from?" she asks.

"Me? Pennsylvania," I say. "Outside Philadelphia."

"Like New Hope?"

"Yes," I respond with a smile.

Mind you, I am not from New Hope, but I have discovered New York people *absolutely adore* New Hope, even if they have never visited New Hope, which I am learning most of them have not. It is just a place they can fantasize about buying a farm and plausibly wearing Hunter boots all day, mucking about in some glorious garden. What they don't seem to know is that, until recently, New Hope was just a lot of tattoo parlors and crystal shops with the occasional swarm of aging Hells Angels clogging up the main drag on two-for-one night at Fran's Pub.

"I hear there are a lot of horses?" she continues.

"Yes, a lot of horses," I respond brightly.

There are no horses where I grew up. Correction: There is an elderly butterscotch pony who limps around a small patch of grass on the short drive to our local mall.

"Do you ride?"

"Not very much these days," I say. "It's a little harder in the city."

"Well, it sounds wonderful," she says. "And L.K. showed me your résumé this morning. It looks like you spent some time at an art magazine. That will be *very* helpful."

This piece of information—namely, that a copy of my résumé still lingers in our office—causes my entire body to seize up. This is the résumé I created with the *fake* job at the *real* art magazine that landed me the *real* job at the *real* fashion magazine. You see, when I was first applying for jobs, I had no luck. That first long month, nobody even called me for an interview. When I asked Allie for advice, she informed me I was unlikely to land a job in New York if I lived in Philadelphia, so I put her mailing address on my résumé instead of my own. She also instructed me *not* to list an apartment number, so it looked like I was someone who came from money. Then, she said I needed more serious work experience than my internship at a community newspaper and my brief tenure working on a regional magazine. Obviously, due to Allie's insane and repeated success, I listened to her every word. She helped me cook up a fake assistant job at a prominent but niche art journal in New York as my most recent work experience.

I know.

But it gets worse.

When the magazine called to check my references after my final bone-chilling interview with L.K. Smith, Allie changed the outgoing voicemail on the landline in her apartment to be that of my "boss" at the "art magazine." I hid under a blanket on her couch as we listened to the voicemail from HR, and when Allie called them back, she provided a glowing review of my work. "It would kill us to lose her," I heard her gush as I writhed in the humid darkness of my self-made protective tent. "She is such an incredible asset to our team."

The call was brief, and when she clicked her cordless phone back on the gray cradle, she took a small bow.

I got the job offer the very next morning, and Allie agreed to keep the outgoing message for an additional two weeks "just in case." I don't know why, but I had assumed that, once I was hired, my paper résumé was tossed into the nearest trash bin and, as such, I was at liberty to invent my professional history anew.

Basically, this is not good news.

"Is everything okay?" Isobel asks, leaning forward with concern.

"Yes, of course," I say quickly, but I am not sure how much time has passed. I clear my throat and desperately cast around for a new topic. "So, your first issue will be June, right?"

"I think so, yes."

"Great," I say, but my ears are still buzzing. "Great."

"I love what my predecessor accomplished with the culture pages, of course, but, between you and me, I would love to give them a little more life, broaden them," she says before lowering her voice. "I'd like to make them a bit more diverse."

While Isobel could mean one of many things with this comment, I am going to assume "diversity" in this context means including people who aren't white (or one of the three Black people we currently cover) in the magazine. Or maybe she means she would like to assign some Black writers? Or middle-class writers? Either way, I wish her well on that very noble journey. MC couldn't even get a Greek singer photographed because her wild, curly hair was deemed (in private, of course) as "too ethnic" and the singer refused to have it flat-ironed just, as she put it, "to make an American magazine happy." I recall how fast her pronouncement had scattered through the halls; it was like dropping a cup of dried rice. The assistants sat wide-eyed and motionless while the senior editors reacted with arched eyebrows and a sad shaking of heads. To them, this singer wasn't making a statement, but rather she simply didn't grasp the fate that befall those who deign to drink from that *particular* chalice. After all, if *we* didn't cover her, *nobody* would cover her.

Well, we can't help her now, I recall one of the editors saying with a light cluck of her tongue.

"That's going to start with bringing in some new writers," Isobel continues. "I'll be having a few lunches."

"I'm happy to set those meetings up for you," I say with competence.

"And I will need to get my office in order."

"Of course. I'll get you the catalog today. You can order anything you want from it," I say before comically dropping my voice to recapture an earlier sense of ease. "That was the big selling point for me.

At my first job, we just had a shared supply closet with a lot of yellow legal pads and those super depressing blue ballpoint pens."

Isobel doesn't laugh. I don't like that she doesn't laugh.

"Remind me. How long have you been at the magazine?" she asks instead.

"August," I say.

"So, you are on the masthead?" she asks. "By, what? The March issue?"

I nod.

We close the magazine and ship it to the printer three months before the issue hits the newsstand. Therefore, the March issue—historically significant as it covers spring fashion and runs well over 500 pages—is the book we were furiously wrapping up with just days to go before the Christmas break. With MC's sudden departure, I knew to stay late each night to proof the final pages with surgical precision, and I found the responsibility to be thrilling.

"So, what do you want to do?" Isobel asks.

"Me?" I say, somewhat startled by the question. "I mean, I just want to do a good job for you."

"Yes, of course," she says kindly. "But with your life? And professionally? What are your goals?"

I smile and look skyward like I am mulling over my options. In truth, I know the answer, but it is not original: It is the same response every other girl in publishing would give if it were not scandalous to do so. I want to be an editor-in-chief. Correction: *Everyone* wants to be an editor-in-chief. Maybe of this magazine or, if that doesn't work out, of another *respectable* magazine. After all, I am only twenty-five years old. Surely there is time to develop the taste and confidence required for such an important and glamorous job? I want to write an editor's letter. I want to choose the stories and select the photographs for each issue. I want to have dinner with interesting people. I want my staff to make a nervous fuss when I enter the room. I want to wear nice clothes that I didn't buy with my own money. I want to have all my clothes tailored. I want to go to the theater every week, and I want to fly to Europe twice a year. I want my picture taken by a Getty photographer when I exit a restaurant or sit front row at a fashion show. I want an assistant to answer my phones and get my coffee. I want a big apartment with a wall of books. Oddly, I want a globe. I want enough money to buy flowers every Monday. I want people to think I am smart. I want people to say that I am tough and decisive, and, if any people don't like me, I want to be wholly indifferent to their judgments. I believe this level of success—and no less than this level of success—will make it clear to everyone who underestimated me that I was strategic in my planning. I want them to understand that I knew what I was doing when I did the things I was doing, even if those things, like lying on my résumé, seemed unsavory in the moment.

Of course, I would be a raving lunatic if I said any of this to Isobel Fincher, so I offer an unthreatening alternative:

"Big picture?" I respond as I employ what I decide is a "cute" grimace. "I want stop to cringing when I hear my own voice transcribing interview tapes?"

Here, Isobel laughs.

"I can't help you with that; it's an occupational hazard," Isobel says, still sort of chuckling. "It's why I pay people to transcribe for me. I hope I can continue?"

"Oh, definitely. They will basically expense anything here," I say. "Like, really. One day I got three Venti soy lattes at Starbucks, went out to lunch, and picked up my dry cleaning at the Hippodrome, which is like an obscenely expensive place to get your dry cleaning done, just to test the system. Nobody flagged anything."

As the words fall out of my mouth, they bounce off the tablecloth like magnetic refrigerator letters. I am dimly aware I have gone for intimacy too fast, but I can't seem to control it: My nerves are a runaway train.

"Oh," she says uncertainly, which prompts me to pull back.

"I heard you wrote a book," I say, and too quickly. "I mean, I *know* you just wrote one. That is so great. It's just great."

Jesus.

"It's a long process," she says kindly, although I suspect she is beginning to weary from the conversational whiplash. "It was a lot of research."

"I can't wait to read it."

"Thank you," she says plainly. "I am really proud of it."

I smile at Isobel like her straightforward acceptance of my compliment (and, frankly, the obvious pride in her work) is normal, but it is *not* normal. Isn't she supposed to say that she *had a lot of help* or that *it's probably terrible*, if only to make me feel more at ease? I steal a furtive glance around the dining room because I would be mortified if anyone overheard me brag about myself in such a manner, but Isobel just sips her coffee, entirely unconcerned.

I find this fascinating.

"So, L.K. has started introducing me around the office," Isobel continues. "I met a woman named Liddy who says she writes for my section?"

"Ah," I say with a pause. "Lydia Saintclair-Abbott."

Isobel narrows her eyes, and I'm encouraged by what I read as a signal she has an abiding interest in office gossip so long as it's gussied up as essential information.

"She's a nice girl," I say before I allow the tiniest wisp of uncertainty to waft across my face like an errant cloud. "I mean, I wouldn't say she *writes* for your section? Marie Clarice tried to assign her a few pieces for culture, but they just never worked out. They were all killed. It was, you know, *a whole thing*. I think, ultimately, she is more of a 'fashion person.'"

"Interesting."

"Don't get me wrong," I continue. Here I place my hand on my heart and try to look earnest. "I don't mean to speak poorly of her."

"Of course not," Isobel says quickly and with a confidential nod. "So is she a *Saintclair-Abbott* of the Saintclair-Abbotts?"

"The very ones," I confirm.

I recall how, as a matter of courtesy on L.K. Smith's urging, Liddy and I had coffee together on that first August morning, and while we chatted politely, it was exceedingly clear after I gave her my background that she suddenly didn't like the looks of me. As I spoke, she let her eyes float around our cavernous office cafeteria. It was obvious she was in search of someone to whom she could more easily relate or, maybe, someone who could be more valuable to her career, and the sheer fact she felt no compunction to even hide her indifference toward me was humiliating. It also quickly led me to fantasize how, exactly, I was going to destroy her. Throwing her under the bus during this lunch with Isobel Fincher, I reasoned, was merely a first step.

"I was also introduced to Gabrielle?" Isobel continues. "I don't remember her last name. What is she like?"

"She is really smart," I say, because, while it would be crazy to give my competition a glowing review, I also need to be mistaken, at least initially, for an upright citizen.

"Well, that's good," she says.

I smile quickly in agreement before I resummon the clouds.

"I mean, I *did* hear she had some kind of mental breakdown over the summer, and then there was 9/11 so, yeah," I say. "It's been a tough couple of months for her."

At this comment, Isobel sets down her cup with a loud clatter, and her giant eyes fill up with a watery, somewhat motherly, sorrow.

"Oh my god," I sputter as the potential horror of my comment becomes apparent to me. "Please tell me you didn't lose anyone?"

"No," she says solemnly. She looks down at her cup.

"Good!" I cheer.

She looks back up at me, and I read her expression as both curious and reproachful.

"I mean, not *good*, obviously. I mean, it's all *so awful*," I spit out nervously. "I was here. At the magazine. It was, like, my second month of work. There weren't a lot of people in the office yet because it was early, and I think there was that crazy Marc Jacobs show the night before."

Isobel sits listening, but her mournful face remains intact.

"The one with the fire boats? Or something? On that pier in Chelsea?"

"Yes, I was there," Isobel says softly. "It was raining."

I nod, like it was the rain that was sad, and Isobel just looks at me, unblinking.

"Anyway, we stood around wondering what to do. We thought the D.C. plane was a hoax, but then somebody heard about the Pennsylvania plane, and everyone started running for the stairs," I say before adding, "I was in a blue skirt."

It is right about here that I realize I am conversationally out of control, like a drowning person who drowns the perfectly nice lifeguard who only swam out to save her. Isobel looks a bit startled, and everything feels fast and hot, like getting lost in a theme park crowd.

"So, Gabrielle . . ." I start, desperate to get things back on track.

Here, I take an audible intake of breath, the ferocity of which triggers an uncontrollable coughing jag that forces me to turn sideways and lean over with my napkin pressed against my mouth. As I hack, Isobel looks quietly concerned, but she doesn't move, and after a minute or two, I manage to recover.

I sit up. I wipe the tears off my cheeks and take a sip of my ice water. "She took a few weeks off from work and seems okay now?" I say. I gently clear my throat one last time. "Although that could have totally been a rumor. There are *a lot* of rumors around here. Anyway, I'm not sure she was the best girl to get off the bench to do people's expenses and get coffee, or whatever. Especially when those expenses are Ronald's, and Ronald's expenses include a *lot* of hotel-room porn."

It is the porn comment, I suspect, that finally prompts Isobel to act. She reaches over to push the plunger down on my coffee pot. I watch as the brown liquid is forced into the bottom chamber.

"It's a French press," she explains.

I look at Isobel.

"Please don't fire me," I blurt out.

This is a desperate and wholly unrehearsed plea. Apparently, it is also incredibly loud. So loud, in fact, that at this pronouncement, the two blonde women seated at the next table turn and stare in our direction.

"Sorry," I whisper, but I'm unsure to whom I am speaking at this point. I look down at my lap, and the waiter arrives with our bill. Isobel and I look up at him—clearly unsure what our individual next moves are—before I extend my hand.

"Yeah, so I'll pay for coffee since you don't have a corporate card yet," I murmur, unable to meet her eyes as I open the padded billfold. "I'll sign you up for a card today. It will take about a week to show up in the mail. I'll have it sent to the office instead of your apartment; it's just faster that way. You activate it by calling the number on the card."

"Thank you," Isobel says.

We walk back to our building in a weighty silence, broken only by Isobel muttering as she generously pretends to do something *very important* with her cell phone battery. As we walk through the lobby, I am about to say something, *say anything*, when I see Mark Angelbeck striding in our direction.

"Isobel?" he inquires. "So sorry, but are you Isobel Fincher?"

"Yes," she says pleasantly enough, but she holds her tiny body warily, like she's ready to fend off a pamphlet should this man turn out to be a Jehovah's Witness.

"I am so sorry for interrupting, but I wanted to introduce myself and welcome you to the company," he says. "I'm Mark Angelbeck, your new publisher."

Mark Angelbeck is easy to recognize: He wears his dark blond hair gently undone, and the deep crow's-feet that radiate from his smiling eyes belie a leisurely life spent enjoying the great outdoors. He dresses in these incredibly binding-looking, perfectly tailored three-piece suits that lend just the right amount of New York polish to his otherwise seductive rumple. Mr. Angelbeck oversees all the advertising sales at the magazine, and he performs his role with such flair that the media columns regularly refer to him as the "heir apparent" to our entire company once the current chairman either retires or dies.

Mark Angelbeck thrusts out his hand. I notice he pokes his tongue against one of his teeth, like he's pleasuring a painfully swollen tastebud.

"L.K. told me to look out for you this week," he says. "And here you are!"

"Here I am," Isobel says, gently shaking his hand. "How do you do?"

They look at each other while I fidget in the wings.

"Have you met Clo Harmon?" Isobel says. "She is my new assistant."

For now, I think miserably.

"I haven't had the pleasure," he says. "It's nice to see you, Clo."

As I extend my own hand, I debate reminding him that we have, indeed, met before, but I reckon it's more beneficial to take this opportunity for a fresh start. I notice his eyes evaluate me the way older men tend to evaluate younger women in the office, but instead of feeling my usual thrill, I feel uncomfortably exposed. There must be something about Isobel's delicate propriety that makes my whorish, manipulative inclinations feel all wrong in this moment.

"Hello, Mr. Angelbeck."

I deliver my greeting in a prim manner that is intended to indicate that, in my limited spare time away from the grueling tasks at the magazine, I edit a parish newsletter. Now, had I been *alone* with Mark Angelbeck, this would be a whole different story. If we were alone, I would avert my eyes in a sweetly subservient manner and touch my hair because I've found that older men respond very well to a shy and fawning register from the young ladies. They want us to be gobsmacked and bashful to receive their attention. Maybe they can help us with something? And maybe we could remain forever in their debt? Honestly, every time I meet an older man, I can almost see the ticker tape of possibilities race across their foreheads. It's wonderfully flattering, and I've never understood why women don't more regularly exploit the power that comes from being wanted in this way? For me, there is no finer feeling than to be handed someone else's self-control. It is a difficult balance, for sure, but if a woman can figure out how to apply just enough tension—by giving up just enough but *never* too much—I firmly believe there is a way for everyone to win. And I like to win. Mark Angelbeck takes me in for another nanosecond before he resettles his interest on Isobel Fincher.

Isobel Fincher is the main event.

"So, when can I take you for a drink? Dinner?" he asks. He does the tongue thing again, or maybe he never stopped doing the tongue thing, I don't know. "Have you been to the Harrison? It's"—and here, he shakes his head like he's got a mouthful of hot brownie batter—"fantastic."

"It sounds wonderful, but my nights are generally busy," she says. "How about a lunch?"

At this suggestion, Mark Angelbeck's eyes go stock-still for a proper second as he struggles to digest the possibility he was just rejected by a beautiful woman who, in some capacity, reports to him. I want to smack him on the side of the head to see if anything shakes loose, but it's clear it would have no effect: Mark Angelbeck is a professional.

"Ah," he says, recovering. "You have children?"

"No," she replies.

He considers her answer for a moment with some confusion and Isobel, to her credit, does nothing to explain herself. She hardly blinks.

"Ah. Well, then... lunch is *perfect*," he says brightly. In fact, he regains himself so enthusiastically, you'd think the whole "lunch" thing was his idea in the first place.

"Great," she says. "I'll have Clo set something up, but you'll have to excuse me? I am on my way to a meeting."

And with that, Isobel starts to walk toward the elevator bank, which is located on the far side of the lobby. Here is what strikes me as unusual: She did not wait for him to end the conversation. I find women usually wait for the man, especially when it's a powerful man like Mark Angelbeck, to excuse them officially (but in a seemingly unofficial capacity) before they exit a conversation. Isobel Fincher, however, all 100 pounds of her, just walked away. I look up at him apologetically, as if I am the one to blame for her poor manners, but I don't think she has poor manners at all.

I think she is magnificent.

Mark Angelbeck's eyes follow her briefly, but then he looks at me.

"I'm looking forward to working with you, too, Clo," he says.

I nod, but then—just like Isobel—I start to walk away. It feels so powerful that my lips immediately ache from suppressing a smile. I move my legs faster and faster, to the point I am almost running, because I want to catch Isobel before she gets in the elevator.

I am desperate to fall in line.

18

At the end of a long week, I am packing up for the day when Davis asks me if I want to get a "quick drink" at the bar around the corner. I had planned to go to the gym, but I would never turn down a proper offer from Davis Lawrence, who leans on my desk and twirls the ends of her hair as she waits for my answer.

"Sure," I say. "Why not?"

"Good." She smiles. Then she looks more closely at me. "We need mascara."

"I need everything," I joke.

"Let's go to the beauty closet."

The beauty closet is an office-sized room that has been retrofitted with floor-to-ceiling shelves on all four sides. The shelves are labeled by beauty brand (Yves Saint Laurent, L'Oreal, Tarte, La Mer, Chantecaille) and meticulously organized by the beauty assistants, who ensure each product stands at attention like a row of ready dominoes. The room is generally locked, but the most junior beauty assistant (currently a girl named Liza) has the key.

"Hi, Liza," Davis says brightly. "Can I get some mascara?"

Wordlessly, Liza hops up from her desk and unlocks the door. She flips on the overhead lights, and then she and Davis begin to walk around, chattering about this product or that product.

"But which one do *you* like?" Davis asks her as she unscrews a tube of mascara and regards the wand in the light. Liza looks delighted to be asked her opinion.

"This one," she says, pulling another tube off a shelf. "Or this Dior one."

She hands over the options, and then Davis begins to poke around for lipsticks, rubbing the colors on the back of her hand.

"What are you getting?" Davis asks me. I am still standing in the doorway. I didn't know I was permitted to partake of the beauty closet yet.

"Do you have any cream for dry skin?" I ask weakly.

"Get some makeup while you're at it?" Davis says lightly, but I worry it feels more like a directive than a suggestion. Liza looks at my face and begins to pull a few products off various shelves. She drops them in a small paper bag.

"Can I get a bag, too?" Davis asks.

A few minutes later, Davis and I are in the bathroom, putting on our new makeup, none of which even remotely resembles the drugstore variety that currently populates my small quilted cosmetics bag. The containers are beautiful—all glass and gold—and I reckon I have just been handed at least two hundred dollars of tinted moisturizer alone.

When Davis uses the bathroom, I press two coarse paper towels into my swampy armpits. When I hear the toilet flush, I quickly throw them into the trash.

"Ready?" Davis asks, sauntering out of the stall. She slips her arm around my waist, and we both look at ourselves in the mirror for a beat.

"Ready," I affirm.

We go outside.

It is still bitter for spring, and the wind slices through my thin coat. We walk briskly toward Jimmy's Corner, which is a dive bar where the junior staff at our company has been known to frequent with great regularity. Tonight, it is populated—as it is always populated—by alcoholic senior citizens and young journalist types. We say hello to a few people we know (or, more accurately, Davis says hello, and I stand behind her feeling about as unobtrusive as an apartment complex) before we split up: Davis goes to the bar, and I set off in search of an open table. The bar, which is festooned with strings of Christmas lights and boxing memorabilia, is laid out like a railroad apartment. As I press through the crowd, I feel nervous, like I am on a first date. I find a spot in the back room and sit down. I decide there is something propitious in the air, the slightest suggestion of a new season. There are a few cute guys drinking pints of beer at the table next to me, and Rosemary Clooney plays on the jukebox. There is also a basket of bar mix, and I absently pick through the little pretzels and salty crackers as I peruse the faded photo collage that has been laminated to the top of the table. It is amazing: If the choice of clothing and hairstyle is to be believed, these pictures were all snapped during the glory days of this bar, which seem to have transpired during one never-ending episode of *Bosom Buddies*. There are perms and mustaches, and everyone looks so happy wearing their patterned sweaters and rugby shirts. Honestly, I find it hard to believe such a simple time in New York ever existed. Davis plunks an airplane bottle of white wine on top of one of the photographs, and I pick it up and unscrew the top. I pour it into a glass.

"Have you ever thought about how many people have already touched that?" Davis asks as she points to the now half-eaten snacks in front of me.

"No," I say, and I feel my neck get warm.

"Like that guy, Clo," she says, and she trains her finger on a grizzled and toothless old man sitting near the bar. "That sad man was eating out of the same bowl."

I look.

The man is wearing a flannel shirt and a mesh baseball cap. His face is sunken around his mouth like a failed soufflé, and he grins at absolutely nothing as he takes small sips from a can of cheap beer. I don't know what she is talking about: That guy looks like he's having the time of his life. I look back at Davis. I know the only way out of my embarrassment is humor, so I drop another fistful of orange crackers into my mouth and give her a crooked smile. A cracker falls out of my mouth and clatters on the table.

"Lovely," Davis sighs as she shakes out of her coat and drapes it over the chair. I notice a few people look over at her and I feel a strange sense of pride, like I briefly possess something that everyone else wants.

She unscrews the top of her own wine bottle and pours it into a glass. She takes a long drink, and sighs:

"This is so much better than what I usually do at night," she says as she stretches her long legs to the side of the table and smiles at me.

I find this exceedingly hard to believe—Davis generally spends her nights on the arm of her mother or with her gaggle of fabulous friends at various parties and clubs—but she regards me so convincingly that I allow myself to briefly consider the lack of structure in my own life might hold some unknown appeal.

We talk a little about work before that one drink magically morphs into a second, and then a third, and, at a certain juncture, I suspect Davis may be on her fourth mini bottle of wine. That's the thing about Davis: She can drink. I mean, I can drink, but she can *really* drink. On the handful of occasions we have been out together, she usually puts down two drinks by the time I have finished my first, at which point she will confide in you about almost anything: her high school abortion, her college anorexia, her college abortion, her summer-camp boyfriend who turned out to be gay, the gym teacher she had sex with in the eleventh grade, the time she was stranded on an island, the shoplifting phase, her old medications, her new, better medications, her brief and entirely unnecessary two-day stay in a psych ward during middle school at the behest of her mother. You name it, and Davis Lawrence has some crazy-ass story about it. Naturally, I find this easy intimacy to be thrilling. I reason there must be something special about me, something that makes her feel safe confiding in me about her deepest, darkest secrets. It does not occur to me that, perhaps, she is this open with everyone. Nor do I consider that, maybe, these disclosures are merely a social smokescreen she regularly deploys, if only to obscure the real rocks she would prefer nobody tries to overturn.

Not yet, anyway.

Frankly, it doesn't matter why she is confiding in me, or even why she wants to spend time with someone like me.

It only matters that she doesn't want to stop.

Somewhere on that third (possibly fourth) drink, Davis receives a call from Harry Wood. While I only met him that night outside the handbag party, Davis talks about him so often—and, by now, I read his blog so regularly—that I feel like I know him in some distant capacity. In a few short years, he has found a way to parlay his job into a *reputation*, which is the model everyone is desperate to emulate these days, and I figure an acquaintance like Harry Wood could be a very useful addition to an ambitious girl's growing Rolodex. I sit patiently while Davis takes the call.

After a beat, she closes her slim Motorola phone shut with an authoritative slap, and I think to myself that I really *must* buy a smaller cell phone.

"Finish up, buttercup," Davis instructs. "We are going downtown to meet Harry."

I gulp down the last of my drink, as directed, and we pull on our coats and head back outside. It's funny: It doesn't feel nearly as cold now. We huddle under the awning and smoke cigarettes while we wait—at Davis's request—for an unoccupied taxi to magically appear in the middle of Times Square at ten o'clock at night. After a few minutes, I suggest we walk to the F train, the entrance of which is right around the corner, but Davis just rolls her eyes and points to the spike heels on her boots. Despite an entire childhood spent in New York City, Davis Lawrence is not a subway person. While I bounce in the chill and despairingly scan the street, Davis remains entirely placid because Davis Lawrence is the kind of girl that knows from extensive life experience that a cab will always appear for her, like the first daffodil come spring. I turn to toss my cigarette butt on the ground when I see him: Oliver Barringer. He is walking quickly down the sidewalk with a few of the guys who work at his magazine. They have clearly just left our offices, and they are headed toward the bar from which we have just made our hasty exit.

"Hey, hey, ladies," Oliver says, slowing to a stop next to us. He smiles his lazy smile. It looks like he hasn't shaved in a while.

"Oliver." Davis giggles with unexpected enthusiasm before she kisses him on both cheeks.

I say nothing. I haven't spoken to him since that night at Bar Tabac, but I do lean over to allow him to kiss my cheeks (because that is apparently what we do, even if they are "total dicks") and I smile at his friends, all of whom I know by sight but have never properly met. They mumble back, the collars of their sun-faded blue button-downs peeking out of the top of their plain Patagonia jackets and car coats.

"Are you guys leaving already?" Oliver asks.

"Sorry to say it, but yes," Davis says and, as usual, she does not elaborate.

She just tosses her cigarette on the ground, and I watch as she makes the rounds with Oliver's coworkers. She always makes everything look so easy: She wraps them in hugs. She rubs arms. She makes eye contact. She tosses around small talk that is laced with meaning. The men, in turn, stammer and shift their weight, all positively delighted to be acknowledged by such a special creature.

"That's a shame you're leaving," Oliver says, and I realize, with some amazement, that he's talking to me. "I was hoping we could hang out again."

"Oh." I feel something in my stomach start to bloom.

"Do you want to get a drink some other time?" he asks.

"Yes. I mean, definitely," I say. "Why don't you email me, you know, whenever?"

"Will do," he says.

Just then, I notice a cab cautiously pull up to the curb across the street. It deposits a middle-aged couple in front of the theater. Davis notices it, too.

"See you later, boys," Davis says, and with a quick wave of her hand, she starts to clatter across the street. I follow behind her, but I can't help but wonder if they are watching us. As we slide into the back seat of the car, I sneak a glance, but they are already gone. I try to process my exchange with Oliver Barringer. Mostly, I am just oddly proud that I was noticed. It doesn't occur to me that, maybe, I am someone worth noticing, nor do I question the validity of what I continue to take for fact, which is that my worth is tied to the unformed opinion of men like Oliver Barringer and his bespectacled colleagues. I find myself wondering if his attention was a brief mistake or courtly gesture for which I should feel grateful. The cab accelerates sharply and as we speed across Sixth Avenue, I want to buckle my seat belt, but I worry it will make me appear uncool, so I just lean back and listen as Davis gives the driver an unfamiliar address.

"So where are we going?" I ask.

"Bungalow," she says as she lights up a cigarette and unrolls the window an inch. "Harry had to shoot something earlier at Happy Ending, but I can't deal with all those social girls trying to get their pictures taken, so he's just going to meet up with us later."

This comment reminds me that, somehow, there is a difference between Davis Lawrence, a society girl who often has her picture taken, and "all those social girls trying to get their pictures taken."

An immense distinction within mere degrees.

"Bungalow?"

Here, I endeavor to sound unconcerned, but I am very concerned. I do not want to go to Bungalow 8 because I feel fat in my outfit, and I don't want to feel fat in my outfit the first time I go to Bungalow 8 and meet up with Harry Wood. I had a larger plan for this moment that involved me being ten pounds thinner and, for some unknown reason, wearing my 7 For All Mankind jeans and a white halter top. Furthermore, I know from experience that pushing it on a night like tonight—a night of bloated self-recrimination about my lack of preparation combined with excess alcohol—will only lead to disaster. We barely travel ten blocks when I feel a sad, sugary exhaustion seeping into the place enthusiasm inhabited mere moments ago. Tonight, I decide, is not my night. I am about to say something about feeling sick to my stomach or claim I have an early meeting when Davis reaches over and rubs my knee affectionately.

"Don't worry, honey," she says. "You will be great."

Here is one thing I know for sure: I will not be great, but there is something about Davis that always makes me want to sublimate myself to her, to transform—at any given time—into the exact thing she needs me to be and, tonight, she needs me to be a game participant in her otherworldly life.

"No, totally," I laugh, somewhat nonsensically before I retrieve one of my new lipsticks from my bag. I finger brush my hair. I unwrap a piece of Trident gum. As we turn onto Twenty-Seventh Street, we slow to a stop, and I look out the window. There are at least fifty people, probably more, in a disorganized line outside a standard issue darkened entrance that, in this moment, reminds me of those scary open mouths from the amusement park rides of my childhood. The men in line are jostling against each other—all weasel-bodied and waffle-shirted—to get a better look at the door, and the women all wear expensive silk tops paired with short skirts or low-rise jeans and squeeze small Louis Vuitton logo bags in their armpits, the combination of which just makes them look trashy and poor.

"Davis, look at the line," I say, and I endeavor to sound sort of bored, like this is the last place people of *our* ilk should be wasting our time. "We are never going to get inside. Can we just go somewhere else?"

Davis hands the driver a fold of cash over the seat, and glances out the window:

"Just follow me," she says with a little laugh.

She pushes open the door with her high-heeled boot and winks in my direction before she rises out of the taxi. I slide across the seat, careful to keep my skirt in place, but by the time I get out and jostle the fabric back where it belongs, Davis is on her way to the door. I hurry to catch up, but I keep my gaze fixed on the sidewalk. I am terrified to make eye contact with anyone. If this was a nature documentary, Davis would be the cheetah. She moves in long, elegant strides with her head held high and no hint of hesitation; she knows from experience that she will capture and devour her prey. I, by contrast, am the towering, clumsy giraffe, following behind her with knock knees, slowly chewing a big, dumb mouthful of leaves.

When we get to the door, we are greeted by a tall Black man wearing a long leather trench coat. He has dreadlocks, and he wears a kindly, albeit somewhat inscrutable, expression. When he sees Davis, he takes a step backward and gives a big nod as he unclicks a short velvet rope, which elicits groans and whispers from the people in line. Davis gives the man a quick kiss on the cheek before *another* man—this one smaller in stature—puts a protective arm around both Davis and me, and while it's nice to feel his arm around my shoulder, I know this is not a personal gesture. It is part of a much larger production in which we all play essential roles. A good doorman must not only make it clear that the elite will be protected, but to theatrically safeguard us in front of an audience reinforces the notion that there is a pecking order and, if you are watching this scene unfold, you do not exist.

The space is hot, but not too crowded at this early hour, and the room is so tiny that it doesn't take long for us to get drinks. Davis puts down her credit card. She tells the bartender to open a tab. A few people at the bar greet Davis with kisses, and she introduces me with such deference, it is almost like I was the one who invited *her* out for the evening. When it's time to find a table, however, even Davis understands she isn't famous enough to procure a seat at one of the black-and-white-striped or -dotted banquettes, some of which sit empty. These are for legitimate movie stars. In fact, she knows the rules so well she doesn't even *try* for a banquette. She doesn't *look* at a banquette. Instead, she perches herself with great intention in the middle of the room on an ottoman of sorts and holds her vodka martini like she is the last egret on earth. I sit down next to her and I try to look both bored and important. I do this by chain-smoking and thoughtfully regarding all the many palm fronds that circle the room: Clodagh Harmon, amateur botanist. I see the famous proprietress—a very tall, incredibly ordinary-looking blonde—seated at one of the tables. Her head is bent forward conspiratorially in conversation as she pulls rapaciously on a Marlboro Light. She fiddles with the pack on the tabletop. She waves someone over.

After one hour, two drinks, and separate but thrilling Sean Penn, Nicole Richie, and someone I think was Famke Janssen sightings, there is still no sign of Harry Wood. The music has gotten louder, and bodies bang into us from all sides. Davis and I now struggle to hear one another over the pummeling din, and two vaguely familiar girls climb up on one of the tables, only to look embarrassed and almost immediately get down. I realize it's late, well after midnight, and I am about to drum up the courage to call it a night when a group of people near the entrance parts like a curtain to allow a tall man to slip between them. He shakes a few hands. He laughs heartily. I see a camera dangling from his left hand and, when he turns in our direction, I notice that his dark eyes are lit like the moon rising over water.

It is Harry Wood.

His face softens when he sees Davis.

"My life is *exhausting*," he moans theatrically by way of greeting, but he looks wide awake to me. He flops down next to us and sets his camera on his lap before resting his head on it. Harry has what my mother would call "a good head of hair on him"—dark brown and wavy, and just a little too long in all the right ways. I wait patiently to see the rest of him again in the flesh because I have only seen him up close one time, and I want to see if my memory matches the reality. Davis rolls her eyes before tapping him on the head.

"Harry," she singsongs. "This is Clo, my friend at work I have been telling you about *forever*."

Harry lifts his head. He smiles sideways at me, and I notice a few pieces of hair are damp and stuck flat on his forehead. He is handsome, with sharp features and perfectly round brown eyes. His long lashes curl back toward his face and his mouth is delicately drawn. He is both striking and a bit feminine, like that boy from the cartoon *Speed Racer*.

"Hi, Clo," he says. "I'm Harry Wood. Nice to meet you."

I smile calmly, but I am surprised that he speaks with a proper Southern accent, mostly because he doesn't *look* like he should have a Southern accent. I definitely didn't pick it up during our first introduction. I am also embarrassed that neither Davis or Harry seems to recall I have, indeed, met him once before.

"Nice to meet you, too," I say back, and I nervously pull a strand of hair behind my ear.

"Did you get the coke?" Davis asks, and she leans forward on her elbows.

"Hello to you, too, Miss Lawrence," he drawls.

She laughs, and he shoots back a suggestive smile so loaded with shared secrets that I instantly feel unwanted in the worst way, like I interrupted a murder in progress, stumbling into a midnight kitchen in search of a glass of milk.

"Sorry," she says to him with a coquettishness that surprises me. "*Hello, Mr. Wood.*"

Until this moment, I had assumed Davis was too pretty to flirt with men, and I find this unexpected register from her to be both perplexing and utterly bewitching. It's like she swallowed some small pill when I wasn't looking and is now supercharged. She runs her fingers through her hair and balls it up at the nape of her long neck before releasing it down one shoulder.

"Oh, hello," Harry drawls.

"So, did you get the coke?" she repeats with a laugh.

I feel my teeth clench. You see, I have done cocaine twice in my life and, both times, after I did the emotional math in the collapsing black hole that was the suicidal hellscape of my morning, I concluded it was a mistake never to be repeated. The hyper-sexualized, insanely confident high cocaine provided me did not compensate, in any capacity, for the anxious, despairing sensation that accompanies holding a fistful of bloody tissues to your nose in a town car at the break of dawn, wondering if the profound depression and memory loss you are currently experiencing is temporary or permanent in nature.

I say a silent prayer that Harry has come up short. Maybe he has been too busy at work, or, quite simply, forgotten her request? Instead, he slaps the tops of his thighs twice in a lively manner, which reads as an utterly charming rallying of the troops, and I know that I am sunk.

"Let's hit the bathroom, shall we, ladies?" He stands up and extends his hand to Davis.

She reaches out her arm, and Harry, with great gallantry, pulls her up from the ottoman. Then, he wraps his arm softly around her narrow waist and draws her body close. I watch longingly as they rest their foreheads together and whisper. The energy leaping between them is tactile, almost painfully so and, yet, I cannot look away.

When he finally releases her, he turns to me kindly with an outstretched arm. As I flop my giant paw into his hand, he wraps his fingers around mine tightly, and it feels immediately reassuring, like the promise of protection. It's sad. I'm so easily seduced by things I should just expect from a man at this stage of my life: a held-open door, a firm handshake, a confidently picked-up dinner tab without having to fumble around about "splitting it" as you snap down two credit cards.

"Clo? Do you want to stand up?"

This question comes from Harry because, as it turns out, I have not moved an inch. I am still seated, and I'm limply holding his hand with my mouth slightly open.

"Oh, sorry," I say absently.

As I stand up to meet him, I can sense the soft heat rising off my cheeks. Maybe it's the way he said my name, with that rocky little twang, or maybe it has just been so long since someone held my hand, but I must look a little dazed because he keeps his hand warmly clasped around mine as the three of us shoulder through the multitudes toward the bathrooms. We arrive, a little dizzy and joyful, and squeeze into a stall, laughing at our own physical awkwardness. I watch as Harry taps cocaine out of a tiny plastic bag and creates a small mound of it on the back of the toilet.

"Do you remember that time we got handed an actual *tray* here?" Harry laughs.

Davis smiles as she rolls up a twenty-dollar bill, and Harry uses his credit card to cut the powder into short lines. At this juncture, I am dimly aware that the two of them continue to talk about something, but I am not really listening. The problem with tonight—like all nights—is I want to make a good impression. I want Harry Wood to like me, or some better, invented version of me. I want him to think I am cool and relaxed and open to life, like a beautiful Italian woman splashing in a fountain, wearing only a negligee.

Davis offers me the twenty first, but I shake my head, so she offers it to Harry. He takes the first line while Davis rubs my back reassuringly. She can sense my discomfort, apparently, but she also has no intention of letting me off the hook. After Harry takes a second line, he pops up and looks directly at me. His eyes are glassy and intense, and there is an appealing mirth radiating from his body now. It is celebratory, but also a bit sinister, and I feel both excited and afraid.

Davis is up next. She lowers her head, and her blonde hair cascades down and covers everything, even the indelicate sound that accompanies snorting something up your nose. Everything around me starts to move more slowly and in this lull in the space-time continuum, I watch Harry lift the camera over his head. He trains it down on Davis, and presses the trigger, which illuminates us all in a white flash. When I look down and blink a few times to force my eyes to adjust, I notice there are two sets of heels in the next stall.

"Captured on film, the beautiful Davis Lawrence blowing lines off a toilet," Harry announces as he takes a second picture from the same angle, his motions now frantic and impatient.

Here is the thing: Davis does not flinch. Why would she? There is no reason to care about this picture, which is surely one of thousands that have been taken without her consent over the years. It will get developed and sit in a pile of prints, somewhere, until it gets lost or destroyed or pasted into a personal photo album. As such, she simply stands up and shakes her glorious hair back before she leans over to do a second line. Without warning, Harry turns his camera toward me. He moves it too close to my face, and I try to take a step back, but I hit the stall door just as the flash blinds me for a moment. I hold my hand up like I am shielding myself from the sun as I anticipate a second attack, and I am surprised to feel a ferocious anger sweep through my entire body.

"Stop," I scream, and too loudly, as my palms fly up to my face. When I open my eyes, Harry is just standing there motionless, his arms limp at his sides. Davis looks at me with concern flickering across her face, and I can't explain it, but her expression communicates to me that this is not the right time to be angry. This is time to be part of the team. I realize my emotions need to find another avenue. I take a deep breath. I can feel my hands shaking.

"No profile shots," I say finally, my voice a hoarse whisper. After a nervous pause, Harry breaks into a howling laughter. He bends over and puts his hands on his knees. I watch his shoulders shake.

"No profile shots," he repeats, still laughing, as he stands back up. "Davis! I love this girl."

"I know," Davis says, and she crosses her hands across her heart. "She's the best."

Let me be clear: Everything about this moment feels wrong, but a strange drive overrides my hesitation. I will be exactly who they need me to be, and, in return, they will be my friends. I decide that is the unspoken bargain they are offering me and, if anything, I am getting the far better end of the deal. I hold out my hand for the rolled-up twenty, and they both nod at me with relieved approval.

A minute later, there is a forceful rap on the stall door. We hear a man's voice boom:

One to a stall. What's going on in there?

We freeze, and only our eyes move. They dart back and forth in a wild, comic manner and then we all crumble into hysterical laughter, a merry trio to which I suddenly feel like I belong.

19

At this point, I feel it is my obligation to reveal that I officially lead a double life.

I suspect this is not the case for most of my colleagues, all of whom earnestly traffic in things like Teterboro Airport, market-price Dover sole, and D. Porthault bedsheets with uninterrupted regularity.

In this secret world, the world I keep well-hidden from my coworkers, I belong to the cheapest gym in my neighborhood, a run-down spot where I climb the elliptical machine and watch *Friends* on the single television mounted to the cinder-block wall. I get my eyebrows waxed for seven dollars at the Korean place on Court Street, shop for nondescript clothes on the sale racks at Midtown Banana Republics and get felt up by drunk guys on the dance floor at Don Hills. Sometimes—an infrequent sometimes—I also get asked on a proper date, which thus far has been a very mixed bag.

I spend a lot of time alone, dancing in my apartment.

There are certain routines, however. For example, every Sunday I take the subway from Brooklyn to Allie's apartment in the West Village to watch *Sex and the City*. Yes, all citizens of New York have sworn a solemn oath to hold *Sex and the City* in broad and biting contempt, but everyone watches it anyway. It's like swimming in the dorky kid's pool on the weekend. Of course I do it, but I am not about to tell anyone at work about it. Instead, I usually roll into the office on Monday mornings claiming to have spent my time wandering the "new exhibit at the Guggenheim" instead of, you know, puking up rum and cokes after a sweaty night at Bowery Bar or half-ass reading a book in a Brooklyn diner, totally alone, and wondering if I'll ever get married. Or, even worse, wondering if I will have any narrative at all.

There is plenty of time, I reason, for the Guggenheim.

On these Sunday nights, Allie and I dine on microwave popcorn, drink too much white wine, and reliably discuss only two topics: work and guys.

In comparison to her grueling hours at the investment bank, Allie's new life as a graduate student seems pretty cushy; in fact, the casual observer may think she reads books all day, prone in her imitation silk bathrobe, and smokes cigarettes. But I know Allie's ambitious undercurrents far too well, and Allie Blum—beautiful, smart, flirtatious, morally questionable Allie Blum—never comes in second place. She has already managed to have drinks with the older, gray-bearded chair of her department (she giddily referred to it as "sexual harassment!") and she recently had a paper accepted at a conference, which apparently in academia, is a very big deal.

For my part, I contribute delightful, preposterous tales from the magazine world to our evenings. This week, for example, a fashion assistant informed me that a famous actress spent an entire photo shoot sucking the coating off Skittles, one by one, all without swallowing a single candy. Apparently, she would spit the gluey innards into a metal trash can, which was promptly and repeatedly emptied by her chubby assistant, and then, when the clean trash can was returned, she would pop a new Skittle in her mouth. I had also been tasked, to my great excitement, with writing a short box for the fitness section detailing the sweat-wicking powers of wool, for which I received a large box of very expensive exercise clothes, all in my size, and all of which I am, apparently, not expected to return. But these were just the opening act for the major moment of my week (and, possibly, my life to date), which is that I saw Joan Didion and John Dunne in person at a small book party I attended on lower Fifth Avenue. They arrived, shoulder to shoulder, and their magnificent faces, which I had only ever seen in photographs, were arranged with both boredom and bewilderment. As they politely circulated, it looked as if they couldn't wait to return to the other (clearly far better) thing they were doing just before they put on shoes to make a mandatory appearance. For my part, I tried to present as calm and not psychotic in their presence. I did this by feigning fascination with the bookshelves that lined the room and not making eye contact with anyone. The idea that Joan Didion and I received the same invitation to the same party was confusing to me in the way a lot of things are confusing to me these days. I didn't know if I should treat it like a freak accident or if, somehow, I was slowly transforming into someone who—solely, of course, due to my association with the magazine—*should* get invited to the same parties as Joan Didion.

Now, while my anecdotes are undoubtedly glamorous, Allie and I reckon that the reason these stories are so enthralling is because they are only on loan; none of this world belongs to us, at least, not in the same way it belongs to other people. We are observers, not participants. The parties, the clothes, and the antics of my more established colleagues are simply a placeholder until our own lives really begin. They are memories we are desperate to collect and stuff into sacks before our time here in New York expires and we must smuggle them out of town.

Which brings us to our next topic: guys. Allie and I have yet to land the elusive New York boyfriend, and because finding a decent guy in this town is another full-time job, we rely on each other for wise counsel during our respective quests. Allie is slightly more demoralized than I am on this front due to her longer tenure in the city. I mean, when we were in high school, we both thought we would be married by now and yet, it is only just recently we settled the debate over keeping condoms in our purse.

It has been decided that we should *not* keep condoms in our purse.

It feels wrong. Like we are asking for it.

This is the era in which the rituals of courtship include trading incredibly long emails in which interested parties intellectually and/or comically attempt to one-up each other in witty back-and-forth missives that run no less than 400 words with the goal of French-kissing in a bar. When these written exchanges are good, it's thrilling. The wit! The vocabulary! The delightful insinuations and arcane references! We forward them to our friends, and discuss, at great length, the adorableness of the author, an almost entirely unknown man who, obviously, will become our husband one day. When they are bad, it's still kind of good because we can pick them apart—right down to the grammatical missteps and predictable affinity for the movie *Blade Runner*—all for laughs.

Furthermore, the fact that almost no one has email at home makes this letter writing a time-bound activity, which adds an additional layer of excitement or despair. Mostly, it's just nice to have something to look forward to when you fire up your computer each morning at work; it's like the salvation of a nearly lost art.

As you can imagine, however, things can get a bit *complicated* when one communicates with paramours in writing. Therefore, Allie and I often dedicate a portion of our Sunday nights to deciphering deeply inscrutable phrases in emails including, but not limited to, *I'm not in the place where I want a relationship right now* or *I think you're awesome, but I have decided to get back together with my ex-girlfriend.* We scratch our heads. What on *earth* could they mean? What are they *really* trying to tell us? Clearly, there is some hidden meaning that requires action on our part. When we are stumped, we constructively remind each other that men are just *intimidated* by us because *we have great jobs* and it's *not the 1950s anymore*, so maybe we should ask them out instead of waiting for them to ask us out. Never mind that our extensive body of primary research that indicates this approach fails 100 percent of the time, we offer it up anyway, again and again, in a dazzling display of our unrelenting girl power. Finally, when all is lost, we provide consolation in the wake of the universally regrettable email one sends in a last-ditch and deeply tragic attempt to restart a conversation with someone who stopped responding to our increasingly desperate overtures: *Hey! I saw this article and thought of you.*

On these wonderful nights, as we get increasingly drunk, we promise our allegiance to each other. We sit cross-legged on the floor with a bottle of wine between us, and we congratulate ourselves for not choosing a boring life. We had the guts to move to the big city. We work hard. We are brave. Most of all, we trust that we will find our way into our own happy endings, and, of course, those happy endings will arrive for us at the exact same moment in time.

We will not abandon each other, we say.

But deep down, I know there is no real safety in numbers.

It's just us girls up against the world.

20

My first six months as Isobel Fincher's assistant are profoundly anxiety-producing, but uneventful in the sense that I continue to have a job when I enter the building every morning. She's more private than MC, often working behind a closed door, and where MC was mercurial and irrational (she once barked at me to tie a ribbon for her "like they do it at Prada!"), Isobel is polite and reasonable and, thus far, has only asked for my assistance on work-related tasks. I mean, she waited for her own electrician the other day, which struck me as a bizarre misuse of the readily available company resources, but there was something noble about it, nevertheless.

On my end, I arrive early each morning with two cups of hot coffee, one for her, one for me. I tidy up her office (but I *never* nose around in the drawers like I did with MC), and I still scour the newspapers and weekly magazines for relevant stories, all of which I clip out with an elegant pair of silver scissors and place neatly on her desk. I ensure she promptly gets phone messages (making copies in the event she misplaces one) and I print out important emails, all of which I save in a file folder I keep inside my desk. Every Monday, I fill out a form for petty cash, and take it up to a window on the sixteenth floor. I slide it under the glass divider and watch the woman count out piles of crisp twenty-dollar bills, all of which I am ostensibly to deploy for Isobel's daily needs (magazines, newspapers, cab fare, coffee) and account for each month in an expense report. Naturally, I use a good deal of this cash for my own personal use (drinks, cabs, cigarettes, drinks) but I have learned there are many inventive ways I can claim these expenses as legitimate. For years, every assistant has participated in this low-level and long-running scam (especially at our magazine, where every assistant is treated by corporate like a father's favorite daughter: spoiled rotten and entirely above suspicion) and since nobody gets in trouble for it, I am not even sure if what I am doing is wrong. So, each night, I follow Isobel to the elevator bank to double-confirm her car number, ask if she needs any cash, and remind her of any early-morning appointments. I, myself, never depart until she leaves for the day, which is usually around seven, and then I hang around for a while just to make sure she doesn't call me on the phone for something and catch me out. I want to do well. I want her to like me. Generally, I think she is impressed by my work ethic and cheerful demeanor, and Davis seems relieved that maybe my "for now" will be "forever" and she won't have to expend the energy required to befriend a new cubicle mate.

Since Isobel started, our section (I call it *our* section now, especially within earshot of Liddy, who has surely gotten wise to my editorial cockblocking) keeps growing fatter. Each page of editorial content is paid for by advertising, for which there is rumored to be a waiting list at $100,000 a page. Apparently, the advertising side gets to pick and choose who gets to pay us for the privilege of appearing in our pages, and—if the procession of wine, flower arrangements, and designer watches and handbags are any indication—they are very skilled at appearing nearly impossible to please.

Basically, we are killing it.

To cover the increased need for the reporting and stories that fill these pages, Isobel, as promised, has brought in new writers, all of whom seem lovely and competent over the phone, and none of whom suffer a cardiac event when I inform them of the enormous sum of money (to me, anyway) they are to be paid for writing a single article. At this moment in time, our magazine pays a freelancer anywhere from two to five dollars a word, depending on the status of the writer and/or the clout of their agent. I fill out cost estimates (how many words we are assigning for a piece and at what dollar amount) and mail out contracts on what feels like an hourly basis, careful to keep photocopies in another very responsible folder in the very responsible filing system I have devised inside my desk. This is to say nothing of our bigger, even better compensated "contributing writers," who are on the hook for a set number of pieces a year in return for a dizzying amount of money and obscene travel expenses. I am also diligent about updating my own Rolodex, adding all new contacts in my best penmanship with a black flair marker. Some nights when I am alone, I turn the plastic dial and, as each card flips by, I marvel at the names inside. These are names—writers, actors, photographers—I have heard my entire life, without ever believing these people to be real. And now I call them directly on their home phones.

A few of the new writers have been kind enough to invite me for a drink to get to know me better, but I always decline. At this stage in my career, I prefer to remain shrouded, for as long as humanly possible, in a hazy cloud of intellectual and/or sexual mystery. I don't want them to realize I am not smart enough to keep up in a conversation. Or to discover I am taller or less attractive than they envisioned over the phone. I don't want them to inquire about where I went to college. Or suggest we meet in a restaurant where I will be required to successfully manipulate a set of chopsticks.

I am so desperate to be mistaken for one of them.

Or, more accurately, fearful that a misstep could result in my banishment from a beautiful land I am just beginning to explore.

Now, while I have not written a proper article yet, only a few short sidebars, I *am* called in with regularity to work on captions and headlines by Isobel, which feels like a step in the right direction. It also turns out to be an exceptionally fun game. Isobel and I have created a long list of the overused puns that should absolutely, positively never be used as headlines in magazine copy (e.g., *Portrait of a Lady*, *Girl, Interrupted*, *The Talented Mr. [Insert Actor's Name Here]*, *Prints Charming*, *Flower Power*) and sometimes, if we have been at it long enough, you can hear our punchy cackles reverberating down the halls. I love these "knock-'em-out" sessions because Isobel lets her guard down and, for all her precision and sense of justice, it turns out she is also wickedly funny. Additionally, these moments make me feel like my job requires skill and talent, as opposed to the *appearance* of skill and talent, and that maybe, just maybe, someone as smart and worldly as Isobel Fincher suspects I possess a talent or two of my own.

It is almost impossible to believe.

She does one vexing thing, however: Several days a week, she will ask me to pull up a chair while she is editing copy or making phone calls to writers. I have no official role in this activity, and the first few times I just sat there feeling like a hulking mouth breather. I keep stealing glances down at my hearty thighs, which careened over the edges of my narrow seat, and comparing myself to Isobel's lovely and fragrant frame. It doesn't help that aside from being pocket-sized and beautiful, she wears the most incredible clothes—oversized tweed blazers, mid-calf pleated skirts, high flat boots, crisp white shirts—all of which make her look like an expensive, off-duty equestrian.

As Isobel taps away on her keyboard during the sessions, she will talk out loud and I dutifully take notes because I am certain there will be some action item for which I am responsible. Sometimes she will place her fingertip on the computer screen and say things like: *You see, this is ultimately repetitive,* or *I am not sure what this adds to my understanding,* or *This entire graph needs to be moved up.*

For a long time, I waited for my instructions, but instructions never came. Instead, Isobel seemed perfectly content to have me sit behind her for hours and watch her work. As the months rolled by, however, and the collection of issues in which my name appeared on the masthead grew more robust, I started to understand things, like why Isobel accepts some pitches from writers and declines others or why she wants to review a certain book or champion a certain movie. In fact, I have yet to see her waffle on a decision or flail around with the indecisiveness that plagues nearly every decision I make.

Under her quiet tutelage, I can now translate the previously inscrutable twists of copy-editing symbols. I learn the definitions of "serial comma," "nut graph," and "TK," which confoundingly means that a missing fact is "to come." I develop a clearer sense of which interview questions procure interesting answers and which ones are too formulaic. As I listen to Isobel on phone calls, I absorb how a supremely talented editor can talk an angry writer off a ledge or coax a lifetime procrastinator toward action, like a magician pulling a happy rabbit out of a hat. With each passing day, I start to feel the bounce of strong writing in my body and understand that proper grammar really does play like music. I can feel—quite literally *feel*—when a piece I am reading is missing a note. It vibrates in my windpipe and hums along the sinew that connects my bones.

It takes me a very long time to realize that Isobel Fincher is teaching me.

It takes me even longer to realize that I have been learning the entire time.

21

As you take baby steps up the ranks—if not by title then by the vaguest misinterpretation of your reputation—you discover there is yet another category of party in New York, and this one I generally define as "literary" in nature. While fashion events are more of a splashy hit-and-run, literary parties are more leisurely affairs that include various "launches" (book, blog, website) as well as all manner of vaguely themed get-togethers (housewarming, thirtieth birthday, ironic Super Bowl viewing) so long as it's thrown by a single male (or bizarre codependent couple) in possession of both a mid-level editorial title and a centrally located two-bedroom apartment in Manhattan or, more recently, Brooklyn. I'm never invited directly to one of these apartment parties, but I have been invited to join by others, namely Davis, on enough occasions that, as far as the crowd at large is concerned, I am a familiar participant. I try to dress a little sexy for these events, but you must be super careful to keep it casual. As such, sometimes I don't remove my striped ski hat *for the entire night* to compensate for my tight tank top or, maybe, I'll toss on a sweater so large that it dwarfs my entire (obviously adorable underneath) body. Once you are appropriately outfitted and armed with a drink, you square-dance around the room and talk in code about who is reviewing what book for what publication and what you *really* think of that person. As it happens, it is never good, and, yet, it is never bad.

This morning, the hangover I combat is courtesy of a party thrown by a rising editor at a major publishing house. I wore my nice jeans and a tight turtleneck, which looked fantastic for a chilly weekend, but felt like a straitjacket because the apartment was quickly overheated by too many bodies. Several girls stripped down to their silk tank tops before the host threw open the windows, all of which overlooked Tompkins Square Park. I spent a good portion of the night trying to inconspicuously pinch the fabric away from my damp armpits. Davis and I each brought a bottle as a gift—vodka and white wine, respectively—and after we theatrically displayed these offerings to our grateful, bespectacled host for approval, we set them down on the fold-out table erected to serve as the bar. By the time we had arrived, the party was well underway, and the tablecloth was already wet and strewn with familiar party detritus: champagne hoods, dead lemons, wine foil, half-empty beer bottles, wadded-up napkins, and a bowl of cashews that looked bloated and gummy. After fishing around for some questionably clean plastic glasses, we both poured a drink (from the bottles we brought, obviously) and settled ourselves in the crowd. To me, the evening felt pleasant and festive, and our host had secured an exceptionally intimidating guest list for anyone who hoped one day to be lukewarmly acknowledged by a terrifically small group of people. As I looked around, I saw all kinds of writerly representation including people (more specifically defined as *men*) from the magazines (the *Nation*, the *Atlantic*, the *New Yorker*, *Harper's*), the literary blogs (*n+1*, *The Millions*), the newspapers (the *Observer*, the *New York Times*), and, finally, the publishing powerhouses (Knopf, Penguin, and Farrar, Straus and Giroux). Additionally, there was mixed-sex participation from book review folks, the short story collection girls, the MFA candidates, and the I-took-one-freelance-reporting-trip-to-the-Middle-East-so-I-can-wear-this-flack-jacket guys. Lastly, there was a lovely cluster of aspiring novelists and academics, all conversing articulately in low voices about Very Serious Things.

Naturally, Oliver Barringer was in attendance—these events fall squarely in his domain—and, just as naturally, I was immediately abandoned by Davis and left to fend for myself within three minutes of our arrival.

No matter: I have a first-rate strategy for navigating these events, which includes being super vague about what I do for a living and drowning all my insecurities in alcohol. When I'm no longer panic-stricken that someone is going to ask me to define *postmodernism* or offer my opinion on *Middlemarch*, I know I have arrived at a safe cruising altitude.

A few other things generally transpire at these parties. For starters, I can be counted on to spill the entire contents of my drink at some juncture and behave as if nothing happened, even though I am aware there are several smirking and slightly disgusted witnesses. Two, I usually indulge in a poetic look in the bathroom mirror when I find myself emotionally undone by the "girl publishing star of the moment," usually a reliably a pretty brunette in heavy glasses who, along with once being a "reader" for the *Paris Review* and a finalist for the Younger Prize, is now publishing a memoir because her life has *already* been infinitely more interesting than mine will ever be. Three, I find I enjoy rounding out a perfectly nice evening by conversing with someone of *actual* influence only to realize with a blurry kind of horror (usually about ten minutes into the conversation and courtesy of their uneasy expression) that I have no earthly clue as to what I have been rattling on about so passionately and, quite frankly, neither do they.

At some late hour last night, I recall drunkenly rooting around the ransacked bar. I ate a few old cashews as I turned over several empty bottles of wine and prosecco before Oliver Barringer, to whom I had not spoken all night, leaned over to pour a little red wine in my plastic cup from his own cup.

"I was sensing some desperation over here," he says. "I think they are out of everything."

"Ha," I respond before I think: *Man, if you only knew.*

"So, you came with Davis?" He tips his grizzly chin in her direction. She is leaning against an open window in conversation with two guys I don't recognize. She has tied her sweater around her waist and is smoking a cigarette.

I nod, but I don't say anything because my tongue is busy prying cashew meat from between my teeth. I also try not to think about the fact that Oliver said he was going to email me months ago, but that email never came.

"I am just pleased she brought *you* and not Harry Wood."

"Why?" I ask. "I mean, what's wrong with Harry Wood?"

"Ugh," he says. "That guy is such an operator. No one wants to talk to him because it will end up on his stupid fucking blog."

"Oh," I say. "Right."

"Are you friends with him?" he asks.

"Harry?" I say, and I raise my eyebrows slightly. "No, not really. I mean, like you said, you can't really trust him."

"Okay, good," he says with such an approving smile that I feel absolutely no guilt for disavowing Harry. "So here is what I find more confusing: Why does Davis enable him? She brings him everywhere."

"He worships her, which probably helps," I say without thinking, although I instantly regret this indiscretion. I take a sip of my drink and despair at the half smile that plays on Oliver's lips. He will most likely repeat this comment and he will attribute it to me.

"Yeah," he says. "I suppose it does."

22

One late winter morning, I find myself inside Oliver Barringer's apartment, and I worry—yet again—that there is something wrong with me. All I keep hearing is that I should be enjoying this—this being *single* and *sexy* in New York City—but I am not enjoying it. That said, I want him to think I am enjoying it. I want him to think I am a sophisticated and modern and deeply sensual woman who has no interest in a proper boyfriend. No, I just want sex. Yeah, that's it. All the sex. *I just got out of something serious*, I assured him, entirely unprompted, over a third and ill-advised drink on our second date. It's no surprise this blatant lie is well received, nor is it that my date—and I use this term hopefully as we are talking about Oliver Barringer here—got me inside his apartment within thirty minutes of this false declaration. He didn't even take the key out of the lock before he pushed me, quite hard frankly, up against the front door.

The first time Oliver asked me out, which was a few weeks after the party on Tompkins Square Park, he posed it like two colleagues grabbing a drink, and I treated it as such, even though I was vibrating with excitement and anxiety in the lead-up to the big event. We met at the Brooklyn Inn, and while the night started out a little stilted, our conversation started to pick up steam after a drink or two. At one point, I stole a glance in the enormous, mottled mirror behind the bar and thought: *Hey, we look good together*. That night, he even went so far as to walk me halfway home, which felt positively courtly, and when he emailed me a few (long) days later about going out a second time, I felt victorious; it was like I was finally being called up to the big leagues.

So, now that I am in his apartment, I do my part. I moan and writhe as he rapidly removes my dress, and the entire time, all (and I mean *all*) I am thinking is: *Why did I wear a dress?* It's a rookie move as there are no stages of nudity when you only wear one piece of clothing: You are dressed, then you are naked. With pants and shirts and skirts and blazers, there is an opportunity to eject yourself from a liaison before you do something you regret. It's like that Mormon underwear. The truth is, by the time I am undressed in these situations, I find it's easier (not to mention a thousand times faster) to have sex with a guy than to explain why, maybe, I don't want to have sex. I mean, I came all the way to his apartment, didn't I? And it would be weird at my age to hold the line at "sloppy third base," right? It would just lead to explaining and rationalizing and cajoling (from him) and apologizing and embarrassment (from me), and then it's just two people who don't know each other very well putting their clothes back on and promising to call each other later. I don't want that. *Nobody* wants that.

Listen, I don't blame the guy. I never blame the guy. I don't blame the alcohol, either, even though it's usually a prominent factor in any of my lousy decision-making. No, I am a grown-ass woman who put herself in this circumstance, and I am not about to pin it on someone or something else. I just wish he was my boyfriend. Or that *someone* was my boyfriend. I want to wear cute sweatpants and feed someone Chinese food out of the container like they do in the movies. I want someone to think I am funny. I want someone to think I am pretty. I want someone to see me as worthwhile so that—maybe—I can figure out how to see myself the same way.

On this particular night, Oliver and I have sex. He has a quick orgasm, and I fake one, as usual, but tonight I decide to trot out one of my favorite variations, which I affectionately call "surprised orgasm." This is when I make breathless little noises meant to communicate that—after a lifetime of substandard sex—this guy (this guy!) is so shockingly good in bed that I didn't see it coming, like a car with no headlights. Afterward, Oliver instantly passes out while I stare miserably at the ceiling with sleep overtaking me in small increments here and there. I am so thirsty I start to panic that my heart might stop beating due to dehydration, but I am terrified to get up and make any bothersome noise. Yes, Oliver Barringer's dick was just inside my body, but I don't want to inconvenience him by, you know, moving that body in any audible capacity for a solid eight hours. Finally, and by the grace of God, a soggy morning light starts to leak through the dusty blinds. He stirs, ever so slightly, and I seize this opportunity to sit up, demurely holding his oily royal blue sheets to my chest. I scan the floor for my clothes, strategizing how to collect each item gracefully because I don't want him to see me naked in the creeping daylight.

Once I have everything in hand, I tiptoe into the bathroom. When I pee (which I try to do quietly by aiming the stream at the porcelain bowl rather than the water) my urine is so thick it feels like my urethra is expelling maple syrup. Then I brush my teeth with a salty finger before I swish a mixture of water and toothpaste around my dry mouth. I finger comb my hair and take a quick look in the mirror before I let myself oh so gently back into the bedroom. He is still asleep, or pretending to be asleep, and I don't know if I should get back into bed or if I should leave.

Leave, I think.

I lower apprehensively to my knees and start patting under the bed for my shoes. I see one and pull it toward me, and this movement unearths a condom wrapper. It is crumpled among the dust and feathers and single socks that reside under his bed. Of course, this condom is *not* the brand we used last night, and this unexpected discovery feels like running headfirst into a brick wall. Everything falls as silent as a new snow inside my body, and I lay down on my stomach and place my cheek flat against the grimy wood floor. I stare at the wrapper. It's red. A red condom wrapper. I had convinced myself that if I impressed the famous Oliver Barringer with my "disinterest in a relationship" coupled with my "wild sense of fun," that he would insist—*absolutely insist*—on becoming my boyfriend. I had so wanted to convince him that I was "not that kind of girl" that I, apparently, was a wild success. I take a few steadying breaths before I pull my other shoe out and stand up. I look down at him and decide he is only pretending to be asleep.

"So," I say as I plop down heavily on the soft bed, "I am going to get a cab, I think."

I think.

Despite my very real and growing humiliation, there remains a distressing part of me that hopes he invites me to breakfast. Or to meet his parents. I want this red condom wrapper to all be some big misunderstanding that we laugh about on our wedding day. On the Brooklyn Heights Promenade. A cool fall day. I wear a short cream dress. He wears a suit. Mr. and Mrs. Oliver Barringer. It receives coverage in the Style section of the *New York Times*, and we pretend to be chagrined, even though we submitted the copy ourselves because it would be good for our careers.

"Go to DeKalb," he mumbles as he rolls over on his side and turns his back to me.

"DeKalb?" Here, I give him a little extra time to realize he should get out of bed and walk me to a taxi like a gentleman.

"Yeah," he sighs with a trace of irritation. "I mean, if you're going home."

"Okay," I say. "Thanks."

Yes, I thanked him at this point.

"And don't worry about the front door," he says, but without looking at me. "It locks automatically. Just make sure you pull it shut tight."

"No problem."

I button up my red coat. I check the pockets for my keys, money wad, and cell phone and, without giving him another look, I walk out the door. A few agonizing minutes later, I am standing on a corner, fully embodying, maybe for the very first time in my life, what is truly meant by the "harsh light of day." I can't stand to be in my own skin. My eyes are sticky and dry, and I can taste semen in my mouth. I squeeze my face as tight as possible to sandbag any memories from crashing over my now severely weakened emotional levees. *Tight. Tight. Tight.* I hold my arm out for a cab, and one glides over immediately—they have recently become more available in Brooklyn—and as we sail toward my neighborhood, I feel grateful that we don't hit a single red light. I want to put as much distance between me and last night as physically possible.

When I arrive at my apartment, I kick off my shoes and pluck out my contact lenses, which I toss on the floor. Then, I take a long, scalding hot shower. I scrub my body with a puffy loofah until my skin turns a somewhat concerning shade of pink, and as I dry off, I start to psychosomatically develop the symptoms of herpes. *Is that a fever? Yes, that is a fever. Is that burning? Oh yes. That is burning.* I debate just how early I can call my gynecologist on Monday for a test, a thought which immediately snowballs into how no one will marry a woman with herpes, and I only have seven more years of peak fertility, and that I will die alone in this studio apartment with herpes and four hundred unread copies of the *Atlantic Monthly*, all piled so high against my door that the police officers conducting the wellness check find it hard to enter. I see them banging the door with their hips: *Something is blocking the door, Frank. Give me a hand, willya?*

I brush my teeth, tap pasty dots of Clearasil on my pimples and coat the rest of my face in drugstore anti-aging cream. I pay special attention to the increasingly thin area around my eyes. Then, I crawl into my unmade bed where I, quite literally, pull the covers over my head to block out the harsh winter sun. I briefly debate having a good cry, but I decide it's not worth the effort; I am too old to cry over milk that I have gone and, yet again, spilled myself. Instead, I fall into a deep, dark, and most necessary sleep.

I wake up thoroughly disoriented a few hours later, unsure if it's morning or early evening. The only thing that locates me is the hot shame, which is slathered thick on my skin, like butter. Well, that and the rhythmic thumping emanating from what I assume to be my inflamed and ragingly contagious vagina. I roll my head over to look at the digital clock on my nightstand: It's almost noon. I remember I am supposed to meet Allie at one o'clock on the Upper West Side for brunch, which will never happen because, as far as I know, no one invented time travel while I was passed out. I sit up and leave her a voicemail that I am running behind ("because I am a disgusting whore") so maybe we should meet in the middle at, say, Broadway–Lafayette, instead? She calls me back to agree and, an hour later, we are seated at a commodious brunch place on Broadway that never kicks anyone out. Along with food, I order a coffee and a mimosa, and Allie gets a Bloody Mary.

I tell her I slept with Oliver Barringer. I say I feel wretched about it, but I also relay that he is funnier than I thought, and he *confided* in me (although now that I think about it, I think he probably just told me) that he is writing a novel. I hope she says that I am overreacting and that he will absolutely ask me on a third date.

She does not.

"Wow, he's writing a novel. Big surprise," she says, bonking her celery around in her cocktail. "Is David Foster Wallace, like, *his favorite writer?*"

"Point taken," I say miserably.

"It's not your fault," she says, but now a bit kinder. "*A Beautiful Mind* and all those people who married Ernest Hemingway made women feel like we should be martyrs for crazy men. That we are supposed to *support* artists rather than *be* the artists ourselves."

"He's not crazy," I protest half-heartedly.

"I think you should date an investment banker," Allie suggests, not listening to me. "That way, *you* can be the crazy one. Like Davis."

Despite all my time at the magazine, Allie has yet to meet Davis in person—my two worlds are kept separate—but she enjoys the stories I share about her life, including the time a private jet was delayed at Teterboro because Davis forgot her headphones at home.

"You know, it's not like I even liked him?" I continue, which I know to be entirely true. "I just really wanted *him* to like *me.*"

I take a bitter sip of my mimosa. The cheap prosecco in it has already gone flat. I have no idea how I can show my face around the office on Monday morning now that I have lost all credibility. The thought makes me want to cry.

"You are worth a guy that likes you," Allie says. "Look at you. You're gorgeous. You have a killer body. You have a great job . . ."

"Easy for you to say now that *you* have a boyfriend," I complain.

It's true: Allie and a guy named Patrick started dating a few months ago, and she even took him to a wedding, which is a big deal by New York standards. He is of medium build and good-looking enough, but he is also a little bland and earnest, like he read a book at some point on how to be a gentleman and is still testing out the techniques. Personally, I think Allie can do better, but I am starting to wonder if the only way a girl can get married is to settle.

"I know," she says as she pops a piece of bread in her mouth and grins madly. "I am the absolute worst."

Oliver Barringer doesn't email me on Monday, of course, but I also don't develop herpes or any other communicable venereal diseases for that matter, so I decide to stick the whole unfortunate situation into my trusty "win some, lose some" file, which is a frothy name for a set of serious topics I don't have the emotional fortitude to tackle.

Otherwise, I am the girl who owns the city.

23

Isobel and I are working out the captions for the next issue. To our considerable amusement, we have just outlawed "The Music Man" as the title for any article that features a male singer when we are jolted back to earth by L.K. Smith's brisk and unmistakable two-tap knock on the door. We quickly straighten up.

"I'm sorry to interrupt, but we will need you to add four pages this month," L.K. says as she slides open the door. She is wearing a pressed trench coat and holding a large alligator skin bag. It's been misting outside all day, and the assistant in me is worried about her hair. I consider fetching an umbrella, but I have no idea how to procure one elegantly. L.K., however, is staring at my feet. Clearly, she is more worried about something else.

"Clo, are those Dr. Scholl's clogs?" she inquires.

"Yes," I respond with a shy pride.

"I haven't seen a pair in ages."

They are orange. I bought them at a vintage store in the West Village, and I thought they were unexpected but in a cool way. However, the loaded way L.K. pauses before she shifts her gaze back to Isobel helps me understand that I should go home, light a fire in an oil barrel under a bridge, and throw my offending shoes inside.

"Did you say *add* four pages?" Isobel asks with some alarm.

"Yes," L.K. responds. "This is tracking to be a very large issue. I just got word from Mark that there are some additional advertisers we need to accommodate."

The opposite side of our floor is the publishing side, which is composed almost entirely of women, but always led by a man, who in our case is Mark Angelbeck. These are the folks who sell the advertising that appears in the magazine. Like their editorial counterparts, these women are always impeccably turned out, but in a more straightforward and less trend-driven manner. They also differentiate themselves by wearing makeup during the day and getting blow-outs with *volume*. They are loud talkers, smell wonderfully expensive, and spend their days successfully wining and dining advertisers on our behalf. At least one day a week, you can hear them clapping and cheering in their own conference room as they celebrate another improbable sales milestone that was reached with ease. They constantly leave the evidence of their success—empty Veuve Clicquot bottles and entirely untouched dessert trays—scattered across their side of the offices for the cleaning ladies to handle.

I don't know anyone on the publishing side except Mark Angelbeck, but that is by design. It is yet another unspoken rule that we aren't allowed to socialize with them, not even in the office. We say it's because editorial decisions should never be influenced by the demands of our advertisers, which makes technical sense, but they are so deferential toward us, and we are so coldhearted toward them, that I suspect this is what it feels like to marry an old guy for his money.

But no matter: Everyone is riding incredibly high.

Isobel purses her lips and turns to the large bulletin board that hangs on the wall. It's where she regularly tacks newspaper clippings, photographs, and printed-out pitches from the writers.

"I'm not sure where I am going to find *four* more pages," she says with a twinge of uncertainty.

"Can't you make the opener two pages?" L.K. says. "All the art was approved."

"I suppose I could."

I sense a window.

"We don't have a dance piece this month?" I offer timidly. "We had that ballet piece?"

"Not the ballet this month," L.K. says briskly, and her words pierce my flesh like a fiery dart.

Apparently, that was *not* a window.

"I think we will be fine," Isobel says, although unconvincingly. "I just want to confirm we still have the exclusive on a few things."

"Can you update the lineup by tomorrow morning?" L.K. asks. "She is going to want to see it before she leaves for the airport at noon."

This is not a question.

"Of course," Isobel replies.

After L.K. takes her leave of us, Isobel spins around in her chair and faces me with a very surprising, *very* mischievous smile. I have not seen this smile from her before, and I glance over my shoulder with some nervousness, wondering for whom it is intended.

"Opportunity just knocked," she says. "Pitch me everything you've got by first thing tomorrow morning."

I feel like I might throw up.

"Really?"

"Really," she affirms.

Oh, I could go into exquisite detail about how I stayed at the office until after midnight, drafting a three-page pitch document fueled by free hot chocolate, vending-machine pretzels, and four cigarette breaks in the dreary, bone-snapping cold of the early spring. Or I could tell you how, as I climbed into my bed that night, I envisioned my finely crafted suggestions being so well received that I was carried around on people's shoulders in celebration, everyone going wild for the genius of such an unlikely, large breasted heroine. But let's just skip to the end of the story: Isobel rejected every single idea and, when the lineup was printed and redistributed the next afternoon by L.K.'s assistant, it was revealed to me—and to *everyone*—that Lydia Saintclair-Abbott had been assigned not one but *two* pieces in *our* section. I feel disgust for myself, of course, but this disgust is paired by the hollowed-out sensation of something even more sinister: Betrayal. I feel like a stay-at-home wife who has just cobbled together the pieces of her husband's infidelity. My mind races with questions: When did Isobel ask Liddy to submit ideas for the section? Where was I? Did she do it intentionally behind my back? If so, why? Do I really come off as that insecure? Or did Liddy seduce Isobel? Yes, that must be it. This must be Liddy's fault because Isobel is too perfect to behave ignobly. I want answers. I want details. I want a play-by-play of the entire, clearly clandestine conversation, and I want Liddy to be very, very contrite about what she has done.

The lineup in my hands is still warm from the printer. I have an ominous premonition that if I allow the paper to grow cool, my fate will be forever sealed. I drop the pages on my desk. Then, I pull on my red coat as I make a beeline to the elevators, careful to keep my head down, fearful of crying. Once I arrive in the main lobby, I walk out the revolving doors and dash haphazardly across the street into the protective embrace of a newly erected parking garage. Once I am out of view, I lean against a wall and burst into tears. I am never going to amount to anything. There must be something core to succeeding in this industry that I simply don't understand, something I cannot seem to be taught, or, even more dispiriting, that I cannot seem to learn. I cry hard, and it's that ghastly, soundless sobbing that dimples your chin and jackhammers your shoulders. This goes on for a little while, maybe a solid ten minutes, before I shove my hands into my coat pockets in search of my spare pack of cigarettes. I light one up and take a deep, emotionally steadying drag. Then I take another. And another. There has always been something about smoking a cigarette that puts me back in my own movie. Somehow, the mere act can provide me with a wider perspective, and I can get a little distance from the fires raging inside me.

I can begin the plot anew.

"Hey, lady!" I am interrupted by a loud voice, echoing from an unknown location inside the cavernous garage. "Hey, lady!"

I turn my head and see an attendant in black pants walking swiftly in my direction. He points to a big sign hanging on the wall.

"What?" I deliver this question like a petulant teenager.

"You can't smoke in here."

He points to the sign again.

"Why not?" I lift my chin and release an inelegant mouthful of smoke into the air.

"You'll blow the whole place up!"

You know, I think as I furiously stomp out the cigarette with the pointy toe of my black boot, *that isn't the worst idea in the world.*

24

In early June, there is a thrilling development: Davis invites me to her mother's house in Southampton. I decide this means we have moved from work acquaintances to friends to, like, basically best friends forever. After all, who wants to host a work acquaintance for an overnight in the Hamptons? The plan is to meet on the Upper East Side at an absurdly early hour on a Saturday to wait for a fabled bus called the Jitney. When I arrive at the appointed corner—I took a town car from Brooklyn because I am billing this as a work expense—there is already a pastel crowd assembled, albeit haphazardly. There is a lot of kissing and waving and earnest plan-making, but I stand alone; I am not entirely sure how to behave without Davis. I fiddle with my bracelet, and it doesn't take too long for me to arrive at the embarrassing conclusion that a black Samsonite roller suitcase is the wrong luggage for this kind of trip. Everyone else has a monogrammed Boat and Tote bag from L.L.Bean resting barely half full at their sandaled, pedicured feet. When Davis arrives, holding an iced coffee and swinging her own canvas bag, I silently despair that, despite great strides in my education, there are still so many little things I don't quite grasp. We wait a few more minutes before a small green bus pulls up. As everyone trundles up the steps with their little bags, I am forced to stow my own giant bag in the dusty compartment underneath. After keeping everyone waiting, I settle most ingloriously next to a blessedly unperturbed Davis and the bus pulls away from the curb.

After three long, bumpy, and mostly silent hours flipping through magazines, playing Hangman, and whispering (the Jitney does not allow loud talking or cell phone use), we pull up to a side street corner, and all I can think is: *This is the Hamptons?* I had been expecting something else, although I realize I am not sure what, exactly. I look out the finger-smudged bus window and immediately spot Barbara, who leans like a movie star against the hood of a buttercream Mercedes convertible. The top of the car is down, and Barbara, in a Pucci headscarf and sunglasses, leans on the bumper with one leg up like a flamingo.

"She can't be for real," I say to Davis, pointing to Barbara.

"Oh," Davis says, looking at her mother with slightly narrowed eyes. "She's for real."

That night, we accompany Barbara to a "little dinner" being hosted "down the lane," which turns out to be a proper party for at least one hundred people, all of whom mill around under a large white tent that overlooks the Atlantic Ocean. The event ticks all the rich-person party boxes: there is a jazz quartet (but they are a little kooky!), an open bar manned by a hot gay guy and a less hot straight guy in a bad mood who smells like rotten cigarettes. There is also a roving photographer with very white teeth who spends the night hustling tipsy middle-aged foursomes into picture-perfect party arcs for the wire services.

Within seconds of arriving, Davis is sucked into a conversation with some grown-ups, and I am left, yet again, to navigate another unfamiliar landscape alone. I immediately spot the bar, but in my haste to get a drink, I walk directly across the lawn. My heels instantly sink into the thick mud of the lush sod and I now understand why Davis and her mother wore flat sandals to this event. Unable to move, I pretend like I am observing the party in a very thoughtful manner as I work to dislodge myself from the muck with the tiniest movements I can muster. I don't want to draw attention to myself. When I am finally free, I tiptoe quickly to the wood floor under the tent. I look down and see my spike heels are matted with sludge and grass, but since I am too exposed to wipe them off, I make a beeline for the bar. I ask for a glass of white wine.

I sip my drink and watch Davis across the lawn. She is now barefoot.

Her sandals dangle from one hand while the other hand is cupped over her mouth as she laughs at something said by an older woman. She wears a long periwinkle silk slip dress. She isn't wearing a bra and, for reasons I can't explain, her hard nipples look upmarket and high fashion in this setting as opposed to trashy, which is how they would look on any other human being. I turn in the other direction where I see something very unexpected: Mark Angelbeck standing in line by the raw bar. He looks strangely childlike, holding an empty plate with both hands as he waits with a middle-aged blonde woman that I assume is his wife. She is wearing an expensive-looking fuchsia shift dress, but her upper arms are heavy, and she gives off the impression that, while they were probably physical equals on their wedding day, she is now nothing but an embarrassment to him professionally. Clearly, the publisher of our magazine should be squiring around a younger, more stylish wife. Or no wife at all. I finish my drink and order another before I ask the bartender where the ladies' room is located. I want to touch up my lipstick and wipe off my shoes before I intentionally throw myself into Mark Angelbeck's line of sight. The bartender points me to the main house.

"Thank you so much," I say graciously.

I pass through a set of French doors off the patio that lead me through the kitchen, which is crowded with staff. *This can't be right*, I think, but I am too afraid to ask anyone for directions. Instead, I timidly walk down a long, excessively bright corridor. The creamy gray walls are hung with art I understand to be significant although I cannot name any of the artists. To be honest, at this point in my life I can only confidently identify Jackson Pollock and Mark Rothko, and I use the term "confidently" with an extreme looseness. Even the most famous of the impressionists—Van Gogh, Monet, Manet—can spin me around with the intellectual uneasiness that accompanies a state school education. I see what I believe is a bathroom door on my right, but just before I enter, my eye is drawn toward another room. It looks to be a study or library of some sort, and it is dimly lit by a fat three-wick candle burning in an enormous hurricane lamp. I check over my shoulder to make sure nobody is watching before I allow myself to drift inside.

Only for a second, I think.

The walls of the room are painted a very dark, nearly black, shade of blue and are lined with floor-to-ceiling bookshelves. There are additional candles glowing from the nooks and a magnificent wooden writing desk sits in the dead center of the room. It has willowy bow-legs, and it is paired with the most ornately upholstered chair I have even seen; it looks like a throne. I try to imagine how pleasurable and productive it would be to write in this room. I would perch at my computer, surrounded by the sounds of the sea. My day would pass punctuated only by the wonderfully sulfurous smell of the low tide intermingling with the dank of old paper and piping hot coffee. I would wear a profoundly oversized white cable-knit sweater. My hair would be wild. My feet would pad the wide-plank wooden floors with the soft grace of a sleepy housecat.

I take in the rest of the decor, which is wonderfully standard-issue for the mid-rung of the uppermost class: There is an Old English Dictionary open (to *D*) on a large wood podium, moody oil portraits of pudgy, pinched-cheek women and strong-beaked men, and, on the desk, I see a square leather cigarette lighter embossed with a picture of a sailboat. I run my finger along the nearest bookshelf, admiring a hardcover collection of books so absurd I start to suspect they are fakes. I open one or two to confirm that, not only do they have pages inside, but many of them are also first editions.

At the end of one row of books, I arrive at a small statue of a horse. It sits innocently enough among some other collectibles (bowls, one of those dreadful blue-and-white Chinese vases) but, to me, this horse is in a different league. While it is only about the size of a hand iron, she possesses a physique so lean and so gloriously muscled, that it reads as a much larger piece. I pick the small statue up and, to my astonishment, it is heavy; it must be at least twenty pounds, maybe more. I had assumed it was hollow, like a chocolate Easter bunny, but it is sculpted out of an exceptionally dense metal. Mesmerized, I run my finger along the horse's formidable flank. It is rough to the touch, like it has rusted slowly and thoughtfully after centuries spent bathing in this fine sea air. As I turn it around in my hands, I find it nearly impossible to comprehend that something so compact could emit such a sense of both ease and power. I glance over my shoulder again to confirm that I am still completely alone. Outside the open doors, I can hear peals of laughter and the joyful clatter of silverware, but in the dark study where I stand, it is as silent as a church. I remember how in college, we used to drunkenly steal little mementos from fraternity house parties—a trophy here, a sweatshirt there—and laugh over our booty the next morning in the dining hall. Without thinking, I open my straw bag and drop the horse inside. The weight pulls dangerously on its cheap leather straps, which dig into the sinew of my shoulder. While I have no real intention of stealing the horse, I did want to see how it would *feel* to steal it, and the sheer spontaneity of this act makes me feel a little high.

Suddenly, I hear a woman's voice out of nowhere, but clearly not *nowhere:*

"Can I *help you* with something?"

I whip around to discover an older, ashy blonde stands not six feet behind me. She has a brisk haircut and surrendering neck. She does not smile.

"No," I respond quickly. "I was looking for the ladies' room. The bartender said it was through the study?"

She folds her arms expectantly across her chest. Clearly, she is wholly unconvinced by my tall tale of bartender incompetence, and I feel myself start to panic.

"No, it's across the hall," she says curtly. "And there are plenty outside?"

While this woman clearly has no idea who I am, nor why I am rummaging around her beautiful house, her breeding only permits her to indicate that angry uncertainty with body language. In return, I earnestly place my palm flat on my heart and open my eyes wide in my own posture of misunderstanding.

"I am *so* sorry, how rude," I say apologetically. "I came tonight with Barbara Lawrence. I'm a friend of Davis's from work."

At this piece of information, the woman's ticking time bomb of a countenance deactivates and her little mouth melts into a deeply relieved smile. She places both hands on her cheeks and opens her mouth in a somewhat convincing display of social recognition despite the fact she has never laid eyes on me in her life.

"Ah, of course!" she says. "It's *so* nice to see you. I'm Susan Goldsmith-Cohen."

As she extends her hand for me to shake, I realize two things: One, she did not see me put the horse in my bag, and two, I have been prowling around the Hamptons estate of Susan Goldsmith-Cohen, the famous New York art advisor and dealer. I know this because her gallery mails me their catalogs each month and her smiling headshot is always on the back cover, although, it's clear they have wisely photoshopped her from the lips down. I talk to her assistant over email all the time.

"Susan," I reply with a breathless smile. "You have a lovely home."

Once I am safely inside the powder room, which, incidentally, is wallpapered with charming little illustrations of Paris, I set my straw bag down carefully because I am afraid to clank the statue too loudly against the shiny white-tile floor. I clasp my hands on the sides of the sink, and I look at myself in the mirror.

I was right: My lip gloss has worn off.

After I reapply a few coats, I lick my finger and rub away the mascara that has melted into the delicate creases under my eyes. I check my teeth and jostle my sweaty breasts around in my dress before I pick up my straw bag and, with the confidence known only to the innocent, I walk back outside to join the party.

The lawn is more crowded now, and I realize I am without a drink. As I shoulder through the bodies, I realize there are some famous faces in the crowd—a broadcast journalist, an actress, a famous director—although most of them are older than me.

"Clo Harmon?"

I turn around and discover none other than my intended target: Mr. Mark Angelbeck. He wears what I imagine are his "weekend clothes": a rumpled white shirt and a pair of light blue pants and flip flops. He is holding a bottle of beer, which is surprisingly understated for him, and I find this more masculine register attractive. His face is tan, and his hair is a little wavier than usual. For an older guy, he looks pretty good.

"Mr. Angelbeck," I say. "What a nice surprise."

"I see you in all the best places."

I smile at him.

"Do you have a house here?" he continues.

"Not *here*," I say in a tone intended to indicate that I have a country house *elsewhere*. "But I am staying with Barbara and Davis Lawrence this weekend."

"Hobnobbing with the elite," he says, holding up his bottle, and from the glint in his eye, I get the sense he is drunk, and about to say something lightly inappropriate when the dumpy blonde wife appears behind him.

"Mark, honey, *there* you are!" she trills as she links her arm under his elbow and tosses me a tense smile. "I've been looking *all over* for you! There is someone I want you to meet."

I can't tell if he is irritated by the interruption. His face remains entirely unchanged.

"Ellen, this is Clo Harmon," he says with his eyes fixed on me. "She works at the magazine. Clo, this is my wife, Ellen."

"Lovely to see you, Ellen," I say.

I adjust my shoulders, ever so slightly, to hollow out my clavicle and, as she glances down, I catch a familiar displeasure flicker across her face. Honestly, I feel bad for women in their forties. Surely, they are still young enough to remember being desired, but they are also not old enough to completely throw in the towel. In this dispiriting gulf, they must feel obligated to preserve some semblance of their former selves, if only a little longer, and it must be exhausting (not to mention expensive) to feel the need to compete—day after day—in a losing game against younger, prettier girls like me.

"So good to see you," she replies, but then she turns back to her husband: "So, mind if I steal you?"

"Not at all," he says. He gives me a small bow. "Have a good weekend, Clo."

After I watch Mark Angelbeck be hustled away, I decide to search for Davis. The property, however, is much larger than I thought: I discover a second pool and a seemingly abandoned garden with super creepy sculptures and Roman columns. When I finally locate Davis, she is standing in a small cluster of adults, including Barbara, and here it occurs to me that there are very few people at the party who are my age. I wonder when Davis will take me to see the Hamptons I've read so much about in magazines and newspapers, with all the valet parking and high heels and poolside parties with deejay music. As I walk toward Davis, my cheeks ache from smiling for *so* long at *so* many strangers, and I enter their sphere quietly. I don't want to interrupt the man who is currently speaking, but Barbara does not share this sentiment. She lights up when she sees me.

"Stephen! Everyone! This is Clo," she announces, cutting off poor Stephen who is dressed, quite unfortunately, in white jeans and a striped shirt, like a gondolier. "She is staying with us this weekend."

"Hello, Clo," Stephen responds. He looks irritated to have to turn away from Davis, with whom he had been speaking, and Barbara uses this break in the conversation to position herself directly between them.

"It's nice to see you," I respond, quite formally, in return.

He offers me a wan smile, like he just learned panna cotta is the only dessert on the menu but says nothing. He just turns his attention back to Davis, only now he has to lean slightly to the side to see around Barbara.

"You should definitely talk to him," he continues. "He could really be helpful to you."

I move in closer.

"Well," Davis begins.

"Let's not encourage her, Stephen," Barbara interrupts with a laugh and a dismissive wave of her hand. "I mean, she has enough on her plate at the magazine. She's doing *so well* there."

Barbara beams over at her daughter and, to my eye, she seems flushed with pride, but Davis just looks down into her drink.

"Is that right?" Stephen asks.

His question is directed toward Davis, but she doesn't answer. It's strange. She seems frightened, like any response is the wrong one, and while I suspect Barbara is the aggressor here (because Barbara is the aggressor everywhere), I find myself, yet again, annoyed with Davis. Sometimes I wonder if her greatest skill isn't the ability to convince people they need to intervene on her behalf. Everyone is always helping Davis with her coat. Everyone is always checking that Davis got home safely. *Say something*, I think, but she doesn't answer. All she does is take another dainty sip from her glass and the conversation is forced to find another trajectory, like a swift-rushing river when it hits a rock. I look away from the group. The party shows no sign of slowing down, and all I can think as I survey the lawn is that, if I had been given half of what Davis Lawrence has been given in this life, I wouldn't be as determined to waste it as she seems to be.

Later, after what feels like a thousand more drinks with all the "friends" from "down the lane," Davis and I decide it's time to head home, but not before arming ourselves with one final glass of champagne for the road. Once fortified, we search the crowd for Barbara to say goodbye, and we find her talking with Susan, who is standing outside the kitchen, flanked by two golden retrievers.

"We are off, Mother," Davis says, and she gives her mother a quick peck on the cheek. "Thank you so much, Susan."

Susan smiles.

"Yes, thank you so much," I say to them both, and then Barbara surprises me by extending her arms for a hug.

I put my bag down, careful not to spill my drink, and Barbara squeezes me in a tight embrace. When she releases me, I wave at Susan before I follow Davis back toward the house. It is dark now, and the string lights hanging over the arbor make me feel giddy, like I am lost in an enchanted forest.

"Clo?" Barbara calls out. "You forgot something?"

I turn around and watch as Barbara leans over to pick up my straw bag, which had been resting at her feet. When her forehead wrinkles at the weight, my stomach jumps into my throat.

I don't move.

"I'll get it," Davis offers.

I watch as she jogs lightly back toward her mother and Susan, but before she gets to them, she is spotted by one of the roaming photographers.

"A picture, ladies?" he asks, and he holds up his camera.

"Of course," Barbara says, and she motions Davis to come closer.

The three women press their cheeks together and smile as the man snaps a few shots; he holds a flash overhead and tells them to put their chins down. When he is done, he asks for one more picture of just

Davis and Barbara and, once he moves on, Davis takes my bag from her hand.

"Why is your bag is so heavy?" Davis laughs as she hands it to me

"Susan seems nice?" I offer as a response.

"My mother *hates* Susan," Davis says as we walk around the side of the house. "They were good friends in their twenties, but that is when my mom was a big deal and Susan was, like, just starting out. She helped Susan get her first clients, and she bought a few pieces off her, but then one of the pieces was misvalued, and that led to a whole thing with lawyers."

"So what happened?"

"She totally vanished when my mom's show ended, like she couldn't be bothered," she says. "They pretend to be friends, but I don't think my mother has ever really forgiven her. I feel like she's always sort of plotting some grand revenge, you know?" She laughs.

"Ah," I say.

Once outside the fence, Davis and I link our arms and sprint down the wide, soft lawn in our summer dresses. We laugh and squeal as gravity pulls our legs down the hill, faster and faster, and we try not to fall or tumble into the imposing hedges that flank the property. Thanks to my idiotic contraband, my bag feels like a lead balloon, and I keep tipping over to the side, which makes Davis howl with laughter. Somehow, we end up on a circular gravel driveway, where we double over, laughing so hard that tears run down our faces. Crickets sing around us, and the crunch of gravel under my feet feels like Christmas morning.

A man's voice pierces a small hole in the magical darkness:

"One more photograph, Davis?" the voice inquires.

We whip around and are startled to discover the party photographer; his face is illuminated in one of the floodlights affixed to the garage. He is boyish, with freckles, and he holds a black milk crate full of cables against his soft chest. He looks to be in the middle of packing up his small hatchback car. The night air is still, and I can hear nothing but the lazy gnash of rocks beneath our bare feet as we shift our weight back and forth.

"Anything for you," Davis responds with a smile.

She holds out her glass, and the photographer gently removes it from her hand and places it on the stone wall behind him. Then he turns back to me with his hand extended. I look at him blankly.

"Drink?" he asks.

"Don't mind if I do," I joke, taking a little sip out of my glass. He smiles, but he just keeps standing there until I realize he wants to take my glass away, too. I hand it over, somewhat petulantly, and rub my wet palm down the front of my dress.

"Why are you taking our drinks away," I whine to him before I turn to Davis to continue my drunken routine. "Why did he take our drinks away?"

Davis doesn't answer me. Instead, she slips her right arm gently around my waist and places her left hand on her hip. She throws her hair back slightly and lowers her chin. She does not look at me. She is giving her full attention to the camera.

"Let me get Davis alone first," the photographer calls out as he takes a few steps backward. "Then I will get a picture of the both of you."

Embarrassed, I quickly step to the side and watch as he shoots a few quick snaps of Davis. When he is satisfied, he just throws up his free hand in a friendly wave and ambles back to his car.

Finally, Davis looks at me.

"He took my drink away because if I ever kill someone in a drunk-driving accident, they will find a picture of me holding a drink and that is what they will run on the cover of the *New York Post*."

I stand there, gaping at her. I wonder why this has never dawned on me before. It's the kind of thing people at a very particular level of society would have to consider when getting their photograph taken.

"And I am sorry to say it, my dear," she says, "but you need to start worrying about it, too."

I roll my eyes like she is being ridiculous, but inside, fireworks are going off.

When we get back to the house, we are so drunk that we bang into all the lovely, wainscoted walls, and Davis knocks down a framed picture as we make our merry way to the kitchen. Once there, we irresponsibly microwave multiple bags of popcorn at the same time and scatter ice cubes across the kitchen floor in our sorry attempt to assemble glasses of water. We think this is hilarious. When we finally make it to Davis's bedroom, we throw open the windows and pull our clothes off over our heads, tossing them in the air. I watch Davis as she stumbles toward her dresser in search of pajamas. She is wearing a gray lace thong and no bra, and her white breasts are small but wonderfully plump and round, the size you just want to cup gently in your hand. Her stomach is flat, but not muscular, and her body is flatter, in general, than it is wide. She has tan lines on her back and when she wiggles into a large black T-shirt, I despair to watch her disappear under the fabric. I rationalize that I don't feel *sexual* toward Davis, but rather the dull ache I experience is scientific: I want time to explore her body. I want her on her back so I can press my hands on her hip bones and run my fingers along the curve of her inner thighs. I simply want to understand how something so desirable is assembled.

I am not assembled like this.

I pull on my own T-shirt and sleep shorts and lie on my back in the queen-sized bed. I listen to Davis putter around in the bathroom before she turns off the lights and climbs in next to me.

"What was that guy talking about tonight?" I ask, and I try to sound light. "The striped shirt guy?"

"Oh," she says. "He knows this director in Los Angeles, and I had stupidly said something about being interested in screenwriting."

"You would be good at that," I say, although I have no idea if Davis would be good at screenwriting.

"Maybe," she says, but unconvincingly. "But maybe my mom is right. It's just not a good time to pack up and move to California."

"Why do you want to move to California?" I ask.

Davis seems to think about this for a moment.

"Because it is a million miles from New York," she says finally.

I say nothing to this, and after rustling around for a bit, Davis gets quiet. In our shared silence, we listen to the ocean. It is so close to the house that it sounds like some otherworldly kind of radio static and, as I listen to it mixed with Davis's breath, I imagine we are waiting for an important broadcast during wartime. I imagine we will be called to an important task. I imagine we will rise to the challenge. I imagine we will emerge patriots. I roll over to tell her this and she tucks her elbow underneath her head and turns toward me to listen. In the darkness, I can see that her bottom teeth overlap just slightly, and there is a permanent retainer affixed to them, which is a private detail previously unknown to me. I find it thrilling to know this about her, and even though I feel drowsy and drunk, I fight to stay in this moment. We whisper and talk and giggle for just a little while longer, and the sheets are so crisp and cool that it feels like I have died and gone to heaven.

25

The following morning dawns so incomprehensibly blue and flawless that Davis and I decide over breakfast (fruit salad and bagels) that our only option is to stay in the Hamptons; we can take the bus home early Monday. That way, we can enjoy a full day at the beach and have time to shop downtown, the latter being an afternoon activity for which I very quickly learn requires nicer clothes than any of the summer clothes of which I am in possession. At the appointed time, Davis and her mother both appear in the foyer wearing linen cover-ups and sandals, and at the sight of my white denim shorts and J. Crew halter top, Barbara can't even hide her disgust. She ushers me into her bedroom.

"Give me a second," she says.

She disappears inside her walk-in closet, and I move closer to her dressing table so I can admire what looks to be a collection of ornate glass perfume bottles. They rest on a large, mirrored tray, and I am surprised to discover they are filled with different perfumes and not just for show like the boxed set that my mom keeps on her own dresser. As I run my fingers along the tops of the bottles, I see the diamond drop earrings Barbara wore to the party last night. It looks like she just tossed them down carelessly at the end of the night. Like Elizabeth Taylor.

I pick up one earring and hold it to my ear. I turn my head in both directions as I look at myself in the mirror, and the late afternoon light makes the stones sparkle like faraway stars.

"This will look so good with your eyes," Barbara says as she emerges with a turquoise blue dress in her hands. I put the down the earring with a nervous clatter, and I spin around.

"I feel embarrassed you have to lend me something," I say.

"Just keep it," Barbara says, handing over the dress. "Honestly, I never wear it."

I hold it awkwardly.

"I mean it," she says.

"Oh, okay," I say. "Thanks."

"So, I see you like those earrings?" she asks.

"I'm sorry," I say quickly. "I shouldn't have touched them."

"You're a woman!" she says with a laugh. "We all want beautiful things."

She peers over my shoulder at the earrings, like they are a newborn baby in a hospital nursery.

"So do you like them?" she asks again. "You should borrow them. Really, I insist. They would look wonderful on you."

While there is nothing specifically sinister in her tone, the question feels dangerous, like, at best, it's a riddle, and, at worst, a trap. There is something I am starting to realize about Barbara, which is she likes to provide people with things, especially things just a little out of reach. She nudges me indulgently, and I run my finger across the cool facade of the diamonds.

"Oh, Barbara," I say finally. "They are a dream."

After browsing the stores on Southampton's famed Main Street (which are inexplicably many of the exact same stores we have in New York City) and eating a trio of gummy yogurt muffins, we return to the house. We settle into the red Adirondack chairs on the back deck because, as Barbara quaintly says, it's time to "see out the day," which, in Barbara speak, means it's time to get drunk. The bluebird sky has given way to a veil of thin, choppy clouds, and I am full of dread for the coming morning. I don't want to leave because, here, I realize that I feel energetically aligned with the universe in a way I never do in the city.

I feel like a child of God.

After Davis grills white fish and vegetables for dinner with an ease and proficiency that stupefies me, she and I decide to take one final swim before an early bedtime. We drag our bodies back into damp bathing suits and drape plush yellow-and-white-striped towels around our necks before descending the weather-beaten steps at the end of the property. The sand feels coarse under my feet, and, as I set my eyes on the horizon, I marvel, as I always do, at how many shades of blue the Atlantic Ocean can be within the span of twelve hours. Evening, however, is my favorite time because—and although I would never say this to anyone—the inky metallic blue of the ocean during this brief window each day convinces me—much like the annihilation that attends an honest heartbreak—that I am in possession of a soul.

Davis wears a black tank one-piece bathing suit, which is a style I haven't worn since I was nine years old, and the spandex coats her body like a second coat of paint. Her hair is wavy and half-up, and when combined with the openness of her face, she reminds me of those old photographs of a teenaged Brooke Shields. Without notice, Davis drops her towel, and she takes off toward the shoreline. As she runs, her long, tan legs move in the powerful, almost mechanical, strides of someone who grew up playing sports. She enters the water at high speed, and her body crashes awkwardly over the first set of breakers; she is immediately submerged in the whip white of the boiling surf. She rights herself and then, after a few more long strides against the current, she takes a smooth, shallow dive under the next rising wave. She disappears under the water for what feels like a long time, and when she emerges from the lather, stumbling and laughing, she beckons me to join her. The sun is dropping below the houses, and it seems to be pulling the remainder of the day's warmth down with it. I suspect I would be happier to remain on dry land, but Davis waves her arms wildly over her head. She is yelling, and even though I can't hear her, I can tell she is happy; she casts it toward me like a spell. I slide the towel off my shoulders and walk to the edge of the ocean, where I let the clear water lap over my toes. I stand there for a minute feeling the pull of goosebumps sprouting across my thighs before I wade into the icy water. I move slowly, so slowly, before I fill my lungs with air and let my body sink beneath the swell. It is so cold that I can feel my heart skip a beat. I pop up like a cork and yelp.

I don't have the same courage as Davis.

When I finally make it out to Davis, she swims closer to me. She regards me curiously for a moment as she treads water, like it's her first time encountering a human being. Then, with an extraordinary swiftness, she encircles my neck with her slick arms and wraps her long legs around my waist. I feel her ankles hook together and her bones push into my spine as she buries her head into my neck. Then, she releases only her arms so she can lean her upper body back and float. I can see the shallow of her belly button pulsating through her wet suit and I feel her leg stubble, which pricks warm against my hips. I put my hands behind her back and try to lift her body up close to me, but she is too heavy. She releases me and treads backward, restoring a safe distance between us, but I follow her. As she swims away from me, I see she has a few pimples on her shoulder, and I find this crack in her physical perfection to be a strange kind of drug.

After a few minutes of playfully battling the waves, we swim out past the break into a smooth patch of water. Here, we both turn onto our backs, and float for a while in a devotional silence. The thin clouds overhead refract the last of the sun's rays like prisms, bending the white light into a nearly impossible combination of colors: searing tangerines and cotton pink, velvety rhubarb, and whispers of blue.

"It's sort of funny that it's the clouds that make it beautiful," I say. "It feels like a self-help book."

"All sunshine makes a desert," Davis responds dryly. "That's one of my mom's favorite lines, anyway."

As the veil of evening continues to descend and the colors fade, creamy-colored lights start to pop on in the houses that line the dunes. I shiver from somewhere deep inside my body.

"I'm really cold," I say.

"Me too."

We splash each other again and try to catch waves and ride them toward the shore. We do backflips and handstands, and, at one point on our long return to shore, Davis swims between my open legs. Her body feels slick and slippery as it glides across my upper thighs and brushes, with a breathless sigh, against the wanting triangle under my suit.

At one point, I place both hands on Davis's shoulders and theatrically dunk her underwater. She pops up and laughs and then she tries to dunk me, but I am too fast. I circle behind her and place my palms, yet again, flat on the round, protruding bones of her shoulders. I push her under the surface. As I hold her there, however, something quiet and curious overtakes me. The sky is dark now, and the waves are coming with an increasing frequency, but here above the water, everything falls strangely silent. I can feel her start to struggle so I lock my elbows and push her down harder, which isn't difficult because I am so much bigger than her. Under my weight, I can feel her body start to tense with panic. She digs her nails into my forearms and tries to pull her knees into her chest, ostensibly to kick me. There is a voice inside my head, and the voice tells me to let her go, but I don't release my grip. I count the seconds as they pass, and then her body goes completely slack. Her back starts to rise in the water, and, with a mix of curiosity and disinterest, I watch her body bob loosely to the surface, shrouded in her long blonde hair.

Just then, I feel something—not *something*, I feel *teeth*—tear into the delicate skin on my bicep. The pain is both unexpected and intense—like stepping on a shard of glass—and I have no choice but to release her shoulders. In that split second, whatever was switched off inside me is switched back on, and I am restored inside my own body.

I watch her head break the surface, and the first thing I notice is her eyes: They are chaotic with fear, like a trapped animal. She flails backward, frantic to get away from me and unable to fully catch her breath. I splash her playfully, like it was all in good fun, and laugh. But she doesn't laugh back. Instead, she starts to paddle away from me, farther and farther, but she doesn't take her eyes off me.

I lift my arm out of the water. There is blood.

"I'm going back," she yells, but only when she has put a safe distance between us, and although I cannot be sure, I think she is crying. She starts to freestyle with great force back to the shore, which looks like it has drifted miles away, and I follow her, but slowly. I don't want to appear as if I am chasing her. Once on land, I jog lightly across the sand. We gather up our towels in complete silence, and she takes the steps back to the house two at a time.

"Is everything okay?" I ask finally as we cross the yard. The grass is wet from the sprinklers.

"Yeah, yeah," she says.

"Are you sure?" I don't know why I am pursuing the topic other than to establish my innocence by playing dumb.

Here, she stops on the lawn and turns to look at me:

"This is going to sound weird," she says slowly. "But I just thought you were trying to drown me."

"*What?*"

"I know," she says, shaking her head. "I don't know what is wrong with me."

"Drown you?" I repeat, now incredulous.

"Yeah," she says. "Let's just forget it. I'm sorry."

The morning comes quickly, and Davis and I must scramble to catch the first Jitney back to the city. As we pack, a weighty silence lingers between us, and I feel like an interloper as I collect my belongings from various corners of the house. Davis lends me a work-appropriate black-and-white-striped dress, which is just stretchy and shapeless enough that I can pull it off, and she makes two travel cups of coffee for the long journey home: one for her and one for me.

I am relieved by this gesture.

As Barbara drives us to the parking lot where she picked us up less than forty-eight hours before, she is apologetic that she couldn't lend us her extra car, which she says is *still* in the shop getting a new battery. The sun has yet to rise, and we are mostly silent as we wait, parched and groggy from too little sleep. Finally, the headlights of the bus sweep across our faces. We get out of the car and stretch our arms over our heads before Barbara walks around to the trunk to retrieve my suitcase.

"Good lord," Barbara hoots as she hauls my bag to the curb. "What do you have in here, Clo? A dead body?"

I say nothing, of course, but—out of the corner of my eye—I see Davis wince from what I can only assume is the intrusion of an unwanted memory from the evening before.

We say our goodbyes and hobble into our seats on the air-conditioned bus. Davis pulls herself into a thick cardigan, and I find myself wishing I had access to my hooded sweatshirt, which rides in my suitcase under the bus. After we pull out of town, the road quickly becomes flat and the horizon opens: At this hour, the sky is blackish blue at the top, but a light peach at the bottom, and I can't help but feel like some unseen hand is slowly revealing to us a brand-new day. Yesterday's stars—all twinkling pinpoints of light—have started to fade, and Davis promptly falls asleep on my shoulder. As I luxuriate in the weight of her closeness, I pray we can both put the swim behind us. After we pull onto the highway, I gaze down at Davis. Her pink mouth has fallen slightly open and—although I cannot be certain—I think I smell vodka on her breath.

26

When I get back to Brooklyn that night after work, the air in my apartment has gone stale. I shove open the nearest window, unsettled that such a brief break from the city can feel like an entire lifetime. I spent my day in the office casually telling anyone who would listen about my little jaunt to the Hamptons with Davis, and (with the exception of Liddy) most of the other girls seemed impressed, if not a little bit surprised. No matter: Superiority—real or perceived—I am starting to realize is a powerful kind of fuel. Instead of burning out with use, it seems to multiply inside your body: Every time I mentioned my weekend, I felt stronger. I felt faster. The tasks of my day seem lighter.

But now, back home, I jack open the last of my sticky vinyl windows, and a flutter of fresh air flushes out the old heat in my apartment. I gaze over my long, unobstructed view of the Gowanus Canal, which stretches all the way to Park Slope. I throw my black suitcase on top of my unmade bed; its heavy contents have been on my mind all day, and even more so now that I have hauled this suitcase up the muggy subway steps. I pull the zipper open along the edge, flip open the top, and push aside the top layer of clothes, all of which are damp from my bathing suit. I unearth my towel cocoon and unwrap the horse statue. Its small, rough body lies on its side, and it's even more beautiful than I remember. At some point on Saturday night, I made several drunken calculations: One, the horse surely wasn't an actual piece of art, and, as such, is undoubtedly worthless and two, my chances of getting busted trying to sneak the horse *back* into the study during the party were far higher than Susan Goldsmith-Cohen ever finding herself inside my apartment in Brooklyn in search of a missing horse. It's funny: While its persistent weight on my shoulder all evening should have filled me with fear, it had the opposite effect. It had been so thrilling to feel as if this horse was some long-lost, loose piece of myself, and it had finally come home. However, in the more sober light of day, I understood that I had made the wrong choice, but it was far too late to remedy my mistake.

I lift the horse up off the towel and set her gently on the edge of my little black walnut desk. Then, I sit down on my chair and, while I know this sounds crazy, I feel like she looks at me with gratitude.

Maybe, I think, she understands that she has come home, too.

A few days later—how many days I cannot recall at this point—I buy a copy of the *New York Post*, as I always do, on my commute to work. I am halfway down the subway steps when my eyes catch the top banner of the cover:

Foal Play: Major Art Theft at Hamptons Soiree

I stop abruptly on the steps, so abruptly, in fact, that the woman behind me bangs her small body into mine, and I grab the railing so I don't tumble the rest of the way down. I paw frantically through the newsprint pages until I find the whole story, which includes: (1.) a party at the home of a famous art dealer, (2.) an A-list crowd, (3.) a missing bronze horse valued at over a million dollars, and (4.) a museum in Germany claiming that the horse was stolen from them and surely ended up with Susan Goldsmith-Cohen through the nefarious back channels Susan, apparently, had been known to travel, all of which has turned my simple theft into (5.) an international art theft and battle over provenance. The article continues to say that it is an "active investigation," but mostly stymied because the party was so crowded and, despite a state-of-the-art security system throughout much of the house, the study, in which Mr. Cohen worked as a lawyer, did not have a camera installed, nor did the adjoining hallway outside the bathroom. Apparently, all the cameras were trained on the mounted art. In the interim, they are interviewing everyone on the guest list.

I was not on the guest list. I was also, I recall now with almost crippling relief, not photographed.

"Until the statue is located and the thief is prosecuted to the fullest extent of the law, we will not rest," Mrs. Goldsmith-Cohen is quoted as saying.

Before I step on the train, I crumple up the newspaper and throw it into a black trash can on the platform.

27

The afternoon of the blackout, it is not the darkness that tips everyone off (after all, it's only four o'clock in the afternoon, and the summer sun still burns high in the sky) rather it's the sudden absence of energy. In an instant, our computers blink to black and the air-conditioning units hush to an eerie halt. Everyone stands up from their desks and, awash in the creepy silence, we wander around the bright halls in confusion. We speculate amongst ourselves: *Do we stay? Do we go? Is this another terrorist attack? Or just an electrical issue?* We aren't quite sure what to do because most of the "grown-ups" have already left for their summer holidays, which reliably occur the last two weeks of August. The timing makes sense: The brutal crush of Fashion Month starts in September, an event which requires a vast amount of mental and physical preparation for the girls fortunate enough to complain bitterly about their mandatory attendance as they instruct their assistants to FedEx a month's worth of luggage to their respective international hotels. This, of course, is to spare them the indignity of carrying anything other than a handbag through the airport. Also, good luck getting someone on the telephone in Milan or Paris this time of year.

After talking to a few other assistants, I return to my desk. Davis—who has recently been promoted from editorial assistant to assistant editor for reasons that escape my resentful understanding—isn't in the office. She has already been in France for a few days on a three-week vacation with her mother for which I am quite certain she didn't fill out the appropriate vacation paperwork.

I always fill out the appropriate vacation paperwork.

As I sit back down, Isobel, who leaves for her own holiday on Friday, comes out of her office wearing a hat and sunglasses. She motions in my direction.

"Let's go," she commands, and I must look unconvinced because she feels the need to emphasize her point with more force. "Let's go *now.*"

"Okay," I say, popping up. "Can I get my things?"

"Quickly."

I turn around and pick up my bag before scanning the area for anything critical which, under Isobel's impatient gaze, strikes me as frivolous and unsafe in a time of potential crisis.

"Let's take the steps," Isobel instructs, and I trail her obediently into the bland concrete stairwell.

We gracelessly descend, our summer mules slapping the soles of our feet before they smack against the steps, faster and faster, in a mixed-media clockety-clock that reverberates unpredictably off the uninsulated walls. I hear feet behind me. I look over my shoulder where I see the assistants from the art department. They are carrying large boxes that contain the negatives for the issues we are laying out; the art director, apparently, does not want to take any chances with the photographs. He holds a large zippered black bag under his arm.

When we finally reach the bottom of the building, I shove open the heavy doors for everyone, and we clatter onto the baking summer street. I cup my hand over my eyes and look around. I spot a group of fellow assistants from our magazine in a small circle, all wondering what to do, and the editors and assistants from the other publications housed in our building start to trickle out the revolving doors, including Oliver Barringer. He looks entirely unperturbed on the arm of a young brunette. As she talks, he leans close and listens with obvious ardor to whatever obviously brilliant story she is telling him. I never heard from him again after the night in his apartment, and I spin around, embarrassed he might see me. My cell phone rings, and I fish it out of my bag. It's an unknown number, but I answer it.

"Hello?"

"Hey, is the power out at your office?"

The voice is Harry Wood's, which comes as a surprise because

Davis has heretofore been the singular, albeit unreliable, conduit of our rickety friendship. I don't even know how he got my phone number.

"Yeah," I say coolly, because I am very cool. "But I am not sure why everyone is freaking out about it."

"Same thing. They told us to go home for the day."

"That seems to be shaping up here as well."

I scan the dwindling crowd, which is starting to disperse in all directions. I crane my neck, but I can't locate Isobel anywhere. I imagine she got a cab, but I feel guilty that I wasn't the one to procure it for her.

That is, after all, my job.

"Let's meet at the bottom of the park on Sixth?" he suggests. "We can hang out at my apartment or something. Maybe it's fine up there?"

"Okay," I say gamely, but my throat starts to bloat with anticipation. This feels like kind of a big deal.

I say goodbye to my remaining coworkers, most of whom are fact-checkers who live in New Jersey, as they organize what strikes me as a deeply tragic carpool home. Once I get a block from my office, I switch into the black rubber flip-flops I keep in my bag before I continue the walk up Sixth Avenue. I make a mental plan to change back into my high heel sandals around Fifty-Eighth Street. I cannot remember a time when heat felt so oppressive, it's like all the air in the city is rotting between the buildings.

My phone rings again: It's Allie. Her classes are canceled, and she is meeting some friends for a drink in the Village. Do I want to hang out? The truth is, I *do* want to hang out, but I know that spending "alone time" with Harry Wood is the capital I desperately need in my quest for greatness. I'm not going to lie: The fact that the news may surprise Davis when she returns from France lends it some additional appeal.

"I can't," I say. "I am going to hang out with Harry Wood."

"Oooh," Allie says. "You fancy."

"So fancy," I agree.

"Don't have sex with him," she instructs.

"I think he may be more interested in guys?" I venture. "The jury is still out on that one."

"Well, then, good for you! I read it is so chic these days to have a gay fashion friend," Allie jokes.

"So chic," I agree. "Although I don't know if I can quite call him my *friend* yet?"

In recent months, I have been, on occasion, invited into Davis's unusual relationship with Harry. In their long-running screwball comedy of sorts, Davis, naturally, plays the ingenue. She is beautiful and witty, but also impetuous and nearly impossible to please. Harry, in turn, plays the handsome, rakish, and seemingly disinterested friend. Despite the professed platonic nature of their relationship, it is Harry who—time and time again—proves he is the only man who really "gets" her. This, of course, makes me the "delighted observer" and all the while, I wonder what the heck Davis Lawrence is doing with Grant, that buttoned-up boyfriend of hers, when she could just fall in love with the clearly more compatible (so long as he's straight) Harry Wood.

Now, there's no denying that Harry plays a very convincing leading man with his sharp features and cartoonish eyelashes. He is also smart, gallant, and well-dressed—he strikes me as the ideal wedding guest—but if you are outside his circle, I have learned he is brutal in his criticisms and commentary. This makes being safely *inside* his circle, as I currently reside to some degree, a downright hilarious place to be most of the time. He always has the best gossip, and he has this wonderful way of making you feel like you are—at great long last—the creature he has been seeking.

I have noticed, however, there is another side to Harry that is more mysterious. He can vanish for days, even a week, and when he returns, he will reveal nothing about where he has been, not even to Davis. I had generally assumed he has a secret paramour, but Davis claims he has never been in a relationship, with either a man or a woman. Not even while they were at boarding school. There is also something performatively offensive about his humor. I mean, the emails he sends Davis and me during the workday have us laughing out loud, but mostly because they are just so inappropriate. Nobody seems safe from his vicious assessments and yet, I never allow myself to believe I could ever be a target.

Even more improbably, it never occurs to me I might already be one.

"By the way, I read your article this month," Allie says, which pulls me back to our conversation.

"*Article* is a very generous word," I say. The "article" she is referencing was 250 words on a fantastically mediocre Swedish girl band with an attractive female singer who likes to wear head-to-toe designer clothes. Despite this, I worked on it so hard and for so long, it was like I was separating conjoined twins.

"I am a very generous person," she replies. "But really! It was good. It's always nice to see your name in print."

I open my mouth to respond when I see Harry Wood striding toward me. His white shirt is unbuttoned to his sternum, and, while his eyes look a little drowsy, he sports an enormous grin. Reflexively, I slap my phone shut without saying goodbye to Allie because, apparently, I am more nervous than I want to admit about this little outing of mine. When he is about five feet away, I watch in what feels like slow-motion as he lifts his camera into the air before he shoots a picture of me from above.

"Seriously?" I deadpan. "Now is a good time for a picture?"

Then, I cringe. I am still wearing my flip flops.

"It's always a good time for a picture, my dear," he says, and he links his arm through mine. "Don't forget: You and I are making history."

As I have never seen the inside of Harry's apartment, I try to project an air of bored detachment as he unlocks the door. For me, there is something uncomfortably intimate about seeing where another person sleeps in New York, especially because it so rarely squares with the image that person projects to the outside world. How could it? It's hard enough to cobble together a more appealing version of yourself. How could you possibly have the time or money at our age to transfer that fabricated ethos to your rarely used living space?

Once I am inside, I am simultaneously confused and relieved to discover that Harry Wood's apartment is not a whole lot nicer than mine. It is a generously sized one-bedroom, compared to my studio, which must cost a pretty penny considering it's a block away from Central Park, but it isn't a palace by any means. Off the living room, there is a tiny galley kitchen laid with black-and-white checkerboard floors. The apartment has dingy walls—I can immediately make out the grayish gum of fingerprints tattered along the narrow trim of the doorways—

and it is sparsely furnished with what looks to be a mix of thrift store finds and heavy French antiques. The one exception is the pine wood IKEA coffee table with four screw-on legs that every new arrival to New York (me included) purchases on their one-and-only trip to the Elizabeth, New Jersey, outpost. *He's straight*, I think. Then, I look at the couch, which is too delicate to be comfortable, and I see that he has adorned it with a set of knock-off Missoni pillows. *Nope, those are super gay pillows*, I think. The door to his bedroom is open, and I can see that his bed, like my bed, is just a mattress on a metal box spring with wheels. It is rolled against the back wall, and it is unmade. The fitted sheet has snapped off one corner, exposing the shiny blue cover of his cheap mattress. *Straight*, I think. He has an ornate Louis XIV–style nightstand, which is piled high with books, and on the far wall hangs an enormous, framed movie poster of something in French with Jane Fonda, which I decide *might* be as gay as it gets. What really fascinates me, however, is his wardrobe. In addition to a closet, there is a rolling rack, on which a great deal of clothing is neatly hung and bagged, and underneath the clothes are clear, stacked boxes filled with folded sweaters. There are rows of shoes, perfectly aligned, and everything has been labeled with a label maker. I once saw Davis throw a lightly stained blouse in the garbage can when she didn't feel like walking to the dry cleaner in the rain; for her, it was easier to just buy a new one than to be forced to stare at the stained one until the weather cleared up. After all, she said as means of explanation, they *never* can get coffee out of silk.

Although I would never say it out loud, it looks like Harry Wood is a Workhorse like me, and suddenly I am suspicious: Why is he letting me see this?

Unsure of what to do next, I ask if I can use the bathroom, which I don't need as much as I need a minute to collect myself. The toilet isn't flushed, and there are expensive grooming products arranged around the sink, the basin of which is crusted with toothpaste, spit, and hair shavings. I count to ten, flush, and run my hands under cool water to kill a little time. I realize there is no towel, so I wipe my clammy hands on my skirt and do a quick check in the mirror. It's very dark in the windowless bathroom, but I think my eyes look more blue than usual.

When I come out, I find Harry is attempting to light the front burner on his gas stove with a floppy little match. Dumbstruck, I listen to the gas as it produces that anxiety-laden tick, tick, tick before he drops the match and leaps back. The stove explodes into yellow and blue flames, just inches from his body, and I scream at the top of my lungs.

"And we have gas," he announces proudly before looking over at me with an entertained expression. "That was quite a noise you made there."

I feel my ears redden as he yanks open the door of his refrigerator. Due to the absence of electricity, it's gray inside, but he manages to produce three brown glass bottles of beer.

"This is all I have to offer you, my lady," he says with a bow of his head. "Should we drink it now or try to buy some more first?"

"Drink the beer now?" I suggest. "It will get hot."

"Good call."

He opens the freezer and examines his plastic ice trays with a frown before cracking a few cottony cubes out on the small but clean countertop. He sweeps them into a metal bowl with a clatter and places the three beers inside.

"Let's sit outside?" he suggests. "I want to see what is going on down there. Crazy, right?"

"Crazy," I concur.

Harry drags two low-slung beach chairs out from behind the couch, and as we move around each other in false familiarity, I realize we have never been alone together.

He hands me a chair, and we head down the stairs.

We settle on the sidewalk, and I feel my skin expand in the unbearable humidity; it's almost as if I wasn't born with enough pores to manage the situation and, soon enough, I will simply split open. I take a large, needy pull of beer. The cold liquid races around the soft inside of my mouth, and as I swallow, I can feel the alcohol dart purposefully through my body, dutifully plumping up my tired, dehydrated veins. Harry and I are both quiet as we drink our beers and watch the sun sink behind the squat buildings across the street. When I hear horseshoes on pavement in the distance, I throw a sidelong glance at Harry.

"Do I hear horses?" I ask.

"There is a horse stable on Eighty-Ninth," he replies, and when he sees my eyes widen, he nods: "I know. It's wild, but that is pretty much my favorite part of the neighborhood. I can hear it from my bed in the morning."

"Wow."

"I think, when I am a hundred years old, I will remember that noise," he says, before adding with a comic shrug. "Alas, I'm just a romantic, I guess."

As the sun sets, the thick heat starts to dissipate, and I slowly relax into what I believe to be a better version of myself. Harry and I banter about the usual nonsense: Who is professionally overrated (as it happens, Harry and I come to the conclusion that we are the most talented people in our vaguely shared industry!), what we are reading (*Yellow Dog* and *The Kite Runner*, respectively), what we plan to read (we both reveal we got advance copies of *Random Family* and, while we don't commit to reading it, it's obvious that we will both *say* we read it at parties), a few theater reviews (*I Am My Own Wife* gets top billing), obligatory yet deeply opinionated commentary about the drama taking place in a foreign country (Liberia something), and national news (George Tenet, Iraq) to make it clear we read the newspaper. Finally, we land on something gossipy, like who got fat, or who slept with someone important, or how we don't understand how a certain blogger our age bought such an insane apartment when they continually insist that they don't come from family money. Those topics exhausted, we rattle a little about the goings-on at our respective offices, careful not to reveal any of our own missteps or insecurities, of course.

There is a long pause before, out of nowhere, Harry takes a deep breath and announces that he's been debating quitting his day job at the newspaper. When I look at him with surprise, he goes on to explain that he wants to focus solely on the website he has been building over the past year on the side. At first, I am not sure if he is serious or—as is far more likely—simply testing this gelatinous idea out on an inconsequential audience. He reveals that he has an angel investor—some rich guy from San Francisco—and this slight influx of capital will enable him to rent a small office and hire a few people. He says it like it's no big deal, but we both know that—if this little lark is successful—it could be a career-making, or at least career-changing, move. We also know it could be an abject failure (after all, we lived through the embarrassment of the bubble bursting just a few years back) but it feels like so much has changed in such a short time, and that, maybe, the collective is wiser now. *We* are most certainly wiser. As I listen to Harry, the thing I find the most perplexing is that, for someone who seems to take life as casually as Harry Wood, he has actually been gritting it out behind the scenes. I had long assumed everything came easy to him—like Davis. Like Allie.

Like everyone.

"Wow," I say. "I am crazy impressed!"

"Don't tell Davis," Harry suddenly says, his body straightening up. "She'd kill me if she finds out I didn't tell her first."

I assure him my lips are sealed, but as I take the final, flabby sip of my beer, I feel important; like I am finally on the inside of something. Furthermore, I can't help but think how good it could be if Harry pulled this off, and I could remain a part of his gang. It would give me access to another corner of society and, once I got into those rooms, I felt certain I could unlock opportunities and capture new contacts. I could accelerate making my way in the world, and maybe I wouldn't need to rely so desperately on the good graces of Davis Lawrence for my survival.

As I don't have any equally exciting news to share, we tumble into the uncomfortable silence I feared was looming just one conversational wrong turn away. As my mind casts around for a worthwhile topic, I pretend to be fascinated by the label on my beer bottle. This is not the time to seem dull; the stakes have just climbed to intoxicating new heights.

Yet, I can find nothing to say.

Just as the lapse in conversation becomes so unbearable that I suspect one of us is about to announce the need for a bathroom trip, I am saved by a group of middle school girls. They approach from the direction of the high-rise housing project that takes up half of Harry's block. They are rowdy and loud, and we wordlessly watch them shove each other and laugh. The girls all seem to be carrying a plastic bottle of soda, which they occasionally employ as a weapon, and I calculate they can't be more than twelve years old, maybe thirteen. They wear low-cut, raw-edged jean shorts and cropped T-shirts. These clothes do nothing to cover their bulging stomachs and meaty arms, and while I envy what seems to be a complete lack of shame about their bodies, I also find myself judging them for not being harder on themselves. By the time I was twelve, I already considered myself fat. I kept a scale in my closet to confirm that assessment on a near daily basis, careful to record the offending numbers on the rainbow pages of my diary. If these girls keep it up, I think, they won't amount to anything.

"Those Puerto Rican chicks," Harry says with a disapproving shake of his head.

I nod in the light affirmative, but I don't say anything because I am not sure what he is trying to communicate to me with this comment.

After a little silence, I can feel Harry turn toward me:

"I'm glad we are hanging out," he says. "Just the two of us."

"Me too," I reply as easily as I can manage.

After a long moment, Harry clears his throat.

"I love Davis, but sometimes she can be a lot of work," Harry says before adding: "Have you noticed that she drinks too much?"

"Uh, Harry," I respond with an unladylike snort. "We *all* drink too much."

"Yeah, no, I know," he says, grinning gamely, but only for a beat. "But with Davis, it's different. You haven't noticed?"

To be honest, I *have* noticed, but her excessive drinking usually serves me incredibly well. There are few things more useful in New York City than a friend who's always up for a cocktail after work (especially now that Allie spends all her time with Patrick), and that is doubly so when that friend invariably picks up the tab because she is filthy, stinking rich. I also find that alcohol can, on occasion, level the playing field between Davis and me. She will get too drunk, and I will heroically manage her in some mature capacity, and in the light of the following day I will (very briefly) have the upper hand for my efforts. Sure, sometimes I suspect she's had a little something at lunch, but that isn't totally unexpected in our line of work, and sometimes she makes a complete ass of herself in public, but I wasn't planning on labeling it as a problem to her (or to anyone) anytime soon. I mean, why would I?

There would be absolutely nothing in it for me.

"She's been drinking too much forever, though," Harry continues as he leans back in his chair. "And she's been nothing but a *rousing success*, so I am not sure why I care."

He delivers this assessment with more than a whiff of bitterness, which I find very intriguing. I lean my body forward slightly to indicate a willingness to engage in a little gossip.

"What do you mean by *forever*?" I ask. This is a careful question.

He shrugs:

"She used to keep those little airplane bottles of vodka in her dorm and field hockey bag at boarding school," he says. He places his empty beer bottle down on the sidewalk and runs his fingers through his hair. "I never called her out, but I used to see them. Like *all the time*. I think in high school we thought it was cool, honestly."

I don't respond to this information immediately because there is an intimacy to it that makes me apprehensive: Why is he talking about this with me? Is it possible he could trust me this much already? It gives me a giddy feeling, like I am a big step closer to being part of the team, but I also know my loyalty, if loyalty should ultimately be required, must remain solely with Davis at this point. While Harry sounds somewhat concerned about her well-being, I suspect he's mostly disappointed society hasn't penalized her for this obvious and repeated failure of self-control, especially when he—apparently—must work so hard for half the success. This type of jealousy is a familiar feeling to me, of course, but I am fascinated to witness it emanate so potently from Harry Wood who, in my mind, was put on this earth for the sole purpose of worshipping Davis Lawrence.

"I guess I would drink too much if I had her childhood," he says. "And I had a shitty childhood, so that is saying *a lot*."

I don't say anything immediately because the less I speak, the more Harry seems to reveal, but all I think is: *What about her childhood?*

"Sorry," he says with a sheepish grin. "I am being a gossip. But she's just very good at making me feel like I need to take care of her, like she couldn't possibly do anything for herself."

I nod, but Harry isn't looking in my direction.

"I have myself to worry about, honestly," he continues, but his voice has drifted a little further away.

I wait for him to elaborate, but he stays quiet. I can almost see my own thoughts tumbling over and over in my head like a bingo ball machine, trying to land on the right next thing to say to keep the conversation rolling along. I turn to look at the street just as a car rolls past, and my vision slowly blurs as I become hypnotized by the pieces of glass embedded in the blanket of soft asphalt. With the headlights of each passing car, the shards light up like a row of lucky slot machines.

I had no idea there was so much glass in the streets.

"Do you think we should *do* something?" I ask finally. "Or *say* something?"

I offer this suggestion against my better judgment. Namely because I am worried that he will say *yes, of course*, but I also want to keep him talking.

"Nah," he says.

"Not even to Barbara?"

"No, definitely *not* Barbara," he says with sudden seriousness. "Barbara is half the fucking problem."

"Oh," I say.

"Be careful with that one," he says after a second. "She suffers from some serious delusions of grandeur."

I don't understand his meaning, but I nod, yet again, as if I agree.

"Yeah," I manage.

"I don't even know why I brought it up," he says with a chagrined little smile. "I'm sorry."

"Is it because I am deeply trustworthy?" I ask. I bat my eyelashes in a comic fashion.

"That must be it," he replies with a chuckle.

He twists the top off the last bottle. I hear it hiss out a little steam before, without warning, it erupts, wild with white foam. The froth races down the glass neck like lava, and Harry takes a panicked slurp off the top. I laugh.

"Share?" he asks.

"Always."

As we pass the lukewarm bottle back and forth, I recognize that the silence between us has morphed; it now possesses a more self-satisfied significance that is fortified, I suspect, by our newly shared secret. *We worry about Davis. There is something wrong with Davis. Davis needs our help.* We don't linger here too long, however: The beer, much like the moment, vanishes quickly.

Harry stands up and stretches his arms overhead. I can see that the armpits of his gray T-shirt are wet.

"Do you want to get more beer?" Harry asks.

"More beer," I affirm.

I am not ready for this night to end.

We pull our beach chairs behind the building trash cans because to abandon them on the sidewalk would be a leap of faith amid the chaos that has been slowly building, around us in the deepening dusk. We toss our empty bottles into a wire trash can before we walk toward Columbus Avenue in search of an open bodega. We move jauntily, our bodies propelled forward with the excitement that comes with witnessing something historic, but as we make our way around the corner, I skid to a halt. While I can't speak for Harry, I am struck dumb by what lays before me, which is a blackness truly exquisite in its totality. Was it this dark just moments before? I cannot remember, but my body begins to metabolize the severity of the situation. I start to break things into compartments. There are no lights anywhere. There are no table lamps warming up apartment windows. There are no illuminated signs beckoning us into the shops. Even the streetlamps and trusty traffic lights have fallen silent, almost doleful, which I hadn't considered a possibility. It's like we are surrounded by dead bodies. There is also this strange juxtaposition of darkness and heat, when darkness, at least in my experience, is usually cold. I look downtown, but an opaque curtain has been drawn down by unseen hands, and it presents the most unsettling effect: It's like there is no New York City *at all.*

In the absence of light, however, my other senses become outrageously amplified; my body feels electric, my fingertips burn with a cool fire. I hear music and voices falling from all directions: There are battery-powered radios issuing news reports from shop windows and people have carried instruments—guitars, horns, harmonicas—out of their apartments. They assemble themselves into temporary trios. They play a few notes. They start a song. They feel each other out. Older kids dart around us in a lawless game of manhunt. They hold flashlights and shout, and I can feel the vibration of their sneakers as they slip across the loose gravel. We step around a circle of young children sitting cross-legged on the sidewalk. They are barefoot and wonderfully unattended, and they write their names with fat chunks of colorful chalk. Up on the brownstone stoops, adults pull popsicles out of flimsy cardboard boxes and quickly try to get them into the right hands before they melt. They laugh and lick their hands as they peel open the sheeny white wrappers. They call down to their children with faces both stoic and magnanimous, like Red Cross workers swarming a disaster zone. Men distribute the household rations of beer and wine to total strangers walking past, all of whom agree to heroically consume the bounty before it spoils or goes warm. There is clapping and singing, and people lean out third-floor windows to wave (or frown) at the merry crowds filling up the streets. Everything smells like cooking grease and propane and birthday candles and hot garbage, which should be an unforgivably offensive mix, but somehow it is full of promise, like that long moment atop a roller coaster, right before the drop. As Harry and I bump through warm bodies, he looks down on me with brotherly affection, a gesture which overwhelms me with an unbearable feeling of tenderness for my adopted city, my adopted people. Harry takes my hand and gives it a little squeeze.

Our search for beer is fruitless. There are long lines at the corner shops and grocery stores, and Harry and I are in no mood to stand around in the heat and wait. The shopkeepers have locked the doors and pulled down the metal grates, which I find strange until I realize they are wary of riots. They know better than anyone else that there is a certain lawlessness to this kind of magic, a hysteria that can infect the unmonitored masses. As such, they will only pass items, mostly water and beer, the occasional bundle of diapers or container of milk through a small, makeshift window in exchange for fistfuls of crumpled cash. The lines for these scant provisions are disorganized and loud, and it is here that I begin to intuit another, more sinister side of the evening.

I see a young mother with nervous eyes waiting in one of the lines. She holds a baby in one arm and her other hand clasps down firmly on the shoulder of a small but squirmy boy. I want to ask if I can help her, but I worry (as I always worry) that this overture would be unwelcome or even worse, offensive. So, I pretend I don't see her, and the guilt hangs, albeit briefly, on me like a dark cloak.

After we walk another block or two, we decide to head back to Harry's apartment. We light up cigarettes and take the same route back, only now several fire hydrants have been popped. The water gushes into the streets with violent force, and while the younger kids have vanished, a few teenagers are jumping in the puddles and splashing water at each other. Harry is quite delighted by this development. He kicks off his shoes and rolls up his pant legs. He leaps into the spray, and then starts to dance in a puddle.

"Come on," he calls to me. "Live a little!"

I am about to remove my flip-flops when a new group of kids descends upon the hydrant. *Kids* is the wrong word: The girls might already be in high school and the guys, all muscled and shirtless with braided gold chains hung heavy around their necks, look to be in their late teens. They hold tall cans of beer, and while the sheer number of them makes me a little nervous, it all starts off innocently enough. There's some splashing and name-calling, some teasing and hugs. But then, one of the biggest guys grabs one of the younger girls around the waist. He lifts her off the ground, and her childlike face twists, savage with fear. She yells and kicks her skinny legs with a terrifying ferocity, and I look around in a mild panic. *What is he going to do?* When nobody intervenes, her motions get more desperate; she thrashes in his grasp and when she screams, he cups his large hand over her mouth. She wrests her head away, but she cannot overpower him. She is completely at his will, and this show of strength and dominance is intoxicating; I watch how it ripples through the other boys. One by one, they start pulling at the shirts of the other girls, grabbing at their midsections and wrists with their mouths open and hands demanding. The girls are hoisted up and tossed into the water before the boys trot back to their friends and offer up high fives. While some of the girls laugh at the attention, there are others that say nothing when it happens; they just walk away with their wet T-shirts clinging to their bodies. The first victim, the youngest girl, pulls her hair in front of her face to hide the fact she is crying. She picks up her pink backpack, which is the backpack of a child, and covers her breasts with her arms.

They taunt her as she walks away, her little body vanishing into the crowd.

I want to get out of here.

Harry has moved closer to me at this point, his face wary. I am about to pull him away when I see a fit, middle-aged woman round the corner. She is wearing a white linen blouse with the sleeves rolled up and tan shorts, and she is being pulled along by a large golden retriever. She must have just taken him for a walk near the park. She has a flashlight.

The boys see her, too.

The energy changes.

I see them exchange glances. There is a younger-looking kid, the smallest of the group, and they elbow him. They chant something I can't quite make out over the rush of the water and, just like that, this poor little kid makes a gritted tooth run at the woman. It's all so fast and unexpected that there is no time to react. There is barely time to think. He just shoves her with his shoulder, like it's a peewee football practice, and she slips in the water and lands flat on her back. The impact causes her to release the leash in her hand, and the dog takes off down the street.

"Harry," I scream. It's all I can manage in my shock, and Harry sprints over to the woman to help her up. As he leads her to the closest set of brownstone steps, I can see that her blouse is wet and blood runs from her hands. She says nothing. Her face is vacant. I figure the guys will take off, but they make no effort to run away nor to conceal their actions. In fact, their bodies seem to grow broader with a newfound power. I turn around to look for the dog when I feel a body bang into me: It's one of the guys. He wears mesh shorts and no shirt and when he runs his fingers through his short, spiky hair and smiles at me, I can see he wears braces. He takes a step toward me, or so I think, and adrenaline shoots through my veins like a sizzling bullet.

"Harry," I yell, which only makes the guy grin wider. "Harry!"

The boy licks his lips, and I realize I have no time to wait for Harry to intervene. I start to walk away quickly, but—believe it or not—I don't want to seem rude or, even worse, somehow racist, in the event I've misread the situation, so I pretend to look for the dog. I do some whistling, but I don't turn around because I sense the guy is close behind me. I shift my brisk walk into a jog, but this awkward increase in pace causes me to lose my balance; my flip-flop nicks a crack in the sidewalk, and I tumble to the ground, catching myself hard on the flat of my palms. I can feel him looming over me, and in my terrified haste to stand up, I fall again, this time on my knees. When I finally right myself, it's like a horror movie: I sprint in the direction of Harry's apartment. People are shouting at me, and I lose a shoe, but I don't stop because I know, deep in my heart, that I am being hunted.

When I finally make it to the corner of Ninetieth Street, I am sobbing and breathless. There is blood running down my legs and the bottom of my foot burns. Finally, I turn around, but there is no one there.

I am all alone.

Harry returns within minutes. His shirt is wet and his face ashen. He looks genuinely concerned in a way that makes me feel like someone, finally, is looking after me after a lifetime of doing everything for myself. I let him hold my hand, and the warmth reminds me of the first night we met. Once we are safely in his apartment, Harry locks the door. He peers out the front window and pulls down the blinds. I sit on the couch, and he gets on his knees in front of me to inspect my bloodied legs.

"I don't think I have any Band-Aids," he says finally.

"That's okay," I say.

"I think you should stay here tonight," he says. "I don't even know if the subways are running."

"Thanks," I whisper. "Do you mind if I take a quick shower?"

This request is uncharacteristic of me. I never ask too much of a friend, let alone a stranger that I am desperate to impress, but I am on the razor's edge of a panic attack, and I need a minute alone. When I step through the plastic shower curtain, I notice the caulking is purple with mold, and there is a light brown ring around the tub, which makes me wonder if Harry takes baths, which would be disgusting in a New York rental. I twist the faucet, which responds with an ear-splitting squeak. I watch the warm water run over my feet, the force of which sends swirls of dirt and blood down the drain. Then, I push the button to turn on the shower, and I rinse off quickly without soap. I am too afraid to touch the withered green bar resting on the metal caddy. I rinse off my palms, which are embedded with little rocks, and I turn around to wash off the droplets of dirt crusted on my pale calves. When I am done, I step onto the grimy bathmat and wrap myself in the thin but blessedly clean-smelling towel Harry handed me. I feel better, but I also wish, maybe more than anything in the whole wide world, that I was in my own apartment, headed for my own little bed. I crack the door and, courtesy of candlelight, I can make out Harry, who is now sitting on the bed with his legs outstretched. He wears only his boxers.

"There is a bathrobe on the back of the door," he says, but he doesn't look at me. He just absently picks at his nails.

I put the oversized bathrobe on, and I tie it tight across my waist to keep anything from inadvertently falling out. The fabric feels rough on my skin, and by the time I emerge from the bathroom fully secured, Harry is laying down with his eyes closed.

It is very hot: I can already feel beads of sweat forming under my breasts.

"Is it okay if I am really tired?" Harry asks. I get the sense he is afraid I am going to feel sexually rejected, which makes me feel, well, sexually rejected.

"No, totally fine," I respond in overly animated agreement. "I am *exhausted*. You sure it's okay if I, you know, sleep here?"

"Of course."

I lay down on the bed, flat on my back, and I hear Harry blow out the candle. The room falls into complete oblivion, but I can still hear voices and car horns on the street. I have gotten what I needed out of this evening, and yet, I don't feel good. The windows are open, but there is no breeze, and, within minutes, the room starts to fill with the dead air of our exhales. I move my head around, trying to find a pocket of freshness, and wonder how long I will lie here before I am dragged back down into the underworld.

I am resurrected the next morning by a throbbing pain in my hip bone. The room is flooded with light, and as I take a quick inventory of my body, I discover the knot in the bathrobe has cut off my circulation. My stomach is squeaky with sweat. I roll over on my side, and there is Harry. He snores shirtless next to me, and his plaid boxer shorts peek out from the sheets. I feel a flicker of relief that I didn't sleep with him, not that I even wanted to sleep with him, and I am equally thankful we couldn't find more beer because I am usually desperate for that kind of approval once I get drunk. I turn onto my back and, as I massage the angry, purple indentation on my hip, I watch the ceiling fan. It is rotating wildly, almost violently, and I become convinced it isn't screwed in correctly. It's about to come loose and crash down on us, and the blades will chop us into pieces.

The fan is rotating.

I bolt upright.

"Harry," I hiss as I shake his warm shoulder. "Harry. Harry! Wake up. The power is back on."

He opens his bloodshot eyes, and there are no earthly words for the tang leaking out of his mouth. I cover my own lips with my hand, worried about how I must smell, and swing my legs out of bed. My inner thighs are sticky with perspiration, and I am uncharacteristically starving, which prompts me to recall we didn't eat anything for dinner. No matter: It is a new day. I grab my phone from the bedside table, and shimmy into the bathroom to put on my bloodstained clothes. When I come out, Harry is sitting up, but he continues to present as profoundly disoriented. I remember that I lost my flip-flop, so I sit down and strap into my three-inch Stuart Weitzman high-heeled sandals.

"I have to get ready for work, but thanks so much for hosting me," I say as I lean over to kiss him on both cheeks. "That was one for the ages."

Here, his tired face positively lights up.

"One for the ages, indeed!" he rejoins, his voice pebbled. "Don't forget: You and I are making history."

It takes him another month, but Harry Wood does, indeed, quit his job at the newspaper, and, right after Labor Day, he officially launches his blog with the help of a publicist and an undisclosed (at least to me) influx of cash. The various media blogs, which everyone now reads religiously on their computers at work, all publish the same photograph of him when they announce the project. It is a picture I know all too well: It was taken at a museum benefit I attended with Harry and Davis the previous spring. In the picture, Harry wears a tuxedo, which is probably why they all chose it, and his trusty camera dangles easily from one hand. His other arm is wrapped, almost too tightly, around the narrow waist of Davis Lawrence, and they are both smiling at the camera. It's funny to have a memento of this event because, less than an hour after this photo was taken, Davis and Harry got into a spectacular argument. I am not sure what caused it, but I do know it ended with Davis sitting on a curb in a beaded dress and sobbing until Harry came outside and apologized. I have pulled up this picture a thousand times on my computer because, if you look a little closer, you can see that I am in the background. It is the first, and only, time I have ever been "officially" photographed, and, as luck would have it, I am standing in profile.

28

One October morning, Davis returns to the office after spending a weekend at Grant's family home in Palm Beach wearing an engagement ring. She extends her hand to me, almost shyly, and I seize it for closer examination. The main diamond is the size of a supermarket green grape, and it is flanked by two hefty side baguettes, all of which are set into a gold band. She explains it is an Asscher cut, which means nothing to me, and I am so envious that I worry I might start to cry.

Fortunately, the news hits the office wires so quickly that I don't have time for a breakdown. Our desks are swamped with editors and assistants, all of whom gush over the ring and ask for a play-by-play of the proposal: *What did he say? Were you surprised? What did you do afterward? When do you think you'll get married? Where?* Honestly, it would be an exhausting conversation for anyone if it wasn't so pro forma. I watch Davis—as I have watched so many of my newly engaged colleagues before her—answer the expected questions deftly and with a bashful, downright virginal grace. At some point, L.K. Smith pays a visit to offer up her own congratulations. I watch as she slides on her reading glasses and leans over to take a close look at the ring.

"Excellent," she says, as she removes her glasses and straightens up. "Excellent, Davis."

She looks over at me. She says nothing, but she doesn't need to say anything to make me feel embarrassed, sitting there in my little cubicle with nary a prospect of my own. It's no secret the magazine prefers the women in its employ to be engaged and married; after all, to be desired and claimed is just another way we are expected to prove our worth.

And I, as ever, am falling short.

Once the crowds settle down, Davis pretends to do some work, but I don't bother; I just sit and stew at my desk in a sad silence. Finally, Davis speaks:

"Isn't this weird?" she says.

"It's not weird," I chirp falsely. "It's exciting!"

"I guess." She looks down at her ring with a closed smile.

"What are you most excited about?" I ask.

Davis does not hesitate:

"Getting an apartment of my own," she declares.

"With Grant," I clarify.

"Oh, yes, right," she says, almost a little embarrassed. "With Grant."

"Well, I think that sounds great," I say. "Did you set a date?"

"My mom is going to want a big wedding, but I told Grant I don't want to wait," she says. "So, we are going to go to City Hall before the new year."

She smiles at me, and while I try to return her excitement, my face must betray me because Davis gets up from her chair. She walks over to my side and sits down cross-legged on the carpet in front of me. Her head is level with my knees, but she gazes upward to meet my eyes. She rests a hand on my leg.

"Are you okay?" she asks.

"Am I okay?" I say, feigning confusion. "Of course."

She looks unconvinced.

"I mean, it was a little bit of a surprise," I admit.

"I know," she says, looking back at her ring. "For me, too."

"Does Harry know you're engaged?"

"Harry?"

Here, she laughs and waves her hand like Harry is entirely insignificant to her, but then she pauses before continuing:

"No, I haven't told him yet," she says softly. "But I don't think Harry's ever been a huge fan of Grant, anyway."

This comment seems to make her a little sad, but I can't be sure. Despite my countless hours of observation and idle consideration, I still have not been able to successfully dissect Harry and Davis's relationship; I'm still not even sure where its beating heart is located. They are completely consumed with one another in one moment, only to be cutting and contemptuous the very next. They are like a beautiful country riddled with land mines, and sometimes I suspect what presents as love is something far more insidious, although what, I do not know.

"Does Barbara know about these City Hall plans?" I ask. "That doesn't sound like something she would approve."

Here, Davis pulls her hand back quickly, like I was suddenly hot to the touch.

"Not yet," she says, her voice rising. "Don't say anything until it's final, okay?"

"Okay."

"She's pretty upset about the engagement," Davis says, but quickly corrects herself: "I mean, she's *thrilled*, obviously, but she is also still processing everything, so I don't want to shock her with any more news."

"Your secret is safe with me," I say.

Davis smiles her grateful smile.

"Anyway, first things first," she says with a clap of her hands. "What do you think about me throwing a big, splashy engagement party in a few weeks?"

"I think it would please your mother," I offer lightly.

Davis looks at me, her blue eyes bright and defiant.

"My thoughts exactly," she says.

29

The morning after Davis and Grant's engagement party, I wake up alone in my apartment. I am on top of my blankets and wearing a fur coat; Barbara Lawrence's chocolate full-length mink-fur coat, to be exact. She lent it to me for the party and apparently, I liked it so much that I slept in it. I dislodge my nightguard from my bone-dry mouth, and marvel I had the presence of mind to put it in last night in the first place. *I should call my orthodontist*, I think, as I slap the plastic arc on my nightstand. *Just to be congratulated.* I sit up in bed and swing my bare feet onto the floor, which causes a headache to ooze down the insides of my skull. I am still wearing a portion of my tights, but the bottoms are ripped at the ankle and jagged. I tear them off and toss them on the floor. Next, I locate my party shoes, which are lying exhausted by the door. I slide them on my blistered feet with a painful grimace, somehow rationalizing this to be less painful than pulling on a pair of sneakers. Then, without consulting a mirror, I walk down the crooked stairs and out onto my street. The old Italian women are nowhere to be found, and as I hobble to the corner bodega, I decide that I am surrounded by too much sadness. It takes the form of everyday objects, like the heap of black trash bags piled upon my neighbor's damp curb. They strain with the elbows of pizza boxes and jangle softly in the winter wind with the sound of empty aluminum cans and glass bottles. *They will be picked up and go nowhere*, I think. But it's not just the trash bags that are sad. I pass a deserted playground with an empty swing that undulates sorrowfully in the breeze. There is an old woman making slow progress with a walker.

An orphaned newspaper page whips into the air before it flings itself with desperation against the leg of a lonely bench.

Everything is depressing.

Inside the bodega, a few men are crowded at the register, scratching off lottery tickets, and I stand on a wet, broken-down cardboard box as I wait in line. The box feels revoltingly soft under my feet, like it has grown bloated and mealy from absorbing the relentless weight of another immutable season.

Or maybe that is just me.

When it's my turn, I buy a large coffee and a pack of cigarettes with my last ten-dollar bill, and one of the lottery guys smiles at me. I like having a fur coat. If you wear a fur coat, you are rich and successful and don't care what people think about you, which is precisely how I want to feel in life. The weather is mild for November, far too mild to be wearing a mink coat, but I don't care.

I am going to wear this fucking coat all day.

Back inside my apartment I take two Advil and wash them down with coffee. I lay on my bed in the coat and interlace my hands behind my head. I feel terrible. It's hard to remember all the details from the night before, but I suspect that is primarily because I don't care to remember. Miraculously, I made it home with my cell phone, which had been safely tucked in my borrowed coat's velvet pocket. I pick it up off my nightstand to learn, with a sinking feeling, that I have four missed calls. They are all from Davis, just a minute or two apart, and they all came in while I was out getting coffee. There is no voicemail. I put the phone back down and turn to the ceiling.

I hate everyone.

Last night, Grant and Davis rented out a new restaurant on the Lower East Side for their engagement party. I spent days shopping for the perfect dress, something that was short and sexy, but also structured and good for winter, like velvet, but, as we are in the middle of shooting the March issue, a furtive pass through the fashion closet turned up nothing seasonally appropriate. I finally found an affordable approximation at the French Connection in Soho, a one-shouldered black dress that hit two inches above the knee, which I wore with black tights and a three-inch pair of suede heels. These are the details from my evening that I can provide with great confidence, but I cannot attest to the accuracy of my recollection for any subsequent particulars.

The party was overseen by a team of professionals, hired by Barbara, of course, who decorated the restaurant to resemble, at least in my opinion, a winter wonderland in the spirit of Slim Aarons. Guests were greeted by a wall of handsome waiters sporting Fair Isle sweaters, all of whom held out silver trays of hot spiced ciders, rose champagne, and cocktails decorated with cranberries and fragrant sprigs of rosemary. The tables were decorated with two-foot-tall vases, artfully crammed with white birch branches and evergreens. There were smaller—although not small—winter arrangements on the bar, and all the doorways and ceilings were strung with tasteful, creamy white little lights.

I had invited Allie to the party with the promise that it would be full of free alcohol and wealthy young bankers, but when we arrived at the appointed hour, the room was sparsely populated. As such, we spent the first hour lingering awkwardly by the bar and hoping someone would talk to us, namely Davis, who I had been dying to properly introduce to Allie. I watched with irritation as a cluster of girls from work showed up together, flush and chatty. Clearly, there had been a pre-dinner, and I bristled that I had, yet again, not been invited and now I had to pretend that I hadn't noticed their arrival or, if I had noticed, I didn't care. As for Davis, she occasionally flitted in and out of our sphere and, while it was completely irrational, I felt angry and ignored. I had hoped that she would make a bigger show of our friendship in front of Allie and that Allie, in turn, would be impressed that I had been so wholly accepted into this rarefied world. Instead, Davis held court by the door with her mother and welcomed guests in from the cold with her electric and grateful smile. I watched her make small talk before graciously pointing the way to the bar.

She wore a diaphanous ivory silk caftan and a turban, which would have looked like a Halloween costume on anyone else, but paired with her glittering blonde hair, which hung loose down her shoulders, it had the effect of making Davis seem like the ideal hostess, completely at ease. You could almost feel a collective discomfort radiate off the other girls who had, when greeted by Davis at the door, found themselves reevaluating their own run-of-the-mill outfit selections.

"The turban is a bit much," Allie whispered sarcastically as she fished around in her Manhattan for the cherry.

I did not laugh.

As the night wore on, there were some toasts and Barbara cried giving her speech, a performance for which she received a wave of rapturous applause from the audience. And when I grew tired of being mad at Davis and Grant for being rich and in love, I decided to direct my burgeoning ire toward Allie, who had been, in my opinion, a disappointing guest. I expected her to be in her usual, wildly flirtatious form, but she seemed determined to stay faithful to her boyfriend Patrick, who was on a work trip to San Francisco. As a result, she was doing a lot of dull nodding and drink sipping and, on more than a few occasions, I caught her flipping open her phone to check if she had a voicemail. As the hours passed, the more agitated I became, especially as I watched people from work drifting in, including Lydia Saintclair-Abbott and her boyfriend, which cast an additional pall on my already near-catastrophic evening. At some point, Allie retreated to a dark corner with the only other single guy in the place and so, with little else to do, I kept drinking. I held on to a dim hope that maybe the right amount of alcohol would flip some recalcitrant switch inside me, and, like magic, I would start to have fun.

At some point near midnight, I saw someone helping Barbara into her own coat, and as she pulled on a pair of long leather gloves, she looked, somehow, displeased. Davis followed behind her as she walked toward the door, almost as if she was trying to catch her to explain something, but Barbara didn't seem to be listening. I quickly ordered another drink, figuring the open bar would surely come to an end with our benefactress gone, but, instead, the DJ turned up the music. People started to dance. I watched as Davis held a glass above her head and sang the lyrics of a song I didn't know.

I turned away from the crowd. I took a sip of my drink.

At some point Liddy slid up next to me. She offered me a quick, seemingly genuine smile, and then she ordered a vodka tonic. There was a red-feather boa around her neck, which looked out of place on her, and she was wearing one of the campy, pink plastic tiaras that some of Davis's friends started to pass out to the crowd.

"Nice crown," I said.

"Why, thank you," she responded, touching it lightly and fluttering her lashes. "Quite a party, isn't it?"

"That's Davis for you."

"I guess you're going to miss her," Liddy said, albeit distractedly. Her crown had become tangled in her long hair, and I watched as she tried to unwind it with a painful grimace.

"What are you talking about?" I asked.

"You didn't hear?"

"Hear what?"

I wince now as I recall my own eagerness because, even in that moment, I knew the information was not going to improve my mood.

"She's moving to California," she said. "Right after Christmas."

And just like that, the ground opened beneath me, and almost like a cartoon, I plummeted into a dreaded, and yet most familiar, darkness.

"Oh, of course, California!" I lied, surprised that my mouth was still moving like the mouth of a normal person.

As I stood there, the weight of Davis's previous offenses—the ones I'd tried to ignore because I was so desperate to remain in her orbit—started to add up. Her strange silences. The easy promotions at the magazine that, when pressed, she herself could not explain. Her complete lack of struggle around topics like money, beauty, and love. Her enormous apartment, her perfect wardrobe, her famous mother. The list kept unspooling in my muddled mind, and now—to add insult to injury—she was moving to California.

And she'd told Lydia Saintclair-Abbot before she'd told me.

It is quite likely Liddy continued to talk, but I could no longer hear; my senses had taken a hasty leave of my body, and the only thing left behind was an empty vessel fermenting chaos and rage.

On certain occasions (and most often in the company of excess alcohol) there can arrive a point where I morph into a woman possessed, and this was one of those nights. I felt myself set off in search of Davis, and thinking back, it must have looked like someone had released Frankenstein's monster into a bar. For starters, I was in heels. Secondly, I'm nearly certain I was mouth breathing. Lastly, I had lost all sense of personal space; I banged into several bewildered partygoers, which sent at least one drink crashing loudly to the tile floor, and when someone touched my shoulder to say hello, I shook them off with such violence that I pulled a muscle in my armpit.

When I finally located Davis—still wearing *that fucking turban*—she was speaking to a couple I didn't recognize, but I was long past the point of social graces. I snatched her arm and whipped her around to face me:

"Why didn't you tell me?" I demanded.

Here, Davis's hand flew to her neck. She stole a nervous glance toward the couple, both of whom looked taken aback by the unalloyed intensity of my vitriol.

"Tell you what?" she whispered back.

"California," I said.

"I just found out," she said, and her eyes grew wide. "*Jesus.* Grant was up for a job, and he just heard he got it this week."

At this point, the couple began to take long, slow backward steps and, to my fury, Davis offered them a helpless smile.

"Am I embarrassing you?" I said.

"No, of course not," she said before whispering: "You just *might* be a little drunk."

"I was here for *like an hour* before anyone got here," I snapped. "You could have told me, but for some reason you were hiding it from me."

"I'm not *hiding* anything!"

"Oh *really*? How does Liddy know?" I barked, and then I realized something even more upsetting: "Wait, does Harry know?"

Davis didn't answer. Instead, she turned lightly over her shoulder and widened her eyes in distress. She was, as usual, looking for someone to swoop in and save her. I grabbed her arm again to force her to look at me, but this time she jerked back angrily. Her eyes flashed.

"That hurt," she cried.

"Why?" I hissed.

"Why what?"

"Why didn't you tell me you were moving?"

"I don't see why Grant and I moving to California has anything to do with you," she said, and here she folded her arms and smirked at me. "I mean, no offense, but it's not like we are close friends."

My mouth opened, but nothing came out. I had heard Davis had a reputation in high school for cutting people to the quick, but I had never seen that register in her—at least not directed toward me—until now.

"I thought you were my friend," I said, recovering my voice.

"Please keep your voice down," she replied. "You are making a scene."

"Who cares?"

"I care?" she offered, her blue eyes narrowing. "This *is* my engagement party."

"Congratulations," I said sarcastically. "Well-deserved."

"Excuse me?"

"No, I'm sorry," I said, and I cringe now recalling my soprano of false sincerity. "You come in every day looking pretty. You're rich. Congratulations! Wow! You should get a promotion! And get married! And get everything."

"Whoa," Davis said, but there was now more than a hint of contempt in her voice. She folded her arms against her chest. "What is wrong with you? Why are you so angry?"

As I stood there, my hands balled into fists, I realized I had no idea what was wrong with me. What I *did* know, however, was that it was critical I appear to be in *complete control of the situation* despite the growing evidence that I had clearly lost the thread. The truth is I didn't work any harder than Davis, but it was easier to blame Davis for my failures than to direct my fury toward some hulking and unchanging infrastructure. After all, I had willingly opted into a caste system, and now I was irate that I wasn't exempt from its predictable dictates?

So, yes, I was angry. I was furious, mostly because I would never be Davis. I would never be a Show Horse. I would always be on the outside, wearing some cheap dress and looking in on a world that would never be mine because, quite simply, I wasn't born into it. The beauty of Davis's life was always going to make mine ugly by comparison, and

I suddenly felt a choking resentment that I was expected to be grateful for her scraps.

Incidentally, I was also really, really, *really* fucking drunk.

Even now, I can physically recall how the room throbbed with light and my body swelled with a heat that frightened me. I realized that I needed fresh air before I started to cry so, without another word, I stumbled away from Davis. I almost made it out the front door before I remembered the fur coat Barbara had loaned me, and so I started to dig through the colossal jumble of outerwear piled on one of the banquettes. I have a memory of people regarding me with worried faces and how my throat started to ache and my ears burned. In frustration, I started throwing jackets over my shoulder, scattering items across the room. When Davis appeared nervously behind me, I started to throw things at her, over and over, until my shoulder gave out from the exertion. Davis just stared at me blankly, and when Grant came over to shield her, I could sense something deep in my chest slowly break apart, like an exhausted iceberg. Was the music still playing? Was everyone looking at me? I have absolutely no idea. All I know is that I somehow managed to locate the borrowed coat, and when I slipped it over my shoulders, I thought I might buckle under its weight. Davis ducked out from Grant's protective embrace and led me to a corner.

"Clo, seriously. What is going on?"

Her eyes met mine and she gave me one of her sweet, inquiring shrugs.

Sometimes I think Davis would shrug her way through life if I let her.

"It's not fair," I managed through angry tears.

At this comment, Davis cocked her head to the side.

"Whoever said it was fair?" she said. Her voice was charitable, but her eyes flashed with anger. "Do you think it's always fair for me? You don't know *anything* about me."

I did not respond, which seemed to embolden Davis. She leaned closer, her voice like ice:

"You're embarrassing yourself, and you're embarrassing me."

"What?" I stammered, but my balance was uneasy. My hand reached for something to steady me, but there was nothing there, and as I stumbled over my feet, I recall how I suddenly became aware that a lot of people were watching this scene unfold. Davis must have realized it, too, because she was just smiling at me, big and easy. It was almost as if she didn't have a care in the world.

I needed to get out of there.

I bolted for the front door and out onto the sidewalk, but I did not make it more than a few strides before I smacked—with incredible force—into Harry Wood. He was smoking a cigarette with a very tall man in a hat.

"Clo," he exclaimed as I toppled over in front of him. "What the fuck?"

"Where have you been?" I sobbed, my body splayed on the cold pavement.

"Wait, are you crying?" he asked, looking more closely at me. I nodded miserably, and he extended his arms down to lift me up. He was frowning with concern.

"Did you know about California?" I had wailed.

"What about California?" he asked.

"She's moving to California."

Harry opened his mouth in surprise, but before he could answer, a door slammed in the background. His eyes shot over my head like a rocket, and I followed his gaze: It was Davis. She had followed me outside and, when she saw me crying to Harry, her face pinched up like an old bird. She stood a few feet away and looked completely undone. She was not wearing a coat.

"Clo, please don't leave," she said before she turned with desperation to Harry. "Don't let her leave, Harry. She's really drunk, and she's having a bad night."

"I'm having a *bad night?*" I asked, incredulous.

"Just stay," Davis pleaded. "Everyone is drunk. I'm sorry."

She started to approach me with her arms outstretched in a posture of peace, but little alarm bells started to ring inside my head. The situation suddenly felt menacing, like that scene in *Rosemary's Baby* when Mia Farrow realizes she is pregnant with the devil, and, to her horror, comes to realize she's the last one to know. I pulled loose from Harry's grasp and stumbled backward a few steps before I lost my footing and landed back on the concrete. I looked up to find Davis and Harry looking down at me. Harry put out his arm again to help me up, but I started to scuttle backward like a crab.

I couldn't trust anyone.

I shouldn't trust anyone.

I rolled over onto my knees, which ripped a hole in my tights, and then I jumped to my feet and took off running indiscriminately down the street.

"Clo," Davis yelled. "Stop!"

But I didn't stop. I ran harder.

I only made it about two blocks, however, before my heart was thumping so savagely, I could not continue. I started to walk. I took a few jagged breaths, but it was almost impossible to get enough oxygen inside my body. I heard Harry and Davis calling out my name, over and over, like I was a lost dog, so I took off my shoes and I started to run again. I jogged right down a side street, my stockinged feet slapping against the sidewalk. I could tell they were gaining on me, so I forced open the rusted gate of a run-down apartment building and I ducked between two overflowing black trash cans. I held my body rigid underneath a window air-conditioning unit, and the ground smelled like urine and onions. I tried to control my breathing, which banged so frantically between my ears that I was sure the noise would lead Davis and Harry right to my hiding spot, like a homing beacon.

This was the moment where I felt myself separate into two people: I was the person crouching behind two trash cans, but I was also the person watching the person crouching behind two trash cans with morbid, judgmental fascination.

Davis and Harry clambered right past my hiding spot, and as I listened to their footsteps fade, I heard laughing. They were laughing, like this was some kind of game, and I felt nothing but a vast emptiness inside. I thought they might double back, so I held my breath as I strained to hear their voices. When I heard nothing for a long while, I finally unclenched my body. I slid down the brick wall, which pulled my dress up over my backside, and I felt my tights soak up a wet residue, best unknown. I have no idea how long I sat there; I may have even fallen asleep, but when I finally lifted my head up, it was still quiet. I could see the blinking red lights on top of the Manhattan Bridge in the far distance. I was about to get up when I heard feet on pavement, crisp and quick. I slunk back down just as Harry walked past my hiding spot alone. He was smoking a cigarette, and from my low vantage point, I could see he was wearing his expensive patent leather shoes. He was heading back in the direction of the party. I sat quietly for another few minutes until I was reasonably sure they had stopped searching for me. They were probably both back inside the party, grateful to be rid of me, shaking their heads in disappointment or disbelief. I have no idea what time it was when I started walking, but I was in no hurry. I moved slowly along the gloomy streets in the direction of Brooklyn, my shoes in my hands, and looked in vain for a taxi. My mind was blank as I made my way up the deserted ramp to the bridge, and as I walked over the entire span, the city laid itself out before me, bright and forever. By the time I made it to my neighborhood, the sky has started to lighten. My thighs chafed from the wetness of my tights, and when the soles of my feet broke through their thin fabric, I ripped them off haphazardly, dropping the thin shards of nylon in my wake.

But in the light of the morning, I am mortified and I don't quite know what to do. I roll back over and pick up my phone again. I don't like to apologize, even when I am entirely in the wrong, so I think of ways to pin last night's breakdown on anything other than my own jealousy, but I keep coming up short. Finally, I just hit the button to call Davis back. I do it quickly, so I can't change my mind, but it doesn't even ring before Barbara answers. This is a surprise, and I am about to say as much when she starts to speak. *Speaking* is the wrong word, though—Barbara is screaming—and the sound is somehow both high-pitched and guttural. It zigs through the phone and hits me like a bolt.

I sit up in bed.

"Davis had an accident," she wails.

Davis had an accident. At least, this is what I *think* Barbara says. Her words are running together, and I am unable, or possibly unwilling, to hear her clearly. I close my eyes and strain to listen. I plug my right ear with my finger to drown out the subway train that has chosen this exact moment to rumble past my window.

"Barbara, what?"

"Davis. We are at the hospital. She had an accident. She fell. I don't know what is going on, but she is in surgery, and the doctors won't tell me anything."

Barbara is sobbing now, and I keep losing her; the receiver seems to have fallen away from her mouth.

"Barbara, where are you?" I demand, but I only hear what sounds like the rustle of clothes and heavy breathing. "Barbara, do you hear me? Put the phone to your ear. Barbara?"

"I'm here," she says, but her voice sounds thick and muffled, like she's lying in a basket of dirty laundry. I can hear sirens in the background.

"Barbara, where are you?" I ask again.

"They didn't find her until this morning," she says, her voice rising again.

I left her with Harry, I want to say. But I don't.

"Barbara, where are you?"

"Columbia Presbyterian."

In this unlikely moment, I hear the voice of Allie's mother, who grew up in the Bronx, say: *No matter where you get hurt, go to Columbia Presbyterian. It's the only good hospital in the city. The rest are for shit.* Of course Davis Lawrence is at Columbia Presbyterian, I think.

The rest are for shit.

"Barbara, I am coming right now," I yell into the phone. "Do you hear me?"

"Yes."

As I pace my apartment, I dial the local Brooklyn car service, who informs me, as they famously do, that they'll arrive in "five minutes." My hands are shaking, but I need to move quickly so I leave on my high heels from the night before, figuring that a fur coat would look ridiculous paired with old Asics running sneakers on the Upper East Side. For some strange reason, it doesn't occur to me *not* to wear the fur coat. I grab my wallet and cell phone, and I turn to the mirror for a quick check. My nose looks swollen, especially at the tip, probably from drinking too much, and my skin is broken out and blotchy. Last night's red lipstick has bled outside the edges of my mouth.

I race back to the bathroom, wash my face, and put on a fresh coat of makeup. I run a brush through my hair. I roll deodorant around my armpits. I take one last look in the mirror. *I am a woman of substance who is gracefully managing a proper emergency*, I think.

When I get to the street, the Italian ladies have finally made their appearance; it is nearing ten o'clock and surely there is a hunk of meat to which they must miserably attend. In their beat-up winter coats, old scarves, and snow boots pulled on underneath their housecoats, they look worn out. When they see me, they make no effort to hide their disapproval of *my* outfit, however. I even catch one woman shake her head. I am about to clack over to explain that I have *an emergency*, and that this coat is *definitely not my coat* as *I could never afford a fur coat*, but the car is waiting, and I lose my steam. I will deal with them later.

"Please take me to Columbia Presbyterian," I say to the driver in what I consider a businesslike fashion as I slide into the car.

"Sure thing," he responds politely, but he checks me out in the rear-view mirror just the same, if only to discern if I am in active labor or intending to vomit all over his car. I've often thought how this must be a constant anxiety for drivers, but I have made it easy on him by wearing a fur coat, a choice that allows me to indicate, without speaking, that I am a respectable fare. As we pull away, I look out the smudged car window at the old women, and I give them all a small, sad wave. I do not know why I want their pity or their approval, but I do.

They do not wave back.

This will be the longest car ride of my life.

Part Two

NEW YORK CITY

2004 to 2006

30

It is New Year's Eve.

It is New Year's Eve, which, incidentally, means nearly two months have passed since Davis's accident, although nobody says that part out loud. Instead, Barbara Lawrence has invited Harry Wood and I to the apartment on Ninety-Second Street as a means of providing her daughter some semblance of holiday cheer. Davis is still recovering from her surgeries, which prohibits her from celebrating in a more meaningful way. Now, I *understand* I should feel nothing but sympathy about her lack of mobility (not to mention her persistent pain, which requires a complicated matrix of pills), and yet I find myself ungenerously irritated that, instead of getting fat from this lack of regular exercise, Davis seems to grow thinner and more beautiful with each passing day. Her high cheekbones are now even more pronounced, and when she turns her head sideways, her jawline looks positively regal. You could wear a near-death Davis Lawrence as a cameo brooch while I morph into an angry sea hag when I contract something as inconsequential as the common cold.

This, my friends, sums up all I deem to be unfair about the world.

The accident.

It could have happened minutes or hours after I last saw her—which was when Davis and Harry ran past me laughing as I cowered behind trash cans on the night of the engagement party—but no one can say for sure. She wasn't discovered until the first light of the following day because, as it turns out, no one bothered to look for Davis when she didn't return to her own party, not even Grant. Instead, she was found by a middle-aged man who *claimed* (Barbara's emphasis, not mine) to have heard some strange moaning as he jogged down Delancey Street on his regular five-in-the-morning run. He didn't have a cell phone on him ("no pockets," he explained, pointing to his track pants, which Barbara, somehow, also found suspicious) and since there were no open bodegas at that hour, he sprinted up the block to call 911 from a payphone. When the officers and ambulances arrived, they reported the man was crouched down over Davis, almost as if he was praying. Her body was lying askew on a pile of flattened cardboard boxes that had been bundled up outside a Chinese restaurant and left under some metal scaffolding. She was still wearing her caftan, which was stained with blood, but the turban had gone missing. She was conscious, but barely.

When questioned over the details of his discovery, the man reported that, after he heard the moaning, he saw what looked like a blonde wig, so he slowed down to get a better look. That is when he saw an exposed arm, so translucent it looked vaguely blue, like skim milk. He said her arm felt cold, too cold, so he checked her pulse and tried to wake her up. He was hesitant to move her body because it was twisted in an awkward fashion so he laid his fleece jacket on top of her as he waited for help to arrive.

She was loaded into an ambulance.

She was rushed into surgery.

The man was placed in the back of a police car to give his statement at the station.

However, because Davis did not have a wallet on her, nor any other form of identification, it took hours for the police to sort out her identity using her phone, which was tucked in the beaded pouch that had hung from her wrist all evening. When they finally contacted Barbara around ten o'clock in the morning, she was confused. She told the officers they must have the wrong girl because her daughter was sleeping at the apartment of her fiancé.

They didn't have the wrong girl.

When Barbara arrived at the hospital, she was given a bag of Davis's belongings, including her purse, and upon finding her daughter's nearly dead cell phone, she frantically called three people: Grant, Harry, and me. We all raced to the East Side from our various apartments, and after some initial small talk in the crowded waiting room, we didn't interact much. I suspect we were all silently blaming the other party for Davis's horrific ordeal and, as we waited for news that might confirm our suspicions, I grew nauseated from the anxiety. The only things my body could tolerate were Diet Cokes from the vending machine and Marlboro Lights, neither of which did anything to assuage my nerves, but both, when in hand, felt like appropriate grieving props.

When I took cigarette breaks outside the busy ER doors, cocooned in Barbara's fur coat, people eyed me with curiosity, and, despite the dire circumstance, I wanted their attention. I found myself eager to look enigmatic, like I was a tantalizing mystery to be solved. Maybe I had just murdered my husband? Or maybe I was awaiting news of my lover, who suffered a heart attack while we were frisking about in bed. Frankly, it didn't matter: Any fantasy was surely better than the potential horrors waiting for me inside the hospital once Davis woke up.

Later that same afternoon, I was standing by the soda machine, from which I had just retrieved my fourth can of Diet Coke, when I saw a guy with ruffled, sandy-colored hair and glasses enter the waiting room. He had one of those long notebooks poking out of the back pocket of his khaki pants, and in an instant, I understood him to be a reporter. I glanced through the revolving doors where I spied another man waiting outside with a long lens camera.

Fuck.

"Grant," I called out nervously across the waiting room as I pointed frantically toward the man, who was approaching the woman at the front desk. "Harry!"

Harry and Grant took one look at the guy and understood—as I understood—that he was a journalist. Somehow, the news of Davis's accident must have gotten out, and this guy was here to report on the story. In an instant, Harry grabbed the bewildered guy by his collar and hustled him out the door. I ran over to the window where, through a dirty plate of glass, I watched him shove the man to the pavement. As Harry yelled over the man's cowering body, frothy spittle flew off his lips, and when I turned to look at Grant, he had his phone to his ear.

"I'm calling my lawyer," he explained, and I wondered what, exactly, Grant—safe inside the hospital—was hoping his lawyer would do, but I didn't have time to wonder for long. Moments later, Harry marched back inside, his face savage with outrage, and threw a disgusted look at Grant. I looked out the window again. The two journalists were gone.

"Nobody will mention this to Barbara," Harry growled. "Understand?"

Grant and I nodded like scolded children, but, as I looked at the three of us, I couldn't help but wonder how anyone outside our little circle could possibly know about Davis's accident after such a short time.

After a few more hours of waiting with no real news, one of the nurses suggested we go home to our respective apartments and get a little sleep.

The following morning, I returned to the hospital to learn from a bleary Grant that Davis had made it through surgery and was awake, which was a relief. A stubbled Harry arrived hours later, reeking of cigarette smoke and hard liquor, and while we all were clamoring to see her, we had to wait until the police were done with their questioning, which took a better portion of the day. Harry and Grant sat in silence a few seats apart, while I paced the grimy linoleum floor, and wondered what details, if any, Davis would be able to provide from the night of her engagement party.

Finally, we were permitted into her room, but not as a group; we had to go one by one because we were not family, a designation that made both Grant and Harry irate, but for different reasons. Grant went into the room first, as he was her fiancé, and I got the second slot. By the time I was ushered inside, however, the sun had started to set, and my first thought was the hospital room was not nearly nice enough for Davis. It was small and exceedingly bright with only a dingy pastel, patterned curtain separating her from another patient, who was listening to a television show in Spanish. The walls were beige, and the black trash can by the door was overflowing with garbage from a fast-food restaurant, clearly left behind by the previous tenant.

And then I saw Davis.

She was propped up in bed by a flaccid stack of gray hospital pillows, and her long arms had been arranged over the sheets. She had a cast on one wrist, which had fractured in the fall, and one leg was elevated. She was attached to a half dozen monitors, all of which hovered around her body like a gaggle of tittering nuns, and she had oxygen in her nostrils. Her eyes were black, a splint ran the length of her nose, and there was a gauze bandage wrapped around her head in a near comic fashion. At a glance, it looked as if she was being treated for an old-fashioned toothache. As I crept closer to the bed, I could see a series of wiry black stitches poking hard out of her swollen upper lip, like an old sailor's whiskers.

She looked worse—far worse—than I had permitted myself to imagine.

Cautiously, I settled down on the edge of the bed and placed my hand on what I figured was Davis's thigh. I looked over at Barbara, who sat indomitable in a chair against the wall, and gave her a weak smile. She was wearing a full face of makeup, including false eyelashes, which I found odd considering the circumstances, but it had done little to improve her appearance. The foundation was caked into the lines under her eyes, and red lipstick sank into the creases on her lips. When she moved her head, however, her hair did not move.

"Thank you for coming," Davis said, but because she had been intubated, her voice came out as a raw whisper.

"Oh, Davis," I said, and unexpectedly my throat caught.

I started to cry.

"You should see the other guy," Davis joked.

For the duration of my short visit, I tried to do most of the talking, but Davis seemed determined to put me at ease. She was gracious and trying to make light of it all, but I couldn't help but feel there was something familiar in this bizarre stoicism. It was almost as if she was reading from a script, gaily insisting—yet again—that everything was *fine*.

At some point, Barbara excused herself to get an update on the status of Davis's private room, and when I turned back to Davis to say something (what, I don't know), her face had puckered shut like an umbrella. She bowed her head and covered her mouth, and as she cried, her body shook so violently that, within moments, a viscous thread of drool hung from her mouth all the way down to the sheets. When her sobs became audible, like a midnight cat in heat, one of the nurses briefly appeared at the foot of her bed.

"She's okay," I said, but I had no idea if that was true.

Between heaves and gasps, Davis told me that, after a certain point, she didn't remember anything about the party. In fact, she could hardly recall the first few hours in the hospital. Sure, there were bright lights and noise and lots of people rushing around, but there was nothing concrete in her consciousness except for a single, completely horrifying moment: A middle-aged woman with short curly hair and wire-rim glasses asking for her to consent to a rape kit.

Davis consented.

The rape kit was negative.

Davis said it wasn't the waiting that was the worst part, although that was its own kind of agony; it was the not knowing.

The not knowing, she said with her sobs softly receding. *The not knowing was the worst part.*

So, tonight, when I arrive at the apartment for holiday drinks—almost an hour late, of course, because the subway was a mess—the first thing I see in the foyer is Davis's wheelchair. It is pushed against the wall and draped with a taupe cashmere blanket and, somehow, alone and unoccupied, it looks even sadder than usual. When I enter the living room, Davis looks up from the couch and gives me a drowsy, sort of self-important smile. She is arranged next to Harry with her legs up on the couch, and she wears a short, oversized mod-style dress. Even though she has a cast on the lower part of one leg, her feet are visible. I see her toenails have been painted in a rich winter red, and the polish is so fresh that it twinkles when it catches in the overhead lights. When Davis motions me to come over, I realize I am not breathing; the visceral reaction I have to her never seems to lessen, no matter how much I steel myself against its eventuality.

"Happy New Year," I call out as I lift a cold bottle of Pol Roger champagne in the air. It cost sixty-five dollars and I put it on Barbara's credit card, but only because I felt sure that Barbara, if Barbara ever found out, wouldn't mind: This is an evening to celebrate her own daughter, after all, and I suspect she would not be impressed with the canned six-pack of Brooklyn bodega beer I could afford.

It was only polite.

"Happy New Year," Davis and Harry sing back in a festive unison.

I smile, but my throat clamps with jealousy at their physical closeness. I haven't seen too much of Harry since the accident. Our friendship, as I suspected, mostly fell apart without the glue of Davis bonding us together, but I find myself hopeful this gathering might reignite our connection. I am glad to see he has chosen a suit and tie for the occasion because, after much deliberation, I decided to wear a long-sleeved, silver sequined dress that I recently unearthed at a vintage store on St. Mark's Place. When I sit down, the sequins slice into my puffy flesh, and the armpits remain faintly perfumed with the onion-adjacent body odor of the previous owner, but I like the way it looks. Even better, it cost a mere forty dollars.

At Barbara's suggestion, I mix a drink in the kitchen before I join the group in the living room. Point of protocol: You always *mix* a drink with Barbara, you never *get* one or *pour* one, even if all that is on offer is a bottle of wine. So, I mix a drink, and for the next few hours, the four of us share laughs and trade stories over cheese and crackers, and a tray of those ridiculously good mini hot dogs from Fleisher's. Harry is as thoughtful and charming as ever, of course: He's attentive to Davis and flirtatious with Barbara in that outsized way most older women seem to prefer, and while Barbara is outwardly receptive to Harry's flattery (I am quickly learning there is nothing Barbara Lawrence likes more than a heap of unvarnished adorations), it's clear she regards Harry with a somewhat sleepy suspicion. Her eyes track his languid movements around the room, like a cat keeping tabs on all her birds, knowing not for when there might be a good moment to strike. As for me, Harry doles out a few compliments, and my heart quickens at the conspiratorial way he looks at me when he speaks, like he wants to be *absolutely sure* he has my attention. He regales us with the wonderfully scandalous stories recently unearthed by the small team that runs his website—primarily New York celebrities and gossip with a little news and politics tossed in for good measure—and while he keeps us well entertained, I can't help but notice that Harry—as handsome as he is—looks drained. There are dark circles underneath his eyes, and, when he isn't smiling, his features seem to slide down his face.

Despite our best intentions, the evening ultimately plays out like a desperate performance, the second act of which we blunt by consuming an obscene amount of alcohol. *Everything is back to normal*, the script reads as we clink our glasses—again and again—with great cheer. *The gang is all here!* And while our hearts are firmly in the right place, we deliver our lines so unconvincingly that it is Davis who, ultimately, saves the show. She behaves as if we are the most brilliant creatures with whom she ever had the pleasure to fritter away an evening. She has trotted out some of the good heirloom jewelry for the big occasion, which includes an enormous diamond cocktail ring on her good hand (the other wrist is still in a soft brace), and she makes certain, with just the lightest tip of her chin, that Marta keeps our glasses refreshed and the hot dogs warm.

Around 11:30, an obviously inebriated Barbara pushes herself up uncertainly from her squat, upholstered chair. We all watch in a silent, shared horror as she pitches over the broad expanse of mauve carpeting toward the large armoire that houses her television. It is painful to bear witness to her obvious struggle; it's always unsettling (for me, anyway) to see a grown-up who is clearly out of control.

It feels unsafe. *I* feel unsafe.

I strain to avoid eye contact with anyone as Barbara briefly fumbles with the large remote control only to hand it off to Harry with a slurring resignation. When she finally makes it back to her seat—a process which was an honest-to-God nail-biter—we all beam in her direction to indicate she has done a *very good job*. She smiles right back and claps her hands like a toddler.

Harry quickly locates the station with Dick Clark, and we watch the flashing screen with palpable relief that someone else is responsible for our entertainment for a few minutes. I glance over at Davis to discover that, once the collective attention shifted elsewhere, every ounce of brightness has leaked out of her face. She looks gray and exhausted, and the furniture that fills the living room seems to have immediately followed suit. The thick drapes, the floral-patterned wallpaper, the glass coffee table, the heavy wood antiques—you name it—everything suddenly takes on a shabby, dated patina.

With about five minutes left in the countdown before the ball drops, Davis falls asleep on the couch. As her heavy head lolls away from us, I can see, with some embarrassment, that there is a wet spot on the neckline of her dress. Her crystal glass, once full of vodka, is tipped over on the carpet, and the square ice cubes have tumbled out. Her bejeweled hand dangles limply over the edge of the couch.

Barbara looks at us blankly. There is no point in staying.

We offer to clean up and, if necessary, help carry Davis to bed, but Barbara declines with a wild waving of her arms because words, apparently, have become too challenging at her heightened state of inebriation. Of course, we carry a few dishes into the kitchen anyway and, as we rinse them in the sink under the tired gaze of Marta, we trade a few loaded looks.

It had been a very long year.

After we gather our coats, I peek into the living room to say goodbye to our hostess, but I am silenced by the scene that plays out before me. The space is illuminated by a single table lamp, and in its amber glow, I watch Barbara place a blanket over her sleeping daughter. There is an incredible gentleness to her movements. She tucks the fringed sides around Davis's shoulders and hips before she settles down on the remaining narrow strip of couch. She lays her palm on Davis's pale forehead and gazes down upon her with a love I don't think I have ever seen conferred upon another human being. As I watch from the doorway, my chest balloons violently with the unexpected reminder that I desperately want to be a mother. I suppose I have *always* wanted to be a mother, and I feel sad that—currently single and without prospects—I am so far from being a mother. In some dim way, I have always intellectually understood that the decisions I make each day are likely burning a daylight I can't fully fathom, but from my quiet perch in the shadows, I get the sense this tableau of maternal affection was something the universe needed me to see.

For my own good.

"Clo?" Harry calls to me softly from the foyer. "Are you ready?"

"I'm coming," I whisper over my shoulder. "I'm coming."

We walk into the elevator without exchanging a word, and as the doors close, I understand that, if called upon to speak, my body will release the barrage of tears building up inside me. I close my eyes and try to will the sensation away.

"Well, there is *a lot* to unpack there," Harry says, and his voice is frosted with a familiar sarcasm.

This is classic Harry Wood: The body is still warm and he's already back to his old tricks. I nod in response, and the motion—however slight—releases a single tear from my eye. It tickles my cheek during its creeping descent, but I must endure the sensation. To wipe it off with my hand would give away my crumbling emotional state.

"I mean, things are starting to go a little *Grey Gardens* in there," he continues. "And I thought it was bad when I lived there."

When I don't respond, I can feel his sidelong glance.

"Hey, you okay?" he asks.

I nod again, but this time, I must look away. I can't believe I am about to bungle a second chance to befriend Harry Wood by crying in an elevator about how I don't have a boyfriend or a baby.

"Do you want to get another drink?" he asks gently.

I pretend to cough so I can quickly wipe away the tears that now hang precipitously from my chin.

"Sure," I manage because another drink is *exactly* what I need, and while Harry seems pleased with my willingness, it really shouldn't be a surprise: I always agree to another drink. I always agree to another drink because, like everyone else in their twenties, getting drunk, chain-smoking Marlboro Lights, or taking drugs (from a short and approved list, of course) are the only coping mechanisms I can somewhat safely operate. Once we make it outside the building, Harry quickly flags down a passing cab, which is easy enough this far uptown, and we climb inside. He gives directions to Bloomingdale's, of all places, which is about thirty blocks south, but I don't ask any questions. I rub my cold hands together as Harry asks the driver to change the radio station and, once he finds a song he likes, he requests the music be turned up to its full volume. He hand cranks the window down and yells the lyrics into the night. I don't know the song—I never know any songs—but I am grateful for the noise.

The cab deposits us on Lexington Avenue, which seems curiously dark and deserted on such a New York holiday, and to my delight,

Harry takes my hand. There is a gusty wind coming from the east, and it whips pieces of trash along the desolate sidewalk. We move faster, the only sound between us being the smack of our dress shoes on cold concrete and, when we round the corner, a plastic bag blows around us tauntingly before it attaches itself to Harry's trousered leg. He stops to untangle it with a little chuckle.

"Want to know something funny?" he asks as he holds the bag between two fingers.

"Sure."

"When I first moved to New York, I told myself that if a piece of garbage ever blew up against my legs, I would know it was a sign to leave."

What a strange thing to say, I think.

"So, are you moving back to Louisiana?" I ask.

He releases the bag into the air, and together we watch it catch in a gust of wind. It wings far above our heads, first out of reach and then out of sight.

Harry Wood returns his brown eyes to me. He slips his arm most gallantly underneath my elbow and winks.

"Not a chance," he says.

The bar that Harry has chosen for us—the Subway Inn—is, without a doubt, the most woebegone joint in all the known world. As we settle into our stools, I look up at the clock. It's approaching one o'clock in the morning, which means it is technically New Year's Day, so I order a drink. I notice everyone is smoking, which, if the news is to be believed, might be illegal come spring. As if on cue, Harry pushes a pack in my direction.

Happy New Year, I think.

I take a long look around room, which is so sparsely lit that it looks misty: There is a checkerboard floor, red walls, and a ramshackle cluster of men in desperate pairs, all of whom are vying for the attention of a middle-aged bottle blonde with poofy hair. She is the only other woman in the bar. She wears a racerback tank top, and the grimy straps of her bra dig into her meaty shoulders. When she leans forward, a spongy bulge hangs over the back of her low-rise jeans and I can see she has stretch marks; they run up her lower back like washed-out train tracks. Otherwise, there is what *looks* to be a homeless person in the back corner with a shopping cart, which makes me afraid to use the bathroom, despite the fact my bladder bulges painfully against my dress.

"This place is perfect," I sigh after a long exhale of smoke.

"It *is* nice to be the most attractive people in the room for once," he says.

This makes me laugh. It's exciting to be alone again with Harry Wood. He has a way of making things feel thrillingly conspiratorial. I take another sip of my drink, which is far too strong, and wince.

"So what are your New Year's resolutions?" he asks.

I pretend to think.

"Get so freakishly skinny that everyone is worried about me," I respond. "The usual."

"Ugh, bitch, you stole mine," he responds.

I laugh at this, too, and a sense of belonging floods my body. I think of all the people packed into expensive downtown clubs or standing behind police barricades in Times Square, and I decide this bar—this little hideaway place—is the *real* New York. It makes me feel like, almost improbably, I finally have a real life.

Harry taps his cigarette into the red plastic ashtray that lies between us, and, with his opposite hand, gently hikes up the cuff of his crisp shirt. In general, Harry's mannerisms are so graceful, so refined, it's like he's the principal dancer in a hand ballet. Honestly, I would be content to watch him eat a bag of potato chips, which, incidentally, he does by placing singular chips on his tongue, one by one, and pulling them into his mouth like the drawer on a well-oiled cash register.

"I don't usually make resolutions," I say finally.

This is a lie. Every year since the sixth grade I have made a New Year's resolution to lose enough weight that people, legitimately, start to worry about me. However, it turns out that I'm either too weak-willed or lack the genetic predisposition for an eating disorder. Either way, I view my repeated nonperformance in the starving-myself arena with great frustration; it feels like a massive failure of character.

"Really? I *always* make a resolution," Harry says.

"You do?" This news is surprising as Harry Wood didn't strike me as one to subscribe to the more mystical notions of self-improvement.

"Yes, and they always come true."

"That sounds more like a wish than a resolution, Harry."

"Call it what you will," he says with a magnificent flutter of his long fingers. "But I'm serious."

"So what's the resolution for this year?" I ask.

"Before I answer, you should know you're implicated."

"Implicated?" I say, but it comes out as an awkward, girlish giggle. Harry gives me an inscrutable look and, instantly, I feel gargantuan and undeserving in his presence.

"For starters, I think it's safe to say that Davis won't be making the rounds this year," he begins.

"What?" I blink, confused.

"Davis," he repeats in a cool, clinical tone. "I don't think she will be much on the social scene. Do you? I mean, she's in a wheelchair, if you hadn't noticed."

While I agree with his assessment, at least in the short term, I find myself taken aback by the brazen manner in which Harry delivers it, namely because I had been operating under the assumption that we were expected to behave as if the old Davis Lawrence—mobile, gorgeous, perfect Davis Lawrence—was right around the corner, ready to pounce.

"I hadn't thought about it," I reply with a light shrug.

"You haven't thought about it?" he asks. He seems surprised. "Not even at work?"

"No," I say. "I just toil away doing fashion captions and fetching lunches."

Now, here is the truth: I have done nothing *but* think about how to best take advantage of the opportunity provided to me by Davis's convalescence, but I can't reveal that to Harry, who I still barely know. At least not yet. In fairness, I didn't *intend* to think about it, but when I was tasked with sorting Davis's mail in the early days of her injury, I was blown away by just how many invitations a one *Ms. Davis Lawrence* received on a regular basis. These were the *good* ones: the intimate dinners for fashion houses, pre-cocktails for the galas, and one-night-only musical performances in abandoned warehouses. It felt like a shame to let them go to waste so I RSVP'd for her, slowly at first, but I figured if anyone working the proverbial doors questioned the switch (which everyone was far too well-bred to do to my face), I would explain I had been explicitly asked by our editor-in-chief to attend in her place during her recovery. What were they going to do? Call her to confirm? Of course not. Furthermore, I reasoned that the magazine really *should* be covering these important events, and I was just being *helpful*.

As it happens, I am learning that attending parties I am ill-equipped to navigate is a mostly excruciating experience. Generally, I get a drink, take two sips, and then abandon it on the nearest tabletop so I can walk to the bar again. I repeat this motion at least five times because I reckon to appear industrious is better than to be caught lingering unwanted on the outside of chattering circles. As I watch other people interact, I wonder if they are really as comfortable as they look or if (as I continue to hope) my regular attendance, as painful as it is, will provide a later benefit, like exercise.

In recent weeks, however, a few people started to recognize me, which I attribute less to my face (which is plain) and more to my still-new bright red coat, which I never remove. To be clear, most people have no idea who I am nor of my larger role in society, but what they *do* know is that I work at the magazine. As such, they will kiss my cheeks or nod dimly in my direction with skeptical approval. After some trial and error, I have discovered that radiating aloof detachment works reasonably well in impressing upon others that what I clearly lack in fashion sense and charisma is intentional because I am a woman of superior intelligence and mystery.

Harry ashes his cigarette and looks at me sideways. He rubs his thumb and forefinger together. He seems to be searching for the right words.

"Well, you *should* be thinking about it," he continues. "It leaves an opening for you."

"An opening?"

"Yes, an opening," he repeats.

I blink at him.

"I think we should work together," he says finally, and I pick up on a hint of irritation in his tone.

"Work together how?" I try to project an air of pleasant naivety.

"I want to up my profile and I want to up the profile of the website," he explains. "I think it has the potential to be huge, and with Davis out of the picture, I'll need a new wingman."

"Why do *you* need a wingman?" I laugh. "Everyone *loves* you, Harry."

I feel my cheeks grow hot as I say this, my flattery perhaps a bit too much, but Harry rewards me with an encouraging smile.

"Well, for starters, it's more fun that way," he replies with a little laugh. "But it's also more effective to join forces, pool invitations, contacts, that sort of thing."

"Like a team sport?" I offer.

"Exactly," he says. "Do you remember how they used to sometimes write about Davis and me? The papers and stuff?"

I nod, but his comment is an overstatement. The reality is that, on occasion, little tidbits would pop up about Davis and Barbara Lawrence in the news—some flattering, some less so—and one time, much to his delight, Harry had been upgraded from "friend" to "paramour."

"Sure," I say gamely.

"That's because it's human nature to wonder what is going on between two people," he explains. "With two people, you can create a *much* better story. You can create mystery, love, scandal . . . you can have a plot."

"Wow, you have really thought a whole narrative through." I laugh, but Harry just looks down at his hands, slightly exasperated. I can almost feel him wonder if Lydia Saintclair-Abbott or, frankly, the piss-soaked guy with the shopping cart in the corner wouldn't be a better partner for his schemes. He stubs out his cigarette and looks directly at me with his enormous brown eyes.

I die a little inside.

"It's all a narrative, Clo," he says finally. "You know that, right? We are both living in the land of make-believe around here."

He wiggles his fingers like a smokescreen.

"Right," I deadpan. "The land of make-believe."

Harry continues to stare at me, and I fluster under his gaze. I don't know what he wants from me, but he clearly wants something:

"What?" I ask, throwing my hands up. "I am just trying to be *funny.*"

"You know I come from, like, nothing back home, right?" he says, and suddenly any jovial frisson between us evaporates. It has been replaced by a disquieting intensity that I have never seen from Harry before; it's like he's worried I am going to snatch something of value from him. I drop my hands to my lap, and I don't know why, exactly, but I feel ashamed.

"Yeah, I know," I mumble quietly, but this is a misrepresentation. The truth is I *don't* know very much about Harry's childhood, and everything I do know is courtesy of Davis, who is always a little vague with particulars. She said he was accepted to Lawrenceville on a full scholarship (which I assumed was attributed to generational wealth and brilliance, not financial need) and that he was beloved around campus for procuring valuable black-market delights like alcohol and cocaine. Additionally, she claimed that he never went home for the holidays, and Davis, unable to imagine him alone in the dorms, would invite him to New York to celebrate holidays like Thanksgiving and Christmas at the apartment. It was in those early years—when they were thirteen, fourteen, fifteen that he became, as Davis recounted, "part of the family," although Harry has never spoken explicitly of this designation with me. For college, Harry went to NYU and, because of some "problems with his housing forms" he lived with Barbara on Ninety-Second Street for his entire freshman year.

This is the extent of my knowledge about Harry Wood's formative years.

"I am going to tell you something that, like, no one knows except Davis and Barbara," he says.

"Okay," I respond seriously.

"I am saying it like it's a big deal, but it's *really* not," he adds quickly, but with a manufactured affability I assume is meant to comfort me. "But I was in the foster system growing up."

"Oh," I say, stunned. I have never known anyone who has been in the foster system. I am not even sure I understand the foster system.

"Yeah," he says. "My mom was an addict, but she died when I was, like, three so I don't remember her, like, at all. I stayed with my grandfather for a while, but"—he searches for the words—"that wasn't a good situation. I was put in the system when I was five."

"What about your dad?"

"No dad," he says, and his tone is so sharp that I know not to press it.

"So, you're . . . adopted?" I ask.

Harry taps the side of the plastic ashtray with his finger a few times but does not immediately look at me. I pick at the waist of my dress and adjust my position. I feel uncomfortable.

"Not exactly," he responds slowly. "I got passed around a few foster homes. I thought one was going to stick but when the couple got divorced, they couldn't figure out what to do with me, I guess."

"So . . ."

"So, I just aged out, technically, when I turned eighteen, but at that point it didn't really matter because I had been at Lawrenceville since I was thirteen. I knew Davis by then, and, of course, Barbara"—here, he rolls his eyes with contempt—"so I felt kind of adopted? I was always there."

"How did you get into Lawrenceville?" I blurt out only to feel immediately chagrined by my lack of tact. "I'm sorry. I didn't mean it like that."

"No, it's fine," he says. "It's a fair question. I was pretty good at school, and I had a good guidance counselor at this totally shitty middle school I went to for sixth grade. He cared about me, I guess. He let me live with him for a while."

"Oh," I say.

"Nothing weird. He had a wife," he quickly clarifies, and I find this urgency odd, until I realize how little I know about what life must be like in the foster system, the regular concessions you must make for your own survival.

"Anyway," he continues. "He knew things were not good so, he helped me apply to, like, every boarding school in the country, hoping for, you know, a miracle. He knew I needed to get out of Louisiana."

Here, he gives me childlike shrug, and I can suddenly make out the ruins of a six-year-old's cheeks.

I am swamped with sadness.

"He died," he says, and his voice drifts away. "My guidance counselor. He died last year, but I didn't find out he was sick until it was too late."

"Oh, Harry," I say weakly.

"His name was Dylan."

He smiles and lowers his head.

"I had no idea," I say. "About any of this."

"That was my hope," he jokes lightly. "It's why I buy all the really nice blazers."

Here, he looks up at me. We smile at each other sadly.

"But to be all alone?" I continue, although I start to realize I am more than a little drunk. "As a little kid? I can't imagine."

I close my eyes and shake my head. I wave for another drink.

"Listen, I'm not telling you this to make you feel sorry for me for being poor or anything," he continues. "I *certainly* don't feel sorry for myself."

"No, I know," I mumble, but my face burns hot. I don't like talking about status or money, and these days, I rarely travel in circles where I am required to contemplate my own privilege, namely because I seem to have less than everyone else. I fumble for the pack of cigarettes that sits on the bar between us; I need something to do with my hands.

"I am saying this to you because I see a lot of similarities between us," he says, and I must frown at this comparison because he clears his throat to continue. "I just mean we are both outsiders, in a way, and you should think about creating your own narrative," he says.

"My narrative?" I raise my eyebrows.

"Yes," he says. "Listen, if I have learned one thing, it is you can decide who you want to be."

"Like fake it 'til you make it?" I offer cheerfully, even though something about this conversation feels sort of pathetic and evangelizing, like Harry is sharing with me something he read in a self-help book.

"Exactly," he says.

"What if I want to become a neuroscientist?" I quip. "Should I start wearing a lab coat?"

Harry frowns.

"I am trying to be serious here, Clo," he says with an irritated shake of his head. "Why don't you *ever* make that easy?"

This comment lands hard, like an intentional insult, but I say nothing in response. For starters, he just told me he's an orphan, so it feels inappropriate to be a total dick with some snarky response. Secondly, he's right: I don't make it easy. I don't like to talk about feelings—not mine, not anyone's—and especially not with someone new in my life. Frankly, I find nearly any kind of intimacy to be almost unbearable, even kissing on television still makes me squirm. On the other hand, I find I am desperate to stop twisting the dial on my life. I just want to land on a real friend, a person who comes through on my wavelength, clean and clear. And so, tonight, with great trepidation, in the dimmest of rooms on the most auspicious of nights, I allow myself to consider if that person might be Harry Wood.

"So what do you think?" he asks, recovering his smile. "Do you want to take over the world with me?"

"Harry, you know I am happy to be of service to you," I say lightly, but blood pounds uncomfortably along my hairline. I try to recall if I have ever been in a conversation that was so transactional, but I wonder if this kind of deal-making isn't the means by which everyone carves out a place for themselves in New York.

"Service to *ourselves*," he says.

"To us, then," I say.

"To us," he says, satisfied, and he raises his drink. "For whom failure is not an option."

We clink our glasses, and I take a sip. There is a part of me that wants to point out that, for me, failure *is* an option. I could always wash up back in the Philadelphia suburbs with only my pride worse for the wear, but I wonder—in the uppermost echelons of the world in which Harry and I now trespass—if this is a distinction without a difference. I do not belong to the world that I so desperately want to belong, and I still do not know if, one day, the tides will change and there will be a clean way into the channel for me. Harry seems to suggest that, for those willing to work for it, all things are possible, and despite a considerable amount of evidence to the contrary, I suddenly grasp how badly I want to believe him. I catch my reflection in the mirror behind the bar, and Harry meets my eyes. We drink our drinks. The jukebox is playing "The Devil Went Down to Georgia."

"You've lost weight," he says after a spell. "It's good."

"That's a pretty inappropriate thing to say to a lady, Harry," I respond lightly, but I am crushed because, clearly, Harry Wood views me as a fat person.

"Don't get me wrong," he clarifies. "You always look great."

"I lost like five pounds," I hear myself admit sheepishly.

"It makes a difference."

His comment, which we both know is not so much a compliment as it is a directive for continued compliance, makes me feel so incredibly stupid and shamed; it's like I was failing, but I didn't know it, and now, apparently, there is no longer room for that kind of failure.

I take a small sip of my drink.

Funny: It doesn't burn as savagely as the last one.

31

Since Davis's accident, I have become what you might call a "known quantity" around the office. As such, people say hello to me in the cafeteria, and I am no longer forced to grope around my handbag in a humiliating search for my work badge each morning. Instead, I am buzzed through the glass doors the moment I step off the elevator.

I am officially on the team.

You see, when I returned to the office after that long, terrible weekend in November, I was surprised to find my desk swarmed by concerned coworkers, all of whom wanted an update on Davis's condition. I was suddenly a mini celebrity, as macabre as it was, and I am not ashamed to tell you that I loved—and continue to love—the attention that accompanies being the local authority on the health and well-being of Davis Lawrence. It has opened the door to potential friendships and won me the light admiration of the senior staff. I have received a few casual invitations to join various groups for lunch or drinks, and even L.K. Smith, who is nearly impossible to crack, has taken to smiling at me (on occasion) when she passes me in the hallway.

I have also been given an increase, albeit temporary, in responsibility. The week following the accident, L.K. asked me to pick up some of the tasks left orphaned by Davis, which included assisting her boss, Kate Dent. Kate is well-known for being best friends with every model on earth and is, allegedly, a direct descendant of Ulysses S. Grant. She is also our fashion editorial director, which means she straddles both the fashion and features departments and is charged with covering things like designer profiles, industry news, and new product launches. Kate is rarely in the office. She spends most of her days at lunch or out on appointments to preview the new, usually top secret, items (shoes, clothes, jewelry) that will exclusively appear in our magazine in the coming months. Kate is tall and blonde with long, blunt bangs, and she has a much looser relationship with what constitutes personal and professional boundaries than Isobel. Translation: I run a lot of errands, some of which are totally legitimate and some, as you might imagine, are not even remotely legal from a workplace standpoint. To be honest, it's been a challenge, code-switching between two wildly different personalities, and while the increase in responsibility doesn't come with any additional money, I am not concerned. I figure that, with enough hard work, I might get a new title on the masthead, which, on its own, would be worth its weight in gold.

When I took on these new responsibilities, I promised myself a few things. After all, if Harry was correct, I had better get busy working on my personal brand. So, for starters, I would keep my desk tidy, which would be uncharacteristic, and, secondly, I was going to decorate my cubicle. So far, I have failed on both points. Despite my best efforts, my desk is always a vague mess. The organization of unrelated objects—pens, paper, mail, personal items—has never been my strong suit. To wit: Just the other day, I discovered a tampon, half wiggled out of its paper chrysalis, had fallen out of my bag. It was just lying on the floor behind my chair for anyone to see. Second, to decorate my little cubicle feels like putting an aesthetic stake in the ground and, as I haven't quite decided what my aesthetic is, I pretend to keep the walls bare in deference to Davis, whose own workstation has remained entirely untouched since the accident, like a shrine. A periwinkle Ralph Lauren blanket is folded neatly over the chair, and her hardbound desk calendar is still open to the first week in November.

This morning, I set down my bag and coffee tray. My voicemail light is blinking, and my desk is heaped with layouts and yesterday's newspapers. I lean over to start my computer and as it loads, my eyes scan the contents. I have six new emails, which is a lot, considering I left my post at 7:30 last night, but now that a handful of the PR girls have gotten Blackberries, they write at all hours. Sometimes, I see them outside parties, scribbling with a stylus, and I can't fathom what would compel someone to embarrass themselves in such a public fashion. After I deal with Isobel's emails, which I can read on my computer, I listen to her voicemail, and I am careful to copy down each message accurately and in my best handwriting before I lay them neatly across her desk.

Then, I start to listen to my own voicemail.

"Good morning, darling," a voice interrupts. It's Kate. She wears a floor-dusting black wool coat that I have never seen before, and that I am quite confident I will never see again.

Kate rarely wears the same thing twice.

I put down my phone.

"Good morning," I say, and I hand her a coffee.

She takes it with a grateful smile.

"So would you see if the film from yesterday is ready in the art department?" she asks. "It would be brilliant if you could get a jump on the captions."

Some notes: Kate is American, but she says things like "darling" and "rubbish" and "brilliant" with such astounding confidence that I not only allow it, but I start to wonder at what stage in my own career adapting affections might become permissible.

I roll the word *rubbish* around my mouth.

"Of course," I say. I push up from my chair.

I love having an official reason to visit the art department. It has more energy than the features department, but is also less chaotic and petrifying than the fashion hallways. Furthermore, this is the only quadrant in our office where the sartorial rules that firmly bind the rest of us are relaxed: Men can have visible tattoos and wear fitted black T-shirts. Women can rock asymmetrical haircuts, be lesbians, and get away with oversized pants and sneakers. Everyone smells creative, like spearmint gum, color printer toner, and cigarettes.

When I arrive, I see the graphic designer who works on Kate's pages is occupied by the beauty editor; they review a new layout on his computer screen in hushed tones. They move images around and adjust the headline.

Hoping to go unnoticed, I turn toward the long black table situated in the middle of the room. It is covered with large-format color printouts from a recent cover shoot, an expensive, logistical nightmare orchestrated in the middle of a desert in New Mexico, the details of which I remember from my obsessive reading of the editorial lineups. A few weeks before the shoot, the actress being featured came to the office with a small entourage to be fit for her wardrobe. While exciting, this is not an uncommon event. I regularly run into various celebrities, athletes, and models as they slowly wander our hallways, being escorted into a fitting or a meeting with our editor-in-chief. In fact, just last week, Kate called me to bring her notebook into the fashion closet, where I discovered a very famous, very blonde actress standing easily in her underwear. She was all smiles as she snapped through a rack of clothes, laughing as she smacked on a gob of pink gum.

I trail my fingertips along each photograph, each of which is so magnificent in its moodiness that I reckon it could have been shot on Mars. I notice some of the pictures are flapped with sticky notes or marked with grease pencil lines that indicate where the actress should be made "more narrow" in the waist or "less tired" under the eyes. At the far end of the table, two photo editors pass a loupe back and forth, and I watch with curiosity as they press the glass eye down on a contact sheet, over and over, and I strain to hear them chat quietly about what they see. While I would love to go on a real photo shoot, that honor is generally reserved for the girls who assist our big time fashion editors. On the days leading up to a shoot, I see them, two by two, in high heels with their faces set in consternation as they push black trunks down toward the mailroom, like they are readying humanity for the flood.

A couple days later, the trunks are followed by the fashion editors, sporting their smart travel valises and big sunglasses, all of whom are heading to places like Paris or Berlin or some island with an airport that has a notoriously short runway.

"What's up, Clo?" the graphic designer calls to me without looking over his shoulder. He is alone now, perched in his tall chair at his even taller desk, which is situated in front of an enormous computer monitor. I start in his direction when all the phones in the art department start to ring thanks to the quick fingers of the three assistants who work in the office of our editor-in-chief. They are calling the attendees of the next meeting, a feat which requires them to dial each number on a long list with the same frantic concentration required to win concert tickets on a regional radio show.

It is a truly humorless affair.

I still don't go to meetings because I am not important enough to go to meetings, but I watch everyone who *is* important pick up their phones only to slam the receiver back down on the cradle without uttering a word. Then they scoop up little notebooks and swap their shoes before they run toward the conference room.

I am not being hyperbolic here: They run.

Once they are gone, I lean next to the graphic designer, who I very much like, and he pulls up the photographs Kate requested. They are of a young, fashionable designer and they were shot in a sunny park in London that the magazine had to cordon off from the public for half a day. The designer looks beautiful, except when she smiles, which causes her to look a little horsey in the mouth.

"I'll bring down those teeth," the designer says both absently and entirely on cue because we all operate by very specific aesthetic principles, all of which we learned (or, in my case, *are still learning*) by observation. He takes a sip of his coffee and clicks open another image when I feel a hard tap on my back.

It's one of the three assistants. She has spindly legs and seems to struggle under the weight of her voluminous brocade skirt.

"They want you in the meeting," she says.

"What?"

"They want *you* in the meeting," she repeats.

I blanch.

"Now," she says sternly.

"Right." I nod. "Sorry."

I follow her down the hall, and when she slides open the door to the conference room, all eyes turn in my direction. Naturally, the only unoccupied chair sits on the far side of the long table, and as I start to lumber toward it, I fret over what to do about my posture. If I roll my shoulders back, my breasts will look too big, but if I hunch forward, I fear I will resemble an overgrown troll. Before I can resolve this issue, the crisp voice of L.K. Smith stops me in my tracks:

"Clo, do you know this piece about the architect in Newport?"

I do not know this piece about the architect in Newport.

"Of course," I say.

"We think it would be perfect for Davis Lawrence because she knows the family," L.K. continues. "But I honestly don't know her status. Do we think she would be up for something by the July issue?"

I say nothing immediately because I have suddenly realized our editor-in-chief—a woman with whom I have never been in the same room—is seated at the table. She folds her arms across her chest. She cocks her head to the side.

"Oh," I startle.

"Clo?" L.K. presses, and I discover with some alarm that I am still unable to speak. My eyes dart with desperation around the table, almost as if I am choking and I must locate the one person who can save me. Instead, I am confronted with the collectively fascinating faces of the magazine's big-time fashion, entertainment, and culture editors—all oft-photographed and legitimately famous in their own right—and they all look at me with eyes full of anxious encouragment. I feel like a young child they hope to coax off the diving board for the very first time.

I want to jump.

I want to make them proud.

Someone coughs. I take a small breath.

"I mean, she would *love* to do it," I say evenly. "But I *think* she has another surgery in a few weeks?"

As far as I know, Davis is *not* having another surgery in a few weeks, but I'm gambling that I have sufficiently covered myself with an intentionally ambiguous sentence construction. After all, I am standing in this room for the very first time and I refuse to let the reason be only because I am informing everyone that—*if they can just hold on a little longer*—Davis Lawrence will be coming back.

I need them to see me, if only for a moment.

"Fine," L.K. Smith responds briskly.

As she jots a note on the paper in front of her, I swear to God, you can hear the entire room exhale; apparently, the staff of our magazine was not keen on watching a gruesome sacrifice so early in the morning. Isobel nods nearly imperceptibly in my direction to indicate I should take a chair, and I curl my hands into fists to stem their shaking. As I sit down, I remember to cross my legs at the ankle, even though I worry it makes my thighs look fat. I blink. I lightly nod. I fold my hands. I realize that I have no idea how to both stand out *and* be completely invisible at the same time, but my sense is that is exactly what is required of all the women in this meeting.

And maybe, come to think of it, of all women in the world.

This thought feels very deep.

For the next ten minutes, the staff goes around the table to discuss their plans for the next three issues. There is very little debate, which I find surprising, and when the meeting is over, everyone files out of the conference room in silence, our faces arranged with a pleasant neutrality.

We know we are being watched.

We are always being watched.

As I pass through the door, one of the senior fashion editors—the coolest, prettiest one in my opinion—sidles up next to me. She has never spoken to me before, but today she squeezes my upper arm affectionately and whispers in my ear:

"Clo, honey," she says. "You really *are* a saint."

32

It is Fashion Week again, which occurs—at least as far as I can tell—with increasing frequency. There are the Fall and Spring shows, of course, and the Couture in Paris, but seasons like "pre-fall" and "resort"—once treated like unpleasant outer boroughs—have taken a rapidly escalating prominence on the collective schedule. Furthermore, the term *Fashion Week* is technically a misnomer. It's Fashion Month. The minute the last runway wraps in New York, everyone dashes to JFK to fly to the shows in London, then Milan, and finally Paris. This grueling routine has ostensibly emerged to accommodate the retailers, who are trying to feed the newly ravenous appetite of shoppers for whom dressing for basic seasonality (fall and spring) no longer cuts the ol' mustard. The impossible pace, however, has started to wear down all the pieces in the machine. Everyone—the designers, the models, the hair people, the journalists, the advertising executives—is exhausted. Not that anyone would dare complain. After all, it's not like there is a better job for those interested in fashion, and should you exhibit any sign of weakness, you are continuously reminded that there are plenty of people more than willing to pick up your ungrateful slack.

It's an old story, but it works.

Tonight, however, I am attending my very first fashion show. I poached the ticket from Davis's mail pile, which I continue to quietly parse through on a daily basis for my own use. I had to choose a night show since there was no plausible way I could go missing from the office during the day, and I figured Davis would be more than supportive of my choice to attend a fashion show in her place and, as such, there was really no reason to let the opportunity go to waste.

The show starts at 8 p.m., so I agree to meet Harry for a drink beforehand in the lobby of the Algonquin Hotel. When I push through the doors at the appointed hour, I see that Harry, as usual, has already arrived. From afar, he looks both expensive and relaxed, which is funny because Harry, while in possession of many noteworthy qualities, is neither of those things. In fact, the more I get to know him, the more I am astounded to discover that he is, quite possibly, the most neurotic person I have ever met. Everything stresses him out—subways, dogs off leashes, tricky paper-straw wrappers, packing a suitcase—to such a degree that I almost feel sorry for him. As I sit down at the table, he tries to peer nonchalantly at my outfit, like maybe my wardrobe could be another thing he could find a way to control. As I didn't have anything in my own closet that I felt was nice enough to wear (and I was still too embarrassed to ask for someone to call one in for me), I put on a nondescript black dress. My working plan was to leave my red coat on for the duration of the night.

"What are you wearing?" he asks finally.

"Don't worry," I said, pulling his drink over and taking a small sip. "I won't embarrass you, Harry."

"Hey," he said, putting his hands up in the air in a posture of surrender. "It's not *my* first fashion show."

"It's just a black dress," I say finally, and I slide my coat down from my shoulders so he can get a better look.

"It's so good," he says warmly, and, as he signals for the waiter to bring me a drink, I momentarily feel like a heel for questioning his motives until he continues: "But maybe just leave on the coat."

We finish our drinks quickly, and then set off on foot down Sixth Avenue. The wind is so strong that we don't say anything, we just keep our heads down and press forward, but, after only a block, my exposed skin starts to burn in the cold. After we skitter up the steps that lead into Bryant Park, Harry turns to look at me. He pushes a piece of hair behind my ear and places his hands squarely on my shoulders.

"You ready?"

"I'm ready."

"If I don't see you inside, let's meet here after the show?"

"If I get inside..." I reply with a nervous look over his shoulder to where the tents loom in the background.

"You'll get in," he says. "Just don't hesitate."

I nod, and then Harry turns around to walk into the tents alone, which I must try very hard not to take personally: After all, nobody wants to back a losing horse.

I straighten up and take a deep breath before I start to stride through the park in the direction of the largest tent. With every step, I endeavor to comport myself like an Olympic gymnast moments before the start of her make-or-break floor routine.

I have trained for this moment, I tell myself.

I will emerge a champion.

As I approach the check-in table, I hand my invitation to a woman with a shaved head wearing a headset. She looks down at it, and then she looks up at my face. I don't move, and after what feels like a dangerously long pause, she checks a clipboard and then writes a seat assignment on my ticket in ballpoint pen.

"Have a good show, Davis," she says, but she is no longer looking at me. Her hand is already outstretched to take the next ticket in line.

I pass through a large opening, and find myself in what looks to be the most glamorous refugee camp in the world. The tent is dimly lit and cavernous, and people are milling about between the seats. I watch a group of photographers crawl over some chairs and line up, shoulder to shoulder, to shoot the celebrities and editors seated in the front row.

As I pick through the folding chairs in search of my own seat, I try to mimic the ease that seems to radiate from the fashion people. I smile with drowsy disinterest, like I just swallowed a handful of Quaaludes in my car service, and I don't make direct eye contact with anyone. When I find my place, which is in the second row, I swiftly stash the overflowing metallic gift bag under my chair, where it will remain, wholly unmolested, for all of eternity. Davis once told me that you never, under *any* circumstances touch the gift bag during a fashion show. It's just another one of those unspoken rules by which we live and die at the magazine. When I look around, however, I spy a few unfamiliar women as they jam their greedy paws into the layers of white tissue paper to dig for the prize inside, and I am reminded we don't all take our cues from the same playbook. I realize Davis is right: It is disgraceful.

One of our senior fashion editors turns around from the front row and catches my eye. We both smile the superior smile of the righteous, but when her brow wrinkles, I start to panic. I look away quickly, my neck instantly hot. *What on earth was I thinking? Will she tell someone?* I hold my breath for a few seconds, surely caught out, but when nobody taps me on the shoulder to throw my bargain-basement ass into the street, I realize I can't keep gawking around the joint like a tourist.

I cross my legs at the ankle and let my knees list slightly to the left. Next, I rest both wrists on the top of my right kneecap, a motion that (I hope, anyway) squares my shoulders and narrows my waist. This posture permits me to display the enormous cocktail ring I borrowed this morning from the accessories department. You see, once you rise out of the lowest rank—you are allowed (although no one explicitly tells you this) to borrow little things like jewelry. It's a simple process: You parse through hundreds of glittering options, which are laid into velvet trays, and once you find something you like, a fashion assistant will snap a Polaroid of you holding your chosen piece. She will write your name on the picture with a black Sharpie and tack it on a bulletin board. This photographic evidence is to ensure that the borrower—at least one day and in theory—will return it, but I have learned plenty of things "fall off the truck" and nobody ever seems to mind.

Time seems to drag on—ten minutes becomes forty-five minutes—and I continue to arrange my face with what I hope telegraphs a stately confidence. As Harry and I don't work for the same publication, we are not seated in the same section, but I can see him on the other side of the runway. He's in a fourth-row seat because only print magazine editors and proper celebrities are seated in the front rows. He listens intently to the woman next to him, laughing occasionally, and from my vantage point, he looks wonderfully bemused, but I am not surprised. For a total type-A misanthrope, Harry Wood has really mastered the art of appearing as if he is having the time of his life.

After ten more minutes of waiting, a convocation of sharp-faced assistants appear, all clad in black. They rip up the white butcher block paper that has been covering the pristine surface of the runway before they vanish into a sudden and total darkness. There is an errant cough and a distant crinkle, but otherwise, the room has fallen into an electric, anticipatory silence. There is a swell of loud music, and the lights come up, and I don't care who you are or how many times you have been pinched into a folding chair or crammed along a wooden bench at a proper fashion show, this, I decide, must be the most exhilarating moment in all the world. I straighten up just as the first model emerges, silhouetted in the illuminated doorway. She starts down the runway in a jilted march. Her legs are preadolescent—her thighs as wide as her calves—and with each heavy step, her feet seem to float in front of her body. She wears a calf-length silk dress twisted at the side. It hangs ripe with possibility on her bony frame, like an unfurnished house, and I feel a million light bulbs go off in my brain. As more models tromp down the runway—shoulders rolled back, fists tightly balled, faces drawn as stern as a schoolmarm—the crowd ruffles and cranes for a better look. The front-row editors jot on the pile of papers and notebooks balanced on their laps; their heads bop up and down, so they don't miss a single look. I don't know if it's the soundtrack or the clothes or the general specialness of this moment, but when the designer comes out at the end of the show and offers a small, grateful wave, I feel dangerously overcome with emotion. As a tear rolls down my face, I realize that I already ache for the day I am cast out and banished, quite rightly, from this beautiful world.

The entire show lasts fewer than five minutes, and when the lights come back on, the hurry and chatter of a more banal reality floods back into my body. People are sliding into coats, and a long line has started to file toward the doors.

"Clo?"

A slightly older girl who used to work at my office is sitting behind me in the third row, and, as she leans forward with a smile, I wonder if she can see I had been crying. After a little small talk, a friend calls to her, and she squeezes my hand and excuses herself. I turn in my seat to see Harry making his way in my direction. His eyes glint with pride.

"Well done," he says, and he leans over and kisses me with such enthusiasm you'd think I had been lost at sea. He extends his hand and, as I rise, I notice a few people from my office look at me with impressed curiosity. Now, while I suspect Harry's public display of ardor to be wholly insincere, it pleases me, nonetheless, to feel a little bit as desirable as Davis Lawrence. As he leads me through the crowd, he stops to talk to people, always sure to introduce me, and then we dash into the freezing night toward the car service I booked for our evening.

We are going to the after-party.

The traffic is impossible around Bryant Park and, as we inch across town, I start to worry when Harry doesn't say much. He just taps his fingers on his knee and looks out the window. These long silences—which I have learned are not infrequent with Harry—never cease to make me feel anxious, like I have stepped out of line. To fill the time, I reapply my lipstick and run my fingers repeatedly through my hair. I find it bizarre that neither of us says a single word about the show except that we both thought it was "good." Despite knowing nothing about fashion in a technical or historical sense, I feel like I have a lot to say, but if New York has taught me one thing, it is this: You never want to have the wrong opinion. Not even among your best friends.

"Why were you talking to Camille Edwards?" he asks finally.

"What?"

"Camille Edwards. Why were you talking to her?"

"I haven't seen her since she took that other job," I say. "She said she's freelance now."

"She didn't leave, Clo," he says. "She was fired."

"What? Why?"

"I heard she was a bad fit," he says evenly. "Which, clearly, she is. She looked like a tranny tonight."

"Wow," I say.

"You shouldn't waste your time on her," he says. "Especially with so many other people watching you."

"I talked to her for one minute," I protest.

"You're an editor, Clo."

"So?" I ask.

He turns to look at me.

"So?" he says, and his voice is tinged with irritation. "Learn to edit."

The party is at the Gramercy Park Hotel and when we pull up, I see a handful of photographers and curious onlookers have gathered on the sidewalk. Harry gets out of the car first and opens my door, which he only does when there is an audience. We are greeted by a young blonde girl holding a clipboard. She wears huge earmuffs and is bouncing in the cold, her teeth chattering. She crosses us off her list, and hands us over to a burly security guard who sports a sleek black suit and an earpiece. We act like this is normal, like bodyguards are part of our daily routine, and once safely inside the party, we head straight to the bar. We both settle on a glass of champagne (although Harry comments with an eye roll that it's prosecco) and we both drink it quickly before requesting a second glass, this one for mingling.

We make a quick round, saying hello to people and kissing a few cheeks, and while Harry is at turns smooth and flattering and funny, I can literally think of nothing to talk about with these people. We have no shared history, nor inside jokes, so I make a few scintillating comments about the weather before Harry takes my elbow and leads me to a couch in the corner.

Harry always finds a corner.

He says you need to make people come to you.

Harry says a lot of things.

"Look at us," Harry says, and he clinks his glass against mine with a wink.

"Look at us," I say.

33

A few weeks later, I pop into Isobel Fincher's office to drop off a proof of one of her pages.

"I am heading uptown to check on Davis," I say. "Do you need anything before I go?"

"That's nice of you," Isobel says distractedly as she pushes her heavy body out of the chair with both arms. "I'm fine. Just heading to the theater."

My instinct is to assist her, but I know better: She is seven months pregnant with her first child, a little detail she has, thus far, refused to let slow her down. This is a standard practice at the magazine where women are expected to have children (to *not* have children makes you look either infertile, lazy, or physically undesirable and, in these parts, those qualities are not the mark of a high achiever), but these same women are also expected to behave as if they *don't* have children. I have heard about this phenomenon many times before, but it's a different thing to see it in practice; the "working mother" is a sisterhood like no other. And while there is the report of the occasional closed-door weeping, most of the mothers in my office behave quite stoically about their situation. They do not complain namely, I figure, because they don't want to call attention to the obvious professional handicap that is a baby. Instead, they employ multiple nannies and housekeepers, which permits them to continue to travel internationally and go out nearly every night of the week for mandatory work events. As a proxy, they get photographs emailed to them by their assorted, reliably Tibetan, childcare providers—child on swings, child making cookies, child in bathtub—and, as a childless woman with exactly zero experience on the matter, I must work very hard not to label this as poor mothering. Mind you, I never have similar thoughts about the men, least of all my own father, who, I am quite certain, despite being a perfectly nice person, never put me to bed as a child.

But, like everyone else, I always judge the women more harshly.

Today, Isobel wears a starched, oversized white shirt over skinny black pants, and her face, which is slightly rounder now, looks to have been brushed with glitter. After she gets to her feet, she pulls out an antique compact, and I watch as she applies lipstick from a gold tube.

"I don't know how you do it," I say. I bend over to pick up her black tote bag, and I hand it to her. "I can barely get myself together every morning."

"When the time comes," she says, "you just do it."

"Words to live by," I say.

After I deposit Isobel safely into her waiting car, I hear my cell phone ring. I bite the top of my mitten and pull it off with my teeth. I rifle through my bag. I answer the phone.

"Hello, Harry," I say, but my voice is muffled. I take the mitten out of my mouth.

"Hello," he rejoins. "I didn't think I'd catch you."

"You almost didn't," I say as I scan the street for my own car, which I find idling down the block. "I am late for a dinner."

"With whom?"

"Davis and Barbara."

"Ah," he says. "You really *are* a glutton for punishment."

"I don't know," I say. I get into the car, and pull the door closed. "I feel bad for her. I feel bad for both of them."

"Well, then I won't keep you," Harry says. "I just wanted to confirm you can still join me at the Cinema Society screening tomorrow?"

"Confirmed," I say, and an excited smile pulls upon my lips. There is something about Harry's attention that makes me feel giddy.

"Excellent," he says before adding: "Say hello to our broken little bird for me, will you?"

"I will," I say.

* * *

In the days and weeks that followed Davis's accident, the police questioned everyone who attended the engagement party. While a standard practice, an investigation was against Barbara's wishes. She did not want the incident to appear in the papers. She didn't want people to talk. She was raised to find it unseemly, not to mention a little low-class, to have her family spoken about in such a public fashion. "Birth and death," she would say, shaking her head. "My grandmother allowed for only birth and death, and I cannot imagine *what* she would think of *all of this*." As such, she spent a good deal of time speaking in terse, whispered tones on the phone with her publicists and managers. She called in favors to friendly reporters, and she threatened unfriendly ones (through her managers, of course) with lawsuits—or worse. Through her family connections, Barbara Lawrence knew many of the old men who financed the newspapers and, while the threats mostly worked, the story of Davis Lawrence's mysterious accident still managed to find a way into the world: The details were handed, person to person, like a hot baton.

We all had our own story. Grant told the police he thought Davis had left with Harry. Harry said he lost her during their search somewhere near Delancey Street, and when he returned to the party, he assumed she had found me, and we had gone home together. He said he stayed for another drink, which several guests could corroborate. Barbara had taken a car home early and was asleep in her apartment a little after midnight, which Marta and Hatch could confirm. Other guests simply hadn't noticed their hostess had disappeared, and those who *did* notice were far too drunk to care. This *is* New York City, after all. People vanish from bars and parties with great predictability, only to turn up in the light of the following day. They leave to buy drugs. They leave to have sex. They drunkenly slip out a side door when they think no one is watching and flag a cab home. There is no buddy system in New York, but, strangely, I've never been fearful that anything properly bad could ever happen to me.

Not until now, anyway.

As for my own interview, I reported that I left around one o'clock in the morning, which was true, and walked home alone over the Manhattan Bridge, which was also true. When asked, I conceded that I was upset when I left (as to be expected, there had been more than a few witnesses to my coat-throwing theatrics) but I claimed to be unaware that Davis and Harry had gone in search for me. I am not sure why I lied about that detail, but I am never entirely sure why I lie about anything.

At the end of the investigation, the police and medical examiners were unable to identify a suspect nor pinpoint the exact cause of Davis's injuries, which, along with a moderate case of hypothermia, included a broken nose and wrist as well as an ankle that had fractured in three places. The best they could say is that her injuries were consistent with falling from an unknown height, most likely the scaffolding she was found lying under.

"My daughter would never *climb on scaffolding*," Barbara had said. "It's the most ridiculous thing I've ever heard."

As for me, I kept waiting for the guilt to set in—after all, I suspect that if it hadn't been for my drunken outburst, none of this would have happened—but, instead, I only felt relief that Davis still seems to remember nothing specific from a large portion of the night, and, as such, my hard work befriending her over the past few years hadn't been in vain. I was still in the game.

Davis stayed in the hospital for over a week before she was transferred to a rehabilitation facility, and while her visitors had been a near constant in the early days, they had begun to thin out by the time she was moved back into her mother's apartment in early December. For those first couple weeks, she slept in a rental hospital bed that Barbara had erected in the living room, and while I remained a dedicated visitor, I could never make out if she was actually happy to see me. She spent most of our time together sleeping or staring out window. She quickly abandoned the novels and magazines I toted over from the office for her reading enjoyment, choosing instead to keep television on at all hours without watching it. At one point, I watched her stub a cigarette into an uneaten plate of fried eggs, and then promptly light up another one. Here is the thing: Despite the circumstances, Davis didn't strike me as entirely unhappy. Quite the opposite. I got the definite sense she was enjoying the solitude that accompanies a proper, clinical depression. She didn't take a single phone call, always sending a dismayed Marta shuffling back the kitchen with the cordless phone in her hand. It was almost as if she had long wished to sink into nothingness, and thanks to the accident, she finally had the cover.

For my part, sitting dutifully by her bedside made me feel important for the first time in a long while.

As part of her rehabilitation, Davis was given a litany of medications, exercises, and general directives from her doctors, the most troubling of which was that she needed to stop drinking, namely because alcohol could interact negatively with her painkillers. Naturally, Davis smiled and nodded and promised her doctors to be a good girl, but once resettled in the Lawrence apartment, she flatly refused to follow any orders. She was like a petulant teenager. She didn't do her exercises. She threw out her newly prescribed antidepressant, which Barbara concurred was the right decision (or, as she so delicately put it, "those things make you fat"), and, despite her doctor's orders, cocktails in the Lawrence apartment seem—to me, at least—to be as plentiful as ever.

"I hardly think a glass of wine will hurt her, do you?" Barbara asked rhetorically one evening as she uncorked a new bottle, before adding in a conspiratorial whisper: "I mean, *she's already in a wheelchair.*"

So, along with managing the regular liquor store deliveries, all of which come up the back elevator with Hatch, Marta has been further instructed to keep short vases of fresh cigarettes on the coffee table and to ensure two large bouquets of peonies—pink only—are delivered every Monday. The linens on the guest room bed are changed twice a week, slept in or not, and we only eat with the real sterling silver, which Marta then must soak overnight in a series of white plastic bins that line the kitchen counter.

I am learning Barbara Lawrence likes things done a certain way.

And, frankly, I find it all to be wonderfully civilized.

34

Twenty minutes after I hang up with Harry, my car pulls up in front of the Lawrence apartment. I see Hatch rocking on the curb with an unlit cigarette in his mouth. When he sees me, he tucks it behind his ear and opens my door with great gallantry.

"Good evening, Miss Harmon," he says, with a comic bow of his head. "You are late! We must get you up to dinner! We can't disappoint the ladies of the house!"

I laugh. He laughs. I like to think Hatch is my people.

"Thank you, Hatch," I say as take his gloved hand. "And you know you may call me Clo, right?"

"I do, ma'am," he says with a little wink.

Up close, Hatch has the ruddy countenance of someone who went at life very hard in his younger days, probably fueled by some visions of grandeur or, at the very least, invincibility. He is tall and lanky with a full head of graying hair, but he has a rough, gently pockmarked face that lacks volume, like a deflated basketball. And while he generally looks tired, I find there is almost a relief to it, like he has landed at his final destination, which could have been much worse, and now he just wants to hang onto it, by any means necessary.

"Did Davis take a walk today?" I inquire as we walk through the lobby.

"I am sorry to report that she did *not*," Hatch replies with *just* the right amount of solicitousness. I respond with a grave nod.

"Did anyone else visit?"

Hatch shakes his head and deposits me in the elevator. He leans inside to press the button for the sixth floor. I have learned from observation that women of a certain class never push a button themselves. Over the past year, I trained myself to stay motionless in all elevators, and, as odd as it sounds, I welcome the rigor. As the doors start to close between us, Hatch tips his hat in my direction and smiles:

"You really *are* a saint, you know," he says softly. "She's lucky to have you."

As the carriage ascends, I turn to look at myself in the mirrored wall. I have not cut my hair since I started at the magazine. This is mostly a failed attempt to replicate the sexy insouciance of Davis's feminine, wavy hair, but I lack her thickness, and my ends don't curl under in the same way. That said, I cannot bring myself to change it, even though it has begun to surrender near death on my shoulders. Not yet anyway. I keep thinking that, if I give it one more day, it will start to perform as expected. Next, I move my lips and gesticulate as if I am responding, with extreme thoughtfulness, to a challenging interview question. I usually engage in this kind of playacting when I am alone, a performative imagining of my future success in a faraway time when people care about what I have to say on some profoundly intellectual topic. However, when the doors ding open on the sixth floor, I quickly revert to regular old Clo Harmon: A friend to many and threat to none. I pull my hair back in a rubber band, and rub the red, workday lipstick off my mouth with the back of my hand. I look at myself one last time, and then I walk down the short hallway and let myself into the apartment.

I have my own key now.

Barbara gave it to me the week following the accident, a small sterling silver Tiffany & Co. heart with Davis's name engraved on the back.

From the entryway, I hear voices rise and fall, but I cannot make out how many voices, nor if they are happy voices or sad voices. To be honest, it's a mixed bag around here most days. I slip off my coat and shoes and as I start down the hallway that leads to the kitchen, I run into Dorothy. Dorothy is one of Davis's physical therapists and tonight, she wears green scrubs and limps along under the weight of the folding table she has expertly wedged underneath her chiseled arm. She offers me a fist bump with her free hand.

"How's it going, Dorothy?" I ask.

"Oh, it's *going*. It's *going*," she says, and her deadpan delivery indicates that it is most definitely *not* going.

Davis has not been a very good patient.

Of all the therapists that cycle in Davis's orbit, Dorothy is my personal favorite. In a world that has heretofore only accommodated Davis Lawrence, Dorothy has zero qualms about giving her an almost comical amount of shit for being lazy about her exercises, which she equates—out loud, no less—with Davis being lazy about her life.

"Where is your fight, girl?" she will bark like a basketball coach while Davis struggles with a set of dumbbells or an elastic band. "You know how many people I work with who would kill to have *your* problems?"

As you can imagine, Davis despises Dorothy.

Davis prefers to be coddled. Davis likes her path swept clear.

I bid Dorothy a good night, and round into the kitchen, where I find Barbara and Davis tucked miserably into the corner banquette. They look up in unison with a weariness that makes me prickle with unease: Am I really *that* late? I glance up at the wall clock: It is 7:25. Their white dinner plates, which hold dainty portions of cold chicken breast and limp asparagus spears, look wholly untouched. I can hear a rattling around in the butler's pantry, so I assume the cook Betsy is on the premises. When Barbara sees me, she sighs with disapproval and presses a barely smoked cigarette into an ashtray from the Sunset Tower Hotel. For her part, Davis holds up a half-full wineglass to toast me:

"How was your day, dear?" she jokes, but her words run together.

"It was fine," I say. "Busy."

Davis takes a sip of her wine. She looks particularly haggard tonight in the harsh kitchen lighting, like when you spot a famous actress buying bananas at a Midtown bodega. Her minty eyes are pink, almost as if she has been crying, and she, too, is long overdue for a haircut. Her dry ends swell like overworked tufts of steel wool, and I can't fathom why Barbara hasn't taken her to the salon where her own hair is so meticulously managed. I take a step toward the table, which prompts Davis to lean forward and shove aside her metal walker with a clatter. She slides over on the banquette and pats the cushion next to her. I settle in and, to lighten the mood, which I see as the main part of my job, I turn to her theatrically:

"Honey, if you insist on doing the whole 'kooky recluse' thing, you really need to invest in a better wardrobe," I say, and I point to her plaid pajama pants.

Davis laughs, which pleases me. I am still the funny friend.

Barbara, however, makes it clear she finds nothing amusing whatsoever in our little exchange. I watch her jam a small fork (Barbara only eats with what I now know are "oyster forks," even at restaurants) into a cube of white chicken, and I can almost feel the steam radiating off her body. She doesn't look directly at me, but I get the sense that she intends to remain angry with me until I offer a proper apology for my tardiness.

"I am *so sorry* I am late," I say.

"Mmm," Barbara murmurs as she chews. She inspects one of her red fingernails.

"Really," I say. "I apologize."

Finally, she looks at me.

"Well, you're here now, I suppose," she says. "Would you like a drink?"

"Sure, but I'll get it," I say with an easy wave of my hand. I don't want to put Barbara out any more than she has *clearly* already been put out by me this evening. "But really, it was a *crazy* day."

"Work," Davis says dryly, and she pours herself some more wine.

"Work," I concur. "We are shipping."

I pull a glass down from a cabinet and settle back next to Davis. I start to pour from the open bottle that sits on the table, but it is practically empty. I barely get a splash, but no matter: I sip gamely on the warm inch.

Surely, this is all I deserve.

"Davis sent Dorothy home again," Barbara informs me.

I say nothing.

"Davis sent Dorothy home again because, *apparently*, Davis is not interested in getting better," Barbara continues.

"Mother," Davis says wearily. "I just didn't feel like it tonight. I'm tired."

"I understand that, Davis," her mother responds evenly. "I really do. I'm tired, too. *Trust me.* But the doctor was extremely clear that if you don't do the work, you won't heal properly."

"Maybe tomorrow," Davis mumbles.

"Maybe tomorrow," her mother mimics.

Here, Barbara looks at me with reproach, as if Davis's repeated recalcitrance is my fault, but this is not new: It seems I am always guilty of some dereliction of duty.

In the days and weeks following the accident, and without discussing my mandate explicitly, nor the expected results, Barbara enlisted my help with Davis. Apparently, she thought my near constant presence would encourage her daughter to take some baby steps toward normalcy, but Davis, thus far, has been wholly resistant to this idea. Honestly, it's almost poetic. While she has been given clearance to resume some of her daily activities, Davis prefers to spend entire days just wandering around the apartment, listening to old music on her mother's record player with a clattering drink in her hand. On the rare occasions she does leave the apartment, it is only to take a short pass in front of the building with the new puppy her mother bought to cheer her up at Christmas. He is a Norfolk terrier, and he was flown in on a private jet from a breeder somewhere in Michigan. Davis named him Captain and when Marta isn't around to take him on his regular walks, he just wets himself on a revolting series of white pads that line the parquet floors.

On some nights, after Davis has a few too many drinks at dinner, she will stumble into her room and plead for me to get in bed with her.

Tonight is one of those nights.

"Lay with me?" she asks. Her voice is childish and whiny. "Please?"

"Davis, you need sleep," I respond with motherly authority.

I help her climb into bed and arrange the silken covers under her chin. I flip off the lamp on her nightstand.

"But I want you to lay with me," she mews, only louder and more petulant now, and I know from months of experience that the only way to quiet her is to comply.

"Of course," I concede. "But just for a minute."

"Just for a minute," she repeats with grave seriousness.

I am still dressed in my work clothes, but I slide easily between the stiff sheets. Davis lays on her back and stares up at the ceiling with her arms folded behind her head, like a ponderous preteen. I roll sideways so I can rest my arm across her warm stomach, and, for a few minutes, I luxuriate in the soothing sensation of her breath as it rises and falls. Her hair smells like cigarettes and her mother's perfume.

Finally, she speaks:

"Tell me a story?"

"Ahh," I say. "A story."

Davis always wants a story. Sometimes she's just digging for news from the office, which is never in short supply, or a play-by-play of an especially outlandish event. I always tell her the funny, embarrassing things that happen to me at work, which she *loves*, and I continuously stress that I am basically a lost cause without her. Occasionally, she will ask me, with some sarcasm, why she so rarely gets a visit from Harry Wood.

"Is his website going *that* spectacularly well?" she asks tonight with a dismissive laugh, but I don't answer immediately because, to be honest, I don't have any idea if Harry's website is a success. Frankly, I am not clear as to what metric a website might be measured, nor do I have any idea how one makes any money. What I *do* know is that Harry has secured a few small businesses to advertise, which he regarded as good news, but I also know he is desperate to get more people to read it.

In the long silence, Davis turns her head to look at me.

"What?" she asks, her eyes searching my face. "Is that it? He's too good for us now?"

"Seems so," I reply with a half shrug.

As I have no interest in sharing the affection of Davis Lawrence with Harry, I generally do nothing to discourage what I perceive to be a rapidly widening chasm between them. Then, I add a little white lie for good measure: "I barely hear from him, either."

This seems to satisfy her.

On the face of it, I don't apprise Davis of any new developments in my life or Harry's life because I don't want to upset her. I mean, nobody wants to learn that life is speeding along just fine without them. However, what is far closer to the truth is that I don't want to poke around too much in her ashes, lest I unearth any smoldering embers. If Davis returned to work, I worry I would lose my status. I would lose my fragile, developing friendships and the general sense of opportunity her absence has provided me. *No,* I think. I have come too far, and I have worked too hard since the accident to be so quickly displaced. I don't need much, I reason. Just a little more time for things to settle, a few more months to cement my position.

So I stroke her hair. I tell her to roll over and hike up her nightgown so I can tickle her bare back. I start my fingers at her neck, and I let them venture to the lowest curve of her lower back. I linger where her breasts swell out along her sides.

"Nothing is the same without you," I whisper.

It's not a lie. Nothing is the same without her.

For me, it's better.

With my arm wrapped around Davis, I briefly fall asleep. It's that deep yet queerly shallow slumber to which it feels magnificent to surrender, even as you simultaneously attempt to claw your way back to consciousness. When I finally emerge, thirsty and disoriented, Davis is passed out cold next to me. I lean close to her face. Her breathing is labored, but it smells like nothing.

I roll over and look up at the ceiling.

I really want to go home.

Gingerly, I slide out of the bed, and tiptoe across the soft carpet toward the door. When I step into the overlit hallway, Barbara is just *standing* there. She's clearly been eavesdropping in some capacity, and I place my finger to my lips to indicate that we should be quiet. She nods and I follow her into the kitchen, where she settles back into the banquette. She lights a cigarette and places her chin on the fat of her upturned palm. As I watch the white cigarette smoke curl slowly past her ear, I get the definite sense that she is posing for an imaginary photographer. This is not a surprise: Barbara Lawrence is always waiting to be immortalized.

"So?" She leads me. "How does she seem to you today?"

"I think she's doing much better," I say cautiously. "She was asking a lot of questions about work."

"Like she's ready to go back?" Barbara asks. She arches one eyebrow, and I move my head side to side slightly like I am considering this question seriously.

"I don't think *quite yet*," I say finally, which I suspect is the correct answer. "But we are getting there."

"Good," she responds. "I don't think we should encourage her too quickly. Do you?"

"Definitely not," I say.

"And Grant?" she asks.

"Nothing about Grant," I reply honestly.

"Good," Barbara says. "It's better that way."

A few weeks after the accident, Barbara informed me that Grant had broken off the engagement. She pleaded with me not to bring it up because she was petrified it would trigger Davis's already unpredictable and fragile state. To say I was shocked by the news is an understatement: Grant had been nothing but dutiful in his caretaking of Davis. He visited the hospital and, later, the rehabilitation facility nearly every day, and he never arrived without an armload of flowers and magazines. He was the one who took charge of the nuts and bolts of Davis's recovery with her doctors while Barbara focused on the softer side of things, which included smuggling little bottles of wine past the nurse's station in her handbag. Although careful not to say it explicitly, Grant seemed to operate under the impression that Barbara was actively hindering her own daughter's recovery. In fact, he was so certain of this malfeasance he tipped the doctors off to Barbara's contraband. This, of course, led to Barbara receiving a most unwelcome lecture from the medical team, which did nothing to improve her relationship with Grant.

When the time came for Davis to leave the rehabilitation facility, Grant arranged for her to move into his apartment, a move that Davis not only approved, but had advocated for with great ferocity behind closed doors. This, of course, led to a horrible row with Barbara, who insisted her daughter be cared for at home *by her mother*. In the end, Barbara won the argument—mostly due to Davis's complete, near childlike, silence on the matter when confronted—and Grant, I surmised, finally understood that he would never be the primary person in his future wife's life. As for Davis, she still wears her engagement ring. It hangs loosely on her thinning finger, and she habitually spins it with her thumb in what I suspect to be a ritual of mourning. On the rare occasions she takes it off, I will sneak it up my own ring finger. I will look in the mirror and pretend I am talking to someone, desperate to confirm this version of myself exists somewhere in a future I cannot yet see.

Barbara peppers me with a few more questions about Davis, and once she feels she has sufficiently covered off on her daughter's well-being, she switches back to her favorite topic: Barbara. She pulls out her *diary*, which I quickly learned is the upper-class word for *calendar*. Barbara's *diary* is a monogrammed, red-leather book from Smython; and it is rarely more than a foot away from her person. This gesture indicates she is ready to discuss her social schedule for the days ahead with me.

Remember: *Not doing is death.*

"What does next week look like?" she asks. She holds a black pen. "There are a few things I want you to attend with me."

During Davis's early recovery, I was asked to attend an art opening with Barbara. She had already promised the artist she would make an appearance, and Davis was more than happy to have her mother out of the apartment for a few hours. The event went well enough—mostly due to the fact I am an excellent wallflower—but it led to Barbara's expectation that I would make myself available to escort her to events several nights a week. I quickly came to understand my role was to accept her invitations in a shocked and delighted fashion, but this has been easy enough because I am, in fact, delighted. Over the past few months, I have been fortunate enough to attend two opening nights on Broadway, a movie screening and dinner (with the cast!) at the Tribeca Grand Hotel, and a big, glitzy gala for Parkinson's disease at Cipriani where I got a gift bag full of Frédéric Fekkai shampoo and that super expensive Elizabeth Arden night serum. When I attend these events, I am dressed by Barbara's stylist, who rolls a rack of options into the apartment, and I am lent a bag and earrings from Barbara's truly insane accessory collection. A trio of women come to do our hair, nails, and make-up, and as I sit on one of the kitchen stools having false eyelashes applied, it occurs to me that I am only one of the hundreds of women for whom this is the only way to get ready for a party in New York.

What's there not to like?

Tonight however, as Barbara goes down her list, I find myself wondering if she had been this businesslike in her interactions with Davis. You see, prior to the accident, Davis would accompany her mother everywhere, which is how I knew who Davis Lawrence was before I had even set foot in a magazine office. She was already a celebrity of sorts, if only for being the daughter of a legitimate star. When she was a young child, her mother would dress her up like a doll, all smocking and pinafores and oversized bows, and then parade her around red carpets and other industry events. At the time, flipping through magazines in my pink bedroom, it all seemed so charming, but from my adult vantage point, I realize it must have been a clear calculation on Barbara's part. She understood nobody could resist the narrative of a working woman who was *also* the perfect mother—and Davis seemed to accept her role with, if not grace, graceful resignation. Even as a little girl, she played the part very well, but now that I actually *know* Davis, I don't think it was an intuitive skill. Davis wasn't *born* this way. She was bred by her mother, who had been bred by her own society mother before her, to excel at the game of exceeding other people's expectations. In public, Davis was forced to shelve her more introverted and unpredictable inclinations; she was to present as the ideal accessory: interesting without being overbearing. You see, the Lawrences come from a long line of old New York money and clout; Barbara's great-grandfather had been involved in the shipping industry in some capacity and, along with his vast fortune came an obligation to create and protect the family's first-class reputation. By the time I met Davis, her performances were nothing short of masterful. She was quiet, appropriate, and delighted. She had a way of smiling at people with grateful relief, like you—and only you—could save her from a roomful of otherwise dull people.

The problem was that Davis couldn't remain Barbara's dutiful, chubby-cheeked child forever. She grew older and more beautiful, and in her later teens, she started to eclipse her mother, whose own star was, most definitely, on the decline. While Barbara had never been a beauty, per se, the passage of time had not been kind to her appearance, although not barbarically so. According to Davis, her mother had her "eyes done" a few years ago, but the work seems reluctant to settle, giving her a vaguely alarmed look. And while she doesn't have wrinkles, her face has started to lack sharpness, her cheeks have grown heavy, like raw chicken cutlets, and her jawline has begun to soften into her neck.

At a certain, uncomfortable point, right around her daughter's nineteenth birthday, fashion designers suddenly wanted to dress Davis in their clothes, and the photographers, in turn, would clamor for a picture of her on the red carpet. It's not hard to see the appeal. Over the years, her braces had been removed, the acne had passed, and she sprouted to a lithe five foot eight inches tall, which was a full six inches taller than her mother.

Invariably, some junior publicist would usher Barbara to the side of a red carpet, entirely unaware of who she was, nor her former place in the celebrity ecosystem, to give the photographers a clear shot of Davis alone. Barbara would be forced to stand with a false smile pasted across her face, laying in furious wait until the flashes that washed over her daughter subsided. Once reunited, Barbara was well-known to show her daughter little mercy. I've heard rumors about Barbara berating Davis under her breath within earshot of reporters, all of whom, thus far, have been kind enough not to write about this unfortunate discord in their columns. For a while, Davis found a solution: When reporters would jam tape recorders in her face for a quote, she would offer up at least one fawning observation about her mother and say very little about herself.

"What do you want her to say?" Barbara would often joke, as she led her daughter away from the panting fray. "She's just a college sophomore!"

By the time Davis graduated from Princeton, however, the media, in general, had become a bit harder to control. The newspapers and magazine editors started to reach out to Barbara's agent to request interviews with Davis (about everything from her wardrobe choices to the particulars of her diet), but by this point, Davis had learned her lesson: She would only provide access if her mother was included in the story. From my vantage point, Davis felt a responsibility to her mother's happiness that was entirely foreign to me. It has been my long-held belief that my own mother was put on this earth solely to drive me places and give me money. It never crossed my mind that she might have had her own dreams and aspirations, let alone a history that did not include me, but I always thought that was normal. So, while Davis's nervous solicitousness toward Barbara could make me feel a little guilty at times, I mostly just found it peculiar. Mothers are not supposed to be jealous of their own daughters, but that did not stop Barbara from dishing out a myriad of side comments and complaints about Davis's failings to which I was often—in the months after the accident anyway—the uncomfortable, yet strangely thrilled, recipient. I liked being trusted by Barbara, although it never occurred to me until much later that these tantalizing offerings might be a test.

Barbara snaps her book closed and takes off her reading glasses.

"Why don't you stay in the guest room tonight," she says. Her tone indicates it has already been decided that I will, indeed, sleep in the guest room tonight.

"Oh, I wish I could, but I didn't pack any clothes for work tomorrow," I say, which I hope sounds convincing. I am homesick for my own little bed back in Brooklyn.

"I'm sure I can find you *something*," she sighs.

She slides off the bench and beckons me to her bedroom. I trudge behind her, only to watch her disappear inside the walk-in closet. I hear soft rattling, and she emerges carrying a few dresses. She tosses them on her impeccably made pink sateen bedspread. Before I can say anything, she trots out of the room, ostensibly to peruse the other closet, which is in a separate room, and half the size of my apartment. As I wait, I count the pillows on Barbara's enormous bed. There are thirteen, all various shades of pink and all different sizes. They are propped up in neat rows against her padded pink headboard, like a mouthful of impotent shark teeth.

It looks like a fusty old lady's bed.

"Okay," Barbara announces as she returns holding several pieces of Davis's clothing. She lays them down on the bed. All the clothes are pinned to pink silk hangers. "What can we do here?"

I select a few reasonable-looking pieces—a dress, a shirt, some skirts—and carry them to Barbara's bathroom, which I have never used before. It's painted a rich mauve, of course, and it has a dated plastic jacuzzi tub (also pink) in the corner, which looks like it hasn't been used in years. Opposite the double vanity, there is a wall of photographs, most of which are black and white and rimmed by gold frames. It is a well-curated mix of candid snaps and professional portraits, primarily of a younger Barbara. The wall reminds me of the collages that accompanied the articles in *Vanity Fair* that my mother and I used to devour about obscure (to me) socialites or the childhood of Jackie Kennedy.

On the wall, there is a photograph of Barbara holding her Tony Award, which she won in her twenties. She wears a spaghetti-strap dress, her hair is pinned up, and she is grinning at something off camera. There is another of Barbara from the same era, wearing a gingham bikini top and high-waisted linen shorts. She sits on the front of a small boat, her legs outstretched, and her fingers play with the gold-link bracelet hanging from her slender wrist. Another: A sepia-toned portrait of a woman in a long lace wedding gown who, by the date embossed on the bottom corner, I calculate to be Barbara's own mother, a long-dead socialite who went by the nickname "Buns." According to Davis, Buns was renowned for hitting a one-handed backhand with a cigarette clenched between her teeth and a penchant for vodka gimlets before dying of liver failure in her early sixties. I keep looking: There is a posed family portrait in which Barbara looks to be about thirteen years old. It is black and white and shot in front of the stone fireplace in a tidy living room of what looks to be a grand house. Barbara wears a modest dress with a Peter Pan collar, and she is so young that her features have yet to spread out, making her look slightly cross-eyed. She is flanked by her equally well-dressed grandparents and undeniably Waspy parents, and a groomed black Scottie dog, all of which remind me that Barbara did not—in any capacity—need to claw her way out of poverty to find herself comfortably situated in a pre-war penthouse overlooking Fifth Avenue.

The photo to which I am most drawn, however, is a framed magazine article. It has been clipped out of an issue of *People* from the 1980s. The page is now sun-bleached, but it features a young Barbara gazing down adoringly on a toddler Davis, perched on her hip. Barbara is dressed like Katherine Hepburn on safari; she wears crisp trousers and a white button-down shirt, and little Davis—blonde, fat, and in a ruffled dress with bloomers—plays with the patterned scarf that hangs from her mother's neck. The article headline is: *How Barbara Lawrence Manages Music and Motherhood.*

"How's it going in there?" Barbara calls from the other side of the door. Her voice is weary.

"Just a second," I call. I turn away from the photographs and quickly disrobe.

As one probably suspected, Davis's clothes are too tight, but Barbara's are too short and, frankly—with all their pleats and big gold buttons and shoulder pads—too matronly for my office. I pull on a short-sleeved cashmere sweater and a long silk floral skirt I have seen Davis wear to the office before. I get on my tiptoes to see myself in the vanity mirror. While the skirt hangs loose on Davis's frame, lending her a sort of unconcerned high-fashion-meets-Bohemia vibe, it bunches along my hips and cuts across my midsection. I pull the sweater over the waistband and shake my hair forward.

It's not great, but it's not a total disaster, I decide.

"Clo?" Barbara calls again, but this time it is clear I am testing her patience.

I emerge bashfully from the bathroom.

"I think this could work?" I say with uncertainty.

"Oh," Barbara sighs. "I *loved* that skirt on Davis."

It's strange: Her tone possesses a wistfulness usually reserved for the dead, but as she makes no further comment, I consider this outfit to be approved. When I return to the kitchen a few minutes later, comfortably back in normal clothes, Barbara picks up her wallet off the marble island.

"Do me a favor?" She plucks out a credit card and holds it in my direction. "Use my credit card to buy a few things that you can just leave here?"

"Oh, Barbara, I couldn't," I stammer reflexively. "Really."

"I mean it," she responds sternly. "You would be doing me a favor. It's nice to know you can just stay over some nights without having to plan *everything* in advance."

She waggles the card at me. I don't move.

"Take it," Barbara says, and I tentatively accept it. While I have been careful to be as vague as possible about my upbringing and financial situation, this offering makes it painfully evident that Barbara has already figured out I am unable to afford the lifestyle I currently pretend I can afford.

Apparently, I can't even *play* rich.

I glance down, and see the card in my hand is a gold American Express card, and it looks just like the one I used to buy my red coat, the one that is still tucked into a hidden slot in my wallet, the one Davis seems to have not realized is missing. We stand silent for a moment, and while Barbara has couched this as an easy favor, it's clear she would like to be celebrated for her generosity.

"Barbara, this is incredibly nice of you," I say.

"Really," she says. "Don't mention it."

Out of nowhere, I have what strikes me as a brilliant idea.

"Is there any chance *you* can help me shop?" I venture, studiously pathetic. "I mean"—and here I force a laugh and point at myself—"I think it's obvious I could use a little help."

The words have barely left my mouth before Barbara's head bobs up like she just heard a strange noise and is trying to discern if it's friend or foe. Then, a toothy grin breaks wide across her face. She clearly hadn't considered this could be an *outing*, and she seems utterly delighted by the possibility of exerting her influence over me in a brand-new way.

"I would love that!" she affirms with a little clap.

"Well, I love it more." I laugh.

"Could we do it in a few weeks?" she asks, opening her red book. "I already have a lot of lunches on my calendar because there are so many people in town."

"Of course," I say, and I hand the credit card back to Barbara. She looks at it for a moment before she accepts it, and by her expression, I know that by returning it, I have passed some kind of test.

And, I am relieved, as I am always relieved, when I please her.

Later, in Davis's bathroom, I wash my face with an expensive foam cleanser that smells like fresh laundry. I brush my teeth and slip into one of her white cotton nightgowns. I debate poking my head into

Barbara's room to say good night—the protocols of intimacy at this juncture are still distressingly unclear—but when I see no light shining from underneath the door, I am grateful that the decision is taken from me. Barbara generally goes to bed early when she doesn't have an event. My best guess is that the physical and emotional toll of taking care of her daughter while simultaneously refusing to pare back on her social commitments proves to be a little more than she can handle at her age. Not that she would ever admit to being tired. Or old, which is what I presume a woman to be once they reach their late fifties. No, if I have learned anything over the past few months, it is that Barbara Lawrence will not show weakness. Barbara Lawrence will not allow herself to be irrelevant. Barbara Lawrence may be in a slump, but Barbara Lawrence will find her way out because—as she is desperate for the world to remember—Barbara Lawrence is a star.

And she will be here long after the rest of us are gone and forgotten.

35

Barbara selects Bergdorf Goodman for our little shopping. She's having her hair cut and colored at their salon, and she instructs me to join her immediately after my workday ends.

Come straight away, she says sternly. *No stops.*

That day, in preparation, I wear what I consider to be my best outfit to work, which is a black wool shift dress from the Gap that is so simple, its provenance could never be discerned with 100 percent accuracy, and the black Louboutin boots I bought with Davis at the sample sale. I stand for the entire subway ride uptown, fearful of getting anything dirty, and when I alight the subway stairs at Fifty-Ninth Street, I dash across the cobblestone plaza toward the entrance of Bergdorf Goodman, stopping only long enough to toss a penny into Pulitzer Fountain.

I close my eyes. I make a wish.

A heavy bronze revolving door marks the entrance to Bergdorf Goodman, and they are so difficult to push that I can only surmise they were designed to keep out the weak. When I finally grunt my way through a full rotation, I find myself on the ground floor of the greatest department store in all the world.

I have never been inside before.

I look around.

The space is bright, and the air is thick with smells and sounds, all of which seem intentionally layered, surely by some retail genius, to create an opposing cacophony of prosperity and lack. I pick up the scent of sharp perfumes and earthy leathers. There is the reassuring tap of high heels across a marble floor, the dull crinkle of thick paper shopping bags, and, in some unknown distance, I hear a series of voluptuous dings as they emanate from expectant elevators.

I want everything, I think. *And I have nothing.*

As I weave through a labyrinth of glass cases, I endeavor to portray a sense of directional and financial confidence, but the truth is that I have no idea where the hair salon is located. I don't want to ask the women manning the counters because they look terrifying. They have thin eyebrows and pursed lips, and they are clearly completely disgusted by all the tourists milling about and gawking over the price of the Marc Jacobs bags. Surely, to ask one of these women for directions would give me away as the impostor I already know myself to be, so I do what I always do: I blink at them like a disinterested heiress who, quite possibly, doesn't speak English. Finally, I corner a male security guard by the bathroom and ask him for directions.

He tells me the salon is located on the top floor of the building.

"Do you know where the elevators are?" he asks.

"Of course," I say with a smile.

It takes me another five minutes to locate the elevators, and once I arrive at the salon, I find Barbara tipped nearly flat over a white porcelain sink. Her eyes are closed, and her hands are daintily folded across her flat midsection. She looks like she is laid out in a casket. A woman is lathering her hair and a short, dark-haired man in a tight black T-shirt stands over her quiet conversation.

"Hi, Barbara," I say softly to announce myself.

"Honey," she replies sleepily. "I am so sorry, but we got started a little late."

"Don't worry at all," I say brightly. "I will read some magazines."

I flicker a smile to the man and turn on my heel toward the waiting area.

"What about her?" I hear the man say to Barbara, and then he looks at me with a smile. "What about you, honey?"

"What *about* me?" I ask.

Barbara croaks one eye open.

"It would be chic a little shorter," she says, but not to me. "She's been growing it too long."

"Mmmmm," the man says, nodding in academic agreement. With his fingers, he pinches up the ends of my hair and rubs them between his fingers with a frown. "*Honey*, you need a trim!"

"Oh," I say.

"Bangs?" he ventures over his shoulder.

"I hadn't thought of that," Barbara says, but her eyes are closed again. "What about her face shape?"

"Oh, she could do bangs," he says. "But not straight because of her cheeks. Maybe a side swipe, but I think I would want to shape her brows first."

At this, I take a small step sideways and I thumb over my shoulder like a hobo trying to hitch a ride on a train car. I have no intention of getting a haircut today, especially now that it has finally gotten to a good length and, even if I did want a haircut, I would certainly not be able to afford one at Bergdorf Goodman.

"I'll just wait for you over there," I say affably, pointing to a series of chairs. "Don't worry about me!"

"We are already here, Clo," Barbara says plainly as her head is squeezed into a towel turban. When she sits up, her eyes look like tired slits. "You might as well fix your hair."

Try as I might, I can't help but notice her choice of words.

One hour later, I have darker, shaped eyebrows, and shorter hair—basically a chin-length bob—with bangs that sweep to the side. I also have a physical sensation I can only describe as a heaving pit of violation. It festers in my stomach like mixing milk and lemon into a cup of hot English Breakfast tea. I can't decide what feels worse: That I hate my new haircut or that I just let Barbara Lawrence have her way with me. I briefly wonder what life was like for Davis as she was growing up under her mother's constantly dissatisfied gaze. Did she only become *Davis Lawrence* by following her mother's orders? Or did she have a say in the matter?

It's an interesting question.

I watch as Barbara distributes crisp twenty-dollar tips to the staff with a truly condescending benevolence; it looks as if she is passing razor blades out to a bunch of desperate inmates. Then, the dark-haired man leads us to the elevator bank where we bypass several carriages with customers inside without comment. I find this puzzling until I realize that someone like Barbara Lawrence cannot ride the elevator with normal people because, well, she doesn't want to interact with normal people in a department store.

Not even one as nice as Bergdorf Goodman.

We finally get an empty elevator and we travel down a few floors where we are met by two smiling women, one young, one much older. They usher us into a private fitting room with light peach walls and plump couches. As we settle down, a proper tea service arrives, and it occurs to me that famous people like Barbara Lawrence shop differently than the rest of us. They can't just flick through the sales rack and shimmy into the dressing room. They need to be treated like, well, celebrities.

After some quick and meaningless chitchat, the more senior of the two women (her name is Pauline) turns to me with that terrifying social-worker smile of hers. She has a few questions: *What's my favorite feature? Do I gravitate toward any designers? How aggressive do I like to be with color? What about prints? Length? Arms?* I try to answer honestly, but I don't make it far: Barbara waves her hand dismissively and removes her reading glasses with a loud sigh.

"Ladies, I think the point is that we are trying to *settle* on a style for her?" Barbara says as she rubs her eyes. "So, I don't understand why we are asking *her* all the questions. That won't get us anywhere. Clearly, she doesn't have a sense of style."

Barbara serves up this verdict with the most incredible display of distracted indifference to my feelings, but nobody says anything. In fact, I don't think a single eye blinks. Maybe another girl would bristle or protest at this unfair assessment, but I stay motionless because I am pretty sure she is right.

"Excellent," Pauline says as she brings her hands together with an efficient briskness and nods to her assistant. "Why don't we pull a few new things we *love*, and we can go from there?"

"Wonderful," Barbara says, but she says it like she thinks they are morons.

"Are there any particular occasions we should focus on first?" Pauline asks.

Sidenote: I find Pauline's pronunciation of the word *occasions* (hard emphasis on a long O) to be incredibly civilized and, for the rest of my life, I will never pronounce it *ah-kay-shuns* again.

"She needs a few things for work at the magazine, and some cocktail," Barbara replies. "Pajamas."

"Nothing formal?"

"Nothing formal just yet," she says. She scans her diary with a frown. "And did that jacket I ordered from Akris *ever* come back from your tailor?"

"I'll check right away," Pauline says apologetically. "And we will be back shortly."

As they hasten out of the fitting area, Barbara leans back in her padded chair and scans the pages of her diary with the tip of her pen. I sit in silent obedience.

"There is a dinner for an opera director next week on Tuesday," Barbara announces as she taps her black pen on a page. "Why don't you come with me?"

"Of course," I say, and she ticks something in her book.

Here, I endeavor to act normal, but let's be serious: This is a bizarre situation. Just as I was getting more comfortable with Barbara, especially since I spend so much time with Davis at the apartment, I am now in the middle of an additional evaluation, the outcome of which feels worrisomely uncertain. All I want is Barbara to feel for *me* a small percentage of whatever pride she feels in her own (albeit far more beautiful) daughter, but I also feel squeamish about Barbara buying me clothes, especially clothes I could never afford myself. I'm sure plenty of women never give this kind of generosity a second thought, but I know myself far too well: I'd rather steal something than be gifted it.

I never like being in someone's *obvious* debt.

The women reappear with two assistants, who are pushing metal rolling racks packed with clothes. Barbara removes her reading glasses and looks directly at me.

"Okay, let's get started," she says.

* * *

I slip behind a long, velvet dressing room curtain where I discover the first rack of clothes is already waiting for me. I know this is immature, but as I undress, I evaluate my body; I can never seem to resist an opportunity to pick myself apart in the name of continuous improvement. I assume this is normal behavior and that self-confidence, whatever *that* really is, emerges in one's midthirties. At least that is what I keep reading in women's magazines.

Today, for starters, I am troubled by how lumpy and unattractive I look in this department store lighting. Why, it's almost as if, despite years of diligent (although possibly low-impact) workouts, I have accumulated exactly no muscle tone whatsoever. I turn to face the mirror and place my hands on my hips. My armpits—once firm bastions of youthful sinew—have begun to look like two tents starting to collapse, and my flabby breasts hang heavy on my rib cage, inching sideways toward the abyss. When my eyes travel farther south, I am forced to confront the thick, shapeless trunk that is my midsection and the coarse mound of pubic hair of which I am still unfashionably in possession. The wiry curls run over the boundaries of my underwear and down the inside of my thigh to a near heroic degree, like soldiers jamming flags into unoccupied territory, and I can't remember the last time I had a bikini wax. Next, I turn around so I can take a good look at my backside. I clench my white cheeks hard, and the pressure spawns at least a dozen dimples of various depth. When I relax, the divots are still present, but softer, like an impatient child's fingerprints on a sugar cookie that has yet to cool.

I really need to start doing squats. With weights.

"Clo?" I hear Barbara's voice. "How are we doing in there?"

"One second," I call back.

For the next hour, I try on linen pants and pencil skirts. I try on A-line shift dresses and long floral frocks with belts. I try on a series of sturdy, mid-length strapless cocktail numbers and a muted rainbow of $400 cashmere sweaters. Each time, as I step out of the dressing room to be evaluated, it's made clear that how I feel about *any* of these clothes is of exactly no import. Barbara is making the decisions and, as far as she is concerned, I have ceased to be a sentient human being. I am called *bosomy* and *wide*. I am informed I have a short torso and no curve at the waist. (*Like Gumby*, Barbara suggests helpfully, at which the sales ladies nod in astonished agreement at her accuracy.) I am praised for my height, my neck, and the length of my legs, but told pinks, oranges, and yellows do nothing for my coloring. I am forbidden from wearing spaghetti straps and boatneck sweaters, but I downright sparkle with pleasure when Barbara *almost* approves of how I look in a gray shift dress. Sadly, directly following this small victory, Pauline presents me with a series of long pleated skirts, and Barbara shakes her head vehemently.

"No. They won't work for her," Barbara decrees. "I mean, she's not built like Davis!"

At this comment, everyone laughs, including me, but mostly because I am trying not to cry. I have spent my life (except freshman year in college, which is a whole other story that involves unlimited access to the dining hall's Belgian waffle maker) being a reliable size six at J. Crew and Banana Republic, but I am learning that designer clothes are a whole different story. Here, I am unable to zip up a pair of size twelve trousers.

Trust me, I didn't need anyone to remind me that I am not built like Davis Lawrence.

At some juncture, I become aware of a whispered conversation regarding my underpinnings. I strain to listen through the curtain. There seems to be some serious concern about not only my bra *size*, but also my choice of bra *style*, and, to remedy this, someone has been dispatched to the lingerie department to retrieve assistance. Moments later, I step out of the dressing room where I am met by a little old woman in an all-black outfit. Her dark hair is scooped into a severe bun, and a yellow measuring tape hangs loose around her sagging neck. She does not say hello, but rather simply requests, in an accent I cannot identify, that I remove my shirt and bra, and stand in front of her (and, thus, everyone in the room) completely topless. Petrified of appearing prudish, I pull my top over my head with a flourish, like I do this sort of thing all the time, and toss it on the nearest chair. The woman stares at my chest for a full sixty seconds, her face devoid of even the suggestion of an expression, and then she turns me around so she can slide the measuring tape around my rib cage.

"Just as I thought," she says thickly.

"What did you think?" I ask.

"What size bra do you wear?"

"A 36C?" I venture carefully, as if somehow this is a test.

At this, she laughs, but it's a mean and mirthless laugh.

"What?" I ask. I am still topless, but now I cup my breasts in my hands. I feel like I am being intentionally humiliated.

"You're not a 36C," she says. "And I know because *no one* is a 36C. The balance is off between the back and the cup."

"So then what am I?"

"34DD," she says, and all I can think when presented with this enormous, pornographic number is that this woman—whoever she is—is clearly out of her ever-loving mind.

Racks are rolled out, racks are rolled in, and a pile of very unsexy shapewear and bras arrives in the arms of yet another assistant. Just as I begin to feel especially demoralized, however, something unexpected starts to happen: The next rack of designer clothes, like magic, starts to fit my body. Apparently, the soul-crushing trial-and-error period serves a proper purpose, which is to first discern what I *cannot* wear. Now, pants slide over my hips and dresses zip with ease. It turns out that shopping at this exalted level is like embarking on a ten-mile run. Sure, your legs feel like painful sandbags during the first few miles, but once the endorphins start to fire, you feel like you could run forever.

Like maybe you were *born to run.*

As I slip in and out of items and parade myself in front of Barbara, I can't help but notice there is a small, but growing rack of items that have received her stamp of approval. I wonder when she will edit it down to the outfit or two that I need for her purposes and maybe a classy set of pajamas. Instead, when I finally emerge from the dressing room, exhausted and back in my own flimsy clothes, I learn that Barbara purchased everything on the rack. My stomach drops because, while I did not keep a full tally, I do know the one dress cost $1,800 while the Manolo Blahnik heels—of which there were two pairs—were each $725.

As we wait for the items to be packaged up, I sip nervously on a cup of cold tea because I'm desperate to have something to do with my hands. Barbara watches me fidget for as long as she can tolerate before she removes her glasses and sighs.

"Clo, you really must get comfortable with people giving you things," she says, and her voice is a disconcerting blend of kindness and irritation, like I just cannot get the hang of riding a bicycle. "It is part of your job now, and to look so unaccustomed to it will, well... it gives away your breeding."

"Oh, I..." I croak, but the word *breeding* hangs between us like a wet towel on a clothesline.

Fortunately, Pauline reappears, which ends our conversation. Her neck is blotchy from what I assume is the aftermath of adding up her commission, and she inquires as to where she should messenger the garment bags. I start to give her my address in Brooklyn, but Barbara interrupts me:

"Send them to *my* apartment," she says firmly. "And make sure to send my jacket as well."

Pauline glances at me, and I nod as a familiar sensation swamps my chest. You see, these magnificent clothes, like all the shiny new things in my shiny new life, are mine, but they won't ever really belong to me.

When we get back to the apartment, Barbara instructs Marta that, when the clothes arrive from Bergdorf, she would like them hung in the walk-in closet, and to make certain they are pinned *properly* to the hangers.

She doesn't want a sloppy job like last time, she barks, and that poor housekeeper's eyes flash with the fear of a powerless child.

36

I knock on the door of Allie's apartment.

Although we no longer meet up every Sunday night, we do try to hang out together several times a month, usually at her apartment on Bedford Street, because it's closer to my office. It's strange: My first years in New York felt like an endless parade of empty hours, but now my schedule feels almost dangerously full. Most nights, I collapse in my bed after midnight, drunk and still wearing my contacts, only to wake up at dawn and start all over again. And yet, despite the glamour of my work parties, spending time with Allie remains my favorite activity. The elements of our long-held routine—polishing off a few bottles of Cavit pinot grigio and eating multiple bags of microwave popcorn for dinner—provide me with a much-needed and soothing consistency in an otherwise inconsistent life. With Allie, I can be myself, which is to say I can be dull, gross, and politically incorrect to an almost heroic degree. I can feel sorry for myself. I can pee with the door open, so I don't have to stop speaking if I am mid-sentence. I can complain about my weight. I can watch television without wearing pants, which is usually the case as my work clothes are so binding and Allie is about six inches shorter than me so none of her pants fit.

When I receive no answer, I knock again, but much harder this time.

"It's open," Allie yells from somewhere far inside. "Come in!"

I try to open the door, but it stops halfway; it's hitting against something. I push against it hard with my hip, but it won't budge so I slide sideways through the narrow opening. I make it halfway through when I hear the distinct tick of a thread catching on the lock. I cringe and close my eyes. I don't look down, terrified I just caused permanent damage to one of my new outfits: It's a $1,500 blazer over a $400 navy cashmere sweater.

Not that anyone is counting.

Allie's apartment is strewn with brown moving boxes, including the one that blocked my entrance. Some of the boxes are neatly labeled and secured with electrical tape (which I am *pretty sure* is the wrong kind of tape) but many more are open and half full. In my rush to get downtown, I neglected to consider that I might be confronted with a fact I had, thus far, been desperate to avoid, which is that Allie is moving in with her boyfriend Patrick. I close the door and lean against it. I can see Allie through the cutout over the breakfast bar. She is on her tippy toes in an unsuccessful attempt to retrieve something from a very high shelf. Her back is turned to me.

"Need some help?" I call.

"Please god," she responds as she settles down on her heels and pops her hand on her hips. "I wish I had your height."

I make my way toward her slowly, stepping awkwardly over boxes and bulging black contractor bags, but she doesn't turn to look at me. Instead, she points up at the object she desires.

"Move aside," I say. Allie smooths the top of her long ponytail in a gesture of hard work, and when she finally turns toward me, her eyes go wide.

"Your hair!" she exclaims. "It looks amazing!"

I smile. Despite initially disliking my haircut, the general reception (especially from the older girls in my office, whose opinions I most value) has been so incredibly positive that I have decided to embrace it. Frankly, the whole thing makes me wonder if, all this time, I have been incapable of seeing myself clearly at all.

"And holy shit!" she continues. "Where did you get those clothes?"

I reach over her head and pull down the item; it's a crystal punch bowl I have never seen in my life. I turn it over in my hands.

"Barbara took me shopping," I say easily. I set the bowl down on the counter, and I add with a wry smile: "At Bergdorf Goodman."

Here, I do a little comic twirl.

"She *sure fucking did* take you shopping at Bergdorf Goodman." Allie laughs, clearly delighted. She walks around me to inspect the whole outfit. "You're like a movie makeover montage!"

"I know," I say. "Apparently, I should have bought, like, ten thousand dollars' worth of clothes sooner. Everyone at the office has been insanely complimentary."

While I deliver this line as a joke, it is entirely true: Everyone has been insanely complimentary, and I suspect the reasons for this are two-fold. One: They are relieved that I have the money to afford such an expensive wardrobe. Two: They are pleased that I am dutifully absorbing and acting upon the raft of lessons to which I have received the most expert tutelage. Basically, I am astoundingly compliant, the wet dream of any group dynamics theorist: I don't want to be me any longer.

I want to be one of them.

"What *is* this?" Allie asks as she rubs her finger against one of the large gold buttons on my magnificently sturdy, nipped-waist black jacket.

"The blazer is Balmain," I say. "And the sweater is Michael Kors. The boots are mine, but from that sample sale."

"Wow," she says as she shakes her head. "I'm so jealous!"

"The blazer cost, like, two months of my rent," I say. "I am not kidding."

"Thank God for the Lawrence largesse, I guess," she says, and she wink-wink-elbows me in the ribs. "When did you go shopping?"

"A few weeks ago?"

"What did Davis get?"

"Davis?" I say lightly. "Oh, Davis didn't go with us."

Allie's eyes flicker in genuine confusion.

"She didn't?" she asks.

"No."

"How did *she* feel about that?"

"I don't think she knows?" I venture. I walk out of the kitchen area and poke around in a box of books on the floor. I pull out a thick, yellowed paperback copy of *Gone with the Wind*, yet another book I have never read. "Can I borrow this?"

"Davis doesn't know?" Allie asks.

"I don't think so?"

"Is that weird?" she presses.

"Weird? I hadn't thought about it," I respond with some shortness. "I mean, it wasn't like I *asked* Barbara to take me shopping. She wants me to stay over at the apartment more to help with Davis, and I never have any clothes."

"Has Barbara not heard of an overnight bag?" She laughs.

"Look, it's *fine*," I say, but I hear the curtness in my tone. "It's not like I have the right clothes for her events anyway."

Allie is very much up to speed on my plus-one status since Davis's accident, and she is generally a very satisfying audience for my stories, so I am surprised by the sudden show of self-righteousness. I mean, of all people, Allie understands what it takes for people—for women—to get ahead: She was sleeping with her department chair less than a year ago, for fuck's sake.

"Wow," Allie says. "That's obnoxious."

"It's not *obnoxious*," I shoot back defensively. "Why are you being so judgmental all of a sudden?"

"I'm not," she protests.

"You are! For starters, I need decent clothes for *my job*, and you know I can't afford them," I say. "Secondly, I don't have time to keep going back to Brooklyn when I am spending so much time with Davis."

"I am not being judgmental about the clothes themselves," Allie replies. "But it doesn't strike you as a little strange that your coworker's mom felt the need to take you shopping for a better wardrobe?"

"Uh, I work at a fashion magazine," I say sarcastically.

"But still," she says, but she doesn't look at me.

"Also, Davis is my *friend*, not just my coworker," I retort.

To this, Allie says nothing. She just starts to wrap the crystal punch bowl in white tissue paper with what I perceive to be a little sneer.

"What's *that* face?" I demand. I feel myself getting hot under my new sweater.

"Nothing," she says.

"Nothing?"

"Nothing."

I stomp over to the loveseat, which is Allie's only piece of remaining furniture, and I shove a pile of neatly folded clothes on the floor so I can sit down. Allie looks at the mess with a frown but goes back to her wrapping. As we stew in silence I entertain, for the first time, if maybe Allie isn't a little envious of my relationship with Davis. This thought softens me to some degree as I pick the thread on one of her throw pillows. Is it possible that, after decades of friendship in which I have been relegated to the passenger seat of Allie Blum's impressive life, I am suddenly the one who is a tough act to follow? The thought hadn't occurred to me, and I wonder if maybe I am being too sensitive about Allie's criticisms. Or, even better, not sensitive enough? Maybe—just maybe—some good, old-fashioned jealousy has taken root in her heart.

The thought pleases me.

"I can't believe it's the last time I will be in this apartment," I offer finally, and while I don't look up from the pillow I am deconstructing, I hope my words are taken as an olive branch of sorts.

"I know," she says. "I feel more upset than I thought I would."

"Me too," I say softly.

It's true. It feels like the end of an era.

We stay quiet for a moment. The only noise is the soft crinkle of tissue paper.

"Will Patrick let me come over to watch TV?" I ask.

"*Of course*, you are coming over to watch TV," she says with some surprise. "*Nothing* is going to change."

"Except your rich banker boyfriend is renting a super sick apartment for you to cohabitate, and I am still eating soup-for-one in my studio apartment?"

"Hey, we are *sharing* expenses," Allie protests.

She, of course, is intentionally missing the point, which is that she is breaking her promise: She is leaving me behind. She is sticking to the script of life while I am still improvising my routine. I know I'm expected to be happy that she found a "great boyfriend" (or, even worse, heartened that her success in dating may lead to my own success one day), but I am not even remotely happy for her: I am so bitter that I can hardly see straight.

"Sharing expenses, eh?" I ask with a roll of my eyes.

"Yes!"

I hold my hands up like a balancing scale.

"He works at Lehman Brothers," I say with fake consideration as I move one hand up and down. "You are in the second year of a PhD."

I continue to adjust my fake scales accordingly. I comically wrinkle my brow.

"I'm in year three," she corrects me.

"Year three?"

"Year three," she confirms with a smile.

That is a lot of years, I think.

Allie keeps wrapping, so I open the battered novel that rests on my lap. I scan the first page.

"Is this any good?" I ask after a moment. I raise the book over my head.

Allie looks up.

"Scarlett gets what she wants in the end?" she offers before adding: "I mean, in a way?"

I close the book: That is good enough for me.

37

The horse statue I stole from Susan Goldsmith-Cohen has always been female, although I cannot tell you why, especially because I don't particularly like most women. Women, in my experience, are far worse than men. They are colder and more calculating, more reliably the falsest of friends. They will lie fallow for years, if necessary, to exact their revenge, oftentimes by dangling a phantom sisterhood that, if we are all being honest here, doesn't actually exist. At least the men are obvious about their evil-doings and swift in taking their retribution. To be honest, I have never understood why society demands that I support all women, just because I am one.

That said, the horse has always been a she, and she continues to sit where I first placed her last summer on the right corner of the little black walnut writing desk in my apartment. Despite the initial sensation the robbery caused, the mystery of her disappearance hasn't popped up again in any newspapers, and, while I have the occasional moment of bone-rattling panic, I have almost stopped worrying that someone is going to reclaim her. The prevailing theory is that, somehow, the horse wasn't actually stolen from the party, rather it was caught up in one of Susan Goldsmith-Cohen's many shady dealings and, as a result, it was mostly her reputation that paid the price. So, the trail, if there ever had been a trail, has long been cold.

And now we belong to each other.

There are nights where I will lay her on a pillow in my bed so I can sleep with her. I will roll on my side and wedge my hands under my ear. I will stare at her, and she will stare right back.

I have a feeling that, if I could only crack her open, I would discover that she contains multitudes.

38

Isobel is pregnant again, but this time it's twins.

As such, she asks me to interview an actress in Los Angeles in her stead because, despite her doctor's reassurances, she is only eight weeks along, and she is too afraid to fly. She got pregnant so quickly after the first baby—far more quickly than planned—and now that she knows it's twins, she refuses to take any chances. She can't ask anyone else because then she would have to explain the situation on the early side to L.K. (and that, as she put it, "just feels like bad luck") but she stresses her firm belief that I can handle the challenge of my very first center-of-book article, which will run a whopping 1,200 words and include several photographs of the actress and her recently retired, enormous football player of a boyfriend, all shot by a very famous photographer. While I am over the moon that she would confide in me about something as personal as her pregnancy, I am even more startled that she is trusting me with this assignment.

I feel I have done nothing material to deserve it.

I do my own cost estimate—which covers flights, hotel, taxis, and all the other general expenses accrued on a reporting trip—and I drop it in L.K.'s inbox. When it comes back signed, I take it upstairs to the petty cash window where I watch in silent awe as the woman counts out 3,000 dollars in cash, all for me to spend—with absolutely no restrictions—on the trip. Two days later, I fly to Los Angeles in the first-class cabin for the first time in my life. The seat next to me is empty so I fill it with my books and journals and magazines. I drink free champagne and eat a hot fudge sundae with chopped peanuts for breakfast that is, improbably, *made-to-order by the stewardess on the airplane.* When I land at LAX, it is magically still morning, courtesy of the time zone change, and a driver greets me at baggage claim. He holds a white sign with my name in capital letters, and when he sees me, he stops chatting with his fellow drivers and breaks into a big smile. *We don't have this smile in New York*, I think, and his ease strikes me as exotic. He takes my bag, and as we exit the airport through a set of automatic doors, everything feels wonderfully warm and unfamiliar.

According to the call sheet (which I have printed out and consulted on nine hundred occasions since I left my apartment in Brooklyn this morning before sunrise) I don't have time to check in at the hotel, so I give the driver the address of a building in downtown Los Angeles. We sail down a highway (sorry, *freeway*) that sprouts billboards, warehouses, and a smattering of palm trees so tragic and gawky that it looks as if they were cast out of a larger, more popular tribe of trees. In the back seat, I put on eye cream, Laura Mercier tinted moisturizer, mascara, and lipstick. I tap a stick of deodorant under my armpits and sniff my shirt. I chew gum and chug a bottle of water. I consult the MapQuest route I printed out at work, just to confirm I am not being kidnapped, and I test out my pens on a piece of notebook paper. When the cab takes the indicated exit, I look out the window as we travel slowly through the streets of Downtown Los Angeles. To my eyes, the city center presents as urban—there are buildings and crosswalks and streetlights—but I spot very few actual human beings. It's like one of those old-timey villages people set up under their Christmas trees: The lights are on, but no one is home. The driver pulls up to an unremarkable office building and, as I step out of the car, I am hit with a wave of dull heat; it's markedly hotter here than at the airport. I take note that the horseshoe driveway is lined with silver trailers and those black Mercedes sprinter vans. They are all idling in the service of our photo shoot, and waves of steam undulate off their baking hoods like a mirage. The driver hands over my bag, and as I walk toward the entrance, I am pounced upon by triple-process blonde lady publicists. They both shake my hand with pronounced enthusiasm before making inquiries about my flight, my need for a bathroom, and my hunger level before they hand me a folder and a bottle of water and escort me to a large freight elevator. They apologize for *the mess* and *the heat* and *how terrible they both look*, and I am confused until it dawns on me that, in my own way, I am also a celebrity. Or, at the very least, above these two publicists in the pecking order of the fashion world. I notice one of the women wears a clownishly large engagement ring. The stone is so cloudy, it looks nearly dead inside, and I immediately think of how Davis would roll her eyes at the garishness of this woman's display; her own enormous ring, of course, is bursting with rainbows. Davis had called me the night before my flight to wish me luck. She told me she was excited for my trip to California, but I don't think she really meant it.

California, I suspect, makes her sad.

The elevator doors thunder open, and the women quietly steer me toward a white and cavernous studio, every crevice of which is drowned in that blown-out California light. When I darken the doorway, it's just like in the movies: Everyone pauses to look at me in judgmental silence before returning to whatever noisy thing they were previously doing. I turn around to ask for support or advice, but my guides have vanished in a deferential cloud of smoke. From the relative safety of the hall, I take a quick inventory of my surroundings in the hope I can plot a safe route to a dark corner.

I do not belong here.

On one side of the room, there are racks of clothes and a line of folding tables, the tops of which are neatly organized with the accessories for the shoot. There are scores of shoes, all lined up with military precision, and rows of black velvet trays full of jewelry. One of our most senior fashion editors, an older blonde woman I have admired from afar for *everything*, right down to the way she holds her reading glasses as she speaks, is going through the clothes in a wonderfully unhurried manner. She is surrounded by assistants, some of whom are taking notes, while others unpack trunks, or steam silk dresses with portable steamers on wheels, or tape the soles of the stilettos with thick blue tape—one by one—to ensure they can be returned to the designer without scuffs. Not that any designer would kick up a fuss about scuffs; it's the price one must pay—among many various tariffs—for this indisputable honor of being featured in our magazine.

In the corner, there is a vanity table, backed by a bulbed makeup mirror, the light from which is so bright that I cannot look at it directly. To the side, there are hundreds of tubes and bottles and palettes and brushes laid out on a series of black towels. The makeup artist is seated in a folding chair, perfectly at ease. She drinks a green juice and twists one of the many gold lockets that hangs from her neck with her fingers as she reads a magazine, which rests on her narrow lap.

From an equipment perspective, this is an impressive operation. There are several cameras on tripods, and a small field of black umbrellas, cracked open like poppies. People carry those pliable silver disks called "bounces" that do something specific with the light, and there are computer monitors, milk crates full of tangled electronic accoutrements, and rolls of colored paper leaning up against the wall. Orange cables snake menacingly across the pine floor, secured by silver electrical tape. On the far side of the room by the windows, I spy a cluster of empty director-style chairs and, when I think no one is looking, I make a break for them. I settle into one quietly, grateful that this little quadrant of the studio seems to be in low demand. This goes well enough, but after ten minutes a group of people settles into all the chairs around me, and I realize I picked the wrong spot.

"What the fuck is going on?" a guy with an unshaved face says. He is wearing black jeans and a black leather jacket, and I feel sweaty just looking at him. I have never seen him before, so I assume he is on the photographer's crew.

"She's flipping out because she says the hairstylist can't do her hair," responds a woman that I *have* seen before. She is a super chic freelance stylist we often hire to assist on our shoots. She is often impatiently jerking racks of clothes through the hallways of our office, and snipping at people about the whereabouts of messengers.

"Why?" the photographer's assistant asks.

The woman glances quickly over her shoulder.

"From what I gather, because the hairdresser is white?"

"Seriously?" he asks. "That is some prima donna bullshit."

She rolls her eyes, and he laughs.

"One hundred percent, but I can't fucking deal with this right now," she says. "We need to get four looks out of the way today, and we haven't even gotten her in one dress."

"There is no way we get them all," the guy says, shaking his head. "I mean, *maybe* two shots with the time we have left. He's not moving too quickly these days."

The woman looks concerned.

"Seriously?" she asks.

"Maybe you should have let her keep the braids," he continues wryly. "It would have been faster."

"Yeah, right," she says. "Just imagine *that* phone call."

I just sit there, a total stranger within obvious earshot of a decidedly, shall we say, *questionable* conversation, but this apparently makes no difference to them whatsoever. As far as anyone here is concerned, if someone is *in the room* then they must be *on the team*. And if I am *on the team*, I have previously sworn a solemn oath to protect all other members of the team, and to dutifully keep everything that happens on today's shoot a secret. As such, they know that whoever I am, I will never say a word about anything I see or hear on the set today, lest it cost me my job, and I can reliably expect the same discretion from them.

Now, maybe it's just me, but as I listen to them talk, it *does* sound like this actress—who I am scheduled to interview after the pictures are taken—is behaving like a diva. I have seen the astronomical budgets for these photo shoots—the day rate for the hair alone is $15,000—so it's not terribly likely they lured today's stylist out of a strip mall. However, this actress *is* also a Black woman, and I reason that, since her hair is simply different than the pin-straight blondes we usually traffic in, she might be irritated by our oversight for a *very* reasonable reason. Not that I would ever be stupid enough to point this out, and call attention to myself. As they keep talking, however, I start to worry about my interview. Will the actress be in a bad mood when I meet her? Is she currently throwing brushes at everyone in a rage? I was hoping for someone media trained to death who would make my job easy. I look up at the clock. It's getting close to lunchtime, and everyone is antsy, especially because New York will be checking in on the progress soon.

To casually vacate the conversation, I drift over to the craft service table. It moans pitifully under the weight of the untouched food and drink that has been heaped without calculation upon it. To wit: There are mini veggie frittatas that look like cupcakes, grain salads with diced carrots, and green salads with salted cucumbers. There are hard-boiled eggs, wedges of carrot cake, and rosy cuts of cool filet mignon. There are finger cookies, roasted butternut squash cubes, and Dannon yogurt cups floating around a sterling silver bowl of melted ice. There are chubby cuts of dill-topped pink salmon, crusty bread sandwiches stuffed with roasted peppers and mozzarella, and a mound of green beans adorned with *teeny-tiny* almond slivers. There are tidy rows of soda cans. There are San Pellegrino bottles and those adorably dimpled Orangina bottles, all set in a charming succession like fat soldiers. There are more than a few silver buckets of wine and champagne that I am quite sure, to my dismay, no one will ever open. There are fruit trays. There are vegetable trays. There are trays of lemon squares, dusted with confectioners' sugar, which are nestled up against a batch of chocolate chip cookies, so plump they look like they might, just finally, exhale.

I pump myself a lukewarm black coffee and, when I think the coast is clear, I jam a cold frittata in my mouth. I cover my mouth with the paper cup, which provides me with reasonable enough cover to deconstruct the condensed brick of salty eggs with my tongue before I swallow it without witnesses. I am still hungry, but I don't dare reach for another; I am petrified someone will catch me out for chewing. I once overheard a fashion editor in our office say to another that there was "nothing more disgusting than seeing a woman eat the appetizers at a cocktail party" and, trust me, that one sticks with you.

Other than that, I have nothing to do until after the pictures are taken so I make myself scarce. I pretend to read the blank pages of my new green notebook. I fake a phone call in the hallway. I reread the articles I printed out about this actress for the hundredth time. I have written out fifty questions. I have practiced my relaxed mannerisms in a mirror. I have practiced my laugh. I have practiced my "serious journalist face." I have done everything I can do to prepare for this interview and yet, I am so nervous that my jaw muscles ache. I glance back over at the bottles of wine.

They are still unopened.

At some point, I hear a bit of hubbub floating over from the set; it seems the photographer has emerged from some private quarter. He wants to test the lighting now that the daylight has started to wane. On his light command, everyone scrambles to attention. His body is frail, but he has dressed beautifully for the occasion and he made the gentlemanly effort to comb his remaining long strands of hair over the moles and liver spots that dot his scalp. He has a large, painful-looking hump on his upper back, and he moves slowly among his assistants, all of whom fall on bended knee like ladies-in-waiting. Upon his quiet instructions, which I cannot hear from where I am standing, they hand him things and they remove things. They dash across the floor and swap cartridges and lights. As I watch him work, I cannot believe I am actually seeing him in the flesh.

Suddenly, the photographer turns around. He takes a long, broad look around the room, which feels uncomfortably intimate; it's like he has broken the fourth wall. Everyone starts to fidget.

Then, he points in my direction.

"You," he says. His tone sounds like I have broken a rule. "Sit."

I stand motionless as, surely, he is pointing to someone else.

"You," he says again, but with more force.

"Me?" I point to myself.

"Yes," he says, but I just keep standing there, completely incredulous. I am sure there has been some mistake, but why is everyone looking at me? My eyes rummage around the room, but when there is no chair to be found, I am at a loss. I start to sink down toward the floor. I am fully prepared to lie prostrate in front of this man if that is what is required of me, but then I sense the flutter of movement to my right.

"Madame, he doesn't mean here," a voice says quietly, and I turn to see that the absurdly elegant older fashion editor has come to my rescue. She places her hand on my back. She smiles at me like I am doing everything right.

"You are going to start walking," she encourages me in a marvelously competent tone, clearly a skill one perfects after thirty years of escorting confused or unwilling people in front of a camera.

I start walking. Her hand remains on my back.

"He needs to test the lighting with someone who is tall and has dark hair," she says. "So you are going to sit down and just do exactly what he says, okay?"

"Okay," I whisper. My heart is hammering in my throat.

"Don't worry," she says, and her voice is so maternal that I am overwhelmed by a desire to hug her. "You're doing great."

She points to a small wooden stool under a large umbrella.

"Here?" I ask.

"Here," she says.

I sit down. The photographer waves his hand, and someone gets me up and adjusts the height of the stool. When advised, I sit back down, and fix my gaze on my gargantuan feet, which, I decide, look hideously oversized in my sandals. I have never had so many eyes on me at one time in my entire life.

"Look up," the photographer says.

I look up.

There is more hand moving and umbrella adjusting and computer tapping, and as all the action swirls around me, I permit myself to feel special, like I was chosen for this important role out of a very impressive crowd. However, as the minutes tick by, the more likely rationale behind my unexpected elevation begins to take its horrifying shape, which is that, in a small sea of sylph-like blondes and short guys with facial hair, I am the closest approximation to a defensive lineman in this entire room.

Before this realization can fully sink in, the photographer approaches me, and, with two fingers, he lifts my chin. He looks me squarely in the face. His eyes are blue and watery, and I decide that, despite his tyrannical reputation, he is a kind man. I imagine that he has grandchildren with whom he loves to play cards. I decide his favorite drink is something soft and unexpected, like a frozen strawberry daiquiri and he likes to watch documentaries about planes and bridges. As he continues to adjust me, I feel a tug in my heart. It pulls and pulls almost as if it wants to warn me that this photographer—and everything else that makes up this truly magnificent universe—won't be with us much longer.

So, I close my eyes.

I promise to remember this moment.

I promise to remember every moment.

The photographer walks back a few feet and someone hands him a Polaroid camera. He snaps a few pictures. He hands them off to an assistant and, while they develop, he shoots a few more. He drops the new ones to the floor without looking at them. Then, without saying a word to anyone, he hands the camera off to an assistant. Then, he hobbles back into his private room, alone and unassisted, and shuts the door.

Everyone looks at each other.

The stylist picks two of the pictures off the floor and examines them.

"I can't change the hair again," she says as she turns one sideways and squints her eyes.

The elegant fashion editor comes to look at the pictures and, after a quick conference with the stylist, she hands two of the Polaroids over to me. I accept them warily.

"You can never tell anyone I gave you these," she says, but her voice is full of the magic that belongs to those who have seen other worlds. "But trust me, you will want them one day."

I say nothing and, once she walks away, I find the courage to look down at the milky images that still develop in my hand.

It's amazing: I can hardly recognize myself.

39

That night, I go to bed absurdly early in a fancy hotel called the Le Hermitage because I don't know anyone in LA, and the team didn't invite me out to the dinner they were all chatting about, for which I am deeply grateful. I am not ready to sit among fashion people and, frankly, I don't think I ever will be. They have an ease I can't mimic on my best days, a clubby kindness that at once feels both truly heartfelt and wholly insincere. I simply don't have enough confidence or experience, although I can't help but wonder if, much like my new photographs, those characteristics might develop over time. So, instead of a proper dinner, I take down an entire can of jumbo salted cashews out of the hotel minibar and drink a bottle of revoltingly oaky chardonnay (minibar list price: sixty-five dollars) while I watch reruns of *Law and Order: Specials Victims Unit*. I don't wear pants or underwear in the bed, but I leave on my bra. I have never been to Los Angeles, so I know I should go out and explore, but I am so worn out that the long list of bars and restaurants Harry emailed me before my departure holds no appeal.

My yet-to-be transcribed interview notes are safe in the green notebook on the nightstand next to me, and the nauseating anxiety of interviewing a famous person—which lasted all of eleven minutes before her publicist announced she was "done for the day"—has nearly subsided. The actress was nice enough, albeit distracted by her team, who kept interrupting us to proffer her with questions and information, but now it is my job to spin those eleven minutes into a multidimensional being who will hopefully be compelling enough to support a six-page spread in our magazine.

I bolt upright, however, at 4:00 a.m. Was that a noise? I am desperate to take measure of the room so I can discern, as quickly as possible, from which direction I am about to be brutally murdered. I come to understand, as my eyes adjust to the dark, that there is no intruder. I am just on New York time. I flop back on the enormous pile of crisp pillows and look up at the ceiling. I have never stayed alone in a hotel room before and there is something airless about it, it feels like being trapped inside a snow globe.

I close my eyes, but I don't fall back asleep.

My flight home is today at four o'clock, but not before a dreaded breakfast with Nana Shaw, a writer and former fashion editor who has been put on what we call (behind the scenes, of course) a "courtesy contract" at the magazine. As far as I can tell from our brief phone conversations and email correspondence, Nana Shaw is an entitled old bat who just happens to be friendly with a lot of older actors and directors in Hollywood. Isobel needs her for Oscar season, and she asked me to meet with her as a "show of deference" on "behalf of the magazine." I agreed easily, of course, but the additional assignment meant I had to be super careful not to mangle or otherwise destroy my one good outfit, an outfit I raced out to purchase, and I hate to admit this, with Barbara Lawrence's credit card the night before I left New York.

Now, while I know this behavior is wrong, I must say that it is such a thrill to buy expensive clothing as if you can easily afford it. If you can find a way to forget, even for an hour, that you are completely broke, there are few activities more enjoyable than playing the role of "rich person" in any high-end department store on a weekday afternoon in New York City. You walk in just a *little* disinterested, and by the time you unhappily examine the contents of a singular rack, an associate stands next to you, ready to accept the armloads of clothes that you, a rich person, want spirited to a private dressing room. As you try things on, she will (confidentially, of course) inform you that *no one* (several A-list celebrities included) who tried on a particular dress filled it out in the same magnificent way. Additionally, she will scurry down to another floor to get you shoes. She will have a young man bring you a glass of champagne. *Of course* she will find out if those pants come in a smaller size, even when it's obvious to all parties present that the last thing you need is a smaller size. *Of course* she will see if it comes in the navy. She will also see if it comes in red. She will find out if the object you desire is available at their other location and, if it is, she will have the parcel bike messengered immediately to your apartment, completely free of charge. The whole time you will comport yourself as both bored and magnanimous—sipping champagne and idly checking your watch—and when you leave with your bags, you will thank her *so much* for helping you.

I think of that expensive outfit now, however, which I tossed on the bathroom floor in my post-photo-shoot delirium, and wince. I claw through my covers and pick up the cordless phone to call room service. I request a large pot of coffee, some newspapers, the thirty-eight-dollar fruit plate, and a steamer, which they kindly inform me is already sitting inside my well-appointed closet. I haul myself out of bed and hang the outfit up on the shower bar. After room service arrives, I sit on the toilet and steam my outfit while I drink coffee and listen to CNN, which I left on high volume in the other room.

At some point, the California sun wedges itself through the thick hotel drapes and it feels safe to get dressed. I conclude that, by reducing the amount of time I spend wearing my expensive outfit, the lower the odds are that I will destroy it *before* I get to the Chateau Marmont. The Chateau Marmont is, naturally, the only hotel in which Nana Shaw would agree to eat a free breakfast with someone as insignificant as me. The only things I know about the place are (A.) that it is an old hotel with cottages, (B.) John Belushi died there, and (C.) if the tabloids are to be believed, Lindsay Lohan is a frequent, albeit deadbeat, guest.

Good enough for me.

The hotel calls me a cab, which takes forever to arrive, and as it winds up an overwhelmed Sunset Boulevard, I am amazed by how unimpressive I continue to find Los Angeles, or Hollywood, or wherever I am to be. I had expected all the roads to wind along the beach, and yet in the 48 hours since I arrived, I have yet to get a glimpse of the ocean. Frankly, it all feels like a lonelier version of New Jersey. However, when the car takes a wide curve on the right, I watch a white, downright Austrian-looking castle rise slowly out of the hillside.

This must be the place, I think.

The sign for the hotel comes into view, and it looks mysterious, like someone carved it out of a magical tree inhabited by talking animals. We turn into the nearly hidden entrance, and after the driver passes through a gate, he drops me at the front door. I bend down to quickly check my hair and teeth in his side mirror before he pulls away.

I pass through the chilly lobby, which despite not being tiled or Spanish, feels tiled and Spanish, and find my way to the outdoor restaurant. I arrive first (assistants always arrive first) and the hostess settles me into a vague sort of rattan chair and a small table in the middle of the room. There are loose tents and umbrellas perched with sweeping generosity over each table, and the entire patio is surrounded by incredibly lush bushes and trees. It feels like summer, and my body starts to untangle in the warmth as I sit and wait for Nana Shaw to arrive.

I look around: I guess it is too early for celebrities to eat breakfast because the restaurant is mostly empty. There is an old guy in a bathrobe talking on the phone at one table, and the only other occupied table is just two guys in business suits. I am little disappointed, of course, but I don't have too much time to dwell; the hostess is leading an older woman toward my table. She is wearing sunglasses, which I expected, and her chin-length hair is matte black and slicked back from her forehead, like an assassin. On her feet, she wears sky-high strappy sandals, and as she walks in my direction, I notice that her body moves in a jittery, stunted way. It's not *quite* like an old lady, but it is also certainly not the horsey gait of youth I have come to expect from fashion editors. She is holding a Birkin or Kelly bag (I can never remember the difference) and she wears a black suit, the skirt of which is so short that it exposes her unsavory pair of pale and pendulous kneecaps.

I rise from my seat to greet her, and she waves me down in an annoyed fashion, as if my courtly gesture is unnecessary. I, of course, remain standing as a mark of respect, and because I'm not *so* new to the game that I still fall for this—or any—ridiculous show of humility from anyone senior to me. I extend my hand and bow my head like I am battling a terminal disease, and this is my one-and-only audience with the pope.

"Ms. Shaw," I say as I deploy my most bootlicking smile. "This is *such* an honor."

"Oh, an honor, huh?" she says dismissively, but I know I have pleased her not only by standing, but by calling her—as we are routinely reminded to call everyone from the old guard—by the proper salutation: *Ms. Shaw.*

The waiter pulls out her chair, and she sits down, but not before she places her bag carefully on the adjacent seat. She doesn't remove her sunglasses and, up close, her black hair looks more red in the light, almost like she colors it herself, which I decide cannot *possibly* be true. She places her palms flat on the tablecloth, which causes the heavy gold men's Rolex on her wrist to clank loudly against the wood, and she quickly scans the room. Disappointed, she turns her attention back to me.

"I am sure you didn't come all the way here just to see me," she says, now ticking through the plastic holder of sugar packets on the table between us. She plucks out a yellow Splenda and starts to shake it. "So, what brings you to LA?"

"Several things, honestly," I say. "And one of them *was* to see you. Isobel was sorry she couldn't come out to LA herself this month."

It is not my place to reveal why Isobel could not make the trip herself, of course, and while Nana doesn't ask, it's clear she's less than thrilled to have been sent the dumpy deputy.

"Well, you can tell *Isobel* I need a bigger contract."

I was prepared for this.

"You're coming out to New York soon, right?" I reply with a smile. "For the gala?"

This seemingly innocent question is engineered to infer that, by simply making an appearance in human form at our annual spring gala, Nana Shaw can remedy her contract, and any other unfortunate misunderstandings, like she's the second coming of Jesus Fucking Christ.

I heard a rumor that one of Nana's former assistants regularly changed the day of the week on the *New York Times* crossword puzzle before she faxed it to Nana; she would turn Monday's puzzle (the easiest) into Saturdays's puzzle (the hardest), and when Nana completed what she thought was Saturday's crossword, everyone had a much easier week.

"Yes, but you should know how *bad* it looks for the magazine that you're asking me to fly in coach. I know a lot of people, and *a lot* of people know me," she says, now scanning the menu. "You'll need to get that changed."

"Of course."

"That *never* used to happen."

"I'm sure."

So, about the first-class thing: L.K. explicitly asked me to book Nana in coach with the clear understanding that Nana would throw an ever-loving hissy fit and be moved to her rightful seat in the first-class cabin. The change will require an additional fee through our travel department, about which no one will care, and I never know why we bother with these cost-cutting theatrics. Then again, I never know the real reason behind any decisions because the intimate details and inner workings of the magazine still remain well above my paygrade. Despite my title change, I have still never been officially invited to a meeting, and every piece of information I receive is, at best, third-hand.

A pretty waitress appears to tell us the specials. As she reads off her little notepad, Nana subjects her to an obvious, protracted, and ultimately unimpressed once-over before she orders grapefruit juice and plate of crisp bacon and potatoes. I order the spinach and Gruyère omelet because omelets are easy to cut and eat without making a total ass of yourself. The tables around us have started to fill up, and now Nana is complaining about her lack of an assistant, which is another longstanding situation about which I must look positively flabbergasted. Nana, you see, is a former "big-shot" editor, a species commonly found in the fashion magazine ecosystem but rarely spotted in the wild once it reaches maturity. In my mind, they are sort of the appendix of our industry: They must have been relevant at some point, historically speaking, but now they serve no clear purpose. Everyone carries on quietly for a while, dancing a deferential dance, because, well, it's easier than going to all the trouble and expense of removing it. However, there inevitably comes a juncture at which the editor feels overlooked or devalued or poorly seated enough that she explodes and—just like that—it becomes an emergency.

And, two things I have repeatedly observed in my short time in this business are: (1.) Like the appendix, people are expendable, and (2.) no matter your grievance, the house always wins.

The house always wins, yet, somehow, everyone thinks the outcome will be different for them. Every editor of a certain age truly believes they are *so* special and their contribution to fashion (and, by extension, the world at large) is *so* great, that they will get to remain on the team in perpetuity.

They never do.

Our breakfasts arrive and I eat what I calculate to be exactly one-third of my eggs before I lay my silverware on the plate and place my hands in my lap. It's time for my prepared text:

"So, Nana," I sigh happily. "You have such an incredible career. I'd love to know what advice you have for me."

Nana doesn't look at me. Instead, she spears a round potato with her fork and slices it in half.

"Advice?" she asks.

"Yes," I say with wide eyes and a sweet, hopeful nod. The point here is not to procure any proper advice, of course, but to make her *think* I care about her advice and, thus, flatter her.

She looks up from her plate and, without breaking her gaze, spears another potato.

"I was surprised when I saw you," she says plainly. "You *really* don't look the part."

Her words are so unexpected that they paralyze me like a poison dart. I sit utterly motionless while Nana Shaw, for her part, is entirely nonplussed. She just moves on to a piece of bacon on her plate. I watch as she cuts it with a knife and fork.

"And when you *don't look the part*," she continues. "You need to work *extra hard* at looking the part."

I say nothing.

"Do you think this"—she points her knife at me and draws an imaginary circle around my face—"is working extra hard?"

"I mean," I stutter. "I think so?"

"Hmmm, I see," she says. "You *think* so."

Here, Nana looks at me with bemusement before she spears another potato with an arched smile. Clearly, this is not her first rodeo: Nana Shaw has dined with a fawning little bitch like me before.

At this moment, a shrill, happy scream ripples through the restaurant. We both turn our heads to locate the source, which is two young blonde women embracing. This is going to sound weird, but as they jump up and down and squeal, they look like they barely know each other, but then again, what do I know? This is LA.

I am just grateful for the brief distraction.

With hesitation, I force myself to turn back to Nana. She rifles through her Birkin/Kelly bag with her head down, but I can see that a satisfied smile still warms her lips. As I wait quietly, her heavy sunglasses slide down to the tip of her nose, revealing that, in lieu of proper eyebrows, she has drawn on thin black arches where eyebrows used to be. This information feels uncomfortably intimate, and I look away with a pit in my stomach. When I turn back, I see she has pushed a lumpy, folded paper bag across the table.

"These are some of my medications," she says. "I want to keep extras in New York for my trip."

"Okay," I say cheerfully, but the way she says the word *medications* sounds so geriatric that something very small inside of my body takes a deep breath, exhales, and then dies.

"Just keep them inside your desk," she instructs. "Safe."

"Of course, Ms. Shaw," I say.

I awkwardly attempt to tuck the mystery parcel into my tote, and Nana just continues to watch me with that same vaguely supercilious expression. She knows this request makes me uncomfortable, but she also knows I will comply to get back into her good graces. In fact, this whole breakfast suddenly feels like a test from the home office, and I feel like a fool for underestimating Nana.

After we say a stilted goodbye in the lobby, I wonder if I should call Isobel for assistance. I don't want to risk a trip through airport security and embarrass everyone at the magazine by getting arrested for smuggling drugs, but I decide against it. If this *is* a test, I have no intention of tipping my hand by exhibiting an utter lack of self-possession and problem-solving skills.

After all, nobody wants to hold my hand.

As it happens, my bags *do* get deconstructed by a mustached TSA agent. He confiscates my face moisturizer for being over the strict three-ounce limit, but he seems wholly unfazed by the brown pharmacy bag full of clattering orange pill bottles—Ritalin, Lexapro, Xanax, Perocet, something called Amox-Clav—all of which are *not* prescribed to someone named Clodagh Harmon. Once I am safely in my first-class seat, I lean my head back and exhale. The cabin smells revolting, like someone just opened a container of yogurt, and as we start to taxi down the runway, I close my eyes tight.

I'll never understand why anyone lives in California.

40

Over the next year, I do some things I know I shouldn't do.
I do some things I know I shouldn't do, but I rationalize that, by doing them, I will surely get promoted and, once I am promoted, I will make good on any indiscretions, financial or otherwise. Absent my near disembowelment by Nana Shaw, my trip to LA was considered a success. My article was approved, mostly thanks to Isobel editing the copy within an inch of its life, and L.K. Smith even stopped by to tell me I had done a "fine job." When the advance copies arrive, I gingerly snip the delicate pages out of the issue with a gleaming set of silver scissors and secure them in a black clip book I bought at the fancy art supplies store in my neighborhood. I mail a copy of the issue to my mother, even though she, of course, pays for a subscription.

For starters (and perhaps at Harry's light suggestion), I have been getting my hair professionally blown-out pin-straight three mornings a week. I charge this service to Barbara's credit card, but I counterbalance the unsavory bits of this behavior with an obvious frugality: I don't choose a fancy, magazine-approved salon. Instead, I frequent an inexpensive chain with a French name situated off Times Square. It is located between a nameless storefront that sells incense and phone cards, and a very popular Starbucks outpost. My "blow-out lady" (as I call her) is a short, perpetually cheerful old Russian woman who, when not wielding a blow-dryer, chain-smokes and reads palms. Despite the wholly transactional nature of our relationship, I find myself regularly troubled about her health. Her cough registers at near Brontë proportions, and her face is perpetually swollen and ruddy from what I decide—thanks to her liberal application of perfume and everything I know about Russia, which is nothing—is chronic alcohol abuse, probably vodka. During my appointments, I talk about things like exercise and vitamins, just to see if she responds in the affirmative, and on the rare mornings she isn't at the salon, I become convinced she is dead, splayed out on the floor of her apartment.

You see, despite my financial situation being less than ideal, I understand there are certain dues—like reliably straight hair, shaped eyebrows, and compulsive dry cleaning—that must be paid to retain your spot on the team. Just like, say, when you join a sorority. However, I am also loath to reveal to my coworkers, or to Harry Wood, the degree to which I am actively struggling with money. People know I am not as wealthy as, say, Davis Lawrence, of course, but I work very hard to paint an otherwise abstract picture of what family money, if any, I may possess. To keep up the ruse, I have been known, on occasion, to use Barbara's credit card, but only to buy things that will either *advance* or *obscure* my reputation. I start small: A lipstick from YSL called Le Rouge. A John Derian decoupage tray to keep on my desk. A classic black Theory blazer. As time goes on, I find I *simply must* buy plane tickets to attend mission-critical events like, oh, I don't know, a coworker's bachelorette party in Tulum, or, maybe, a quick trip down to Art Basel in Miami with Harry to network. I go to a holistic doctor and get something done called cupping, which costs $400 and leaves me with nothing but biscuit-sized black bruises on my back. I participate in the office-wide juice cleanses and shit my brains out in the unventilated office bathroom for days. I do barre classes in Soho at thirty-five dollars a pop, and buy the "barre-specific" socks (ten dollars) every week because I continuously misplace the pair I purchased just the week prior. I endure something called a Brazilian bikini wax at a truly terrifying place in Midtown called J. Sisters where my furry nether region is nothing but a sickening disappointment to the gruff Russian women employed there, and I once tried a spray tan, which—aside from feeling like the wrong end of a firing squad—turned my pale skin an unnatural, carroty hue, like one of the more frantic Muppets.

Okay, there *is* another thing, which doesn't look great on paper, but is industry standard to such a degree that it is, quite possibly, nothing but white noise. This would be the compromising of any semblance of journalistic integrity (although it may be debated if fashion magazines are held to the same standard as, say, the *New York Times*) in exchange for super awesome free stuff. What kind of free stuff, you ask? Well, to name a very limited few: free dinners at new restaurants; microdermabrasion treatments; deeply discounted, custom-made Manolo Blahniks that arrive in sheeny white boxes directly from Italy; Broadway tickets (two on the aisle!); shopping bags full of expensive makeup and night creams; handbags from Marc Jacobs; and silk scarves from Hermès.

Now, at the top of the glittering pyramid during this moment in history is the "press trip," which is an obscenely luxurious vacation for a handful of important editors that is paid for by a brand in exchange for possible coverage in said editor's respective magazine. So far, I have skied in Jackson Hole, attended the opening of a boutique hotel in Miami, and enthusiastically participated in a wine tasting in Sonoma where I drank too much and slept with a newspaper editor named Stan from the *LA Times*. Say what you will, but press trips are wildly effective. After all, we toil in an industry where relationships are *everything*, and there is no better way for a reporter to amass reliable contacts than to spend a weekend drinking endless bottles of expensive wine in a rustic hot tub, all in the name of journalism.

In this period, there is also what's called a "media rate," which is the dumpy second cousin to the press trip. However, what the media rate lacks in immoderation, it makes up for in versatility as a media rate is not time-bound, and it can be applied to nearly any hotel in the world.

To procure a media rate for personal or professional reasons, the conversation with the press representative of the property you would like to visit goes like this:

Magazine Journalist: "I have heard so much about your hotel, and I would love to check it out. Can I book a room with you? Or should I call the main reservations number?"

Public Relations Woman: "Oh, no. Someone like you doesn't call reservations! It's unnecessary as we would *love* to have you stay with us for free!"

MJ: (pause) "Oh, I couldn't accept a free room. We aren't allowed to do that from an ethical perspective."

PR: (knowing pause) "Of course! I forgot to mention we also have a media rate for working journalists."

MJ: "Oh, wonderful. I'd be happy to pay the media rate. What is it?"

PR: "Uh... it's fifty dollars a night. Would that work?"

Would that work? The room she is offering me for fifty dollars costs over $2,000 a night *during the offseason*. While I am there, I can also expect a boozy dinner with the PR team, during which someone will get inappropriately handsy with me under the table, and at least one spa treatment or excursion, which generally involves a helicopter or wooden boat that I am to understand is rare and expensive.

Yes. That will, indeed, work.

Finally, I occasionally use Barbara's money to play the role of generous benefactor to Harry Wood. After the accident, I rationalized I was simply taking Davis's place by performing regular good deeds like paying for Harry's cabs, cigarettes, and the occasional, late-night cocaine delivery from his drug dealer, an affable guy named Raf who pedaled around the city on a BMX bike. After all, Harry was a poor orphan who invested his own savings, however meager, into his website, and I am a champion of a free press. The truth being, of course, I am delighted to provide for Harry Wood because I am very keen to stay in his glamorous, well-connected circle and the best way to do this, I reckon, is to appear both glamorous and well-connected myself. In recent months, we have been spending a lot of time together, and although it can sometimes feel more like a business meeting than an official friendship, it is the closest I have ever come to being in a popular crowd. When we aren't at parties, we meet up at wine bars or his apartment to go through our invitations for the week, sorting out what events we should attend and what events we can safely skip with no damage to our emerging reputations. In truth, most of the events are mine; I have started to get invited to things—here and there—in Davis's wake, but I am only too happy to share this bounty with Harry.

To have easy spending cash on hand for my endeavors, I have devised a system where I use Barbara's credit card for things my company continuously and inexplicably is happy to expense (coffee, magazines, shoe repair, blow-outs, dry cleaning, drinks) and I diligently turn in my receipts for reimbursement, as directed. Once those receipts are processed (without question by some mysterious entity headquartered in another state), the money is deposited directly into my personal bank account at Citibank, at which point I am free to withdraw the money and spend as I see fit, which, on several occasions, has been my rent in Brooklyn.

In my defense, I am not *totally* irresponsible here. I maintain a detailed accounting of Barbara's money in a small black notebook I keep in my handbag. I know, down to the dollar, how much I have spent, and I fully intend to pay back every penny once I start to make some real money, which I suspect is right around some approaching (and hopefully not imaginary) corner. Like Davis, I am careful to keep my purchase amounts under five digits to avoid setting off any alarms with Barbara's accountant, and thus far, there has only been one occasion where I thought, for the briefest of moments, that I might get caught out. Harry and I had dinner downtown at Butter on Lafayette Street with a small group of people that included an impossibly cool girl DJ and a small, start-up fashion designer with whom Harry had recently been spending a lot of time. It was one of those nights where my clothes felt too tight and, conversationally, I was unable to find my footing. Despite all evidence to the contrary, however, I kept telling myself I was having fun because I *should* be having fun. When the waiter brought the check to the table for me to sign, he said: *"It's been a pleasure to serve you, Barbara,"* and I stole a glance at Harry to see what, if anything, he had heard, only to discover his expression was entirely neutral. Nevertheless, as I slipped the card back into the secret compartment in my wallet, I had to remind myself to be more careful.

Overall, I would say my system, at least so far, has been successful, but despite my diligent record-keeping and good intentions, I am also not stupid: I recognize that things have gotten out of control. I have spent more money than I can ever reasonably hope to repay on my current (or even slightly increased) salary, but I have no idea how to remedy this problem in the short-term. Furthermore, the longer I go without getting caught, the more I can disassociate the action (bad) from me as a person (good). So, in the absence of a plan, I just pray every night that I will be saved by some turn of luck or twist of fate, and then I wake up and start all over again.

As they say: The only way out is through.

41

Because Barbara Lawrence refuses to have a second summer derailed by Davis's injury, and Davis still seems to enjoy my company, I am invited on a semi-regular basis out to Southampton during the *season*. These days, I am occasionally offered a ride by some of the girls at work—all of whom are happy to drop me off on the way to their boyfriends' houses on Gin Lane or a dinner with their parents in East Hampton at the Maidstone Club—but I find small talk in cars to be excruciating, not to mention dangerous. There are too many ways to tip my hand, too many signals I am likely to misinterpret. As such, I prefer to take the Jitney. It allows me to spend three hours alone, happily reading whatever new novel I promised Isobel I would read by Monday, my sandaled feet resting on the stiff canvas of my monogrammed bag. I don't speak to anyone, but it's not too difficult as nobody speaks to me. Instead, as I watch the spires of Manhattan slowly sink into the horizon, I allow the bricks of stress to slough off me, if only for a few hours. When the little bus trundles onto the now-familiar streets of Southampton, I know I am back on duty. Barbara and Davis always pick me up in the cream Mercedes convertible, although they generally keep the top up these days, much to my dismay. Some nights, I try to sell Davis on going out on the town—maybe to a club or even just for dinner—but she always declines. In some ways, I understand. In the eighteen months since the accident, there have been a few setbacks, mainly from complications surrounding a second operation on her ankle that left her with pain so severe she was prescribed some kind of painkiller that can render her a little unpredictable. She can seem disoriented or drowsy, and sometimes she loses the thread of a conversation, and while I would find this handicap infuriating, Davis seems oddly relieved to shelter behind whatever thick cloud the pills reliably provide her. As for Barbara, she makes no comment on the matter, preferring to view Davis's troubles like a beautiful ghost that temporarily haunts the house. Here is the thing: Davis is *not* fine—not really—and I find it perplexing there seems to be a mammoth effort to ignore her struggles, but hardly any thought put toward solving them. Sometimes I worry I should intervene, but I find I can quickly absolve myself from even the *perception* of culpability because I am just an outsider.

After all, I am quick to reason, I am not her *mother*.

With Barbara's blessing, I don't pack a bigger bag for my summer weekends because I keep some clothes at the house. I was assigned a few drawers in Davis's room, which is where I sleep despite the existence of two exceptionally well-appointed guest rooms. I have filled my drawers with bathing suits and exercise clothes and my dresses, skirts, and white jeans are pinned to pink satin hangers by Marta.

This Friday, because of an accident on Montauk Highway that backed up traffic for miles, it is nearly dark by the time I arrive at the Jitney stop. When we get back to the house, Davis makes popcorn. She pours a glass of white wine for each of us, and we collapse on the couch, snuggling ourselves under the same blanket. As we debate what movie to watch, Davis tips two round, white pills in her mouth. They are smaller than the chalky-looking Vicodin she used to take, and she washes them down cleanly with a sip of wine.

She catches me looking at her.

"My foot," she explains, but she looks embarrassed, so I rub her arm. I nod like I understand.

"You have been through so much," I coo.

At the comment, Davis smiles at me like I am the only woman in the whole world. Then, she rests her beautiful head on my shoulder, and I ruffle with contentment.

The next morning, I roll over to discover Davis is not in the bed. I turn my eyes toward the painted white beams that run across the vaulted ceiling, and I just lie there for a good, long while. I close my eyes and try to force myself back asleep, but it proves a lost cause. A singular seagull makes one of those throaty, staccato calls you only hear by the sea; it's as if he is endeavoring to warn us all of something dire, but to his frustration, no one will pay him any mind. The gull goes on for a while, repeating the same call, and I slowly come to realize the house is otherwise quiet.

Too quiet.

I suspect I have been left alone.

I get out of bed and stretch my arms over my head, which triggers some bone in the middle of my chest to audibly pop in disarmingly geriatric fashion. I pull a hooded sweatshirt over my head, and heel-toe barefoot over to the kitchen, where I discover Davis sitting alone, reading a magazine. She absently dunks a teabag in a proper teacup—no saucer—and when she hears my footsteps, she looks up with a smile. She is wearing an old, oversized pair of tortoiseshell eyeglasses and her hair is tangled.

"Good morning, sunshine," I chirp.

Before she can respond, a screen door slams, like a close-range rifle shot. I wonder why, for a house so meticulously turned out, no one bothered to install springs on a single door. Every time I hear one of the doors yawn open, my entire body seizes up in anticipatory horror. Davis, of course, is reliably unperturbed by the noise because, as it happens, old money loves a full-bodied smack from an old screen door. It is yet another component of a larger, most secret code for which I still, despite my best efforts, have no legend.

There is a second smack, and Barbara sweeps into the kitchen. She wears a gargantuan pair of black sunglasses and cradles a precarious tower of newspapers topped with a cardboard coffee holder full of cups. She places everything in a jumble on the table, including her car keys and wallet, and immediately sighs with irritation at the mess, as if it's not of her own making. I watch as her neck cranes around, almost reflexively, for Carmen, her longtime housekeeper in the Hamptons. She's in her white tennis clothes, but the shirt is too tight; I can see a pad of fat bulge over her bra strap. This is very uncharacteristic for Barbara who, when not relentlessly exercising with her trainer, is relentlessly tailoring her clothes. I am suddenly thunderstruck by a previously unconsidered realization: What if there is a point for every woman in which diligence can no longer save you?

Aging is a horrifying thought.

"Ah, coffee," Davis says. She pushes her teacup aside and reaches for a paper cup. "Much better."

Davis removes the lid and blows on the coffee lightly before she takes a sip and makes an unhappy face. She pushes back her chair, limps to the island, and dumps two spoonsful of sugar from the dish on the counter into her cup.

"Too much sugar, Davis," her mother murmurs, but Davis just shrugs and settles back into her seat. She separates the sections of the *New York Times*, passing Arts and Leisure and Metropolitan to her mother and sliding Sunday Styles to me. She keeps the *New York Post* for herself, and I am mesmerized by the slow and thoughtful way she turns each oversized page, like she has all the time in the world. I crack open my section and, as I do every Sunday, I thumb straight to the wedding announcements where I scan each vignette for a single piece of information: the age of the bride. This week is an upsetting assemblage of girls in their mid-to-late twenties, all of whom are *not* keeping their name. Last week was much better. It featured a bunch of women who were over thirty-three, which is my magic, you-are-not-yet-tragic number. I close the section and decide to depress myself with the Real Estate section instead.

We all read in a lovely silence for a good long while.

"Well, well, well . . ." Davis says.

Her voice cracks the protective shell around us, like a brisk spoon smacking a soft-boiled egg. Barbara and I look up, lightly sedated, from our reading.

"What is it?" I ask.

Davis says nothing. She just slides the open newspaper in my direction. I look down to where she points, and my heart muscle seizes: It's me. Right there, in the middle of Page Six, is a photograph of me. It is a small group shot, and I am wearing a borrowed Carolina Herrera dress. It was so tight that the fluttering, gauzy armpits split open during cocktail hour, and I had to spend the rest of the evening with my elbows pressed down my sides. I can easily recall the exact moment this image was captured, which was during a garden party held earlier this week in a museum. I had taken Harry as my guest. In the picture, his arm is wrapped tight around my waist, and my arm dangles down languidly.

I look wonderfully bored.

Like Davis.

As I have never been on Page Six before, my first instinct is to leap up from the table screaming with joy and call Allie so she can buy up all the copies from her local newsstand, but I understand—from the lack of celebration in the room—that I have done something very, very wrong.

"God, I look awful," I groan.

That's right: I cannot think of anything *else* to do other than to put myself down in the hopes that my clear inferiority will bring everyone else in the room back up to a comfortable altitude.

Barbara cranes her neck to get a closer look, which causes her reading glasses to slip slightly down her nose. She stares at the photo for a few seconds before she returns to her own perfectly folded piece of newspaper.

There is a long, freighted pause.

"You've looked better," she says, finally, her voice flat. "Your arm looks fat."

At this comment, I steal a glance at Davis.

Her face has gone completely white.

How strange, I think. *Mess of your own making.*

After breakfast. Davis and I go down to the beach. We sunbathe and read magazines in an uncomfortable silence before I suggest a short walk. Davis agrees, and we pull ourselves up drowsily from our striped towels and head toward the ocean. Nothing further has been said about my photograph in the paper, and although I understand I am in trouble, I get the sense there is little I can do to remedy the situation. I must wait for the storm to pass. As we move slowly down the sand, I feel emotionally exhausted, like one half of a perfectly lovely couple that, despite their very best efforts, remains on the brink of divorce. We come to a stop at the water's edge, and the sand feels cool and gelatinous under my bare feet. With each receding wave, I watch a scattering of tiny, pastel-colored clams dig frantically for cover. Once they are safe, I unearth them with my toes, over and over. I want to watch them struggle for salvation.

"Do you want to swim?" I offer tentatively, looking back at Davis.

"No," she says. "I don't really swim anymore."

I recall the black maillot I saw hanging in the outdoor shower this morning.

"Oh," I manage.

"I mean, because of my injuries," she says quickly, almost as if she read my mind. "That's why I don't swim."

No, I think. *She doesn't swim with me.*

We meander a little farther down the beach, our only communion found in the brief moments our bodies touch as we sidestep the unseasonably icy water. It is high summer, and there are people everywhere, spread out on towels or sitting on chairs underneath umbrellas. At a certain point, Davis stops again, and I watch as she draws circles in the wet sand with her big toe. The air is warm, but not hot, and an irksome wind scatters the intermittent patches of sun that toast my shoulders. Davis wears enormous sunglasses, and her tangled hair whips in every direction, but she makes no effort to contain it. The ocean waves thunder in my ears and I can see whitecaps start to peak past the swell.

"I am sorry my mom said that about your arm," Davis says finally.

"It's fine," I say with a half shrug. "I mean, it did look fat."

Davis snorts lightly, and we stand together a little longer.

"So," she begins, but there is a cautiousness to her approach, like she is trying to find the right words. "You and Harry seem to have become good friends."

I don't respond immediately. Instead, I watch a wave crest in the far distance. There is something in her tone that signals me to tread carefully.

"I guess?" I reply, finally.

"I am not mad or anything," she quickly clarifies. She tosses me a tepid smile. "I just got the impression you didn't see that much of each other?"

"We really don't," I say. "We just happened to show up at the same party, but I can see how it's weird."

"It's okay," she says. "Harry is a very good guy."

"Yeah," I respond, but maybe a little too wistfully. "I mean, he seems like it."

"So, are you two a little bit *more* than friends?" she inquires, her eyes wide.

"What? No!" I blurt out, even though I feel wonderfully validated by the accusation.

"I wouldn't be mad," she says, but I am unconvinced.

"Davis, trust me," I say. "He makes it *very* clear I am just a placeholder."

"Placeholder?"

"For you," I say. "He is just waiting for you to come back."

This seems to brighten Davis, but only briefly.

"The whole world is just waiting for you to come back," I add.

Davis rubs her wrist.

"But come back to what?" she asks.

"The magazine?" I venture. "The world?"

"I think about coming back to work all the time," she says. "But it feels overwhelming."

"Do you miss it?"

"Miss what?"

"I don't know," I say with a shrug. "Being in the world?"

"Sometimes?"

"Hmmm," I respond unhelpfully.

"To be honest, it's been a bit of a relief," she says. "Before, my mother was always on my case, upset with me about something, and now it's like she's lost all interest in me."

Her comment surprises me, mostly because she cannot possibly believe it, but I say nothing in response. She grabs a fistful of her hair and pulls it away from her eyes. She turns to look at me directly.

"That's terrible, isn't it?" she presses, but I get the sense she doesn't think it's terrible at all. She seems proud, like an amateur magician who has, after countless failed attempts, finally wrestled free from a pair of of underwater handcuffs.

"Davis, your mother has not lost all interest in you," I protest with a snorting laugh. "Trust me. You are *all* she talks about."

"Davis Lawrence," she says.

I look over at her quizzically.

"Have you ever noticed I am never Davis? I am always *Davis Lawrence*."

I think about this for a second; I had not noticed, but she's right.

"Listen, I understand that she wants me to reflect well on her," she continues. "I mean, I am her only child."

"You do reflect well on her," I insist. "I mean, everyone wants to be *Davis Lawrence!*"

Here, she laughs, and I laugh, too. It feels good to laugh.

"Well, I have been very well trained," she says. "Do you know I had my first skincare consultation when I was nine?"

She laughs again, but I say nothing.

"I mean, at the time, that seemed normal, but now that I am older, it feels sort of strange?"

"In your mom's defense, you do have great skin," I joke.

"Of course, I do," she responds, and, while she smiles, her voice curdles slightly. "It's important that everything be great. Just not *too great*, of course."

"Not *too great?*"

"No greater than the *great* Barbara Lawrence," she clarifies, and her tone is theatric.

"What do you mean?"

"She always needs to be the star," she says. "Don't pretend you haven't noticed."

"Sometimes, I guess?" I venture, benignly.

"Listen," she says, and she looks at me sideways, her tone quietly serious. "You need to be more careful about things."

"What things?"

She seems to think for a minute, and I start to feel the blood drain out of my face.

"There is an invisible line that you *cannot* cross with my mother," she says. "But it's not easy. I never know exactly where it's drawn because she is always moving it."

"I am sorry about the newspaper thing," I say.

"It's not *just* about that, although that wasn't great," Davis says. "It's bigger than that."

"What happens when you cross it?" I ask.

She turns back to the ocean.

"I mean, have you ever crossed it?" I press, and I hear my voice falter. Davis nods, but when she says nothing else, my mind starts to race.

"Anyway," she says, recovering with a simple wave of her hand. "It's all fine."

"It doesn't sound *all fine?*" I manage.

Here, she smiles cheerlessly.

"It's better than when I was a kid," she says. "Let's just put it that way."

"What happened when you were a kid?"

She doesn't respond, but I remember what Harry said to me, years ago, during the blackout: *I guess I would drink too much if I had her childhood.* In this moment, I find it strange that I never asked him to elaborate. It's almost as if I didn't want to know because knowing would complicate something I had no interest in making complicated.

I want everything to be as easy as it looks.

Davis glances over her shoulder. The house looms watchfully in the high, pale dunes.

"Let's go back," she says. "I've walked too far already."

42

That evening, Barbara has a cocktail party and, naturally, it has long been decided that I will attend, which means Davis will be left home alone for a few hours. Generally, I love nothing more than to network at society functions with Barbara, but the atmosphere in the house still feels so profoundly ominous that I am afraid to be alone with her. As I put on makeup in the bathroom, Davis sits on the toilet and pages through a magazine. I lean toward the mirror to wing some mascara on my lashes, and a soupy anxiety starts to congeal in my chest.

"Does it bother you?" I ask Davis.

"What?"

"That I am going to another party with your mom and leaving you here?"

I am angling for an out.

"No," she says without looking up from her magazine. "Honestly, if she doesn't go out, she just paces around the house, and it drives me crazy. She's like an English hound."

"Okay," I say. "But just so you know, I would *much* rather stay here."

"I know," she says.

"I'm just not sure how to say no to her?"

"Don't worry," Davis says as she presents me with a wan smile. "No one knows how to say no to my mother."

✻ ✻ ✻

The party is being held at a private home on the bay, which is on the other side of town, and, at Barbara's request, I drive her in the convertible with the top up because she doesn't want to ruin her hair.

As I pull out of the gravel driveway, the air is luxuriant with the stench of a dead low tide, and I wish—maybe more than anything—that I was driving with Davis, or, frankly, with *anyone* my own age: I want to put the top down and howl with youthful rapture into the collecting night.

Instead, I am the responsible party. I must drive slowly and carefully along the roads with both hands on the steering wheel. For her part, Barbara is curiously silent, and after about five minutes, she speaks:

"She's very attached to you, you know," Barbara says. "I'm sure you realize that."

"Who?"

"Davis," she replies.

"Oh," I reply uncertainly.

"And you have been so good to her," she continues. "And so good to me, and I want you to know how much we appreciate you."

"Of course," I say. "I am so happy to help."

"She's a weak girl," Barbara says with a soft shake of her head.

I grip the wheel tighter. It's strange: Her delivery of this assessment is so inscrutable that I'm not sure if she is conveying pity or contempt for her daughter, but I also don't think it matters: She simply wants to discern where my loyalty lies.

"Turn here," Barbara says, and she points me down a half-paved lane that runs along the water. After a quarter of a mile, she instructs me to slow down across from a small, shingled cottage. I slide the car into park and gaze across the street, but I can barely make out the shape of the house. It is hidden by overgrown pine trees and a maze of holly-like brambles.

"I want to give you this," Barbara says, and she hands me a small black velvet jewelry box. "They are the earrings you admired so much last summer."

"Oh, Barbara," I exclaim, embarrassed by the gesture. "This isn't necessary."

"It's just a little thank-you," she says. "It's nice to know I can trust you to take care of her."

I open the box.

"Put them on," Barbara says with a smile, and I comply, slipping them on with the help of the visor mirror. When I turn to show her, the earrings swing slightly, and the diamonds pull down heavily on my lobes.

"They suit you," she says, with a satisfied nod. "And... Now you will never forget us."

Here, Barbara gets out of the car, and I follow quietly behind her. When we reach the open front door, we are greeted by a mellow, ungroomed Airedale, who we follow down a short hallway and into a high-ceilinged living room. We are right on time for the party, but the room is already elbow to elbow with people, all of whom seem wonderfully drunk and untroubled by the wicked ways of the world. It's the kind of crowd that makes me look forward to being old one day, so long as I am also in possession of a beach house and a tremendous amount of money. When we pass through the threshold, nobody seems to notice our arrival. I look at Barbara, and her face twitches like a discontented cat. Clearly, she thinks she has somehow been *excluded* from some VIP start time, and I know from experience this is not an auspicious beginning. She exhales; this is somehow my fault.

"Did you get the start time wrong?" she hisses over her shoulder.

"No," I say quickly. "You said it was seven o'clock."

"I hope you're right," she replies through a gritted smile. "I don't need to be embarrassed in front of my friends."

"You said seven o'clock," I repeat, but this time, I feel uncertain. *Was I supposed to check the invitation?*

However, within fifteen minutes of our arrival, things start to pick up. I have completed my daughterly duties: I escorted Barbara into the room and procured her first cocktail. As I delivered said cocktail, I made a big, fawning fuss about something Barbara had *said* or *done* that day to no less than three people, making sure one of them is a man with whom Barbara could flirt. Finally, I have answered with great solemnity some questions about Davis's health and lauded Barbara, yet again, for her tireless work as a mother. For my efforts, she smiles bashfully and gives my arm a little rub while our audience nods at me with cloudy-eyed approval. They call me things like "lovely" and "delightful," and I am somewhat ashamed by how much this pleases me.

With Barbara momentarily content, I am free to retreat to the bar and get a drink for myself. I settle on a vodka and club soda, and finger my new earrings as I take little sips from the tall glass. I look around the room to see if there is anyone I know or, more importantly, anyone I should meet that could be useful to me. This is an older crowd and quite distinguished, although I am never entirely sure who's who among playwrights and novelists and historians that flitter in and out of Barbara's larger world. Of course, one of the people I *do* recognize is our hostess, Greta Greer. Greta is an older woman, maybe in her sixties, and she was once the very famous editor-in-chief of an equally famous fashion magazine. This is her party, and this is her house. Greta is tall with thin arms, and her long graying hair falls loosely down her back. There are freckles on her face, and, even at a distance, she smells like sandalwood and sage. She exudes that mystical brand of quiet self-assurance that I suspect cannot be manufactured. Whatever she has, she was born with it. As I watch her gesticulate with a stubby cigarette between her fingers, I am bewildered by her hands, which are brown-spotted and run wild with bulging blue veins. They are the hands of a properly elderly woman, and yet, they look marvelous to me, fearless and free. On her ring finger, she wears an enormous square emerald surrounded by diamonds and her nails are painted the same orange red as my mother's potted geraniums. I look down at my own hands self-consciously, and realize I must look like a blank envelope in comparison to this woman. I watch her kiss a man on both cheeks before she turns in the direction of the kitchen and vanishes—much to my chagrin—from sight.

I continue to take in these most unfamiliar surroundings. Much like our hostess, this old house is a wonder. According to Barbara, it was erected long before the Hamptons became, well, *the* Hamptons, and it has been in this family for generations. The walls and the ceiling are constructed of honey-colored, knotty wood planks, so porous that you can see light peeking through from other rooms, and the living room is decorated with old rattan and wicker furniture. There is no air-conditioning, and the cushions, which are upholstered in a faded floral pattern, are gently speckled with mold. Despite this being the summer season, a single log burns in a stone fireplace so cavernous that you could literally roast my entire body inside it on a pike. The fire perfumes the air with the festive, nostalgic scent of wood smoke and barefoot summers, and, for a moment, I feel like a happy child.

People crowd around the fireplace mantel, which is littered with beaded clutch bags and empty glasses, and everyone interacts with an ease I don't usually come across at Barbara's events. To begin, there is a lively foursome playing gin rummy at a round table. They holler and throw cards while empty high-ball glasses rest in puddles of condensation at their elbows. Near the kitchen, a tipsy older couple sways to music I cannot hear, while another twosome huddles conspiratorially on the couch. They whisper with their foreheads pressed together, and I imagine they are secret lovers, trading incendiary gossip and sweet nothings, right under the noses of their unwitting spouses. This party is fun, and it strikes me as a gathering of *friends*, not the usual "acquaintances" or "former colleagues" with whom Barbara congregates in an unyielding (and increasingly desperate-seeming) effort to remain top of mind. But these people also don't seem like Barbara's friends; they are too sloppy and unguarded.

At some stage, the couple's three children appear briefly from points unknown. It is two boys and a girl, and they look to be in their twenties. They are uniformly tall, tan, and blond with that rugged beauty I've only ever seen in a Ralph Lauren advertisement. The youngest boy, who looks to be in college, stays after his siblings depart. He wears a faded rugby shirt, no shoes, and a dingy, sea-soaked sailor's wristlet. He moves with remarkable ease among these adults, all of whom he has, no doubt, known since he was a towheaded toddler. He shakes hands and laughs and accepts a good-natured hair rumpling or two, and I find myself longing for a family and house and life just like this one day. I want to be old and happy, and in these moments, I wonder if I blew my only chance at this kind of future the day I packed my bags for New York.

Too late now, I think.

I scan the room to confirm Barbara remains occupied before I get another vodka and soda. The room has grown warm, and I walk toward a set of open French doors when I see her: Susan Goldsmith-Cohen. I have not laid eyes on her since the party at her house the summer before Davis's accident—the summer of the stolen horse—and I am startled by how much older she looks after the passage of only a few short years. As I stand there, paralyzed, Susan looks up from her conversation, and when her eyes meet mine, they pass over me in a dim, frowning recognition. Quickly, I push my way through the crowd, and stumble onto the back patio. Once I confirm I am alone, I lean against a shingled wall, and I cover my face with my hands. I sink down to my heels and scream silently into my palms. It feels like a rickety dam is breaking apart inside my chest and flooding my entire body with poison. I think of the horse, which currently sits on the desk in my apartment, and wonder what possessed me to show my face at this, or any, party so close to the scene of my crime. My hands shaking, I pull a cigarette out of my bag, and light it quickly. I take a few deep drags before I stand up, but my legs are disjointed and unreliable so I lean against the house, and look out over the vanishing bay. The sun is well below the trees at this hour, and in the newly green gloaming, I make out the silhouettte of an old wooden dock. It extends with great trepidation into the lapping water, its graying railings are hung with crab traps and multicolored buoys. There is a flagpole at the end of the lawn, and the cleats bang loudly against the metal, like a lonesome boat at sea. Suddenly, I hear footsteps behind me.

This is it, I think.

"Sometimes, I need a break from these things, too," an unfamiliar voice says.

I turn my head and discover, with more than a little relief, that it is Greta Greer. She bows her head and, with a flick and a hiss, lights up a cigarette with a gold Zippo lighter. She snaps the lighter shut and exhales. I say nothing and she looks up to the sky.

"My husband says I should stop throwing so many parties if I tire of them so easily, but, as they say"—and here, she exhales smoke into the air—"old habits die hard."

"It's a beautiful party," I say.

"Thank you," she says, and then she looks at me a little closer. "You came with Barbara Lawrence, right?"

Her smile is warm, but I worry that Barbara would say I shouldn't trust her. Barbara doesn't think it's wise to trust anyone.

"Yes, I am a friend of her daughter Davis," I say. "From work."

"A magazine girl," she says approvingly. "One of us."

"Yes," I say sheepishly. "I mean, I guess?"

"I am Greta," she says, and she extends her left hand for a light shake.

"Yes," I say. "It's so nice to meet you."

"So, how *is* Davis these days?"

"She's good," I say. "She's mostly better."

"Terrible what happened to her," she says. "Wasn't it?"

I nod, and Greta takes another deep inhale on her cigarette.

"I have heard about you," she continues, her voice pinched. She exhales with a little cough.

"You have?" I ask.

"Yes," she says. "You're the surrogate daughter. *Everyone* knows about you."

Her smile is wholly unchanged, but I don't like this designation, which is strange as it is exactly what I have been working so hard to become.

"Oh, hardly a surrogate daughter," I say, and I force my tone to remain buoyant. "I am just happy to help where I can."

"Of course," she responds with a kind nod. She drops her cigarette to the deck, and when she doesn't stomp on it, I notice she is barefoot. "Like the boy."

I wonder if she means Harry, but she does not elaborate. Instead, she points down to her smoldering, half-smoked cigarette.

"Those things will kill you," she says, and I get the unsettling impression she isn't talking about the cigarette. "You are young enough to quit."

"I know," I mumble.

I feel stupid and bashful and fat.

Here, Greta Greer turns away from me. She leans her elbows on the railing of the deck. I move gingerly next to her as she points across the water.

"Do you see all those houses over there?" she asks. Across the bay, I can see yellow lights glinting from a handful of windows.

I nod.

"When I grew up, there was nothing but darkness," she says. "Now, they are building a hotel."

"It must have been beautiful," I say. "Quiet."

"Oh," she says softly. "It was."

We fall into silence.

"I read your magazine all the time when you were the editor," I say finally. "It was one of my favorites."

"And here you are now," she says. She waves her arm in an arc above her head.

"And here I am now." I smile, then add: "When you left, I read you were going to start your own magazine?"

"Hmm," she murmurs with wistful amusement. "I thought I would, too."

"What happened?"

"Well, once I left the magazine, it was hard to get anyone interested."

"Really?"

"I quickly learned there was a very big difference between 'Oh, this is so-and-so calling from the magazine' and 'Oh, this is so-and-so calling from . . . my apartment.'"

"That's surprising," I say, but she only shrugs.

We both gaze over the bay for another minute, and then Greta pushes herself upright and turns toward the door.

"I'm sorry," she says. "But I didn't get your name?"

"It's Clo," I say, and I clear my throat: "Clodagh Harmon."

"Clodagh Harmon," she repeats. "I'll remember that one."

After she disappears inside, I watch her discarded cigarette slowly burn down on the deck. It looks like a week-old umbilical cord. I worry it will smolder between the planks and the house will burn to the ground, and I will wake up in the morning to learn that this entire world was lost, and it was all my fault. I consider extinguishing it with the toe of my sandal, but I do not. Standing there, I feel tired of doing what everyone expects me to do all the time.

I am just tired.

My drink is empty, and I jangle the ice in my glass. I am unsure if getting a third drink is a good idea, especially as I am required to drive Barbara home at some currently unknown point, but I figure it can't hurt to see what is going on around the bar. As I turn toward the French doors, however, I am stopped short by what I see through the windows.

It is Davis.

She stands in the middle of the living room wearing a long white dress. She looks frail, but glows ethereal, like the ghost of a dead, much-beloved child. Her lips are finger-dabbed with a rich diamond gloss and her clean, brushed blonde hair topples down her shoulders like a shipwrecked mermaid. Her wide eyes search, as ever, for someone to save her, but there is no desperation in her manner.

Naturally, Davis is not adrift for long because girls like Davis Lawrence are never adrift for long. She is quickly approached by several people, mostly men, and the gentle intensity of the swarm that builds around her is unlike anything I have experienced in my life. As I watch the scene unfold from my perch on the patio, I feel jealous, like I'm playing a plump, petulant Scarlett O'Hara, forced to bask in the wispy goodness of her Melanie Hamilton. I steal an apprehensive glance around the room to locate Barbara, and I am relieved to discover she remains coquettishly engaged with a good-looking, younger man in the corner. He looks exactly like one of those sculpted, financially secure men with hair like a beaver pelt that one generally sees featured in luxury watch advertisements. I met him earlier during my duties. He is a movie producer who is visiting from LA, and Barbara wasted no time in cornering him, no doubt in the hopes of landing a job. I watch as she leans forward conspiratorially to whisper something in his ear. He laughs, but it's not a real laugh. His eyes sweep the room in search of a plausible exit, and when he doesn't immediately pick up on the arrival of Davis, I exhale.

This reprieve, however, is extremely short lived.

He spots Davis.

In a move that one could reasonably argue was simply good, old-fashioned chivalry, he kindly excuses himself from Barbara. I want to intervene. I want to beg him to stay put, if only to spare the rest of us the rod, but I am powerless to do anything other than watch him move with incredible purpose through the gaggle of unsteady guests in the direction of Davis Lawrence. With each step, I feel the atmospheric pressure holding the room together start to plunge, although surely this is my imagination. Everyone else is oblivious. Everyone else is just having a wonderful time. When the handsome man reaches the place where Davis stands, he bows his head slightly and extends his hand, and Davis, in turn, offers up her delicate fingers with a shy smile. Her cheeks warm as if the mere touch of his hand makes her blush. They talk briefly before he escorts her to a couch where she will, I imagine, hold court for the rest of the evening.

I look back in Barbara's direction to see that her benign perplexity at the handsome man's hasty departure has given way to a seething clarity. Her fingernails curl earthward like talons, and she doesn't move; she just stares at Davis for a good, long while. Finally, she takes a long swallow of her drink, and slams the glass down on the nearest tabletop. Then, she moves briskly, unknowingly, in my direction on the patio. When she thuds through the open doors, she looks surprised to see me:

"What are *you* doing out here," she barks. "I have been searching for you."

She has not been searching for me.

"I was just checking it out," I mumble. I point in the direction of the bay where a singular, flaxen light illuminates the end of the dock. It looks like an Edward Hopper painting.

"I don't bring you to these things to have you *disappear*," she snaps angrily. She starts to fish through her clutch bag for her cigarette pouch, but her hands are shaking.

"I'm sorry," I say. "It was only for a minute."

She lights her cigarette but says nothing.

"Did you see Davis is here?" I ask innocently, my hasty calculation being that Barbara can use this opportunity to pretend she regards Davis's arrival as good news and, thus, save face.

"Yes," she says flatly.

"It's *great* she came," I continue with as much innocent good nature as I can muster. "You must be so pleased to see her out and about!"

"She's in no state to be here, and you *of all people* should know that, Clo," Barbara says, her voice rising with each syllable. "If she was in any condition to be here, don't you think I would have brought *her* instead of *you*?"

"I'm sorry," I say. "You're right."

Barbara lifts her chin with petulance toward the sky and a single porch light falls harshly upon her upturned face. While her forehead is waxy and smooth, the skin on the lower half of her face has started to sag down and puddle, like when you kick a lumpy comforter to the bottom of an otherwise well-made bed.

"Can I get you a drink?" I offer.

Barbara shakes her head, and—with nothing else to do—we stand together and watch Davis. I want to go inside, but I am too frightened to move a muscle. Barbara's emotional inconsistency always makes me uneasy, but tonight I find her particularly terrifying.

Through an open window, I hear Davis's laugh rise above the din of the party. She must be amused by something the producer said because she leans closer to his face, and her bare shoulders rise and fall with delight. Her cheeks are pink, downright flush with possibility, and it occurs to me that, maybe, it is not simply Davis's youth or beauty, per se, that Barbara wants to destroy or, at the very least, hide away. No, it is that Davis hasn't even *begun* to live her life. Unlike Barbara, she is an entirely blank slate. She has no narratives to correct, no haunting mistakes, no eye circles to spackle over. Davis Lawrence has come into her full beauty and, as a result, she could become anything she wants, including a star, while all her mother can do is cling to a formidable past that less and less people can even recall. As I watch Davis, I understand she knows we are watching her. She wants to be watched. As she runs her fingers through her long hair, it dawns on me that, despite her proclaimed innocence, Davis Lawrence knows exactly where her mother has drawn her invisible line.

And she has just willingly entered a battle she cannot possibly hope to win.

The next morning, Barbara rips open the curtains and shakes me awake. She informs me that plans have changed, and she needs to drive me to the Jitney right away. I sit up disoriented and look at the clock on the nightstand: It is 6:30. The space next to me in the bed is empty.

"Where's Davis?" I ask. My voice is scratchy.

"She went on a walk," Barbara says tersely as she glances down at her watch. "Now, come get your things. We don't have a lot of time."

I throw a few things in my bag and run a wet toothbrush over my teeth. There is no coffee waiting for me this morning, and when I look out the front door, I see that Barbara is already sitting in the car. The exhaust is rumbling angrily out of the tailpipe and a pair of white hands grips the top of the steering wheel. I get in the car, and as Barbara backs down the gravel driveway, something calls at the corner of my eye. I look up at the house.

It's Davis.

She sits alone in a third-floor window, which is a part of the house I have yet to fully explore. She gazes vacantly down upon the driveway. I nudge myself forward so I can get a better look at her through the windshield, but when our eyes meet, she lets the curtain flutter closed.

And then she is gone.

When I get back to the city, I immediately call Davis from the street, and while I am relieved that she answers on the first ring, I am surprised by just how cheerful she sounds.

"Hello, my dear," she says. "I hope there wasn't too much Sunday traffic."

"Are you okay?" I ask.

"Me?" she replies, and her voice remains light. "Yes, honey. Why?"

"Well, I mean, your mom?" I grind my teeth together, suddenly afraid to be more specific.

"My mom?" she says, but then laughs. "Oh, honey. You can't let her get to you."

43

It is late September, and I am barefoot atop a carpeted riser at the Vera Wang store on the Upper East Side. I am wearing a pastel blue satin bridesmaid dress. It has a periwinkle sash and an unflattering square neckline.

"Put on the shoes," the attendant says.

When I fail to wedge my enormous feet into a pair of black pumps, Allie glances down and smiles. Apparently, I do *not* have a sample-sized foot at Vera Wang.

"What do you think?" Allie asks. We both look at the dress in the three-sided mirror.

"It's definitely my favorite," I say.

In truth, I've hated every single dress I tried on to the depths of my soul, but this is the best option among all the dresses I hate.

"Okay, mine, too," she says, clearly relieved by our shared choice, especially because I am the maid of honor.

She turns to the other bridesmaids, which include Patrick's two short, strawberry-colored sisters from Ohio. They are seated expectantly in the padded chairs that line the room with their blunt legs crossed at the knee.

"So did you feel good about this one?" Allie asks as she points to me with a hopeful smile.

Of course, all the girls agree with wild enthusiasm, even though the dress flatters exactly no one, but I reckon this agreeability is attributable to one of two sources: One, they are already married, and someone wore an ugly, expensive bridesmaid dress on their special day, or two, they hope to have their own wedding one day and would like to be at liberty to inflict a similar sartorial injury upon others.

I fall—with overwhelming bitterness—in the latter category. Allie is getting married in the spring.

The long-standing plan has been to try on dresses at Vera Wang and then go out to dinner as a group to "get to know each other" before the wedding. However, in recent days, Isobel assigned me a short interview of an up-and-coming actor who I would meet at a small dinner in honor of his latest film. Of course, once Harry got wind of my invitation, he very confidently requested to be my plus-one. While I initially demurred, he sweetened the pot by saying there was a guy he wanted me to meet, a new editor at his website named Matthew.

"Why don't you pick me up on your way?" he suggested. "He will be at the office, so I can make a casual introduction." Here is the thing: I am learning that, when someone asks for something directly, it is almost impossible to say no. Now, while my own long-standing approach (i.e., hem and haw, act like I am not interested, heavily hint but be indirect about my desires) has not been a terribly successful acquisition strategy, I truly cannot imagine being as blunt as Harry. It's not simply that I find it embarrassing, which I do, it is also that I have yet to see a woman succeed in this manner. After all, there isn't a lot of power or gratification to be found in rewarding a pushy woman with the exact thing she wanted in the first place. Apparently, it's far more satisfying to bestow her with something she pretends not to deserve.

As I shimmy out of the stiff bridesmaid dress and back into my even stiffer work clothes, I search for the right way to break the news of my early departure to Allie, although I think it would be quite unfair for her to hold it against me. After all, her life is sorted out: She has a job, a fiancé, and a two-bedroom apartment, while I still get urinary tract infections and live alone, quite literally, under a train.

It is time to get my own life sorted out.

By any means necessary.

As we walk toward the front doors, I touch her elbow.

"Listen," I whisper, and I lean close. "I have not-great news."

Her face clouds over.

"What? You can't get the discount on the dresses?"

"What? No, that's fine," I reassure her, although I feel a flicker of irritation. I *had* offered the discount as an engagement present, but I feel like Allie has yet to be sufficiently grateful or impressed by this gesture. "I just can't go to dinner tonight. Something at work just came up."

"Something at work?" she asks. "But we planned tonight around *your* schedule. I wanted to do this a month ago, but you couldn't because of work."

"I know," I sigh with false remorse. "It *just* came up."

"Can you skip it?" she asks. "This is really important to me."

I feel myself bristle at this comment because, for the past few months, *everything* has been "really important" to Allie. When she got engaged to Patrick, she wanted me to organize a celebratory dinner with friends, which I did with a considerable amount of good cheer and efficiency, despite wanting to slit my own throat open at the news that she was getting married in the first place. That dinner was followed by a proper engagement party at a duplex apartment in Tribeca, hosted by all the happy parents, and now I am in the throes of organizing not *only* her bridal shower, but her bachelorette party, which she wants held at the Raleigh Hotel in Miami over a holiday weekend. This is not to mention all the little details tacitly assigned to the maid of honor around the rehearsal dinner, bridesmaids' gifts, hotel gift bags, and the wedding itself, the care and keeping of which is wrapped up in my daily, nearly debilitating anxiety around the probability that I will be attending Allie's wedding completely single.

I have nobody to bring.

"I am sorry," I say. "I can't skip it."

Allie looks away for a moment and then turns her eyes back to me.

"Well," she says with a shrug. "I hope it's worth it."

"I'd so much rather stay here," I say.

"It's not Davis, is it?" she asks.

I am taken aback.

"No," I say. "It's not Davis."

I give a quick parting hug to the bridesmaids, all of whom stand frowningly on the corner of Madison Avenue in deference to Allie, and I slink into my car service. I direct the driver to Harry's new office, which is located on Greene Street in Soho, and with nothing to do for the duration of the ride, I look out the window. It's still warm outside, and the streets are full of people. At every red light, I watch pods of younger girls skitter across the crosswalk. They wear short dresses and high heels and as I watch them collecting the pieces of their lives like a scavenger hunt, I suddenly feel very old. If you live in New York City long enough, you can find clues about your own existence on almost every block. Despite how often the city changes, it also doesn't change at all, and every time I pass certain storefronts and street corners, they can sucker punch me with an almost unbearable nostalgia of the times, good and bad, that are lost to me forever.

When I enter the lobby of Harry's building, I retrieve a mirror from my handbag and check my makeup. I look more haggard than I did in the softly lit dress shop, and it's funny how I always believe the worst version of myself. A good photo is an accident; a terrible photo is simply how the rest of the world sees me. I pull out a tester of perfume and spray the air in front of me so I can walk through it. Once I am inside the elevator, I flip my head upside down and shake it with my hands to give it a little volume. I smooth out my wiry eyebrows. I dab on a little lipstick. I roll my shoulders back.

The elevator doors open directly into Harry's office space, which never ceases to feel weird, but I step out with a manufactured confidence, nonetheless. There is no waiting room or receptionist, just a medium-sized room with fluorescent overhead lighting and with a few desks with computers. On the far wall hangs a very large whiteboard covered with numbers and words as well as a really good cartoon of a dog with the word *dick* in a thought bubble over its head. It's nearing eight o'clock, but the office is full of people, and I wonder which one is Matthew. When Harry sees me, he waves me over to his desk.

"So, do you make *everyone* burn the midnight oil?" I ask as I absently drop my bag on his desk.

Harry looks down and grimaces. His personal workspace is completely barren, except for an Apple laptop, which is closed and positioned in the dead center of his desk. There are no pens, crumpled papers, or days-old coffee cups. We both stare at the bag for few seconds before I pick it back up. Then, Harry replies:

"It's only eight o'clock," he says. "And, unlike *you*, we are on a twenty-four-hour news cycle."

"Sounds exhausting."

"It *is* exhausting," he says. "Those guys will be here until one."

I look over at the small group of Harry's employees, a handful of men, all dressed down in jeans and hooded sweatshirts. Some of them are wearing oversized headphones around their necks. They sit on the edges of their desks in a motley circle.

"Are they kidney transplant surgeons?" I ask dryly.

"They are having the overnight meeting," he answers. "They are figuring out what stories will be ready to go live tonight, and they are here for any breaking news. A few of them just do the uploading into the CMS and the HTML code."

"Ah," I manage, and while I have no idea what those acronyms mean, I *am* a little disappointed someone like Harry is using them. It feels like letting the terrorists win.

"And over there," he says, pointing in the opposite direction, "is my engineer."

"You have your own engineer," I say with mock delight. "You have most certainly arrived."

Harry smiles, but it comes off as forced, like he thinks I am an idiot. I briefly wonder if I am an idiot.

"So," I say casually with a little wave of my finger. "Which one of these guys is the *Matthew* you want me to meet?"

"Matthew?" Harry looks confused.

"The new editor?"

"Oh, yeah," he says, recovering himself. "Sorry. He's not here."

"Oh," I say, and I look down at my shoes. "I thought . . ."

Harry straightens up with a reassuring smile.

"Last-minute thing, but I told him *all* about you, and I gave him your email address," he says, before quickly adding: "He said he's going to write you. He sounds *very* interested."

"Okay," I say, but a syrupy disappointment coats the inside of my body, as I realize he was never planning to introduce me to a Matthew.

In fact, it occurs to me that a "Matthew" probably doesn't even exist, but if anyone knows how to manipulate my obvious weak spots, it's Harry. I am not sure if I feel embarrassed or duped, so I pretend to fish for something in my bag.

"Give me five minutes to wrap up, and then we will head out?" Harry says.

"Perfect," I say, but I don't look up, fearful my expression will betray me. "The car is waiting downstairs."

Harry walks over to the group by the whiteboard. They all look at him intently and, although I cannot hear what he is saying, his employees seem to hang on his every word. There is a pocket of laughter. Harry leans over the shoulder of a Black guy with a shaved head. He peers at the screen of his computer and points to something and, for the very first time, I wonder if Harry Wood sees a world that the rest of us cannot see.

44

Early the next morning, the overhead lighting flickers ominously as my subway train rumbles under the East River. I check my watch and wonder, for the umpteenth time, where Harry ended up last night. When we first arrived at dinner, he hovered attentively at my side, but once he made the acquaintance of the actor and his publicist, he moved on to another circle of guests. When it was time to leave, I couldn't find him. Finally, I saw him sitting at a back table, talking in a very animated manner to a group of people, including the actor. The waitstaff was cleaning up around them.

"Are you ready to go, Harry?" I had interrupted with an easy smile.

Harry stopped talking with a frown, and everyone looked at me blankly, like I was his nagging wife. I was tempted to point out that the man they were all *so* entertained by had not even been invited to this little party, but I bit my tongue.

"Not yet," he said. "But you go ahead, and I'll call you in the morning."

"Are you sure?" I pressed, entirely expecting him to change his mind and escort me out of the restaurant.

"I'm sure."

He did not call me in the morning.

I get off the subway, and as I walk slowly in the direction of my office building, I check my phone. I have no missed calls. As I slip into the nook where I swap my shoes, I realize that something inside my body feels broken. It rattles around, like a mouse in the walls, and while I know it's there, I just can't seem to locate it.

I take the elevator up to my floor, and I still love the way the office smells so early in the morning, like a sealed-up summer house at the start of the season. There is an uneven pile of layouts from the C+E section that include the approved text and display copy, which is our lingo for headlines and captions. I shuffle through the pages quickly. A few headlines have been killed—which means I will have to think of new ones before lunch and distribute them for approval. I push the papers aside.

Next, I launch my email and scan my inbox with an almost embarrassing degree of hope. Spoiler alert: I do not have an email from someone named Matthew, although I do check twice to be certain. While this is not exactly *surprising*, I am gutted, nonetheless. Not only did I want to believe that Harry Wood had been telling me the truth, but also because I was *very careful* not to step on any cracks during my walk from the subway this morning. You see, in moments of uncertainty, I need to believe I can control the direction of the universe with my actions. I decide to believe that this *Matthew*, whoever he is, is a real person. I reason that he probably overslept or that, maybe, he can't quite figure out a good thing to write to a lady as impressive as myself.

Reluctantly, I start to transcribe my notes from the interview with the actor.

About an hour later, people slowly start to arrive at their desks. I can hear them throw out tired greetings and set down their expensive handbags and Starbucks cups. For a moment, I long for Davis. I miss waiting for her to arrive each day, my body near electric with anticipation. I miss having someone to talk to about my night or, more broadly, my life. There is a shared happiness that comes with arriving at the magazine each day. You can hear it in everyone's voice, this sense of having something wonderfully new to share, but that is the thing about this city. It is always unfolding itself to the people who are willing to pay attention.

And to pay attention is the job.

To procrastinate on the actual writing of my piece for Isobel, I answer some personal emails, wander around for an Advil, and check my voicemail before I summon the courage to open a new Word document.

As much as I like writing, and I *do* like writing (the solitary nature of putting together a large jigsaw puzzle without a guiding picture feels both rigorous and soothing to me), my mind is, as usual, completely empty. Even though I have written several stories to midrange fanfare, this initial feeling of falling into the abyss never fails to unnerve me. I stare at the cursor pulsing on the blank page for a few minutes as I try to arrange a good opening line in my head. Generally, there is a formula to magazine articles: You open with a catchy line that is just inscrutable enough to keep the reader interested (e.g., *Bobby Jenkins never fancied himself a pig farmer*), and ultimately deliver on its relevance in the final, punchy sentence. This opening line is followed by a quote, which is the easy part because even the dreariest interview subject manages to choke out one decent soundbite. It's the third sentence that takes more arranging, and this is generally the moment I begin to beat myself up. I chastise myself for being stupid, overweight, and undisciplined. I remember I'm a terrible writer with a drinking problem and no husband and that I will, quite literally, never make it past page forty-five in *Ulysses*. More painfully, I start to panic that Isobel, upon reading whatever garbage I ultimately hand her, will discover that I am, indeed, the complete impostor that I have always known myself to be.

My fingers tap on the keyboard.

The words fill the page.

That is the thing about this place, I realize.

You travel and travel and travel.

And yet, you never arrive.

45

Davis is having trouble with her shoes. We are in the foyer of her apartment and, with a swallowed consternation, I watch as the buckle on her heeled Mary Jane continues to resist her many advances. Finally, and with mock exasperation, Davis plops down on the floor and lets her legs splay out like a ragdoll. She sticks out her tongue.

"Help me," she giggles.

Quickly, I kneel to fasten her shoes like I am tying a toddler's sneakers.

"My hero," she says, and she extends her thin arms into the air. I pull her up, and as she titters into the wall, her unsteady, oversized motions remind me of those videos of a horse being born. When she finds her bearings, she flips her blonde hair back with a laugh, and points both of her of her index fingers at Harry, who has been watching the whole scene unfold with no expression in his eyes.

"Harry," she sings in a baby voice. "Where have *you* been?"

"I'm right here," he says before he shoots a worried glance in my direction.

Davis is wasted, and while I am very familiar with Davis being wasted, Harry still only floats occasionally (and opportunistically, in my opinion) into her life and, as such, he seems shocked by her condition. He coughs loudly in my direction and shakes his head.

"Honey," I say, taking his cue. "It's so cold out. Would it be more fun to stay here?"

"Absolutely not," Davis responds, and while her voice is suddenly clear, she now seems confused by the mechanics of the clasp on her clutch bag. "It's *October*. How cold can it possibly be?"

I look at Harry and shrug: It *is* October. The second week, in fact, and all over the city, the leaves have begun to burst forth in reds and yellows and oranges.

It is also Davis's birthday, and Harry and I are taking her out to dinner at La Grenouille. Harry had initially suggested a more modern, recently opened downtown brasserie for our little celebration, but Davis wanted to stay closer to home. She still didn't seem to have any real interest in being social; the scene, such as it was, still held no appeal. While she had gone to a few parties, and had allowed her mother to drag her to the occasional event, she told me she found them confusing: Was this supposed to be fun? Was this ever fun? Furthermore, Barbara always seemed to have something ungenerous to say about her performance—she talked too loud, her dress was too showy, she didn't talk enough—so she mostly liked to keep to herself.

With some effort, we wrangle Davis into a coat, and when we get her down to the lobby, Hatch frowns at her condition. He offers to call a driver, but we decline. The night is damp, but tolerable enough and Davis, we silently concur, could clearly use some air. So Harry takes one arm, and I take the other, and we head out together for the first time in a very long while. As we slowly take in the blocks in the direction of the restaurant, we talk and laugh, yet amid this pantomime of normalcy, I can't help but think that if Davis Lawrence were a wishbone, Harry and I would not hesitate to rip her in half.

After ten minutes, Davis is a little steadier but with nearly thirty blocks to go, Harry flags down a passing cab. While we arrive a half hour late for our reservation, the maître de seats us right away in a soft banquette. You see, the Lawrence family are no strangers to La Grenouille. According to Davis, her grandfather, aside from being a most regular diner, used to hold his annual company Christmas party at the restaurant. Davis would twirl around, no doubt to the delight of the crowd, in little tartan numbers sewn by her mother's dressmaker.

"I think that was the first time I tasted wine," she once told me. "I would skip around and takes sips from all the abandoned glasses."

Sometimes I try to imagine Davis as a child.

I wonder if she was lonely.

Once we are settled, Harry orders a bottle of champagne and, as the waiter fills our glasses, I look around the restaurant. I have never eaten at La Grenouille before, and I marvel at the serenity conferred by the old guard. This is the way people *should* eat, I think. There is no DJ. There is no woman in a crop top wielding an apple martini, no twenty-something banker with a Caesar-style haircut drinking a Red Bull and vodka.

The Dover sole is reassuringly market price.

Harry offers a toast.

"To Davis," he says. "On her birthday."

"To Davis," I say, and we all tap our glasses and look each other in the eye.

I take a sip, and regard Harry across the table. He is wearing a black suit with a white shirt and no tie, and his hair is gently undone. I feel conflicted about tonight. In one way, I am happy we are all together, but a larger part of me feels like I am in the middle of a competition that is not rigged in my favor. While I often wonder (with great bitterness) if Davis will ever tell Harry that she is angry (or at the very least upset) that he abandoned her so completely, there is something that tells me she feels this injustice less acutely than I do. If anything, she seems to glow in his presence.

Harry orders several plates of appetizers, but to our shared dismay, Davis barely touches the food. Instead, she drinks champagne and pleads with us to tell her stories, but every time I try to squeeze a word in, I am interrupted by Harry who seems intent to keep the conversation centered around (A.) his website, and (B.) their relationship *before* I came into the picture. *Do you remember this? Wasn't it funny when we did that?* And Davis, for her part, is blinking and childlike; it's almost as if she is desperate for his approval, which gives me the uneasy sensation of being edged out, which is a feeling that rarely needs much encouragement. And at some point, I stop talking. I just want to see if anyone pulls me back into the conversation, but when that doesn't work, I intentionally dump a hefty piece of salmon down the front of my borrowed dress. It lands on the shelf of my breasts, but I don't pick it off. I sit completely still and silent. I want to see if Davis or Harry take notice, but they don't even look in my direction. After a few minutes, the hunk of bright pink flesh begins to slide down my chest before it tumbles, with a thud, into my lap. I glance down at my dress. There is an oil stain, and a large portion of sheeny silver skin is stuck to the fabric.

"The fish is delicious," I say loudly.

Still, they say nothing. They just smile and nod, before Davis goes back to listening to Harry.

Finally, I excuse myself to the bathroom. As I angrily blot the stain on my dress with a damp paper towel, I look in the mirror. I search my face, but I am not sure, exactly, what I am hoping to find, especially because everything is *exactly* as it should be: My forehead is wonderfully smooth and my red cheeks have been lasered, albeit temporarily, into submission. My eyebrows (which, in college, were as thin as a length of bucatini) are now fat and feathered, each hair is tweezed and tinted by a lovely woman with an even lovelier atelier space on the Upper East Side. My morning blow-out has yet to succumb to the heft of a burgeoning rain and my breasts are corralled by a minimizer bra that boasts five wonderfully geriatric snaps along the back and cost a whopping $150. As I stand there, I wonder if this is the most beautiful that I will ever be—we Harmons being renowned late-bloomers—and, if so, why it feels nothing like I thought it would.

Then again, nothing does.

When I finally emerge from the ladies' room, Davis and Harry have inched so close together that their noses nearly touch. Davis nods as Harry seems to emphasize the same point, over and over, making crisp motions with his hands. From the shadows, I strain to see what, if anything, I can distill from their body language before they notice me. If, that is, they notice me at all. I start to move slowly to the table, and when I am about six feet away, Davis's eyes flutter up, and she pushes herself away from Harry reflexively, like she has just been caught doing something naughty.

"What are you two gossiping about?" I ask casually as I slide back into my seat and return my napkin to my lap.

"Nothing," Davis sings sweetly, but her eyes dart nervously in Harry's direction.

"Correction," Harry adds. He rests his chin on his steepled index fingers and smiles at her: "Nothing *interesting*."

He raises an eyebrow, and Davis laughs, but just barely.

"Harry, that is *not* true," Davis exclaims before turning to me with a nervous smile. "Harry was telling me what's going on with the website."

"Ah," I say, and I take a sip of champagne. "Which is?"

"Some venture capital guys in San Francisco might want to invest in it," she says. "Right, Harry?"

I look at Harry. This is the first I've heard this news.

"It's early days," Harry says, shaking his head. "Nothing even remotely concrete, but I think some people are starting to understand there is a real opportunity to monetize content online in a way they just can't with print."

"Monetize content," I repeat archly. "Well, *that* sounds positive."

"Potentially," he says, ignoring my sarcasm. "But they want me to double my traffic, which means I will have to hire more people, and then prove that content at scale is valuable to advertisers."

"If anyone can do it, you can," Davis coos, and I am suddenly overcome with the horrible impression that they are holding hands under the table.

"Well, I am just glad to hear you weren't talking about me," I say with a little laugh.

"Now, I know I said the topic wasn't *interesting*," Harry begins, but he keeps looking at Davis like she's a new bride. "But it *was* more interesting than you!"

Here, Davis giggles, but when she realizes that I have not joined her, she drunkenly clamps her hand over her mouth. Her eyes turn pleadingly to Harry who, in turn, throws his arms across the white tablecloth. He gathers up my hands and looks me directly in the eyes. His expression is both chiding and sweet.

"I was kidding, Clo," he says. He pulls my fingers against his lips and gently kisses them. "When did you get so serious all of a sudden?"

"So serious," Davis parrots, but her words sound sticky.

After dessert, which nobody eats (even though the waiters put a candle into a pile of profiteroles), Harry and I try to hustle a now downright sloppy Davis out of the restaurant. We move slowly, careful not to make too much of a scene, but when we pass the bar, Davis throws her arms over her head and calls out "happy birthday" to all the patrons assembled at the stools. The men, of course, all wave back and smile (after all, who can resist the attention of a beautiful, happy blonde?), but their tight-lipped wives do not share this sentiment. They radiate molten disapproval, smacking their husband's suited shoulders with light hands and shaking their heads. By the time we get to the corner of Fifty-Second Street, Harry must hold Davis up by her armpits while I try, without much success, to hail a cab.

"We should sing," Davis suggests loudly. "Should we sing?"

She attempts to pantomime a tap dance with her feet.

"We should absolutely *not* sing," Harry says.

When a taxi finally pulls up to the curb, I hear Harry quietly instruct Davis to "act normal" as he settles her into the back seat, which, incidentally, is the exact moment I realize that they will share a cab uptown while I will take my own car—alone—back to Brooklyn.

I don't like this arrangement. Especially not after the secret conversations during dinner. It makes me feel paranoid. And, incidentally, being paranoid also makes me feel paranoid.

"Thanks, Harry," I say, lightly. "I can take her home."

"We are both going uptown so, it's fine," he responds with a quick wave that I read as dismissive. "It makes more sense."

"But I have clothes at the apartment," I chirp. "I can sleep over and you would have to go *all the way* across town after you drop her off."

Harry looks at me with irritation, but I just smile a knowing, vaguely dippy smile because *surely* Davis would prefer that I take her uptown. I bend down to talk directly to Davis, who is slumped in the back seat of the car with her eyes closed. I speak in slow and soothing tones, like a kindergarten teacher:

"Honey, do you want me to take you home?" I ask before adding for good measure: "And get you in your pajamas."

Now, in my mind, this is not really a question, so I am perplexed when Davis treats it as one. She lifts her chin and looks at me with tepid consideration for a few seconds.

"No," she says finally. "I want Harry."

"What?"

"I want Harry," she says firmly, and there is no consolation in her voice. "I don't want you to take me. I want Harry."

I rise, shocked, and watch wordlessly as Harry slides into the cab. With his fingers around the handle, he looks up at me with a pitiful smile, like I just tried—and failed—to secure a seat at the cool kids' table.

"I've got this, Clo," Harry says. "Get home safe."

He pulls the door shut with a loud slam and turns toward Davis, who snuggles under his arm.

I watch the cab pull away, but I don't move for a long time. My eyes just follow the pink taillights of the taxi until they are absorbed by the night. While I am gutted, there remains a hopeful sliver inside my body that they will drive around the block—laughing that it was all *just a big joke*—and come collect me in the cab. So, I continue to stand there, marking time as my trench coat flutters in the spring wind, but they do not return.

Harry pulled harder. He broke off a bigger piece of the bone.

Finally, I start to walk downtown. I listen to the sound my high heels make on the wide sidewalks of Fifth Avenue. It is the slow cadence of defeat. How could I have been so blind—no, not blind, *stupid*—as to only see in Davis and Harry's relationship what I wanted to see?

I am thirsty so, when I pass an open newsstand, I slow down and unzip my wallet. I never carry cash these days, mainly because I am trying to dissuade myself from buying cigarettes regularly as they have now shot up to an unfathomable seven dollars a pack, so I am relieved to find it contains a mangled ten-dollar bill. I pull a bottle of water out of the illuminated minifridge, and hand my money to the man behind the plexiglass divider. He talks loudly on his cellphone in a language I do not recognize. As he counts out my change, I scan the dozens of magazines that hang from clips around the perimeter of his little booth. All the covers are sun-bleached and weather worn, but there are also neat stacks of fresh newspapers and magazines in front of the candy display. I quickly locate a copy of our magazine and pick it up. It is the new issue, which is the one with my interview with the actor from the dinner party. The dinner party after which Harry went missing for a few days, only to emerge with no explanation. I flip through the pages.

"Sir?" I say, and the man looks up. He places the phone against his chest and raises his dark eyebrows.

"Yes?" he asks.

I turn the open magazine to face him. I point to my article.

"Can you read that?"

"Yes?" he says. "It's four dollars."

I shake my head in frustration. I jab my finger hard on the page.

"No, here," I say. "That's me."

When the man fails to look impressed, I tuck the magazine under my arm. I rifle through my wallet and produce my driver's license. I slide it under the plexiglass divider. Then I hold the magazine up again:

"That's me," I repeat. "I am Clodagh P. Harmon. I wrote that story."

He hands my license back with a toothless smile.

"Congratulations," he says, and then he puts his cell phone back up to his ear.

I stand there with the magazine in my hands.

"That's me," I whisper.

For reasons I cannot explain, I buy that copy of the magazine, even though I have at least five sitting on my desk, before I crawl miserably into a taxi. I lean my head against the window, and by the time I am sailing over the Brooklyn Bridge, I have lathered myself into a nonsensical frenzy. I am convinced that Harry and Davis are sitting in her living room, meticulously planning my eventual demise. Or, at least, making fun of me in some capacity. As the familiar parks and brownstones of my neighborhood blur past, my stomach sears, like I just swallowed a thimble full of hot acid. When I get to my apartment, I realize I have forgotten (or lost) my house key, an unfortunate fact I confirm only after I dump the entire contents of my bag onto the sidewalk in front of my building. This happens with some consistency, the misplacement or loss of important things, and unsure of my next move, I flop down on the stoop in my stained party dress. I kick off my high heels and rub my feet as I listen to a train rumble over my head. The night is colder now and because I am not wearing underwear, the concrete stoop quickly numbs my backside. In my growing despondency, I feel physically angry, like I want to punch a giant pile of pillows, when I spot a woman walking down the street with her dog. I can tell she doesn't see me, so I chirp an intentionally creepy hello, mainly to enjoy the violence with which her body startles. It doesn't help. A light flips off on the second floor of the brownstone across the street. Someone sails past me on a ten-speed bike. The pleasant grumble of a television wafts down from a half-open window. I look down and I spy a barely smoked cigarette lying on the sidewalk. It is most likely one of Saul's, I reason, so I dust it off and light it. It's unfiltered and unpleasant to smoke, but I smoke it down to my fingers anyway.

When I am finished, I sniff my nails and allow my body to sink into a more intuitive dimension. I decide that I am not, in fact, breathtakingly drunk, but *rather* I am now privy to a spiritual realm that mere mortals can neither access nor understand. I, Clodagh Harmon, can see where the universe begins and ends. I can manifest my own destiny. I conclude that my insecurity—both acute and in general—is only because I am more brilliant than I realize, and that—even on my worst days—I am surely more interesting than someone like *Harry Wood*. I conclude that, going forward, I should only commune with my fellow geniuses, all of whom, thus far, have been frustratingly hard to find.

Yes, this all makes sense.

At some point, I look up and see two full moons glowing in an otherwise black sky, and even in my severely inebriated state, I recognize that seeing two moons is *not* a good thing. As I haul myself unsteadily onto my stockinged feet, I start to sing a little song about two moons. I suspect the song is quite good, and I remind myself to *write down the lyrics* when I get up to my apartment. *Maybe I could be a lyricist?* I think. *Is that someone who writes regular songs? Or is that just for Broadway musicals?* I turn the word around in my mouth like a loose marble: *lyricist*. Once fully upright, I smooth the wrinkles out of my outfit and pat down my hair before I buzz the door.

One must keep up appearances.

A light turns on inside, and I say a prayer that it is Saul and not his wife. I am in no mood for a lecture, especially one loud enough to wake the whole block, and when the door opens, I am relieved to see it is, indeed, only Saul. He is bleary and wearing a blue bathrobe, and I find myself, quite unexpectedly, curious as to what kind of pajamas a man like Saul Rothman wears to bed each night.

"I forgot my key," I say.

"Again?"

"Guilty as charged," I say with a salute, although I have no idea for what reason.

"You need to get your shit together, Clo," he says as he makes room for me to squeeze past. He is sort of joking and sort of serious.

"I know," I respond, and I, too, am sort of joking and sort of serious.

I pitch up the steps with my shoes in hand, and I hope he doesn't notice I am drunk. He notices.

"Are you okay?" he asks.

"I'm so sorry," I say, and, for a second, I think I might start to cry. "It won't happen again."

46

I wake up the following morning to the sound of *The Today Show* coming from my television. Apparently, I had not turned it off (nor any lights in my apartment for that matter) when I stumbled into bed the night before. I flop my head back down on my pillow, which is humid with perspiration, and when I run a fingernail along my teeth, a light brown sediment is dislodged.

I sniff my hair. It smells like cigarettes for the first time in a long while, and I am flooded with nostalgia for the time when everyone smoked, and I didn't have to hate myself so incredibly much for every social misstep, no matter how minor. I miss hungover Sunday brunches full of stories—who lost an item or kissed a stranger or threw up in a taxicab—and I don't know when the stories stopped. Slowly, there were more marriages and serious promotions and even the occasional baby, and I somehow did not notice I had been left behind, holding a lonely balloon.

I look at my phone. I have no missed calls.

Nobody cared if I got home okay.

I roll to my side so I can look over my apartment. There seems to be a fly buzzing over the sink, and my salmon-stained dress sits on the floor with my heels nested so perfectly inside that it looks like I was lifted out of my outfit last night by a UFO.

You need to get your shit together, Clo.

I crawl out of bed, drink from my gallon of water, and pull on my workout clothes. I walk fifteen blocks to the gym where I complete the same, basically useless, exercise routine I have done for years, regardless of my physical condition, because I need to prove to myself that I am fine. After all, I have repeatedly read in magazines that if you can keep your routine then you don't have a drinking problem. It's when you break your routine or make excuses for why your routine has become "unmanageable" that you are supposed to worry, and I have long carried this information around with me like a tin of balm.

After my workout, I round back onto my block with a fresh cup of coffee, only to discover it is lined with ambulances and police cars. While their red lights flash frantically, the sirens are curiously silent. There seems to be no urgency coming from the police officers and firemen who mingle in the gathering crowd, and, so, I assume I have missed the action. My apartment is situated at the far end of the street, so I keep walking, but when I get a few feet from my front door, one of the police officers turns his body sideways to block the entrance. I glance down at his gold name tag, which reads M. MCNELIS. I find this reassuring even as the sweat on my back begins to chill.

"Can we help you, miss?"

"I live here," I say.

"Are you the daughter?"

"No, I'm the tenant. I live upstairs." I point up at my window. "Is everything okay?"

The police officers glance at each other.

"Is everything okay?" I repeat, only now with a fretful lilt.

"The homeowner had a heart attack," McNelis says.

"Which one?"

He looks down at his notebook.

"Saul Rothman?"

"Oh my god," I exclaim as I slap my free hand over my mouth. "Is he okay?"

The officers exchange looks again, and in that moment, I know that Saul is dead. I look down at the breathtakingly expensive cup of coffee in my hand—a cup of coffee I just purchased from a guy sporting a waxed mustache and red suspenders, the coffee Saul Rothman would invariably despise—and I know that he is dead.

"But I saw him last night," I say.

I offer this piece of information like it's a hot tip that will aid in their nonexistent investigation, but they don't seem to grasp the significance of what I am telling them: Saul Rothman cannot possibly be dead because I saw Saul Rothman *with my own two eyes* last night.

"Like *after* midnight," I add, more loudly now, but they say nothing. The radio on McNelis's chest starts to crackle, and he steps away to answer it.

"Definitely," I say again. "It was *definitely* after midnight."

I wait for a response, but the other officer only offers me a sad smile before he joins McNelis so they can converse, apparently, about something more pressing in private.

As I stand there, my eyes fall on the smattering of cigarette butts scattered across the pavement.

This is the shortest delta between someone being very much *alive* and someone being very much *dead* that I have ever experienced and, while I don't know it in this moment, I will carry the nagging kernel of that possibility close to my heart for the rest of my life.

47

For some idiotic, misguided reason, I agree to join my mother for a fundraiser over the Christmas holiday in Philadelphia. It has been organized to benefit the Catholic grammar school in her old neighborhood, and since I am home, I figure: Why not? I have officially watched enough romantic comedies about city girls moving home and finding true love to gently investigate the possibility of my own success should I manage to squeak through that uncertain escape route. I doubt any mothers will set me up with their sons, however, not that anyone my age in my family's social orbit remains unmarried in Philadelphia. Historically speaking, people are generally taken down by a singular, hysterical wave of confirmation bias around the age of twenty-eight that sends them all trotting up the stairs of the nearest Catholic Church, usually with a few hired guys from the Mummers string band in tow.

After my mom and I get dressed for the event, we spritz our outfits with Norell, which is the only perfume my mother has ever worn, with the exception of a brief Giorgio Beverly Hills flirtation in the 1980s, a scent that still transports me to the arrival of a newly permed babysitter wearing a pair of white Keds with no socks.

My mom takes our usual route to Northeast Philadelphia down Roosevelt Boulevard, and we roll down our windows as we drive past the Nabisco factory. We poke our noses eagerly into the night air, searching for the scent of baking cookies, and when we pull into the neighborhood, my mom parks a block away from the school gymnasium. She doesn't want anyone from the old neighborhood to know she drives a Mercedes because (as it is for all Irish Catholic girls) to be outwardly successful is unseemly; it must be hidden away and disavowed, like an unwed mother. As we scurry down the cold, cracked sidewalks, she says my hair looks nice, and I tell her I love her outfit, which is true. She looks classic, as usual, but tonight she is studiously understated. I, of course, have taken the exact opposite tact because, unlike my mother, I have a different definition of protective armor. I am wearing a black silk top and medium-wash, high-waisted bell-bottom jeans from Marc Jacobs, a pair of which was gifted, as far as I can tell, to every single magazine editor in New York this year. They look amazing, but the hemline is so long that they are downright dangerous without that assistance of three-inch heels, even for someone as tall as me.

I have decided that tonight I shall play the role of Davis Lawrence. I will be the local celebrity. I will be the most interesting person in the room, a willowy beauty projecting a kindness and ease that is, in reality, entirely foreign to me. I will be distant yet magnanimous. I will not be awkward. I will not be loud. I will not fill all conversational silences with funny stories about myself. I will not mimic people's speech patterns or affectations in a weird attempt to make them like me more. I will not get fall-down drunk.

My mother and I enter the gymnasium through a set of double doors and check in at a long table. After some pleasantries, we agree to buy raffle tickets, which are being sold by the arm's length. As a matter of tradition, we always measure raffle tickets against my mother; it is an odd point of family pride that, along with her perfect nose, my mother has exceptionally long and lovely arms.

Suffering arms, we call them.

We get a lot of tickets.

They are red.

The gymnasium is as bright as an operating theater; it hums with conversation and the squeak of sneakers is amplified by the basketball court's shiny maple floors. The space is outfitted with dozens of folding tables, each of which is covered with a blue plastic tablecloth that has been sprinkled with gold confetti. There are clusters of balloons tied to the backs of metal chairs and the netted hoops have been hand-cranked back deferentially for the occasion. I tuck my reams of tickets into the back pocket of my jeans and head to the bar where I pour myself a plastic cup of room-temperature chardonnay. My mother drifts off to talk to a friend, so I peruse the buffet dinner, which is comprised of aluminum foil trays of sausage and peppers, Caesar salad, and a basket full of round, dusty white rolls. On the raffle front, there are "baskets of cheer" and family portrait sessions; there are gift cards to local restaurants and the opportunity to win a two-person blow-up boat with plastic oars. I take an exceptionally long time deciding what plastic beach bucket to toss my tickets inside because I, quite unexpectedly, find myself feeling exposed and the buckets provide a plausible cover. There are a few girls I vaguely recognize, but otherwise, I only know the grown-ups, many of whom have been in the periphery of my life since the day I was born.

I toss my tickets in a few baskets, and then I locate my mom. She is across the gym with some friends; she is doing a lot of nodding, and she has her own plastic cup in hand. I walk in her direction because, quite frankly, the adults seem safer.

"Look at you!" my mom's friend Eileen exclaims when I approach her. "You look wonderful."

Reflexively, I lean to kiss Eileen on both cheeks, but she looks so genuinely startled by this gesture that I quickly reverse course by patting her on the shoulder. Then we both take a broad, smiling step backward; we will need space to recover from such intimacy.

"Oh, thank you," I say.

"And look at your shoes," she exclaims. "My god, your mother and I would be in the hospital if we tried to wear those things. Wouldn't we, Mary?"

"Oh, absolutely," my mom agrees kindly, and I feel overwhelmed with shame for wearing such ridiculous shoes. I am embarrassing her.

"Now tell me," Eileen says as she dips into a just-us-girls register. "Is your life just like *Sex and the City*?"

"Oh, not *exactly*," I demur. Fun fact: This is a weird thing literally *everyone* asks single women who live in New York.

"Oh, I'll bet it is!" she gushes, and my muscles unexpectedly relax at the intensity of Eileen's enthusiasm. She seems genuinely interested in me, and I realize I cannot recall the last time anyone was genuinely interested in me, as opposed to, say, the idea of me. As she smiles kindly at me, I feel my chest swell with gratitude.

"I don't know how she does it," my mom says.

"Boy, don't I know it," Eileen hoots before turning back to me. "So how's the love life? Any boyfriends?"

"I just broke up with someone," I lie. The truth is that I have been single so long I stopped counting the months.

I sneak a look at my mother, but—bless her heart—she does not react to this blatant fabrication. Her face stays neutral, like the mossy surface of a long-neglected pond. For her part, Eileen endeavors to look both compassionate and upbeat about this piece of unfortunate news:

"Oh, hon, who has time for a love life with that crazy career of yours," she exclaims. "It must be so exciting."

"Oh, it is," I say. "But very busy."

"Have you met any celebrities?"

"All the time," I respond, which is true, but I must be careful. I don't want to come off like I am bragging or feel, in any way, superior to this once-familiar crowd. "And they are all just as crazy as you'd think."

"You see, I *knew* it!" Eileen says with a feisty snap.

It's like I am playing Sad New York City Lady Bingo—and I am killing it: *High heels?* Check. *Sex and the City?* Check. *Still single?* Check. *Prioritizing my career over motherhood?* Check.

I want to die. I also want to tell Eileen that I would give it all up for a nice guy, but since I can't control the finding of that nice guy, I focus on what I can control, which is the direction of my career. I really want her to understand this about me for some reason, but I say nothing.

I feel a light tap on my shoulder.

"Clodagh?" a voice asks. "Is that you?"

I turn my head to discover the voice belongs to a girl I knew loosely from childhood. We were friendly more by circumstance than choice; our brothers used to play for the same inner-city soccer league, and we would ride our bikes in the church parking lot or make dandelion necklaces in the open fields during weekend games. She was the first person to tell me about how condoms work, and I recall not believing her; it sounded too ridiculous.

Tonight, I give her a quick once-over: She has a small, dull diamond engagement ring and matching silver wedding band (marital status being the first thing I confirm about people these days), and, otherwise, she is short and dressed like a TGI Friday's waitress. She wears a red shirt that strains against her large bosom and a pair of ill-fitting khaki pants that, because they are a few inches too short, reveal she wears white socks with her chunky black shoes.

"How are you?" I ask.

"I am doing good," she says kindly. "Are you still in New York?"

I nod.

"I don't know why I asked that," she admits with a tiny guffaw. "Everyone knows you are in New York."

"Yep, still in New York," I say before adding: "I just bought an apartment."

"Where?" she asks.

"Where?"

"Yes," she says, but now she enunciates, as if I don't speak English. "*Where* did you buy an apartment?"

I raise my eyebrows. I am surprised by the specificity of this question. To look at her, I would assume her understanding of New York City geography consisted of the four blocks that ring the American Girl Store in Times Square but if she can be a bitch, I can be one, too.

And, trust me, I am better at it: I am on the fucking varsity team.

"On Central Park," I say. "The east side? *Upper* Fifth Avenue?"

We nod at each other, but I can tell she is impressed.

"Are you married?" she asks.

"Not yet."

"I'm sorry," she responds, which is another dig, although this one is far more successful. It lands like a small sandbag on my chest.

"I don't see what there is to be sorry about," I reply. "My boyfriend wants to get engaged, but I have a lot I want to accomplish before I start a family. I said I want to wait a year, so we *just* started ring shopping."

Oh my god. What the fuck is wrong with me? First, I lie about an apartment, and now this? Why is it so hard to admit I don't have a boyfriend? Why do I see this as a terminal failure instead of just, say, a passing circumstance? Then I remember: It's because, in the world I currently inhabit, we women must be good at everything.

"Ah," she says with a little smirk. She takes a sip of her drink. "I love it. That is *so* New York."

I feel my body start to fill with anger. *So . . . New York?* Is that supposed to be some kind of insult? How does this girl not comprehend how different—and how much *better*—my life is than her life. I want to roll my eyes at her lousy, ill-fitting outfit and parochial worldview. I want to inform her that flying to Orlando and Las Vegas is not what people mean by "traveling" and drinking a Miller Lite before dinner does not constitute as "cocktail hour." I want to disclose that my handbag costs $4,000 and that I ate dinner with Sofia Coppola (once, in a group; we did not speak). I desire to inform her that, just last week, Annette de la Renta told me—in passing, at a benefit—that I had a fantastic figure, as I was wearing one of her husband's (borrowed) dresses. I am desperate to rattle off the litany of serious books I've read and the number of articles I have authored for the magazine. I want to pull out my passport and show her the stamps, proof of the countries to which I have traveled, the faraway sights I have seen. I want to reveal that Ralph Lauren is, indeed, pronounced phonetically while Loewe is not.

And while I yearn to put her in her place, whatever I deem that place to be, I cannot find the words because the truth is that I wholeheartedly agree with her assessment of my failures. After all, I am completely bungling the one task God (or some benevolent being) put me on this earth to accomplish, which is to be desired enough by one man to produce at least one additional human being.

The rest of it doesn't mean anything.

Not really.

Apparently, this admission of my "singleness" is all the encouragement she needs to find her footing. She starts telling me how—*against all odds*—her forty-year-old cousin got married last fall. She assures me I won't always be unlucky in love, which is a label that makes my eyes involuntary twinge hot with tears. I look around for my mother, but I don't see her, and so, I imagine myself sinking to the bottom of a deep and soundless swimming pool, just like they do in the movies.

This is the real reason I stay out of church gymnasiums: They make me feel sad.

They make me feel sad because everyone else always seems so happy. They seem settled and content, and I fear that, if I visit church gymnasiums too often, I will prove a terrifying hypothesis that has haunted me for years: What if New York doesn't build up, but rather it destroys? Every year, a million girls, just like me, move to New York City. We are the girls that believe success can only be attained via the harshest of training grounds. We are the girls that distrust things that come too easily, the girls who believe life, an interesting life, must be painfully earned. What they don't know—*what I did not know*—is that, if you are not careful, the path home can become overgrown. With a slowness nearly impossible to detect, there comes a point when you cannot find your way back and, so, your only choice is to move forward toward a destination utterly unknown.

The girl continues to speak to me, but I stay at the bottom of the pool, relieved to be deprived of my senses until I feel the energy in the gymnasium has shifted. I can make out the grumbling vibration of a man's voice; it booms over a crackling loudspeaker, and, like a siren's song, it lulls me in the direction of the horror that surely awaits me on the surface. I break through the plane and look around. There is, indeed, a man standing on the stage (the gymnasium doubles as an auditorium) and he gleefully fishes his tattooed forearm around in a plastic, red pail. He retrieves a small ticket and holds it up in the air.

The room cheers.

The raffle has begun.

I watch people gravitate toward the stage. They assemble into an expectant half-moon and strain to listen as the man slowly calls out the numbers on the first ticket. Someone shrieks and, amid a smattering of applause, I see a young woman run up to the stage to accept her gift, which is nestled in a white wicker basket. As she walks back to her cheering table with a mad grin, I realize someone has turned the music off. I look back toward the stage just as the man plucks out another ticket. There is more yelling and clapping and, one by one, people race up to the stage to collect their prizes. There are hugs and cheering, and when I finish my wine, I crane my neck in the direction of the bar. I hear the man call out another number, but, this time, it is met with nothing but silence. He calls it out again, which reminds me to pull the tickets out of my pocket. It becomes clear that he will continue to repeat the number until someone claims the prize. I look at my spoil of tickets, and I listen harder this time. I have the number.

In an instant, I feel entirely found out.

The man calls out the number again. The confused chatter grows more insistent.

"It's me," I say, feebly and to no one in particular. "I have the number."

At this news, the girl to whom I've been speaking looks up from her own reams of tickets, all of which she has laid flat on the table in front of us. Her expression is such a bizarre mix of both awe and disdain, you'd think I'd been awarded the last berth on Noah's Ark.

"Does anyone have the number?" the man asks. "Going once..."

The girl continues to stare at me wide-eyed, but I say nothing.

"Going twice..."

The room starts to buzz with delighted curiosity.

"Say something," she hisses.

"I can't," I whisper back.

She shakes her head in annoyance, and throws her thick arms in the air:

"Clodagh Harmon has the number," she yells over the crowd. "Clodagh Harmon has the number!"

At this proclamation, every head swings in our direction, and a few mouths fall agape. There is a slow build of whispers, and the sound fills the cavernous room like a swift, summer rain.

"Clodagh Harmon," the man says, and he blows up his cheeks with air and widens his eyes, unable to make out where, exactly, in the crowd he should look.

At this point, people have started to look in my direction.

"Where are you?" he booms heartily. He smiles. "Come on up and claim your prize!"

The girl nudges me forward and I begin to walk toward the stage. I don't know if it's my imagination, but I am pretty sure the entire gymnasium nose-dives into a reproachful silence as my heels (which I now understand to be ridiculous) click across the basketball court. I feel guilty and stupid and proud, like a frosting-smeared Marie Antoinette, and by the time I hoof it up to the stage, the man has been joined by a woman I don't recognize. She seems to be the prize master. She has short hair, small gold hoop earrings, and a crucifix rests upon the freckled crepe of her décolletage.

"There ya go, hon," she says. "Congratulations."

She points to a white plastic laundry basket on the floor. It is crowded with alcohol bottles, the slim necks of which are adorned in colorful, curly ribbons. Standing there as someone takes my picture, I realize with horror that I have won the basket of cheer, which was the big prize of the night.

I won the thing that everyone wanted.

"Wow," I say. "Thank you!"

I bend down to hoist the basket with both my arms, but it is too heavy. I can only lift it a few inches before I drop it with a clattering thud. I scan the crowd for assistance, but everyone has drifted back toward their friends. The music has been turned back on: Steely Dan plays over the speakers. After a few painful moments standing alone, two teenagers with bushy hair and acne hop up onto the stage and carry my bounty, such as it is, to the nearest table. I thank them.

Finally, I am joined by my mother and Eileen. My mother looks stricken.

"Well, this will last you the next ten years," Eileen says as she pokes through the basket with approval. She shows the more expensive bottles to my mother, who grimaces as Eileen continues: "It's the good stuff, too! Look!"

She hands me a green glass bottle of Tanqueray and I look down at the label. I calculate that in ten years, I will be thirty-nine years old, which feels like a lifetime away.

And yet, I can somehow see it: One morning, I will wake up alone and discover the future sitting at the foot of my bed. It will gaze upon me with immense sadness, and I will prop myself up on my elbows to get a better look. I will try to untangle what has brought it such sorrow only to realize that it mourns, as I will one day mourn, the moment it all went so irrevocably wrong

Part Three

NEW YORK CITY
2006 to 2009

48

In the strange haze of the holiday season that directly followed Saul's death, there was a shiva (his family), a Catholic ceremony (his wife's family), and an endless stream of foil containers full of lasagna and noodle kugel were stomped up the stairs by assorted neighbors and relatives through the New Year. As I wasn't invited to attend any of the services, I laid on the floor of my apartment and pressed my ear against the hardwood floor. I guess I had hoped to hear a comforting word or a reassuring pocket of laughter. Maybe a prayer or an unfamiliar song. I was looking for something, anything, that might make me feel even a little bit better.

But nothing did.

In the middle of January, Saul's wife, now widow, knocks on my door. She informs me that she has put the building up for sale. This is a possibility I had not (idiotically, in retrospect) considered in the navigation of my own potent and unsettling grief over his death. She says she intends to move in with her sister near Jacksonville, Florida, and that I need to be out by the end of the month. This isn't a question: The market is hot, and she wants to take advantage quickly and so, the very next day, there is a chattering cavalcade of painters, contractors, and real estate agents marching through all the rooms to get the property ready to list. While I am at work, they paint my apartment a muted shade of what Allie labels "gentrification gray" and when I see it, I feel the serrated pang of a missed opportunity: I have lived here for over four years. Why didn't I paint the walls of my apartment? Why did I never get curtains when

I hated the blinds so much? The truth is that I hoped my single days in this studio would be brief, and when my *real* life began, I would decorate my home, wherever it was, in magnificent earnest.

The building sells in two days to a young, married couple from Tribeca. I only know this because I meet them by accident on a cold Saturday as they prowl around with an architect and interior designer. After we exchange pleasantries, they offer me their life story unsolicited: They met in college! They got married in Italy (but had a big party for friends in the city!) and their dog died recently, which was super, *super* sad. They have a one-year-old baby (named Ava Grace, like everyone else's baby) and a new baby on the way, which—trust me—is abundantly clear, if only by the way the woman relentlessly molests her barely rounded stomach. She wears Tod's driving loafers, a pair of which I have always wanted but are so expensive that I cannot justify buying, skinny jeans, and an oversized, nautical striped sweater.

Naturally, I detest her on sight.

She informs me she is an event planner and the husband is—wait for it—an investment banker, the likes of which have slowly started to descend upon my formerly unfashionable neighborhood, only to convert all the multi-unit buildings into single-family homes. I think back to my early days at the magazine, when I told some of my coworkers that I lived in Brooklyn only to watch their beautiful foreheads wrinkle with pity. It was as if the recipient of this information was *very sorry* to learn something had *happened to my trust fund*, but they sincerely hoped it was *sorted out in short order*. As the couple walks the house, I linger outside the doorway of my little studio on the top floor and eavesdrop as they discuss what walls can be torn down and how quickly they can rebuild the "nightmare" staircase. For some reason, I find it galling that they want to change the stairs: How do they not understand that the stairs being lopsided is what makes the apartment so charming? I go down to the street and smoke a cigarette, which makes me feel sad about Saul. The Christmas lights still hang in the windows across the street, and I think about how much life I have lived inside this little apartment. I throw my cigarette butt angrily into the street, unable to stomach that the little world I so painstakingly built is about to disappear into the hands of an event planner with Tod's driving loafers.

Even worse, I only have two weeks to find a new place to live.

Back at the office, I spend the bulk of my days scanning Craigslist only to learn that the rent in Brooklyn has gone up to an appalling degree since I first moved in, and my salary, despite two separate, although minuscule, "cost-of-living" increases, has not followed suit. After all, people working at magazines are paid in perks, which had been fine with me until I realized that, to get a new apartment, I'd have to call my dad to pony up a security deposit, and my first and last month's rent. He might also be required to sign as my guarantor, because my salary remains too low to legally rent a decent place on my own. I know my parents would do it, but I just don't think I can stomach being a disappointment. After all, I have led them to believe I am making a *killing* in New York. How else could I possibly explain my wardrobe, the labels of which give my mother a near cardiac event every time she is tidying up my piles when I make a visit home.

"Oscar de la Renta?" she will say, holding a limp garment in her hand like she just discovered a *Playboy* under my bed. "Can you *really* afford this?"

Harry makes some suggestions—he knows a guy who needs a roommate in Williamsburg—but I just don't think I can do that, either. I am too old to move in with a stranger, and especially one who plays guitar in a band called FiveHead. At the height of my early despair, Allie unhelpfully suggests I tap into my retirement account, in which I discover that I have only been socking away three percent of my salary. When I call my benefits department hotline for more information, I learn that, even with the company match, the penalty alone would nearly wipe me out. Please don't misunderstand me: I most definitely see the irony in the fact that I am *regularly* photographed wearing $4,000 dresses and I have flown to Nantucket on a private plane, but I still don't have a proper savings account. To be honest, until now, I hadn't been troubled by the massive discrepancy between my image and the reality because I reckoned two things. One: I was still on the climb to the top and I couldn't expect things to truly settle until I reached the summit. Two: The summit would be permanent, a well-padded tuffet from which I would, after years of struggle, spend the remainder of my days looking down with disdain upon everyone else.

For the first week of my search, there remains a hopeful part of me that believes I'll magically stumble across the perfect apartment in my current neighborhood. Listen, I have read enough literary fiction to know a special affinity for Brooklyn is no longer an original or defining characteristic. It's like saying you like puppies or a seventy-five-degree day. That said, in my first uncertain months, alone in a brand-new city, Brooklyn saved me. Unlike Manhattan, it struck me as a place where you could really *have* a life instead of just borrowing one, and I recall the desperation with which I wanted to stuff it up my shirt like a big secret.

I shouldn't have to leave.

I am finally broken, however, in the second week of my search when I am shown a dusty studio on Amity Street. The listing boasts an alcove, which I have learned from recent experience translates to "bay window" but I allow myself to feel excited about it anyway, especially because it's on the parlor floor, which always boasts the most desirable apartment in a brownstone. When I arrive, however, I quickly discover they have clearly split the floor in half, which makes it considerably smaller than my current apartment. Even more depressing, the refrigerator covers about three inches of the bathroom entrance which, aside from looking bizarre, prevents the door from closing properly.

I point this out to the agent.

"It's not great," she admits as she taps two acrylic nails together. "But you're living alone, and who spends time in their apartments anyways?"

I mull over the word *anyways* as I turn away from the kitchen and walk toward the soft curve of windows that overlook the street. The trees are bare, and no people walk on the sidewalk below, but I remind myself that everything is gray in November, and by springtime the block will come alive again: There will be flowers and children and ice cream trucks playing music. It is also an apartment I could reasonably afford. Frankly, there is no good reason *not* to take it, other than I have slowly permitted another idea to incubate over the past two weeks, which is to parlay my misfortune into an invitation to stay at the Lawrence apartment. I run my hand along the glass, and when I pull away, my finger pads are black and tacky with some strange substance.

I turn from the window, and I thank the agent for her time. As she locks the door behind us, she says she will need a decision no later than five o'clock because she has a long line of interested renters—Brooklyn, she says, is starting to attract a whole new class of people—and I promise to get back to her.

Then, I promptly walk to Court Street and call Davis. When she answers, I burst into tears.

Less than a week later, I pack my small lot of furniture and books into a storage unit in downtown Manhattan. Then, I messenger two racks' worth of designer clothes and six cardboard boxes (filled with toiletries, books, socks, and shoes) to the Lawrence apartment on the Upper East Side. I stuff the rest of my life into three large suitcases and one tote bag, all of which I place together on the curb in front of my building as I wait for my car service to arrive. The tote bag was a last-minute addition. As I packed up my things, the only item subject to internal debate was Susan Goldsmith-Cohen's horse statue, to which I had developed an odd, anthropomorphic affinity. I couldn't bear to abandon her to the grim loneliness of some random air-conditioned storage unit near the Financial District nor could I toss her body—as I briefly debated—into the Gowanus Canal. No, I decided, she had to stay with me. So, I wrapped her in a clean towel, which I tucked deep inside the tote. I figured I could deal with her when I arrived at my new, albeit temporary, home. As I suspected, when Davis learned of my predicament, she insisted I stay at the apartment until I could find a place of my own, and after some rehearsed, tearful refusals, I was only more than happy to take her up on the offer. It's funny: I never asked if Davis had cleared the arrangement with her mother, but I wasn't worried. I figured if anyone would find the idea of an additional audience appealing, it would be Barbara Lawrence.

After I get everything to the curb, I take one final dash up to my apartment. It's strange: It looks smaller with nothing to fill up the space, and I try to remember my first night, sleeping all alone in a brand-new bed, the trains rumbling overhead. As I walk across the floor, a few dust bunnies get caught up in the draft. I watch them skitter along the filthy baseboards where my small couch used to sit. I wonder if I should partake in some mourning ritual, but my throat aches to such a painful degree that I can't bear to stay another second. So, I trundle back down my wonderfully crooked, soon-to-be-straightened steps for the very last time, and duck into the waiting car under the watchful eyes of old Italian women of the neighborhood.

I don't look back.

Davis is standing on the sidewalk when I arrive.

While I had sobbed for the entire ride into Manhattan, I am surprised that, when I see her, something starts to soften inside of me, some palpable loosening of my dread and grief. I was so distraught over losing my apartment that I didn't really consider what it might be like to fully *gain* Davis Lawrence. And here she stands, waiting for nobody in the whole wide world but me.

I did not, however, account for the dreaded dog in my calculations, who lays panting at Davis's feet on a leash. When I get out of the car, he barks wildly and pulls her in my direction, knocking her slightly off-kilter. She laughingly allows him to drag her to the curb.

"Welcome to the Thunderdome," she says dryly. She holds out her cashmere-gloved hand for one of my bags, but I shake my head.

"Hatch can handle the luggage," I say.

Davis raises her eyebrows.

"Making yourself right at home, eh?" she asks.

I feel myself redden.

"I didn't mean it like that," I stammer. "Just because of your wrist."

"I know." She smiles. "I'm *joking*."

"I promise it will only be for a few weeks," I say. "I'm sure I'll find a place soon."

"Stay as long as you'd like," she responds, and she bumps her shoulder against mine playfully. "You might be saving my life."

During my first Saturday in the apartment, I tell Barbara and Davis that I am going to grab a few toiletries at Duane Reade, but, instead, I walk directly to the Dempsey and Carroll stationery store on Lexington Avenue. I have long admired its facade, which is painted a rich colonial blue, but, until today, I never had the nerve to venture inside because, quite frankly, it's very expensive, and I would have been too embarrassed to walk out empty-handed. You see, having the right personal stationery is very important and, in my opinion (which is the opinion conferred on me by the magazine, of course), Dempsey and Carroll make the very best stationery in all of New York.

When I open the door, I am immediately embraced by the smell of fresh flowers, old paper, and a fragrant, unknowable smoke, which twirls off a large, clearly expensive candle. I unbutton my hefty coat. The store is tiny, and the heavy mahogany bookshelves that line the walls make it feel even more intimate and more exclusive, like a private club. I am the only person in the store, and as I browse my options, my shoulders warm under the patient gaze of the preppy blonde woman behind the small counter. She gives me *just* the right amount of space before she joins me, and, with competent ease, helps me select the perfect set. It's a smooth cream cardstock, sturdy as a credit card and with a navy blue border. My name, which we decide should be *Clodagh P. Harmon* as that mimics my byline, will be set across the top of each card in a downright aristocratic font. The envelopes, for an additional cost, can be lined with a corresponding navy paper.

"Would you like to add your return address?" the woman inquires.

"Of course." I give her my new address, and she glances up briefly to offer me a neighborly smile.

We are all friends here.

"And how would you like to pay today?" she asks.

"Do you take American Express?"

Without waiting for an answer, I slide Barbara's gold card across the countertop.

"Now, do you want two sets of stationery or just one?" she asks. "I would say you go through one pretty quickly, especially this time of year."

"Two sets, please."

Despite my claims to the contrary, I have already decided that I am not going anywhere. There will be no more scouring Craigslist. There will be no more sad tours of filthy and misshapen apartments. There will be no more tacky real estate agents. There will be no more Brooklyn.

After all, I have come to the conclusion that Harry Wood is not to be trusted.

And Davis Lawrence, it seems, must be very closely watched.

49

Within one month of moving into the Lawrence apartment, several notable events occur.

For starters, Harry Wood shows up unannounced one evening gripping the necks of two bottles of expensive champagne. It's only my first week in the apartment, and he claims he's come to celebrate the collective cohabitation of "his favorite people in the world." Now, while this seems all fine and dandy, I intuit something sinister, or at least self-serving, about this little intrusion, especially because he wasn't particularly supportive when I first told him about my plans.

"Isn't that taking it a little too far?" he had asked.

"Taking *what* too far?" I asked irritably.

"This whole Talented Mr. Ripley thing?" he had said, swirling his finger around me in the air, his mouth turned up in a knowing smile.

"Oh, please. You are being ridiculous," I had protested. "It's only going to be a few weeks until I find a new apartment."

"Well," he said with a dismissive shrug. "Don't say I didn't warn you."

Now, while I am annoyed by Harry, Davis is in the opposite camp: she seems positively overjoyed by his surprise arrival. Harry flatters and teases her as he unwraps the foil on the bottle and, when the cork pops, Davis hoots and hollers, and I join her, if only to hide my uneasy displeasure. As for Barbara, she is polite to Harry as usual, but she is also watchful, and I get the sense there is still something about him that she doesn't quite trust.

As we sip our drinks, Harry asks if I will be staying in *his* bedroom. He reminisces about events that predate me, including a small apartment fire and something *hilarious* about an escaped parakeet. Of course, this all makes me feel wretched at first, but as the night wears on I detect an odd shift in Harry. He goes from gregarious to a little manic, moving around the room recklessly and lighting one cigarette off the next. He drums his hands and feet as he talks, and excuses himself on at least two occasions to use his cell phone in the hallway. I start to wonder if this recent turn of events hasn't destabilized him in a more serious way than simple, good, old-fashioned jealousy. There is something desperate about him, and while I cannot place it, I reckon it is something I need to keep my eye on.

The second event of note is that I run into Mark Angelbeck outside the local Gristedes grocery store on a gray Sunday afternoon. He is walking an old yellow Labrador, and has a copy of the *New York Post* tucked into his armpit. One side of a plaid shirt hangs haphazardly out of his wool sweater.

"Oh, hi, Mr. Angelbeck," I call out shyly as he passes me.

He stops. There are crumbs in his stubble.

"Clo, what a surprise," he says. "I didn't know you lived up here."

"Oh, I just bought a new apartment."

"Where?"

I name the building, and he lets out a little wolf whistle.

"That's a swank spot, my dear," he says, and then he adjusts his position and cocks his head to the side. It's almost like, now that he has learned I am in possession of tremendous wealth, he can finally place me. Placing people—be it through your college or summer town or street address—I have learned, is very important to a certain class; they need to know exactly where you fit within their world, and they need to unearth this information as quickly as possible. As I have no intention of disabusing him of any of these assumptions, I stand there and smile the untroubled smile of the elite.

Of course, I live up here.

"We should have lunch sometime," he ventures.

"I would love that."

"I'll have my assistant set it up after I get back from Europe," he says before pausing to add, "You look great, by the way."

"I do?" I reply, careful to make sure my delivery is both saccharine and bashful.

"Indeed, you do."

The final thing is that New York gets hit with an unexpected snowstorm. It starts while I am at work, and as I watch the doughy flakes tumble out of a bland sky, I am filled with an almost childlike happiness. All through the day, the snows spins outside my window in taunting, playful circles before it blankets the sidewalks at an astonishing clip. I choose to view this meteorological event as an exceptionally good omen, a clean slate of sorts.

Everything will be fine, I think.

As I walk back to the apartment that evening, the freshly laid snow groans and squeaks under my weight. Children in snowsuits race toward the park dragging colorful sleds and dogs on leashes leap around and nip at the cold air with delight. I reach down and try to make a snowball, but the snow is too loose to pack properly. I toss my failed attempt limply into the street in front of the apartment, and then I clod into the lobby. Hatch is resting on a shovel and watching the news on his small television.

"They are saying it could be a foot," he says.

"A foot?" I exclaim, and Hatch laughs at me as I jump up and down.

When I get up to the sixth floor, I stomp my boots in the hallway, and I wonder if Barbara would ever let me make a fire in the apartment's pristine, entirely untouched fireplace. I place my hand on the doorknob, but, to my surprise, I can hear yelling coming from inside the apartment. When I press my ear against the wood, I can tell it's Barbara, but the door is so thick, I cannot hear what, exactly, is being said, only that it is angry. I let myself into the foyer. I close the door behind me as quietly as possible.

"I just need, like, five minutes," Davis says. Her voice sounds tight.

"You don't get five minutes, Davis," Barbara yells.

I hear the whinny of a blow-dryer starting but the sound is immediately muted by a pair of high heels running furiously across the parquet floors. Suddenly, there is a loud smashing sound, and the blow-dryer goes silent.

"When I say you don't get it," Barbara screams, "it means you don't get it. Who do you think you are?"

There is more noise, and more loud words exchanged, and while I don't know what is going on, I certainly know enough to feel frightened. I take a few steps back and as I lean against the wall, my hands search frantically along for the doorknob. Then, I hear the high heels again, stomping in the direction of the foyer—I know it is too late to make an escape. I force a big smile across my face just as Barbara marches into view. She is wearing a long, white fur coat, and her face is flushed.

She looks surprised to see me.

"You? How long have *you* been standing here?" she barks accusingly. "Are you *spying*?"

"No, I just walked in," I stammer, but Barbara isn't listening. She turns to look in the ornate oval mirror that hangs over the entryway table. She pats a stiff, stray section of hair in frustration.

"My hair," she says angrily. "It's wrecked."

I sneak a look down the hall just as Davis emerges warily from the bathroom. Her hair is soaking wet, and it has soaked the silk fabric of her dress, rendering it translucent. I can make out some of the freckles that pepper her chest. As she gets closer, I see she isn't wearing makeup, and, despite the weather, her legs are bare. She is holding a pair of heels in her hand and when she bends over to set them on the floor, I notice her dress is unzipped in the back.

"Mom, I *said* I am sorry," Davis says, and while her tone is that of light frustration, it's clear she has been crying. "See, I am ready."

She slides her feet into her shoes and throws her hands up in the air, but Barbara says nothing. She just regards us both in the mirror as she pinches a clump of mascara from her lashes.

"It's like you go out of your way to sabotage me," Barbara says finally, her voice low and angry. "You have known for weeks how important this night is to me. To my career! Everyone will be there."

"Mom, I swear, I thought it was eight," she says. "I wouldn't do this on purpose."

Barbara turns away from the mirror and gives Davis a quick once-over, and I am mystified when she makes no comment about her daughter's disasterous appearance. I thought, for certain, she would tell her to put on a different dress or find some lipstick, but she just pulls open the front door.

"Let's go," she says. She walks into the hallway.

I look at Davis.

"What is going on?" I hiss.

"Nothing," she says weakly, and while she tries to shrug it off, I watch her eyes fill with embarrassed tears.

"Well, you can't go out like this," I say, pointing to her outfit. "It's snowing."

To this, Davis says nothing. She just looks in the mirror and tries to finger comb her mangled hair. Then, she presses her fingers into the corners of her eyes in a futile attempt to stem her crying.

"Davis?" I whisper. "Seriously. You're scaring me."

She turns to look at me directly.

"Can you clean up the bathroom before we get back?" she asks, her voice pleading. "I made a mess."

"Sure," I say, but the whole exchange feels loaded with meaning.

"Thanks," she whispers, and she starts for the open door.

"Davis, you need a coat," I say.

"I'm okay," she says vacantly.

I wiggle forcefully out of mine, and as I am about to lay it on her shoulders, I remember her dress is still undone.

"Davis," Barbara shouts angrily.

"You're unzipped," I whisper, and my voice is now full of panic.

"I'll deal with it later," Davis responds. She grabs my coat with both hands and, pulling it over her shoulders, vanishes into the hall.

I stand motionless in the foyer for what feels like a long time, my heart beating wildly. Then, I softly close the front door and rest my head on the wood. The apartment is very quiet—almost suffocatingly so—but after a few beats, I make out the sound of running water. I walk to the bathroom where I find the faucet gushing into the sink at full volume. I turn it off slowly and regard myself in the mirror. I look pale. On the floor, I see the shattered blow-dryer. I kneel on the wet tile floor and gather the large plastic pieces in my hands. I put them in the trash can, but then I worry Barbara will see it and, somehow, the memory will trigger her again. I pluck the pieces out of the trashcan and tie them up in a plastic bag. I go back hallway and shove the bag into the bottom of the recycling bin before I return to the bathroom. I hang the wet towels on hooks. I straighten the shower curtain. I pick up the makeup scattered across the vanity area, and as I turn the delicate pieces over in my hands, I find myself thinking back to the scene Davis made at Greta Greer's summer party—how Davis, in an instant, captivated an entire room—and wonder if Barbara hadn't given Davis the wrong time on purpose, if only to ensure that Davis would look ugly and undone. I tuck the stray items neatly in a side drawer. I rinse Davis's toothbrush and put it back in the holder. I wipe down the sink with a small pink sponge.

I feel like an unwilling accomplice to a crime.

When I moved to East Ninety-Second Street, I wasn't prepared for how much I would miss the simple joys of living alone, the piddling around my studio apartment, sorting mail and making photo albums and pairing socks. This evening however, as I wander the apartment as a resident instead of a guest, I don't luxuriate in the stillness. I feel spooked. The rooms, generally familiar, feel sinister amid such silence. The chairs and tables regard me with reproach. I hear cabinets creak open and closed.

There are ghosts in this house.

Reflexively, I walk in the direction of Barbara's study. The door is open, and behind the desk, there is a bookshelf, which is attached to the ceiling by very intricate crown molding. This is not uncommon, of course, because at a certain level of financial or intellectual accomplishment, everyone has the same style bookshelf in New York. They are a cultural calling card of sorts, and I have always been surprised that someone as image conscious as Barbara Lawrence tucks her own book collection inside a barely used office. It feels like a missed opportunity for someone who never, *ever* misses an opportunity for self-promotion.

I let my eyes roam the shelves: There are neat rows of books, both those I can imagine she has read (*The Corrections, The Great Gatsby,* and, quite possibly, every book ever written by Mary Higgins Clark, all of which are perplexingly in hardcover) and a smattering from the snobbish, "intellectual-class" canon I'd bet hard money she has yet to crack open (*The Power Broker, Memoirs of the Duc de Saint-Simon*, the dreaded *Ulysses* again). The books are broken up by Barbara's extensive ashtray collection, all of which I have been told were pilfered over the years from wonderful places like the Crillon in Paris and Raffles in Singapore. Every ashtray comes with a *simply marvelous* story about a similarly *marvelous* evening during which a young, famous Barbara was able to abscond with the memento amid high society hilarity and chaos, her narrow waist nipped into a crinoline-lined frock, a vodka gimlet at her hip. Her ashtrays make me feel bad about myself, like I am not really *living* my life, but this is not a huge surprise: The high bar against which I measure myself shifts like the wind.

I often wonder if Barbara ever looks at this bookshelf or if it's nothing but white noise in an otherwise frantic life. I mean, how often do we really *look* at the things we have accumulated? Either way, she has not detected one new, undoubtedly consequential addition: During my first week in the apartment, I placed Susan Goldsmith-Cohen's horse statue on the third shelf. I tucked her between a framed photograph of Barbara and a lumpy ceramic bowl, and I adjusted her several times before I was satisfied with the final position. Now, every day and without exception, I crack open the office door to confirm that my beloved, longtime companion remains exactly where I need her to be.

She is always there.

It turns out that clichés are clichés for a reason.

The best place to hide something really is in plain sight.

50

My plan was to arrive early for my lunch with Mark Angelbeck. For starters, I have been taught I must always—and without exception—arrive early for work-related meetings. That said, I also wanted a little extra time to position my body for maximum impact. I had spent all of February shopping for the right dress for this long-delayed occasion. I wanted to wear something that made me appear both sophisticated and capricious, like a frosty debutante who, without warning, might slither out of her silk knickers and offer herself to you in the coat closet when no one is watching.

I bought the dress, a silk jacquard number with a low neckline, at Saks Fifth Avenue with Barbara's credit card, but since I can wear it to at least one of her upcoming events, I conclude it's some variation of fair game. Despite this rationalization, I enter the price in my little notebook (nearly $3,000, but it *is* a McQueen) and force myself to do the overall math, which informs me that I have spent over $100,000 of Barbara Lawrence's money.

This lunch, I decide with a panicked resolve, must go perfectly.

However, when I arrive at the restaurant fifteen minutes early, the hostess informs me that my party is already seated. I peek over her shoulder to see that Mark Angelbeck is, indeed, tucked into a table. He is wearing glasses and looks to be reading something on his lap. When he sees me in the doorway, he quickly stands up, and I feel my knees wobble with uncertainty. *Was I ready for this?* I put so much thought into *how* I would look at this lunch that I didn't dedicate enough time to practice all the charming and intelligent things I might say, and now it is too late. I didn't even read the newspaper this morning. The waiter pulls out my chair, and once I am settled, Mr. Angelbeck takes his seat. He smooths down his tie, and I notice there is an uncorked bottle of white wine tilted in the silver ice bucket between us.

It bobs before me like a life raft.

"I took the liberty," he says. He gestures to the bottle with a smile before he glances up at the lingering waiter. "It *is* Monday, after all."

"It is, indeed," I say with festivity as the waiter fills my glass.

I take a small sip, and the wine tastes wonderful, like clean dirt and white grapefruit. I smile and take another and, with this one, I feel the crimp in my shoulders start to release. I find it fascinating, in the absence of the distractions that usually accompany my drinking (loud music, people with better jobs than me, worrying about looking fat, saying something catastrophically stupid), how swiftly the alcohol hits my bloodstream this afternoon. It swims in elegant circles around my head before it flows down to my chest, leaving me awash in the sensation of well-being. My nerves soften and the room slows down. I starts to recall the steps to this dance.

"The wine is delicious," I say agreeably.

"I'm so glad you like it," he replies with a smile. "It's been a while so tell me: How was your weekend?"

"It was very good," I reply. "*Quiet.*"

This comment—like most things that come out of my mouth lately—is a half-truth. Barbara and Davis had flown to Palm Beach, and while they invited me to join them, I declined. I was desperate to enjoy the lost pleasures of an empty apartment, if only for a couple of days. I envisioned flipping through trashy magazines and drinking a lot of water, but after only a few hours alone in the apartment, I felt strangely unmoored, like I was floating between worlds with no real place to call home. After one day of piddling around the Upper East Side, I started to feel sorry for myself, so I called Harry to see if he wanted to join me.

"I didn't know you were around," he said when he answered the phone. His voice sounded raspy and exhausted.

"I am around."

There was a pause.

"Does Barbara still have the color printer?" he asked.

"I think so?"

"Perfect," he said. "I'll be over in an hour."

When Harry arrived, he looked boyish and rumpled, like he had spent the past few days in matching pajamas and drinking chocolate milk. He had a leather overnight bag slung over his shoulder, and a white laptop tucked under his arm. He gave me a big hug before walking directly to the kitchen table.

"Thanks for letting me work here," he said absently as he plugged in his computer.

"Oh, sure," I said easily, but I was dispirited that I was, indeed, being passed over for unlimited access to a color printer. I had hoped that maybe the "printer" thing was just a ruse to spend some quality time with me, but within minutes of his arrival, Harry was bent over his laptop. As he worked, I lingered around the kitchen, grateful to be thrown the occasional conversational bone. For example, he told me he was working on an investor deck, and he showed me a few pages—mostly charts and graphs—before he solicited my opinion on a few writers in our distant circles. I tried to be useful, but at a certain point, the conversation stalled out. I laid flat on my back on the banquette and lit a cigarette. As I blew smoke into the air, I listened to the light clack of Harry's fingers on the keyboard until I couldn't take it anymore.

"Can you take a little time off?" I whined. "It's Saturday. I'm bored."

"Only boring people get bored," he replied, and, finally, I took the hint.

I drifted into the living room alone, and as I dropped down on the couch and flipped through the television channels, I felt more undesirable by the minute. Surely, if I was Davis, Harry would have dropped everything to join me, but, as the world often likes to remind me, I am not Davis. And yet, despite understanding this in some capacity, I still believe there is something I could do or say, some lipstick I could wear or alliance I could broker that would make me shiny to Harry Wood all on my own.

I must have drifted to sleep, only to be awoken by the sound of Harry rattling around the kitchen. When I opened my eyes, I felt disoriented;

the clock said it was only 4:30 in the afternoon, but the apartment was already bathed in the curious murk of early winter. I got up off the couch, and wandered into the kitchen where I found Harry parsing through the wine fridge. He was checking the labels on the bottles and sliding them back in place until he found one that seemed to satisfy him.

"Is it cocktail hour?" I asked.

"Domaine de la Romanee-Conti Echezeau," he said, and he held up the bottle. "1982."

"Is that good?"

"Oh, my dear." He smiled. "It is very good. Like giant cliché good." He fished a wine opener out of the silverware drawer.

"Won't Barbara kill you?" I asked.

"Please," he said. "Like Barbara would ever notice."

"She will probably think I drank it," I mumbled, but my objection had come too late. Harry had already started to wrest open the bottle.

"Put on the record player, will you?" he asked.

"What do you want?"

"You decide," he said.

I walked back into the living room and put on the Dinah Washington record that I heard Davis play countless times. My Irish grandmother had a record player. It was built inside a large wooden credenza and, because she had arthritis and didn't walk very well, she taught all of her grandchildren how to switch out the records. We had to lean over the edge on our tiptoes to reach the turntable, our tongues poking out of our mouths with concentration, and, all these years later, I still find the hoppity hop static bump of a needle hitting vinyl to be one of the most promising sounds in the world.

With the music playing softly, Harry and I laid on the carpet in a shared silence for a long time. Our hands were only inches apart, and as I felt the energy leap between our bodies, I marveled, as I always marvel, over how Harry Wood can infuse nearly any situation with a near religious significance.

"I always loved this apartment when nobody was home," Harry sighed finally. "It was the only time it was peaceful."

I had rolled over on my stomach to look at him.

"I know," I said. "Sometimes, I don't know why you moved out."

To this, Harry says nothing. He just raises his eyebrows.

"Do you know what I realized?" I said as I pushed myself up into a seated position. "You never told me your New Year's Resolution this year."

"Get so skinny that everyone worries about me," Harry deadpanned, his eyes still closed, and I had laughed.

"No," I pressed after a moment. "What is it, really?"

Harry opened his eyes. He looked at the ceiling for a long minute.

"I would like to really *be* someone, you know?" he said, and then he turned to look at me with a smile. "Is that corny?"

"Breathtakingly so," I had replied.

"I know," he laughed.

We moved on to a second bottle of wine. When Harry started flipping through the record collection for something more upbeat, I tottered unevenly into the kitchen in search of crackers or cheese, something we could eat that might soak up all the alcohol. When I came back holding a lone box of Triscuits, Harry was nowhere to be found.

"Harry?" I had called out.

"I'm in here," he yelled, and his voice sounded like it was coming from Barbara's bedroom.

I recall how I padded recklessly down the hallway, red wine sloshing over the side of my glass and landing in fat drops on the carpet.

"Harry?" I called. "Where are you?"

"I'm in here."

I found him in the bathroom. He was barely waist-deep in Barbara's enormous pink hot tub, pouring a bottle of fancy shampoo into the running water. He turned the jets on, which caused the bubbles to lather with a dangerous swiftness. He scooped up a handful of foam and blew it limply in my direction.

"Harry." I laughed.

"Get in," he said.

"Are you naked?"

"No, I am in a three-piece suit," he said. "Of course I am naked."

I looked around uncomfortably. This was not where I expected the night to take me.

"Clo, if you don't want me to see you naked, I'll cover my eyes," he said.

"I don't want you to see me naked," I said firmly.

Harry closed his eyes and covered them with his hands.

"No peeking," I said.

"Please," he replied. "I can see a naked girl if I want to, Clo. I am not *that* hard up."

I turned away as I slipped out of my clothes. Then, I tiptoed toward the tub and, after throwing my thick leg over the side without even a whiff of femininity, I slipped heavily into the churning water.

I quickly slumped down to my neck.

"Okay," I said, once I was comfortably covered with bubbles. "You may open your eyes."

Harry opened his eyes.

I recall how we sat facing each other, the white froth swiftly swelling to our chins, and, when it finally threatened to cascade over the side of the tub, Harry leaned over to turn the water off. As he settled back, however, his smooth body slipped against mine in a way that felt equal parts exhilarating and revolting, and I froze, curiously unsure if I wanted to feel that strange sensation again. In the new silence, I could just make out the music playing from the living room, and there was a gentle hiss of bubbles, all snapping and sizzling around my ears.

I leaned back and closed my eyes.

"I think we look very elegant in this bathtub," I said.

"Mmmm," Harry murmured. "Do you know what I think?"

I lifted my head and looked at him.

"No, what do you think?" I asked.

"I think this whole world looks good on us."

When I woke up the following morning, I checked the room that Harry had slept in, but he was gone.

"Well, a *quiet* weekend sounds lovely," Mark Angelbeck replies, bringing my attention back to the table. "My kids always have a million things going on, and now we have spring break in a few weeks."

I smile sympathetically. We both pick up our menus.

"And how are things on the editorial side?" he continues. He slides his reading glasses back on his face.

"Things are going very well," I say. "And on your end?"

"*Insane*," he says with a light laugh as he sets down the menu. Then, he ruffles his hair with both hands. "But the good kind of *insane*."

"That would be a good title for a memoir," I joke.

"Indeed," he says, raising an eyebrow in approval.

As Mark Angelbeck and I proceed through the paces of small talk (the weather, our order, the contents of the next issue), I find myself surprised that someone who sells people intangible things for a living is not more facile in conversation. He seems awkward, even a little nervous, but this unexpected lack of sure-footedness gives me the confidence to do the one thing I do well: shape-shift in response to whatever the person sitting in front needs the most in that moment. For Barbara, it is gobsmacked fawning and obedience. For Davis, admiration and enablement, which I garnish with the constant confirmation of her choices. For Harry, it's an endless game of playing the fool; I must pretend he's gotten the better of me, but without my knowledge. As for Mark Angelbeck, I quickly discern that all he wants is my encouragement to slide back into the past. With me, he would like to revisit a happier time, a time not so long ago, when he was young and on the cusp of something unknown, but surely extraordinary. Incidentally, I imagine this was also the time of his life when a "drinking lunch" with a member of the opposite sex held wonderfully predictable possibilities. So, I shift my body again, and I gaze at him with my lips parted in wonder; I want him to feel he's the oracle I have climbed so many mountains to find.

After he talks about himself for a good, long while, he leans back and looks at me with his head cocked to the side.

"So, how about you? What do you want to do next?"

"Next?" I ask.

"Well, I'm guessing you don't want to assist Isobel Fincher for the rest of your life?"

"Oh, I love Isobel," I say, which is true, but I straighten up. We have reached the most important moment in our conversation, and I need to play it perfectly. So, I lightly shrug my shoulders and put on a pondering expression. "I guess I haven't given it much thought."

"Surely there is another job at the magazine you might want?" he prods. "Or, maybe at another one of our magazines?"

"Of course," I say.

"And what job would that be?"

"Well," I say slowly. "I think I *might* make a good editor-in-chief."

To be clear, I have practiced this response countless times—making sure I deliver it with a dainty self-assuredness that communicates that while I am *talented*, I am also not a *threat*—and, yet, when I hear myself say these words out loud to another human being, I wince at how completely absurd it sounds.

"Editor-in-chief, eh?" he says, and I instantly blanch at his tone, which is both amused and reproachful. "You know what they say about 'Shooting the king,' don't you?"

"Oh, I don't mean *now!*" I exclaim, and too loudly. I feel my face redden. "Or for *our* magazine, just *any* magazine."

"Any magazine?"

"Yes, sure," I say quickly, desperate to backpedal. "Like *Dog Monthly* would be fine."

"*Dog Monthly*," he repeats, and while he clearly doesn't get this feeble attempt at a joke, he is kind enough to chuckle. I look away, hoping to find a respite from my climbing humiliation only to be confronted with an even greater horror. The pretty hostess is leading our editor-in-chief through the crowded dining room with two companions. I watch as she settles into the corner banquette and places her clutch bag on the tabletop before her eyes take a long sweep of the crowded dining room.

They land on me like a dark cloud.

She does not look happy.

"Oh god," I gasp reflexively. I whip my head back around and stare down at my lap. "Oh god."

"What?" Mr. Angelbeck asks.

"Nothing," I whisper.

He conducts a slow and obvious scan of the entire restaurant.

"Stop it," I hiss with my head still down. I feel my composure scattering like little birds. "It's nothing."

"Your boss?" he asks, but it's clear that my discomfort is a source of amusement.

I pause. I think about an appropriate response.

"Yes," I say miserably.

"What about it?"

"I don't know," I say. I meekly lift my head a few inches so I can look at him. "I mean, she's probably wondering what I am doing having lunch with *you*."

"Why?"

"Uh, I'm a *nobody*," I say. "You're the publisher?"

"You're not a nobody," he says. "You're, what? An associate editor?"

I roll my eyes.

"Don't worry," he assures me. He cuts another bite of his salad.

"How can I not worry?" I ask. "You didn't see her face. I bet they are packing up my desk as we speak."

He looks at me without blinking. The way he chews suddenly feels very naughty.

"So you want to be an editor-in-chief, huh?" he asks.

Before I can answer, he gives my knee a little squeeze under the table. It happens so quickly that I don't have time to be surprised, but I do register that his fingers feel both warm and rough as they linger on my bare skin.

I try to recall the last time I shaved my legs.

"Well, then, my dear," he says, and his eyes twinkle with a kind of menacing glee. "If that is what you *really* want, *she's* not the person you need to make happy."

Within seconds of returning to my desk after lunch, the phone rings. It's L.K. Smith's assistant calling me to come to her office. As I walk down the long hallway, the other assistants, including Liddy, glance up from their computers, their pale faces arranged in an uneasy curiosity. This isn't a surprise: Everyone pays attention when someone is summoned to see L.K. Smith, but today I feel more paranoid than usual, like there is a plot unspooling to which I am wholly unaware.

When I enter L.K.'s office, she is bent over the final proof of our cover story, which is due to ship to the printer today. I know because I checked the fashion credits for Kate earlier this morning. Without lifting her head, she indicates with her free hand that I should take a seat on the white couch. She keeps reading for what feels like an eternity, making small marks with a red, tacky pencil, and I sit with my head down. I pick the dead skin around the cuticle on my thumb until it starts to bleed.

I press my hand into my skirt.

I have a bad feeling.

Finally, L.K. puts down the pencil and removes her black reading glasses. She fixes me directly with those gorgeous, glacial blue eyes.

"You had lunch with Mark Angelbeck today," she states.

Fuck.

"Yes, I did, but . . ."

L.K. holds up her hand to silence me.

"I know you had lunch with him," she continues. "Because I asked you to have lunch with him."

I sit completely frozen. Of course, L.K. Smith did not ask me to have lunch with Mark Angelbeck, but in her unending tactical brilliance, she has already created a cover story for me to placate our editor-in-chief.

"Correct?" she prods, her eyebrows lifted.

"Yes?" I reply meekly. My left armpit starts to heat up.

"May I advise you in the future to let my office know when you plan to have lunch with the publisher of this magazine?" she says. "As a courtesy?"

"Of course," I stammer. "I'm sorry."

"I really should not have to babysit you at this stage, Clodagh."

Here, L.K. puts her glasses back on and returns to the proof, which is my signal to leave. Apparently, there are more pressing things to which she must attend than my grotesque stepping out of line. I am to understand that, while I will not be fired for my indiscretion, I have been—quite officially—put on warning. Now, L.K.'s reasons for protecting me on this occasion are obvious: The magazine is a battlefield, and I am a well-trained foot soldier in the highly specialized army that she has invested considerable time and energy to assemble. She trusts I would take a bullet for her (which I absolutely would) and she also understands that protecting her own troops is how she retains her power. She has a twenty-year track record of success, and she isn't stupid enough to waste a good soldier by throwing me into some other, less beneficial, line of fire.

Not yet anyway.

You see, once you are on the team, every single person at this magazine will die for you.

That is, until your actual value or perceived power no longer serves them.

At that point, they will rid themselves of you, quickly and without hesitation.

They will not mourn you.

But it's easy enough, I figure.

I just must make certain they do, indeed, die for me first.

51

For the next few months, I take the stairs instead of the elevator to avoid running into Mark Angelbeck. I hold my heels in my hand as I hoof it up the nine floors to my office each morning and back down nine floors each night, but it feels like a small price to pay to stay in L.K. Smith's good graces.

As Kate is often traveling for work, and she never bothered with hiring a new assistant, I am often asked to cover her slate of appointments, which, from a time-management perspective, works just fine with my schedule. I spend my days with Isobel, and my late afternoons being shuttled across town to various showrooms and studios to preview any new clothes and accessories that might be appropriate for the magazine. The actual mechanics of the job are straightforward. I take digital photographs of the presented product, and, when I return to the office, I print out color pictures, which I then cut out and paste to white boards for Kate to review. When a particular item is chosen from the boards for publication—let's say, a pair of shoes to be worn by a celebrity or a beaded clutch for our annual gift guide—there is a fashion credit, which tells the reader where to purchase the item and at what cost, although more often than not the item is so expensive that we simply state you can only learn the price "upon request." This might not seem like a big deal, but to the designers and larger labels, it is the holy grail, a measure of success that everyone in our industry seems to understand. By this point in my career, I know most of the PR girls at the various houses—we attend the same parties and send snarky emails back and forth—and so, while these appointments are "working" meetings, they are also fairly social. There is a lot of air-kissing and gossiping and the occasional glass of champagne. Generally speaking, the items I am shown—shoes, earrings, coats—are under embargo, which means they cannot be released to the public until an agreed-upon date, which usually coincides with the publication of our issue.

So, one early summer afternoon (after I take the stairs to the lobby), I go on four appointments. When I am done, I tuck Kate's digital camera safely in my bag, and kindly ask my driver to take me downtown so I can catch the tail end of a dinner a few of the other mid-level editors organized earlier in the week at DaSilvano in the West Village. When I arrive, there are groups of people sitting on the sidewalk benches, all waiting for a table, and two paparazzi photographers smoke on a nearby curb. I am whisked to my table on the patio, and after I kiss a series of cheeks, I order a glass of rosé. I look around: The night air is wonderfully warm, and the crowd tonight is buzzing and festive. Smiling, I turn back to the table only to discover everyone is staring at me expectantly.

"What?" I ask. I pull Margot's drink toward me to take a small sip.

"So, we have been talking about Liddy . . ." Trent from the art department begins, his eyes flashing across the table.

I look up, my lips still attached to the rim of Margot's glass, and my heart sinks. *Oh god*, I think miserably. *Don't tell me Liddy got a promotion.*

"I mean," Margot says with a light roll of her eyes, "are you shocked?"

"I *am* shocked," Hadley, one of the beauty editors, chimes in. "I mean, it was all so . . . unceremonious."

"What were they going to do?" Trent asks. "Throw her a party? It's always unceremonious."

"Wait, what are you talking about?" I ask, confused.

"Liddy," Margot says, and she slices her hand across her neck. "*Gonesville.*"

"What?" I stammer.

"Liddy was fired," Trent says, and almost too gleefully.

"What?" I repeat.

They nod in unison.

"This afternoon," Margot says, but she has lowered her voice to a whisper. "While you were out."

I sit back and press my hands gently against my cheeks, which suddenly feel very warm. The waiter puts down my drink and I take a grateful sip.

"What happened?" I ask.

"Do you want the *official* story or the *real* story?" Trent asks.

"Both?" I manage, but weakly. I know this is not going to be good news.

"The *official* story is that she lost a dress for a cover shoot," he says. "It was one of a kind, and there wasn't enough time to make another one."

"Not great," I say, and I look around the table for confirmation. "But are you saying that's not the real story?"

Trent glances over at Margot and Hadley, like a little boy confirming he can eat a second dessert, and Margot shrugs with studied disinterest.

"She's not really a Saintclair-Abbott," he hisses, and then he makes a motion with his hands like a bomb is exploding.

"What?" I exclaim, but it comes out like a little dog's bark. I slap my hand over my mouth, and my eyes dart around the crowded space, searching for eavesdroppers.

"Apparently, Liddy spent a summer in Dallas during college working at the same country club where the Saintclair-Abbotts were members," Margot begins.

"One summer!" Trent laughs, and Margot shoots him an exasperated glance.

"And during that *one* summer," she continues, "she dated one of the sons?"

"And?"

"He dumped her, I guess?" Margot ventures. "I don't know, but a year later, she turned up in New York with a brand-new name."

"More like a brand-new life," Trent says.

"I don't understand," I say.

"Bottom line: She's *not* from Dallas," Hadley says. "And she is not a Saintclair-Abbott. She's from Maryland."

"Like gross Maryland," Trent adds.

"But clearly, she took very good notes," Margot says. "I give her credit. She had everyone fooled."

"But her apartment?" I sputter. "It's been photographed."

"Have you even been invited to her apartment?" Hadley asks.

"I mean, no, but..."

In this moment, I am overcome with the strangest urge to count my fingers and toes, if only to confirm that, in the aftermath of this revelation, I am still intact. Honestly, it never occurred to me to doubt Lydia Saintclair-Abbott's story of origin, but how often do we ever question someone's story? To me, she was New York Perfect: A case study in the unassailable power of personal diligence, privilege, and academic credentials. I hated her so much for hating me, but I hated myself even more for caring what she thought about me in the first place. And now what? Now she is just gone, and I have no recourse? No moment to gloat? As I sit there in stunned silence, an unsettling thought that would have been ridiculous to entertain even a moment before flutters through my brain: What if Liddy didn't so much dislike me as fear me? After all, wasn't I a fellow grifter of sorts? I mean, if anyone was going to see through her little act, shouldn't it have been me? And, yet I suspected nothing. Suddenly, I think back to how often she came to the office early to use the printer, or how she made enormous lunches in our cafeteria, only to barely nibble at her plate before boxing it up. I had always assumed it was her cover story for not eating. In fact, I used to joke she probably threw the box out the moment we weren't looking because, I mean, how else could she so reliably fit into so many sample-sized dresses. What about the countless times I saw her in the fashion closet, late at night, parsing through the racks of dresses that were slated to be returned, gently plucking a few out for personal use.

I see all these things differently now.

"Wow," I manage.

Everyone nods in a way that is both shocked and callous, like children of war, and I pull the sleeves of my dress down over my wrists. I am too big for the space I inhabit suddenly, too exposed. I finish my drink quickly.

"It was all the galas that did me in," Trent continues. "It was like she never grew out of the benefit committee stage and, you know, got a life."

"Who figured this out?" I ask.

"One guess," Margot says as she signals for the bill.

"L.K.?" I ask.

Trent nods gravely.

"She has eyes everywhere, that one," Hadley says as she stands up. I watch her slip a new Balenciaga bag over her bare shoulder. "She made a comment about my late arrival time last Friday. She was like: *Oh, how was your doctor's appointment?* And then she just stood there. She was waiting for me to, basically, lie to her face."

"She told me that yellow V-neck sweater I wore last week was *interesting*," Trent offers.

"Now, that was just her being *kind*," Hadley says.

Margot snorts with laughter, then signs the check, which she will expense in her next report, as she is the most senior of our group. As I half listen to them debate which bar or party we should go to next, I worry that I am too rattled to be good company, although I don't say anything because a part of me is always worried that if I bow out early, I will miss something important. We leave the restaurant and link arms as we clamor toward an open cab on Sixth Avenue. Since there are four of us, I offer to take the front seat, but I instantly regret my decision. The cab has a plastic divider, and while I can hear everyone laughing in the back seat, I have no idea what is being said, and to turn around would seem a little desperate. So, I lean forward and turn up the radio with a quick flick of my wrist, and I start to sing. I sing louder and louder and louder, if only to drown everything else out.

When I wobble into the apartment a couple hours later, I realize I neglected to call and say I wouldn't be home for dinner, which is one of those things that can set Barbara off under the right circumstances. I gently place my keys on the front table and strain my ears, but when I hear nothing, I glance at the grandfather clock: It's eleven o'clock. Davis is generally home at this hour—frankly, Davis is generally home at all hours—so I kick off my shoes and check her bedroom. I want to tell her what I heard about Lydia, but her room is empty. I check her bathroom and the living room, but I only find Captain, who is tucked into the corner of the couch, snoring softly. When I see Barbara's bedroom door is closed, I go into the kitchen to drink a glass of water and parse through the envelopes and catalogs that have been piling up on the kitchen island. There is an open bottle of white wine on the table, so after I locate the cork, I place it back in the fridge. Then, I sweep the twisted foil into my palm, and deposit it in the wastebasket. I wash the two finger-smudged wine glasses with soap, and place them upside down on a cloth to dry. I take a final survey of the rest of the kitchen, namely because I want to be reestablished as a thoughtful roommate. I wipe a damp paper towel along the countertop, neatly pile up the magazines and newspapers and collect a few tea-stained teacups and saucers. I empty the ashtray. As I bag up the trash, the house phone rings, but when I look up to answer it, the cordless receiver is missing from the charging cradle. I lift the banquette cushions and peek under an errant flap of newspaper, but after a few rings the automated voicemail message triggers. It is followed by an exceedingly long beep:

"Hey, Barbara, it's Tony," the caller announces with a little cough. "Sorry to call so late, but I just wanted to give you a heads-up that I am sending some tax documents from the trust early tomorrow by messenger. So, hopefully you're home or the housekeeper can sign for them. I need you to review them and, if everything looks in order, initial them where I put little tabs. I think they are yellow tabs, but it doesn't matter. They are the only tabs. Anyway, I can send a messenger to pick them up but just call my office to let me know."

Tony coughs again:

"And, um, listen. I transferred money to the *other* personal checking account because your one Amex bill has been high for a while, which is not a *huge* deal, but the bank has been hitting you for the overdraft fees, which I just noticed. *It's all fine now*, so don't worry, but let me know if you want to discuss in our next meeting. Again, there is no action necessary, but I wanted to make sure you were aware. Okay. I hope all is well. Call me with any questions."

There is another short beep and then the machine produces a click that sounds, almost improbably, like it just swallowed the message for safekeeping. I stand motionless in the dim kitchen and watch the red light blink for what feels like a lifetime.

Let me know if you want to discuss in our next meeting.

She wasn't really a Saintclair-Abbott.

My body takes over without consulting my brain.

I walk to the machine.

I press the delete button.

The light stops blinking.

With a ferocity that alarms even me, I clutch the countertop, and my brain jumps into protective action. I swiftly churn up strategies, explanations, and scapegoats. I scratch out various, yet plausible escape routes in a rapid succession. Since childhood, it has been my experience that there is a way out of everything, so long as the lies you tell have the tiniest attachment to the truth. What my brain does *not* consider—nor has it ever considered—is that the salvation for my sins might be found within the bounds of a confession. Why? Because if I confess, I will be fully exposed. With a lie, there is the chance, however slight, that I will get away with my crimes and misdeeds.

Suddenly, I hear a noise behind me. I startle like a nervous bird.

It's Davis.

"Hey," she says easily, but her expression is hard to read. I can't tell how long she has been standing in the doorway.

"What are you doing here?" I say, but my tone is too severe.

"What am I doing here?" Davis asks, and her sleepy eyes widen. "Uh, I live here?"

"No, I know"—I force a laugh as I catch myself—"I just didn't hear you come in the front door, that's all."

I need to look untroubled, so I gently cross my arms across my chest and lean against the countertop. I kick one foot across the other. I smile.

"I didn't come in the front door," she says. "I was in the hall bathroom."

The hall bathroom is right next to the kitchen. From the hall bathroom, you can hear everything. You can hear toast pop out of the toaster.

"Why?" I ask.

"Why was I in the hall bathroom?" she asks. She tilts her head sideways in confusion. "It's the only good light for tweezing your eyebrows around here."

She holds up a set of black tweezers.

"Ah, good tip," I say.

Suddenly, I hear a small thud in the foyer, and while my own head turns reflexively in the direction of the noise, Davis doesn't seem to register it.

"So how do I look?" she asks instead.

She waves the fingers of her left hand in front of her eyes like a game show hostess.

"Utter perfection," I manage.

She beams at my assessment, and by the way she smiles, I can tell that she is high or drunk and, if she is high or drunk, I reason, she probably didn't hear the voicemail. I feel the block of ice on my chest slowly start to melt.

"So where's your mom?" I ask.

"I haven't seen her since this morning," Davis says. "And I cannot begin to tell you how nice it is to have the apartment to yourself."

"I can imagine," I say.

"So, where have you been?"

"I was working late . . ." I trail off.

"Oh, honey," she says, and she makes a little sad face. "I feel like you are working all the time."

Later, as I am washing my face before bed something flickers and grabs for a soft corner of my attention, some critical detail I overlooked in the heat of the moment. I close my eyes and try to reassemble the scene in the kitchen. For one, there were *two* wineglasses on the island, which I had initially assumed were left behind by Davis and Barbara before I learned that Barbara hadn't been home since the morning. Furthermore, when I put the wine bottle back in the fridge, I now recall it was clammy with condensation, as if it had been recently opened *and* recently abandoned. What about the strange noise I heard? Which, now that I think about it, sounded like the front door closing. I look up into the oval mirror. My face is covered in foam. I close my eyes and let hot water run over my hands as I try to access something I saw, but didn't register, and then it hits me:

Someone else was in the apartment when I arrived.

52

I know I need an escape plan, but many months pass before I am alone in the apartment. Barbara has gone to a breakfast, but according to Davis, she's really gone to yet another audition. Not that Barbara would admit it was an audition, Davis explains, because *Barbara Lawrence is a major star* who doesn't need to *audition* for *anything*, and, as such, Barbara Lawrence is simply attending a lunch meeting.

After Barbara departs in a cloud of cigarette smoke and Jardin d'Amalfi, Davis takes Captain on a long walk in Central Park.

After I hear the door close, I get out of bed. I trod into the kitchen, and I pour a mug of coffee. I walk over to the windows that overlook the park and press my forehead against one of the screens to see if I can see Davis and Captain. The leaves on the trees have just started to change, and as I watch people scurry along the sidewalk below, I stick out my tongue and gently tap the black mesh. It tastes searing and salty. I lick it again.

The grandfather clock in the main foyer chimes ominously.

It's time to get to work.

I decide I am in a good position, but only if I act fast. The money I have saved on rent has started to add up, and before I spend it, I need to find a way to (A.) figure out from which account Barbara's American Express credit card is automatically paid, and (B.) get the account number and passwords, so I can make a cash deposit and pray that when a considerable hunk of money lands from an unknown source, that no one is the wiser amid a sea of innumerable accounts and an untold millions of dollars. My general plan is to pose as her assistant and go to the bank under the guise of an errand. After all, who would suspect anything was amiss about a deposit? At some level, I recognize this to be an absurd plan, an astounding exercise in suspending disbelief, and yet, what other choice do I have? It's not like I can march into the kitchen one day and say *Oh, here is a partial reimbursement for the money you didn't even notice I have been slowly stealing from you.* Furthermore, the truth is that I have not squirreled away *that* much money, barely a dent against what I have borrowed, but I staunchly refuse to accept there isn't a way out of my situation. A few weeks ago, I calculated that it would take me about another five years (maybe more) to pay the debt off entirely at my current salary if I incurred exactly no further expenses. Of course, this is to say nothing about the emotional toll that keeping secrets of this magnitude can wreck on a person. I feel squeezed from all sides, and yet I am employed twelve hours day in an environment in which perfect composure is a core requirement. Every time my cell phone rings with an unknown number, I freeze, and when I let myself into the apartment each night, I worry I am walking into a much-deserved inquisition after which I will find myself tossed, quite rightly, out to the street.

On this morning, I begin my search for Barbara's bank information in her bedroom. Marta, once a constant tidying presence, doesn't arrive until the afternoon these days so the bed is still unmade. It's an unfamiliar sight, but I have noticed that a lot has started to slide around the apartment in recent months. Dirty dishes in the sink, dog hair balled up on the couches, and—perhaps the greatest horror for any girl with an Irish Catholic upbringing—the baseboards have accumulated a visible layer of dust and grime. I am tempted to fill a bucket with warm water and Murphy' oil soap and get to work with an old washcloth, hopeful that action—any action—might alleviate my growing fear that money is not as plentiful as I need it to be. Today, however, the toss of sheets in Barbara's room makes me feel at liberty to lay down on her mattress and pull the comforter over my shoulders. I close my eyes and sniff the flat pillow under my cheek. It smells stale, like an old person. I roll over to Davis's side of the bed, which smells like laundry detergent. It makes sense: Davis doesn't sleep with her mother very often, at least not since I moved into the apartment.

More often, she sleeps with me.

As I don't have time to waste, I sit up and slide open the drawer of Barbara's nightstand. I parse through the untidy jumble of items but turn up nothing except some Episcopalian mass cards for dead people, boxes of matches from Sant Ambroeus, gold Uniball pens, and various glass jars of expensive creams. Next, I pick through the drawers of her armoire and low dresser. This task takes far longer than I anticipated, mainly due to the fact I must leave each piece of clothing as meticulously folded (and often tissue-papered) as I find it. While my fingers are clumsy, my body is tuned like an electric fence, ready to react to even the slightest of provocations. Every few minutes, I think I hear footsteps or the grind of a key in the lock, and I sprint back to the couch, heart pounding, until I can confirm the coast is clear.

After I complete a full search of Barbara's bedroom, I head toward her home office, which remains a rarely used part of the apartment. I tiptoe across the thin, oriental rug toward Barbara's writing desk, which is a delicately constructed wood antique with heavy brass handles. The drawers are almost impossibly sticky; they squeak miserably as I struggle to nudge them open. I rifle through a smattering of papers and documents, but I don't come across anything from her bank, not even a lone box of checkbooks. This is when despair, which is a feeling I've been reasonably adept at staving off thus far, starts to rise in my body. I can't fathom how such profoundly analog information could be so incredibly difficult to find especially since a third grader could steal my identity in ten minutes. Barbara's large desktop computer hums softly to my right, and I lean over to tap the keyboard quickly with my index finger. To my relief, the screen lights up and there is no prompt for a password. I click quickly through the three folders that sit on her desktop, and review her browsing history, but I find nothing of use. There isn't even anything of *interest*, which I find downright stunning. My own search history is—at any given point—a cornucopia of neurosis. My searches in the past week included, but were not limited to, the following: symptoms of ovarian cancer (I had a backache), an "Am I an Alcoholic?" quiz (I chose to answer by "drinks" instead of "alcohol units" and, thus—trumpets, please!—I am *not* an alcoholic), vintage fur coats (shockingly expensive!), the schedule at Alliance Française (before all the financial meltdowns started this year, my company would reimburse French lessons), Match.com (horrifying to even contemplate), plane tickets to Paris, and "Can you get HPV if the guy wears a condom?" The answer to that last one is yes, which, frankly, strikes me—like all things related to sexually transmitted diseases—as incredibly sexist.

Defeated, I sit down in the overstuffed leather chair in the corner, and I look up at the bookshelf. The horse is still exactly where I placed her, and while I consider taking her down, if only for a moment, I don't dare. I am not sure what, exactly, is still holding my world together, but I know not to take any chances.

I have taken far too many already.

53

On a personal note, I have *sort of* been seeing a new guy, and while I pretend it's going well, I generally feel horribly ill at ease in his company. I blame myself for this discomfort because clearly if I just *do the right thing* or *say the right thing*, the sensation of inadequacy will subside. I do not—for one second—allow myself to consider that maybe we are simply a bad match or even worse, that he is not particularly invested in the trajectory I am secretly planning for our relationship, which may or may not include a daughter named Charlotte. I don't have time for missteps. Apparently, I must go along to get along because I didn't settle on another man already, and, at the not-so-ripe old age of thirty-one, the Lord is punishing me for my hubris.

However, God forbid I talk about marriage or children with any of the men who have made cameo appearances in my romantic life. Instead, I must pretend that I *don't* want them because to display headstrong indifference to love is the tactic by which the girl in all the movies gets to live happily ever after. Furthermore, such admissions could earn me the back-alley designation of "psycho" or "desperate" and, thus, I must remain cheerfully silent on the issue which, infuriatingly, seems to leave the whole ridiculous proposition of my future up to the men. In a way, it's like everything else in my life. I can't ever seem to shake the terrible sense that I am just hoping to be picked out of a crowd and that, even if I am eventually recognized for something, I must act surprised and bashful. I must pretend my success—even if it was hard-earned and well-deserved—was gifted to me out of pity or as a prize for consistent good behavior.

I can't own anything. I never get to make the call.

Some nights, however, I lie in bed and run through a terrifying waterfall of calculations regarding my love life. Like, if I meet my future husband *tomorrow*, we will likely date for one year (minimum) before we get engaged and then it will be *another* year until we get married. That means I will be thirty when I start the process of trying to get pregnant, which is sailing a little close to the wind, especially if I have any fertility problems. And that is if I meet him *tomorrow*.

But I am getting ahead of myself.

The new guy: We are "early stage," which means it's only been about four weeks so we are still wrapped in that gauzy and forgiving cocoon of a fledgling New York courtship. We meander through Prospect Park and share a cup of coffee. We go to the Metropolitan Museum of Art and sit in thoughtful silence in front of the big Jackson Pollock. We plan a trip to Storm King (I know, gag), but we miss the train and spend our day drinking Bloody Marys instead. We go to the movies once (he chooses) and dinner twice, but mostly we talk about books and music over beers in the handful of dive bars that are equidistant from our apartments. Interestingly, the venues he chooses always seem to contain at least one of his ex-girlfriends, all of whom are named sexy things like Delphine and Esme. I have not met most of his friends (except for one night, very briefly, when we went to a bar in Williamsburg so he could play a video game called *Buck Hunter*, about which I pretended to look delighted) and I have no idea if he is seeing other women, but I wouldn't dare to inquire, even though the notion gives me a stomachache. He's an editor at a political website, which makes him smart, and either super rich or super poor (journalism, I am swiftly learning, is not a profession intended for the middle class), although I suspect, by the positively disgusting apartment he shares with four other guys off Driggs Avenue in Williamsburg, he falls, quite soundly, in the latter category. The fact that I have seen his apartment, of course, also means that we have had sex. It was fine, but also a little awkward, and now I feel like he expects to have sex every time we see one another which, to be honest, I really wish wasn't the case. I worry some essential connective tissue is missing, that soft, wonderful thing that binds two people together. But no matter, I know my role: I'll limp along and try to ignore the grind in the hope my pain and forbearance will—one day—pay off.

So, this morning, which is a Thursday, the new guy walks me to the corner coffee shop in his neighborhood before I head home to get ready for work. As I have not been invited to leave personal items (toothbrush, change of clothes) at his apartment, I must take the G train across Brooklyn, but this does not bother me quite yet. In fact, this morning I am positively giddy as we stroll together past the row houses and chain-link fences that run along Bedford Avenue. It's nearing summer, but the morning air is still cool, and when the new guy deposits me at the café with a kiss, my cheeks bake with happiness. I watch him meander back in the direction of his apartment, and when he is finally out of sight, I slip into the shop and take a spot at the end of the short line.

A deep voice drawls:

"Hey, lady."

I look up from my reverie, and I can't believe it: It's Oliver Barringer. He looks good. He wears a machine-battered gray T-shirt, jeans, and sneakers. He clutches a large coffee in one hand and his mangled black headphones in another. I notice that a softly bloated, younger blonde girl with dark roots and unfortunate bangs hovers uncertainly in the background. She is clearly *with* Oliver, but she has not been invited to join our small circle, nor introduced, and so she stands there in last night's makeup looking indifferent, even though I know (mostly from personal experience) she throbs with shame.

I bet she's a writer, I think with salted amusement. *Or has a blog.*

Oliver's hair is shorter than the last time we spoke which, at this point, was when I slunk out of his apartment a literal lifetime ago. At some point, he left his full-time role at our company and is now a prolific and very well-compensated freelance writer who regularly appears on various morning news programs. He looks me over this morning as if I had been trotted out solely for his entertainment.

"Oliver," I say as calmly as I can muster. "How are you?"

"I'm okay," he says before adding quickly, "How is Davis?"

I am great, I think. *Thanks for asking!*

"She's fine," I say.

"I'm glad to hear it," he says, and now we both just nod at each other.

"So," he starts. "Do you live around here now?"

"No," I reply before adding: "My boyfriend does."

"Ah," he says, his eyes tinged with skepticism. It's almost as if he can't believe that, once he passed me over like a dented avocado, there would ever be any further interest.

The line moves, and I take a grateful step forward. To my surprise, Oliver follows. He moves his body closer to mine, even though the café isn't crowded, and I inch myself backward, irritated that I still find him attractive.

"Hey, I am heading up to your office this week," he continues.

"You are?"

"Yeah, I have a meeting with L.K. Smith," he replies. "I am doing the piece on the governor?"

"Right," I say, although this is news to me.

"It's my first piece for you," he says. "I just got put on contract. For the book, but they also want me to start contributing to the website."

"Congratulations," I say, but this is terrible news. The prospect of running into Oliver Barringer in my office on a regular basis makes my body slowly start to deflate; I can already see him sitting on the edge of some shiny new assistant's desk, teasing her about something.

"Maybe we can grab a coffee?" he asks.

"Next?" the barista calls out.

I glance quickly in her direction and give her an apologetic half smile.

"If I am around..." I trail off, but I don't dare look at him. I am fearful my body will wither.

"Jeez, say you will at least consider it," he says with a little self-deprecating chuckle. "Please?"

I finally turn toward him. The way he fashions this request has a great gentlemanlike quality to it, almost as if I am a woman worth courting. I momentarily envision him in jodhpurs and a top hat. Then, I remember that we had sex and I never heard from him again.

He does not think I am a woman worth courting.

"Sure," I say, and he smiles.

It's because I said I had a boyfriend, I think. Guys like Oliver Barringer are always looking for novel ways to test their skills on girls like me, if only to sharpen them for their real targets.

"Next," the barista calls, although with a little less hospitality this time, and I move toward the counter. Oliver, seemingly satisfied, gives me a little wave, and starts to walk toward the exit. The girl follows him. When they get outside, Oliver looks right. Oliver looks left. Then, just like that: He is blown away like a dry piece of tumbleweed, snatched up in the whirl of the wild city streets.

54

I don't go to benefits very often at this point in my career—that's a younger girl's game—but when I *do* go, I generally only stay long enough to be photographed for the wire services. However, there are a few exceptions, the most obvious one being the annual gala thrown by our magazine inside the Boathouse in Central Park. After years of lingering around awkwardly like the last kid chosen for kickball, a miracle occurred: I was finally put on the list of girls who were approved to work the event. After I survived training camp (a meeting the weekend before the gala in which we were warned by a senior staff member not to chew gum, paint our own nails, arrive late, talk loudly, faint, have to use the bathroom, or socialize with the guests), I was dressed by the fashion girls and, the morning of the party, a team of professionals came to my desk to do my hair and makeup.

At the appointed hour, we were all shuttled to the park in a fleet of town cars and given our marching orders. While I was a few years older than most of the other girls, I didn't let this bother me. After all, this may be the only time I find myself here, I figured, so I might as well try to enjoy it.

My main job was to move guests from one location to another by gently placing my hand on their lower back and whispering things like: "Cocktails are on the other side of the veranda" or "May we invite you to move to dinner?"

At one point, moments before the guests were to move to dinner, I was dispatched with great urgency to remedy a place card that contained an unfortunate misspelling. I raced toward a curtain near the front doors, behind which a calligrapher sat with pens across a tabletop. She is present at every event we host just in case we catch any misspellings, or a card needs to be swapped out for a missing guest, or a quarrel or love affair about which we are unaware requires a quick shuffle of seats.

She quickly makes up a new card, and after I deliver it, I am strolling, quite proudly, across the room when I run into Mark Angelbeck.

"Clo," he says kindly as he places a kiss of both my cheeks. "Where have you been hiding?"

"Mr. Angelbeck," I reply meekly.

"You look lovely," he says.

"Thank you," I say, and as I feel him place his hand on my lower back, my eyes sweep the room for L.K. Smith.

"Well, I am looking for someone so . . ." I start.

"I have been thinking about our lunch," he says.

Our lunch was months ago.

"Really?" I ask. "How so?"

He says nothing. He just chews an ice cube.

"Want to ditch this place?" he asks.

The last thing I want to do is ditch this place, of course, and especially not with Mark Angelbeck, but I worry there is no choice but to agree because, well, he's legitimately my boss. "I'm working," I say. "I'll get fired."

"I can assure you that you won't get fired."

I glance around again before, entirely unsure of what to do, I tell him that I am going to go outside and get in my car service, and he should wait ten minutes before he comes out to join me. Of course, less than two minutes later, he slides into the back seat with a pilfered tumbler of whiskey and lopsided smile.

"I am terrible at waiting," he says, and then he instructs the driver to take us to a new, yet already impossible to get inside restaurant tucked into a corner of the West Village. I don't like this choice of venue; it's too popular with the publishing crowd. I am worried about being seen, but I don't say anything, namely because there always remains a part of me that wants to be seen, no matter how dangerous or stupid.

Or both.

"I am surprised you don't stay for the whole event," I say casually as our car pulls onto Central Park West. I glance out the back window—just to get a last glimpse at the Boathouse—before I resettle forward. I place my hands on my lap.

I feel terrible for leaving.

"That was the whole event," he says. He sounds a little bored.

"Oh," I reply. "Isn't it only, like, ten o'clock?"

I look down on my wrist for an imaginary watch.

"Don't tell me you haven't been to the gala before?" he asks.

"Okay," I say with a sly smile. "Then, I will not tell you that."

"Ah, a newbie." He settles back on the seat with an understanding smile. "So, after dessert, everyone leaves for the after-parties. And what after-party you attend is far more important than the seating chart."

"Blasphemy," I cry. "People died over that seating chart."

"I come only with the truth," he says, and as the car bounces over a pothole, the thin shards of ice tinkle in his glass.

"So, am I to understand that skipping the after-parties is the real power move?"

"Clearly, my work here is done." He laughs, but as he takes a pinch of his drink, I sink a little inside. I had been invited to two different parties, which felt like a big deal. I know all the juiciest stories thrown around tomorrow (not to mention the best photographs) will be the by-product of the competing late-night events, and now I will be forced to trudge into the office with nothing but empty pockets. I wonder if, after this little lark with Mr. Angelbeck, there will be enough time for me to get back uptown. I have no idea how late these parties go.

When we pull up to the restaurant, I ask the driver for a voucher, and Mark chuckles:

"You still have *vouchers?*" he asks, and he leans forward to inspect one, like he's come across an old photograph. "Wow. In my day, we all just kept a brick of those in our apartments. I would give them out to anyone who needed a ride."

"And I thought we had it good. What do you use now?"

"At my level, my dear," he says, "you don't need vouchers. I have my own driver."

"Well, where is this driver of yours?"

"I left him at the gala." He laughs as he slaps his forehead in mock horror. "Poor guy! Should I call him?"

He gets out of the car and walks around to open my door, which would feel delightful if I didn't, in some way, feel like a hostage. We walk down a short flight of stone steps, and when we pass through the door, the hostess's face lights up in a thouroughly performative recognition. As we are led through the snug, dimly lit dining room, Mark says hello to a few people seated nearby, and they smile at me like I am important. There is a proper celebrity eating pasta at the table next to us in a tuxedo, and I realize that he, too, must have been at the gala.

Sometimes, I cannot believe New York is so exciting.

"You sure have a lot of friends," I observe once Mark settles back down.

"A lot of them are from the glory days," he says. "When I was an editor, like you."

"The glory days, eh?" I laugh before adding: "I didn't know you were on the editorial side."

"It was ages ago, before I got married, when money didn't matter," he says as he takes a nip of his contraband whiskey. "You know, when I was an assistant, they still had the drink trolleys?"

He pantomimes pushing a cart.

"Stop it," I cry out, incredulous. "You are not *that* old!"

Here, he rattles his nearly empty tumbler, and grins at me. His eyelids sag under the weight of his drunkenness.

"Okay, I am not *that* old," he concedes. "But I'm close. And look at you! So young that you missed the real heyday."

"Wait, I thought *this* was the heyday?" I exclaim, but I also allow myself to luxuriate, ever so briefly, in being called young because I am patently unsure where I fall in the spectrum of desirability at the age of thirty.

"Oh, no," he says with mock sobriety. "Everyone is so serious these days, it's become impossible to have any fun. Now, the nineties? The nineties were fun. In the nineties you could do anything."

"This is fun?" I venture, and I put on a little sad face. "Right?"

"True," he says. "This *is* fun. But, alas, you'll never fly on the Concorde."

"You flew on the Concorde?"

"Honey, we *only* flew on the Concorde," he says.

"Well, I guess I'll have to rely on your stories to delight me," I say admiringly.

He lifts his arm over his head and shakes his glass, which triggers a young waiter to trot in our direction. I feel ashamed by this obnoxious gesture, but Mr. Angelbeck takes no notice. He just orders another drink and then he points to me:

"And for the lady?" he asks.

I order a vodka martini.

"A martini, eh?" he says. "I always knew you were one of us."

I smile, but there is something about the way he says "one of us" that makes me feel queasy, like he is warming me up for some big ask, but he doesn't elaborate. Frankly, I have been in such an anxious state over my money worries and Lydia's termination, that this would be the perfect time for Mark Angelbeck to ask me for a favor. I would gladly give him anything he wanted if he could provide me with some sort of salvation in return. But he just sits there, sipping his drink and making small talk. He has started to look a little sweaty and his face swells scarlet. I keep waiting for him to loosen his black bow tie, but he doesn't. I also wonder when, if ever, I will start feeling like a grown-up. While there is no doubt my coquettish gratitude is effective with Mark Angelbeck, it has stopped feeling like a thrill to me. I have recently begun to suspect I am not getting away with anything, which is how I long measured my success. I am simply getting what I deserve. Or, at the very least, what I have been led to believe I deserve after so many years of service and subordination. I keep reading that I should be negotiating my salary and "advocating for myself" in the workplace, but I still feel like a little girl who is just lucky to have received an invitation to the party. I still can't imagine there will be a day in which the direction of my life is not dictated by the benevolence of another person.

And I wonder: *How can that possibly be?*

Drinks come. And then more drinks. Suddenly, Mark leans across the table.

"Can you keep a secret?" he whispers.

The frankness of this question tips me off-balance: I thought we were engaged in a standard corporate flirtation—the outcome of which might lead to special treatment for me in the future, of course—but now I am unsure of the game. My dress suddenly feels like a tourniquet, and I worry I have underestimated how dangerous it is to be on the field when you don't know the rules. I think about how Isobel Fincher would never in a million years have left the gala with Mark Angelbeck. Isobel Fincher would never be so pathetically obvious.

"I don't know," I respond blandly. "Can I?"

"A lot of changes are about to be announced," he says.

"Oh," I say calmly. "Like what?"

"Organizational."

"Oh," I say again, but now my mind is racing. "Do I need to worry?"

He smiles at me with satisfaction but when he says nothing, I get the distinct impression he is, yet again, enjoying my unease.

"Well?" I press, but I remember to keep my tone playful. I don't want to come off as grubby or difficult.

"No, you're fine," he says finally, and I watch his body deflate a little.

"Well, that's good!"

"I think," he says, and here he wiggles his pinkie at me with the rest of his hand wrapped tightly around his glass, "the changes could be very good for you."

Before I can respond, the waiter places two large plates of pasta on the table, both of which Mark insisted we order and eat with an expensive bottle of cabernet. I want to press him for details about these alleged organizational changes, but a few more people stop by our table, and, as I listen to them talk, I realize I am very drunk. As one of the women eyes me, I realize that I have long forgotten my manners. My fork, which is covered with red sauce, lays askew across the white tablecloth, and I have bitten into a bread roll—my second bread roll, mind you—like it's a fat éclair. I am gossiping about people I should not be gossiping about, and I am letting Mark Angelbeck occasionally brush his hand across my knee.

At some point, the waiter puts down another bottle of wine, and in my surprise at its arrival, I drunkenly elbow it straight off the tabletop. It smashes on the floor with incredible force, and the entire room—once loud and clattering—falls into a perfect silence. I look down. The wine has splattered on my shoes and soaked the gauzy hem of my dress. The heavy glass shards from the bottle bob gracefully in the sea of red wine that puddles on the floor, like boats clipped to their moorings. Immediately, two small busboys come over to sweep it up, and while I am entirely mortified and genuinely apologetic, Mark Angelbeck just starts laughing, which makes me start laughing. When the owner sends over a brand-new bottle, we laugh even harder.

On the car ride uptown to our respective uptown apartments, Mark sits close to me. I say nothing as he slides his hand up my skirt. He keeps his eyes on the road ahead. I lean back on the seat, let my knees fall apart, and let out a soft sigh.

It doesn't occur to me—it doesn't occur to *anyone*—that this just may be the last good time.

55

For the entire month after the gala, I go back to taking the stairs to work each morning, fearful I will run into Mark Angelbeck and be forced to acknowledge the waves of shame and self-loathing that wash, with great regularity, over my body.

In my darker moments, I replay how I got out of the car that evening with a bright smile and a little wave, only to cover my face in a hollowed-out kind of horror once I made it to the safety of the lobby. "Did something happen, miss?" Hatch inquired, following me with concern as I made my way to the elevator.

"No," I replied, shaking my head, my eyes down on the floor. "Everything is perfectly fine."

One night, however, when L.K. is away and the office is quiet, I decide to come home early from work. I take the subway back to the Upper East Side, and stop briefly for two glasses of white wine in a dark Irish bar, which somehow both amplifies and soothes the deep sadness that has taken root inside my body. It is dusk by the time I arrive back at the apartment, but I am surprised to see all of the lights are out. I kick off my shoes and when I snap on the table lamp in the living room, I let out a little yelp.

Davis is on the couch.

"Jesus," I exclaim. "You *scared* me."

She is wearing her bathrobe, but it is untied, and her pale breasts are fully exposed. It takes me a long second to realize she is holding a bag of frozen corn against her mouth. There is a small mound of bloody paper towels crumpled in her lap.

In an instant, I sober up.

"Davis, what happened?" I exclaim.

Davis says nothing, and I fall on my knees beside her.

"Can I look?" I ask.

She shakes her head.

"Davis," I say gently, like I am speaking to a child. "Just let me look?"

I reach gingerly toward the bag, which is no longer cold, and pull it away from her face. Her upper lip is swollen and split, and blood is starting to clot, although just barely, around the wound, which runs about a half an inch in the direction of her nose, like a cleft palate.

"What happened?"

"I fell when I was walking Captain," she says. Her eyes are pink and bloodshot from crying.

"You were walking Captain? Tonight?"

She closes her eyes and nods. A single tear rolls down her cheek.

"Did you hit something?" I ask, and I peer closer. "It's pretty deep."

She wrinkles her nose.

"Do I need a plastic surgeon?" she asks.

"I don't know, maybe?"

I have no idea what requires the expertise of a plastic surgeon, but I do know we have moved past the Neosporin and Band-Aid phase; this isn't the kind of cut that heals entirely on its own.

I stand up.

"Let's get you to the hospital," I say. "I think you might need stitches."

"It's fine," Davis says quickly.

"It will literally take us five minutes," I say as I start toward her bedroom. "Let me get out of this dress, and I'll get you some clothes."

"No," she says, but this time her voice is uncharacteristically firm. "No hospital."

I turn around and throw my palms up with annoyance.

"Davis, seriously, you need to get that checked out," I say. "It's not a big deal. I will take you."

"I'll call Phillip," she says. "He will know what to do."

"Call Phillip?" I ask, disbelieving.

This makes no sense: Phillip is Barbara's agent. He is a short, nervous man with thinning black hair and a small mustache. He is often around the apartment—perpetually rubbing his wrists like he was released from handcuffs after a misunderstanding with the police—and while he's been Barbara's theater agent for as long as I have known her, I have never been clear on why she is so loyal to him. He doesn't seem to be very good at his job.

"Yes, Phillip," she says. "Please. His number is in my phone."

"Where is your phone?" I ask.

"I think it's in the kitchen," she replies. She puts the bag back on her lip.

I walk into the kitchen where, after some searching, I find Davis's phone on the floor. I open the freezer, and fish out a bag of green peas, before I return to the living room and hand her the phone. She turns it over in her hands for a moment before she raises her eyes.

"Can you give me a minute alone?" she asks. "To call him?"

I find this bizarre. Why does she need to be alone to call her mother's agent? Also, where is Barbara?

"Where is Barbara?" I ask. I hand her the frozen peas.

"She fell asleep," Davis says, but she doesn't look at me as she puts the new bag against her lip and winces. "She's asleep."

I spin on my heel and walk in the direction of Barbara's bedroom with great purpose. I fully expect to knock on her door and inform Barbara not only of Davis's dog-walking injury, but of her refusal to go to the hospital. If I know one thing about Barbara Lawrence, it is that she will get her daughter to a plastic surgeon if a plastic surgeon is warranted, even if she must carry Davis to the hospital herself. However, when I turn down the hall, Barbara's bedroom door is wide open, which is unusual. I approach it swiftly, but when I get to the threshold, I stop:

Barbara is sitting on the far edge of the bed with her head down. She looks to be breathing heavily.

"Barbara," I say.

But Barbara doesn't move.

"Barbara?" I say again, and she turns her head in my direction. Her face is blotchy, nearly distorted with rage.

"What do you think you are doing in here?" she growls. "Get out."

When I don't move, she makes an unexpected jerking movement, like she is going to chase me. It is so startling that I involuntarily take a step back, and hit the back of my head against the doorjamb. A bolt of pain shoots across my forehead.

"Get out," Barbara screams, and I stumble backward into the hallway so quickly that I fall over my own feet and land hard on the carpet. I start to crawl away, clawing against the floor in panic, and then, fearful I cannot outrun her, I push myself against the wall. I pull my knees into my chest and lower my head, trying to make myself as small as possible. I sit there motionless for what feels like a long time, afraid to breathe, until I hear new voices in the apartment. I stand up and sprint into the living room where I find Phillip standing over the couch. He wears a pair of baggy tan pants and a gray Notre Dame sweatshirt. I have never seen him in anything but a navy blue suit and I find myself unsettled by how feeble and inconsequential he looks when stripped of his usual, more powerful vestments. He has brought along an unfamiliar young Indian man with an obscenely thick head of black hair. As he shakes my hand, he introduces himself as a doctor. As I watch him examine Davis's face, I notice Hatch lingers in the doorway with his gloved hands balled into fists at his side. He won't make eye contact with me, which I find strange; he just stands at attention like a toy solider.

"She should go to a hospital," I say loudly, but to no one in particular.

Phillip raises his open palm in my direction, like a crossing guard.

"Please," he snips. "Can you give the doctor some privacy?"

I look at Davis for confirmation. She nods at me.

Reluctantly, I go to my bedroom, but I don't close the door. Instead, I take off my dress and drop it heavily to the floor. I put on jeans and a sweater, furious to be cast in the roll of the anxious husband who is barred from the delivery room. I wait twenty minutes, but when nobody comes to update me, I go in search of the information myself. As I pass Barbara's bedroom, I see the door remains open, and I glance inside. The doctor and Phillip are standing in front of her, and she is blubbering like a child, although I am not entirely convinced that she is fully awake. Her arm has been pulled out of her pajamas, and the doctor is on his knees at the foot of the bed, drawing a syringe. I peer closer, but when Phillip catches me lingering, he strides in my direction with a frown. He comes into the hallway and softly pulls the door closed behind him. He ventures a strained smile.

"Davis got eight stitches," he says to me with a light pat on my arm. "And something for the pain."

"Okay," I say uncertainly.

"She's going to be fine," he says reassuringly, and he gently turns me away from the door and pushes me, ever so slightly, back down the hall. "And don't worry: There won't be a scar."

56

I don't sleep well that night, and in the morning I take a quick shower before the sun comes up. When I step onto the bath mat and wrap a towel around my body, I listen for signs of life, but to my relief, the apartment is still quiet.

I dress in the darkness. When I get down to Fifth Avenue, the light has yet to rise above the buildings, and everything is cast in the cool blue of an unlived day. It's so early, that the street sweepers are still making their rounds. I stop to watch them as they rise ominously over a gentle slope, their battle-worn bodies as nameless and faceless as tanks. As they thunder past me, a light wind picks up and the brushes swoosh in frantic circles against the pavement like faraway static.

When they pass out of sight, I call Harry.

"Did you hear?" he asks in lieu of a salutation. He sounds breathless.

"Hear what?"

"Mark Angelbeck was just promoted to the president of your company."

I stop short on the sidewalk.

"Shut up," I hiss.

My mind starts to race.

"I will *not* shut up." Harry half laughs. "Because it's true. Do you seriously never read the news in the morning?"

"I read the papers when I get to work," I reply.

"That's wonderfully Amish of you, sweetheart," he says.

"I just had dinner with him a few weeks ago," I say absently. "The night of the gala."

I think about his hands on me in the back seat and squeeze my eyes tight with shame.

"You did?" Harry asks, and his voice sounds excited. "What happened? What did he say?"

I say nothing. My mind is entirely somewhere else.

"Clo?"

"Harry, can I ask you something?"

"Of course."

I pause. I am not sure where to begin.

"It's sort of private?"

"Is it Davis?" he asks, and the knowingness in his tone is both disarming and a relief.

I take a deep breath.

"Honestly, things are a mess," I say. "But I have no idea if it was *always* this bad and I didn't see it, or it's gotten worse since I moved in."

There is a long pause.

"Harry?" I ask. "Can you hear me?"

"Listen," he says. "I'm heading into a meeting, but why don't we meet for lunch later today so we can talk. Could you swing that?"

"That would be great," I say, and I am surprised when I hear my throat catch. When we hang up, I feel something akin to gratitude ripple through my veins, and for a moment I don't feel so alone.

A little after one o'clock, I meet Harry at a bar near his office. It's in Soho on the corner of Prince Street. A neon sign hangs over the double wide doorway, and through the glass, I can see Harry is already inside. I pull the handle on the door and I press myself inside the lunchtime crowd.

"It's weird," I say to Harry as I kiss him over the small table. "I have walked by this place *a thousand times*, but I have never been inside."

"It's not bad," he says. "It's been here, like, over a hundred years."

"And to think, now it gets to share the block with an Apple Store!" I joke.

I sit down. I run my fingers through the front of my hair, which is an affectation I have long borrowed from Davis and look down at the menu. I can feel Harry's eyes appraising me.

"The burger is good," Harry says, his arms folded across his chest. "And the chicken club."

He apparently has no need for the menu, but quite frankly, neither do I. The idea of eating anything with such an uncertain churn in my throat feels dangerous.

"How's the beer?" I ask.

"The beer is also good," he says gamely, but I feel strangely foolish when he doesn't indicate he intends to order one. Once we inform the waiter of our order, Harry puts his elbows on the table. He rests his chin on his knuckles and looks down at me. I notice he is wearing a very expensive-looking silver watch.

"So," he leads.

"It's about the apartment," I start.

"What about it?"

I realize I hadn't quite rehearsed what I was going to say, and I worry that, in the light of a new day, my fears were a little dramatic.

"Well, not so much about the apartment as the apartment's inhabitants?"

"They are a special breed," Harry says. He unfolds his napkin. "Is Davis still taking the pills?"

"The pills, the alcohol, the smoking . . ." I throw my hands up with light exasperation.

"Not that *you* would be one to judge," Harry says, and while his tone is teasing, he never misses an opportunity to remind me that I, too, am a little ugly inside.

Like I needed a reminder.

"Never to judge," I respond. I force a laugh. "But I worry she might need some proper help."

"Like rehab?"

"Maybe?"

"It won't happen," Harry replies plainly.

"Why not?"

"Barbara sees it as a temporary circumstance, which it probably is, you know," he says. "Davis has had her little spells before."

"Little spells?" I ask. "She's taking an oxy before breakfast, Harry."

"Probably better to keep *that one* quiet," he says with a light roll of his eyes. "But trust me, she always snaps out of it."

"I am not saying we should put a billboard in Times Square," I protest.

"I know, those things always get out," he says. "And I don't think that would benefit anyone, do you?"

I find the use of the word *benefit* to be strange, and when the waiter reappears with our food, I order a beer.

"And one for you, sir?" the waiter asks.

"None for me, thanks," Harry says.

Naturally, this makes me want to order two beers and pound them in rapid succession until I remember there was an actual reason that I called him here in the first place:

"But there is something else," I say.

Harry looks up from his sandwich.

"I don't know how to say it," I say. "I am sure I am completely crazy."

"What?"

"When you lived there..."

"Clo," he interrupts me gently. "That was a very long time ago."

"No, I know," I say quickly. "But when you lived there, did Barbara ever *hit* Davis?"

Harry stops chewing.

"I know," I say, and I feel my face redden. "I'm crazy, right?"

Harry puts down his sandwich and rests his palms on his lap. He glances around our table apprehensively before he leans forward:

"What happened?" he asks softly.

I tell him what happened—or, at least, what I *think* happened—and when I am finished, he turns away from me. He looks out the window for a long time, and when he swallows, I notice for the first time he has an enormous Adam's apple.

"Harry?" I prod. My pulse thumps in my wrists. "What?"

He turns back to me.

"Sorry," he says with a little shake of his head. "I am sure it's nothing."

"Then why are you acting weird?"

"I'm not," he bristles.

"Uh, you are," I say.

"I'm really not," he says sternly, and then he glances down at his watch. "But I have a meeting that I totally spaced on, so I have to go."

"What?" I stammer incredulous, but Harry just stands up. He grabs for his coat, which is slung over the back of the wooden chair, but his movements are uncharacteristically sloppy. The chair tips backward and hits the ground with a loud smack. As Harry leans forward to wrest it upright with his free hand, he shoots me a dirty look, like I am the reason he has lost his composure.

"Harry, what's going on?" I demand, my skin is pricked with fear. I half stand up, but he waves me down.

"Can you get the check?" he says. "I'll pay you back."

I don't have time to respond before Harry pushes through the bodies and out the front door. I manage to wave down a waiter and hand him Barbara's credit card. I don't even ask to see the bill. I don't have time. I need to catch Harry. I quickly sign the receipt—leaving our food almost entirely untouched—but I pick up the pint glass and take a long pull of the beer. Then, I grab my own bag and coat and run onto the street.

"Harry?" I yell, and I spin in a circle, trying to locate him in the crowd.

But Harry Wood is nowhere to be found.

It rains for the rest of the day.

I have plans to see a new play with our theater critic, after which we will undoubtedly end up at Orso, where people will stop by our table all night just to get a word with him, and I won't get to bed until midnight.

It all sounds exhausting.

But, on the other hand, maybe a dark theater is a good place to hide.

It's been a strange day.

I haven't been able to shake my lunch with Harry, nor have I been able to get him on the phone to explain his hasty departure. However, I have little interest in racing back to the Lawrence apartment, especially because there will be no discussion of what happened last night, and I don't possess the wherewithal to perform like everything is normal.

Everything is *not* normal.

The office is dark and empty at this hour. I put on some lipstick and unsheathe the expensive umbrella the company gifted to me on my first anniversary. It's funny: There was a time not so long ago when I carried around one of those spindly numbers they hawk outside Penn Station, but that was before I understood how a good umbrella, much like good shoes and a good bag, lends one a sense of respectability in New York. It's another secret signal that you belong to a certain, far superior, world. I take the elevator to the main lobby. I push through the revolving doors and onto the sidewalk. I stand under the overhang for a moment, trying to sort out just how hard it is raining, and then I see him: Harry Wood.

He makes no effort to seek cover from the downpour. Water drips from his dark hair, and I wonder how long he has been outside in this weather.

"Harry! What are you doing?" I exclaim as I motion to him frantically. "You're soaking wet. Come under here!"

Harry shakes his head, which sends him slightly off-balance, and he must steady his shoulder against the closest brick wall. I can't see his face in the darkness, but I can tell he is laughing by the way his shoulders bob up and down.

"Are you drunk?" I ask, but this is a rhetorical question: Harry is clearly drunk. He can hardly stand up straight. When a group of people leave my building, they all give him a sidelong glance, and I look away like I don't know him. This is not a good place for Harry Wood to be caught blind drunk.

It's not good for either of us.

"I tried to call you," I whisper once they are gone, but it comes out an accusation.

"Oh, I know," he replies in a bitter singsong. "I know."

"Why didn't you answer?"

"Because I was getting drunk," he says, and he smiles with his eyes closed. "Drunk. Drunk. Drunk."

Here, his body sways unexpectedly, and I dart forward to catch him. I grip his upper arm and try to hold the umbrella over both our heads; the raindrops sound like gumdrops falling from the sky. When I look down, I see there is a flat, clear bottle in Harry's suit pocket. It has a red cap.

"Harry, we have to get you home," I say. "You're soaked."

The umbrella is not big enough for the both of us, and I worry that, if my hair gets wet, it will curl before I make it to the theater. I tilt the umbrella back in my direction, and Harry wiggles free of my grasp and walks backward into the storm with his arms wide and mouth open to the sky. I grab his arm and hustle him toward the parking garage across the street. Once inside, I close my umbrella and shake it out with force while Harry just melts thickly onto the pavement. He pulls the bottle out of his sopping jacket, unscrews the cap, and takes a sip.

"Harry?" I kneel on the wet concrete to look at him. "You are *not* okay."

"No," he agrees. "I am not okay."

"Care to elaborate?" The knees of my jeans start to feel damp, so I shift back to my heels. "I feel like you wanted to say something at lunch."

"No," he says with a sorrowful smile: "I most certainly did *not* want to say anything at lunch."

He puts the bottle down so he can rub his eyes with the meat of his palms. I pick it up to take a quick sip: The lukewarm liquid sears my mouth like pouring peroxide on an open wound. I turn it around to see the label.

"This is really shitty vodka, Harry," I say. "How much did you drink?"

"Who cares?"

"I care?"

"I know," he says sarcastically. "You always care."

I roll my eyes and take another small sip.

Harry sits up straighter:

"There was one night when Davis and I were home for fall break," he begins. "And Barbara beat her up pretty bad."

He delivers this information so casually, so unexpectedly, that I gag as I try to swallow my mouthful of vodka. It burns in a straight line down my throat.

"What?" I bleat, coughing.

He motions for the bottle, and I hand it back to him.

"It was bad," he says, and he takes a sip. "Like we-had-to-take-her-to-the-hospital-and-get-her-twenty-five stitches-in-her-head bad."

"What?" I repeat.

"There was blood everywhere, and when we finally got her down to the lobby, Hatch had to help Davis into the car," he says. "And the entire ride to the hospital, Barbara kept telling us the story."

"The story?"

"She wanted us to say that Davis got jumped by some guy in Central Park, but she didn't get a good look at him. She wanted us to say he stole her wallet. Here is the best part: She wanted us to say he was Black."

"Black?"

"She said it was more believable."

I say nothing, namely because my brain cannot seem to locate the next right word.

"She was so calm," Harry says quietly.

"Who? Davis?"

"No, Barbara," he says. "That is the part I remember the most. She was just so calm."

I stare at Harry's face. The fluorescent lights in the parking garage are so intense that I can see the pores on his nose are clogged with blackheads.

"The thing is," Harry continues. "When you go to the hospital and you're a beat-up kid, the cops come."

"They do?" I manage.

"It's a little thing you learn in foster care, my dear," he says, and here he pretends to tip an imaginary hat.

"Harry," I chide.

He looks away and swallows hard.

"After they, you know, fix you up, the police take you into a room alone. They ask you a lot of questions," he continues. "They want to make sure that, you know, it's not child abuse or anything."

"Oh."

"The police questioned me, too," he starts, but before he can say anything else, he covers his face, and I realize he is crying.

"What did you tell them?" I ask, but he doesn't respond. He just wipes his eyes with the bottom of his shirt.

"Harry, what did you tell them?" I ask again, but now more firmly. He looks at me with confusion.

"What do you mean?" he asks. "I told them she was mugged by some Black guy in Central Park."

"Why?" I can hear the judgment in my voice.

"Why?" he says, and he sounds genuinely confused, "Because that's what Barbara told me to say?"

"But that was a lie."

"Of course it was a lie, but I figured you would understand."

"Understand what?"

"That I was young?" he shoots back. "I thought they were the only family I was ever going to have, and Barbara, the way Barbara looked at me was . . ." Here, he trails off.

"It was what?"

"I knew if I said anything, we would *all* lose everything," he says, and now his anger toward me is rising. "Not just me. Barbara would lose everything. Davis would lose everything. Can you imagine if that had gotten into the newspapers?"

He slumps over in the gaping doorway and stares out at the street.

"When we got home, Barbara gave me Davis's wallet," he continues. "She told me to take the cash out of it, and to throw it in Central Park."

My face must betray me.

"I'm sorry," he says quietly. "You must hate me, but I didn't have a choice."

"I don't hate you," I say carefully. "I just don't know what to think. This is a lot of information."

"Do you want to know the worst part?" he says. "It was Davis's birthday."

I say nothing.

"And when we got home from the hospital, Barbara made this big show of lighting the candles on her cake, and we all sang like, well, like nothing happened?"

"Even Davis?" I ask.

"Especially Davis," he says.

"Oh, Harry," I say. "I am so sorry."

"There were a few other times," he says. "More yelling than anything else, but nothing as bad as that one time."

"How many other times?" I ask.

"I don't know," he says. "Davis and I never really talked about it, but I thought it had stopped?"

"Maybe it did?" I say earnestly. "I didn't see anything. Honestly, I am sorry I even brought it up."

"Still," he says miserably. "I feel like this is all my fault."

"If this is anyone's fault, isn't it Barbara's fault?"

Harry says nothing.

"Is this why you always feel like you have to protect Davis?" I ask, and—believe it or not—in this moment I find myself annoyed that I did not experience some childhood tragedy that I could now parlay into Harry's unrelenting affection.

"I guess," he says.

"Harry, you cannot beat yourself up," I say. "You aren't perfect."

"You are," he says.

"Harry," I exclaim. "You—*of all people*—know I am not perfect."

"I mean, you're a conniving little bitch, but . . ." Harry starts, and he manages a little smile.

I laugh, too, but it is a phony laugh. I need a minute alone to digest this exchange, but first I need to transition Harry out of the public sobbing phase and into the anonymity of a car service, namely so we aren't spotted by anyone from my office. I fish my phone out of my coat pocket, and when I flip it open, I see it's almost eight o'clock. I cannot be late to the theater, which is a few blocks away. I dial our company car service.

"I'm ordering you a car," I say.

"I am sorry," he says, but it comes out more garbled now.

"Stop it, Harry," I say. "We all make mistakes."

Here, Harry lifts his head up from his knees.

"Yeah?" he asks.

"Of course," I say. "It's not like I've never made a mistake."

"Like what?" he asks.

"I don't know," I say, but I am distracted by the dispatcher. I cover the bottom of my phone and whisper. "Stupid shit."

He looks at me expectantly, and I get the sense that, in the wake of his own unburdening, he now desires a corresponding chunk of my flesh. Even more strangely, I find myself wondering if, by revealing some previously unknown vulnerability, I can use this moment to bind myself even more tightly to Harry Wood.

"I have not returned, like, three dresses I borrowed from work?" I offer.

"Scandalous," he says with a raise of one eyebrow, and I smile.

I pretend like I am thinking.

"I've used Barbara's credit card a few times?" I finally offer, although the moment it comes out of my mouth, I regret it.

"Yeah, I know," Harry says.

"You know?" I look at him, confused.

"You do it *all* the time," he says. "I'm not blind."

"Oh," I say uncertainly. "How come you never said anything?"

"I was waiting to see if you would tell me," he says. "I was trying to figure out if it was approved or if you were keeping a little secret."

I pull back.

"Like some kind of test?" I say, incredulous, and I feel myself start to get angry, but Harry only looks at me strangely.

"Oh, Clo," he sighs. "Don't you know by now it's all some kind of a test?"

I say nothing in response, but I suddenly feel unbearably foolish, like Harry just tricked me into committing an irredeemable error of judgment, the magnitude of which will be wholly unknown to me until, I reason, it is known to everyone.

I am usually more careful.

"So what are you going to do if she catches you?" Harry asks.

"It's not that much," I lie, desperate to backpedal. "I am going to pay it all back."

"How?"

I don't respond.

"Don't bother," he says, but he's started to sound drowsy. "She's so rich that she will never even notice. *Trust me.*"

As I search the street for the car, I wonder if what Harry says is true. And, if it is true—that I will never get caught—does that mean I don't have to feel guilty? Can something be empirically wrong or, as I have long suspected, are crimes relative to the circumstances? As I sit next to Harry, I allow this thought to comfort me as I spot a pair of headlights creep searchingly up the street. I wave my hand in the air.

"The car is here," I say, which rouses Harry to some degree.

After I help him into the back seat and give the driver his address, I remind Harry to change out of his wet clothes when he gets home.

"Clo," he says. "Please don't say anything to Davis? I don't want her to know I told you."

"Of course," I say.

I slam the door and, as the car pulls away, I feel my body shudder, like it's trying to rid itself of some unwanted virus.

The rain is slackening, and as I race along the sidewalk in the direction of the theater, I desperately search the faces of the people who pass by for some sort of sign. But sign of *what*, I wonder. I have no idea.

I only know that I have trusted far too many people in a land where no one is ever to be trusted.

57

It's March in New York, which means that it is too cold to eat lunch outside, and yet Harry has, apparently, decided we will eat lunch outside. Not that he bothers to inform me of this plan. When I arrive at the restaurant, which is a corner café in the West Village, I search the overheated interior before I spy him through the window. He is sitting at a table on the sidewalk under the weather-beaten awning. His legs are crossed (quite campily, in my opinion) at the knee and he taps on his iPhone. When he sees me, he offers a quick smile, but he doesn't stand up. This isn't surprising (he doesn't rise to greet me these days unless there is an audience), but I also don't care. He has been distant for months, claiming it's the pressures of work, and I have grown tired of performing somersaults to reassure him—over and over—that I am of value. I pull out my own chair, sit down, and glare at him from the other side of my enormous sunglasses as he pretends to read the menu.

"It's too cold to eat outside," I snip finally.

"You're late," he says without looking up. "And Benjamin Franklin said the cold air is good for you."

"So where is this mystery person you want me to meet?" I ask, instead of taking Harry's bait.

I decide this is very mature of me.

Harry lays his phone on the tabletop. He checks his watch.

"They should be here any second," he says. He straightens out the cuffs of his coat with his signature grace and takes a sip of his wine. The glass is almost empty.

"They?" I ask. "I thought it was one person?"

"Does it matter?"

"I suppose not," I sigh as I place the cloth napkin on my lap, and lean closer to the overhead heater, which glows orange, but doesn't seem to produce much warmth. "I just don't have much time today. We are closing, and I still need to come up with something for the website."

"How modern," he says dryly. "You're embracing the internet."

"*Embracing* is probably too strong a word," I say as the waiter arrives to fill my glass with wine. I take a grateful swallow. "We continue to tolerate the internet."

"Well, I am grateful for your disinterest," he says. "It has allowed guys like me to flourish."

"I wish I could take full responsibility," I return with a wry smile. "But our disinterest seems to be corporate mandate."

Here, Harry lightly chuckles.

"It shouldn't take too long," he says. "I already have them on the hook."

In recent months, Harry has asked me to join him at several business-related meetings and other, more social, events because, in his estimation, having a well-known magazine editor as a close friend lends him additional clout as he builds out his operations. His website is now a big deal—a household name in our rarefied circle—and I usually get pulled in when he's wooing a new advertiser or, more recently, an investor. My job, as far as I can tell, is simply to reflect his brilliance back upon him, and wear an intimidatingly fashionable outfit. Historically speaking, I don't mind these little outings because I generally enjoy an element of theater amid the drudgery of my daily existence, but lately I have started to feel a little bored or, more accurately, like there is something better I should be doing with my time, something ownable. After all, Harry has built a legitimate business while I am still desperate to figure out what my *something* might be.

I still don't feel special on my own.

A woman and man cautiously approach our table; they wear corporate clothes and have nearly identical sets of oversized white teeth. The man is short and bland as a pebble while the woman has a rough, tomboy aura to her, like she spent her childhood running around without sunscreen, but not in the freckled Greenwich way. She is more Arizona, all leather and unfiltered cigarettes. She is also more businesslike than the women at the magazine. When Harry introduces us, it's almost as if she doesn't care what I think of her, which, naturally, makes me dislike her on the spot.

"This is a lovely restaurant," the woman says after the waiter takes her drink order. She requested a glass of pinot grigio once she saw that Harry and I were drinking, and she's behaving as if the unexpected allowance has put her in a giddy mood. She also doesn't seem to mind the cold. "And how nice to finally meet you in person, Harry!"

"No," Harry says, and I marvel at the way his eyes start to twinkle, like he's flipped some internal switch. "The pleasure is all mine."

From their conversation, I quickly understand they are executives at a major mass retailer based in the Midwest. They are good at things like electronics and kitchenware, but they are expanding their operations into clothing and accessories, and eager for advertising and partnership opportunities that would lend them, as the man puts it, "fashion credibility." They think Harry's website would be a good fit. So, for twenty minutes, as I pick through an arugula salad with poached pears, Harry talks about his company. He employs an *aw-shucks* demeanor that suggests his website is just a hobby—a passion project if you will—that *happens* to perform ridiculously well. However, once the woman starts asking him pointed questions, he quickly exhibits a keen understanding of relevant statistics and can speak authoritatively on topics like month-over-month growth, page views, and cost per customer. While I have borne witness to this presentation before, I never cease to marvel at Harry's unexpected aptitude as a businessman, especially because, for me, the mere launching of an Excel document can trigger a seizure of insecurity. However, after taking several rounds of funding over the past few years (who provides this investment, I am never clear, nor is Harry forthcoming), Harry has transitioned from editor-about-town to executive-about-town (although he prefers to call himself a "founder") and, as such, he has decided to move his website to the big leagues. He's shopping around for a proper acquisition, partly because he claims he can't possibly continue to run it at the current rate without the capital of a parent company. He needs more people. He needs more space. He needs upgraded technology.

At a certain point during the meal, I am surprised when the woman turns her attention to me, although she doesn't quite look at me directly.

"So, Harry says you go to the appointments?"

I don't know what she means, and I say as much.

"To see a new product? Before it is released? Sketches, prototypes?" she inquires.

"Yes," I say, but uncertainly.

The man and woman exchange looks.

"You know that information could be very valuable to us," the woman continues. "We are always looking for ways to bring luxury products to the *real* woman."

"Oh," I say.

I glance expectantly at Harry. I am certain he will jump into the conversation and explain how magazines work, namely that everything I preview as an editor is under embargo or an NDA or, most often, an unspoken contract of silence, but he just smiles placidly, like a well-trained flight attendant during turbulence. I tap him under the table with my boot, but he doesn't flinch.

"Of course," the woman continues, sensing my unease. "In addition to the advertising dollars we would allocate to Harry's website, we would compensate you for any information that might help guide us in our own design and production process."

I pause with my fork midway to my mouth.

"Oh," I say again.

I look down to see a wet flop of lettuce dangling from the prongs so I set it down gently on my plate. I dab the sides of my mouth with the rough napkin and venture a little cough in Harry's direction.

"What my colleague is trying to say," the man interjects with a paternal guffaw. "We pay for this kind of work."

"Pay?" I ask.

"Yes," he says. "We generally structure it as a consultant's fee, usually ten thousand a month, but for you—considering your access and your point of view—I think we could certainly go higher."

The woman nods in agreement.

"Definitely higher," she says.

I sit in a bewildered silence for a few beats before the executives—bright smiles intact—shift their eyes anxiously toward Harry: *Who the fuck is this woman you brought us?*

Harry rearranges his body so he can look directly in my eyes, and he offers me an easy smile. Too easy. It makes me instantly suspicious, like I'm a beloved pet being soothed before the euthanasia.

"It doesn't sound like they need too much, Clo," he says gently, and he glances at the executives, who vigorously bob their heads. "They just want the photographs you take on your appointments anyway."

"We would *never* disclose our agreement with any third party," the man says. "If that is a concern?"

"Just the photographs you take anyway," the woman repeats, and she places her hand on the tablecloth. "Again, we just want to bring a little affordable luxury to the *real* woman."

When lunch ends, we part ways with the executives, and, without saying a word to me, Harry takes off toward Sixth Avenue. He walks so swiftly that I need to chase him down the sidewalk in my high heels for half a block before I can grab his elbow. He turns around with exasperation, but he doesn't look at me.

"What the *fuck* was that?" I hiss.

"What?"

"That," I say. I thrust an angry finger down the street.

He finally looks at me, but his expression makes it clear that he is displeased with my behavior.

"A business opportunity?" he responds with a shrug of his shoulders.

"I'm sorry, but am I *a prostitute?*" I spit out.

"You're making a big deal out of *nothing*," he says before adding, "That was embarrassing. *You* were embarrassing."

"I thought I was meeting someone for lunch," I say. "You didn't tell me you were going to pimp me out to some corporate assholes, so they advertise on your fucking website."

"I was just trying to help you," he says. "Why do you always see the worst in me, Clo? I am trying to *help* you! Isn't that what friends do?"

"Help me?" I cry. "You mean help *you!*"

"I don't know how many times I have to say it, but I really need you on my team for this stuff, Clo," he says. "I saw it as a good opportunity."

"If it's such a good opportunity, why don't *you* do it?" I snap. "Don't drag me into it."

"I would be happy to, but I don't see the same products that you see," he says. "Your magazine has more access than anyone else. You know that."

"So, you were just going to use me?"

"You should just forget it," he continues with a sigh. "You are always overreacting about the most basic stuff."

"I'm not overreacting," I say. "But why would I want to do this? I could get in so much trouble."

Harry slips his hands into his coat pockets and looks up at the sky.

"We all need different things in life," he says. "Some people need excitement, I guess."

"Is that what I need, Harry?" I demand. "I need *excitement?*"

"No," he says, plainly enough.

"Thank you," I say pointedly before I turn to the street, quite cinematically, in my opinion, and raise my arm for a taxi.

"But Clo?" he asks.

I turn around to look at him.

"Yeah?"

He looks at me, his face inscrutable.

"Don't you *really* need the money?"

When I return to the office, I am still reeling from my outing with Harry. My unease is not so much tied to Harry's assertion that I need money to pay Barbara back—that is empirically true—but more because Harry's offer, such as it was, felt more like an expectation, or even a demand. I shake out of my coat, which I throw haphazardly over the back of my chair. I look over at Davis's empty desk, which remains oddly preserved, even after all these years, and I find myself longing for the time when she felt faraway and exciting to me. It's strange: I feel like the closer I get to everyone, the further I am from truly knowing them; the early horse trading of our vulnerabilities did not seal our commitment, rather it has left us all exposed in dangerous ways. When I sit down and reach into my black bag to retrieve my wallet, the white business card pressed on me by the woman at the end of our lunch flutters cheaply to the floor. I frown. Our business cards don't flutter, I think. They fall to earth like a weather-beaten cedar shingle. I pick it up off the carpet and snap it down flat on my desk. I look at the card for a long while.

Ten thousand dollars a month.
For you, we could certainly go higher.
It's just the pictures you take anyway.

When I get off the subway that night on Eighty-Sixth Street, I slip into a row of gray payphones on the corner. I pick up the black plastic receiver, which feels oily between my fingers, and hold it an inch from my ear. There is pink gum smashed above the coin return and a small sticker that encourages me to STOP ORGAN HARVESTING. I slip two quarters in the slot, and I dial the number on the card. The woman answers.

"It's Clo Harmon," I say. "From lunch?"

"Ah, Clo," the woman says. "I was hoping you would call."

58

It turns out Harry was right: Maybe I *was* overreacting. As it happens, the little side hustle he devised is not only mutually beneficial, but it is also incredibly easy. So easy, in fact, that, on my good days, it is hard to feel like I am doing anything wrong at all. To begin, Kate is manifestly delighted to pass off any real work to an eager beaver like me, including her many appointments. I simply forward the pictures I take with her digital camera to the Midwestern woman via email with my notes, as well as things like pricing and materials. Per Harry's suggestion, I am careful to use my personal email account for these exchanges, and for additional security, I delete all messages within seconds of sending them, although I do bcc Harry in the event something gets lost in the transfer. The big retailer, in turn, deposits a consulting fee into my checking account on the first of every month.

For the big retailer, the benefit of our arrangement is two-fold. One, to see new product and designs in advance enables them to offer a less expensive version of the exact same product, and two, they can capitalize, without cost, from the marketing and PR spend put forth by the actual designer to introduce their product to the world. So, at the same moment you see an amazing dress on a celebrity in your favorite magazine or marching down a runway in Milan, you can drive to your local strip mall and buy a nearly identical knock-off for less than fifty bucks. Now, if the Midwestern retailer *waits* until the style is released, it will take months of supply chain bottlenecks to get their copycat product to market. By that point, the customer will have moved on to something else, which would leave the retailer with not only a missed opportunity, but piles of unwanted inventory. As it happens, this retailer is using this strategy with everything lately—fashion, beauty, school supplies, electronics—because "bringing luxury to the *real* woman" in this cheap, expedited, and tacky-ass manner is making them all incredibly rich. It's making me rich as well, relatively speaking, but I have yet to spend a dime of the money they have paid me. These funds are earmarked for Barbara Lawrence and, more broadly, the saving of my tattered soul.

My compliance has other benefits, too, namely that Harry seems to find me interesting again. We have resumed our weekly lunches, parsing through our invitations for the coming week, and he is usually the last person I talk to before I fall asleep at night, my cell phone wedged between my ear and the pillow. While I am somewhat ashamed of the lengths I have gone to for his approval, it feels so nice to be regularly in his company again that I try not to overthink it.

The other thing I try not to overthink are the men in suits that have been lurking around the hallways of our office building in recent weeks. They have laptops tucked under their arms, but don't say much; they simply stride the hallways with great purpose. When I arrive at work each morning, I watch them congregate in the downstairs lobby. They talk too loudly for my taste, but they dress to impress: crisp white shirts, no ties, expensive leather bags, the big, banging silver watch. They also have razor burn and wedding bands, both little details that signal a stability I find inexplicably sexy these days. There is only one woman in the group. She is built like a high school cross-country runner—gangly, tall, flat as a nine-year-old boy—and I suspect her to be a few years younger than me. Every day, she wears a skirt suit and pantyhose with her open toe, block heel slingbacks. I can't help but envision her in the hosiery aisle at Duane Reade each week, desperately hoping the most popular size and style (size B, control top) is still in stock, lest she be forced to wash out an old pair for work. The issue with the pantyhose, aside from being completely hideous, is that no one at our magazine—at *any* magazine—is going to take her suggestions seriously dressed like that, which is probably why they brought in all the young, well-dressed men. My bet is this woman does a lot of work but has yet to utter a word during the proceedings, such as they are, because when it comes to the big decisions at our company, we defer to the men. We don't have much of a choice: There are no women in the executive ranks of our company.

The rumor spreads quickly that these men (and one woman) are consultants who have been hired by the newly annointed Mark Angelbeck at an enormous expense to help the company streamline operations and, thus, lower our (currently astronomical) expenses. Their sudden arrival seems to be of great concern to everyone, and while I intellectually understand it, I find I don't share in their unease. Even after it is announced by Mark Angelbeck that our company will cease publication of two of our longest-running magazines and move a third magazine to an online-only edition, I still don't worry about my own future. For starters, I figure I am still low-level enough to be considered cheap labor. Furthermore, I work at the most profitable magazine at the company, a status achieved and retained through our meticulously executed outward display of wealth and superiority. As such, I simply assume those magazines were sacrificed for our benefit.

It's not like we can suddenly walk around looking poor, I reason.

After all, this is the land of make-believe.

59

Isobel Fincher is leaving the magazine.

Isobel Fincher is leaving the magazine after six years of service, and, in my shock and grief, I decide to take her decision personally. I feel mad. I feel abandoned. But mostly I suspect I am so ridiculously overwrought because I am about to lose my only real advocate, and despair that, without Isobel, I will cease to exist. What I know for certain is that everyone in the features department will stop learning how to be a better writer and editor because, as far as I can tell, Isobel is the only person who still offers a technical apprenticeship around here. Sure, we all have our knuckles smacked for failures of taste from time to time, but Isobel, in conjunction with L.K. Smith, is one of the last bastions of journalistic rigor. She does not tolerate sloppiness, be it grammatical or factual in nature, and if a writer turns in a final draft that does not meet her standard, she will kill it, no matter how much the writer howls. And they do howl—writers, of course, being famous howlers—but in the end, they generally end up apologizing to Isobel, promising with a chagrined earnestness to do better the next time.

Of course, Isobel's standards, well learned and long practiced, stand in direct contrast to what is slowly becoming of value on the other side of our floor where you will find the two-person staff of our small but allegedly growing website. They prowl around the office asking for ideas and distribute traffic reports so each editor can see how much traffic their print content is generating online. While there is an unspoken pact to barely humor them, I still find it depressing:

We used to be the hot girl, but now we are letting anyone with a few bucks peek up our skirt.

As such, I am convinced Isobel's decision to abandon the ship—which I view as abandoning me—must be related to her discomfort with these changes, which is sometimes referred to (in hushed, superior tones, of course) as "the shift from class to mass," although everyone is reasonably confident this tacky phase will pass quickly, like Lucite sandals. The official story Isobel has given to L.K. Smith for her departure is that she wants to "spend more time with her family," but I fear it is only a matter of time before she announces some amazing new job or another bestselling book, and I am sent back to writing photo captions and mailing packages to hysterical women with dairy intolerance all over the globe.

When someone resigns from the magazine, we inexplicably throw them a champagne toast at ten o'clock in the morning. During these uncomfortable events, the entire staff amasses in the conference room and, to some fanfare, presents the soon-to-be-former employee with an expensive designer gift (usually pilfered from the accessories closet) and then we all stand around awkwardly for exactly eleven minutes and pray for our own death. We were spared the indignity when Liddy vanished under the cover of night, but at Isobel's gathering, it is a full house. I petulantly pound three plastic flutes of Veuve Clicquot on an empty stomach, and when I get back to her office, I burst into tears.

"I don't know everything yet," I weep nonsensically. "You can't leave."

"You know plenty," she says kindly, but I can tell she is amused by me. I can generally be counted on to amuse Isobel.

Today, however, I can find nothing funny as I look around her empty office. Her beautiful portraits have been shipped to her apartment, and the brass lamps are gone. I recall the late nights we spent together, bathed in their scholarly glow as we worked on the pages for our section. The bulletin boards are bare, save a few white thumbtacks gummed into their flesh, and the whole thing strikes me as so unbearably sad that, when I start to cry harder, Isobel gets up and closes her door. She gently drags her chair next to mine. As usual, she smells earthy and floral, like an English garden after a warm rain.

"Clo," she says gently. "You have talent. You have guts. You are a hard worker. What are these tears? You are going to be *fine*."

"I don't have the right talent," I mutter miserably.

For her part, Isobel seems to consider this for a moment. Her warm hand fans soothingly against my back.

"It's an important distinction," she says, finally.

"What is?"

"Between talent and the appearance of talent," she says. "Both can work, but in different ways."

"So what do I do?"

Here, Isobel gives me a sad little smile.

"You have to decide that path for yourself," she says.

I wipe the tears off my cheeks with the back of my hand.

"But what if I can't decide?" I ask.

Here, I feel her hand lift from my back. Then, she turns me around by my shoulders so I can face her.

"You must decide," she says, and there is a sternness in her voice that takes me entirely by surprise. "Otherwise, they will eat you alive."

60

I invite Allie to try a new restaurant in Brooklyn with me. There is a tasting for magazine and website editors, which is a rarity these days, and the place is close to my old apartment, which I have been longing to see for months, although I never seem to find the time. Allie is newly pregnant, so I send a car to pick her up before it comes to collect me at the office. When it pulls up outside my building, I can see Allie laughing in the back seat as the driver walks around to open the door for me.

"You have your own car now?" Allie asks, wide-eyed, as I slide beside her.

"Oh, I'm big-time," I joke.

"I'll say," she replies.

In the days following Isobel's departure from the magazine, I was very careful. I made not even the slightest indication that I was interested in her job because—as I have learned through years of observation—any such overtures are categorically disqualifying for a woman in my position.

When I finally got the call to come down to L.K.'s office, I was quickly settled behind her closed door—and with about as much fanfare as that which attends cracking open a can of soda—L.K. informed me that I would be taking on the bulk of Isobel's responsibilities on a "probationary" basis. She didn't quite use the word *promotion*, nor did she indicate the specific change to my salary (it was mutually understood I could do the backward math when I received my next paycheck and that it would be profoundly unimpressive), but these details are beside the point. I was now a senior features editor. At the end of our conversation, L.K. tacked on two thrilling additions: One: I could move into Isobel's empty office, and two: I was permitted to hire an assistant.

I thanked her for the opportunity. I promised I would not let her down.

"We shall see," she said softly, but her mind seemed like it was elsewhere. "We shall see."

As I walked out of L.K.'s office that day, I recall feeling a sense of guilty elation, like someone I loved died unexpectedly, but I was just informed they left their shockingly vast fortune to me. Of course, while I knew it would be indecent to celebrate openly, especially if the position was, indeed, probationary, I also knew I needn't bother. The news would be spread around the office in minutes, and, at least for the next few days, I would be an object of widespread envy and scorn.

In short order, I moved my things into Isobel's office, and I tacked my first tear sheet up on her old bulletin board. I bought a lamp. I hung a picture. A few congratulatory bouquets arrived, the largest one from none other than Isobel Fincher herself, and L.K. Smith had the accessories girls send me over a new Yves Saint Laurent bag.

I hired an assistant, a recent Barnard graduate named Sarah, although finding the right kind of girl was a disconcertingly challenging process. Overall, I have noticed that the incoming class of assistants is a strange new breed. They present as entirely devoid of basic manners; things like shaking hands, eye contact, and deferring to their elders seem genuinely foreign to them. Furthermore, they exhibit very little tolerance for trial and error. Instead, they ask for explicit instructions for *everything*, and they expect those instructions to be delivered in the spirit of equality, respect, and, most horrifyingly, mentorship. When they don't understand something, they ask their superiors for clarification instead of mousing around among the other assistants for the information they seek. They wear a dizzying rotation of cheap clothes from H&M and Forever 21, but instead of this being a shameful secret, it's a bizarre point of pride, even as their satins fray and seams rip. They cook hot dinners in their apartments. They drink in moderation. They wear flat shoes. They get tattoos on the insides of their forearms that say things like *breathe* in their own cursive handwriting.

It's all very deep.

It's not that they aren't smart or hardworking because they are *very* smart and hardworking, but they also firmly believe their generation has something special to offer, a secret language that will be valuable to humanity for generations to come simply because they grew up with unlimited access to the internet. Furthermore, somebody must have told them that life would be just and fair and that, if it ever failed to be just and fair, it was their obligation to remedy the situation, regardless of their lowly station.

I don't think most of them will last, however.

This is the land of harsh winters.

So far, however, *my* Sarah is the ideal assistant and, even better, she is highly coachable in any areas where she does not possess a natural aptitude. Early on, I had to teach her to answer my phone in a more cheerful manner because she was my "front of house" and to have a mumbling assistant does not reflect well on me *or* the magazine. In return, I reminded her that she would be dealing with some incredible writers, all of whom presented a once-in-a-lifetime opportunity to learn how to be a better writer and build up her network. She smiled when I said this, but I had the sense I had offended her, although I cannot imagine why; it was the exact same thing Isobel said to me when she first started, and I had lapped it up like a runaway cat.

That aside, my biggest concern with Sarah is that she isn't having any fun. She's only twenty-two, and yet, she is a serious girl; always punctual and fresh-faced each morning. Her nails are filed round and painted in a rich cream polish, and her black hair is blown straight with a few curling-iron twists. She always smells the same, like fresh-scented drugstore lotion and department store perfume. She changes her earrings each day. She takes SoulCycle classes. I wonder if—for some brief shining moment—I ever came off in the same way? I certainly worked hard to *appear* as if I had my act together, like I hadn't woken up in a stranger's bed and had to wait outside the chain clothing store across the street from my office—tapping my high-heeled foot in impatience—until it opened so I could buy new clothes for the day.

I want to call Isobel and ask about her first impressions of me, but I don't, namely because in her unfailing politeness she would surely say that she couldn't remember.

When Sarah first started at the magazine, I tried to employ some of Isobel's regal distance. I wanted to be admired by Sarah, but from a slight and breathless remove. I endeavored to be an empowering leader who was measured and kind, a steady hand in a most tumultuous sea but—as luck would have it—I spilled a scalding cup of tomato soup on my crotch on her third day of work. I was on an important call when it happened and poor Sarah, after she assessed the root cause of my screams, had to scurry to the Gap to buy me new underwear and a skirt. After she handed me the blue plastic bag of clothes through a crack in the door, I had to hop inelegantly around my office on speaker phone as I tried to writhe out of my soppy lace thong and into the tiny black cotton bikini that Sarah, surely with an unfathomable amount of distress, had to hand-select for me. As I tried to pull the skirt over my hips, I realized it was a size two which, even at the Gap, is a solid size too small. Instead of being annoyed, however, I felt nothing but pride in my selection of my Sarah. To buy me the smallest size was a smart, strategic bet: It was her way of nonverbally communicating that she sees me as skinny, which was impressive for her to intuit as something I would want to hear after just a few days on the job.

However, it proved to be somewhat hard to claw back respectability and awe from Sarah after such early buffoonery, so I end up doing with Sarah what I always do: The ol' self-deprecation dance. I want her to like me. I just cannot seem to help it. I want everyone to like me, even if I don't like them. So, I confide too much, too quickly. I make jokes at the expense of others to get the laugh. I make a big deal of her birthday. I text her at inappropriate hours about something funny I see on TV or a passage in a book that reminds me of something we have previously discussed.

With me, there is no regal distance.

I am whoever you want me to be.

But tonight, it feels so good to be alone with Allie. It always feels good to be with her, like I am permitted to cast off my emotional buoys and float out to sea. As we fly down the West Side Highway toward Brooklyn, we talk about the usual things, but I find I am only half listening; I am desperate to confess my sins. There is something about the two of us, together in a warm car that feels safe, like a confessional. I figure that if anyone would understand the holes that I have dug for myself over the past few years, it would be Allie. Since middle school, Allie has been the least black-and-white person I have ever known, ruthless in her own ambition, and a firm believer that the ends always justify the means. She is the perfect place to stash my secrets, and yet, I cannot seem to bring myself to reveal the whole sordid story, not even to her. It stays tangled in the top of my throat. I suppose I am worried that, because Allie is on the path of the righteous with her marriage and baby on the way, my junior varsity antics will disappoint her. There is a larger part to my hesitation, however, which is I suspect that, if I string the entire tale together for a third party, it will sound far more hideous than I have, thus far, allowed myself to believe.

So, I swallow down the sourness that sloshes around my stomach and I tell her, instead, about the ridiculous things that have most recently transpired at the Lawrence apartment. This week alone, Barbara had a laser treatment that burned her face so badly that she stayed in bed for three days, barking at Marta for ice packs and aspirin, and Davis purchased a new area rug for her bedroom that cost $17,000. Over the years, I have confided in Allie about more consequential things, too, primarily because I have learned that to live too deeply inside the world of Ninety-Second Street begins to distort my thinking, and Allie provides a much-needed reality check. For example, she knows that Davis had a pill problem, and that Barbara is a nasty drunk who is still under the impression she is famous, but I don't tell her everything. I haven't told her about the night Davis got stitches in her lip, nor have I mentioned what Harry revealed to me in the parking garage, namely because I am ashamed that I did absolutely nothing with the information other than stuff it deep inside my body. Most days, I tell myself I am a better friend than Harry. I tell myself that I will deal with Barbara's misdeeds in a righteous manner when my own life is more settled, and I have a little more to give.

Right now, I reason, I shouldn't intervene: There is just too much to lose.

I look out the window. The car is driving up Smith Street. I place my fingertips on the cold glass, and watch familiar storefronts fly past like old movie reels from a happier time.

"God, I miss it here," I say.

"Really?" Allie says with surprise. "You don't seem to be looking for a new apartment."

"I know," I say. "But it's also nice not to pay rent."

"Oh." Allie laughs. "I am *pretty sure* you're paying rent."

"Fair point," I reply. "But when I do move out, *which I will*, I am coming back to this neighborhood."

"I thought you were an Upper East Side girl now," Allie says.

"Nah, I think they are onto me," I say. "Plus, everyone is like a hundred years old up there."

We drive in silence for a few blocks.

"Sometimes I am so jealous of your life," Allie says, and, at this comment, my head whips in her direction. I pantomime a shocked face.

"I'm serious." She laughs. "Don't look at me like that!"

"Why?" I am genuinely confused.

"I don't know," she says with a shrug. "I mean you have this great job and get to travel and meet all these incredible people, and I just feel like . . ." Here, she trails off. "I might as well live in, like, North Dakota or something."

"They would die for you in North Dakota," I joke, but she doesn't laugh.

"I am really scared to have this baby," she says, and her voice breaks, but only slightly. "It just makes everything feel so permanent."

"Is permanent a bad thing?" I ask gently. "I mean, sometimes I wish anything in my life was permanent."

"It's just scary," she says. "I feel like you grow up with all these questions you really want answered, like, you know: Where will I go to college? Am I going to get married? Or will I have kids or a good job or whatever, and then when you start to get the answers, it feels sad?"

I nod at her.

"I guess I didn't realize how much energy there was in the wondering," she continues. "And the answers feel kind of flat. Or final?"

"I get that," I say.

"Anyway," she says. "It's just a thing I think about sometimes lately."

The car pulls up to the restaurant.

We step onto the street.

Allie gently takes my arm and we walk together toward the door. The hard ball inside my sternum starts to loosen and fray. I find myself unsure of just how long it has been since I was wholly myself. Am I even myself when I am alone anymore, I wonder? I discover it is disconcertingly hard to say. My phone rings, and I look down at my hand: It's an unknown number. I debate ignoring the call, but something tells me to pick it up.

I answer with a roll of my eyes. Allie smiles.

"Hellllooo?" I sing.

"Hello," a man's voice says. "Is this Barbara Lawrence's daughter?"

"Excuse me?" I say, and while I am still smiling, I don't like the tone of his voice. I stop walking.

"Pardon me for calling," the man says, but his voice drops to a whisper. "But your mother asked me to call you. She has"—here, the voice pauses—"She has possibly had a *little* too much to drink, and we think someone should escort her home. To be safe, of course."

"Of course," I reply. "Where is she?"

"The St. Regis, miss," he says before adding: "Please hurry."

"Wait, why do I need to hurry?" I ask.

When there is no answer, I know the line has gone dead.

"What was that all about?" Allie asks.

"I don't know," I reply honestly. "Something is wrong with Barbara."

"Big surprise." Allie laughs sarcastically.

I look at the slim phone in my hand. It feels warm.

"I should go," I say.

"Seriously?" Allie asks. "I'm sure she can fend for herself for once in her life."

"I know," I say, but my mind is already trying to recall where in Midtown the St. Regis is located. "I'm sorry."

Allie looks down the street. Her mouth is pressed tight.

"We can go to dinner another time?" I offer. "And you should take the car home."

"Yeah, sure," she replies, but she doesn't look at me.

"Allie, I am really sorry," I say.

"You can't keep running to them every time they call you," Allie replies sharply as she pushes her hands deep into her coat pockets. "You have your own life, you know."

"Do I?" I ask.

"Just because you aren't married doesn't mean you don't have your own life," she says. "It's not like one thing is your whole identity."

This is easy for Allie to say, of course, because Allie has Patrick. Allie has a baby on the way. Allie has an apartment with a working fireplace, tenure at her university, and money in the stock market. Allie gets her teeth cleaned twice a year. Allie, dare I say it, owns her own life while I am still borrowing mine, unsure if there will ever be a lasting variation. I can't throw everything away over one stupid dinner with Allie, especially when Allie has amassed a slew of priorities that have replaced me. At least I am actually *needed* by Barbara and Davis. There is a certain point—even in freewheeling New York—where it becomes unseemly to be a single woman. People start to wonder what is wrong with you and I can feel myself inching dangerously close to the lost-and-found bin. Furthermore, while personally depressing, my marital status should, in theory, have absolutely no bearing on my career prospects. However, there comes a point for women at the magazine where not being married is a dead end. After all, how can I possibly write about the ideal—love, wealth, style, status—if I cannot attain it for myself?

It is not fair of Allie to judge me.

"I don't *run* to them," I retort, but the moment I am out of Allie's line of sight, I sprint toward a taxi idling at a red light like my life depends on it.

Because it does.

61

I call Davis several times during the long ride back to Manhattan, but, each time, it goes right to voicemail. By the time I am scrambling out of the cab in front of the St. Regis, my heart strains so painfully against my chest that I wonder if I am having some kind of stroke. I walk into the lobby, which is hushed and sparsely populated, and I lean on the wall outside the King Cole Bar for a moment to comport myself. As I fish around my handbag for lipstick, a deep voice interrupts me:

"Miss Lawrence?"

I spin around and see a man in a suit standing in the doorway. When I say nothing, he looks at me quizzically.

"Are you Davis Lawrence?" he asks.

"Yes," I say, recovering myself with a light shake of my head. "Yes."

"Your mother is back here," he says kindly.

As he leads me through a smattering of circle tables and past the enormous mural behind the bar, he speaks in hushed tones:

"She came in for a late lunch," he says. "And when her companion left, she stayed at the table. I am so sorry I didn't notice the situation earlier before things"—and here he breaks off with an uncomfortable cough—"took a turn."

"That's okay," I say, and I look around the room, but I don't see her.

"We did manage to move her to a more private area, however," he says.

We pass into a smaller restaurant space where, behind a white curtain, I see Barbara seated at a small table. She is spinning a metal cocktail stirrer around the ice in an empty rocks glass with her cheek propped up on her palm.

"Your daughter is here," the man announces with a great gentility, and Barbara looks up sleepily.

"Wonderful," Barbara drawls sarcastically. "My daughter is here."

She pulls a cigarette from her chain-mail pouch, and looks around aimlessly for her lighter, which rests on the edge of the table.

"Here," I say easily as I light the cigarette for her. She takes a hearty puff and settles back in her seat.

I look at the man with an apologetic smile.

"Would you mind calling us a car?"

"Of course," he says.

"And do you have a back entrance? I wouldn't want anyone to see her."

"Of course," he says again, and I watch as he walks in the direction on the maître d' stand.

I turn back to Barbara. She is fiddling with the neckline of her dress, and the lit cigarette comes dangerously close to the fabric. I gently move her arm away from her body, but she doesn't seem to notice.

"I've got a car coming," I say reassuringly. "Did you call Davis?"

She looks up and blinks strangely. One of her false eyelashes is partially dislodged.

"I called Davis," she spits out, and while it is clear she is angry, she is so drunk that her delivery is mostly comedic. "Ten times. But she's not picking up."

I sit down across from her at the table, and arrange my face with compassion.

"Not picking up," she repeats, but now her voice sounds like she is speaking through a mouthful of applesauce. "Not even *for her own mother.*"

When I say nothing, she takes a long drag of her cigarette and just stares at her nails with irritation.

"I didn't want her, you know," she says.

"Who?" I ask, confused.

"Davis," she replies.

"What do you mean?" I ask.

"I wanted to get an abortion," she says, and now she looks directly at me, almost as if she wants to shock me with this admission. "I was *supposed* to get an abortion. In those days, you just got an abortion because everyone said a baby would ruin your career. So you got an abortion."

Here, she shrugs and widens her eyes in such an exaggerated fashion that I almost burst out laughing because, well, this unexpected ragdoll routine is just that comic. Or rather, *it would* be, if it wasn't so sad and scary. I shush her in a way I hope communicates she is saying things she might later regret, but I am also oddly fascinated. I don't think I have ever heard the word *abortion* so many times in one conversation.

"Do you know who her father is?" Barbara asks me.

I say nothing.

"Of course, you know," she snips, and her voice is suddenly seasoned with contempt. "You know. I *bet* you know."

I stay silent, but *of course* I know the presumed identification of Davis's real father.

Everyone knows. It's been in the fucking newspaper.

"Well, I thought *her father* would leave his wife when he found out I was pregnant, but he didn't," she continues, and while now her voice is bemused, it feels forced. It's clear this memory remains a suppurating wound, picked over so many times that it has never had the chance to entirely heal.

"We were in love, you know," she continues. "Everyone likes to leave that part out of the story. Everyone just likes to say I was some kind of homewrecker."

"I'm sure," I respond nonsensically. I just want to keep her talking until the car comes. I have seen this on television. You are supposed to keep them talking. "That sounds hard."

"So I went to get an abortion because there was no point in having a baby if he wasn't going to marry me, but they said I was too far along," she says. "They said it was too late. Whoever the hell *they* were."

She looks at me like a confused child.

"Who were *they*?" she asks. "I can never remember."

"I don't know," I answer.

Somehow, this response seems to satisfy her, and she puts her head down on the table.

"Once she was born, she was so beautiful," she says, her voice muffled. "Have you seen pictures? So beautiful."

"She was beautiful," I reassure her. "She *is* beautiful."

"I flew all the way to LA to show him his baby," she continues. "I went to his house. I knocked on the door."

Here, I wince.

"I went to his house, and I knocked on his door," she repeats as she pushes herself upright with great effort. "The wife answered, you know. She was just a *housewife*. She still is a *housewife*."

Barbara spits out the word *housewife* in a tone usually reserved for terms like "child molester."

"What happened?" I ask.

"Well, he didn't leave his wife," she bitterly informs me. "I guess Davis isn't as beautiful as I thought, huh?"

"Barbara," I chide. "Shush."

"They didn't even invite me inside the house," she says bitterly. "They left me on the fucking doorstep. I was holding Davis in a blanket and standing on the *fucking doorstep*."

"That's terrible," I say.

Because it is.

The car arrives, and with the help of the maître d', I manage to help Barbara through a side door, but not without a few people on the sidewalk turning their heads in hesitant recognition. As we head uptown in silence, Barbara rests her head on the window and, after a few seconds, she seems to fall asleep. I watch her jagged breath for the entire ride, but the way her mouth hangs open unsettles me; she looks like a corpse. When we get to Ninety-Second Street, Hatch helps me get her into the hall bathroom. We prop her up over the toilet, and she immediately throws up.

"There you go," Hatch says, as he hands her a box of tissues, and I'm surprised at how calm he behaves, like he's done this a hundred times before. "You'll feel better now."

After Hatch returns to the lobby, I dash to the kitchen in search of soda or crackers, something that might help Barbara sober up, but as I stand in the pantry, she starts to cough. It doesn't sound like the sick kind of coughing; it sounds more like choking or distress. I run back toward the bathroom, and find Barbara is now splayed across the tile floor on her stomach. The back of her dress is somehow halfway unzipped, and her bra digs into the soft, freckled flesh of her back. I stand frozen in the doorway as she tries to pull herself over the side of the bathtub. She grips and pulls, but then her hands slip, and her chin smacks the porcelain. She howls in pain.

"Barbara," I gasp.

I drop to my knees and try to pull her up, but she is shockingly heavy for someone so small. I can hardly move her. As I try to get a solid grip on her body, she feels both firm and fleshy in my hands. Like a baby walrus.

She moans like I am hurting her, so I stop. I check her face, and while there is no blood, I can see a bruise starting to form under a red bump on her jawline.

"Barbara, where is Davis?" I ask, and I hear the alarm in my voice.

She says nothing.

"Davis?" I yell into the air as I struggle to unhook Barbara's arm from the tub. "Davis?"

There is no answer.

Once I manage to lay Barbara flat, I unzip the rest of her dress. Then, I peer down the darkened hall in both directions. The apartment is silent. I want to check the other rooms, but I am too afraid to leave Barbara alone, so I sit on the toilet, and place my head in my hands. My mind is racing, but my body is paralyzed.

As I had long suspected, I am entirely useless in a crisis.

"Davis," I yell out again, but now louder.

"Davis. Davis. Daaaaaa-vis," Barbara starts to mimic in a high-pitched, slurring singsong. It's hard to hear her clearly, however, because the words are muffled by her forearm. "Davis, Davis, Davis."

I slide off my perch on the toilet and sit cross-legged next to Barbara. The back of her hand is covered with slobber, and I can now see there is brown bile splashed on the tub basin. My stomach heaves unevenly, and I search for somewhere else to put my focus. I see a lone toothbrush hanging in the old wall-mount. It is pink, and I stare at it as I listen to Barbara dry heave over the floor. Finally, she stops.

"Barbara, where is Davis?" I ask gently, but I keep my eyes on the toothbrush.

"She was such a beautiful baby," Barbara says, and she lies back down on the floor.

"Mm-hmm," I mumble.

I am terrified that Barbara's heart is about to stop beating or she will choke on her own vomit or do whatever people do when they overdose. I want to fetch my phone from my handbag in the foyer and call an ambulance, but I remain afraid to leave her alone, even for a second. On the other hand, I also worry that, should this not be the life-or-death situation I presume it to be, Barbara will never forgive me for the headlines.

This is how famous people die, I think. Pride.

Correction: Pride and being surrounded by idiots.

I notice Barbara has closed her eyes.

"Barbara," I say, and shake her shoulder. "Try to stay awake, okay?"

Here, she turns her head toward me. Her black eyeliner is smudged and she has officially lost the lashes on one eye, which makes her look creepy, like she's in *A Clockwork Orange*. She looks at me for a long time.

"She always finds somebody just like you," she says finally.

"What do you mean like me?"

"Some *nobody* to worship her," she says. "She's too trusting, too stupid, and then it *all* falls apart, and I am the one who is left picking up the pieces."

This is the point of the evening where I become convinced—probably from too many made-for-TV movies in the 1980s—that Davis has been murdered by her mother, and her decapitated body is stuffed in a black trash bag somewhere in the apartment. I abandon Barbara to take panicked inventory of all the rooms in the apartment. I turn on the lights. I lie down and look under the beds. I look behind the shower curtain in Davis's bathroom. I push back the dresses in the closets.

I do not find a body.

Suddenly, I hear Captain's collar jangle and the front door slam. I run toward the foyer where I find Davis in matching workout clothes, alive and well. Her white headphones are still in her ears. Her blonde hair is pulled up in a perfect ponytail.

"What are you doing here?" she asks, as she wedges out of her sneakers. "Didn't you have dinner with Allie?"

"Where the *fuck* have you been?" I demand. "Your mom has been calling you for hours."

"I know," she says.

"You know?" I exclaim. "Why didn't you answer?"

"I took a quick walk," she says.

"You took a walk?" I bark, incredulous. "Your mother is a fucking mess, and you *took a fucking walk?*"

Davis looks at me blankly.

"She's in the bathroom," I say. "I don't know if she's drunk or took some pills, but we need to call an ambulance *now*."

Davis calmly unhooks Captain's leash, and he darts toward the kitchen. She lays her house keys and phone down on the foyer table. She unzips her jacket with an almost laughable amount of disinterest.

"I'm serious," I exclaim, and here, I flap my hands like a landing mallard. "She needs help!"

Davis removes her headphones and tucks them into the pocket of her fleece, and while I am entirely confounded by her lack of action, I am also so relieved to no longer be the responsible party that I cover my face with my hands and start to cry.

"Oh, Clo. She's *fine*," Davis responds, and despite the cool indifference of her tone, she pokes her head into the bathroom. When she turns back around, she rolls her eyes but says nothing; she only lightly motions for me to follow her into the kitchen.

I follow her.

"She didn't get the part," Davis says as she pulls a glass down from a cabinet. "She went out afterward and drank too much with God knows who, and now she's home."

"What part?" I ask. I realize my hands are shaking.

"I am not even sure this time, probably Broadway something, but she will be fine in the morning," she says. "She always is."

She fills her glass with water from the refrigerator door and takes a sip while I drop unsteadily onto the banquette. Then, Davis sits across from me with her elegant fingers wrapped around the tall glass. I don't say anything for a minute because the aftereffects of the adrenaline have left me dizzy and disoriented. I wipe my eyes on the sleeve of my coat, and Davis pushes over a box of tissues. I pull one out and blow my nose.

"Where was she this time?" Davis asks. "Wait, let me guess. The Carlyle?"

"The St. Regis," I say.

"Ah," she says with an impressed raise of her eyebrows. "That's a new one."

I must look wretched because her face softens.

"Oh, Clo. I am so sorry," she says, and she sounds genuinely sad, like I just discovered there is, in fact, no Santa Claus. "I know how much you idolize her. I didn't want you to see her like this, but I promise she will be okay."

I look at her, and I realize, maybe for the first time, the fog that has hung around her since the accident seems to have entirely lifted. Her cheeks are pinched pink, and her eyes are clear and bright. She looks radiant, albeit a few years older than the Davis I first fell in love with, but it lends her a more refined aura. As she sits there smiling, it becomes clear to me that my early arrival at the apartment was not a surprise to her; she had orchestrated the entire thing. Despite her claim to the contrary, she wanted nothing more than for me to see her mother in this condition. She wanted someone else to take the frazzled phone call from a point unknown. Someone else to find Barbara, tucked into the back of some dark bar, too drunk to get herself home. She wanted someone else to make the embarrassed apologies on her behalf. Someone else to load her into a waiting car service and to rub her back as she vomited.

She wanted someone else to be the dutiful daughter.

And, apparently, she wanted that someone to be me.

"Are you okay?" she asks finally.

"I don't know," I reply honestly. "Is this . . . normal?"

Here, Davis pulls her ponytail loose and runs her fingers through her golden hair. She offers me a rueful smile.

"Depends on how you define *normal*," she replies.

I realize I have no idea how I define *normal* anymore. Normal used to be something else entirely.

"Do you have a cigarette?" I manage weakly.

She hops up quickly and grabs a pack off the island. She flips open the top and takes one for me and one for herself, and then she lights them in that order. We take our first drags and exhale. The silence between us is tactile; I could claw it out of the air like biscuit dough.

"If I had any money, I would get the fuck out of here," Davis says finally.

"You have tons of money," I say, and this time, I don't flinch at my straightforward assessment of the obvious. "Not to mention your mom's unlimited credit card."

She looks at me with confusion as she stubs out her cigarette. I notice, with irritation, that she only took one drag.

"For 'emergencies'?" I do air quotes.

I wait for her to laugh, but she doesn't laugh. Instead, she searches my face, entirely baffled, but in a sad way. It's almost as if she cannot believe that—after *all this time* and *all this first-rate training*—there remains something fundamental about money I still don't understand.

She finishes her glass of water in a long gulp and stands up:

"Any chance you can help me put Mom in bed?" Davis asks. "I usually do it by myself when Marta isn't here, but it's a lot easier with two people."

Against any rationality, I warm at the way she says "Mom" instead of "my mom" and I stand up dutifully.

"Of course," I say.

We manage to rouse Barbara enough to walk down the hallway, and then we haul her onto the mattress together. After we get her dress off, I watch Davis gingerly strip off her pantyhose, her face set in concentration as she peels the gauzy fabric down her mother's vein-splatted legs. We pull the duvet over her naked body, and once she is settled, we look down at her for a long moment. Then Davis, with an automatic efficiency, rolls Barbara on her side and props pillows in front of her stomach and at the base of her back. She looks like a s'more, I think, and I almost make a joke until I realize it isn't funny: Davis must be arranging Barbara in this way so she doesn't choke on her own vomit, and I wonder how young (and under what horrible circumstances) Davis must have been when she was forced to learn this trick of necessity.

Davis snaps off the bedside lamp, and the room falls into complete blackness. A car alarm goes off outside. We stand unmoving, and while I cannot see Davis, I feel her energy all around me.

"Please don't tell anyone this happened," she asks. "Especially Harry."

"Of course," I say, but I realize that I have lost count of all the secrets I am supposed to be keeping for other people. We continue to stand for a while in silence.

"Do you really want to get out of here?" I ask finally.

"Yes," Davis replies without hesitation. "I've wanted to get out of here my whole fucking life."

"So what are you going to do?" I ask.

"Don't worry," she says. "I have a new plan."

62

It is only two o'clock in the afternoon, but I am rushing to leave the office because Harry called: He needs me to attend a last-minute preview at the behest of the Midwest retailer, and while he is vaguely apologetic about the inconvenience, I get the clear sense my attendance is non-negotiable. I shut down my computer, and pull on my coat, and as I skitter into the lobby, still shoving things in my handbag, I run into L.K. Smith. She is waiting for the elevator. While she makes no comment about the hour, I feel compelled to explain that my departure is *work-related*, but this unprovoked oversharing is not uncommon from me. There is something about L.K. Smith that kicks my mouth into high gear, generally to my own embarrassment or detriment, and I am baffled this affliction doesn't seem to strike the other girls, all of whom are perfectly comfortable to stand with her in complete silence.

I wonder if it's a boarding school thing.

"I have an appointment," I say with a smile.

"With whom?" she asks, which I hadn't been expecting and, thus, had no ready answer at hand.

"Ralph Lauren," I say, which is the truth.

"Why are you going to Ralph Lauren?"

She blinks at me, but I can't quite tell if her inquisitiveness is laced with suspicion or simple curiosity. Since my "promotion," I no longer split my time between fashion and culture and, as such, these types of appointments have been removed from my purview.

"Oh, I . . ."

"Shouldn't Kate's new assistant be seeing things at Ralph Lauren?" she presses. "Is it for a shoot? I'm confused."

This straightforwardness is classic L.K. Smith.

"Oh, no," I say, and I flutter my hand as we step into the elevator. "I am thinking about pitching something about him for spring, and I am just doing a little research."

"But for the fashion section?" Her eyes narrow. "We really need you to focus on bringing your section up to the level, Clo, including the website."

"Not for the fashion section," I stammer. "I mean, not *technically*, but honestly, it is probably a terrible idea."

"What is it?"

"The idea?" I feel my body start to wilt.

"Yes," she says. "What is your idea?"

"Oh," I say, and I hear my voice lilting dangerously. "I don't want to waste your time with it now, especially if it turns out to be nothing."

As the elevator descends, L.K. and I stand in a weighty silence, and when the doors ding open, she exits without a word. As I follow behind her, my mind is racing: *What does she know?* We push through the doors, and our heads swivel in search of our cars. A dispatcher holding a radio jogs toward us, his mouth drawn in a beleaguered smile. He helps L.K. to her car, and then points to mine, which is down the block. I offer her an innocent wave before I duck inside.

My hands are shaking.

As we pull into traffic, I sneak a look behind me to confirm that L.K.'s car is directly behind mine. At the end of the short street, we wait at the light and, when I see her turn signal indicates she is heading downtown (instead of uptown in the direction of Ralph Lauren), I close my eyes and lean back on the seat. *What? Did I think she was going to follow me?* Will she dispatch someone else to check up on me? In this moment, I can fully register that my life is completely out of control, but I also feel powerless, like I have screwed up so tremendously that there will never be a way out. I press my forehead against the cold glass and watch the ashen streets fly past the window, like an invisible hand shuffling a deck of cards. I no longer think it's safe to go to the appointment, nor can I imagine having to endure the performative small talk of deception, my body screaming inside a stranger's skin.

I want to disappear.

At least for a while.

Like Davis.

I lean forward and tell my driver there has been a change in plans. I ask him to take me back to the apartment on Ninety-Second Street. He looks in the rearview mirror with a minuscule nod before he turns the corner to round the block. Once we are on Park Avenue, the car moves slowly through the Midtown rush-hour traffic, and when I pull up in front of the Lawrences' building, I see, with some surprise, that Harry Wood is walking out of the lobby. I am about to crack open the door and yell for his attention, but there is something about his manner that stops me. I slink down in my seat so I can observe him unnoticed. He clutches an envelope to his chest, and he glances over his shoulder like he is worried someone is following him. I sink down further and tuck my chin into my coat.

What is he doing here?

He disappears in the direction of Madison Avenue, and when I am reasonably confident the coast is clear, I dash into the lobby.

When I get up to the apartment, Davis is in the living room; her face is slack and illuminated by the flickering blue of the television. The pink end of her freshly lit cigarette swells and recedes in the darkness.

"How was your night?" I call gaily from the doorway as a means of announcing my arrival. I coolly slide out of my coat and lay it across a chair. Then I remove my leather gloves finger by finger, just like women do in the movies when they are trying to pretend nothing is wrong.

"Fine," Davis replies, but there is a falseness to her voice that puts me on high alert.

"What did you do?" I strain to get a better look through the dense film that coats the room.

"Absolutely nothing," she says. "I just sat here and watched all kinds of garbage."

"Davis, are you *smoking*?" I ask. "I thought you quit."

"I mostly did," she says. "I just got bored."

"You know, you should invite people over from time to time," I say. "Or come out with me more."

"Yeah, I know," Davis says with a tiny shrug, but she remains transfixed by the television. "You're home early."

I linger for a beat in the doorway, curious if she will say anything about Harry, or invite me to join her under the blanket, but when she says nothing else, I go to my bedroom. As I unbutton my skirt, I dial Harry. He answers on the first ring, and I can tell by the background noise that he's walking along a busy street.

"How was your appointment?" he asks.

"I didn't go," I say.

There is a pause.

"What do you mean you *didn't go*?" he asks finally. "Did they cancel it?"

"No," I say before adding, "I just didn't show up."

"What?"

"Listen, I think people are starting to get suspicious at work."

"What do you mean?"

"There was just a thing today with L.K.," I say. "I feel like she knows something is up. She was asking questions."

"What kind of questions?" He sounds both annoyed and concerned.

"Just things," I say. "People talk, you know? I just think I should cool it."

"It's not really a great time to cool it," he says.

"Why not?"

"I am still trying to close the deal with the private equity firm," he replies. "They are right in the middle of due diligence."

"What is due diligence?"

"It's when they go through my numbers and projections," he says. "They want to make sure I am not a bad investment."

"Are you a bad investment?"

"No," he says. "But part of the appeal is having a robust advertising portfolio, and I really don't need anyone dropping out right now because you don't hold up your end of the bargain."

"My end of the bargain?" I ask, flummoxed.

"Yes," he says. "You made a deal with pretty serious people."

"What does that mean?" I ask. "Serious people?"

"Well, they have paid you a lot of money for certain expectations to be met," he says. "And I can't control them."

"Is that some kind of threat?" I ask.

"No," he says with an impatient sigh. "It's not a threat."

"It sounds like one."

"I just wonder if you aren't overreacting?" he offers.

I sit down on my bed and chew at the skin around my thumbnail. Harry always says I am overreacting, of course, but there is something unsettling in his tone tonight, something disassociated, and I know better than to pick a fight with Harry Wood without a decent plan of attack.

"Maybe I'm just tired," I say instead. "It's been a long week."

"You have to be careful, Clo."

"I know," I say. "I will call them and apologize, but we really need to discuss this arrangement."

"Okay," he says.

I pause.

"So where are you now?" I ask.

"I am walking to the bodega to get cigarettes and, quite possibly, chocolate milk."

Here, he laughs at himself like everything is normal, and I stand up and walk over to my window.

"The one by your apartment" I ask.

"Yeah," he says carefully. "Why? Are you around?"

I pull back the curtain, and look down to the street, half expecting to see Harry lurking in the shadows.

"No," I say. "I am back home."

Harry doesn't immediately respond, but I can hear the city sounds so I know we haven't been disconnected.

"Ah," he says finally. "And how are big and little Edie?"

"Fine," I say before adding, "They miss you. Davis says you haven't come by in ages."

"I know," he says. "I'm a total louse. Tell her I'll come visit this week."

63

If you have ever gone properly crazy, you understand that it is difficult, if not impossible, to pinpoint the exact moment you became an unreliable narrator to your own life. I suppose it starts with the little things: You see two people talking in a conference room and become convinced they are discussing your obvious incompetence. Your assistant loses a few pounds and starts wearing a leather jacket and, suddenly, there is no doubt she is *not only* after your job, but wildly better qualified to do it. Friends fall silent or smile too broadly when you enter the room. A colleague doesn't return your call. You are left off the list for a meeting. People are cheerfully tight-lipped about their evening plans.

Now, what can be especially disconcerting is that it's generally unclear if these troubling scenarios were always there (and, thanks to your previous confidence, you didn't notice them) or if they are, in fact, new and nefarious developments. If you have ever—even by accident—built your entire identity around a very small, very structured world, there comes a time when a thick, suffocating haze settles, and you no longer can remember that other options exist.

Once someone falls into the grip of this particular kind of insecurity, the grip of this haze, there are countless ways to cut them down, to make them feel undeserving or, even worse, remind them they are replaceable. I have learned from experience that, no matter how hard you work, there is always a way to be not good enough, and that paranoia is like English Ivy, invasive in ways from which is it nearly impossible to recover. It grows slowly—perhaps a fragile sprout will stretch through the warm soil and blink in the light—but with the proper care, those seeds can grow up tall and strong.

They can spread like wildfire.

They can block out the light.

It can make even the most level-headed of people do irrational, dangerous, stupid things.

64

Harry has gone missing again, and while I am familiar with his absences, this one feels different, although I can't say why. It's only been two days, which is standard, but I still find myself regularly refreshing my email at work between meetings, wondering when he will resurface and, more pressingly, if this particular walkabout doesn't somehow pertain to my recent insubordination. When my desk phone rings in the afternoon, I glance hopefully at the number on the little screen, but it isn't Harry. It is one of my writers. I can hear Sarah answer, and when she comes into my office to announce the caller, I silently shake my head.

I can't talk to any writers right now.

You see, when I was awarded Isobel's title, albeit on a probationary basis, I thought the transition would be a simple one. After all, I had known her stable of writers for years, and so it made sense that of all the people at the magazine, I would be the person to take up her illustrious mantle, even just for ease and continuity. However, the writers do not seem to see it that way. Instead, they are appalled and offended that someone they perceive as "junior" is now the person badgering them about their deadlines or trying to shuffle around their sentences. They wonder aloud why we didn't poach someone from *British Vogue* or the Arts and Culture section of the *New York Times.* They complain about the recent reduction in word counts, an unfortunate reality that, of course, has nothing to do with me. They go on to grouse about how nothing is shot on location anymore. They sigh when I tell them their choice of hotel is no longer approved by corporate. When I reject their ideas, they never take it up with me. Instead, they call L.K. Smith, and have a conniption fit of epic proportions. They hang up on me when I ask them if they will write a story for the website. They will condescend to me—to great effect—over a comma being added or a sentence being cut.

But who can blame them?

I used to be the girl who booked their plane tickets, including their upgrade requests and fabricated dietary restrictions. I used to procure their envelopes full of petty cash and send them confirmation numbers for car services and pedicures. Perception aside, however, it's become clear to me that I also, unfortunately, don't possess the magic Isobel seemed to wield with ease. I wanted to be good at this job. I wanted to be respected by the people that I have idolized for so long, but I worry—as I struggle to remember what, exactly, to do with punctuation around a clause—that I have overinflated my abilities. *They will settle*, L.K. assures me, but I am not convinced. Each morning, I am confronted by a new pile of rejections from our editor-in-chief—stories killed, headlines redlined, and my personal favorite, a pitch I submitted which was returned to me with the word *banal* written across the top in capital letters.

I tacked that one on my bulletin board.

Around four o'clock, I tell Sarah I am going to take a quick walk.

I say I want to clear my head.

When I get down to the street, I duck into an abandoned storefront and light up a cigarette. Where I stand reeks of urine, but I can't move out into the open because it is no longer appropriate to smoke on the sidewalk. Cigarettes, once the most sophisticated and cinematic accessory a girl could wield, have been relegated to the trashy masses, and while I understand smoking can kill you, I find myself longing for the days when we were too young to care about what might kill us.

With my free thumb, I dial Harry for the third time today, but when he doesn't answer, I don't leave a voicemail. I hang up and am about to tuck my phone in my pocket when it vibrates in my hand. I don't even look at the screen before I slap it to my ear:

"You've been a hard man to track down," I say.

"Clo?" a familiar voice says. "It's Allie."

"Oh, hey," I say. I flick the butt of my half-smoked cigarette to the ground.

"Who is a hard man to track down?" she asks.

"What?" I ask. I pinch the bridge of my nose and squeeze my eyes shut; I try to put my thoughts in order.

"Who is 'a hard man to track down'?" Allie repeats.

"Oh, I am just waiting on a quote from this designer..." I begin before I trail off. "What's up?"

"Well, I am sure you are busy tonight, but our babysitter just canceled, and I thought *maybe* you might want to watch your goddaughter for a few hours?"

"When?"

"Tonight? Like at seven? I know this is a long shot, but we wanted to go to dinner."

"Sure."

"Sure?" she repeats like she misheard me.

"Yeah, sure. Why not?" I say, and Allie squeals. She hollers the good news to Patrick, the simple sound of which makes my chest constrict. The degree to which I long to holler good news to someone of the opposite sex really cannot be overestimated at this stage of my life.

I go upstairs and finish off my workday with no word from Harry. I bid Sarah a good night, but as I walk toward the subway, the punchy, dislocated chaos of Times Square does little to assuage my rippling anxiety. By the time I get out of the subway on Ninety-Sixth Street (Allie moved to the Upper West Side when the baby was born), I am awash in a thousand new conspiracy theories about what, if anything, is going on with Harry Wood. The truth is I am desperate to avoid the most obvious one, which is that I have made it easy for him to hold something over me, should holding something over me be what he desires. Miserably, I head in the direction of Allie's apartment on Riverside Drive, but I only make it a block before I decide to make a quick pitstop in the first run-down-looking Irish bar I pass on my route. As I enter the dark space, I rationalize this choice is downright artistic of me. After all, isn't this what journalists do? Don't they explore their city? Don't they share a drink with its denizens? Why, I feel just like Joseph Mitchell, certain whatever interesting person I meet tonight will someday make the subject of a fascinating little article for which I will be rightfully lauded. I settle on a tippy wooden stool at the bar and order a vodka on the rocks with lemon; I don't want to waste any time with soda or tonic. I try to start a conversation with the middle-aged man next to me, but he mostly watches a basketball game as he plows through a few bottles of Coors Light. There used to be a time when I could make an old guy like that turn away from a basketball game, but aside from a few grunts and niceties, he pays me no mind. Furthermore, he does not provide me any interesting anecdotes. As I sip my drink, I can't help but wonder if my looks, such as they are, have faded more than I might allow myself to admit. I finish the drink in less than five minutes. I leave a twenty on the bar.

    I continue down the sidewalk, but all the lights burn a little bit brighter now.

65

Despite my detour, I arrive right on time to babysit for Allie and Patrick, which, even in my agitated state, makes me feel that, by dint of my punctuality, I am not an entirely lost cause. Allie is clearly giddy to be getting out of the house. So giddy, in fact, that she gives me only the briefest rundown of the essentials (bottle in fridge, video monitor on coffee table) and assures me it will be a quiet night. Apparently, her daughter Penelope (known colloquially as Penny) *never* wakes up in the middle of the night. She is only five months old, but Allie can safely say that it's "not in her nature."

I assure them that all will be fine, and I shuffle them—like the kindly spinster aunt I am—out the door for their dinner.

"Have fun, kids," I say, and then I close the door, lock it, and head back to the living room to watch TV.

Allie's apartment is nice. It's not as spacious as the Lawrence apartment, of course, but it also feels less claustrophobic. It's a pre-war building so it has high ceilings, ornate molding, and two proper bedrooms. It also has real furniture (albeit matching and from Pottery Barn, which feels disappointingly off-brand for Allie) and a working fireplace, the mantel of which is lined with framed photographs of Allie and Patrick. As I examine the display of pictures more closely, my sternum pulls earthward as if it is weighted down by some imaginary stone. I have no idea what it might feel like to mingle my life with another person. The biggest photograph on display is a beautiful black-and-white candid from their wedding reception. Allie looks so happy in her strapless dress and Patrick—the dull idiot that he is—looks handsome. I must say, I put on a brilliant job at that wedding. Not that anything less than a brilliant performance was expected at the wedding of my very best friend. My parents were in attendance as were our childhood friends and New York friends and, despite being one of the only girls without a date, I was smiling and gracious in my blue Vera Wang dress. I didn't make eye contact with anyone for the entire day, fearful a single knowing glance would dissolve me entirely, and I waited until I got off the shuttle bus to cry in the bushes that lined the vast parking lot of the cheap hotel chain where there had been a block of rooms.

I turn away from the mantel and flop on the couch. I turn on the television and put my feet up on a leather ottoman. *This feels nice*, I think, but after ten minutes of domestic bliss, I get restless. I check my phone. I change the channel. I flip through a magazine. I look through Allie's medicine cabinet for a tweezer. I poke around her bedroom. Finally, when I can no longer stand being in my own body, I open the refrigerator in search of wine. My vodka buzz is dulling, and I just need a quick top-off. I am relieved when I find an open bottle of chardonnay with about a glass left. I figure Allie won't mind. However, when that glass goes down too quickly, I return to the kitchen in search of another bottle. I find two bottles of red on the counter, and I decide to open the one with the less expensive-looking label. I can always replace it tomorrow, I reason, as I easily locate the corkscrew nestled in Allie's wonderfully wide silverware drawer. I stand over it for a moment and tick down its contents: four different sizes of spoon, three kinds of fork, three kinds of knife.

This drawer makes me miserable.

I retreat to the couch with the bottle and new glass. I pick up the video monitor: All I can make out through the grainy, ghostly haze is a lumpy, motionless pile.

I take a long gulp from my glass.

I don't usually like red wine, but this one is wonderfully sharp and spicy, so I pour myself a little more. I check Facebook on my phone. I pop a bag of popcorn and freeze in horror when the microwave beeps. I have no idea what sounds wake up a baby, but Penny, bless her heart, stays quiet. Back in the living room, I shovel popcorn into my mouth and sloppily answer a few work emails, which I know I shouldn't do at this hour, and especially on my phone after a few drinks, but my new iPhone makes this urge nearly impossible to resist. I softball texts out to my friends, including Harry, who continues to be suspiciously unresponsive. I change the channel again, and I try to recall the time in my life when I could watch a TV show and be totally immersed. Now, television feels too slow. It doesn't feel like enough.

Nothing feels like enough.

I pour another glass of wine, and I pick up my phone again. I call Davis, and when she doesn't answer, I call the apartment.

Marta answers on the first ring.

"Hi, Marta," I say. "Can I talk to Davis?"

"She's not here," Marta says. "She went out a few hours ago."

"Ah," I say. "Do you know where she went?"

"I don't know," Marta says. "I just know she was all dressed up."

"Okay," I say, but I sit up straighter on the couch. "Can you let her know I called?"

After I hang up, I go to Facebook, which I was loathe to download for this exact reason, and I look up Harry's profile, thinking maybe it will provide me with some clues. I am surprised to see he has posted a new image of himself wearing a tuxedo. When I look at the image closer, I realize that he is holding someone's hand, but the woman (and I can tell it's a woman because her short nails are painted cherry red) is cut out of the frame. Her arm is thin and pale, and on her wrist hangs a gold Cartier bracelet, which is the same bracelet Davis has worn all the days I have known her. It was a gift from her mother on her thirteenth birthday. Apparently, it had to be screwed on at the store on Fifth Avenue, and while Davis got the bracelet, it was Barbara who kept the screwdriver.

Everything stops.

I think about Davis's increased absences from the apartment, and the new clothes that recently arrived from Bergdorf Goodman via messenger. There is also the running regime and closed-door phone calls. The two empty glasses of wine, Harry sneaking out of the apartment. It all starts to bind together in my head, like a fresh cone of cotton candy.

Something is going on behind my back.

I look back down at the picture. Harry mentions the location in his caption. It's a newly opened high-end hotel bar on the Lower East Side, which, geographically speaking, is as far away from Allie's apartment as possible while remaining on the island of Manhattan. I glance down at the monitor. The baby hasn't moved an inch. I gulp down the rest of my glass of wine in one warm mouthful. I pull on my coat.

When I get down to the lobby, I find an elementary school–aged girl doing jerky, inelegant laps across the tile floor in pink roller skates with giant pom-poms affixed to the laces. She wears kneepads and a unicorn helmet, and the doorman pays her no mind. Her shirt says: WE SHOULD ALL BE FEMINISTS.

Good luck with that, I think.

"Hey," I call out, and I clap to get her attention. She flings her skinny body against the wall to stop. The doorman looks up from his copy of the *Daily News*.

"Me?" she asks.

"Yeah. You. Do you babysit?"

Her little gap-toothed mouth breaks into a gigantic smile.

When I get out of the cab on Delancey Street thirty minutes later, I slam the door with such force that the small group of early twenty-somethings turns to look at me wide-eyed, like I should apologize for bothering them. I say nothing. In fact, I cannot discern anything distinct about any one person in the mix as I walk past them; I only see a blur of bodies and hear the hum of their late-night chatter. The air feels colder than it did uptown, and the night sky, more caliginous. There is a short line outside, but I bypass it with such aloof swiftness that the man who works the door looks at me twice, but he does nothing to prevent my entrance.

I am the right kind of girl.

Once inside, I am surprised to discover this establishment is more of a lounge, and the space is loud and dark, which serves only to magnify my intoxication. The walls are painted a robin's-egg blue, and there are potted plants and clusters of threadbare couches. As I look around, I marvel that I used to find this sort of place appealing or, even more absurd, promising. The corners are hazy with smoke, which is something you never see these days. I realize it must be coming from various vape pens, the aesthetics of which I will never understand: Everyone looks ridiculous, like they are tooting into a contraband kazoo. As for the patrons of this party, the girls all have long hair, parted down the middle, and no bangs. They wear skinny jeans, tall black boots, and blazers, and they bob straws in vodka sodas as they subtly appraise the competition. If you ever desire to differentiate between female species in the wild, you only need to know this: Well-bred girls don't fidget. They move with an equanimous, happy confidence through a world in which trains never get delayed, and the guy *always* calls. The lesser girls are more ill at ease. They exist in a state of constant motion, as if some combination of repetitive tasks will dilute the thick solution of desperation that chugs through their unworthy bodies. They fiddle with their expensive handbags. They pick at the place where their shirt is tucked into their jeans. They check their phones. They reapply lip gloss. They laugh at nothing, and just a little too loud. I know this performance all too well. These motions are the hopeful overture to New York's most beloved romantic fable, which is that your life will change—for the better, of course—in an instant, when you meet the man who will become your husband at a bar in New York. What they *don't* know—what I didn't know—is that you can burn through an entire decade in search of a single night. I want to tell these girls to go home, that their future is not, in fact, standing somewhere in this bar, but I don't.

They must learn the hard lessons themselves.

I gently navigate my way through the crowd in search of Harry and Davis, although I am entirely unsure of what I will do when I discover them: Will I act happily surprised? Or bubble over with fury? Will I accuse them of something? If so, what? And, while I cannot fathom what I will say, I know for a *fact* they are in this bar. I can feel it in the gristle of my bones. I keep pressing through bodies, over and over, but with each subsequent second, my search feels more frantic than the last. I am grateful, as always, for my height as it gives me a better view of the room, but as I devour the space, inch by inch, I grow increasingly agitated that I have failed to locate them. After a few wrong turns, I find a set of stairs, and I race up them, two at a time, to the second floor. The bar has no line, so I order a glass of white wine. I rationalize that it must look weird, stomping around empty-handed, but the truth is that I feel tired, and I hope that another drink will restore my energy and confidence. Glass in hand, I continue to scour the space, but—just like in the movies—the walls start to contract and expand like a funhouse mirror. I quickly forget where the stairs are located, but I see a bathroom in the far corner. I go inside, and when I don't *see* Davis, I call out her name like there is an emergency. The girl putting on lipstick over the sink stops to look at me.

"Are you okay?" she asks. She looks concerned, but also a little repulsed. I worry she thinks I am one of those middle-aged ladies from the suburbs who has come to spend the night with her girlfriends in a going-out top and I feel myself die a little inside.

"I'm fine," I say, but as I turn to walk out, my heel nicks on something unseen, and I fall, fast and hard, onto the wooden floor. I catch myself with my hands, but the side of my head smacks against the wall. My wineglass shatters, and the pieces skitter wildly across the floor.

"Holy shit," I hear the girl say. She runs over to me.

"Are you okay?" she asks, and in my humiliated haste to get up, I bang into her. She holds me by the elbow with one hand.

"Careful," she says kindly. "Careful."

Once I am on my feet, I shake her loose. I don't need her help.

"I am fine," I snap. "I just tripped over the step."

We both look down at the floor. There is no step, of course, but the girl nods reassuringly as she steals a peek over my shoulder.

She's clearly looking for assistance.

Or an escape hatch. Or a witness.

I can't tell.

"I am just looking for my friends from the magazine," I say, as if this piece of information will allow her to place me in some kind of imaginary cool quadrant, but when she only nods with sympathetic concern, I start another unsteady pass of the room. I am certain I overlooked some tidy nook in which Davis and Harry are tucked away, but when I don't find them, I start to doubt myself. *Why is nobody wearing tuxedos?* I wonder. I squeeze my eyes closed and try to think clearly: Do I have the wrong bar? Or, even more worrisome, the wrong night? I had forgotten that Harry would *never* post a picture on his Facebook page that he hasn't had sufficient time to Photoshop. *How would he do that if he was still at the party?* I think. I try to remember the other parties happening this week, but my mind is entirely empty. I have started to feel dizzy. I start to search for the exit, a cold sweat collecting on my lower back, and when I finally stumble, gasping for air, onto the sidewalk, I see that my palms are bleeding. I look more closely and see there is a small sliver of glass arcing out of the fat of my thumb. I pull it out with my teeth and press my hand against my shirt, which is warm with perspiration. I raise my free hand and flag the first passing cab.

When I am about five blocks from Allie's apartment, I look down at my phone for the tenth time to confirm, with some relief, that it is not yet ten o'clock. Allie is not due home until closer to eleven, but I bounce my toes and drum on my thighs with a gagging anxiety every time we hit a red light. I am certain my sides will split open from the pressure that is building inside me, and when we finally reach her block, I ask the driver to drop me at the corner. I reason this will make my reentry less obvious, but to whom, I am not sure. I pay the fare with my credit card, and sprint down the block and up the short flight of wide stairs into the lobby.

The doorman is still reading the *Daily News*. I take this as a good sign.

After I wait an intolerable minute for the single elevator carriage to return to the lobby, I decide to take the steps. I only make it two floors before I hear a baby screaming. The noise is unmistakable; it is shrill, and it bounces off the concrete walls like a police siren. I race up the last two flights, burst into the hallway, and dart in the direction of Allie's apartment. There is a woman standing in her open doorway with her arms folded, but I don't stop. I turn the knob, which I dimly realize is unlocked, and run directly into Allie. She's in her coat and hat and she holds Penny, who is nearly purple from screaming, in her arms.

I freeze.

"Where the *fuck* have you been?" Allie demands, but her voice is full of a fury so potent that it knocks the wind out of me. I stand with my hands on my chest, completely unable to move, and my coat, which is wide open, feels buttoned up too tight.

"Answer me!" she screams when I don't respond. "We got home twenty minutes ago, and the apartment was empty. The door was unlocked. Penny was just screaming in her crib."

Here, her voice catches, and she starts to cry. It's almost as if, by saying it out loud, she made the unthinkable true. I swell with tenderness: Allie does not want this to be true. Allie wants to believe in me.

"I...I had to run out," I stammer. "But Penny was sleeping, and I was just going to be a few minutes. You said she never woke up?"

"So you just left her alone?"

"No," I protest. "I left her with the kid next door. I paid her twenty bucks."

Allie's eyes flash with an incredulous confusion, and the sky breaks open. I suddenly understand how completely insane that sounds, but I also think that—in this exact moment—that if I spin the perfect lie, I can get out of it.

"What *kid next door?*" Allie demands.

My hands ball at my flanks, and I feel the blood drain out of my cheeks. I have gone entirely blank; I cannot remember the name of the kid on the roller skates. Alex? Liz? Erin? This is the moment I see Patrick. He glares from the doorway, and his wide chest heaves in a way that frightens me; if I were a man, he would have already beaten the ever-living shit out of me.

"I don't remember her name," I admit finally, and the shame overtakes me, hot as an oven.

"Lily?" she offers.

"Yes, Lily!" I exclaim. I smile, as if the problem has been solved.

"Lily is seven years old!"

"Oh."

I want to explain myself but can't think straight. I am battered in a sea of Penny's screeching cries and my own thundering heart. I watch in a kind of slow motion as Allie's eyes fall to the coffee table in front of her couch, which is still littered with my drunken detritus: There are two empty bottles of wine, a few empty glasses, and popcorn is scattered along the carpet. The television is still on.

"Are you *drunk?*" she demands.

I don't think I am drunk, but I don't respond. I am not entirely sure I can assess my own level of inebriation.

"What the *fuck* is wrong with you, Clo," she hisses. "How much did you drink?"

"I didn't drink that much." I try to state these words as clearly as possible, if only to regain some footing, but I can tell I am failing. "I am not drunk."

"Patrick was about to call the police."

"The police?" I exclaim, genuinely confused. "No, you don't understand!"

"What is there to understand? You left my five-month-old daughter alone," she screams. "You're fucking wasted."

"There was a work emergency, and..."

"What?" Allie demands. "What *emergency?*"

All the noise reactivates little Penny, who had just started to settle. She starts to screech, and Allie turns her eyes to her child.

"Clo, you need to leave," she says, but she does not look at me.

"No, please," I plead. I move toward Allie, but she takes a protective step backward. She holds Penny tighter to her chest, and her eyes flicker with fear, like she's terrified I am going to snatch her baby. "Allie, listen. You don't understand."

Allie looks at me strangely, and then her eyes widen:

"Do you have blood on you?" she cries out, and Patrick straightens up. "Is that blood?"

I look down and see there are a few large spots of blood on my silk shirt. I look down at my palms, which are now caked with dirt and dried blood.

"Get out," Allie screams. "Get out!"

"Allie," I say. "Let me explain."

"Get the fuck out of our house," Patrick interjects, and his voice is so loud and terrifying that, without warning, I start to cry. They are frightened tears. Patrick yanks open the front door and points to the hallway where a handful of concerned neighbors have gathered in silent, shocked reproach. Patrick's hands shake, and I begin to absorb the seriousness of the situation. "Get the fuck out of our house and don't you *ever* come back."

I turn around to look at Allie in desperation. Surely, she will call him off, if not to preserve our lifelong friendship, then to punish Patrick for this wholly unimaginative dialogue: *And don't you ever come back?* Isn't this banality from Patrick the *exact* thing that makes her occasionally question her marriage in the first place? But Allie doesn't intervene: She bounces poor Penny gently, whispering into her translucent, little baby ear. *Hush.*

"Allie?" I whimper.

But Allie, my Allie, she does not look up.

I have zero recollection of walking through the mob of angry neighbors or riding the elevator, no memory of passing the doorman in the cavernous, art deco lobby or making a left off One Hundred First Street. I don't recall cars or traffic lights or the sound of my own breath. I regain consciousness, such as it is, in the middle of Central Park. It is pitch-black, and the wind channels sharply down the manicured pathways; it sears any skin that is unprotected, like my neck and wrists. I know it is not safe to be in the middle of Central Park alone at this hour, but I also don't care if anything bad happens to me. In fact, I hope something bad happens to me, something truly terrible. If something happens to me, everyone will have to forgive me, right? I think back to Davis in her hospital bed all those years ago—all tubes and monitors, bruises, and swabs—and I wish it upon myself. I close my eyes and move my lips in a silent prayer, and I am just drunk enough to believe I can manifest my own demise. I stand there for a long time, but nothing happens, no violation or tragedy befalls me. I even make a few girlish noises to sound like easy prey, but the park stays silent. The bushes don't even rustle with menace. Finally, I put my head down and allow my feet to continue eastward. My coat is open, and the hem waffles in the wind.

When I get home, I discover with some surprise that Davis is sleeping in my bed. I have no feeling in my hands or feet, and as I undress clumsily, she stirs in the darkness.

"Clo?" she murmurs. "Is that you?"

"Yeah," I say.

"You woke me up," she whines, but, as always, it sounds playful and sweet. I feel compelled to comfort her, but I fight the impulse. She is the enemy now, I decide. I throw my bra on the floor. I pull on a nightgown. I think about saying something about my suspicions until I realize they have yet to congeal into a coherent accusation, let alone a fair one. When I get into bed, Davis sits up halfway to adjust her pillow.

"I tried to call you," she says.

"You did?"

"My mom got a job," she whispers. Her eyes are glistening and intense, like a child who wants my approval. "I took her out for drinks to celebrate."

"What do you mean your mom got a job?"

"She's going to be the star of a new play," she says. She shakes the pillow and lays her head back down. "On Broadway. It's a musical revival. A big one."

I am about to say something when Davis lays her perfect hand across the top of the duvet. It is there, in the half-light of a most terrible night, that I see Davis Lawrence's nails are not, in fact, painted red.

They are bare and buffed up to a seashell shine.

66

In the months leading up to the previews for Barbara's show, there is rarely a time when the apartment is not filled with people. There are assistants and press agents, stylists and voice coaches, and there is even someone who stretches Barbara's body after rehearsal each day. She takes dance classes in the mornings and has rehearsal downtown every afternoon.

Overall, Barbara appears to take these changes in stride, which baffles me until I remember that Barbara Lawrence used to be a major Broadway star. I had only had the pleasure of being acquainted with the Barbara Lawrence who was rich, but mostly washed-up, stomping her foot when she was denied the good table at Michael's. My Barbara Lawrence spent her days furiously shaking the trees in the hope some acorn of recognition would fall into her greedily upturned hand. But now that new Barbara (or *old* Barbara) has been returned to her rightful perch, she is positively magnanimous to everyone who enters the apartment. She is punctual for rehearsal. She practices her lines. She gargles salt water. She ices her shoulder. She doesn't drink unless she has the day off and, even then, one skimpy little martini suddenly seems to suffice. She goes to bed on time with a silk eye mask strapped to her professionally plumped and blasted face. She loses ten pounds. She sings in the shower.

I notice, however, that, as Barbara grows bigger and stronger, Davis slips deeper into the shadows. She seems fearful that one false step will siphon the attention away from her mother, and she refuses to take that risk. She is often absent from the apartment, and when she is called upon to make an appearance, it looks as if she put a great deal of effort into looking unattractive or, at the very least, plain. She wears her glasses and oversized sweatshirts, and while she is polite to everyone in Barbara's orbit, she says very little about herself.

As for me, I observe everything from the edges because, while nobody has made an explicit comment, I suspect, courtesy of this reversal of fortune, I am officially taking too much space in the apartment. To make myself smaller, I tidy up the bathroom, consolidating my items to one drawer, and make sure I don't leave clothes or books laying around in the common rooms. I spend a lot of time at the office or attending events, hoping, in some way, I will be forgotten. I know I have overstayed my welcome, but every time I start to think about my fate, I stop. It's too impossible to contemplate.

Furthermore, and if I am being honest, there is something else that is keeping me in the apartment. Since Barbara's casting, Harry has started to make more regular appearances, and I am not willing to cede my territory to someone who, in my opinion, is only a reliable friend to Davis when there is something in it for him. One night, when I walk into the kitchen after work, I find Davis and Harry eating sushi out of takeout containers and drinking wine. There are some papers and notebooks between them, and when Davis sees me, she gently closes one and smiles:

"We ordered extra for you," she says, pointing to the tray of sushi.

"Thanks," I manage.

"Did you know that Harry just *bought* a new apartment?" she says.

Here, Harry smiles.

"You did?" I ask, confused as to where he got the money for a new apartment considering I just paid our last dinner tab. "Where?"

"Great Jones Street?" he says.

"Downtown?" I say with surprise. "I never thought I'd see the day."

"Please." He laughs. "It's closer to the office, and it was *definitely* time to get out of my shithole apartment."

"You should see it," Davis says as she pops a roll of sushi in her mouth. "It's absolutely enormous."

"Then, I want to see it," I say amiably, but all I can think is: *When did Davis see the apartment?*

"I am going to throw a housewarming party," Harry says.

"After opening night, please," Davis deadpans. "I'd like to live to see another birthday."

"After opening night." Harry laughs. "And I'll expect you both to be there."

A week before opening night, Davis shows me where her mother hides the "good" jewelry. It is not locked in a safe hidden behind an oil portrait of one of Barbara's forebears, as I had long suspected, but rather it is in Davis's closet, stuffed inside a kid's gym bag from the 1980s. The nylon bag, which is green with rainbow straps, sits along a pile of nubby stuffed animals, extra blankets, and a graying collection of Cabbage Patch Kid dolls.

"Why does she keep this in your *closet?*" I ask, horrified, as Davis pulls the bag out of the pile.

It turns out that the apartment was robbed when Davis was in elementary school, and the only room that wasn't ransacked was hers, as it was, clearly, a child's room. Even the safe had been opened, and its valuable contents (she doesn't elaborate) were never recovered so, as a result, Barbara relocated all her sensitive documents and expensive material to Davis's closet. So, this explains why Davis's room is still papered in little pink flowers and why there are dolls artfully arranged on an untouched wooden rocking chair in the corner. It's funny: What I assumed was Barbara's unhealthy reluctance to let her only child grow up is just a ruse to keep her fine jewelry collection and notarized copy of her will away from burglars.

There has *got* to be a metaphor in there somewhere.

"Shall we take a look?" Davis asks.

She unzips the bag, which is crammed with black velvet and cream sateen boxes, and the jumble spills forth like a sea full of icebergs. She dumps the contents out on her pink comforter.

"We'll need something to wear to the premiere, right?" she says.

As Davis balls her hair on the top of her head with a tie, her shirt rises a few inches, revealing a deliciously flat stomach. She has taken up yoga and she recently started wearing a stack of colorful crystal bracelets on her left wrist; they clatter as she moves her long arms. Intellectually, I find this choice of accessory to be disappointing, but they look so elegant on Davis that I have debated, on occasion, buying a few for myself.

"Ready?" she says.

We greedily start to snap open the boxes. There are real pearl necklaces draped on black velvet, diamond drop earrings affixed in satin cases, and handfuls of gem-laden necklaces. There are at least two dozen rings sunk with emeralds, rubies, sapphires, and onyx, each one more enormous than the next, and a brooch shaped like a harp with diamonds dotting the strings. Davis shows me a pendant that is shaped like a frog at rest upon a bejeweled lily pad, and there is even an art deco–style headband composed of thousands of teeny-tiny little diamonds. There are proper tennis bracelets, Cartier and Rolex watches, and generations worth of gold signet rings and plain wedding bands.

We start to unhook the jewelry, piece by piece, and lay it out on the bedspread for closer inspection. We face each other with our legs crossed and heads down like two children playing cards, but we need to keep scooting back to make room on the bed. The boxes, and the attendant baubles they contain, seem endless.

After we sit together in awed silence for a while, Davis proposes that we try on our favorite pieces, which I, of course, was hoping she would suggest.

The first thing I choose is a pair of diamond clip-on earrings. I hold them up to the midday light before I clamp them onto my tender lobes. Next, I parse through a pile of ring boxes. As we continue to sort and experiment, we continuously hop off the bed to see how we look in a long mirror before we scurry back to try on something else.

At a certain point, I am wearing so much jewelry that I feel legitimately weighted down; my earlobes stretch under the weight of a pair of diamond chandelier earrings and my knuckles are swollen from trying on so many rings.

Davis plucks the biggest tiara off her bedspread. She places it on her head and walks to the mirror where she adjusts it gingerly. I watch her from behind.

Once she has affixed it low along the top of her forehead, like a flapper, she turns to face me. All I can think is, for the first time in a long time, she looks exactly like the old Davis Lawrence.

"What do you think?" she asks.

"I think you look like a blonde Cleopatra," I reply agreeably.

She turns to regard herself one more time, and then she sits back down on the bed. She picks at the edge of a necklace, frowning slightly.

"Everything okay?" I ask, but I find myself feeling apprehensive. I wonder if she is going to inquire about the diamond earrings her mother gave me, which, at least thus far, I have kept a secret.

"I'm fine," she responds, but her voice sounds a little nervous. "There is just something I've been wanting to tell you."

I turn toward her, but before she can say anything, we hear the unmistakable slam of the front door.

Davis leaps up off the bed.

"Shit," she hisses, and her eyes flash. "She's back early. Quick, help me clean this up before my mom sees it."

I must not move because she smacks her hand on the bedspread.

"Hurry!" she growls, and I leap to my feet as Davis starts throwing boxes into the gym bag. "I am not allowed to play with the stuff in the closet."

As I pull off one of Barbara's rings and shove it back into the velvet valley of its tiny box, I can't understand why Davis isn't allowed to touch things in her own closet. Even her phrasing—*I am not allowed to play*—is strange. It sounds like something you might say to a careless, grubby-handed toddler, sure, but not a full-grown adult. Nevertheless, I swiftly snap off my earrings and I draw a necklace over my head. However, there is one ring that I cannot get off—a beautiful diamond and aquamarine number—but it's small so I spin it around and hide in my fist. I'll rub soap on it later, I think, as I pinch pairs of earrings off the bedspread and drop them safely into their satin bags. I look over at Davis. Her neck is red and her hands shake as she tries, without success, to clasp a triple-strand pearl necklace back into a flat box. Finally, she gives up and shuffles the remaining boxes inside the gym bag. She pulls the zipper closed and kicks the entire collection off the far side of the bed with her bare foot just as the door swings open.

It's Barbara.

"Hi, girls," Barbara says, but despite her movie-star smile, it's clear she thinks we are up to something. Her hair is pulled back in a tight band and spiked with bobby pins, and her lined face is caked in stage makeup, which, up close, looks at least two shades too dark. I watch her brown eyes dart with great suspicion around the room, but I can't really blame her. After all, Davis and I stand shoulder to shoulder with our hands clasped behind our backs like two naughty children.

She narrows her eyes.

"What are you two *doing* in here?" she inquires.

"Just chatting," Davis says sweetly.

"Okay," Barbara responds slowly. "I am going to change my clothes, but let's meet in the kitchen in ten minutes for dinner?"

"Yep," Davis says. "Be right there!"

Barbara walks out of the room, but she does not close the door. I look over to Davis, and she stares down at the pink carpet.

"Davis?" I ask.

But she doesn't answer me.

She just walks out the room.

Once Davis is gone, I sit down on the bed and twist the ring stuck on my finger, but it won't budge. Someone told me that Windex makes a good lubricant, but I'm not sure this is the right moment to rifle around the laundry room in search of cleaning supplies, especially because I am not even entirely sure what just happened. After a few minutes, I start to hear more voices ring through the apartment: Barbara's entourage has arrived. I roll over and dig through Davis's nightstand in search of one of her fancy tubes of lotion, which I slather on my finger before I pull at the ring again. This time it slides off, but too quickly. I watch it bounce along the pink carpet before it disappears under the bed. I drop down on my knees and stretch my arms to retrieve it. Then, I crawl over the gym bag, which lays on it side behind the bed. I put the ring inside its box, and then I give the bag a quick once-over, just to make sure everything is neatly in its place before I zip it up again. As I put the bag back in the closet, I discover large carboard boxes, all sitting in a row, tucked behind Davis's lower row of pants and skirts. The boxes are marked PRIVATE in large letters, which, naturally, makes me curious, especially in the aftermath of Davis's revelation that the closet was off-limits. I glance toward the door. The voices are now faraway in the kitchen, so I walk across the room. I close the door and softly turn the lock. I listen for a few seconds before I return to the closet. If anyone knocks, I reason, I can just say I was changing my clothes. I get back down on my knees, and I pull one of the boxes toward me. I lift off the lid and set it gently on the carpet. I look inside. The box is filled with standard files, and the tab of each folder is labeled in Barbara's distinctive handwriting. The categories are both expected (tax returns, bank statements, pay stubs, insurance information) and less expected, but sort of charming (copies of Davis's college applications, thirteen years of private school report cards, a hand-painted Mother's Day card from 1989). I feel a little disappointed, although I don't know what I was expecting to find. In the second box, there is a neat row of black three-ring binders, their spines neatly labeled with dates. I pull out the binder labeled 1990–2000 and open the cover. It contains sheets and sheets of Barbara's blank checks, all of which are printed—as all checks are printed—with both her bank number and her routing number along the bottom. My spine snaps straight. I wonder if there is any way I can use this information to deposit the money I have saved into one of Barbara's accounts. I leap to my feet and grab a pen and piece of paper from Davis's desk. I copy the information down and slip it into my back pocket. Maybe I could go to the bank and act confused, like I can't remember into which account my boss wanted me to deposit her money, and could they let me know my options? In the moment, this seems slightly less implausible than some of the other ridiculous scenarios I have cooked up. When I return to the binder, I keep turning the pages, only to discover the back half contains duplicates of every check Barbara wrote in that ten-year period. I haven't balanced my own checkbook in ages, instead trusting the bank to accurately manage that task for me, and I marvel at Barbara's financial diligence. Every check—dry cleaners, babysitters, electric bills—is in her handwriting. She isn't quite—as Davis once claimed—someone who "couldn't be bothered" with the more granular elements of daily life. Quite the opposite: She seems to be counting every penny.

How odd, I think.

I am about to close the book when my eyes fall on a familiar name: Harry Wood. I peer closer. It looks as if Barbara Lawrence wrote Harry

Wood a check for $5,000 on October 18, 1992, which I quickly calculate would have been the day after Davis's fifteenth birthday. I feel my scalp start to tingle. I quickly flip through the rest of the pages, and by the time I reach the last page of the binder, I see that Barbara Lawrence wrote Harry Wood a $5,000 check every month for nearly a decade.

I lean back on the side of Davis's bed, and I count on my fingers. If I am doing the math correctly, that is close to $600,000 dollars, which explains, at the very least, Harry Wood's wardrobe. Next, I calculate that we are more than halfway through another decade and wonder if Barbara is still writing checks to Harry. If so, for what reason? Does Davis know about these payments, or is this a secret that Harry Wood has long been sworn to protect? I pull out the next binder, which starts at the year 2000, but before I can open it, I am startled by a loud rap on the door.

"Clo?" Davis calls. "Dinner's ready."

"Sorry," I say, as I scramble to my feet.

I hear her jostle the knob.

"Why is the door locked?" she asks, and she sounds alarmed.

"I'll be right there," I call back as I slip the binders back into the box and replace the lid as quietly as I can manage. I slide the box across the carpet and push it far behind the row of Davis's dresses.

I open the door.

"You know how my mom hates waiting," she says, and she narrows her eyes as she looks over my shoulder. "And why was the door locked?"

"Sorry," I say cheerfully, before lowering my voice. "I locked it so I could clean everything up."

Here, Davis's face softens.

"Thank you," she whispers. "You're a saint."

67

It is opening night for Barbara's Broadway show, and the after-party—which Barbara's team decided should be an intimate, invite-only affair to create the sense of Barbara being a "scarce resource"—is being held at the apartment.

I attend the performance with Davis and Harry, of course, but somehow, after the triple curtain call, I get separated in the sold-out crowd, which flows like late-stage lava out of the theater. Out on the street, there are several editors from our office, all breathless with praise. There are also men yelling from pedicabs, offering people a ride, and a line of theatergoers by the stage door, all holding playbills and pens. I spot a boyish photographer on a bicycle as he snaps the celebrities—of which there were many in attendance—as they step into taxis and town cars. I see a circle of girls, all tapping wildly on their phones. I walk to Eighth Avenue, which is where we asked the driver to wait for us, but when I get to the appointed location, there is no car. Clearly, Harry and Davis left without me.

It is warm, and my silk dress flutters in the wind. I rise on my toes and look downtown. Traffic is at a standstill for blocks, and so, with no clear plan of action, I just stand on the sidewalk and toy with the diamond drop earrings Davis lent me from Barbara's collection for the night. I start to replay the past three hours in my head.

Barbara Lawrence was electric onstage.

Despite months of preparations, not to mention her long history as an *actual* actress with a degree from Julliard and a raft of awards, I had honestly not considered the possibility that Barbara Lawrence was talented. In fact, earlier that night when I settled into my seat at the theater, I thought we were there to humor her, as one might indulge the ensemble cast of an elementary school production.

Instead, Barbara Lawrence had been so good in her role—so brittle and sly, so hilarious and knowing—that at a certain point, as she sang and danced, I could no longer remember the characteristics or even expressions that belonged to the real Barbara Lawrence. The woman onstage, whoever she was, had eclipsed my memory as completely as a new moon.

It was astonishing.

So astonishing, in fact, that I don't quite know what to do with the information; I just hold it carefully close to my body, like a handful of marbles.

And now, I am alone, and there are no cabs. I'll have to take the subway.

When I arrive in the lobby of the building, there are two girls in black cocktail dresses holding clipboards and checking off guests. I get in the elevator with a few other people, and I can the hear music and laughter long before the doors slide open on the sixth floor. The entrance to the apartment is propped open, and people fill the front foyer, which means Barbara must be throwing quite a party. As I pass through the threshold, I find it difficult to parcel through the crowd and I must admit: This feels like a real party. The din is festive, and the air hangs with laughter and spice and cigarette smoke. Someone is playing a show tune on the grand piano and although I recognize the tune, I do not know the name. I can hear the cinematic crackling of ice in a martini shaker and the squeal of greetings. Quickly, I press my way into the kitchen, which, as I suspected, was cordoned off for the catering staff. I wedge past a tall metal bakery rack, which is slotted full of trays of appetizers, and pour myself a vodka from the bar. I add no mixer, I just dump a handful of ice in the glass and take a small sip. It sears my throat. I take another. I take one more.

Just as I realize I could spend the entire party alone in the kitchen, happily getting drunk by myself, Barbara appears in the doorway.

She is in a floral dress that pinches at the waist and flairs out to her knee and black heels. At some juncture between her curtain call and the party, her pancake stage makeup was sloughed off and a new, more subtle coat was applied to her face. Her hair, however, remains stiff and unmoving.

"What is going on with the appetizers?" she demands, and two women, both of whom have been frantically scooping little quiches off a hot baking sheet, dash out of the room with round silver trays. Barbara's dark eyes follow them, and, to my horror, she shoots off a brisk series of claps to indicate they are not moving quickly enough. Once they are gone, she notices me by the bar. First, she looks surprised, but then she softens:

"When did you get here?" she asks.

"Oh, I just walked in a few minutes ago and I wanted to collect myself for a minute," I say before adding: "Because you were *incredible* tonight. My head is spinning."

Barbara smiles blandly but says nothing; she just checks her hair in the reflection on the microwave door. I take another sip of my drink, and realize I have not eaten all day.

"It looks like quite a celebration," I continue, and I hold up my glass. "It's very, *very well*-deserved."

Barbara finally looks away from her reflection.

"It is," she says. "Isn't it?"

The living room is crowded, so crowded that I find it hard to make it to where Davis stands in a small circle of her mother's guests. A few familiar faces try to engage me in conversation, but I point to my ears and pretend I can't hear anything over the bang of the piano. When I finally arrive at Davis's side, she lights up. She wraps her arm around my waist. Her hair, which is clean and styled like Veronica Lake's, smells like coconut, and she wears a clingy white silk dress. Frankly, the dress is so tight and so sexy that I can't believe Barbara let her get away with something so attention-grabbing on her big night. I hadn't noticed it under her coat at the theater, but then it dawns on me that Barbara, who left the apartment before noon, probably didn't see it, either.

"Can you wear underwear with that?" I ask.

"No, I cannot," she responds, and we both laugh.

This is the best I have felt all day.

I survey the room. I remember a study from freshman year psychology class about tip jars. The theory was that, if a bartender filled their tip jar with money *before* the shift began, they would receive more tips over the course of the night than if the jar was empty when the shift began. It's called "seeding"—the professor said—and it works because people tend to do what other people do. We are just that impressionable or, more accurately, just that fearful of backing the wrong horse. It's funny: For the past few years, nobody in this room would even return Barbara's calls—she had been cast out so completely—but now the room is crammed with the same people, all hoisting up glasses and calling out her name. It would make me furious, the unabashed fair-weather-ness of it all, but Barbara seems delighted by the attention.

Suddenly, Harry appears. He holds two glasses of champagne.

"Madame!" he says to me heartily. "You have arrived!"

"Monsieur," I rejoin, but I feel a little irritated that neither Davis nor Harry have made any comment about abandoning me at the theater. "I have, indeed."

Harry extends his face in my direction, and I gamely kiss his cheeks, but I find—in light of recent revelations—that I look at him a little differently now. He hands a glass of champagne to Davis, and he keeps the other one for himself. I watch him take a sip, and he eyes me quizzically over the rim.

"You okay?" he asks.

"I'm fine," I say easily before turning to Davis with a sarcastic smile. "So is Barbara over the moon?"

"You mean to have everyone falling all over themselves for her?" Davis responds with a roll of her eyes. "Yes."

I laugh and Harry laughs and, for the briefest of moments, I allow myself to think that maybe—just maybe—everything is fine, and I have just fallen victim to my own catastrophic thinking again. My eyes search the room for the waiter with the tray of champagne. I wave him over. I decide to enjoy my night.

"Harry, of course, had to move heaven and earth to keep the announcement out of the papers," Davis continues, but with some distraction. "I mean, could you imagine the news hitting on the same day as my mother's reviews? We would all be shot dead in the street."

Here, she laughs a little.

"What announcement?" I ask reflexively.

Harry tilts his head up to the ceiling with a grimace.

"What announcement?" I repeat. My skin prickles.

Davis glances questioningly at Harry, like a confused toddler.

I turn toward Harry.

"Harry?"

"I was going to tell you tonight," he says.

"Tell me what?"

"The website is going to be acquired," he starts. "The deal went through."

"When did this happen?" I demand.

"Last week."

"Last week?" I repeat.

"I thought you told her, Harry," Davis whispers, and her tone is both bewildered and tinged with reproach.

"I wasn't allowed to say anything," he replies. "It's business."

"Oh, right," I say sarcastically. "Business."

"Clo," Davis interrupts, her voice soothing. "We should be *excited* for Harry, no? Isn't this good news?"

"I just don't know why he didn't tell me," I reply, and I keep my eyes trained on Harry. "I mean, have I not been part of this process?"

Davis looks at Harry with confusion.

"It was under wraps until the contract was signed," he says. "We had some personnel issues to sort out before we could finalize the agreement."

"What personnel issues?" I ask.

Harry and Davis exchange looks, and then Davis breaks into a big smile.

"Ta-da!" She laughs and does a little curtsy. "I told you I had a plan."

I must look confused.

"This is what I wanted to tell you the other night," she says. She bobs up and down and presses her hands together.

"What?" I ask.

"Harry hired me to be the editor, but I am going to be based in LA, so I can cover more of the entertainment side." she says. "We have been working on it for a while, and I have been dying to tell you."

I feel my stomach bottom out.

"What?" I demand, and I turn toward Harry. "Is this true?"

"Wait, are you mad?" Davis says, and her brow wrinkles with concern. "I thought you would be happy for me?"

I open my mouth, but nothing comes out; my head feels like it was just bashed in with a baseball bat. Suddenly, I feel the kitchen vodka hitting me all at once and, without another word, I move as fast as I can in the direction of the front door, careful not to knock over any famous people or trigger a stampede with my panicked urgency. I need to get out of this building and as far away from Harry Wood and Davis Lawrence as I can before I do something stupid, and catastrophically so.

When I get to the elevator bank, I push the button with such force that I snap my finger joint in the wrong direction. I look down and am surprised to see how quickly it turns purple. I push the smooth, round button again, over and over, but now with my thumb. I look up at the brass plate and see that the carriage isn't moving; it just sits in the lobby. I push the button again, and I can feel my panic rising. I debate taking the stairs.

"Come on," I whisper in a desperate attempt to coax the elevator upward. "Come on, come on..."

The apartment door slams. I know it is Harry, but I refuse to turn my head.

"Can you just listen to me?" he says, but his voice doesn't sound apologetic; it sounds annoyed.

"Stay away from me," I respond.

"Can you let me explain?" he asks. "I wanted to tell you myself."

I push the elevator button again.

"I didn't have a choice," he says.

"You didn't have a choice?" I repeat, unbelieving, but now I turn to face him. I see he has pulled the door shut, and we are alone. "I could have gotten fired for what I was doing! I took all the risk for you, and *this* is how I find out?"

"Clo, that's not fair," he says sternly. "I am sorry you feel left out, but I wasn't allowed to say anything until the deal was signed."

"Except to Davis?" I press. "Apparently."

Harry looks down at his shoes.

"Did you ever think that I might want to be your editor?" I ask.

"Why? I thought things were great at the magazine?"

"That's not my point," I respond. "My point is you didn't even bring it up with me."

"You know how these things work, Clo," he says.

"What does that mean?" I snap.

He puts his hands in his pockets. He seems to think for a moment.

"I needed a name," he says, finally.

"A name?" I repeat.

"Yes, *a name*," he says. "These investors are finance guys. They don't know anything about fashion, so they wanted a big, fancy name to attach to the project."

"I don't get it," I say.

Harry says nothing. He just looks at his shoes, and, suddenly, a wave of humiliation ripples through my body. I close my eyes. "Oh," I whisper. "Like a Davis Lawrence."

Here, Harry simply shrugs.

"I have a question," I say finally, my voice brittle.

"What?"

"If Davis was still working at the magazine, if the accident had never happened, would you have asked *her* to meet with all your executives?"

Here, Harry meets my eyes. He looks both vacant and defiant.

"No," he replies.

"Why not?"

"Davis couldn't do it."

"She *couldn't* do it or *wouldn't* do it?"

He looks away from me again.

"Both," he says quietly.

"Ah," I say. I feel tears leap to my eyes. "But you could make *me* do anything because I am, apparently, just a nameless nobody."

"Hey, wait," Harry interjects, now angry. "I didn't make you do anything! You did everything on your own, and do you know why? Because you got something from it, too."

"What did I get from it?" I demand. "Money?"

Here, Harry laughs.

"Give me a break," he says. "You hung around the apartment after Davis's accident out of the goodness of your heart?"

"I wanted to help Davis," I reply weakly. "She is my friend."

"Please," he says, and his voice is now full of spite. "She wasn't your friend. She was your opportunity."

"What do you mean?"

"You barely knew her," he says. "But you knew what *someone* like her could do for *someone* like you."

I take a step back.

"Someone like me?" I exclaim. "What are you trying to say?"

"I am trying to say that you are just as calculating as anyone else," Harry says. "But at least I am honest about it."

"Harry . . ." I start, but I trail off.

We stand in silence for a few seconds.

"Listen, I'm sorry I didn't tell you sooner, but I am just not sure why you can't see this as a *good* thing," Harry says, and, to my surprise, he laughs. "I mean, why are we fighting about this? This was our plan, wasn't it?"

"Our plan?"

"Just two workhorses taking on the world?" he says, and he holds his palms up and pantomimes a funny shrug. "Remember?"

"Right," I say, and Harry must see an opening because he leans forward and takes my arms. He pulls me into his chest. My instinct is to scream and yell like I am being attacked, but, instead, I allow him to wrap his arms tightly around my body. I close my eyes and remember the first time I met him, all those years ago, and the way he held my hand as we walked through the club. It made me feel safe and he led me to believe I was, in some way, desirable. *How badly I wanted to be seen,* I think. I rest my cheek on his shoulder. His tuxedo jacket gives off that chemical smell of new fabric, and I wonder if he bought it just for the occasion. I breathe in more deeply, and I am able to detect a more familiar scent underneath; the almost visceral mix of Irish Spring soap, dry-cleaning fluid and cigarettes that, should I live one hundred years, will always remind me of Harry Wood. I press my face into his chest with a strange and ferocious hunger, like if I can get enough of this moment inside my body, then it will belong to me forever.

Harry Wood, I realize, is a question I don't want answered.

Finally, I pull back.

"What happens next?" I ask.

"Don't worry about it," he says, and he tucks a lock of hair behind my ear. "I can handle them from here."

Suddenly, the elevator doors trundle open, and a few more well-dressed guests spill into the hallway. Harry and I take a bashful step apart, like secret lovers, and as they head into the party, I notice that Harry does not take his eyes off me. He just keeps one hand on the elevator door, and when we are finally alone again, he does something unexpected: He steps into the open elevator.

"Where are you going?" I ask. I suddenly feel a little frantic.

"I am going to leave while the party is still fun," he says.

"But Davis will kill you if you don't say good night," I say.

"She will be fine," he says. "I am just glad you and I had a chance to talk."

Harry presses the button inside the elevator and takes a step backward. I watch him slide his hands into his pockets and look up toward the ceiling. Then, the doors close, and I am alone, looking at my own warped reflection in the dinted brass doors.

I return to the party.

The air in the apartment has grown thick and stuffy, and the music, louder. There are more guests and more laughter, and, when I finally wrangle my way into the living room, I discover a large group is crowded around the piano, glasses in hand.

They have started to sing.

It is another song I do not know.

Davis is among them, and I watch her, as I always watch her. She stands a foot behind her mother who, naturally, is leaning on the piano like it's her own cabaret. Davis sings along gamely, her ruby lips move along to the lyrics, and she smiles with great encouragement at anyone who works up the courage to join the fray. Her hair is so golden and her body so wonderfully slight that, in this exact moment, I almost do not believe she is real.

It's hard to believe any of it has been real.

When Davis sees me, she stops singing and her worried eyes stripe across my face like searchlights. She wants confirmation that Harry and I have set things right in the hallway, and that order has been restored to our shaky little triangle. I give her a thumbs-up, and she rewards me with an electric grin before she turns, with visible relief, back to the piano. She starts to sing again, but bolder and brasher now, and I swell with longing for a girl, for a world, that will never belong to me.

Slowly, I walk to my room only to discover that the bed is piled high with other people's things. Apparently, Barbara turned my bedroom into the coat room, and as I kick off my shoes, I hear someone start up on the piano again. I climb onto the bed, and, within seconds, everything fades to black.

68

When I wake up the following morning, the coats are gone. I have the vaguest recollection of disappointed whispers and the sensation of things being pulled, with considerable effort, out from under my heavy frame.

I roll over and look at the ceiling.

The party is over.

Still in my dress, I walk barefoot through the apartment, which reveals itself to be a mess. There are nuts scattered across the floor, and ashtrays overflow with soft piles of dead ash. I collect a few glasses from the top of the piano and wince at a large red wine spill on Barbara's pink rug. Clearly, there had been some attempt to clean it up, a dry sponge lays abandoned on the carpet next to the stain, curled up like a dead beetle, but it was mostly a failure, and so, like everything else, it will be sorted out today. I turn into the kitchen, where Barbara and Davis are huddled over a stack of newspapers at the table. Barbara's assistant is typing on her iPhone by the coffeepot, and I can hear Phillip on the phone in another room. Marta is tying off a white bag of trash.

"Good morning," I say.

"The reviews are incredible," Barbara replies in response, her eyes glinting as she waves a paper over her head. "Everyone loves the show."

"Everyone loves *you*, Mother," Davis says, to which Barbara extends her hand to cup her daughter's cheek.

"I know," she says with a squeal. "It's true! Everyone loves me."

She laughs.

I gently place the dirty glasses in the sink.

"Listen to this," Davis crows, and she starts to read the review from the *New York Times* on her phone. It is only when I see her looking at me expectantly that I realize I have not heard a single word.

It doesn't matter, of course. I know my lines.

"Barbara," I say. "You are a triumph."

The weekend comes quickly, and when I wake up on Saturday morning, my skin feels swollen and itchy, like I am reacting to some unknown irritant. As I pace the apartment, I cannot recall the last time I had so little to do. Barbara is at the theater, and Davis is meeting Harry for a working lunch (to which, of course, I have not been invited), but I lob a few calls and texts in his direction, anyway. I mostly want to garner a sense of his mood, but by the time I pull up to my office on Monday morning, he has yet to respond to a single overture, which I know is not a good sign. I try one more time:

Morning! Let me know if you need any help with the party on Friday.

When I get to my office, I find Sarah's desk is empty, and her computer is dark. I check my watch: It's nearing ten o'clock in the morning, but I already know she will arrive entirely nonplussed with a tall tale that involves an exercise class or an entirely avoidable transit delay. My office phone rings. I scoop the receiver up off Sarah's desk.

"Clodagh Harmon's office," I say.

"L.K. wants to see you," the voice says on the other end of the line before adding: "Now."

Of course she does, I think, and despite the fact I have played through countless variations of this scenario throughout my career—this mysterious, career-ending summons from L.K. Smith—I never thought it would ever really happen to me. Like a plane crash. Or an unplanned pregnancy. I look at my watch again and wonder how Harry could have gotten to her so quickly.

"Thanks," I say.

When I get to L.K.'s office, her assistant gestures for me to go inside.

"Good afternoon, Clo," L.K. says when she sees me. "Sit down."

I sit down.

"So, I have something that has come to my attention," she begins.

I look at the floor.

"Susan Goldsmith-Cohen," she says. "Do you think we should do something on her?"

My head snaps up.

"What?" I ask.

"Susan Goldsmith-Cohen?" she repeats. "The art advisor?"

"Why?"

"She's dead," she says. "She died last night."

At this piece of information, the room tilts to the side.

"Of what?"

"Some kind of cancer," L.K. says as she holds her reading glasses up to the light and inspects them for smudges. "She had been sick for a while."

"Oh," I manage.

"That story is going to be *everywhere* again," she continues. "Honestly, I am glad she's dead because I don't think she could go through the humiliation again."

To this, I say nothing. Instead, my body feels like it's been unhooked from the mother ship. *So this is not about Harry*, I think, and although there is some relief to this thought, there is an ache deep in my gristle that tells me I have not made it to the safeness of another shore. Suddenly, I remember the horse in Barbara's study, and how the apartment was just filled with people at the opening night party on Thursday, all milling in and out of her rooms, commenting on her art collection, her wallpaper, the estimated expense of the flowers. I turn to look out the windows, and my eyes settle upon the dull blue line of the East River, which is hardly moving, in the distance. I imagine tossing the statue into the water like a small boulder. I can almost feel it sink into its unknowable depths before being pulled along in its brawny current to nowhere.

"It was all such a shame, really," L.K. says, and she looks out her window like she's remembering something from a faraway time. "She always seemed like such a smart woman, and with such incredible taste. And to think: It was all a house of cards. Do you remember it?" she asks.

"Vaguely," I lie.

"So what do you think?" she inquires, but now she eyes me with impatience. She clearly finds my garbled half answers wildly insufficient.

I take a breath.

"I don't think it makes sense for the book," I say finally. "But I can ask Sarah to do something short online? I am not sure it will get much traffic, but it might make sense to at least register it."

"I think that sounds right," L.K. says before adding, with a wry kind of smile: "I guess it's a good thing the pursuit of glamour is so seductive."

"Why is that?" I ask.

"Well," she says, looking up at me. "We would both be out a job if it wasn't."

When I return to my office, I see Sarah has arrived. She is drinking an iced coffee and talking to a few other assistants, all of whom have congregated around her desk. When she sees me, she gives me a sad little wave:

"So sorry I was late," she says. "But I just found out on Facebook that my ex-boyfriend is dating someone."

"Oh," I say.

"I just wish I hadn't joined it," she continues, and one of the other assistants nods. "I just feel like there is nowhere to hide, you know?"

I look at her for a long minute before I shake my head.

"Right," I say, and while I try to look solemn, I can sense a smile forcing its way across my face. "There really isn't anywhere to hide."

That night, I lay awake in bed for hours, the endlessness made marginally less terrifying by the rhythmic lull of Davis's breathing, which is as thick and indulgent as a fattened king. Despite the time, the sounds of the city outside my window—rumbling delivery trucks, car horns, the occasional low-flying plane—have not died down, but they do sound lonelier now, like an alley cat mewing mournfully over an empty tin can. I think about how many unknown lives there are in New York. *I can pack a suitcase*, I think, *I can walk out the door of the Lawrence apartment at daybreak and never be heard from again.* I roll over and look at the wall. I wonder what feels worse: To actually be betrayed by someone you trusted, from which I imagine you can, at least one day, recover, or to live within the raging haze of its possibility, an uncertain and dangerous place from which there is no respite.

* * *

Around three o'clock in the morning, I finally slide out of bed. I go to the bathroom and retrieve a large white towel from the linen closet before I slip silently down the hallway and into Barbara's darkened office. With the towel draped across my hands, I stretch on my tiptoes and pluck the horse down from her shelf, like I have just successfuly apprehended a housebound bat. From there, I carry the pile back to the half bathroom, and lock the door. I stretch the towel across the floor, and lay the statue on her flank. I haven't been this close to her in such a long time and as I run my finger along her rusted sides, I feel strangely emotional in her presence, like she can see the very insides of my body. Upon closer inspection, I notice that dust has collected in her delicate nooks and crevices. I ball up a paper towel and run it under a quiet stream of water from the faucet. Then, I wipe the entire statue down—partially because I have been remiss in her caretaking, yes, but also to remove any fingerprints. I find a Q-tip and twist it gently into the hard-to-reach places. Once she is clean, I wrap her tightly in the towel and tuck the soft parcel into my monogrammed L.L. Bean tote.

Then, I quietly climb back into bed. I glance at the clock. It is almost two o'clock in the morning.

I fall asleep in seconds.

69

The following Saturday night, I take the subway down to Harry's new apartment with my tote bag wedged between my ankles. It is his big housewarming party, and, while I am late, Davis has already been there for hours. She went early to help him set up with the caterers.

I get off the subway at Astor Place and walk slowly down Lafayette before turning onto Great Jones Street. When I get to the address listed on the invitation, I look up at Harry's building. I can see the fourth-floor windows are illuminated, and the gentle noise of a party drifts down to where I stand on the street.

This is it, I think.

The elevator doors open directly into Harry's apartment which, to my astonishment, seems to be a full-floor loft. The floors are light pine, and the air smells like fresh paint and sawdust. As I move through the rooms, I realize the walls don't reach the ceiling, which gives me the not-altogether-unpleasant sensation of being a mouse trapped in a luxurious maze. The apartment is crowded with people and sparsely furnished, and I nod at a few people I recognize. It's a strange mix: There are the expected models, editors, designers, and a handful of not quite A-list New York actresses, but there are also men in business suits—some balding, some short, and none particularly appealing—who I assume are part of the investment team that Harry just spent the last year so enthusiastically courting. They look to be having a wonderful time.

Welcome to the land of make-believe, I think.

What's left of it, anyway.

Suddenly, Harry appears. He looks flushed and happy.

"You're here," he says, and he gives me a big hug.

"I am here," I say, and I wing my index finger around. "And I won't ask how much this ridiculous apartment cost you."

"Always a lady." Harry laughs. "Let's just say I am very lucky this acquisition went through because I was leveraged to the hilt."

"Well, it was worth it," I say. "This place is going to look *very* good in photographs."

"These days, there is no other reason to buy it, my dear," Harry whispers in my ear, as he waves to someone across the room. "Other than shameless self-promotion."

I smile and hold up my bag.

"Anywhere I can stash this?" I ask.

"Yes," he says. "Check out the library in the front hall. I think you'll be impressed."

With that, he drifts into the crowd, and I am left alone to ruminate on the blatantness of his declaration, and how—in my short lifetime—there has been a shift so massive that it was almost imperceptible in the day-to-day. I spent years trying to figure out how to make myself legible to other people—how to make them see me in the way I wanted to be seen—so they would choose me. Maybe they would choose me to become a part of their crowd. Or select my picture for inclusion in a party roundup. Or seat me at the good table. To succeed was always about being accepted, being championed by some mysterious, superior entity, but not anymore. You used to have to work for decades to become a CEO. Now you can bake cookies in your apartment and call yourself a CEO or start a street style blog and refer to yourself as an editor-in-chief. Seemingly overnight, the gatekeepers I worked so hard to ingratiate myself with abandoned their posts, and I feel unmoored to realize I am not entirely sure of who I am in the absence of their gaze.

I carry my bag to the library and, when I am sure nobody is watching, close the door. I turn the lock softly and lean my back against the door so I can look around. He's right. I am impressed. I wiggle out of my heels before I tiptoe over to his newly built bookshelf. I remove a few books, and I stack them in a neat pile on the floor. Then, I pull the white towel out of my tote bag, and I unwrap the horse before I place her in the open spot. I take a long step back to make sure I like her positioning.

I put the towel back in my bag.

I stash my bag next to the door.

I leave the room.

I get a drink.

For the next hour, I watch the party from the sidelines as Harry leads Davis around the room. She is wearing a seafoam, one-shoulder cocktail dress and her hair is pulled back in a slick ponytail. I can see her mother's yellow diamond earrings sway from her lobes.

With his arm firmly around her waist, Harry introduces her to his guests, including the gentleman from the venture capital firm. Davis, for her part, of course, plays it perfectly. She shakes hands. She leans forward and listens. She smiles her electric, well-bred smile.

It feels like I am watching a scene from a future that does not include me.

Probably because I am.

At a certain point, Harry and Davis drift in my direction. They are whispering about something, and Harry has his fingers wrapped around Davis's perfect wrist.

"Hey," I say loudly to get their attention. "I need to get a picture of you two."

"Where?" Davis asks, she looks around with a light frown.

"Not here," I say. "It's too crowded and the light is weird. Come with me."

They follow me down the hallway and into the library.

"So," Harry says, waving his arm across the space. "It's not done, but what do you think so far?"

"I love it," I say, and I hold out my hand. "Give me your phone."

Harry fishes his iPhone out of his pocket and hands it to me.

I motion for them to stand in front of the bookshelf.

I take a picture

I take a few more.

"Is it good?" Harry asks when I am finished.

I pretend to look at it.

"It is perfect," I say.

I hand over his phone, and he immediately begins to pinch the screen and swipe through the images.

"These *are* good," he says, and Davis peers over his shoulder. "Should I post one right now?"

Davis shrugs, and I look at him and smile:

"You definitely should," I say

Thirty minutes later, I am riding the subway uptown alone.

I have my work tote wedged between my ankles again, and while I want to report I feel tainted and sick, like I just swam through an oil spill, the truth is that I feel nothing. Just the curious emptiness of a free fall.

You see, on the way out of Harry Wood's brand-new apartment, I took the horse off the shelf and wrapped her back in the white towel. I returned the books to the shelf, and I turned off the light. Then, without saying goodbye to anyone, I tossed Barbara Lawrence's gold American Express card on Harry's new entryway table, and I walked out the door. I did not look back.

After all, you must make certain they do, indeed, die for you first.

70

"Harry was arrested last night."

These are the first words I hear early Sunday morning, two days after the party. Davis stands at the foot of my bed, her eyes wild with panic.

I push myself up to my elbows, and pretend I was asleep.

I haven't slept in two days.

"What?" I ask.

"Harry was arrested last night," she repeats. "His assistant just called me."

"For what?" I ask.

"I have no idea," she says. "But there was something online about an art theft? I can't get any real details, but we have to go to the police station now."

I sit up straighter.

"Where is your mom?" I ask.

"She just left for the theater," she replies. "She only has a matinee today."

"Davis, you can't go to the police station," I say. "What if there are photographers or something? Your mother would kill you."

Davis considers this for a moment.

"Why don't we call Phillip?" I suggest, and I swing my bare legs out of bed. "Maybe he can find out what is going on?"

We both go to the kitchen, and I watch as Davis paces the pantry with the cordless phone to her ear. When she comes out, she puts it back on the cradle.

"He says he will call us back as soon as he has more information," she says, her brow crooked with worry.

"Okay," I say. "Whatever it is, I am sure it's a misunderstanding."

When a few hours pass with no call from Phillip, I go across the street to Central Park. I think about taking a walk but, instead, I settle on the bench nearest to Fifth Avenue so Davis can find me.

I sit in silence with my legs outstretched in the sun. I watch a robin peck around my feet.

Finally, a dark shadow casts across my body.

"Phillip called," Davis says.

I shield my eyes and look up at her.

"What happened?" I ask.

She tells me what she knows: Harry posted some photos from his party on Facebook, including the picture I took of him with Davis in the library. Since images of Susan Goldsmith-Cohen's missing horse had, indeed, been nearly everywhere in recent days, it didn't take long for an eagle-eyed follower of Harry Wood to notice the horse in the background. They took a screen shot and posted it online. It was shared. At some point, someone sent it to the police. Within hours, the picture was everywhere. When Harry caught wind of it, he took the photo down, but it was too late.

"It's ridiculous," Davis says as she sits down next to me, and chews on her thumb. "Harry wasn't even at Susan's stupid party."

"No," I say.

"Well, then it must have been someone else," Davis says. "Right?"

I look straight ahead, but I don't reply. It feels like the last of my life force has begun to leak onto the sidewalk. I suppose I had long hoped that escaping my predicament would provide me some semblance of relief, and I am surprised to find there is no comfort in this moment.

I turn toward her:

"Davis, can I ask you a question?"

"What?" she says.

"The night when you fell with Captain," I begin. "You didn't really fall, did you?"

Davis's face twists in surprise.

"Of course, I fell," she snaps, and she points at her face. "I got eight stitches in my lip to prove it."

"I don't think you fell," I say quietly.

"Why would I lie?"

"Because your mom hit you," I say.

Davis stands up quickly, and takes a fast step back, like I slapped her across the face.

"What are you *talking* about?" she exclaims, her voice incredulous.

"Harry told me about your fifteenth birthday," I say.

"What about it?" She arranges her face in a studied confusion.

"About having to go to the hospital."

"I honestly don't know *what* you're talking about," she sighs with annoyance, and her delivery is so genuine, I start to wonder if the story Harry told was a lie.

"A mugger in Central Park?" I offer, and, here, I watch her beautiful face drop like a tossed sack.

She turns away from me, and I am overwhelmed with the desire to pull her into my body, to tell her that nothing was her fault. But I can't.

"It's not what you think," she says finally, and she recovers herself with a strange breeziness. "Harry is always so dramatic, you know? You have to take him with a grain of salt."

"So, was he lying?" I ask.

"It's just more complicated. You don't know what it's like to be a single mom," she says. "And *trust me*, I wasn't an easy kid."

"Why didn't Harry help you?" I ask.

"Harry?" she asks.

"Yeah," I say. "I mean, he lived with you. He saw what happened."

"Trust me, if there was *anything* he could have done, he would have done it," she says solemnly. Here, she sits back down next to me. "He's my best friend."

"Best friend, huh?" I mumble.

Davis narrows her eyes.

"Yes," she says slowly. "Why? What are you trying to say?"

"He's a shitty best friend, Davis," I retort. "That's what I am trying to say."

She gives me a contemptuous snort.

"Why have you have always been so ridiculously jealous of our relationship?" she throws back. "You have no idea what he has done for me. You have no idea how much he cares about me."

"How much he cares about *you*?" I spit out, and, here, I laugh.

"What's so funny?" Davis strains to look unperturbed.

"Can you think of any reason your mom would have written him a check for five thousand dollars the morning after your fifteenth birthday?"

Here, Davis just looks at me. I continue:

"I saw the canceled checks in those boxes hidden in your closet," I say as means of explanation. "I didn't mean to, but I saw them when I was putting back the jewelry."

"Oh, god. Who knows?" Davis responds, and she shakes her head. "I mean, it was probably something to do with school. He was always about to lose his scholarship."

"It wasn't just one time," I say.

"What do you mean?"

"She still pays him five thousand dollars a month," I say. "Every month."

"That's ridiculous," Davis says.

"You can go look for yourself," I say.

"But why would she do that?" Davis asks, and she sounds genuinely confused.

I raise my eyebrows but say nothing, and Davis stares at me blandly for a beat before her face hardens into understanding.

"How dare you?" she says, her voice rising. "Harry would *never* do that to me."

The rest of the day passes with no word from Harry. All we know is that he was charged with possession of stolen property and released on bail, but we have no idea where he is staying, no sense of his plan. Despite the anxious mood in the apartment, Barbara had decided earlier in the week to invite people for dinner on Sunday as Monday is her only day off and, quite predictably, the news of Harry's arrest did not dissuade her.

Around six o'clock, Davis and I are getting ready to perform for

Barbara's guests, albeit in a strained silence, when we hear Hatch buzz up from the lobby. Davis, hopeful it is Harry, runs toward the foyer in her bare feet, and I follow her.

"Don't tell me people are early," Barbara sighs as she walks to the intercom.

"Ms. Lawrence," Hatch says. "There are two agents here to see you?"

"Agents?" Barbara asks, her voice unconcerned.

"Police agents," Hatch says uncertainly. "They say they are with the FBI?"

Barbara glances with irritation at Davis and me—her inconveniences in life perpetually remain our fault—before she tells Hatch to send them up. She finishes her martini in one gulp and reapplies her lipstick, turning her face back and forth approvingly in the hallway mirror. She calls for Betsy to put on a pot of tea and, when the officers arrive, she escorts us into the formal living room. The younger officer lets out a little wolf whistle as he looks around.

"This is some place," he says.

"Thank you," Barbara says. "Now, what can we help you with? We are having people over in about an hour so this will have to be quick."

She looks down at her gold watch and then looks up with a smile as she folds her hands. Her nails are round and crimson.

The FBI agents introduce themselves. They tell us they are with the Art Crimes Unit and that they are working in conjunction with local police to investigate several pieces of artwork stolen from Susan Goldsmith-Cohen, including the horse statue that was photographed in Harry Wood's apartment. The young one is Martinez, and he is short with muscles. He quickly informs us he has a master's degree in museum studies. The old one is O'Malley and he has snow white hair, and a red face splattered with ruptured capillaries. He lets us know nothing. Under any other circumstances, I would have already cracked a joke.

"We are here regarding the alleged art theft perpetrated by Harry Wood," Detective Martinez says in a very official-sounding voice.

"We are all shocked by the news," Barbara responds.

She gives us a quick glance, and we nod in return.

"I can imagine," Martinez says, and he pulls out a notebook. "Do you mind if I take notes?"

"Not at all," she says.

"And who is this?" he asks, tipping his chin.

"This is my daughter, Davis, and her friend, Clo, who is visiting." The detective nods at us.

"Now, am I correct that you and your daughter are close acquaintances of Mr. Wood?" Martinez continues.

"Yes," Barbara says.

"And is it true he lived here with you on occasion over the years?"

"Yes," Barbara says again, but now her voice is pricked with irritation. "He didn't have a family of his own, so he stayed here for periods of time during high school and college."

"And holidays," Davis pipes up, before adding: "Birthdays."

"Yes," Barbara says stiffly. "And holidays."

"And why did he move out? Did you have a fight?"

"A fight?" Barbara says with a laugh. "No, there was no fight. He was a young man. It was time for him to move on and start his own life. He had saved up to get an apartment, and, well, off he went. Honestly, it was more than a decade ago. I don't really see how any of this is relevant."

Here, Martinez exchanges a look with O'Malley.

"What makes it relevant, Ms. Lawrence," Martinez continues, "is that of *all* the people who attended the party in question at the Goldsmith-Cohen residence, you are the only one with a financial connection to the main suspect."

I steal a glance at Davis. She sits with a bland smile.

"So," Martinez continues, "I suppose we find that interesting."

"Interesting how?" she asks, crisply, and O'Malley leans forward on his elbows with a smile.

"For starters," he says, and his ears flush pink against his white hair. "I would be remiss if I didn't say that I was a huge fan of yours, Ms. Lawrence."

"Thank you," Barbara replies with a smile.

"But, as for Harry Wood, we know he came from unfortunate circumstances," he says.

Barbara nods.

"But he also seemed to live pretty well," he continues. "Nice clothes. Trips to Paris. Expensive dinners. That sort of thing?"

"Harry is a very hard worker," Barbara says.

"No doubt," O'Malley says with a kind nod. "But it turns out he had gotten himself into a bit of financial trouble over the past few years. He owed a lot of people quite a bit of money. Serious people."

Serious people.

"I'm sorry to hear that," Barbara replies, but she doesn't sound very sorry.

"As part of the investigation, we took a look into his bank accounts, of course," O'Malley continues. "It looks like you have been paying him a monthly stipend? Or a fee? Is that right?"

Barbara says nothing.

"How much was it?" O'Malley asks Martinez with a pantomime of forgetfulness.

"Five thousand dollars," Martinez replies, and he slides a photocopy over of a canceled check. Barbara glances down briefly, and then turns the paper over.

"Five thousand dollars," O'Malley repeats, and he shakes his head in a sort of grandfatherly disbelief before he lays both his hands on the table, and leans forward kindly, like he has a secret.

"We also found your credit card in Mr. Wood's possession when we searched the apartment," he says gently. "An American Express?"

At this information, I catch Barbara's eyes flicker.

"Now, you're welcome to do what you want with your own money, of course, Ms. Lawrence," O'Malley says, leaning back. "But we do have some questions."

"Such as?"

"Well, were you helping his business out?" he offers. "Was this a fee for some type of service? Or were you just giving him an allowance?"

"It was," Barbara starts, but she must clear her throat. "More of an allowance."

Martinez writes something in his notebook.

"With money being such an issue, maybe he took the horse to sell it?" O'Malley muses. "These highly publicized pieces usually go cold for a while, but they often turn up as collateral, and much of the time it is for debts."

To this, Barbara says nothing.

"Here is the part that gets me," young Martinez interjects, much to the pretend dismay of his counterpart. "How did Harry *get* the statue? He claims he didn't steal it. He told us that he has no idea how it ended up in his apartment."

"Well, Susan was fairly loose with other people's money and other people's art," Barbara says with a smirk. "Trust me, I should know."

"That is true," Martinez concedes. "But as far as we know, Harry wasn't at the party at the Goldsmith-Cohen residence." Here he licks his thumb and pages back in his notebook to read from scribbled notes. "When we interviewed Susan in the summer of 2003, she said she didn't invite him, and there aren't any photographs of him. He also *says* he wasn't there, and none of the guest we interviewed recall seeing him."

"But you were there," O'Malley says to Barbara. "And you are a close connection of Harry Wood."

"Are you suggesting I had something to do with this?" Barbara asks, her voice rising. "Or is this coming from Harry?"

The agents exchange looks but say nothing.

"It's typical," Barbara scoffs. "But I don't know what to tell you. After all, you found the statue in his apartment."

"See, that is the thing," O'Malley says. "There was no horse in his apartment."

Barbara and Davis look surprised at the information, and I can feel my heart pick up speed as I watch Martinez reach under the table. He pulls a folder out of his bag. He opens it, and slides a piece of paper in Davis's direction. It is a color printout of a photograph taken of her at Susan Goldsmith-Cohen's party: She is standing on the gravel driveway and laughing, probably at something I said. I recall the photographer, and the way the garage light illuminated the deep creases in his otherwise young face. He had been holding an orange milk crate full of wires when he called out to Davis for just one more photo. He put down the crate, picked up his camera, and relieved us of our drinks. I can still feel the humidity of Davis's body when she wrapped her arm around the waist of my dress.

I can still recall the cheapness of that dress.

"We know this is when you"—and here he points at Davis—"were leaving. You seem to be outside the party in this photograph."

I lightly crane my neck to look at the picture.

"Yes," Davis says. "I was on the driveway."

"The part that really jumps out at me is that you aren't holding anything. You don't have a drink. You don't have a purse."

"She doesn't have a horse," I intone, following the beat of his language. I can't seem to help myself. He looks at me and smiles:

"That's correct," he replies. "She doesn't have a horse."

For the first time, I lean back in my chair. Maybe these men are not here to accuse us of anything? Maybe they simply came to conduct interviews in good faith. This is a soothing thought.

Until, that is, Martinez flips over another image and pushes it in our direction. It is of Barbara and Davis, and it was taken earlier in the evening. I am confused about the relevance until Martinez drums the image with his pointer finger—over and over—as he points out one small detail: Barbara is holding my straw bag. She has it partially tucked behind her long skirt—she was probably embarrassed to be seen with it—but, even in the photo, you can see it is heavy, and something bulges out of the side.

"Boy, what I wouldn't pay to know what was inside that heavy bag of yours, Ms. Lawrence," he says.

Barbara looks down at the picture again, but she says nothing. Instead, she straightens in her chair and reaches for her cigarette pouch which, in my experience, is how Barbara signals she is getting into a character. She holds up a cigarette, and O'Malley leans over the table with a lighter.

"Thank you," she says, but she fixes her eyes on the young detective as she exhales.

"Detective . . . I'm sorry, what was it again?" she asks. She leans on her elbow and taps her ring finger against her thumb.

"Martinez," he replies. "Agent Martinez."

"Yes, of course, Detective Martinez," she says. "Are you married?"

Officer Martinez does not flinch.

"Yes, ma'am," he says.

"Well, then surely you know what women carry around in their handbags?"

When he does not answer, she takes another drag. She exhales. She waits. Her eyebrow is slightly arched.

"Well?" she presses him, finally. "Do you know what women keep in their handbags?"

"I suppose I do, ma'am," he concedes. "But would you mind if we took a look at that bag?"

"I would be happy to show it to you, but I don't even recognize it."

"Do you normally not recognize your own purses?"

Here, Barbara just smiles at his ignorance.

"Do you think it's here?" he asked.

"You're welcome to look in my closet. You're welcome to look anywhere you want, although I am not quite sure what you're hoping to find."

Here, Detective Martinez stands up, he cranes his neck to look around the room.

"There is one thing," Barbara says, crushing her cigarette into her ashtray.

"What's that?"

"Well, I am not a lawyer, but don't you need a warrant?"

"Technically, yes," O'Malley says. "If we don't have your approval."

"Well," Barbara says, and she rises up from the table without breaking her gaze. "As I said, we have people coming for dinner, so why don't you get a search warrant and come back?"

"Come back?" Officer Martinez asks.

"You can tear the place apart, if you'd like, just not tonight," she says lightly, as she moves into the direction of the foyer, and we all push out of our chairs to follow her. "After all, we want to get this sorted out as quickly as you do. Susan was a *very* dear friend."

At this, Barbara opens the front door, and smiles. The agents thank us for our time, and they hand us their business cards. We bid them adieu with the most darling little handshakes, like we have been called upon by potential suitors, rather than interrogated by the Federal Bureau of Investigation. Once they are safely inside the elevator, Barbara closes the door. She rests her hand on the thick wood and lowers her head.

"We have to get Phillip on the phone," Barbara says, her voice tinged with madness. "We cannot have them coming back here and searching the apartment. Can you imagine?"

When Davis and I say nothing, she continues:

"Could you imagine if the producers got wind of this?" she says, and she walks back and forth in the foyer. "Or the press?"

"Mom?"

Barbara turns around to look at her daughter.

"What?" she snaps.

"Why did you give all that money to Harry," she asks, but she keeps her eyes on the floor.

"Davis, please," she sighs. "Not now."

"I'm serious," Davis says, and she looks up.

"I did it to protect you, Davis," she says.

"Protect me?" Davis fires back. "How?"

"Your whole life, you're always bringing home strays. You are always trusting the wrong people."

"How was Harry the wrong people?" Davis asks.

"He is poor, Davis. And he comes from nothing," Barbara replies.

"So what?"

"So what? Poor people do desperate things, especially when their backs are up against the wall," Barbara says. "I have seen it all my life."

"But Harry is my friend," Davis protests.

"Harry would betray you for a dollar," Barbara snaps. "And I was just trying to shield you from it."

"By paying Harry?"

"The money gave him a reason to stay quiet, not to mention a reason to stick around," she says.

To this, Davis says nothing, and Barbara turns back to the mirror.

"And tell me this, Davis," she says coldly. "I know you want me to be some kind of monster here, but if Harry was such a good friend, why did he take it?"

Davis stands frozen, and when the door buzzes with the dinner guests, Barbara points at us, her eyes blazing:

"Not a word," she hisses. "Not a word."

71

Early the next morning, I wake up to find Davis on the edge of the bed. She has dark circles under her eyes, and I can see she has put on makeup, including a red lipstick, but she does not smile.

"Good. You're awake," she says, but her voice is lifeless. "I need you to come with me."

"Where?"

"Just get up."

Dutifully, I swing my legs out of bed. I hop into jeans and a sweater, but my clothes have started to pull and pucker; nothing fits the way it used to fit. Quickly, I wash my face, put in my contacts, and run a brush through my limp hair. I open the foyer coat closet and run my fingers along my options—I must own at least ten winter coats at this point, most of them gifts for PR girls and designers, but the decision is easy: I snap the red one off its wooden hanger. When we land in the lobby, I realize I didn't brush my teeth, but Hatch is waiting by an idling car, so I don't say anything. I just run my tongue over my teeth as Hatch ushers us into the back seat. His head moves around in jerking motions, like a scrawny bird, and it occurs to me that Hatch must be approaching seventy by this point.

"Nineteenth Precinct, please," Davis says to the driver, and then she pulls her sunglasses down over her eyes.

"Why are we going to the police station, Davis?" I ask nervously.

Davis doesn't say anything.

"Can you *not* be dramatic right now?" I say, and she turns to look at me, although it's impossible to see what is going on behind her large black shades. "You're freaking me out."

At this, Davis presses the button that opens the window, and the car fills with a fast, thick wind. My hair whips around wildly and Davis floats her arm outside the window, like she is trying to catch something. I check my watch. It's almost nine o'clock in the morning. I remind myself to call Sarah when we get to the station. I can tell her I have a family emergency, and I will be late to work.

We arrive at the police station, and I chase Davis up the stairs and through the arched doorway. I watch as she walks directly to the front desk. With efficient crispness, she gives her name to the female officer who sits behind the desk. She signs a sheet on a clipboard and sits down on a padded chair in the waiting area. I sit down next to her.

"Do you want coffee?" I ask.

"No."

We wait in silence for about ten minutes before the female officer shows us to the cubicle where Detective Martinez sits. His chair is empty, but as we wait, I look around: He has several photographs of two young kids tacked to the spongy wall of his cubicle, and a framed photograph of himself on a motorcycle. He also has a wall calendar with nothing written in the squares.

"Good morning, ladies," I hear.

Officer Martinez drops his compact body down hard in his chair and lays a thick folder down on the desk.

Davis looks over her shoulder.

"What can I help you with, Miss Lawrence?"

Davis taps the desk like she is thinking about something, namely if she wouldn't prefer to wait for the kinder, gentler officer who she can expect to be nice to her, but she removes her sunglasses.

"You were wrong about something," she says finally.

"And what was that?" he asks.

I feel my blood run cold.

"Harry Wood was at the party at Susan Goldsmith-Cohen's house," she says. "I saw him, *and* I spoke with him."

Detective Martinez looks bewildered, and more than a little bit disappointed, like this was the closest to celebrity crime he was ever going to get, and he had hoped to drag it out a little longer.

As for me, I am thunderstruck.

Martinez clicks the back of his pen and writes something in his narrow notebook.

"And you just *suddenly* remember this?" he asks, his tone unbelieving.

"No," she says crisply. "I didn't *suddenly* remember it. You never asked me directly and, to be honest, I had wanted to protect him because he is such a good friend."

"But you don't want to protect him anymore?" he asks.

"No," Davis says. She briefly lowers her gaze. "Not anymore."

At this comment, Martinez looks at me. I close my eyes and lower my head in what I sincerely hope looks like a posture of grief and, with my eyes squeezed tight, all I can hear is the incessant, hideous clacking of his plastic ballpoint pen.

"How do you think he got into the party," he asks Davis. "It was a *pretty* high-end crowd. There was security."

"Harry?" Davis asks with a surprised little laugh. "Oh, Harry knows *everyone*. Frankly, I am surprised to hear you say Susan claimed she didn't invite him. She knew him quite well."

Officer Martinez looks up:

"Really? That would be new information," he says.

"Oh yes," Davis insists with a confident nod. "They were quite close."

"If that is true, then I can't understand why he wasn't on the original guest list?" he says.

"I have no idea," Davis says.

"Do you think he was going to sell it?" Martinez asks. "He was in serious financial trouble. He took out a lot of loans, and he had a lot of investors. He owed a lot of unhappy people."

Here, Davis shrugs.

"Harry and I never talked about business."

Martinez seems to think about this for a minute, and then he writes something else in his book.

"Do you have any idea where he might be hiding it?" he asks.

Again, Davis shakes her head.

Martinez seems to think for a long moment.

"We are going to need a written statement," he says.

"Of course," Davis replies before adding: "You can get one from Clo, too. She was with me when I talked to him."

An hour later, we walk out of the police station and get into the waiting car. Davis ruffles her long, glittering hair and folds her hands on her lap. I wait for her to say something to me, but she stays silent. When I sneak a look over, her jaw juts out, but I can't tell if it's in defiance, or sorrow, or preparation. Somehow, I know better than to ask.

Finally, she speaks:

"Thank you," she says.

"For what?"

"For letting me know about Harry," she says. "I feel like such an idiot."

Suddenly, my throat fills with a thick paste. I cough hard, but nothing is dislodged, and I briefly wonder if this is my punishment for lying.

"You're not an idiot," I say.

"I have never had anything make me feel so angry and so sad at the same time," she says. "Not even the accident."

"I am sure," I manage thickly, but my head swims.

"I was so close to a new life before the accident," she says. "Do you remember?"

I nod, but I can still recall how, at the time, I had resented her. I didn't understand why someone like Davis Lawrence was in pursuit of a new life in the first place. I begrudged her restlessness and thought her ungrateful and spoiled.

"I didn't want to marry Grant, you know," she says, and I turn to her in surprise.

"What do you mean?"

"I thought getting married would be a good way out of my situation," she says. "It was respectable, you know? Something my mother couldn't take personally. It was all part of a grander plan."

"Davis," I say slowly. "What was your new plan?"

"Ah, yes, my plan," Davis says, and here she lays her head back on the seat and closes her eyes.

"I asked Harry to give me that job," she says.

"You did?" I ask, and I feel something rise in my throat. Harry had led me to believe he simply needed a Show Horse to push through the deal. It never dawned on me there could have been other forces driving this decision, and it certainly never occurred to me that Harry might have just been trying to do something good for someone, deep down, he knew he had wronged for too long.

"Yeah," she says softly as the car pulls up to the building. "But who knows what is going to happen now."

When Hatch sees us enter the lobby, he jumps up from the chair, but we just shuffle wordlessly past him like we have been out dancing all night. We ride to the sixth floor in silence, and I watch from behind as Davis unlocks the heavy front door and presses it open with her shoulder. She hangs up her coat. She lays her sunglasses on the table in the foyer.

"Davis?" Barbara's voice trills suspiciously. "Is that you?"

Barbara sits on an upholstered chair in the living room with curlers in her hair and a short glass of Alka-Seltzer on the table next to her, which strikes me as almost performatively hungover. She is thumbing mindlessly through a magazine. A woman sits on a small wooden stool, buffing her feet over a wooden bowl of soapy water.

"Where have you been?" she asks, and while she smiles, it is terse and expectant. Not that I am surprised: We are all raw from the night before, and, today, it feels like everything hangs in the balance.

"We took a walk," Davis responds plainly. "Around the reservoir."

"At this hour?" Barbara questions. "With your leg?"

"Yes," Davis says softly. "I'm fine."

"If you say so . . ." Barbara trails off disapprovingly. "But I can't fathom why you didn't take the dog."

"Did you talk to Phillip?" Davis asks.

"I hung up with him five minutes ago," she begins.

"And?" Davis asks.

"And I absolutely lost my mind, of course."

"But, what did he say?"

"Apparently, there is some new information," she sighs, as she rests the magazine on her lap and places her fingers on her temples. "And, of course, he made a few calls to some of our friends, so I don't think they will be coming back."

"That's a relief," Davis says.

"I hardly slept a wink last night, Davis," Barbara says, and she picks her magazine back up. "You owe me one for this nightmare."

"Is there any fruit left?" Davis asks.

"I think so," Barbara says, but she doesn't look up. "Ask Betsy."

I follow Davis to the kitchen. As she opens the refrigerator and rifles around, I cannot, for the life of me, understand how they intend to continue to play their roles, especially now, but I also know that I can no longer serve as a dutiful spectator. While it's too dangerous to linger around the scene of my crimes, I realize it would also be too sad. I find myself wondering if this is how Harry Wood once felt, to love and need someone so desperately that you can no longer be near them and survive. Davis pours coffee into two mugs and sets them down at the table. Captain twines hopefully around her long legs, and she shoos him away.

But then I have an idea.

"Davis," I whisper, jolting up in my seat. "Why don't we get an apartment together?"

"What?" Davis lifts her head.

"We can get an apartment together," I say, but now with more confidence. "*You* can get out of here."

Davis seems to consider this for a beat.

"Where would we go?" she asks.

"Wherever we want."

"With what money?" she inquires.

"I have money."

Now, my mind is racing with possibility.

"How do *you* have money?" She cocks her head to the side.

"I got promotions," I answer. "I am a good saver. I buy things on sale. You know, the way *normal* people have money?"

Here, Davis smiles.

"Are you suggesting I am not a normal person?" she asks with a little smile.

"Davis, you have *never* been a normal person," I respond. "Which is precisely why the entire world is madly in love with you."

At this comment, she sinks down to the floor and extends her long legs. She picks at a button on her sweater, and I kneel next to her.

I see a smile play on her lips.

"If I say yes, can we move to California?" she asks. Her voice is small, but hopeful.

"*Of course* we can move to California," I respond, and I allow myself to feel excited, like this something that might really happen. "Let's move to California."

I put my hand on her leg, and she places her long, beautiful fingers on top of mine.

"California," she whispers.

"California," I say.

This moment dangles precariously before us, like a spider on a web. I want all of this to be possible. I need all of this to be possible. And yet, even as I watch it unspool before my own eyes, I know it is not to be:

Davis Lawrence isn't going anywhere.

"Davis?" Barbara yells from the other room. "I need you for something."

Davis looks me directly in the eye.

"You can't ever say anything," she implores. "Ever. About anything."

"I won't say anything," I assure her.

And I never do.

72

$223,197.07.

That is nearly a quarter of a million dollars.

It took years to accumulate, but when I walked out of the Lawrence apartment on Ninety-Fifth Street for the very last time, I had nearly a quarter of a million dollars sitting in my checking account, all saved up for a greater purpose, which was the saving of my soul. Perhaps I should have revealed its existence and returned it to Barbara. Or given it to Davis as the financial means to make an escape. Or made an anonymous donation to a deserving charity, but I didn't do any of those things. No, I decided to keep the money for myself. Every single dollar.

At a certain point, I no longer desired absolution for my sins.

After all, I've learned the world is full of sin.

The money I stole was more than enough to rent a new apartment in my old Brooklyn neighborhood. In short order, I bought some nice furniture, and transferred my mail and magazine subscriptions from the Upper East Side. I bought a Mac laptop computer. I got a brand-new iPhone, and requested a new number, which confused the girl working at the AT&T store on Atlantic Avenue.

"You sure?" she asked. "I've never had anyone trade a nine-one-seven for a six-four-six before."

I was sure. I couldn't wait any longer for calls that were never going to come.

Finally, I took a cab to my storage unit to retrieve all my books and the little black walnut writing desk. After I lugged everything up the stairs to my new apartment, I unwrapped the horse and placed her back in the space she had inhabited so many years ago.

Sometimes, when the nostalgia was too much for my body to bear, I would put on Barbara's fur coat and a pair of high heels and I would walk all the way to the promenade in Brooklyn Heights. I would stare searchingly over that great, muscular body of water, but it was no use: I stopped recognizing the skyline of the city long ago.

I saw them in person once, Davis and Barbara.

It was about a year after I moved out of the apartment. It was a slow week at work as my section had been cut down to three pages, and I was meeting two editors from another publication for a drink at Bar Centrale on Forty-Sixth Street before they headed off to the theater. So, with nowhere to go and no one to meet, I decided to take myself for an early drink at Bar Centrale. I arrived a little before 4:30, and I sat on the stoop in my black cocktail dress, listening for the click of the lock. Once inside, I sat at the tiny, horseshoe-shaped bar and ordered a Vesper from the gray-haired bartender. I smiled at him, and he smiled back, but I don't think he recognized me. I was first introduced to this bar by an older journalist who invited me for a drink to discuss my career during one of my many manic networking phases. He was incredibly smart and, in my opinion, being absurdly generous with his time; this was a writer whose work I had long admired, and he was bothering to take me seriously. We had an entirely appropriate conversation and, as we sipped our drinks (two cranberry juices), I remember thinking that I must be *really* good at acting. I do not remember thinking that maybe this person saw some something in me that I, even on my best of days, simply could not see in myself. I can recall how the minute we parted ways, I skittered toward the subway, like a weighted-down shoplifter escaping the scene of the crime.

It makes me sad to think about now.

Like maybe I had been enough after all.

That night, however, the small space filled with people, and while most of the patrons were older than me, there was one foursome that looked to be in their twenties. They were dressed casually—too casually for my liking—and they were making their way through a fleet of amber Manhattans and typing on their phones. Just catching sight of them, I remembered my own long-ago evenings here, all of us spun around the same zebra-striped banquettes. The world kept no records in those years. We were all traveling the same uncertain path at the same uncertain time and making our decisions without a map. Maybe we did not know exactly what lay ahead for us in those early years—those years when our own greatness seemed like a foregone conclusion—but to be completely irrelevant was never something any of us had considered. In those years, the rooms were dark, the silverware clanked like a song, and for what we did not know was only to be a moment, the entire world spun in the palms of our hands.

At 7:45, I watched the twenty-somethings pay their bill. They rose from their seats in conversation and tucked their iPhones into the pockets of jeans. All across the room, there was the sliding on of coats and little waves and plastic pens being laid down on signed credit card receipts, and, just like that, the entire bar emptied out.

I was alone.

"No show tonight?" the bartender asked me.

"No show," I responded.

As I finished my drink, I watched the waitstaff tidy up the tables for the post-show rush. I paid the bill, and when I stood up to put on my red coat, I glanced out the tall windows that overlooked Forty-Sixth Street. The street was swarmed with people, all excitedly scurrying in the direction of some play or show or dinner, and, for a moment, I remembered all the reasons that I loved New York. Directly under my window, I saw a group of people coming up the stairs of Joe Allen, and that is when I saw them: Davis and Barbara Lawrence. They were in conversation with another couple (well, more accurately, Barbara was in conversation, and Davis was just standing there) and I pressed my forehead against the glass. Davis was still frail, but it no longer lent her the air of nobility it once had; instead, she just looked brittle, like an unremarkable piece of driftwood. Her long neck pulled with beams of sinew as she strained to hear the conversation, and her hair was much shorter than the last time I saw her. The once-brilliant yellow-gold strands looked more muted now, almost gray, like she had shampooed with a bucket of dirty mop water.

I had done this to her, I thought.

I had destroyed the most beautiful thing in the world.

But for what, I cannot remember.

I watched her for a long time, and when I was unable to bear the sight of her any longer, I turned away.

I sat back down.

I ordered another drink.

I reminded myself to be careful, that the money wouldn't last forever.

Nothing does.

As for Harry, I don't know. I heard he was living in Astoria, Queens, but I also heard he was in Los Angeles working for a producer. Someone said he moved back to Louisiana, but I can't imagine Harry would ever have moved back to Louisiana. All I know about what happened to Harry Wood is what I learned from the media coverage and office gossip, all of which was as brisk as it was brutal; it was big news for a few days, but then Harry Wood was collectively and completely forgotten. Sometimes I sooth myself by remembering that Harry had misplayed his hand. He had to know it was coming; it's the fate of all Workhorses, after all. We carry the loads so well and for so long, that, one day, we go lame. We will grind down our own bones before we realize it has all been in service of someone else.

Someone better.

But I tell myself a lot of things these days.

I just wish I could tell him that I was sorry for what I did to him.

But I can't.

The bartender places a gimlet down. I try to smile, but my mouth doesn't move. Suddenly I feel desperate to hang onto Davis Lawrence, desperate to live inside my old life, if only for one more minute. I shove my stool back with a startle, and I rush toward the windows with my arms outstretched.

But the street outside is empty.

Acknowledgments

First and foremost, I want to thank my three children—Charlie, Margaret, and Holland Nagy—who not only lived alongside this project for a very large chunk of their childhoods, but who were also my biggest (often funniest, sometimes neglected) supporters. Yes, the book is finally done. And I love you more than you will ever know. Secondly, not a single page of *Workhorse* could have been written without the patience, wise counsel and many sacrifices of my husband (and fellow writer), Estep Nagy, to whom this book is dedicated.

An enormous debt of gratitude goes to my agent, Mollie Glick, who (along with forever reminding me of that Cuba Gooding Jr. line at the end of *Jerry Maguire*: "You're militant . . . but I got nothing but love for you . . .") stayed by my side during every step of this process. And, in the event she ever needs to hear it: You are doing everything right. Also, to Dana Spector, who just may be the world's most straight-talking voice of reason. Thank you.

I would be nowhere without Megan Lynch at Flatiron who, in addition to being a talented editor and cunning businesswoman, gets extra points for not batting an eyelash when I ordered an extra shot of vodka with my vodka gimlet on the first night we met. It has been an absolute dream to work with you, and your incredible team at Flatiron, including Kara McAndrew, Morgan Mitchell, Emily Walters, Ryan T. Jenkins, Marlena Bittner, Kate Keating, Cat Kenney, Maria Snelling, Drew Kilman, Hayley Jozwiak, Jaime Herbeck, and Rachel Bass. Thank you for seeing me so expertly (and so patiently) over the finish line. And to Keith Hayes and Leslie Graff, who created this unforgettable cover: Way to nail it.

A debt is also owed to my parents, Edgar and Patricia Palmer, for their unfathomable yet unending belief in me (and my mother for trying to instill in me her excellent fashion sense); my brothers, Michael and John Palmer, for ensuring I developed a thick-enough skin required to withstand the scrutiny of writing a novel; and to Erica Barth, Allison Deutermann, and Liz Grant: Without you, my world would cease to spin.

I would also like to thank: Joselin Linder for never giving up on me; Jeffrey Clifford and David Heyman at Heyday Films for working so hard to bring Clo to life; Helen Laser for giving her a voice; my brilliant team in the UK, including my agent Karolina Sutton, and Hope Butler, Katie Bowden, and everyone at Fourth Estate; Garth Risk Hallberg, Elise White, Frank Rich, Valerie Steiker, Joanne Chen, Laurie Jones, Julia Ruttner, Eileen and John Kerrigan, Rita and Edward Grant, Alex Kolbe, Cathy Beaudoin, Jonathan Van Meter, Adam Green, Eve MacSweeney, Alexandra Kotur, Tonne Goodman, Matt Dellinger; OG's Sarah Haight, Maggie Bullock, Esme Rene, Tara Gallagher, Lauren Collins, Megan O'Grady, Silvia Sitar, Lauren Santo Domingo, Meredith Melling, Jill Demling, Sylvana Ward Durret; and YG's Amy Stoddart, Jaime Henderson, Lisa Bieber, Christina Hynoski, Ricki Rubin, Karyn Whytedog; the indispensable Bradford Elementary moms, my forever families in Avalon and under the tents at BBTC, the Point O' Woods community, and Angelbecks liquor store in Montclair, New Jersey, for whom Mark Angelbeck is so fondly named. And, of course, to Megan Salt.

Finally, I did not start writing this book until I was in my mid-forties, which surprised nobody more than me. After all, I came of age in an era rife with "wunderkinds" and all those "20 Under 20" lists, and then (somewhat despairingly as the years rolled by) the "30 Under 30" and "40 Under 40" lists. I suppose I was long resigned to the fact that with a job, three kids, and a profoundly impressive collection of ruched one-piece bathing suits, any dreams of a more writerly life were officially part of a distant past.

I write this only because, if you are reading this, I want you to know one thing: It is not too late. Whatever it is, it is not too late.

This has been one of the great joys of my life.